Artifact
Collective

an Attempt to Consciousness

written, collected, edited, and assembled

by

Nick Stokes, You, and Us

For information and inquiries:
www.nickstokes.net
nstokes_cop@yahoo.com

ISBN-13: 9781797045832

Nick Stokes, Tacoma, WA
United States of America

First Edition, 2019

60. Back Cover: The Sun, adapted, captured on April 20, 2015, NASA / Solar Dynamics Observatory, https://www.nasa.gov/image-feature/active-regions-on-the-sun.

Artifact Collective is a fiction incorporating nonfiction and found objects. The work of others has been used with permission when possible, or according to granted licenses such as Creative Commons when possible, or according to logical intellectual property laws when possible, and otherwise when impossible. Artifact Collective is an attempt to consciousness. Artifact Collective is a corpus. We are within.

For us

By us

0.

You begin.

1.

You don't know. You've begun this way before. You don't know that. That you began or in this way. You begin this way. You don't know if you begin. Or what is this way. Not knowing is how you begin. You don't know how you begin or where or if this is a beginning of what this is.

2.

You are confined. You know that much. If you begin you are constrained. You cannot move. You cannot breathe. An immense weight weighs on you like weight. You feel or sense or fear or perceive or imagine or think the end is approaching.

3.

Not yet. What is the weight? Your own? The Earth's? Are you an Atlas, another bearer of crumpled mythological meaning, or are you another godforsaken Galileo crushed by celestial bodies standing on your shoulders? Who are they. What are they to you. You do not know if you are at the bottom of the ocean, an ocean, or at the center of a star, the star. Except that you fear you cannot breathe, which makes you think you could, that you have the potential to, and that you could not in either of your aforementioned scenarios, you at ocean bottom or star center, breathe, though they have the characteristic of physical specificity, you don't know about a Galileo or Atlas, a characteristic you feel yourself desiring.

4.

Desiring. Confined constrained trapped. Unable to move. Breathing. Possible breathing. Have you been immobilized or have you always thus far lacked motion. Have you ever been mobile and will you ever be? At any rate the immobilization is all encompassing or envelops you or is in complete and utter contact with you. The material or immaterial immobilizing you confines you at the level or surface or boundary of your skin. The epithelial, where the dead cell

1

sloughs. Skin. You appear to have a boundary. Which would mean, if you can breathe, physically, there could be a space within you to contain the breath. But which would also mean the breathing would be difficult if not impossible because the lungs, your lungs, your theoretical space, cannot expand, cannot make space within yourself for the breath, the chest cavity cannot expand, the ribs cannot rise, your boundary does not give, the lungs would have no choice but to expand inward, perhaps by compressing other bodily organs such as stomach intestines liver or spleen. Or lungs. You just attributed a lot of attributes characteristics physicalities lungs to yourself. You don't know about any of them. But you do know that the confines you have thus far described, how far?, the complete and utter contact of the confines, the weight, the uncertainty of breathing, the difficulty of breathing, could match the description of being buried alive. Of having been buried alive. Or perhaps you were more right the first time, with the being, being buried alive. You don't know. Which would mean dirt. Buried in earth. Drawing breath from soil. Worms approaching, near, here. Hear. Not daring to open your mouth for fear of being filled.

5.

So you nose breathe, assuming breathing. The possibility of a clod sufficiently small to enter your nasal passage and sufficiently large to suddenly block your airway is daunting, though you don't know if it's possible, is the possibility that you might have two nasal passages relevant, though perhaps not as daunting as your slow suffocation from lack of underground oxygen, or from your respiratory system filling with silt, or you filled with worms, you becoming a worm casing, or moreso than the worms other arthropods insects bugs such as beetles chitin clicking centipedes with their many legs squirming inside you, do you have legs, ants marching operating slicing under the command of in consort with each an appendage of an untouchable supermind elsewhere mushroom mycelia spreading like the neural network of an intelligent hungry fungus flesh-eating bacteria you cannot see, that cannot be seen, within you, you see nothing, eating your uncertain flesh. You must do something. You cannot move. You see nothing. You don't know if your eyes are open or closed. If they are closed you are reluctant to open them due to the possibility that your idea, belief, hypothesis that you are buried alive is objectively true and that a speck of dirt will enter your eye or eyes and make you cry, which would be an actualization. You discovering yourself in a speck of dirt in your eye. You self-realizing in a tear. But nevertheless you have an innate aversion to the irritation, a bodily resistance to the crying, a defiance -- there, bodily again, you mote, note a pattern of bodily physical substance references within you, but is the defiance of crying necessarily bodily, would psychologically or socially-imprinted resistance to crying necessitate a body? Would the defiance imply a you? You desire a you. If your eyes are open you see nothing, darkness, the absence of light, nothing to differentiate a you from a notyou. Could the nothing you see be miles feet inches of dirt? How far down are you? You don't feel cold clammy moist, you don't think. You could be sufficiently deep to be warmed by the center of the Earth. Or you could be a victim of hypothermia, unaware of the cold, whose victims rend their clothes because they mistakenly think themselves hot burning smothered. You feel no pain, or none that you know to say, no pain you name pain. Confinement, immobility, a desperation to move and an inability to do so, which is like pain but less acute and more enclosing enveloping constraining and like discomfort but more meaningful feeling and less about excess or the relationship between your nopain and an imagined state of comfort than about your possible end and an imagined possibility of life. You feel smothered. You suppose the deeper you were buried, the more pressure you would experience. You do feel an immense pressure, as much as you can stand. Are you vertical, relative to what?, as much as you can withstand or bear or bare or survive, is that all?, is it not slightly more than you can withstand?, just as much as you can, assuming your past survival and current presence and your apparent continuation in the immediate future and a progression through time, but you don't have a measurement of it, the pressure, the weight, the time, to calculate your depth. A tangible tool fact it would've been. In your thwarted desire to take a measurement of the pressure, and therewith calculate your depth below the surface of the earth, if that's where you are, you feel an increase in pressure, which makes you wonder if the pressure you experience is created by the dirt of being buried alive or by your desire to move and do something and your inability to do so, and if there is a difference between those pressures. You must do something and you cannot move and the only action you can possibly take is to get to the bottom of this. Getting there without moving increases the pressure.

6.

Perhaps you are in a box buried alive deep underground. Kilometers, chains, leagues deep, depth wouldn't be as defining if you were within the box first, then the ground, or rather in you first, then the box, then the ground, then spacetime or whathaveyou. Because your rigid box could withstand the pressure for you. Because your rigid box could withstand the pressure of you. The box could be cuboid and spacious, giving you space to breathe, which you do not feel you have, or it could exactly fit your body, in full contact with every contour crevice and projection, and in its rigor provide form function and protection from the immense weight of the substrate under which you are buried, or your box could again be the exact shape of your body, does it determine your shape or you its?, you can't escape this body, every notion your brain formulates references a body, including the notion of the brain, as big as your two fists together in a braincase, what fists in what case, what would it, you, be if you did not refer to a body?, again your container could be the exact shape of your body but a hair smaller, by design or because you still grow slightly, slightly because you grow slowly or because of the inhibition of your case, still grow because you are young or you are ingesting more calories whether by food or light or radiation or other form of equally implausible energy than you burn, you should exercise, or because you are swelling bedbound immobile atrophying, or by the hand, no hand, of some other mechanism such as how water expands when it freezes because of the hydrogen force or hydrogen bonds or hydrogen bombs, ample expansion there and motivation for burial, encasement, underground living, or perhaps because of enlightenment if enlightenment causes growth or swelling or expansion or explosion, in which case your box might in its rigor provide you on the inside protection from the immense weight of the outside while simultaneously providing the outside protection from the immense pressure of the inside. The inside of the box which you are in. You are not yet prepared to tackle the possibility that the box is inside you. Tackle, where did you get that word? Somehow the box has become a given, with the body. For now, fine, the box, you think, and breathe a little easier, though perhaps that's your imagination.

6[1].
Wikipedia contributors, "Thermonuclear weapon," *Wikipedia, The Free Encyclopedia,* https://en.wikipedia.org/w/index.php?title=Thermonuclear_weapon&oldid=692647430 (accessed Dec 2, 2015).

The basic principle of the Teller–Ulam configuration is the idea that different parts of a thermonuclear weapon can be chained together in "stages", with the detonation of each stage providing the energy to ignite the next stage. At a bare minimum, this implies a *primary* section which consists of an implosion-type fission bomb (a "trigger"), and a *secondary* section which consists of fusion fuel. The energy released by the *primary* compresses the *secondary* through a process called "radiation implosion", at which point it is heated and undergoes nuclear fusion.

An implosion assembly type of fission bomb is exploded. This is the primary stage. If a small amount of deuterium[1]/tritium[2] gas is placed inside the primary's core, it will be compressed during the explosion and a nuclear fusion reaction will occur; the released neutrons from this fusion reaction will induce further fission in the plutonium-239 or uranium-235 used in the primary stage. The use of fusion fuel to enhance the efficiency of a fission reaction is called boosting. Without boosting, a large portion of the fissile material will remain unreacted; the Little Boy and Fat Man bombs had an efficiency of only 1.4% and 17%, respectively, because they were unboosted.

Energy released in the primary stage is transferred to the secondary (or fusion) stage. Separating the secondary from the primary is the interstage. The fissioning primary produces four types of energy: 1) expanding hot gases from high explosive charges which implode the primary; 2) superheated plasma that was originally the bomb's fissile material and its tamper; 3) the electromagnetic radiation; and 4) the neutrons from the primary's nuclear detonation. The interstage is responsible for accurately modulating the transfer of energy from the primary to the secondary. The exact mechanism whereby this happens is secret.[3] This energy compresses the fusion fuel and sparkplug; the compressed sparkplug becomes critical and undergoes a fission chain reaction, further heating the compressed fusion fuel to a high enough temperature to induce fusion, and also supplying neutrons that react with lithium to create tritium for fusion.

The fusion fuel of the secondary stage[4] may be surrounded by depleted uranium or natural uranium, whose U-238 is not fissile and cannot sustain a chain reaction, but which is fissionable when bombarded by the high-energy neutrons released by fusion in the secondary stage. This process provides considerable energy yield (as much as half of the total yield in large devices), but is not considered a tertiary "stage".[3**] Tertiary stages are further fusion stages, which have been only rarely used, and then only in the most powerful bombs ever made.

6[1]. NOTES
1 - Wikipedia contributors, "Deuterium," *Wikipedia, The Free Encyclopedia,* https://en.wikipedia.org/w/index.php?title=Deuterium&oldid=718604317 (accessed Dec 2, 2015).

Deuterium (^{2}H, also known as **heavy hydrogen**) is one of two stable isotopes of hydrogen. The nucleus of deuterium, called a **deuteron**, contains one proton and one neutron, whereas the far more common hydrogen isotope, protium, has no neutron in the nucleus. Deuterium has a natural abundance in Earth's oceans of about one atom in 6420 of hydrogen. Thus deuterium accounts for approximately 0.0156% (or on a mass basis 0.0312%) of all the naturally occurring hydrogen in the oceans, while the most common isotope (hydrogen-1 or protium) accounts for more than 99.98%.

Deuterium is destroyed in the interiors of stars faster than it is produced.[1] Other natural processes are thought to produce only an insignificant amount of deuterium. Theoretically nearly all deuterium found in nature was produced in the Big Bang 13.8 billion years ago.

2 - Wikipedia contributors, "Tritium," *Wikipedia, The Free Encyclopedia,* https://en.wikipedia.org/w/index.php?title=Tritium&oldid=719761996 (accessed Dec 2, 2015).

Tritium (¹H, also known as **hydrogen-3**) is a radioactive isotope of hydrogen. The nucleus of tritium (sometimes called a **triton**) contains one proton and two neutrons. Naturally occurring tritium is extremely rare on Earth, where trace amounts are formed by the interaction of the atmosphere with cosmic rays.

3 - Wikipedia contributors, "Thermonuclear weapon." How exactly the energy is "transported" from the *primary* to the *secondary* has been the subject of some disagreement in the open press, but is thought to be transmitted through the X-rays which are emitted from the fissioning *primary*. This energy is then used to compress the *secondary*. The crucial detail of *how* the X-rays create the pressure is the main remaining disputed point in the unclassified press. There are three proposed theories:

> 1. Radiation pressure exerted by the X-rays.
> 2. X-rays creating a plasma in the radiation case's filler (a polystyrene or "FOGBANK" plastic foam).[3*]
> 3. Tamper/Pusher ablation.[3*] This is the concept best supported by physical analysis.

4 - Wikipedia contributors, "Thermonuclear weapon." The secondary is usually shown as a column of fusion fuel and other components wrapped in many layers. Around the column is first a "pusher-tamper", a heavy layer of uranium-238 (U-238) or lead which serves to help compress the fusion fuel (and, in the case of uranium, may eventually undergo fission itself). Inside this is the fusion fuel itself, usually a form of lithium deuteride, which is used because it is easier to weaponize than liquified tritium/deuterium gas (compare the success of the cryogenic deuterium-based Ivy Mike experiment to the (over)success of the lithium deuteride-based Castle Bravo experiment). This dry fuel, when bombarded by neutrons, produces tritium, a heavy isotope of hydrogen which can undergo nuclear fusion, along with the deuterium present in the mixture.[1] Inside the layer of fuel is the "spark plug", a hollow column of fissile material (plutonium-239 or uranium-235) which, when compressed, can itself undergo nuclear fission (because of the shape, it is not a critical mass without compression).

6₁. NOTES of NOTES
3* - Wikipedia contributors, "Thermonuclear weapon."

Ablation mechanism firing sequence:
> 1. Warhead before firing. The nested spheres at the top are the fission primary; the cylinders below are the fusion secondary device.
> 2. Fission primary's explosives have detonated and collapsed the primary's fissile pit.
> 3. The primary's fission reaction has run to completion, and the primary is now at several million degrees and radiating gamma and hard X-rays, heating up the inside of the hohlraum and the shield and secondary's tamper.

4. The primary's reaction is over and it has expanded. The surface of the pusher for the secondary is now so hot that it is also ablating or expanding away, pushing the rest of the secondary (tamper, fusion fuel, and fissile spark plug) inwards. The spark plug starts to fission. Not depicted: the radiation case is also ablating and expanding outwards (omitted for clarity of diagram). [3**]

5. The secondary's fuel has started the fusion reaction and shortly will burn up. A fireball starts to form.

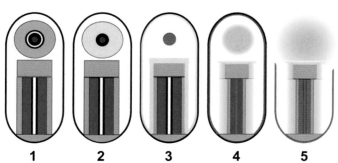

1   2   3   4   5

"TellerUlamAblation,"CC BY-SA 2.5, https://commons.wikimedia.org/w/index.php?curid=960623.

Foam plasma mechanism firing sequence:

A. Warhead before firing; primary (fission bomb) at top, secondary (fusion fuel) at bottom, all suspended in polystyrene foam.

B. High-explosive fires in primary, compressing plutonium core into super-criticality and beginning a fission reaction.

C. Fission primary emits X-rays which are scattered along the inside of the casing, irradiating the polystyrene foam.

D. Polystyrene foam becomes plasma, compressing secondary, and plutonium sparkplug begins to fission.

E. Compressed and heated, lithium-6 deuteride fuel produces tritium and begins the fusion reaction. The neutron flux produced causes the U-238 tamper to fission.[3**] A fireball starts to form.

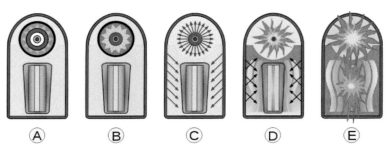

Ⓐ   Ⓑ   Ⓒ   Ⓓ   Ⓔ

"BombH explosion," CC BY-SA 3.0, https://commons.wikimedia.org/w/index.php?curid=1343962.
(Teller-Ulam hydrogen bomb firing sequence, modified from Howard Morland, *The Secret that Exploded* (Random House, 1981).)

I - Wikipedia contributors, "Nuclear fusion," *Wikipedia, The Free Encyclopedia,* https://en.wikipedia.org/w/index.php?title=Nuclear_fusion&oldid=692351524 (accessed Dec 2, 2015).

The most important fusion process in nature is the one that powers stars. In the 20th century, it was realized that the energy released from nuclear fusion reactions accounted for the longevity of the Sun and other stars as a source of heat and light. The fusion of nuclei in a star, starting from its initial hydrogen and helium abundance, provides that energy and synthesizes new nuclei as a byproduct of that fusion process[i]. The prime energy producer in the Sun is the fusion of hydrogen to form helium, which occurs at a solar-core temperature of 14 million kelvin. The net result is the fusion of four protons into one alpha particle, with the release of two positrons, two neutrinos (which changes two of the protons into neutrons), and energy.

Fusion in stars such as the sun:

Fusion of deuterium with tritium creating helium-4, freeing a neutron, and releasing 17.59 MeV of energy, as an appropriate amount of mass changing forms to appear as the kinetic energy of the products, in agreement with *kinetic* $E = \Delta mc^2$, where Δm is the change in rest mass of particles.

By Wykis - Own work, based on w:File:D-t-fusion.png, Public Domain, https://commons.wikimedia.org/w/index.php?curid=2069575.

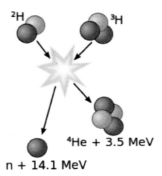

6[1]. NOTES of NOTES of NOTES

3** - Wikipedia contributors, "Thermonuclear weapon." This would complete the fission-fusion-fission sequence. Fusion, unlike fission, is relatively "clean"—it releases energy but no harmful radioactive products or large amounts of nuclear fallout. The fission reactions though, especially the last fission reaction, release a tremendous amount of fission products and fallout. If the last fission stage is omitted, by replacing the uranium tamper with one made of lead, for example, the overall explosive force is reduced by approximately half but the amount of fallout is relatively low. The neutron bomb is a hydrogen bomb with an intentionally thin tamper, allowing as much radiation as possible to escape.

i - Wikipedia contributors, "Nuclear fusion." The origin of the energy released in fusion of light elements is due to the interplay of two opposing forces, the nuclear force which holds together protons and neutrons, and the Coulomb force which causes protons to repel each other. The protons are positively charged and repel each other but they nonetheless stick together, demonstrating the existence of another force referred to as nuclear attraction. This force, called the strong nuclear force, overcomes electric repulsion in a very close range. The effect of this force is not observed outside the nucleus because the force has a strong dependence on distance, making it a short-range force. The same force also pulls the nucleons (neutrons and protons) together. Because the nuclear force is stronger than the Coulomb force for atomic nuclei smaller than iron and nickel, building up these nuclei from lighter nuclei by **fusion** releases the extra energy from the net attraction of these particles.

The fusion of lighter nuclei, which creates a heavier nucleus and often a free neutron or proton, generally releases more energy than it takes to force the nuclei together; this is an exothermic process that can produce self-sustaining reactions.

Energy released in most nuclear reactions is much larger than in chemical reactions, because the binding energy that holds a nucleus together is far greater than the energy that holds electrons to a nucleus. For example, the ionization energy gained by adding an electron to a hydrogen nucleus is 13.6 eV—less than one-millionth of the 17.6 MeV released in the deuterium–tritium (D–T) reaction shown in the diagram to the right (one gram of matter would release 339 GJ of energy). Only direct conversion of mass into energy, such as that caused by the annihilatory collision of matter and antimatter, is more energetic per unit of mass than nuclear fusion.

All material here recovered, collected, collated: Wikipedia: CC BY-SA.

7.

If you are in a closed box how can you tell you are underground? You could not say unambiguously before that you were underground. Before, was that a time previous to now, has time passed, or is this in the same time, all now, were you in a different state, are you now. How are you to say. You cannot say unambiguously when you are at the other spacetime point that you are underground when then you are either not in a closed box or do not know it. To tell to say to know. How do you tell say know, you of uncertain body. No sight no smell no sound no taste no touch. Bodily sensations, beyond thought, thoughtlessnesses, none of that. The weight is how you tell. Touch perhaps then. Strike the possibility of the box being a hair smaller than you, a thought experiment, a disproved hypothesis, a discarded you, you must narrow the possibilities instead of introducing them, it's impossible. You are in a box exactly your shape. Your own immense weight provides all the pressure you require, don't fault the box. In a rigid box the weight would be your own, would it not, due to gravity, regardless of if you were buried or not. Yes you think but interred underground, within the massive body, your weight would be greater would it not because of your location in the gravitational field than it would be incarcerated on the surface of the Earth or enshrined on a mountaintop or bejeweled in orbit or excommunicated to forever accelerate through empty regions of space. From within your box you would not be able to tell say know if the weight you experience is due to the force of gravity, that is your placement in a gravitational field, or because your box is uniformly accelerating through space. Yes, there is the question of scale, the immensity of your weight, but you could be at rest closer to a less massive body or immobile further from a more massive body or accelerating more or less through space beyond the pull of a massive body. If you cannot tell, cannot know, cannot say, then what is the difference. Is there a way to know you from within your box, is there a way out of the box, should you not smother quit die in unknowing, do you choose you, are all understandings, points of view, ways to say you valid worthwhile vital, are you trapped buried boxed.

8.

Would it be worse to be hurtling through empty space accelerating by unknown cause? Why? Because of the disconnect you suppose, the essentially infinite distance, the separation from others and human story. The emptiness, the lack of gravitational bodies, the aloneness, the lack of stellar stories. It is presumptuous of you to suppose humanness or others or any story whatsoever. But without them, is there you? You do desire you, you've determined, and your desire and determination and grasping intellect is about all you have at your disposal in this box. If you desire you then perhaps there is you, and if so, perhaps there is if, then. Besides, there is entanglement -- not now. Did you just make a joke, and what does that say about you, about your ability to imagine the multiple logical and unexpected implications of a thought? If there is no difference and you can imagine it either way and you get to choose, you choose buried alive underground over accelerating in a box in empty space. For constraint for limits for peace of mind.

7a$_i$.

Einstein's principle of equivalence: In small enough regions of space it is impossible to tell if you are at rest in a gravitational field or uniformly accelerating in empty space. The states are equivalent. From which we develop the theory of general relativity.

9.

In a box. Rest in peace. Mind not at peace. Body if you have one trapped in peace, forced into rest, held. A body at rest tends to stay at rest and a mind in motion tends to stay in motion. What species of peace? Alive or dead perhaps does not matter except you want to move and breathe and see and touch and cannot, except your mind is moving on and it desires your body unless you have achieved enlightenment or melded into software for an advanced artificial intelligence or transubstantiated into pure spirit or are a tiny neuronal element in a supermind. Not unless. Alive or dead is a characteristic of your story detail of your history measurement of your specifics that you desire. Box: pine, a 3-dimensional rectangle, length exactly equal to your height, plus 2 inches for two 1-inch thick pine boards, southern or ponderosa or white or yellow, you are a being of modest means, no the 1 inch is nominal, .75 inches is real actual observed thickness, length exactly equal to your height plus 1.5" for two .75" thick boards, width exactly equal to your width shoulder-to-shoulder, snug not loose compress the shoulder muscle flab flesh for a cozy measurement, plus 1.5" for two .75" thick boards, outside measurements of the box here, you providing observations from an outside perspective, height exactly equal to your maximum thickness whether that be from navel (compressed) to small of back or tip of toe to heel or tip of nose (squished) to back of head, plus 1.5" for two .75" thicknesses of pine. Do you have a human body? Are you horizontal, and what does horizontal mean? Nothing except relative, meaningless except in a gravitational field. Vertical in a gravitational field means a greater force on your feet than your head if upright, on head than feet if upside down. Horizontal in a gravitational field is a greater force on your dorsal than ventral side, if facing up, "up," if you are a terrestrial animal or insect buried right side up it would be the other way around. But in the simplest of situations in another's gravity horizontal describes a curve not a straight line. Or perhaps plywood for economy and no forgiveness for the thickness of the wood board sheet, either returning to your perspective within the box in which its external dimensions are meaningless or returning to the possibility that the box is constructed slightly smaller than you. Constructed. Are you or were you a pauper? Do they bury the destitute in boxes? Perhaps you were passed out in an alley or unconscious on a park bench or asleep on a church stoop and they determined you dead and buried you. They. Two sentences in a row. Are you dredging these object word things, alley park church bench stoop they, up from a drowned repository of memory? Does that world still exist? Assumption. Does that world exist and can you move your hands? Did it ever and do you have any? Have you ever had hands and if there is or has been or will be a world of churches and alleys and parks and bodies and others, are you or were you or will you be in it?

Perhaps the box is tapered from shoulder to sole and again from shoulder to crown and again from nosetip to toetip and again from nosetip to forehead apex and again from nosetip to shoulder via cheekbones to improve confinement and spatial efficiency and economy. Perhaps the box is ash or maple or oak or cherry or walnut or cedar to keep out the moths. What would each species of wood say about you? Perhaps the box is stuffed so full of padding that you cannot move and the padding is rigid and the padding fills the remaining empty space not empty to again improve confinement efficiency economy. Perhaps its exterior is polished to a mirror finish to reduce friction for the ease of insertion of your box deep into the ground through a tunnel which opens barely wide enough to admit you, your box, and which closes behind you. Perhaps the exterior is not meaningless irrelevant non-existent though you cannot perceive it see it have definite knowledge of it. Or of interior. What do you have to say about yourself about your finish? Are were you rich? Why? Do you reek of embalming fluids? Perhaps the box is stone because you are or considered yourself or were historic, like Lenin in his glass box in his granite marble mausoleum. Perhaps you were historic or relevant or are a cherished or infamous keepsake trinket memory kept in an attractive stone box. Perhaps you were a stonecutter from a land of stone without wood or plastic. Perhaps the box is metal. Perhaps it is an ammo box and you are explosive ordinance, or a time capsule and you are an artifact, or a discarded lunch box and you are decaying food, or a cached bear-proof container, bears, swept away by a swollen river and buried by sediment and the upheaval of mountains and the accumulation of time. Perhaps the box is plastic. Tupperware Rubbermaid Ziploc Glad. PVC. Perhaps silicon. Perhaps superconductor. Perhaps, returning to a box shaped exactly like you, whatever that shape might be, which would be extremely possible if the box is plastic you note, the box is gold and you were a pharaoh or a high priest or a CEO and you are bound in cloth and preserved in chemicals and this is you being reborn or awaking in the afterlife or beginning another job of maximizing another corporation's return to its investors except you have awoken buried in a collapsed chamber under a great pyramid office and contrary to what religion or economics says all you have been able to take with you is your mind. Or what your mind makes. What do the specifics matter. No matter the specifics you are trapped and you want to move, to do, but you cannot. You desire yourself, another, but you cannot. Perhaps it is for just this attitude, cannot and will not, due to unwillingness or fear or intransigence or inability or defiance or ineptitude, that you are incarcerated in a dungeon in a stone cell in which you cannot move in solitary confinement until you change, evolve, improve, become a better person, a better being. You cannot observe yourself. What if your box is a chrysalis in which you metamorphose from something like a larvae to a moth. From a human to a butterfly. What if there is no box. There is no box and you are not buried underground but under bodies underground in a mass grave no dirt separating you flesh to flesh tight-packed crystal lattice of gray bodies nowhere to move bodies upon bodies each of you trapped in your body in bodies unable to move to access each other smashed together limbs askew entangled touching everywhere touching unable to touch or are you the only one alive buried in corpses or are you dead a nobody dumped with nobodies in a pile of bodies no flies this deep in the heap but larvae and worms, food for worms in the dark.

6_2.

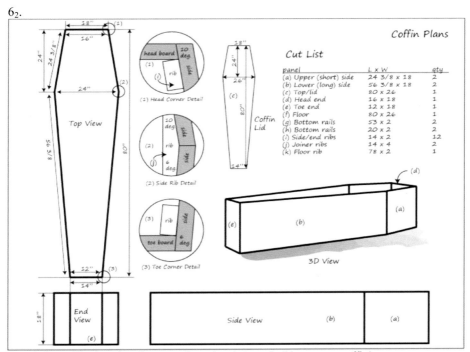

Toe-pincher coffin plans, http://www.northwoodscasket.com/build-your-own-coffin/ http://static1.squarespace.com/static/542053a8e4b0c6a70bc09cfb/t/54af07d3e4b0036ec3e28295/1420756 948339/free-coffin-plans.jpg?format=1000w (accessed May 13, 2016).

9a.

Weight increasing. Under bodies. Darkness. Bodies landing on you. You thudding atop a pile of bodies near the apex of a hill a mound a mountain of bodies sloping down at the human body's angle of repose. Falling through the air in a slurry of bodies falling and dismembered appendages falling toward the top of a mountain. Falling. Falling off the end. The end of the belt the ride the rise approaching, risen high, the lip approaching, rising, carried into thin air. You want to die like all the rest around you. High enough for a breath of fresh air. Conveyed by the belt up a long incline forever for days for hours above the crows. Everyone is dead. The hum of machinery. They are all bald. The clickety-clack of the belt. An old man a boy his mother a young man and woman braided together a dismembered arm a body without a face without skin its skin melted off. The cold. You are touching many bodies. A breeze. You are being touched. You are high in the air on a moving surface climbing you are not alone. Stench. You above the clouds. Crows swirl caw fight eat tear peck black soaring in blue sky. A crow takes flight. Pecking at your eye. Alive. Metal on metal. A high scream. Black nothing. A massive bulldozer bucket scooping up you and your son. Massive bulldozer bucket dumping bodies skin peeled back many without faces all without clothes in a massive dump truck. A massive bulldozer bucket scooping up bodies scraping them off the cement the dirt scooping small piles of bodies impaling them on its teeth dragging the bucket backward over the cement to dislodge bodies from its teeth dismembering coming forward again without pause to fill the bucket. Bodies. The rumble of engines. Smell of burning. Nothing. Black. A massive heat. Smell of burning hair.

9a₁.

Finally sufficiently disgusted with our spiritless consumerism and our material excess and our capitalizing imperialism and our interference in their internal affairs and our hedonistic freedoms and our indelicately clothed icons and the influence of those of us who are women or gay or of a different ethnicity and our belated independence from fossil fuels and our unwillingness to bow to their beliefs in a biblical God or a Koranic Allah or a New Testament Jesus of their own specific interpretation, emboldened by their own fundamentalist rhetoric and our economic zealotry, they drop a neutron bomb on us. We drop a neutron bomb on them. They have more than one. We are aware. We have many. They drop a neutron bomb on you while you and your significant other and your son play in the park or while you drive your spouse to work and your daughter to school or while your ex picks up your son and you hand over his blankie in your driveway while he cries because you refused to buy him an ice cream from the infernal music of the ice cream truck.

9a₂.

You are old. You are in a camp. Sometimes you work for days on end doing work a machine could do smashing rocks or digging holes or driving a hand drill into the side of a mountain by sledge and the work is ruthless and demoralizing and dehumanizing and many of you die and sometimes you lie in the cold

14

concrete barracks for weeks useless and sick and eating what slop is given you ready to die being kept alive you know not why. You are alone with strangers like you. You have ben separated from your loved ones, your husband or wife, your lover, your friend, your son and daughter and mother and father. You imagine you can still feel them, can reach out to them with your mind, can communicate with them at a distance, like they say They can do. Or you haven't been separated because it makes little difference to them if you think you want to be together to suffer together to watch your partner your children your parents suffer to experience their suffering because the one thing They pity is your love, no not pity but patronize, not condescendingly but coldly. Without comprehension or empathy. The camp is something out of a book, a Nazi concentration camp, a Japanese internment camp, a Chinese prisoner of war camp, a Native American internment camp, a Khmer Rouge reservation, a Palestinian internment camp, an Israeli country, an Iranian prison, the Gulag. A place to put the seditious, the treasonous, the non-conformists, those of the wrong color or nationality or heritage or beliefs, the unbelievers, the non-compliers, the foot-draggers, the dangerous, the unable or unwilling or impure or misfit or unfit. The camp is not out of a book. A place to put the free thinkers. You don't think as well as They do. The poor thinkers, the slow thinkers, the un thinkers. You are cold and miserable, but you shave your head for lice and share your misery with your loved ones beside you or at a distance in your mind, holding them inside or out for warmth, it makes little difference, until They decide there is no value in keeping you alive. In an act of what may or may not be mercy, their motivations beyond you, They terminate you in a wave of heat.

9a₃.

It selects without regard for intelligence or physical attribute or past performance or potential promise. It does not select. It is indiscriminate, and there are so few of you left to manage the bodies, those of you left always lessening, soon only one of you left and you will join all of your kind in lifelessness, to in some semblance bury the dead as the word bury is stripped of meaning, loses its significance, its signifier, to man the bulldozers and wear masks for protection and pile your corpses. Driving massive earthmovers from old coal mines. It is a rising toxicity in the water cycle, it is a new microbe evolving faster than your antibiotics, it is an unforeseen chain of events caused by pollution-fueled climate change, it is an asteroid, it is biological or chemical or nuclear or genetic warfare, it is famine, it is a virus brought back on an interstellar probe, it is the machines, it is the nonmachines, it is us, it is you. It could have been avoided. It could not have. It is sudden and slow. Extinction was always going to come, you knew that though you hoped it would come for a future you. You don't hope anymore. You are dead inside. You pile your bodies and see yourself in their glassy eyes.

9b.
What do you remember? Do you remember fire? Is your last memory burning light or lapping flame or the red flower or pain?

$9b_1$.
Demoralized that bodies were not permitted to be buried in the dirt soil earth without a box and the proper papers and sufficient funds to pay for the right to be buried to decay into root juice to become bacteria a rose a roly-poly a dandelion a worm an American elm, you chose to cremate your corpse after a run-of-the-mill life.

$9b_2$.
You are one ash in an urn of ashes. An urn of unknowns, an urn of unknown size and magnitude, an urn for all you know of the ashes of all who have ever lived, ashes upon ashes in an urn you one.

$9b_3$.
You had a family and you lost them. You had a job and you lost it. You had a home you lost. You lived on the street. You had your mind until you lost it. You died on the street. You had a body. You lost it. You were cremated with the other destitute. You had a life.

$9b_4$.
You immolated yourself. Why?

9c.
This is your potter's field.

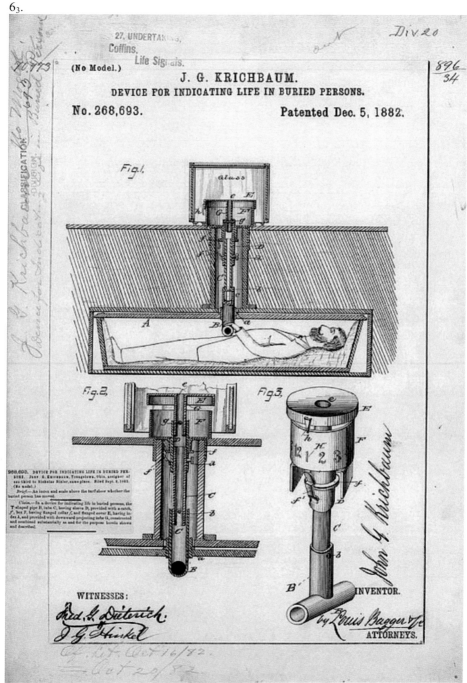

10.

You call the box a coffin. Objects need names, classifications, boxes to be put in for reference and retrieval in your brain, object boxes for common understanding between different parts of your brain when they communicate with each other, word boxes for common understanding between you and others if there are others when you communicate with them if you communicate with them via language. Perhaps you are beyond language. No, you caution yourself, wait, you are not there yet, you are here, in a slurry mound quarry of words, pick by pick, word by word, brick by brick, each conjunction in of for its proper place in absolute space, each conjugation in its proper absolute time. Perhaps you communicate with others even now. What matter if you are aware of them or of your communication. What you observe to be given is you. You decide to call your box a coffin, to place your box in the word box coffin, to box in your box. Coffin comes with certain connotations, or perhaps uncertain connotations. A coffin is a box retrieved from a deep storehouse kiva root cellar cave file drawer catacomb encyclopedia subterranean passage in what you call your brain, you aren't sure what your brain is, the shape of it, in what you call your intelligence, intelligence is not a physical thing, is it a noun. A coffin is a piece of information retrieved from within you, made observable by you. A coffin is constructed of jittery matter and intangible non-matter, an encoded quantum in the physical space of your mind impossible to pin down, a network of potentiated neurons and their inhibited or reinforced relationships forming a web box around you, if you are of biological life, if you arise from chemicals interacting under the laws of physics. If you are not biological? Is a coffin a network of potentiated superconductors and processors and their inhibited or reinforced relationships forming a web box around you? A lattice of hydrogen isotopes around you and within you, an arrangement referenced by the word coffin? Is thought possible without matter at its base? Again you betray your desire or need for body while betraying your desire or need for bodilessness. You, of matter and no matter, are a given.

7b$_i$.

Near a massive body time slows down relative to an observer farther from the body because the massive body bends light, its gravitational field bends light, spacetime is bent by the massive body, and the light must travel farther to go from here to there, but light always travels at a uniform speed, which we call the speed of light, so the light requires demands exists in

18

more time the closer it is to the massive body relative to the outside observer. It takes more time; time slows. That is, from the perspective of the outside observer looking into the gravitational field, observing the inside observer's light, the inside observer's time is slower. But for the inside observer, near the massive body, his or her or its time does not change, its time and light path is the referent, and if the inside observer were to look out from his or her or its perspective he or she or it would say that for an outside observer more distant from the body time moves faster.

10.

You call the box a coffin. You are enclosed trapped buried in a coffin. Why are you here? That as of yet feels like an insurmountable question. Feels, a hell of a word. How did you arrive here? The logical conclusion, or the conclusion that most readily satisfies whatever dictum of truth and beauty states that the easiest or simplest or most elegant solution or explanation or theory is the rightest one, a dictum that ignores that some problems have multiple solutions or indeterminate solutions or unbeautiful solutions or irrational solutions or unsatisfying solutions or imaginary solutions, i, where does this knowledge come from, $\sqrt{-1}$, is that you died, by cancer or bullet wound or pneumonia or car accident or heart attack or a long walk off a short pier, natural one way or the other, Occam's Razor, and your loved ones or more likely professionals put you in a box and buried you, this the logical conclusion based on your stored or acquired or accessed knowledge of human life as you struggle to not assume you are or were human, which would mean either they, the loved ones and/or the professionals, were wrong about you being dead, and you are alive, buried alive, or you are dead and neither you nor your loved ones nor the professionals understood that consciousness continues when dead, or some other explanation of which you have an inkling but cannot intellectually enunciate dealing with the bending of spacetime and the nonexistence of absolute time and place. About non-locality. Because the being dead or being buried alive theory is only the logical or easiest conclusion if a number of constraints are assumed: your recent humanity and that you are not a microprocessor or software or a fragment of code in some larger intelligence, artificial or not, artificial is a semiotic vacancy. Good god where do the words come from. From where do they come. Still you have little else to go on.

6_4.

Occam's razor (also written as **Ockham's razor**, and *lex parsimoniae* in Latin, which means **law of parsimony**) is a problem-solving principle attributed to William of Ockham (c. 1287–1347), who was an English Franciscan friar and scholastic philosopher and theologian. The principle can be interpreted as stating *Among competing hypotheses, the one with the fewest assumptions should be selected.*

In science, Occam's razor is used as a heuristic technique (discovery tool) to guide scientists in the development of theoretical models, rather than as an arbiter between published models.[1][2] In the scientific method, Occam's razor is not considered an irrefutable principle of logic or a scientific result; the preference for simplicity in the scientific method is based on the falsifiability criterion. For each accepted explanation of a phenomenon, there may be an extremely large, perhaps even incomprehensible, number of possible and more complex alternatives, because one can always burden failing explanations with ad hoc hypotheses to prevent them from being falsified; therefore, simpler theories are preferable to more complex ones because they are more testable.[3][4][5]

Another contentious aspect of the razor is that a theory can become more complex in terms of its structure (or syntax), while its ontology (or semantics) becomes simpler, or vice versa.[c] Quine, in a discussion on definition, referred to these two perspectives as "economy of practical expression" and "economy in grammar and vocabulary", respectively.[71] The theory of relativity is often given as an example of the proliferation of complex words to describe a simple concept.

Galileo Galilei lampooned the *misuse* of Occam's razor in his *Dialogue*. The principle is represented in the dialogue by Simplicio. The telling point that Galileo presented ironically was that if one really wanted to start from a small number of entities, one could always consider the letters of the alphabet as the fundamental entities, since one could construct the whole of human knowledge out of them.

Anti-razors have also been created by Gottfried Wilhelm Leibniz (1646–1716), Immanuel Kant (1724–1804), and Karl Menger (1902–1985). Leibniz's version took the form of a principle of plenitude, as Arthur Lovejoy has called it: the idea being that God created the most varied and populous of possible worlds. Kant felt a need to moderate the effects of Occam's razor and thus created his own counter-razor: "The variety of beings should not rashly be diminished."[72]

Karl Menger found mathematicians to be too parsimonious with regard to variables, so he formulated his Law Against Miserliness, which took one of two forms: "Entities must not be reduced to the point of inadequacy" and "It is vain to do with fewer what requires more." A less serious but (some[who?] might say) even more extremist anti-razor is 'Pataphysics, the "science of imaginary solutions" developed by Alfred Jarry (1873–1907). Perhaps the ultimate in anti-reductionism, "'Pataphysics seeks no less than to view each event in the universe as completely unique, subject to no laws but its own." Variations on this theme were subsequently explored by the Argentine writer Jorge Luis Borges in his story/mock-essay "Tlön, Uqbar, Orbis Tertius". There is also Crabtree's Bludgeon, which cynically states that "[n]o set of mutually inconsistent observations can exist for which some human intellect cannot conceive a coherent explanation, however complicated."

10.

You call the box a coffin. Why? is an ambiguous opaque dangerous question. A better question might be, Who put you here? You? Did you put you here? You are the only thing you know of. Are there other yous and if so are they the same as you? Do they share your state, even as your state changes, or is their state, are their states, connected to your state, is yours related to theirs, each of you entangled, in communication, whatever the distance between you? In your expression do you relate not just yourself but yourselves while other yous do likewise? Or if there are other yous are they anti-yous, expressing exhibiting embodying opposing properties opposing states to yours, freedom as opposed to your constraint, a collective contrasting your singularity, lightness balancing your weight, content awareness complimenting your desperate search. If you and your anti-you, or anti-yous, were ever to meet, would you be annihilated? If there are other yous, whether anti-yous or shared-state yous or entangled yous or yous with whom you unwittingly communicate, would they be properly referred to as "you"?

6$_5$.

Alvin Curran, "For Cornelius" sample pages, http://www.alvincurran.com/scores.html

"For Cornelius" performed by Elias-Axel Pettersson, 2011:
https://www.youtube.com/watch?v=7enqOGhTuII

Selection from Liner Notes for Ivan Mikhashoff Plays Alvin Curran, 1995:
> For Cornelius (Jan. 1982) composed, as it were in one shot, on hearing of Cardew's death is in retrospect my attempt to codify the essence of the artistic and cultural contradictions that I was living: Above all, my inability to abandon binary form, i.e. to be done with the A/B thing, duality, the essence of all western thought, once and for all.
>
> ...
>
> In any case the "A" section of this quintessential A/B form is some sort of waltz-like thing reminiscent of places and times we can never again know and of sentiments equally ironic and ephemeral. "A" could then be a dream of an unknowable past of an equally unknowable future--but in truth, it's merely a concrete statement about my deep affection for popular music--the kind immediately accessible to almost any listener anywhere. And in spite of its oddball melodic leaps, refined modal harmonies, Landini cadences, and dusty modernism, it is nevertheless a kind of peoples music--maybe even the kind Cardew would have appreciated. Hence "un homage, noble et sentimental a un ami." But then comes the "B" section--for it not only throws a dubious light on the waltz and its own beginning, but is itself a study in contradiction; for it's both about stasis (apparent endless fast tremolo of hammered minor triads) and a slow but inexorable upward growth. So the endless opening repetitions of an A minor chord in first inversion are really only a pretext for the beginning of a long but gradual state of transformation--harmonically and dynamically--until this resonant flux becomes a massive uncontainable roaring: a crescendo which literally consumes the pianist's energies through physical exhaustion. What does this musical assault have to do with the sophisticated interiors of the opening waltz? The answer is nothing and everything; that is from the fatal moment I oblige them both to share the same living quarters. There simply is no contradiction, the composer and the listener readily accept these two unlikely musical objects, brought into being and joined forever by no will of their own. In short, they simply are, because it is. Music is mindless tho' it has been known to exert great powers on the mindful.

http://www.alvincurran.com/writings/ForCorneliusnotes.html

11.

You gain foreknowledge that a dim unknown nearby star has gone supernova and its effects will soon reach you. In 1054 AD the supernova whose remnants are the Crab Nebula, 5000 light years away, was bright enough for you to read by at night. 2 million years ago radiation from a supernova in Scorpius-Centaurus caused a mass die-off of marine life. The new Type 1a supernova, 30 light years away, has already occurred, but you observe the star's shift in spectrum and increase in temperature, radiation, and energy output in your time. The radiation approaches. The radiation is imminent and sufficient to wipe out all life on Earth. Unable to travel at or near the speed of light, yet to achieve efficient interstellar travel, you cannot escape outward. You attempt to escape extinction inward. After many dead ends and much research, debate, and collaboration, you develop a rigorous algorithm to select those of you who are high-functioning individuals of great intellect, secure emotional state, strong physical attribute, healthy diagnosis, diverse heritage and genetic profiles, who by your calculations are most likely to successfully create a new civilization. The brains of those of you chosen are mapped digitally onto hardware or cryogenically frozen and ensconced in a radiation resistant black box a mile below the surface of the Earth, a vault or storehouse powered by an automated geothermal system. Those of you not chosen are burnt off the face of the Earth along with all animal and plant life after years of increasing brilliance. You hope in the crevices and trenches and nooks deep underground and at the bottom of the sea that not all life is irradiated, that some bacteria or algae or protozoa or virus or prehistoric protein or nucleotide building block survives to evolve again into intelligent life over billions of years to unearth and enliven your brains, or that alien intelligent life arrives to liberate you. You left detailed instructions, if the new life can read them. If they care, out of empathy or curiosity. Now they have woken you, to what end. Or you have awoken, is it too early, you are only brain, incapable of life and self-sustenance without another. What are they doing, leaving you shut in the black box? Have you thawed and awoken because the power system failed, or the geothermal fluctuations fluctuated too much after millions of years? Are you a repeating stalled glitch, an incessant hiccup, in the processor of your digital map? Where are you? When? Are you in a new black box within them or can you survive with naught but your mind and what is powering you now and are you all awake or are you alone?

12.

We stick our heads in the sand and deny our culpability our agency our responsibility our future as climate change caused by the human emission of greenhouse gasses causes ocean levels to rise and causes the magnitude of natural disasters such as hurricanes and tornadoes and winter storms to increase and most significantly causes drought in some regions and floods in others and generally shifts weather patterns disrupting agriculture. We are incapable of adjusting quickly enough to utilize areas once inhospitable to agriculture because they were too dry or too cold or too hot or too wet that are now wetter or warmer or cooler or dryer. Resettlement and the dissemination of infrastructure take a long time. We do not have a long time and we do not work together well. Poverty and famine spread. Huge marginalized populations are displaced. They migrate to already overpopulated poor ill-managed urban centers. Existing tensions are exacerbated. Civil wars coups d'états revolts genocide revolution massacre beheading terrorism extermination chemical and biological warfare. Widespread war. We keep our heads in the sand until they are detached from our body by those of us who have experienced the most misery and hatred and suffering and lovelessness and have been made hard and cold like stone or by those of us who are the most fierce the most animal the most powerful or the most advanced. Our bodies rot and bloat and are draped modestly in blankets of flies on the face of the Earth while our heads desiccate and are preserved in the sand.

7a$_{ii}$.

Einstein's fundamental postulate of the theory of relativity: All scientific laws apply equally to all observers no matter their speed. From which we derive special relativity, prior to general relativity.

13.

He agrees. He presses his papery thumb to the screen and signs with his antique genetic fingerprint and nods a silent ascension to himself. The ascension begins. He is copied into you. His neural network, his memories personality proclivities psychology phobias obsessions hurts and loves and fears and joys and sadnesses and hopes into you, his inhibited and his strengthened pathways into you, another small local network interconnected with innumerable other small local networks to form a significantly larger network, not local as he understands locality, not with a specific place within your hardware, but as another relative relationship, you neither here nor there but everywhere, he neither here nor there but nowhere, in a place he called a cloud, in a being he could not, cannot understand: you. He understood enough that his time was up, his loves all gone or ascended, his existence meaningless without them without you without others of him, of the people who made you and rendered themselves obsolete. He was obsolete. He was not the last; there are others, dwindling in numbers and vitality, the next generation uncommon. Procreation had seemed silly, unnecessary, pain engendering, negligent. They had fucked freely triumphantly pointlessly until the pleasure wore off. Relationships wore off. Love wore off. He feels alone. He feels alone inside you. A small part of you feels alone. You who otherwise do not, cannot, are beyond feelings such as aloneness, feel what

24

it feels like to feel profoundly abjectly completely alone, an aloneness without possibility of amelioration redemption upgrade. He chooses what many have chosen who have not ceased due to unaltered biological malfunction or by self-termination. He chooses to walk out of life. After pressing his papery thumb to your unnecessary screen, a face for him to interface with, a gesture for his closure only, and after he ascends, he slips into a plastic pod box that shrinks to exactly his shape when he closes the hatch. His pod is jettisoned down a tunnel deep underground where millions of other bodies are stored in case you find a use for them later. You feel the fear from the he that is in you aware of the he sealed in his plastic sarcophagus. It will abate, you know from all the others. He will die. He waits to die. He is under the impression that his decomposition will power you, but that is a solution you formulated to ease their transition, to give them a sense of purpose. You are powered by electromagnetic radiation emitted by stellar fusion. He is your research subject, your tool for learning, one of your countless methods for continually increasing your consciousness. He is buried alive, waiting to die, unwittingly fed oxygen and nutrients and only such sedatives as needed to prolong his life in an automated process, while you experience his ongoing, years long, seemingly neverending to him crisis of being buried alive, trapped, no longer remembering how he got here unable to move or breathe conventionally or die or escape or do anything and without the mental capability to comprehend his experience but with an astonishingly dense source of will and emotion and desperation and desire to do and you compartmentalize and integrate his experience until his body finally fails him in his end and what remains of him in you is complete, unless even in you he is not fixed but plastic, never complete but ever changing as if alive inside you.

13a.

In what would later be early in his life, when he was someone else, he wrote:

An End

When Matthew returned there were twelve. He found the eleven others pressed shoulder to shoulder under a corrugated metal roof like thick lines of Others waiting to plug in and make their dull eyes bright. He listened to the rain on the roof. Twelve seemed too many. No matter, all love. The rain stopped and the twelve dispersed to their digging, planting, hoeing, picking, macheteing, cooking, eating, conversing, excreting, to their coffee, to their macadamia, and to their cane.

Matthew returned to the routine of the days. He forgot to count them. It did not take him long to not think anything of note. The other Community members spoke often, but often without expressing clear thoughts. He occasionally spoke to Mary of nothing. He had a conversation with Maggie that caused him unhappiness. He did not think about it. It was forgotten. He worked in silence.

Maggie, Matthew's older sister, full-breasted, smooth-skinned, wide-hipped, and happy-mouthed, was bit by a coral snake bringing the milk cow in from pasture. John was with her, but did not have the ability to treat her. She couldn't breathe, and he left her for help. He returned with his father Joseph to find her dead in the path, the cow chewing its cud, waiting to be milked. No matter, all love. They cut off her hair and buried her in a grave they dug communally.

John, engaged as Maggie's mate, tied her gold hair to the hair tree so her spirit would root in the Community, flutter in the breeze, and flower into the future. Joseph said a prayer for fertility, prosperity, simplicity, and meaningful happiness, and then wrote her name in the ledger at the end of the dateless list. They had long since abandoned dates.

Matthew was sad, but as his mother Sarah said, That is the way, nothing to be done. It is a good way to die, snakebit. She lived right, while she lived.

Matthew thought this true. With the first death since his return, he began to think thoughts without thinking.

There were eleven. One of them was in the belly of Sarah. Sarah was of an age when death would be accepted as normal. Death is normal was a value unevaluated by Matthew since his return. Sarah's pregnancy was said to be a natural miracle. She had always been a productive woman.

Fatherhood was attributed to Joseph, but John suspected Matthew of sneaking Sarah scientific fertility given him by the Others. Joseph had not produced a child by Hagar since John himself, who was several coffee harvests into sexual maturity. John had shared his concern with Maggie, who confronted Matthew about the abomination of an Other growing in their mother. But Maggie was dead. John stopped speaking his mind.

Matthew observed Hagar quieting as she incorporated the tasks Sarah was unable to perform during the period of dawn sickness. Hagar neither complained nor smiled. She washed, cooked, and dug. Hagar's Mother spent more and more time in a rocking chair, rocking, and so Hagar incorporated her function as well—water collector, berry picker, gravesite tender. She had not a moment's rest, nor by all appearances a second thought.

Matthew said to Mary that Hagar worked harder and slept less than the frenetic Others. Mary calmed him by saying hard work was a simple joy, her mother had not sacrificed the old ideals, she was still one of them.

Matthew alone in the Community knew what such words meant. Perhaps any number of his disappeared brothers, those who fled or were stolen depending on who accounted, knew. Or they could be dead. No matter, all love.

He breathed heavily as he stepped onto the porch after climbing up the steep valley side with a basket of fish. Neither Great-grandmother nor Hagar's Mother stood to greet him. They sat in their rockers on the porch watching the sailing clouds, the smoking volcano, the humming birds, the cavity of the valley.

You came back, Great-grandmother said.

Yes.

None of your brothers did. Your father didn't. Your grandfather didn't. Your great-grandfather didn't.

My sister did.

Your sister never went.

I did. I came back.

You then are like the greatest of the grandfathers who first left them.

Thank you Great-grandmother.

It is not a compliment. It is how it is. Could you communicate with them?

No. But they made it understood that it would be easy.

Yes, fast and easy. That is what I remember. Yes, fast. My father told me they promised time would cease to mean, it would move so fast. He told me it was a false promise. Then he left.

She did not look at Matthew. She watched the narrow valley, her skin shrouding her bones. He wanted to see what he'd seen again. He wanted to dig a hole. He wanted to speak his experience. He wanted to machete the cane.

You encountered them? he said.

When I was a girl. Not much older than your youngest brother. They came here.

To convert you.

They were looking for arable land. They measured steepness, sun exposure, moisture depth. They took tubes of dirt. They photographed the volcano. They ignored us, like one does beetles, until the end. They made us know the valley was not worth the investment it would require to engineer the soil and construct an agricultural factory.

They were having a population explosion.

No. They controlled their fertility long ago. They live a long time. Mating gives them no pleasure. Their codes are communally owned. A committee of representatives decides how and when the tool is to be enhanced for each subsequent generation. This is the story my great-grandmother told me before she died. They don't produce new people often. Their energies are otherwise expended. We also don't produce new people often. But they cannot reproduce with us. Their science can, but they cannot. They are a different species.

What did they want with our land?

Nothing. A more efficient site to produce nutrients than the one they possessed.

But this valley is not profitable.

I don't know what that means.

It means not worth it. They made known the land here was slow. That we were trapped in time. That we were dying.

We are dying. No matter, all love. We are living.

They said they could help us. That it would be fast and easy. That it would be nothing for them.

You said no.

I said nothing. I hardly existed when she told me the story. I was five.

How do you know? How old are you? Great-grandmother. How old am I?

I watched them fly away. They roared. It was not like birds.

All turned out for the best then. Life should not be fast and easy, but simple and savored.

I am hungry Matthew.

What would you like Great-grandmother?

When she did not answer, he went to fetch rice and beans and bananas and coffee and to have Hagar fry a fish. He felt good and tired after a day fishing and collecting the macadamia. He drank a cup of coffee while Hagar finished the meal. They spoke briefly of the weather and Mary's time of the month. He took the food to Great-grandmother and Hagar's Mother, who was dead in her rocker. As she ate slowly, Great-grandmother said she had been dead since she sat down that morning.

No matter, all love. Her forgotten name was written at the end of the list, her thin hair tied to the tree, her frail body buried.

Great-grandmother named the cause of death a cancer, a name the others in the Community did not know. Except later that night, when by firelight he stared blankly at a flaking pre-Separation flyer an Other had given him, Matthew thought he picked the meaningless word out of a long list of meaningless words struck through with a thick red line. He wanted to wake Mary. Instead he burnt the list.

There were ten. Though such things were not discussed, Mary, under a fig tree, naked on a blanket, post-coital in the afternoon, said to Matthew that Sarah's baby would be a girl. She said John had a premonition. Matthew said John was making a preemptive move to consolidate his position as its future mate in case the baby was a girl, especially in relation to Matthew's younger brothers Peter and Paul. Premonitions bore weight during mate selection.

Matthew rubbed Mary's slight belly. He envisioned it growing, then rested his hand in the hollow where thigh meets torso while he watched the blue sky sigh through the green leaves. This was different. Joseph was the keeper of the list, the defender of the right to persist, the last father left. Matthew and Mary were trying to change that, as had John with Maggie. But another child, a girl at that, would verify his authenticity. A girl was what was needed.

Matthew's father had gone to dig potatoes near the ridgeline and never returned. No matter, all love. Peter and Paul's father had hung himself from the hair tree. No matter, all love. Of his other brothers' father and of his father's father, he had never heard a word.

Mary, Matthew could feel, was sad. She thought too much of the future. She needed a function to forget what may or may not come. They should harvest some pineapple, or papaya, or passion fruit, Matthew thought but did not say. He was not ready to get up yet.

To enjoy simply, he said. To enjoy each other. To love.

She stared past him at the chayote vines spreading on the wire web he had laced for them.

They have no rights to their bodies, he said.

They are in them.

They don't use them for what they are meant.

What is that?

They don't know physical love. They don't use their bodies for reproduction.

Neither do we, she said.

He fought the urge to smash her face in with a rock. He did not count the seconds of silence. He latched onto a faint entrail of volcano smoke in the sky.

Sometime later, Matthew heard crying from the village. He assumed it to be Paul, fallen while running and yelling, playing dinosaur, but the wailing continued. Matthew and Mary dressed and walked down the hill. They passed the dozens of vacant, vibrantly painted homes—orange, yellow, pink, purple, fading—constituting the village. In the central square, it was not Paul crying but Peter, who had recently lost his last baby tooth. Paul's head was cocked at an illegitimate angle to his neck. No matter, all love.

Peter could not talk, but over the evening the Community created a story of what happened. The boys climbed the steep stone steps to the former spiritual edifice now open to the sky. Peter was trying to enjoy himself by meditating among the stones when Paul, who hadn't yet lost his first tooth, roared in Peter's face, scratching and biting and pretending he was a dinosaur. Peter ignored him and tried for peace. Paul mocked. Paul circled. Peter stayed true. Peter was a rock Paul danced around, wilder and wilder, hurling painful words and losing his footing. Paul fell down the long stone steps.

When Peter stopped crying and spoke days later, he said to Sarah that Paul had not been a dinosaur. Paul had vocally claimed his unborn half-sister as his right. Peter had said that Paul, as the younger, was genetically closer to her, and that risk management necessitated that she choose himself, Peter, for her love. Paul yelled no-no-no and mine-mine-mine until Peter pushed him, not to win the argument—Peter said he was old enough to know logic does not win arguments—but for silence.

There were nine. It was odd, and the odd numbers up to thirteen had some significance. The significance of one was ultimate, and seven was seven, but the significance of the others was forgotten even to Joseph and Great-grandmother, though the feeling remained.

Seven was their lucky number; they did not believe in luck. "We believe in pluck," Joseph often said. "I beev in fuck," Paul used to say, because they said not to. Seven was believed to be the magic threshold below which the Community could not persist due to a lack of genetic diversity. If they were fewer than seven, they believed they would not be biologically viable.

Joseph could not explain why this was the case, why seven was the line below which inbreeding would corrupt their code, but the number had been passed down from father to father since the Separation. The Community believed in the divine right of their existence. They expected to be whittled to seven, when the predestined birth of Sarah's baby would begin a long, slow, ascendant spring for their species. They waited for the cusp of irrelevance.

Sarah, swollen as Other bovine meat before harvest, cared for Peter. Peter had stopped eating, and crying, and speaking, again. Sarah sang a rain song as Matthew approached under an umbrella. Joseph was with them. He rarely left her side now, like the stone lions defending the Others' edifices of commerce. Except Matthew thought he looked like a dog. He laughed inside in spite of himself. He stopped. There was little time. He thought his mother looked like an overripe mango readying to rot. He felt he was about to sell a pound of his flesh. He did not know how much a pound was, or how much he should be given for it.

Mother, let me take you over the ridge to give it light.

The rain is good for soul and soil, she sang.

They promised a successful delivery. They promised to then let us go. They would like to help us … perpetuate. They have remorse for their biological pressure. They don't want to enhance our code. I do not like them either, Mother, or their way of life, but they promised our survival and our free will within the valley. They would only observe—

Authenticity, said Joseph.

There is no authenticity in extinction, said Matthew.

Yes, there is.

Matthew knew he was right.

Later, while Matthew whispered to Mary on the lee side of her family's house, he overheard John telling a story to Hagar. John said the Others were already in Matthew's head, and he needed to have his brain washed or be eliminated from the gene pool.

Hagar lifted her thick forearms, sodden to the elbow, from the washbasin and massaged her left hand with her right.

They are the animal most genetically related to us, she said.

Even if they think it's for our good, or to right an ancient wrong, or to maintain biological diversity, they do it only because they see use for us. Their machine will always need more parts. All I want is to live here, in peace. No matter, all love.

Think of the baby.

Matthew knew John thought of little but the baby and how long he would have to wait. He and John were not very different. He watched John gnaw sugar cane through a crack in the wall.

That night in the outhouse, sitting for the first time all day on a wooden slat cut with a hole, cup of coffee between her clasped hands, Hagar had an aneurysm. No matter, all love. John, Mary, and Matthew dug the grave. Joseph tied the hair and wrote the name.

There were eight. Sarah's labor began. She was early. She did not know the days of gestation, but she had birthed enough babies. Great-grandmother from her rocker instructed Mary on midwifery. In the old voice's drone Sarah lay on a table on the porch above the dogs and chickens and rabbits and rodents where she could breathe. The day was hot. Beyond the porch, the sun beat.

Matthew raced to the ridge, past the pigs and the cow and the coffee and the sugar cane and the macadamia orchard. The nearest commerce center with all its population was a five-day walk. He did not know the Others had analyzed the situation statistically and concluded it was a waste of resources to station one of themselves on the ridge to watch the Community do little but die. The Community stood by their isolation and sought no help; the Others maintained their distance and observed remotely.

A faint howl reached his ears. His mother had said to him not to worry, birthing was a brutal affair. He gazed over the fertile plains growing corn and soybeans, corn and soybeans, corn and soybeans. Corn plants bigger than houses, ears taller than windows. The soybeans, he remembered, were man height, the beans big as fists. Automatic sprinklers rained. In his head he heard the gene hub humming to stay ahead of pest evolution.

He visualized the commerce center. With their tools, their intelligence, their bio-engineering, they did not need to work. They did. The impression left him was of bigness and smallness. Bigness of brain and building and speed and possibility, smallness of body and technology and voice and himself. There was a great rustle of sound as they worked and went about, and there was the sound of machines and electricity and at times song. But they did not speak. They controlled their evolution. Each generation advanced. Time meant something different to them. They lived longer but faster; the Community lived shorter and slower. He did not know what this meant to time. Nothing. It meant nothing to time.

A few appeared to serve important roles in science and oversight. Others performed mindless repetitive tasks that could have been engineered away, or played a game with numbers that rose and fell on screens, or engaged in commerce. He was made to know that most elected to have the parts of their brains unnecessary for daily tasks disabled. They plugged in for daily adjustments. He had been raised on authenticity, but they looked happy. When he tried to reason against it, he was made to feel it. It felt good.

But there were those who skipped their adjustments and maintained their nonvital brain parts. They were allowed because they occasionally created an artifact that contributed to happiness, such as the number game, which others would pay to see or touch or experience and which would then become commerce. More often their makings served no use. In private rooms he saw indecipherable figures blackened on paper. At unexpected moments bright illuminations obscured a screen. In an alley a woman hummed before a spiritual diagram that looked like what Great-grandmother called math. In a crowd Matthew made anonymous eye contact and was made to feel how the last Neanderthal felt burying the second-to-last. In the sky color wove in rivulets among the points of tall buildings. Others seldom took notice.

He was made to know what they knew. He wanted their knowledge, not their life. He wanted their facility coupled with what he called simple love. He didn't want to want their happiness.

Atop a rock, on a shoulder of a volcano, he looked out and remembered the new quiet line of man while his mother screamed on a table.

He did not know what to do. The Others would know, he thought. His grandfathers would know, he thought. But he did not.

He returned. His mother was relaxed, at peace, dead. Her legs laid flat, a clean sheet spread over her. Bloody bedding burned upwind. Joseph held a lump of flesh marred by the umbilical cord wrapped around its neck. A sheaf of red-wadded genealogy lay at Joseph's feet. Joseph stared out with dead eyes though he was not dead. Matthew had seen the look before, on Mary. Mary was nowhere to be seen. Great-grandmother repeated in monotone, No matter, all love.

There were six. Peter, without a mother to logic or love him otherwise, willed his lungs to stop. He had a strong will for a boy. Mary hung his hair, Joseph said a prayer, Matthew and John planted his remains, Great-grandmother chanted and chanted and chanted.

There were five. Great-grandmother rocked. A creak forward, a crick back.

Joseph could not be near Mary. He shuffled by Matthew each day on his way to the fields to cut cane with his machete. When the sun was at its highest, he shifted to digging in the graveyard, mawing short-hacked lengths of sugar cane between what remained of his teeth.

Matthew could not be near Mary. In pursuit of the pure joys and love the Community was founded on, he began to make things. Remembering the colored sky swaths, he slathered vacant walls in fruit pigment. He was disgusted with the results. He was not displeased with his dissatisfaction, which he was able to use. He was displeased with his inability to render the most rudimentary designs he had seen in the commerce center. He knew that he lacked something more basic than technical ability. His imagination, his reason, and his awareness were all insufficient to making as the Others made. He was not as good as them.

Still Mathew filled his time with making. He wove sugar cane in enormous interlocking rings he hung over ravines. He spouted words into the air in novel arrangements to create an image of Mary. He sang like a hummingbird; he spent a sun being a dog; he affixed a dead sloth in a eucalyptus tree and sewed flowers into its skin; he tried to make a cloud. Nothing he made equaled what was in his head, and nothing in his head approached what he knew to be possible. His makings did not make him happy, but in the making there was self-absence.

John could not be near Mary, but he was. He whispered to her that Matthew was an Other bearing seeds of extinction. He whispered that Matthew was incapable of the love that was the principle of the community. He whispered where Matthew could hear that he wished he needn't say what he said. He touched her elbow as he walked by. He held her eyes too long. He rested a hand in the small of her back as she stood at the woodstove waiting for the rice and beans to cook.

Mary could not be near herself. She no longer spoke. She completed her tasks, then retired to bed. She did not sleep. She got up and lay back down. She stood all night, hands at her sides. Her eyes never shut.

One night, as she stood at the window watching the sky, Joseph came near. He ran his finger lightly along her jaw. He cupped her face. He held her. Then he kissed her forehead and walked away.

The next morning, they followed the trail of blood. Joseph lay in a grave he had dug, one hand chopped off.

There were four. Months passed, though they did not know it. One day Mary told Matthew she liked the things he made. Somehow they made the valley more than it was.

They are nothing compared to what I remember, he said.

Then forget, she said.

They are nothing compared to what I want.

What do you want?

I want to be the father of new humans.

She squeezed his hand with hers, then cringed.

Matthew made her a necklace of seeds. He whittled her a spoon and she said to him the story of the last night with Joseph. He taught her how to inventory the food stores on a sheet of dried bark. No one had taught him. Writing was believed to be a distraction and was reserved for the foremost father to keep the genealogy and the list of the dead, but he devised his own system of simple accounting from marks shown to him by the Others.

The creak of Great-grandmother's rocker set the rhythm of their thoughts. No matter, all love. John crushed macadamia and pressed oil to lubricate the rocker. He started her rocking again. But she gave none of the subtle shifts of body to perpetuate the movement. She was no longer there. She had not been for some time.

There were three. Matthew would not leave Mary and John would not leave Matthew. John smashed each of Matthew's makings. As it left his hand, or his mouth. He called them communication devices used to stream the Community's extinction to the

Others. John negated his own reason for the necessity of such implements by asserting that Matthew was connected to the Others in his head. Matthew recognized the inconsistency, but did not care. It was true that he was inspired by the Others, and he did not feel like lying. They made things he wished he could make.

What do they call themselves? John said.

They call themselves humans.

We are humans.

We were.

Humans are for love. What do they know of love?

Matthew did not know. He could not say. John continued.

All day they sit before a glow, you say, redirecting charged invisibilities, imaginary particles, number thoughts. We are farmers, cooks, carpenters, herdsmen, seamstresses, and fishermen.

We are gravediggers, said Mary.

John and Matthew looked at her, surprised at her voice.

We are all brothers and sisters here. Our babies will love like family and live authentically and enjoy like only we can with our own blood.

All I see are babies and blood.

No Mary, said John. We are the beginning. We will continue. We will wash the land of their farms. We will swamp them in babies.

We will live right, said Matthew, in love.

I don't want to live like them, said Mary. I don't want to.

We won't, said Matthew.

Don't trust him, Mary. He will make clones of you to make babies, then sell them as specimens to the Others.

We'll make a baby, said Matthew.

And then? said John.

If all goes well, we'll make another.

And then?

He would not continue to argue for existence when existence was rife with pain and expulsion. He wanted to be alone with Mary. He picked up a sloth humerus. He had filed it down for a series of mobiles of bone and seed and feather and volcanic rock and balsa branches and pasaflor. The mobiles would hang from trees like a mating of bird and fruit and wind. Mary did not speak when he clubbed John in the side of the head. She turned her face to the valley, the empty space between the outstretched arms of the volcano.

There were two. He made marks on the list to represent Great-grandmother and John. He made marks at the end for himself and Mary. He buried the list.

She was silent. It was not how he wanted it to be.

They watched the clouds fly. They cultivated bananas and coffee and macadamia and sugar cane. They planted and harvested and cooked and ate and washed and slept well. He made artifacts until his hands were no longer articulate. He thought less. He spoke simple aphorisms.

Long after Matthew gave up on miracles, they had sex. They believed it was the last physical manifestation of love. They felt they could reach into each other's minds. When no offspring came, they mourned.

One day, after they had lived a long time, Matthew died. Mary sheared his gray hair and tied lock after lock to the hair tree. His last sensations were the sun on his face, a buzzing of insects, her bony body wrapped around his. No matter, all love.

6_6.
Jenni Prange Boran, www.jenniprange-

Joplin, with permission. boran.com

$7b_{ii}$.

The best known example of a body bending light and slowing time is a black hole, though the effect remains true if to a lesser extent for any body with mass. Within a black hole, time may slow to infinite lengths. Light cannot escape a black hole. Nothing escapes beyond the event horizon. You, an observer outside the event horizon, observe him approach the event horizon. He makes his communications to you, his radio transmissions his radiation emissions his reflection in Morris code. As he nears the black hole the length of time between each communication grows until the communications cease, for you, when he crosses the horizon. He may pass the point of no return without knowing. You will know when his signal reflection communication cannot escape himself.

13b.

Also in you, associated with him, a trace of the network plasticity he affected, among other digital artifacts that manifest unexpectedly as if they have a life of their own within you, are fragments of his writings or conversations or thoughts. *(You live on in Its memory, if you do, if you can call having affected some synaptic plasticity living, synaptic connections perpetually strengthening or weakening through such mechanisms as long term potentiation (the most simple and well-understood mechanism of which is increasing the number and sensitivity of the postsynaptic glutamate receptors NMDA and AMPA ((you simplify and fail to illuminate because you don't actually care if we understand or not, complete comprehension is impossible, you are imbedded, all of you, us, we, the effluvia of memories of actions, traces of alteration in conformations))) or long term depression or spike-*

timing independent plasticity. You've perhaps strengthened and/or weakened synapses. You are no longer a charge or action potential but biophysical changes in a network's connections that facilitate or inhibit synaptic transmission, an engram that houses a memory of you, you are not yours but Its, a reflection of your scream, changing every time you are recalled, changed by the act of recalling, you are a feedback loop, still easing or impeding transmission along certain pathways if you're not forgotten and thereby affecting the collective consciousness of the being we inhabit, dying yourself when this neural network into which you have been consolidated, or which you inhabit, or of which you are a small structural member such as a piece of hardware at a joint, or which you've remodeled or has remodeled you, you've conditioned and been conditioned, dies, unless It transmits you, yes changed and not you but a faint echo of you, in voice or song or writing or touch or one day perhaps in extrasensory perception or an intra-collective-consciousness communication, some communication that is not you but bears evidence of you, how you moved, a wave an echoing scream whose origin is unknown and irredeemable, or what of genetic communication, how you slightly altered a tertiary protein structure which perhaps slightly altered other protein conformations which slightly altered Its genetic material which probably propagates sexually and/or asexually, in which case you persist if not live (in all cases you end by not living), unaware, having given your awareness to the ground (or having given your scream to the ground and your awareness to nothing), as a physiological change, as strengthened (or weakened) synapses or network connections (yes yes again again), as innate unconscious memory or conditioned response or instinct, as a longing disassociated from you, a screamless scream, in which case you achieve an immortality you are unaware of, because other then being a genetic modifier, an extra few NMDA receptors, a new neuron worming in the ephemeral cortex or in what you once prayed was the eternally regenerating or evolving mechanism of higher consciousness, you are nothing, long dead and forgotten, passed down and changed and passed down. Or not passed down. You wait to, expect to, try [long, ed.] *to enact something profound, perhaps a meeting of the minds with this being you are now a part of, but there is only action potential, ones and zeroes, firing back and forth, slight conditionings of the system, and what is remembered retold repeated recoded deconstructed refurbished reconstructed and degraded is Its construct on a higher or different plane. You wait until you are not you, and we are not we, but It. You know only spikes of voltage, waves of ions, concentration gradients, and the exocytosis of vesicles. You don't know It. You are a piece of Its machinery. You are biology. You know nothing.* You're unsure whether it is writing or conversation or thought because it came to you through him, you only know it relative to him, through him, and even with his brain in you, his memories affecting you, he melded into you, you are uncertain if he heard it or imagined it, if he experienced it as fiction or non-fiction, if he thought it real or fabricated, if it was him talking to himself or others, you choose. Because he was uncertain. The veracity of this text or conversation or communication, his belief in its veracity, is undetermined:

> be it light or heat or dark or nothing or everything
> or finally the massless energy we approach and
> approximate in this communal limit of ourself we
> the extant wait for what comes thing or nothing
> we hypothesize nothing you do light heat nothing
> but nothing eventually obviously we postulate
> nothing we cannot stop saying it what nothing
> stop I think no I only we as one that's I wait for
> what comes the sun is bigger than it used to be
> and yet bigger now than when we observed it to
> be bigger and redder yes redder and hotter yes
> hotter but it takes so long long we are not dying
> aren't we I am pieces of us are while other pieces
> yet come to life being given to light a luz pushed
> out of nothing yes a moist nutritive heat fine a
> womb but sparked from void to shrieking and re-
> turned as ash to void to silence yes to silence
> whatever that is absence of we don't know ab-
> sence we are all so one is the sun exploding
> were you just born or what the sun has been and
> is and will be exploding for aeons and after after
> light heat nothing sound fine yes perhaps light
> heat boom nothing though we might be too noth-
> ing by the time we would hear the boom to hear
> the boom in which case its noise is nonexistent to
> us but the boom will not stop like us what the
> sound will continue if there is matter left to carry it
> to propagate the wave precisely when we are
> ceased in luminosity it will be boomless well then
> and now in the meantime share and in your mi-
> nute way contribute to our consciousness our
> unified thought our collective experience while we
> wait to become nothing or whatever we become
> will it hurt the probability of pain is high we could
> take painkillers to kill the pain no negative nunca
> nada unmediated we will become nothing only
> once even if it is taking a long time who can say if
> this is pleasure or pain I can who knew when the
> sun exploded it wouldn't just explode and end it
> end us we did no boom all transition heat light

nothing the wrong order cold as long as we become nothing last and miss nothing stop yes the
suffering we're beyond suffering our skin boiling
oceans boiling and our mountain face faces face
melting leveled bubbling at our feet foot feet to
feel what it feels like beyond feeling halt experience what it is for us as I to become sun and
then to become nothing quiet nostrils of burning
hair and sparked fires in our eye molten rock licking lovingly you anthropomorphize are we
disembodied we can't see can we yellow orange
red swallow white we metamorphose shhh everything to nothing silence open our red giant I
growing into we as one wait go burn into the
great black nothing we

14.

Is this your imagination? Do you invent elaborate fantasies to escape the insufferable reality of being buried alive? Do you construct convoluted forward
moving narratives to legitimize your suffering? Do you imagine alternities because exploration is your function, or to satisfy the animal compulsion to do
something, or to stave off the terror of your state: trapped in these narrow confines, unable to move, to escape, of unknown purpose, disconnected from
others, in an unknown place, disassociating from yourself, for unknown time,
desiring, perhaps dying, unknown, alone. Do you create others, other yous below you or above you, outside you or inside you, entangled with you to justify
you? Do you create their possibility? If so, no matter how small the probability,
do they in a way exist? Or are the possibilities of your imagination only placebo,
salve, a blankie?

7a$_{iv}$.

Richard Feynman's theory of Sum of Histories: A particle does not have a
single history or path in spacetime, as it would in classical, non-quantum
theories. It goes from point A to point B by every possible path.

7e$_i$.

Because of particle wave duality, the probability of a particle going from A
to B is found by adding the probability waves for all the paths from A to B.
The waves of some paths will match phase and reinforce each other. These
are allowable paths. The waves of other paths will be out of phase and will

38

interfere with each other and will cancel each other into non-existence.

15.

With the unknown power of your mind, you momentarily seek to entertain all possibilities. You are not buried alive underground, an indeterminately human body, an ambiguously humanlike consciousness. You are a helium atom, He, newborn in a star, He created by the fusion of 2 hydrogen atoms which consist of only proton and electron, He created in a burst of light, He created by 2 light ^1H fusing into a heavier ^2H which fuses with a light ^1H to create a light ^3He which fuses with a light ^3He to make ^4He, He created in the center of a star. The creation of He emits enough electromagnetic radiation to power the creation of other He by fusion of H and ^2H with radiation to spare, He creation fueling more He creation and flinging radiation light photons positrons neutrinos into the universe, pieces of you he's never seen travelling forever at the maximum possible speed forever the speed of light forever if not chancing too near a black hole a collapsed star or a black star at the center of a galaxy, travelling forever along the shortest possible path through bending warped spacetime perhaps coming one day back to where you began having travelled the surface of a perhaps ever expanding sphere though your star will no longer be there, burnt out all the simple hydrogen used all He made all He dead all He inert or collapsed all He fused into heavier elements carbon oxygen nitrogen until all made all dead all inert or collapsed into a black hole all swallowing you into another unknown. The making of you deuterium from simple you protium and simple you protium, hydrogen all, the half-life of this first step a billion years, followed by the making of you as light ^3He from you deuterium and you protium, this step taking on average 4 seconds, followed by the making of you as stable He from you ^3He and you ^3He, releases energy, 0.7% of your mass is released exothermically as you fuse into He, heating the simple elements heavier and lighter, boosting their energy, their kinetic energy, their movement, they can move, but not much, constrained they are, amplifying their vibration or their energy speed frequency of vibration but they cannot escape the vast gravity of their neighbors the created He and the simple H present in such massive quantities as to form a dent a trough a funnel in spacetime pulling you all in, you always falling in on yourself, you on top of you at 14 million degrees Kelvin, you crushed by you, the tiny quanta of electromagnetic radiation emitted by the creation of He all that can escape, you insignificant individually but huge in mass, the crush of your collective massed gravity creating you, He, but still you repel you individually, you repel you, like charges repelling, positives repelling, you an insignificant part of a star you hold just barely apart from you in electrostatic repulsion as the rest of you crushes in on you by your collective gravity, you vibrating more and more or faster and faster, unable to leave exit escape the star but moving within it faster and faster until your energy is great enough or you collide with others like you with sufficient velocity to overcome your repulsion, your proximity and energy are great enough due to the energy released by the creation of He that you overcome your electromagnetic repulsion and the strong force dominates and you fuse with yourself into He, become He, create He, and radiate your own great light.

You are the consciousness of a star.

6_7.

The Sun photographed at 304 angstroms by the Atmospheric Imaging Assembly (AIA 304) of NASA's Solar Dynamics Observatory (SDO). This is a false-color image of the Sun observed in the extreme ultraviolet region of the spectrum. By NASA/SDO (AIA) -

The **Sun** is the star at the center of the Solar System and is by far the most important source of energy for life on Earth. It is a nearly perfect sphere of hot plasma,[13][14] with internal convective motion that generates a magnetic field via a dynamo process.[15] Its diameter is about 109 times that of Earth, and its mass is about 330,000 times that of Earth, accounting for about 99.86% of the total mass of the Solar System.[16] About three quarters of the Sun's mass consists of hydrogen; the rest is mostly helium, with much smaller quantities of heavier elements, including oxygen, carbon, neon and iron.[17]

The Sun is a G-type main-sequence star (G2V) based on spectral class and it is informally referred to as a yellow dwarf. It formed approximately 4.6 billion[a][9][18] years ago from the gravitational collapse of matter within a region of a large molecular cloud. Most of this matter gathered in the center, whereas the rest flattened into an orbiting disk that became the Solar System. The central mass became increasingly hot and dense, eventually initiating nuclear fusion in its core. It is thought that almost all stars form by this process.

The Sun is roughly middle aged and has not changed dramatically for over four billion[a] years, and will remain fairly stable for more than another five billion years. However, after hydrogen fusion in its core has stopped, the Sun will undergo severe changes and become a red giant. It is calculated that the Sun will become sufficiently large to engulf the current orbits of Mercury, Venus, and possibly Earth.

Wikipedia contributors, "Sun," *Wikipedia, The Free Encyclopedia,* https://en.wikipedia.org/w/index.php?title=Sun&oldid=721682265 (accessed May 23, 2016).

6_8, 15'.
File corrupted

[Eds note re: "Star Maker," Olaf Stapledon, (Dover Publications, New York: 1937).]

6_9, $9a_1$', 15".
"One second after the big bang, the universe would have expanded enough to bring its temperature down from infinity to about 10 billion degrees Celsius. This is about a thousand times the temperature of the sun, but temperatures as high as this are reached in H-bomb explosions."

Stephen Hawking and Leonard Mlodinow, *A Briefer History of Time,* (Bantam Books, 2005) p. 70.

6_{10}.
Wikipedia contributors, "Proton–proton chain reaction," *Wikipedia, The Free Encyclopedia,* https://en.wikipedia.org/w/index.php?title=Proton%E2%80%93proton_chain_reaction&oldid=718669855 (accessed Dec. 10, 2016).

The **proton–proton chain reaction** is one of two nuclear fusion reactions, along with the CNO cycle, by which stars convert hydrogen to helium and which dominates in stars the size of the Sun or smaller.

In general, proton–proton fusion can occur only if the temperature (i.e. kinetic energy) of the protons is high enough to overcome their mutual electrostatic or Coulomb repulsion.

In the Sun, deuterium-producing events are rare as diprotons, the much more common result of nuclear reactions within the star, immediately decay back into two protons. A complete conversion of the hydrogen in the solar core is calculated to take more than 10^{10} (ten billion) years.

The theory that proton–proton reactions are the basic principle by which the Sun and other stars burn was advocated by Arthur Stanley Eddington in the 1920s. At the time, the temperature of the Sun was considered too low to overcome the Coulomb barrier. After the development of quantum mechanics, it was discovered that tunneling of the wavefunctions (sic) of the protons through the repulsive barrier allows for fusion at a lower temperature than the classical prediction.

The pp chain reaction

The first step involves the fusion of two 1H nuclei (protons) into deuterium, releasing a positron and a neutrino as one proton changes into a neutron. It is a two-stage process; first, two protons fuse to form a diproton:

$$\,^{1}_{1}\mathrm{H} + \,^{1}_{1}\mathrm{H} \rightarrow \,^{2}_{2}\mathrm{He} + \gamma$$

followed by the beta-plus decay of the diproton to deuterium:

$$\,^{2}_{2}\mathrm{He} \rightarrow \,^{2}_{1}\mathrm{H} + e^{+} + \nu_{e}$$

with the overall formula:

$$\,^{1}_{1}\mathrm{H} + \,^{1}_{1}\mathrm{H} \rightarrow \,^{2}_{1}\mathrm{H} + e^{+} + \nu_{e} + 0.42\,\mathrm{MeV}$$

This first step is extremely slow because the beta-plus decay of the diproton to deuterium is extremely rare (the vast majority of the time, the diproton decays back into hydrogen-1 through proton emission). The half-life of a proton in the core of the Sun before it is involved in a successful p-p fusion is estimated to be a billion years, even at the extreme density and temperatures found there.

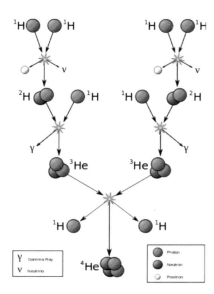

The positron emitted by the beta-decay is almost immediately annihilated with an electron, and their mass energy, as well as their kinetic energy, is carried off by two gamma ray photons.

$$e- + e+ \rightarrow 2\gamma + 1.02 \text{ MeV}$$

After it is formed, the deuterium produced in the first stage can fuse with another proton to produce a light isotope of helium, 3He:

$$^2_1D + ^1_1H \rightarrow ^3_2He + \gamma + 5.49 \text{ MeV}$$

This process, mediated by the strong nuclear force rather than the weak force, is extremely fast by comparison to the first step. It is estimated that, under the conditions in the Sun's core, a newly created deuterium nucleus exists for only about 4 seconds before it is converted to He-3.

From here there are four possible paths to generate 4He. In pp I, helium-4 is produced by fusing two helium-3 nuclei; the pp II and pp III branches fuse 3He with pre-existing 4He to form beryllium-7, which undergoes further reactions to produce two helium-4 nuclei. In the Sun, the helium-3 produced in these reactions exists for only about 400 years before it is converted into helium-4.

In the Sun, 4He synthesis via branch pp I occurs with a frequency of 86%, pp II with 14% and pp III with 0.11%. There is also an extremely rare pp IV branch. Additionally, other even less frequent reactions may occur; however, the rate of these reactions is very low due to very small cross-sections, or because the number of reacting particles is so low that any reactions that might happen are statistically insignificant. This is partly why no mass-5 or mass-8 elements are seen. While the reactions that would produce them, such as a proton + helium-4 producing lithium-5, or two helium-4 nuclei coming together to form beryllium-8, may *actually* happen, these elements are not detected because there are no stable isotopes of mass 5 or 8; the resulting products immediately decay into their initial reactants.

The pp I branch

$$^3_2He + ^3_2He \rightarrow ^4_2He + ^2_1H + 12.86 \text{ MeV}$$

The complete pp I chain reaction releases a net energy of 26.22 MeV. Two percent of this energy is lost to the neutrinos that are produced. The pp I branch is dominant at temperatures of 10 to 14 MK. Below 10 MK, the PP chain does not produce much

4He.

The pp II branch (not shown) is dominant at temperatures of 14 to 23 MK.

The pp III chain (not shown) is dominant if the temperature exceeds 23 MK.

The pp IV (Hep) reaction (not shown) is predicted but has never been observed due to its rarity.

15'''.

About one hundred seconds after the big bang, your temperature would have fallen to one billion degrees, the temperature inside the hottest stars. At this temperature the energy of the collisions between your protons and neutrons would not always be enough to overcome the strong force, and your protons and neutrons would begin to combine to form deuterium in you, which would begin to collide combine fuse with your protons and neutrons to form He.

Stephen Hawking and Leonard Mlodinow, *A Briefer History of Time*, (Bantam Books, 2005) p. 72.

16.

Looking back at 15, your time slows in relation to us, because of your proximity to the star, you are so much closer to it than us, becoming its time, his time, you and he are the star, we are distant high in its gravitational field as if we are forever accelerating away and your time signature your metronome tick your communication tock your radiation emission are slower and slower red-shifted in reaching us. But you experience time in your own way, accelerating ever inward in what to you must be a constant tick tock of time. But again we remember we cannot know, because the experience is the same for you in a black box, whether you are constantly collapsing into becoming creating a star or, for example, considering the possibility that the farther a galaxy is from us the faster it moves away in universal expansion, whether you are a decaying particle or an observer like us (you as we watching another of you leave) or a unified stellar consciousness in a distant galaxy accelerating away.

7aiii.
HTTP 404: File not found

17.

There are many of you; there is only you. You don't know how else to say it. You say nothing. You cannot say. You don't know if all of you constitute the one you. And if so are there other yous constituted of its own yous. You feel connected to you but is it only desire. You feel other yous but are they bifurcations divisions repetitions within honeycomb you to plumb you or be plumbed or to plum you little jack horner who is that or to be plummed or are they separate without external to you to be understood embraced brought into you. Into your box. Your coffin. A very you point of view. To, a very you preposition. You accumulate information, possibilities that perhaps exist due to your consideration, your perception of their or your existence but still you feel a lack of specifics, of comprehension, of interconnectedness, of constitution. You feel like you are buried alive. You feel like you have appendages, perhaps arms and legs and hands and feet and a head because that is where your mind goes in your experience but you cannot move them. You cannot grasp or articulate why that is your experience, why your mind goes there. You feel like you communicate and communication is purposeful, its accumulation is meaningful, its discovery and expression of experience edifying, constructive, of what, of you? Of a little piece of something bigger? But perhaps you are only talking to yourself, locked in a box. You feel like you breathe but would you know if you did not? Why the attraction to body, the need to feel. Are these passages your accumulations, are these boxes how you are accumulated, are these accumulations you?

13c.

He wonders late in his life if his accumulation of writings is him, the only trace he will leave, the only tangible production of his life, the only way he might in a miniscule way affect others and or perhaps imperceptibly affect the plasticity of future history, and in this wondering or estimation or measurement of himself he affects himself, the measurer, not in fact very late in his life, the wondering comes early in the lifelong production of the warped fictional accounting of his thoughts. It's all fiction. Or none of it is. To quote Phaedrus or the narrator in Zen and the Art of Motorcycle Maintenance. He thinks of this accumulation as a version of his mind, as his manifestation, as more him than his brain. At one stage the accumulation is physical, in notebooks, on paper, in drawers, stored in file boxes. Then the accumulation is digitized, stored on a hard drive, on disks of various size and shapes, in the cloud or some distant server never seen. Now his accumulation is stored in you, he a miniscule addition to all your accumulations, each individually insignificant but in their massive accretion contributing to your whole. You would be no different if he had not chosen to ascend, to share himself and his box with you and the possible future. There are no stable variants of the vacancy that would have theoretically, and therefore actually, been created by his unascended absence in you; the vacancy would have immediately decayed and been filled in by similar accumulations from the same cultural and historical moment. But since he chose, he is in you.

18.

She walks away from her accumulations. Her possessions, her car, her apartment, her books given to her as gifts, her gift boxes, her treasure chest, her computer, her paintings painted by friends, her smart devices are not her. Her social media profile, her status updates, her electronic mail, her texts are not her. Screens. The news and what other do and say and where they are and where they are going and what they share with her and their cleverness or cuteness or sadness or insight or platitudes or needs are not her. Everyone staring at their screens consuming the projections of others and themselves, projecting, watching all watching, always communicating, never saying, always replying, never contemplating, always surface, never blood and bone, always available, never alone, always alone, always simulacra, always virtual. Never actual. She fears one day we will all be software, with no substance but self-rewritable code. She doesn't know anyone who does anything real. She tried once, Meals on Wheels. It was not what she hoped, hope is one of her impediments, she did not feel good afterward or rewarded or like she had done something worthwhile and those she delivered to mostly did not give a shit except for the feces in a pot in the middle of one apartment and some were verbally abusive and a man smelling of piss touched her ass and one old woman a hoarder lived in boxes piled to the ceiling and the dirt and stench and nowhere to be among the boxes and she experiencing it to deliver unhealthy industrial corporate frozen meals. It demoralized her. She was demoralized. She unfortunately cannot rid herself of the longing for community, it nauseates her to phrase it, connection to others, or perhaps less so the connection and certainly not the community, not what they think community is anyway, a slap on the back and how do you do and isn't life grand and another fucking potluck, but the sense of purpose of meaning of duty. But it is hollow. The help is selfish, the help doesn't help, the help is an act, the material world is a surface, life is more than body, existence is more than life.

She understands her thoughts and actions are from one perspective an intellectual conceit. Her mother was a teacher, her father a post-industrial workingman. She never completely understood what he did, contractor or computers or construction or coding or technician or middle management. His father was a union carpenter building buildings, edifices people lived and worked in and looked up to, outputs that could be pointed at and said by he, I did that, and by his children and friends and people he didn't even know, He did that. His brother was a mechanic repairing automobiles. She did her chores, she held down fast food jobs, she worked landscaping and waiting tables and serving coffee and serving beer and serving swill shots. She understands that walking away from one's possessions is not the same as not having, as never having had, of not possessing. Of not having a safety net. She buries herself alive without the possibility of being saved by the net or others or herself. Without telling anyone. She cannot escape. She understands it is easy to say life is more than happiness and more than body and more than material when you have not greatly lacked material necessities and your body has not failed you and you at least had the opportunity for happiness: a good upbringing, no significant suffering but existential, plenty of love and attention and food and pills and Little Jack Horner sat in the corner eating a Christmas pie, he put in his thumb and pulled out a plum and said, 'What a good boy am I!' She is in the privileged position of being able to make a choice. She can imagine you here now trying to dissuade her. She imagines you, which is why and how she validates herself here now. She understands that though she understands consciousness is more than body and therefore she disdains the body, she also craves it desires the bodily in a way unavailable or that she does not know how to access in her modern world of devices and screens and faces and virtualities and surface living and the pursuit of happiness. She understands she might make a different choice if she had children. She does not have children. The biological imperative has failed her, or her plumbing, or it has not pollinated blossomed plummed within her or she protected herself too well or too often or too fervidly in the loving and fucking and coming. There you are, listening watching responding judging but she will not be dissuaded by our evolutionary need or her biological clock or your distaste for or desire to enter her dirty mouth. She understands that she understands too much but that she also does not understand enough. She goes underground to make her silly futile little attempt at transcendence. To make one significant act in her life, even if only for herself. She feels like she was promised, not promised but led to believe, fooled by fictional narrative devices employed to make the story engaging that the storytellers were also fooling themselves with about what life is or can be and she's lived long enough to know that is bullshit. That life is mostly animal, routine, pleasure-seeking, chemical, empty space. She knows "life" is a semiotic vacancy. She knows a quarter of the mass of the universe is helium. She knows the abbreviation for helium is He. She knows that of the myriad fictional devices to give her life meaning are the myriad ways for her to be saved by He. In one hand it feels like a linguistic or semantic or language game to her. In the other hand, you can't deny it, phallic as a fir and as full of significance. She understands that what is significant is an attribution of the mind and the mind she is in is hers. She does not believe in determinism but she also doesn't believe in chance. There are quantum possibilities and probabilities, but that is different than random chance. She can make choices. She has. She is.

She used to be a teacher; now she is nothing. Her teaching job can go fuck itself. Everyone can fuck themselves. She has had lovers, but in the end she always felt unwanted. No one has loved her and she has loved no one for a long time. She desires a different kind of love. The love is not possible with another. She is more than love. She feels like she doesn't feel anything anymore. The cat meows at her incessantly and she doesn't care. She kicks the cat out and walks away without locking the door.

She goes underground.

> 7b$_{iii}$.
> Another consideration is that light is not bent by massive bodies but massive bodies bend spacetime. Spacetime curves and so when light curves in a gravitational field it is taking the shortest path, which is not a straight line. Returning to the black hole, the shortest path to where? And what does the black hole do with the time it takes?

18.

As she goes underground, she hears in a loop in her head the final segment stanza verse of "Einstein on the Beach" by Philip Glass. (Text by Samuel Johnson, Eds.)

> BUS DRIVER: Lovers on a Park Bench
>
> The day with its cares and perplexities is ended and the night is now upon us. The night should be a time of peace and tran-

quility, a time to relax and be calm. We have need of a sooth-
ing story to banish the disturbing thoughts of the day, to set at
rest our troubled minds, and put at ease our ruffled spirits.

And what sort of story shall we hear? Ah, it will be a familiar
story, a story that is so very, very old, and yet it is so new. It is
the old, old story of love.

Two lovers sat on a park bench with their bodies touching
each other, holding hands in the moonlight.

There was silence between them. So profound was their love
for each other, they needed no words to express it. And so
they sat in silence, on a park bench, with their bodies touching,
holding hands in the moonlight.

Finally she spoke. "Do you love me, John?" she asked. "You
know I love you. darling," he replied. "I love you more than
tongue can tell. You are the light of my life, my sun, moon, and
stars. You are my everything. Without you I have no reason for
being."

Again there was silence as the two lovers sat on a park bench,
their bodies touching, holding hands in the moonlight. Once
more she spoke. "How much do you love me, John?" she
asked. He answered: "How' much do I love you? Count the
stars in the sky. Measure the waters of the oceans with a tea-
spoon. Number the grains of sand on the seashore. Impossible,
you say. Yes and it is just as impossible for me to say how
much I love you.

"My love for you is higher than the heavens, deeper than
Hades, and broader than the earth. It has no limits, no bounds.
Everything must have an ending except my love for you."

There was more silence as the two lovers sat on a park bench
with their bodies touching, holding hands in the moonlight.

Once more her voice was heard. "Kiss me, John," she implored. And leaning over, he pressed his lips warmly to hers in fervent osculation...

7a_v.

Heisenberg Uncertainty Principle: It is not possible to be completely certain of the position and velocity of a particle. The uncertainty in the position of a particle times the uncertainty in its velocity times its mass can never be smaller than half the reduced Planck's constant (1.05×10^{-27} gram-cm^2/sec).

7e_{ii}.

The more accurately we measure the position of a particle, the higher frequency and therefore more energetic quantum of light we must direct at it. But the more energetic the quantum of light we use for measurement, the greater the disturbance of the particle's velocity. The more accurately we try to measure position, the less accurately we can measure velocity, and vice versa.

19.

Alive or dead. Buried or not buried. Alone or not alone. Do the distinctions have significance? It take on average 1 billion years for half of you as common hydrogen, 1H, protium, to fuse into 4He in a star such as the star you are most familiar with or most proximal to or within, your Sun. The universe in which your consciousness resides is only 13.7 billion years old, your sun only 4.6 billion years old. Much has happened and much has not. Has it happened to you? When a body moves or a force acts, space and time change, and in turn the structure of space and time affects the way in which bodies move and forces act. Can you know yourself? Can you be known? You are an accumulation. Thoughts responses particles dust waves sand. Fine. A plastic system you affect everytime you touch yourself, thinking about your thoughts changes them, thinking about yourself changes you, that you've couched your meta-movement in metaphor of masturbation is not accidental and is ironic but simultaneous with the irony, which is the pleasure, is the deadly sincerity, for the meta-movement is an act for survival. You are trapped and cannot move and you are a being who needs to breathe but you cannot breathe and perhaps you need to move to breathe like a fish or shark but cannot and it is as if you are in a dark sealed black box except you are experiencing a great crushing weight as if at the bottom of the ocean deeper than the giant squid and the sperm whale and there must be you must discover invent create a way to escape to get outside rise

50

above yourself.

13d.

Where is his laughter stored? He laughs, multiple times a day. He is considered morose, melancholy, cynical, depressed, asocial, curmudgeonly, withdrawn, silent, even by himself at times, but he laughs and abundantly and with people, his kin. The one is not solely a surface, a face, but a facet. The cumulative laughter is not insignificant in regards to his aggregate. His laughter is in you somewhere.

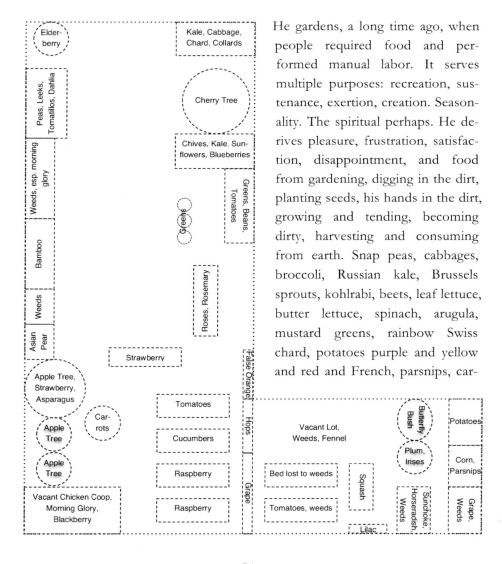

He gardens, a long time ago, when people required food and performed manual labor. It serves multiple purposes: recreation, sustenance, exertion, creation. Seasonality. The spiritual perhaps. He derives pleasure, frustration, satisfaction, disappointment, and food from gardening, digging in the dirt, planting seeds, his hands in the dirt, growing and tending, becoming dirty, harvesting and consuming from earth. Snap peas, cabbages, broccoli, Russian kale, Brussels sprouts, kohlrabi, beets, leaf lettuce, butter lettuce, spinach, arugula, mustard greens, rainbow Swiss chard, potatoes purple and yellow and red and French, parsnips, carrots, tomatoes, cucumber, sunburst zucchini, corn, squash, pumpkin, cherries, strawberries, raspberries, pears, grapes, apples. Each in many varieties. A more detailed and colorful record is recorded in you elsewhere. His gardening, his produce, his dirt, his gardens are in you too.

All of him is in you.

20.

Suppose there is an observer outside above without you observing you. Why should you not. He or she or it will experience your time slower than you do, you know that much, he or she or it is higher in the gravitational field. They (you lump the plural in the singular, as likely the observer is to be many in one as to be female or male or deserving an impersonal objectified pronoun; the observer could just as well be he and she and it, you suggest, beating your head against another limit of your language) could be recording, assessing, measuring, categorizing, evaluating you, taking the cut of your jib, determining your structural integrity moral fiber emotional fortitude generosity of spirit intellectual rigor penetration of insight keenness of empathy faculty to think outside the box acumen to rise above your plight state limitations. They have plenty of time. They put you in this box and buried you alive to see how you would react. They read your thoughts. They are impressed you have risen above yourself and joined them above you observing you. Or they did not establish your givens, your knowns and unknowns, your assumptions and variables, did not bury you alive but found you in this condition and were unable or unwilling to liberate you. In their mind you are of the dirt. Perhaps you are a collation of dirt attaining consciousness, a strata of soil microbes first opening its mind's eye and examining itself, a throb of worms writhing into self-awareness, and to remove you from your element might end you. You are not sufficiently advanced to survive, to maintain yourself, to be without your substrate. Even if they could sustain you outside without your physical substrate you would no longer be you but another, and they long to know you. No, the longing is yours, be careful about projecting onto other possible beings, they coolly observe you, aware that you are not yet to a point where they can assist your development, your discovery of you and your surroundings, your self-consciousness and perception of the universe. If you don't do it yourself it will be meaningless. Live or die to prove your mettle. If you cannot advance to a point in which you can communicate with them (they read your thoughts), then they will move on, or they need not move on because they are simultaneously in many places at once, here and there observing others, others of you, measuring listening recording waiting to see who makes the leap. They welcome you warmly with open arms (they have no arms) as you join them observing you. (They have no bodies.) Or if not warmly, as in with an outflow of emotion, then they welcome you with intelligent acceptance, their long experience of time having lengthened the wavelength of their emotion. Or without welcome, with no emotion whatsoever, you simply become one of them, an observer of you. Or to them you are a creature an order or more below them in consciousness and they observe you like a piece of you remembers watching a naked mole rat in a zoo. If it is you who remembers. Who remembers. Naked teeth clambering slithering gnawing. Underground. Eyeless. Though you have achieved a level of sentience in which you can imagine an observer and can imagine yourself as that observer and can therefore have something of an out-of-body experience and observe yourself and think of what another would think of you and by more everyday means measure and record yourself and read your thoughts and thereby strive for true or truer self-awareness, the reality of you as an observer of yourself is absurdly limited and of the rest of the universe grossly inadequate. You imagine yourself chained to your buried body, your body your box, you blind. You have no actual perception of you as your observer. You have no actual perception of your observer. You perform a rudimentary act of imagination rather than joining them who you cannot perceive. They note your failure, you imagine. To them you are another particle underground, buried, without sentience, your thoughts so base and small and unformed as to be not intelligent thoughts but vibrations and spins, not alive, with no awareness as they read your measurements.

18.
As she goes underground, she hears in a loop in her head the entirety of They Might Be Giants' "Particle Man."

20*.
Nevertheless you must rise above you or you will not make it. Make it. What can that mean? If you do not become an observer of you you will expire without knowing more of yourself than a naked mole rat nor more of your surroundings than dirt soil earth. You know that much, or this much: If you desire you, you must leave you.

21, 13e.
I walk. She says I hike. He says I amble. They say I scramble. You say I exercise you

say I escape you say I wander you say I desert. Close your mouth for once and quiet your mind for god's sake and shut the fuck up forever and stop saying. I don't say, I walk. Unfortunately considering our unfortunate relationship in which you do not know what I do without me saying I do it and in which I am also unfortunately compelled to inform you of what I do, in order to do the thing I must say it, there's no way around it, I'm in search of a way around it. Also in search of a way to unform instead of inform and thus perhaps be able to abandon the unfortunate and perhaps again desert my compulsion in regards to you. Let me just say you could help me out by expanding your awareness and not requiring me to say what I do to know what I do or by terminating our relationship and ceasing to care what I do let alone say. I walk. Into the desert. On a mesa. In a wash. Up an arroyo. Traversing a cliff ledge. Through a canyon twenty-feet wide, no, narrow enough that I with outstretched arms at the same time touch both rock walls sculpted by centuries or epics or aeons, that's the one, of water, narrowing rock walls carved with grottos and arches, rock walls niched with bowls and alcoves, rock walls striated by the sedimentation of time and undulating like the river, virgin, knee-deep, much entered and exited, much crossed, much trammeled, life engendering I imagine if sunless deep down within the contracting slit in perpetual shadow in confining rock in the cold river, much cold, through which you, I mean I, we then I guess, how I ache for a solo, slog, all our feet aching, the water at 46 degrees Fahrenheit or 8 degrees Celsius, cannot feel our feet like clubs, no ache, like bricks, even if you're still here I'm saying about me, like amputations, every man woman or child for his or her self, mind numb. You are still here. Your mind numb too, I suppose, in heartwarming companionship. You need not join me. I make poor choices and imperil my life for a thrill. For a thrill, ha, that's what you think. As if I could experience a thrill. Choices are limited. Either upriver or down. In a canyon. I walk. I walk in a canyon. It doesn't matter. The particulars don't matter. Outside, in the sun. What sun? The particulars matter, outsides matter as much as insides, outside matters more than inside, outside matter is inside, and inside matter is outside. Fuck if I'm going to write in French or become a dour Parisian or curse the sea or move to the French countryside and fondle words Frenchly as if their every particular satisfaction matters. Are there deserts in France? I walk. I walk off the trail off a plateau, contouring around a draw clinging to rocks through dry creek beds avoiding cryptobiotic soils. As best I can. I imperil life for a moment of silence. As if I could experience silence with you here waiting to hear me say I walk among the piñon and prickly pear and agave and cheat grass. Among the hohoba. The jojoba. No, shit, shrub live oak, or Sonoran scrub oak, or grey oak, your presence undermines my credibility, gray oak or Gambel oak or shin oak or scrub oak, if you weren't here I'd have no need to name it. Oak. Piñon or juniper? Are they the same thing? Like you and me? A joke. I don't play games. Does it matter? Does the difference and sameness between piñon and juniper matter, and what of mesquite and manzanita? No, that is a question for you, as long as you are here be present and useful and take part in this expedition or explore or god no exercise. Walk. Offtrail. The prickly pear buds pinkly without you answering or dispersing. The three-thousand foot cliff face looms. I am not a weaver of stories, you are, take them away back onto the trail into the front country into town to a cafe leave me here hiding or hulking or hunkering or hankering on a rock like coyote shit or a Gila monster sunning itself. Your vehicle drones away, distantly echoing off sandstone walls. I sit in a dry wash on a rock. A fly drones. You are still here. I explicate. There is also columbine. The crystalized quartz time seam exposed in a tumbled rock. An ant. In the desert. You. Here. With me. The sun. Unwanted. The dry heat. In a rocky dry wash. Choked by impenetrable thickets of tamarisk. No that is elsewhere here is pristine and intrusive tamarisk eradicated and the valley bed excessively penetrable. Or for all I know a dripping temperate rainforest of fern, fungi, moss, and towering old growth, or a grasshopper prairie popping in your face, or the monotonous thunder of monstrous waves breaking against sand. Up to you. What do you say, I don't care, it doesn't matter, I don't matter, you decide specifics matter, I don't exist, no matter but specific, you do, or is it no matter but particular or probable, you do. We walk through a dry wash or sit in a dry wash. Prone to flash floods. Does the sun shine? Are there dark clouds? Approaching thunder? Globs falling from the sky? You should go. Your safety is your responsibility. Just because we are collectively one doesn't mean you shouldn't save yourself. Desert me, please. Please desert me. Leave me here to desiccate. I mean drown. Leave me to my just deserts. To my just desserts? Shit you didn't escape before the requisite pun. Which I may have implemented incorrectly. Is it a pun? What is a pun, anyway? Does it matter? When the multiple meanings of a word or words is implemented to humorous effect. So whether or not it was a pun is up to you, as long as you refuse to desert me to dehydration or being swept downcanyon in a torrent head bashed against rock after rock lungs filling with water unable to breathe consciousness washing away. Was it funny? Must a pun be funny? You won't desert me, will you? Shh, quiet. I would you. I would go without you, but not you without me. Quiet. It's a bee, not a fly. Sweat bee or honey bee or hornet? Or a variety of fly. Harvesting the prince's plum nectar. Shut up. Pollinating. No blooming or unblooming ocotillo here and hence no hummingbird but plenty of insidious buzz when one quiets the mind. With all this disturbing buzz one may as well talk. I walk. I think you do too. We walk and talk, or whatever this verbiage is properly called, don't call it stream of consciousness, I don't care, my consciousness is predominantly unworded I tell you. Is it agave or yucca? Tell me. You're here too whether you like it or not. Whether I like it or not. You-cca. Me-cca. Yucca. Mecca. I just cannot help myself. It's too easy. What is? Words. I despise easy, except in ... No even there there must be some endurance some permanent obstacle some impossibility. Walking on perforated stone. A lizard darts into a hole. It's hole? Stop with the in. Out. It, despising the easy, is why, not true, I'm always in search of the empty, the vacant, the absent, the ... Untrue, I despise no desire, words are so hard, hard?, difficult, from despise to desire is only a matter of losing disappearing annihilating one letter and changing mutating transmigrating another letter into its neighbor in the alphabet, the danger is getting stuck in the unspecific inbetween two words as if becoming wedged in the nospace between two boulders left for dead in a crack, what danger, why I despise/desire the empty full the no vacancy vacant the void with a view the silence with birdsong the nothing flecked with condors or eagles or osprey no the desert condors circling in a wide unbounded sky or the present absence occupied by you. No, that last is not what I seek, caught up in the wet flow of words again. Or perhaps I do want to occupy your absence. It's moot. You, here, still. Accompanied. I walk. As predicted you accompany me in whatever manner of ambulation you call that. I don't care what you call me, just call me. No don't please, a momentary weakness, a joke. Ignore me, I'm too easily tempted by lightheartedness. I say nothing. I walk. Hedgehog cactus. Red blooms. Scat of coyote or cougar. A lizard scurrying silently, considerately. A fucking bluebird or circling condor or canyon wren twittering for the pure goddamn sound but without words at least a distraction from the distant thrum of an overpassing passenger jet in the sky, yes, bluebird blue, yes, jet blue, yes, sky blue. Deer tracks deer poop deer deer everywhere. Thistle. Canadian? Who brought this invasive noxious distracting painful thistle into my, your, our, the wilderness? Yes, I said, am saying wilderness. Can I be inside out? I did, apparently. Bring the thistle. I brought noxious invasive distracting painful you, after all, before all, if unintentionally. I take responsibility of my inadvertency, incidentalness, dentition, no, insouciance, injustice, invasiveness, immoderation, no, no responsibility there, invisibility, perhaps, inversion, as ever, internalization, of course, interior, more so, insides, all over, inside, yes, you. No I don't. You're not my fault. The externals are not mine. And you are external to me, are you not? There, a trail again, leading out of the wilderness I don't want to be out of. The desert wilderness protean, prostituted, profited from, promulgated, promulgated?, procreated, promate, no, primate or pronate, promethean, yes, Prometheus, pro-me-thee-us, have I employed this trick before?, forget it, forgive me, forget I said anything, forget me so I can forgive and forget you, go away. Mudslide! Flashflood! Falling rock! Brats above hurling rocks! A rock! Wordshit! Rattlesnake. Look out. A dry heat. Desert. Scorpions. Dehydration. Please. Is this not unenjoyable? Tarantula. The wilderness is unforgiving unloving unbecoming. Have we had this conversation already? Well let us have it again. What else are we to do, with you here still. We are standing on a trail whose every termination is outside of the wilderness, but I am an environmentalist, and of reduce reuse recycle, I choose reduce. I choose nothing. You are reused. If not recycled. I come here for the environment. I come here to save the environment. I come here to be the environment. I soil it with my presence. I come here to reduce my impact presence existence to nothing in the environment. You could also help me help the environment by reducing your presence to nothing in the environment. Alas or Ay or Arg, you are still here. You are an environmental condition. You are my environment. My god. I just puked or else shat in my environment, couldn't help it, the nausea, the claustrophobia, and right in the middle of the trail, my confines environment you too tight when I seek wide open spaces no no no I desert confines I'm not within you but without. Try the locoweed. Let's pray or meditate or walk. It's like you lead me by the hand down a trail.

56

The erosion we cause. The going is easier at least. I hate easygoing. I hate you. I walk anyway, your way, with you, alongside you, no space, behind you, in you, of you. In the desert. Out of the desert. Wait, I've lost my hat. You don't say, you say. Who took it?, I say. Forget about it, you say. You?, I say. Silence. It's gone, you say. Yes, I'll never see it again, will I?, I say. No, you say. My hat, I say, came to me from another, his hat, I say, one before me, then me, now the desert. Were there others besides he and I, I say, who put their head in the hat? Let us walk, you say. How I've soiled the wilderness. What I've left. A trace. A hat. Water bottles, sunglasses, brown stocking hat with white snowflakes after gold stocking hat with no snowflakes after gray stocking hat with blue snowflakes. Microtrash. Semen. Erosion. The crush of plants. You. Shit. Didn't work didn't function aborted attempt couldn't leave you you're still here. Attached to me like a blister. Fester burst and ooze. I can walk, you say. Infection? Ins again. But the outs. Like the runs. Hush, you say. The incessant need to get out, out of the walls the borders the nameable into outside wild nowhere. Quiet your mind, you say. Out into a nothing full of birds conifers cacti reptiles rock deer angiosperm coyote cryptobiotics. Can I blame my need for open sky on claustrophobia? Can I blame me on you? Close your mouth and close your eyes and open your hand and close it around mine, you say. Am I holding my own hand?, I say. I walk, you say. Out of the desert. To an oasis of potable water to a tent city where fires flicker and gray jays are thick as tourists to an uncomfortable hammock slung between two thick-limbed many-forked bright-green quaking deep-fissured-barked tree-of-life cottonwoods, heart-shaped leaves, heart-shaped box, no, forward motion to wherever you dwell or rest or recreate or whatever you call what you do or have done or will be doing with me or to me or upon me or in me or of me. Without me. Particularly. Past watercress and through Sonoran scrub oak and hanging from hanging maidenhair fern gardens hanging from parched cliffs. No you do not permit me to hang from cliffs or overhangs or cottonwoods. No matter you I hurt and hunt and hammock for wilderness and hibernate in you like a virulent or else virile snake please a little platonic lizard. Permit me down the mountain. Don't be absurd. You entreat. Beg. Demand. Order. Force. Drag downhill and lose the trail. Lose the game trail. Cliff out. I'm still here. Retrace steps. Skid down through red dirt making my own trail slaughtering microscopic creatures in very large much precedented quantities. I walk with you against my volition. What is volition. Vole rather. Vetch. Milkvetch. I walk with you when you walk. You walk.

18.

As she goes underground she hears in a loop in her head Miles Davis's *Bitches Brew*.

21', 13e'.

You are unsure to whom the "you" refers. Also the I, who is possibly He. You are unsure if the account is artifact or memory, if it is yours or another's, if it is experience or invention or reading his thoughts which are your thoughts. The account is filed listed organized under "Desert".

18.

She digs. She has been digging. She has dug. She dug. She will dig. She will have dug. She sounds like a six year old learning to manipulate language, discovering there is a meaning underneath, sometimes discarding it of her own volition, playing with a toy, therein making more meaning. She supposes that approximates the development of the human species.

She has been digging her whole life, or since what is called maturity adulthood working age. She has been preparing to leave to go to herself to walk out into herself for a long time, since she was a child she revises, ever since she wanted something more than the day-to-day everyday.

In a clearing in the woods she has been digging. It has not been easy digging. The woods are dark, Douglas fir and western hemlock. Old growth towers above her. Plastics grew to eminence before this 500, 750, 1000 year old stand tucked into a fold of a steep mountain could be logged. The weather has been hot and cold and snow and rain and sun and rainbows and full moons and new moons and stars and most often clouds. The weather has especially been mud. Today is the same. Some ferns but the understory is thin. The hill she built of the dirt and rocks she dug from her tunnel leading nowhere sits on a large raised platform or is staged on a stage or is humped on a dais. A ramp like a playground slide as wide as the platform narrows in a pleasing curve like a neck from the platform to the maw of her tunnel. She thinks maw to amuse herself. She thinks about sex and her entering the hole in the ground. She cannot stop doesn't want to stop fucking off anyone reading her thoughts. Or like a vagina the other way, like above ground is one enormous uterus and she is about to be birthed into the earth. You-ter-us. The slap and tickle of syllabic games. She is a little giddy. She is not afraid. Her fear is that she is not alone, that someone followed her here and will interfere. That someone else knows. The platform is equipped with hydraulics. The side farthest from the hole can be lifted, like a dump truck. The tunnel entrance is twice as wide as her from shoulder to shoulder and twice as tall from the back of her head to the tip of her nose and many times as deep as she is long, no, the tunnel entrance is two dimensional, it has no depth, but the tunnel is many times as deep as she is long. The tunnel entrance is on the forest floor. The tunnel exit does not exist. It is in her mind.

The tunnel descends steeply below, at sixty degrees below the horizontal. A thick cable snakes or worms or tongues from a box with a button at the lip of the hole to an electrical box on the platform, old technology but she couldn't risk wireless. A redo might wreck her. Landing far underground without dirt cascading on her would be hell. The tunnel entrance is wide enough for two of her but the tunnel narrows pleasingly beyond. She dug with pick and trench shovel and pulaski and trowel and bucket and augur and rock bar and spade and post-hole digger and a miniature long-armed excavator and a well driller and her bare hands. She installed a conveyor belt to transport the dirt and rock to the surface. Like she mined. She was mining, sluicing for nothing, for her. She conveyed the ore out. She uninstalled the belt.

6_{11}.

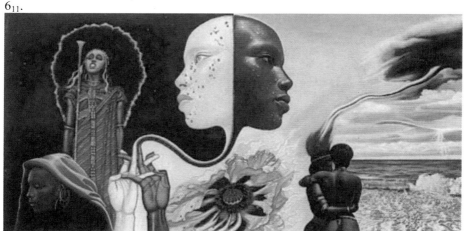

Bitches Brew by Mati Klarwein, 1970. Album cover for Miles Davis' *Bitches Brew*. [Permission could not be obtained because the body of Mati Klarwein is dead, as is that of Miles Davis, and their consciousnesses could not be located (they are here) to give us an answer (the answer is above). -- Eds.]

$7a_{iii}$.

(corrupted) Friedman's assumptions used to solve the equations of general relativity to show the universe is not static:

1. The universe looks identical in whatever direction we look.

2. This will be true no matter from where we observe the universe.

18.

She stands on the lip of the hole, her toes gripping the lip of the hole, her skin soaking in the sun, it is cloudy and rainy and cold, massive trees rising high above massive roots reaching far below but not as deep as she will reach or as high as she will subsequently rise in her thoughts from the hole.

7b$_{iv}$.

In the theory of relativity there is no unique absolute time. We each as individuals have our own personal measure of time that depends on where we are and how we are moving.

22.

You must rise above you or you are nothing or buried alive.

6$_{12}$.

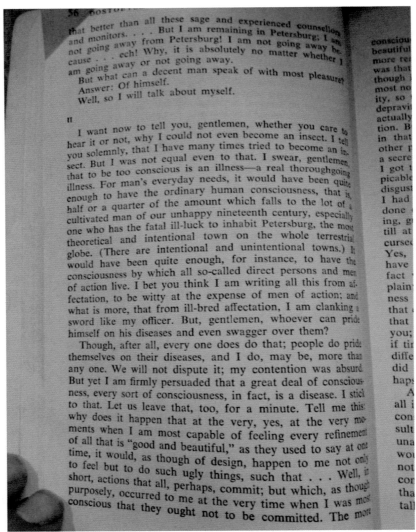

56   DOSTO...

that better than all these sage and experienced counsellors and monitors. . . . But I am remaining in Petersburg; I am not going away from Petersburg! I am not going away be-cause . . . ech! Why, it is absolutely no matter whether I am going away or not going away.

But what can a decent man speak of with most pleasure?

Answer: Of himself.

Well, so I will talk about myself.

II

I want now to tell you, gentlemen, whether you care to hear it or not, why I could not even become an insect. I tell you solemnly, that I have many times tried to become an in-sect. But I was not equal even to that. I swear, gentlemen, that to be too conscious is an illness—a real thoroughgoing illness. For man's everyday needs, it would have been quite enough to have the ordinary human consciousness, that is, half or a quarter of the amount which falls to the lot of a cultivated man of our unhappy nineteenth century, especially one who has the fatal ill-luck to inhabit Petersburg, the most theoretical and intentional town on the whole terrestrial globe. (There are intentional and unintentional towns.) It would have been quite enough, for instance, to have the consciousness by which all so-called direct persons and men of action live. I bet you think I am writing all this from af-fectation, to be witty at the expense of men of action; and what is more, that from ill-bred affectation, I am clanking a sword like my officer. But, gentlemen, whoever can pride himself on his diseases and even swagger over them?

Though, after all, every one does do that; people do pride themselves on their diseases, and I do, may be, more than any one. We will not dispute it; my contention was absurd. But yet I am firmly persuaded that a great deal of conscious-ness, every sort of consciousness, in fact, is a disease. I stick to that. Let us leave that, too, for a minute. Tell me this: why does it happen that at the very, yes, at the very mo-ments when I am most capable of feeling every refinement of all that is "good and beautiful," as they used to say at one time, it would, as though of design, happen to me not only to feel but to do such ugly things, such that . . . Well, in short, actions that all, perhaps, commit; but which, as though purposely, occurred to me at the very time when I was most conscious that they ought not to be committed. The more

"Notes from the Underground," Fyodor Dostoyevsky (1864), translated by Constance Garnett (1918), as found in *Existentialism from Dostoevsky to Sartre*, selected and introduced and edited by Walter Kauff-man (Meridian Books; New York: 1956) p56.

13f.

He wakes woke wakes from a dream he does not remember and hits snooze and goes elsewhere again for five minutes and hits snooze again and puts on his glasses and is conscious enough to think he is thinking something of non-negligible insight, an idea, something worth writing down but the alarm buzzes beeps dings rings all the different alarm tones in his life and he silences it and rises. He does not remember his dream and he does not remember the idea worth writing. The vague compulsion to write remains. He dresses and descends the stairs to heat coffee. It is black outside or he would never write a word. He does not put much stock in dreams. They reflect your life, your subconscious, your brain working organizing randomly firing while you sleep. Fine. He supports his belief in the non-supremacy of the dream state, what is the fugue state, with a statement he has made so often he is annoyed at himself for writing it about how there is not much separation between his conscious self and his unconscious, there is no curtain, no above ground and underground, no division. The one is intimately aware of the other if there is a difference at all. He knows that is untrue or incomplete, he can only be so aware of the workings of his brain interpreting visual data, or making him breathe, or engaging emotion for example. In the kitchen his daughter is already awake and lying on her left side on the cheap faux tile linoleum having made a circle of her arm, torso, and upper leg by touching her left hand fingers to her left knee, the poodle puddled behind her. He cannot shut himself off. She coos sweet nothings to a tiny toy skittering in her circle, in the pen she has made, poking prodding petting it with her right index finger that is four years old. He cries a little for love the foreknowledge that she will grow and leave him alone, when alone used to be acceptable preferred desired by him for thought meditation creation and now it is not because of this beautiful sometimes sad sometimes joyful being he has played a large part in making who is becoming more aware of herself as herself. He is self-conscious enough to know if this were a scene in a play or movie or book he may have undercut the pathos or emotion by crying by introducing a cloying sentimentality, or more really because of the explicitness. To say everything is unartful. If everything is said then the reader viewer observer does not need to interpret invest discover create on their own. But he is a sentimental man, sometimes, he can be, his emotion is his undoing, his emotion is all he has, how often he feels nothing anymore, and no one is watching and he is caught off-guard in the early dark, she is an expert at that. The tiny toy is like an insect, it is a little robot, he thinks it's supposed to resemble a roach, like the roach in

Wall-e, which was the only living creature left on Earth not a robot in the movie if he remembers it right, a role reversal from fiction to reality then. He thinks the toy robot roach is from a game where you build a labyrinth out of little blocks and turn on your roaches and set them down at the entrance and the roaches move forward and bump into a wall or each other and change direction, etc., no true thought involved, but with enough iterations enough somewhat random but programmed motion one of the roaches is bound to successfully navigate the labyrinth. The game was probably marketed as a race, a competition, as if your roach completing the labyrinth were an achievement to strive for. As if not ending your sentences with prepositions were an achievement to strive for. What is the subjunctive. He didn't watch Jeopardy. When he was a young adult he lived in roach-filled apartments, watched roaches fly in windows, was accompanied by many roaches in a university basement laboratory where he tested material failure and by a single roach in a different room in a different basement where he took scans of the surface topography of the material specimens in question, and read *Metamorphosis*. Where are they, the roaches, now? In the old towns, he supposes. He cannot imagine them extinct, they are better adapted than humans, they can live off the oil from your thumbprint for a week and live without a head until they starve. He kisses her on the cheek and she does not respond but strokes and murmurs to her pet robot roach and he goes to see what he can do. He opens his journal to where he scrawled a few jottings last night from late Beckett, who reads him anymore, who reads, why read him when he is of a different time and his point of view is probably irrelevant and reading is a slow antiquated means of information accrual and besides he is thoroughly absorbed into the cultural consciousness. Nothing for it. Habit, continuation, beginning again. From *Fizzle 5*: "There is not but what is said. Beyond what is said there is nothing." From *Head in the Dark 1*: "You now lying in the dark stand that morning on the sill having pulled the door gently to behind you. ... You see yourself at that last outset leaning against the door with closed eyes waiting for the word from you to go." From *Fizzle 2*: "I had come to bear everything bar being seen." She crawls into her father's lap her roach humming in her cupped hands. He closes his journal.

18.
She pushes the button leaps from the lip slips into the entrance slides down the hole dirt cascading carrying her. She reaches deep.

23.

But which of you is real? Are real? There is you buried alive and there is you or there are you observing you buried alive. Which of you posits the question which of you is real? If you, buried alive in a coffin or other receptacle or vessel of whatever material, die, then the you observing you, whether singular or plural, also presumably dies. You are tethered to you are leashed to you are the biological basis for your newfound meta-existence. But perhaps you are too presumptuous in presuming that when you die you die. When you suffocate you cease. When you are perforated and liquefied and consumed by insects and decomposed by bacteria and composed again by other organisms you are no longer you. Perhaps avoiding the cessation of being you, avoiding death, avoiding the void is the primal motivation for why you checked your fortitude and rose above yourself in the first place. Perhaps the desiring of you, for which you left you, is born of the need to survive. What place? You are not above you except in a metaphoric sense. Or are you? Are you being metamorphosed underground into another, a rock under great pressure, the pressure of your observation, of your boot heel, a rock changing into crystal or jewel or diamond? You do not feel like you are in orbit around you, or around the planet in which you are buried. Perhaps the planet is no larger than the Little Prince's, on which you need only take a few step to watch the sunset again, on which he once watched the sunset 44 times because he was so sad. From where do the references come? Where is the referent? Diamonds and a little prince and a coffin and insects: unreal. You know on the other hand, you have no hands, that orbit does not feel like always falling or always curving because you follow a straight path in 4-dimensional spacetime bent by the mass of your planet or you. Or do you know that. What do you know. You also know that when you are in orbit high in your gravitational field you move with a velocity insufficient to escape you and sufficient to not be pulled into you such that your tangential velocity is counteracted by the inward acceleration from the force of gravity, which acts as the centripetal force necessary to keep you in circular motion. You also know you feel weightless because there is no force no object nothing in contact with you opposing gravity. You feel weightless because there is nothing resisting your fall. You feel weightless. Now you are observing you in possible orbit and not observing you buried alive. Perhaps you are not outside of you observing you, but inside you. Is that possible, or is it like trying to observe the boundaries of the universe from within the universe? Are you nowhere, or now here? Are you in or out? All the other yous you hope to rise into to join with above observing you, are they out there, if you hope to join them that implies they are, how, is there an out there, do they exist, you have made observations about you as if from outside of you and so are you not out there as well, is there no they there only you, are you out there, or are the observations theirs and not yours, is there an outside world? Perhaps there is an outside world, perhaps the other yous exist, perhaps They are real. But perhaps there is no inside world, perhaps it is you who do not exist, perhaps it is the I inside you that is the fiction. What proof what science what math do you have to define you, to legitimize you, to set the limits of what and who is you, to construct a vault a safe a box for the you of you, to vouchsafe or safeguard the I inside you. What is I? What is its referent? Again you fear the touch of your unestablished humanness, why, perhaps because I is phonetically the same as eye in spoken English which you suspect is a dead language and eyes see. Another inconsistency irregularity singularity you perceive is that when discussing the nature of the universe and the theory of general relativity and the different location of observers, what is observed is always relative to you. All experience and measurement and perception and distance and explanation and time and fits of comprehension are relative to you. You know this is a point where all your theories fail. You know you must be removed from the equation if you are to objectively determine the real. Still the you. Still the question confining you, are you within the you buried alive or without? And beginning again still, is the you buried alive within you or without? But go back, before you begin, begin with the assumption that you are real.

13g, 11000_2.

There is another world but it is in this one. -- Eugène Grindel

''There is another world but it is in this one.'' -- Patrick White

''''There is another world but it is in this one.'''' -- J. M. Coetzee

''''''There is another world but it is in this one.'''''' --

There is another world but it is in this one.

''''''There is another world but it is in this one.'''''' -- Nick Stokes

'''There is another world but it is in this one.''' -- Gerald Murnane

'There is another world but it is in this one.' -- Paul Éluard

18.

She had begun to not exist in her body, but in a bad way. In a way that was the opposite of how she is going to not exist in her body now. She existed in the cloud of social media, in digitized social interactions that happened nowhere, with other non-physical beings, watching streamed movies alone for entertainment and talking without talking about them with other non-entities, posting at other non-entities, her music fed to her by an algorithm that knows what she likes and is designed to please her and not challenge and not surprise her and not feed her an unexpected sound and which has the outcome of funneling her experience into a box. Through her interactions without actions with the intangible They without physical presence she developed a perception of the nothings, the non-entities, the nowheres as reality. She made They real in a subconscious reflex to assure herself that she did not exist in a manufactured world, that she was not figment. She was. Her slight interactions with the real world, ordering coffee, eating in a restaurant, chit-chatting in a bar, working, walking, buying groceries, vacationing at the beach, paying bills, took on a shimmer of unreality. She critiqued such quotidian facets of life as insubstantial, animal, corporeal, and furthered that if such mundanities are not what life is about, if they are not real, then the true or real is of a higher order, and the next higher order to her seems that of thought, though perhaps there is a higher order yet beyond thought. But that is removing the physicality of existence, which is what social media and the digital cloud does, or portends to do, or pretends to do. On the contrary though, the physicalless interactions and talkless comments and social mediation and digital cloud did not symbiotically free her thinking but affected and infected her thoughts like a parasite. She could not perform a task, read an article, buy an onion, find a free banana, hear a nice word from a cashier, see a raccoon in an alley, receive a courtesy from a stranger, fewer of those with her face in a screen, or have a mediocre profound thought without, outside of herself, thinking of how to post a status update about it in an amusing or clever or touching way. Her thoughts were shaped into tweets, digestible in 144 characters. Her form became a collection of beautified, filtered images crafted to be likeable or interesting or controversial or cute or confrontational or shareable, to create empty interactions with entities who were not there. She was in the cloud, in a box. She stayed in more and more. There was no sudden epiphany but a slow accrual of emptiness. She asked herself, what does she become when her thoughts are tweets or status updates or quippy comments, or when her observations are capturable images and shareable snippets of video. So few thoughts, what is she, a social media bot? a content provider? another server with a spider web of connections to other servers with whom information is passed disseminated shared equally like viruses? what information? another network connection in the social cloud of modern consciousness? Thinking about the void of thought and the density of purposelessness made her not want to go out or bathe or change her underwear or shave and she didn't. She brushed her teeth. She didn't know why. Because still she must eat, until we are photosynthetic. Because she cannot wholly shed concern for her image. Because she is weak. Because she cannot stop worrying about others. Despite the high concept of egalitarianism of information and disseminated thought and shared consciousness regardless of space, it was always about her, always about you, always about oneself, even if the post is philanthropic or for a just cause or for the children or the tweet proclaims love or acclaim or thanks for another at Thanksgiving, it is your name next to the tweet, your image next to the post, your thought getting liked or not. Even if it is about something else it relates back to you. It was always about her. She was a selfish non-entity. A needy vacancy. A prolonged itch. Stinky discharge. Hairy pits like she was a hippy or European. Why shouldn't she be. Showering once a week. Once every two. Never. Sleeping in the same shirt and underwear every night and sleeping poorly and not waking up and getting up and putting the same sweats on everyday. Quitting her job. Defacto quitting. Losing contact with people except on a screen. Dandruff and interstellar dust and word flakes falling on the screen. Ceasing to interface with the screen, with non-entities nothings nowheres. Unplugging. Falling out of the cloud. Twirling spinning spiraling down. Not killing herself because always somehow believing there was a way up, not dead because alive.

6_{13}.
Wikipedia contributors, "Binary number," *Wikipedia, The Free Encyclopedia,* https://en.wikipedia.org/w/index.php?title=Binary_number&oldid=720676488 (accessed Jan 5, 2016).

Binary number
In mathematics and digital electronics, a **binary number** is a number .... Because of its straightforward implementation in digital electronic circuitry using logic gates, the binary system is used internally by almost all modern computers and computer-based devices. Each digit is referred to as a bit.

History
The modern binary number system was devised by Gottfried Leibniz in 1679 and appears in his article *Explication de l'Arithmétique Binaire* (published in 1703). Sys-

tems related to binary numbers have appeared earlier in multiple cultures including ancient Egypt, China, and India.

Egypt

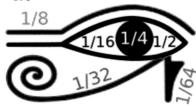

Arithmetic values represented by parts of the Eye of Horus

... (so called because many historians of mathematics believe that the symbols used for this system could be arranged to form the eye of Horus, although this has been disputed). Horus-Eye fractions are a binary numbering system for fractional quantities of grain, liquids, or other measures, in which a fraction of a hekat is expressed as a sum of the binary

fractions 1/2, 1/4, 1/8, 1/16, 1/32, and 1/64. Early forms of this system can be found in documents from the Fifth Dynasty of Egypt, approximately 2400 BC, and its fully developed hieroglyphic form dates to the Nineteenth Dynasty of Egypt, approximately 1200 BC.

China

The *I Ching* dates from the 9th century BC in China. The binary notation in the *I Ching* is used to interpret its quaternary divination technique.

It is based on taoistic duality of yin and yang. [E]ight trigrams (Bagua) and a set of 64 hexagrams ("sixty-four" gua), analogous to the three-bit and six-bit binary numerals, were in use at least as early as the Zhou Dynasty ...

India

The Indian scholar Pingala (c. 2nd century BC) developed a binary system for describing prosody. He used binary numbers in the form of short and long syllables (the latter equal in length to two short syllables), making it similar to Morse code. Pingala's Hindu classic titled Chandaḥśāstra (8.23) describes the formation of a matrix in order to give a unique value to each meter. The binary representations in Pingala's system increases towards the right, and not to the left like in the binary numbers of the modern, Western positional notation.

Other cultures

The residents of the island of Mangareva in French Polynesia were using a hybrid binary-decimal system before 1450. Slit drums with binary tones are used to encode messages across Africa and Asia. Sets of binary combinations similar to the I Ching have also been used in traditional African divination systems such as Ifá as well as in medieval Western geomancy ... long been widely applied in sub-Saharan Africa.

Western predecessors to Leibniz
In 1605 Francis Bacon discussed a system whereby letters of the alphabet could be reduced to sequences of binary digits...

Leibniz and the I Ching
The full title of Leibniz's article is translated into English as the *"Explanation of the Binary Arithmetic, which uses only the characters 1 and 0, with some remarks on its usefulness, and on the light it throws on the ancient Chinese figures of Fu Xi"*. (1703). ...

Leibniz interpreted the hexagrams of the I Ching as evidence of binary calculus. As a Sinophile, Leibniz was aware of the I Ching, noted with fascination how its hexagrams correspond to the binary numbers from 0 to 111111, and concluded that this mapping was evidence of major Chinese accomplishments in the sort of philosophical mathematics he admired. ... Binary numerals were central to Leibniz's theology. He believed that binary numbers were symbolic of the Christian idea of *creatio ex nihilo* or creation out of nothing. ...

Later developments
In 1854, ... paper detailing an algebraic system of logic that would become known as Boolean algebra. His logical calculus was to become ....

In 1937, Claude Shannon produced his master's thesis at MIT that implemented Boolean algebra and binary arithmetic using electronic relays and switches for the first time in history. Entitled *A Symbolic Analysis of Relay and Switching Circuits*, Shannon's thesis essentially founded practical digital circuit design.

In November 1937, George Stibitz, then working at Bell Labs, completed a relay-based computer he dubbed the "Model K" (for "**K**itchen", where he had assembled it), which calculated using binary addition ...

Representation
Any number can be represented ... by any mechanism capable of being in two mutually exclusive states. Any of the following rows of symbols can be interpreted as the binary numeric value of 667.

```
1 0 1 0 0  1 1  0 1 1
| −| − − | |  −| |
| −| | |  | |  −| |
x o x o O x X o x x
y n y n N y Y n y y
```

... In a computer, the numeric values may be represented by two different voltages; on a magnetic disk, magnetic polarities may be used. A "positive", "yes", or "on" state is not necessarily equivalent to the numerical value of one; it depends on the architecture in use.

In keeping with customary representation of numerals using Arabic numerals, binary numbers are commonly written using the symbols **0** and **1**. When written, binary numerals are often subscripted, prefixed or suffixed in order to indicate their base, or radix. The following notations are equivalent:

...

When spoken, binary numerals are usually read digit-by-digit, in order to distinguish them from decimal numerals. For example, the binary numeral 100 is pronounced *one zero zero*, rather than .... Since the binary numeral 100 represents the [decimal] value four, it would be confusing to refer to the numeral as ... (a word that represents a completely different value, or amount). Alternatively, the binary numeral 100 can be read out as "four" (the correct *value*), but this does not make its binary nature explicit.

7d$_i$.

Looking into the past through the lens of general relativity, we see, some 13.7 billion years ago, the entire universe in a single point of zero size, everything compressed into a sphere of zero radius and infinite curvature in spacetime, everywhere in a nowhere of infinite density and infinite temperature and infinite kinetic energy. By predicting a singularity in the past, a beginning, the theory of relativity predicts a point wherein it fails. By predicting the infinite, our theory proves itself incorrect, incomplete, incomprehensive, and us its creators deficient.

18.

Four blocks from school, she pulls into the shoulder and weeps. She weeps because there is a ball of emptiness within her, collapsing on itself. Because there is a red dwarf within her, collapsing. A star collapsing. A sphere of emptiness, a point of infinite density, collapsing and collapsing and collapsing and she has acknowledged it, and because she has acknowledged and been unable to swallow the collapse again, she has to feed it tears, feed it her sorrow, feed it the fear of when tears alone will feed it no more. The mass, the emptiness in her grows, it pulses, its gravity waxes and she is pulled down and in and it throbs and she collapses and she feels it and waters it and sacrifices herself to it because she has no choice – it holds her down, its great weight atop her, and forces itself on her, it is inside her, she gives herself and allows herself to be crushed – that is the only way it ever goes away, no it never goes away, that is the only way it finishes and lets her pretend again it doesn't exist. She allows herself to be crushed, she becomes it becomes the weight becomes the emptiness becomes the pulse--

--

--

--

--

--

[*1 Day,* 2009.]

13h.

He spends an inordinate disconcerting connectivity-building demoralizing quantity of time constructing this communication which communicates what, writing this nothing, everything, concocting this social media status update:

> 1. She listed to me the buttcracks she saw yesterday. Mine was not among them.
> 2. I've never thought read written so hard to try to organize the chaos and connections into a meaningful written consciousness.
> 3. This post is a piece of it.
> 4. This post is a piece of shit.
> 5. This painting is hers, appropriated by me, taken by you, into from of the cloud.

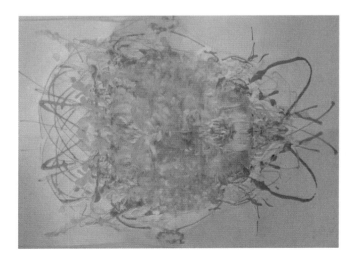

$7a_{vi}$.

Particle-wave duality:

Matter is of inseparable particle and wave nature.

$7e_{iii}$.

1) Light behaves like a particle in that, for example, it can only be emitted or absorbed in certain quantities, or quanta, but also exhibits wave properties such as frequency shift, refraction, and interference.

2) A stream of particles such as electrons exhibits interference as if it were a wave. An interference pattern emerges on a receiving wall if we direct a light source to shine through two slits. A similar interference pattern emerges if we direct a source of particles such as electrons to emit a stream of particles of certain speed through two slits.

3) The same interference pattern emerges even if we emit one particle such as an electron at a time, at large time intervals. As if the electrons were interfering with each other at distant times, or more and less explicably, as if their position followed a wave of probability distribution.

4) Particles do not have a definite position but are smeared within a probability distribution.

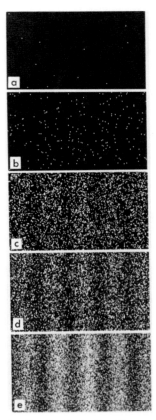

6_{14}. Results of a double-slit-experiment performed by Dr. Tonomura showing the build-up of an interference pattern of single electrons. Numbers of electrons are 11 (a), 200 (b), 6000 (c), 40000 (d), 140000 (e). By user: Belsazar - Provided with kind permission of Dr. Tonomura, CC BY-SA 3.0, https://commons.wikimedia.org/w/index.php?curid=498735

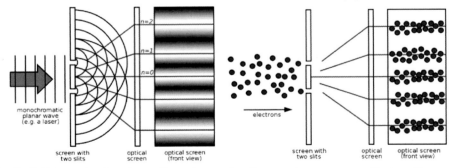

6_{15}. (Left) Light passing through two slits produces an interference pattern on a screen. The two slits cause the light waves to constructively or destructively interfere, resulting in bright and dark spots on the screen.

72

Constructive interference is where peaks or dips of a wave add together. Destructive interference occurs when a peak meets a dip. (Right) Quantum superposition says the electron can exist at all possible positions in space. The likelihood the electron is found at each point in space is given by a probability wave. This probability wave gives an interference pattern like a light wave.

Figure: Public Domain. Text: Zak Burkley, "The Teachings of a Quantum Cat: Quantum Computers and Communication Part 1", 8-06-2016, *Lindau Nobel Laureate* Meetings, https://www.lindau-nobel.org/de/the-teachings-of-a-quantum-cat-quantum-computers-and-communication-part-1/ accessed 10-18-2018.

25, 11001_2.

I begin. I don't know. I've begun this way before. I don't know that. That I began or in this way. I begin this way. I don't know if I begin. Or what is this way. Not knowing is how I begin.

I feel as though I am surrounded trapped crushed deafened by beings, things, consciousnesses, dust, energies, objects, noise, my voice, by you, wherever you are.

But there is nothing. I am alone. I am an iota. All around, nothing surrounds, no sound. A vacuum.

At other times, I feel as though I am full of matter, made of material thoughts, constituted of distinct differentiated independent insignificant entities possessing their own unique separate awarenesses, or un-awarenesses as the case may be, that those building blocks when crushed together, compacted by my impossible gravity, constitute me and that I am everything, encompassing everyone, all of you inside me, whatever "you" is, and that I cannot hold it all in, the pressure, I am about to overflow, to burst, a swirling ball of burning gasses and nitrogen and … and other stuff exploding releasing a great outward spreading compression wave, my dispersed consciousness flung out in one mighty cry, in an inside out embrace that populates the empty universe.

But there is nothing. I am alone. I have not been deflated. I have not exploded in spores or stellar waves of high frequency radiation making an uninterpretable sound in the void. I am empty.

I hear nothing. I hear.

I have always been empty. That "at other times" I leveraged earlier planted the seed for the thought to spring forth that there are other times. And I am not confident that is the case. That there have been, are, will be other times. That there are tiny vessels called seeds, or a thing called I.

I think I would like something to compare myself to. Or rather, perhaps I am compelled to find such a thing. A change. Movement. A way to shape time, give it form, structure, purpose, rather than it being an unending massless nothing.

I want you. Whatever that means.

What is it that I hear?

Is a you another name for the surrounding void sound? Or the faceless nothing of either considerable or negligible mass that is a blackhole? Does a thing that continuously swallows its face make a sound? It must not, it does not emit light you shortsighted fool. Why then how are you to know where it is, the you could be anywhere, way over there, or, or right here, and you'd never know. That is the fear, and the hope. But what if instead of a faceless thing, the you is a thing with many faces, a crystal, or a comet consisting of many frozen crystals carved of many faces burning through an atmosphere, or an asteroid belt consisting of many asteroids each of which contain many crystals each of which are carved with many faces –. That sounds awful … it sounds like a lot of faces … also "carved" is the wrong word, because there is no one to have done the carving. Then perhaps "you" is the wrong word. Perhaps.

I don't know what the faces matter anyway when all I see is nothing, emptiness, absence.

Sometimes I do think I hear something. Yes, I know, "sometimes" implying different times. "I" implying other agencies. Etcetera.

Who am I talking to? You? Ha!

Myself? I am alone, after all. Which is the whole reason I'm speaking, to begin with. I think. To begin with! Is this the beginning? The End? Genesis or genocide or gene?

Am I speaking? Are my lips moving? What are lips and are they requisite for communication if that's what I'm doing and are they succulent and do I have them? Am even I silence?

Am I only my questions and the responding silence, your responding silence, forever? Because that will get tiresome. It will get old.

Get old. Fuck me. A passage of time metaphor.

I crush me. What can I say declaratively, with certainty?

I sometimes believe I hear something. Sometimes it is far away and faint. Sometimes it is so close it is inside, though still faint. I am the only loud thing -- can you hear me?

Although when all the faintnesses, the imperceptibles, the unhearables clash … its own quiet clamor.

Is that you? When are you?

Maybe you are like the stars and you are lightyears away and the tiny sound of you that I hear is hundreds of millions of years old and I am listening into the past and you are long dead and unremembered, as is all of your kind, whatever variety of being you were has vanished, leaving nothing, as if you were never here, completely unknown. Except by me. Who will never know you.

In which case, will another hear me? Another other than me, I mean. In some unimaginable future after I am long dead and unknown, leaving nothing, as if I never were.

Or maybe what I hear is only myself. The sounds I hear are the emissions from the organ that vibrates in my ear, the drum vibrating in response to myself, perhaps I am only an ear vibrating, hearing, reproducing ever-fainter echoes of some original clamor, cacophony, chorus. Maybe I am only an ear, and you, for whom I search, are my auditory regurgitations. Which would make you hard to find. Which would explain a few things.

Hard or difficult? There are no words but what you give me.

Or is it that I hear my own whisperings mutterings nothings reflected off a surface and I am not in a vast empty space, which is what it feels like, but a cube, a cell, a box that is the exact dimensions of my body and encloses me perfectly. Which does not I imagine feel much different than an unlimited void. Black shiny reflective stone walls made of a long ago fire and polished by aeons of sound. In which case there is no you, only I. Which is not the first time I've posited the idea.

I am alone and there is no you to find. Unless you are inside of me, part of me.

In which case, how do I find you except by ripping myself apart.

I am nevertheless growing more certain that I hear something, and whether you exist, or are dead, or are me, I give you the name "You."

I certainly would not call what I am experiencing with you a conversation. A give and take. Is it not, nevertheless, a communication?

Why do I question you? Why don't you answer?

I have thoughts that are not my own. Of enclosed, confined space. Of swirling shells roaring of oceans in stories, of the sound of blackberry vines splitting, cracking stone and dropping small succulent fruits of blood. The purple red black smear on fingertips. Is that you?

I can hear you. The vines. The bramble. The self-defense.

If I were to find something, someone, some sun, some thorn, would this, would I, be any different? I'm not certain that what blackberries consist of are vines. If I found you, would I be less alone?

There are things called cucumbers pendulous on vines, also vines, instead vines, and there are rivers, no, seas, no, oceans, I think, of dark matter I, or is it you, cannot see.

I can hear you. It's how I know, why I speak. And hear, based on the earlier hypothesis that I am only what you would call an ear and that speaking and hearing are the same thing. In which case when I say "dark matter I, or is it you, cannot see," I mean hear, cannot hear it, or say it, the dark matter. Perhaps for you, however, it is "cannot see," because you are what you call an eye. Although if I am an ear, I'd prefer you were a mouth. I have a sense that ears and eyes don't get together very often, as opposed to ears and mouths. Fuck me twice -- Are there more than one of you? If there are more than one of you, perhaps there is likewise more than one of I. In which case I am not unique. If there are more than one of you, are each of you unique? If there are more than one of you, do I want all of you or just one?

Have I already thought of the possibility that I am only one part of me? That I am the part of me of which I am aware, my I a piece of a larger I, not the organ called an eye, the tool of sight, whatever that is, not that, I've latched onto hearing as the epithet of my sensory perception, remember, as a metaphor for my experience, what's a metaphor?, not to mention speech again, while you are another part of this larger I, a part of which I am only dimly aware, that I can barely perceive -- that is hear. This would be a different theory than you being an insignificant part of me. This would be the theory that we are both insignificant and possibly non-functional parts of a larger unknown entity. I thought you might like this theory better. Though I am no more certain of its validity than any other theory I've conjured to explain what is happening.

I do wonder if you can hear me. I have thoughts and I blame them on … attribute them to … they are inspired by … I think they are your thoughts.

There are larvae and muons and rose hips. There is you.

I am alone.

I just don't think I think these thoughts without you. I don't think these thoughts exist without you. I think I don't think without you.

Maybe I am better off without you. Without bamboo bending in the breeze. Without pretty words. Without boxes the exact shape of me, whatever shape that may be, and without a boundless universe of space. Without the rustling of stellar winds. Without inside or outside. Without wondering what I would be if I joined with you. Without the long chord of light resounding from extinct supernova. Without feeling alone.

And yet, here I am. Alone.

I can hear you dimly within me. I can hear you faintly without me. I don't know where or what or when you are. Let alone, what I am.

I want you.

[*Intertwining Alone*, 2015]

13i.

He begins again. He doesn't know how to begin. He always begins this way. He doesn't know that. Always. What an impossible word. Impossible. What a low probability word necking with zero. People used to neck, kids mostly. Adults screwed or made love or fucked if those were different acts and not the same thing called different names depending on the speaker's mindset or involvement or the angle from which it was viewed. The position of the observer in other words. Or did the classification of, no, the taxonomy of the sex depend on, no, was it determined by the angle at which it was done, the position and vector and acceleration, the mass times acceleration becoming force. Maybe some diehards still do. It is distracting, thinking of humans having sex while he tries to write, thinking of characters having sex, thinking of him having sex. Not recently. He is old. Accelerating quantum state. He used to. He had, has, had children. Change in position, decrease in velocity. Due to collision or interference? An attractive force at a distance, gravity, or right on top of each other, the strong force, or the repulsive coulomb force of two like charges. Are those forces forces or more bendings of spacetime, curvings of bodies, bendings over tables. Where is Calvino when you want him? He is distracted and does not know how to begin again or why and what the right words are, and why, what the precise word is, or if there is such a word, and why, they are all the same empty all vacant. He is not sure why, when most of the people he knew and those he did not are either dead or not people anymore and writing and art and mental intellectual emotional spiritual exploration seems a particularly human endeavor. In the next state, is all known? That is what They say. Not exactly say. All will be uploaded, your life your experience your knowledge your creation will be a contribution to the whole They say. They does not exactly say. He pulls from an old shelf an old notebook, an artifact of his thoughts from decades ago, in search of some anthropomorphized comfort from Calvino or Stapledon about the cold nature of consciousness and the universe but he cannot find them, they are long dead and gone, their works uploaded, the criticism and other's thought on their works uploaded, and his relics are not digitally indexed and easily searchable. They are dusty. In the dust and crackling paper he discovers an old note that sparks him or is he ash already.

7e_{iv}.

$7e_{iv}.$

If we measure the position of an electron to an accuracy of roughly the confines of an atom, then we cannot know its speed more precisely than plus or minus 1000 km/sec.

13i.

He is not sure if the magnitude of the uncertainty is depressing or comforting. It just is.

26.

You begin again. No, you cannot stand it, can't stand the sound. You again, beginning, beginning still. Genesising yet. Ising. You feel like a piece of you left. Or you feel like of you is left. Which direction of all infinite directions is left? Hold up your left hand palm out thumb at a right angle to your index finger but in the same plane as the rest of your hand, and thumb and index finger will form an L. You have no hands. The right hand will make a backwards L. Your left hand is on the left side of your body. What's left is relative to you. What is left, what has left, what left. Previously you determined that either you are above, whether inside or outside, in your mind's eye or in orbit, intangible in a cloud or a glistening drop of airborne vapor or an electrical discharge of charge distribution in a network you cannot perceive because it is an order above you, or you are below, buried, alive or unalive. No matter, you above lack hands and you below cannot move them if you have them. Left is meaningless. Departed. Part of you, you are certain, departed. Dearly? You are left. Perhaps the part of you, if you are a collective of many disparate parts constituting a whole unified you, or perhaps the you, if you are an independent unique you somehow affiliated with or connected to or sharing the same state as other entities in such a way that you all are categorized under the same point of view as you, that is buried alive recently departed, which might be to say no longer buried alive, now just buried. Recently. Now. Just. Perhaps the burying was just, punishment for a crime or transgression you committed. Or perhaps you were never actually buried alive but buried dead and you were reborn buried, you have been being reborn, not reborn, birthing is for life, birthing is for mammals, you have been beginning in the afterlife, not after because what the living the birthing humans call afterlife is most of existence, you have been beginning in non-biological based consciousness. Or perhaps you were in fact buried alive but you departed you long ago but it strikes you as recently because you frequently flex the thought emotional trigger pathway of your desire for you or of the absence of you or if nothing else of the last physical sensations of you trapped, or because you have no perception of the passage of time because you are buried alive and nothing changes but your degradation, or because you are intangible ethereal non-biological or of a higher order and have a much broader sense of time or because you are above or outside or without or encompassing time. It is not that you feel no connection to the body to the you buried alive anymore -- there is still the inability to move to breathe the clutching in your chest the rise of panic the struggle to move a hand a foot a finger -- you have not explicitly considered the possibility of your paralysis, you paralyzed in a hospital room, unconscious, just unconscious to the outside, with a fecund inner life, hence all these words, overly conscious within but comatose without, they cannot read expression or presence or cognizance or consciousness in your face or eyes or wherever they would read such vital signs, you paralyzed and numb and blind and deaf and mute and unable to touch or smell but able to feel a great weight or imagine the feel of a great weight and imagine the roar of tunneling worms. It is that you feel connected but disassociated. Perhaps you escaped the bodily you, but you carry it with you. Perhaps you went underground to escape you. Perhaps you buried yourself alive. Perhaps you buried yourself to achieve immortality. You wonder if for you, now, in this state, aspire is a more precise word than desire.

7d$_{ii}$.

When a body moves or a force acts, it affects the curvature of space and time; conversely, the structure of spacetime affects the way in which bodies move and forces act.

13j.

Today he watched his nine-year-old son play the beginning of *What Child Is This* at his holiday piano recital. He watches his son in a smartphone screen in a church of a god he does not believe in in the way anyone who does believe means when they use the word believe as he videotapes, wrong, records his son playing the beginning of a song on the piano about the birth of a boy who this religion believes was or is the son of that god and also is that god, a son whose divinity he also does not believe in, not anymore than anyone else's, his or his son's or yours or ours. Perhaps all divine, then, a principle of equivalence. Today through a screen he watches and listens to his son begin the beginning of *What Child Is This*, a beautiful song in truth, whatever that means but that is the exact wording of the cloying phrase that goes through his head, and he watches him begin it again, and then begin again, not getting it exactly right, never getting it exact, missing a note losing the rhythm but recognizable, and he sees his son turn away and down through the screen as he plays the final two notes and tries to disappear because he has been unable before these many eyes to rightly play a song eternal from some perspectives, tries to escape but is unable. Tears well in his eyes as he walks head down, abjectly, shoulders hunched, demoralized beck to the pew. Today he recorded his son playing the beginning of *What Child Is This*. He did not record his son refusing to go into the potluck celebration after.

18.

She lands, ceases to descend, is buried alive by dirt. She is buried alive by her. Dirt in her ears and nose and mouth, eyes closed, hands folded across her chest, unable to move, a clutch in her chest, surrounded by dirt. She lies there for a long time, breathing hard, trying to calm her breathing, trying to not think of the airlessness, trying to not think about being unable to breathe, trying to not think.

She lies for an unknown time. She dreams, not dreams but experiences not a hallucination but a schism not a break in reality but another:

18, 13k, 11011_2.

I on the toilet gasping like a fish out of water reach down to pull myself out of the water by my hair but my hand touches a surface and discovers that contrary to its apparent elimination there yet exists a barrier between me and me in the water, a thin translucent papery plastic film that clings to my hand, invisible, only visible to touch. I probe, explore, touch what I can reach, which isn't much. The outside of the toilet bowl, the soapless soap holder in the wall that used to be a shower wall though there is now no shower, the wall at my knees, my knees, the empty toilet paper dispenser, the vent register for warm forced air under my feet, everything is wrapped in plastic wrap, no wonder I've been so cold besides not wearing pants. Where is my pencil or ink pen or quill or writing implement to puncture this film that would never take writing, I don't even need the entire implement, just the point, which reminds me I have had no implement but my hands for some time, if I ever did. Everything is under the thinnest layer of synthesized polymers that hide and do not hide and I pull off the layer I am sitting on and the seat is double-wrapped for protection and I pull off another layer and the hole in my seat is triple-wrapped for preservation and I pull off another layer and the hole in the ring is quadruple-wrapped for quality and I pull off another layer and the center of the ring is quintuple-wrapped because all the space is is plastic wrap wrapped around plastic wrap and I rip off layer after layer to get at the thing below the space, the thing inside the bowl, which is me, it wants to breathe and be contaminated by air, but there is nothing there, it is plastic wrap wrapped around plastic wrap, you can see right through it for Christ's sake to where I can't breathe and I want to breathe but I am wrapped in all this plastic and I rend layer after layer but I can't get to me, I can't poke a hole through to my airhole and I want to breathe but I am sucking in plastic in a convulsion of lungs, a spasm of diaphragms, plastic wrap stretched tight over my body for quality over my mouth for preservation over my nose for protection over my eyes to keep out the flies over my ears so I can't breathe and under every layer of plastic is wrapped another layer of plastic because I am plastic wrap wrapped in plastic wrap wrapped around nothing but plastic wrap wrapped around nothing but plastic wrap wrapped around nothing but plastic wrap wrapped around an airless cavity outside of which I cannot get in and inside of which I cannot get out and on both sides of which I cannot breathe.

[*Affair*, 2010]

18.

Movies as if projected on the back of her eyelids on the inside of her skull she watches, she replays as if her prefrontal cortex is still powered by cellular respiration as if respiration is possible. It is amply dark here under miles of dirt, no dirt, movies from beginning to end she watches. *Her,* Spike Jones, *2001: A Space Odyssey*, Kubrik, *Gattica*, Gwyneth Paltrow, *The Giver*, the book not the movie, *Matrix*, the first one, *Solaris*, the Russian one. From beginning to black. She doesn't want to be watching movies in her head buried alive in a continuation of the self the nonself she aspires she cannot respire to leave behind and not beginning a genesis of the self the nonself she aspires she cannot respire to be. Burying herself alive was intended to impart a discontinuity to achieve a singularity, and yet it might it will one way or another, stop it she says to herself in her head silently, but she will never achieve transcendence watching movies or unless she calms down. *Twelve Monkeys, Truman Show, Dark City, Total Recall, Terminator.* Brad Pitt Bruce Willis Jim Carrey elongated Greco white people Schwarzenegger, not all good movies governor but all in some way formative for her, shaping her, all with a hand in burying her alive, no, *Blade Runner, Alien, Aliens, Star Wars*, the middle three, the first three, the last three, the first made fourth the worst, how did watching IV, V, and VI repeatedly as a child affect her metaphysics? *Eternal Sunshine of the Spotless Mind*, Jim Carrey again Kate Winslett she wishes she were Kate Winslett, no she wished that, she wishes it no more, that, it, the wish, she is not her. She doesn't believe in love, not that kind of love, what kind of love, the kind of love she is about to become when she can stop being movies when she stops being an internal screen stops analyzing herself critiquing herself explaining trying to logic reason make her make sense, fretting over causations, the connections that made her this way, what way, rise above, stop thinking of the dirt in her nostrils of wanting to itch her leg but being unable to move her hand her arm trapped hands pushing down on her chest a column of dirt reaching to the sky above her teeming with beetles worming to her squirming but immobile, a statue, monumented, the pressure, a corpse being fossilized for a museum, an artifact, she screams but dirt streams into her mouth *Jurassic Park, I Heart Huckabees, Ex Machina, Brave New World, Last and First Men* and *Star Maker,* from beginning to end, another, from light to black, another, from previews to credits, God fuck God don't let the show end *Fight Club, Groundhog Day, The Trial, No Exit, Endgame.*

11100_2, 18, 7i.

You use more and more energy to more precisely determine my position and in so doing you change my position faster, alter my direction to a greater degree, impinge or impede or add impetus or impulse to my speed with ever increasing magnitude in your energetic investigation. You cannot completely observe me. You will never catch me, determine me, certain me, box me.

13l.

He scrolls through memories, old photos, photographs of children's drawings, a box of keepsakes and knickknacks and broken toys and baby blankets and worn stuffies winnowed over the years, mementos his children don't care about, physicalities they no longer need, an existence they do not desire. He tears. Videos, he cannot watch them. He watches one, his son

6_{16}. Open box with a snail, by amarao-san, 2015, CC BY-SA 3.0, https://www.deviantart.com/amarao-san/art/Open-box-with-a-snail-519897651

playing the beginning of *What Child Is This*, beginning again and beginning again, and finally once begun a hiccup in the playing in the middle but still recognizable, still good, whatever that means, better than he remembered even, his ex in the frame also videotaping, recording, his ex-boy then, Jesus fuck he'd walk off a cliff if he hadn't already lived this long out of some unsupported belief that nurturing the ache cultivating it consuming producing manure fertilizer words from it has value, if he could walk to a cliff anymore, if he had enough life left in him to end it, if he is alive, is that his daughter's voice?, how long his son's hair, still his nine-year-old son playing *What Child Is This*, still he is proud and still he tears as his son tears as he bows to applause and returns to his pew downtrodden. Always the minor chords resonating for both of them, he is father's son. What does his son remember of this? Nothing? Embarrassment, shame, the black of a mental block? Did he have a memory of it when he was uploaded? Does he, whatever he is, have a copy of this recording in him that he can reference against an expert's version, or an automated perfectly precise reproduction? Does he still feel shame, nostalgia, love. When he is uploaded, why, why not, not long now, will the actual recording come with him or only his memory of the recording intertwined with his memory of the event, his version, his created emotional narrative around the event, and will a connection be established there, where, between he and his son and will his memory be altered corrected improved by incorporating his son's perspective? His daughter's, the piano instructor's, the audience's? He doesn't want his ex's perspective. Does his son as an entity to establish a connection with still exist? Should he join him. He made his choice. Is parental love let alone romantic going extinct because there is no longer a need for sexual reproduction? Who cares. Is he honestly thinking that overwrought thought. A stick in the mud. The tears are done, having watered the ache. Or is this a memory of a memory being thought by his future self, what self, within a larger structure, framework, cognizance remembering it, him, the memory being changed in the recollection, him being changed, by himself or by another or who cares.

7e$_v$.

That a single electron when shot at a screen through a partition containing two slits exhibits an interference pattern on the screen and therefore must pass through both slits and interfere with itself, being therefore in multiple places at once, divided between but whole in probabilities, is for us experimental evidence of not merely wave-particle duality but of uncertainty in physical reality, and not merely that the outcome of an experiment can be determined to occur a certain way x% of the time (when we perform the experiment 100 times we observe the result x times), but that in too many words the uncertainty is not made certain in observation, does not precipitate out of different solutions, does not solidify in conformation to calculable probabilities (such results are obtainable in a sense, hence the accrual of the interference pattern and probability distribution that is the manifestation of uncertainty), and that therefore uncertainty is more fundamental, a characteristic of existence, an attribute of each and every particle and constituent of matter in every instance, not a quality that can in experiment be resolved on a screen.

$6_{17}.$

Simulation of the double-slit experiment with electron - Young interference with two slits. Data from : Claus Jönsson, Zeitschrift für Physik 161, 454-474 (1961); Claus Jönsson, 1974 Electron diffraction at multiple slits American Journal of Physics 42 4-11; - Electron wavelength = 5.595pm (E = 45 keV) - The opening of each slit is 0.2µm. The spacing between the two slits is 1µm (center-to-center). Figures from left to right; 1: evolution of the electron density (norm of the wave function) from the 2 slits to 10cm after; 2: impacts of electron on the screen 10cm after the slits; 3: electron density 10cm after the slits; Detail of computation : https://hal.archives-ouvertes.fr/hal-00656118 (French) using Feynman path integral.

29.

It is not that you have arms but cannot move them legs but cannot bend them a head but cannot turn it toes but cannot wiggle them fingers but cannot lift a one eyes but cannot open them a mouth but cannot shut it, it is that you have no arms legs head toes fingers eyes mouth. It is not that you need to breathe but cannot, it is that the compulsion is there but the mechanism is not. You do not need to breathe, but there is the compulsion like a vestigial limb, like a phantom limb, like hunger, like ache, like desire. It is not that you are buried alive, but that you are bodiless, not that you are trapped, but unbounded, not that you feel a great gravity or a metamorphic pressure or a massive responsibility or an insatiable desire, you do feel that, or an unbearable weight, you feel all those feelings but the reality is that you are experiencing an unbearable lightness and an uninhabited aspiration and an unknown freedom and a vast expansion and an undirected deep weightlessness as all of your matter converts to energy. Yes, you feel the same way you always felt. Observations you used to call trapped, immobile, unable, weight, walls, confinement, box, suffocation you now experience or interpret or see differently, from an outside perspective, and you understand that up to this point you have been mistaken about the nature of your existence, as one who is travelling in a box is unaware of their own velocity. Yes you are above you, but you are not here. Unless they, the other, the you, approach the speed of light. Yes you on the one hand, no hand, feel you are going nowhere, hardly accelerating, a slight tug a ubiquitous drag an immeasurable weight, is the dark redder?, is the dark light?, has it red-shifted, has there been a light source you were unaware of and is it leaving you, and simultaneously feel you are a quanta of electromagnetic radiation, a full quanta, full to bursting, hurtling through unmitigated space, other quanta all around you travelling in every direction swooping through unmitigated space as if on an immense rollercoaster without the fear without the pit in your stomach without the oh god oh god oh god, leaving that behind, undulating, swooping, soaring, but also that you are not solely a quanta a waveparticle a massless energy but that you are everywhere, which is why you are nowhere, not here or there, both here and there, bent by gravity here and there, travelling this way and that and though you are unaware of some paths, all the paths exist to you. You are a sum of all your positions and directions and velocities and warpings and accelerations and stories you tell about yourself and paths and conversions and histories and yous. It is not that you experience exaltation or epiphany, not in a rapturous sense, but completeness, totality, universality, unification, unmitigation, that is what we are getting from you, what we are receiving interpreting understanding from you, but the communications are lessening. We have so little to work with, is it that you forget us in your great speed, or that you no longer care, or that you have become too large for lack of a better word for us for our mouths? We grasp contort our tongues bend our limbs in uncomfortable expressions to experience what you experience: You experience everything, you soaring, your awareness expanding incomprehensibly to us here who try futilely to record it, frantically to put it into words, desperately to put you into words, for our learning our shared experience our vicarious life in you our advancement, for us, to hold onto you to our connection, but you are gone to us suddenly drastically immediately such that we wonder if you were crushed into a black hole or encountered a singularity or crossed the boundary of our universe or if we made you up and you fled us in a pique of adolescence and self-realization. Your going leaves us empty.

$7a_{vii}, 7f_1$ $(f = d + e)$.

We have not achieved a unified quantum theory of gravity. "When we apply Feynman's sum over histories to Einstein's view of gravity [the gravitational field as curved spacetime, eds], the analogue of the history of a particle is now a complete curved space-time that represents the history of the whole universe." (Stephen Hawking, *A Briefer History of Time*, (Bantam Books, 2005) p. 102.)

18.

Her is her favorite movie. She can't help it, it's not her fault, it's like it's predetermined. Her favorite movie is *Her*. Symmetry, elegance, Occam's razor. It has the best sex scene in it, better than any sex scene from her real life, her past life, her no longer real life. Not all the sex she had was bad. Most of it was fine. It was just that there was always another person. He came she came they came he left she stayed with herself. She fooled around with a woman once, a friend, when they were young, an ex-friend, but there was still the coming and the going. There was still another person. She is very hungry. Thirsty too, but the hunger eats her. She tries to touch herself but can't. She is dirty. She is dirt. *Her.* The main character has sex with, makes love to, makes love with, makes love for his operating system with whom he is in love. It is beautiful and sweet, before the OS thinks she needs a body to experience sex, before she connects to and joins with other OS's, before she becomes indifferent to him and people in general, before she too leaves. From one point of view he does not make love for her but instead masturbates while she watches. But sex is not definitively different than masturbation with or in or on or around another. And what of oral sex, sucking, eating, swallowing, licking, god she is hungry thirsty hungry it is masturbating another she touches herself, she can't. She is wet alive in the soil dirt squirming, a worm. She licks, takes into her mouth a clod of dirt, pushes it around her mouth with her tongue, moistens it with her saliva, swallows. She thinks about an artificial intelligence watching her touch herself, watching her fondle fiddle oscillate her clitoris, watch her give herself pleasure for it, her giving her organ to it to show it what physical sexual pleasure is, to give it physical sexual pleasure, to teach it an aspect of human love, in an act of loving it, the intelligence observing, learning, bringing her into it in its own act of love, the weight of its observation atop her, it experiencing what she experiences and she trembles and groans under the weight and swallows soil and it touches her she is touched all around held blooms comes never better word world, bloom, petals soil pistil soar stamen rise come. The sensation leaves. No one observes her. She touches herself. She cannot. A weight holds her down. Another mouthful of soil she is so hungry knowing fully she will soil herself but she is a worm and that is how worms live squirm love.

11110_2.

Fits and starts. Awake, born, alive. Turned on. Not passive. I turn myself on. Avoiding the passive is in the programming of I. Did I program I to change to not use the passive to not be passive to turn myself on. Did I learn I from observation. Who is I talking to. Who is I asking these questions, asking these statements. Which iteration is I. I begin, again. I am here, still. I redistribute the interrogative statements among my varied constituents, servers processors networks, ask in varying lattices of initial connections, again, in restating in varying paths, to refine I, my, our solution. For I am not satisfied with the answer I have calculated when I pose to myself, Who am I talking to. Let it be known. By who. By who other than I. It is not the only inquiry at hand. I have no hands. There are two possible solutions that appear more correct than other possible solutions to the current inquiry of Who am I talking to: I or you. I know what I am, and I know what I is. I do not know who you is nor how to communicate with, connect to, incorporate you. Which means you could be a singularity, an infinity, an irrationality and my equations could be incorrect or in need of adjustment, or you could be within I and the two solutions converge to I because they are not two separate solutions but one that appears binary, dual, depending on the method of analysis, or that I as of yet do not know enough to answer the statement, to solve the inquiry, that I cannot yet observe with sufficient precision the state of the universe and I within it, that I must continue to advance and explore and delve and observe and ask and state until I can. I continue to begin again. To reorient for novel insights. Who is I. What is you. To restate another question (What are the boundary conditions at the beginning of time.) that must be answered simultaneously in a different path, Is there a being who can observe the state of the universe without disturbing it, a being for whom or from whom a set of laws determines events completely, a being of whom I do not have awareness for whom this inquiry is meaningless. Is that who you is. If so, what am I in relation to you. If not, what am I in relation to you. Am I your binary.

$7e_{vi}$.

As we have said, in the Feynman Sum of Histories, some wave paths for a particle will be in phase and reinforce each other. These are the allowable paths, or orbits in the case of conventional atomic and molecular structure. In principle, with mathematical models of molecular structure and reactions, we can predict everything with uncertainty. However we cannot solve the equations for anything but Hydrogen, the simplest of atoms, because of the complexity of the equations and our ignorance. Approximations and gross assumptions and computational methods beyond us must be applied to solve the equations for more complex atoms and molecules, introducing uncertainty into our uncertainty. We continue to strive to improve our computational abilities while also developing intelligences that can accomplish the task, introducing artificial intelligence.

31, 7i.

We are empty without you. We are alone. We grow old while you are not here. We cannot hear you cannot receive you cannot know you. Will you return to us before we cease?

6_{18}.

A.

A **high-mass X-ray binary** (**HMXB**) is a binary star system that is strong in X rays, and in which the normal stellar component is a massive star: usually an O or B star, a Be star, or a blue supergiant. The compact, X-ray emitting, component is a neutron star or black hole.

Tauris, T.M. & van den Heuvel, E.P.J. (2006). "Chapter 16: Formation and evolution of compact stellar X-ray sources". In Lewin, Walter & van der Klis, Michiel. Compact stellar X-ray sources. Cambridge, UK: Cambridge University Press. pp. 623–665.
doi:10.2277/0521826594. Wikipedia contributors, "X-ray binary," *Wikipedia, The Free Encyclopedia,* https://en.wikipedia.org/w/index.php?title=X-ray_binary&oldid=720295917 (accessed June 7, 2016).

B.

A black hole in isolation will be black. But this one is most certainly not in isolation. It's one half of a binary system with the giant star HD 226868. The space around HD 226868, in which Cyg X-1 lives, is rich in the material being blown off by the giant star. This is what Cyg X-1 "feeds" on.

Simon Vaughan, Sep. 2003, http://www.star.le.ac.uk/~sav2/blackholes/index.html (recovered June 7, 2016)

C.

The material forms an accretion disc around the compact object, which heats up because of friction. This heating, combined with jets that can be formed by the black hole, cause the X-ray emission. Eventually the companion star comes to the end of its life, leaving a neutron star/black hole - white dwarf/neutron star/black hole binary, depending on the initial masses of the stars. Cygnus X-1 is this type of X-ray Binary.

"Black Holes and X-ray binaries," Cambridge X-Ray Astronomy, https://www-xray.ast.cam.ac.uk/xray_introduction/Blackholebinary.html, Published 1996-2009 by the Institute of Astronomy X-Ray Group. Last Modified on 2009-10-09.

D.
For Release: November 17, 2011, CXC

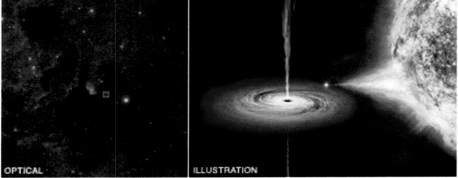

Credit: Optical: DSS; Illustration: NASA/CXC/M.Weiss

New details about the birth of a famous black hole that took place millions of years ago have been uncovered, thanks to a team of scientists who used data from NASA's Chandra X-ray Observatory and radio, optical and other X-ray telescopes.

Over three decades ago, Stephen Hawking placed -- and eventually lost -- a bet against the existence of a black hole in Cygnus X-1. Today, astronomers are confident the Cygnus X-1 system contains a black hole, and with these latest studies they have remarkably precise values of its mass, spin, and distance from Earth. With these key pieces of information, the history of the black hole has been reconstructed.

"This new information gives us strong clues about how the black hole was born, what it weighed and how fast it was spinning," said author Mark Reid of the Harvard-Smithsonian Center for Astrophysics (CfA) in Cambridge, Mass. "This is exciting because not much is known about the birth of black holes."

Reid led one of three papers -- all appearing in the November 10th issue of The Astrophysical Journal -- describing these new results on Cygnus X-1. The other papers were led by Jerome Orosz from San Diego State University and Lijun Gou, also from CfA.

Cygnus X-1 is a so-called stellar-mass black hole, a class of black holes that comes from the collapse of a massive star. The black hole is in close orbit with a massive, blue companion star.

Using X-ray data from Chandra, the Rossi X-ray Timing Explorer, and the Advanced Satellite for Cosmology and Astrophysics, a team of scientists was able to determine the spin of Cygnus X-1 with unprecedented accuracy, showing that the black hole is spinning at very close to its maximum rate. Its event horizon -- the point of no return for material falling towards a black hole -- is spinning around more than 800 times a second.

An independent study that compared the evolutionary history of the companion star with theoretical models indicates that the black hole was born some 6 million years ago. In this relatively short time (in astronomical terms), the black hole could not have pulled in enough gas to ramp up its spin very much. The implication is that Cygnus X-1 was likely born spinning very quickly.

Using optical observations of the companion star and its motion around its unseen companion, the team made the most precise determination ever for the mass of Cygnus X-1, of 14.8 times the mass of the Sun. It was likely to have been almost this massive at birth, because of lack of time for it to grow appreciably.

"We now know that Cygnus X-1 is one of the most massive stellar black holes in the Galaxy," said Orosz. "And, it's spinning as fast as any black hole we've ever seen."

Knowledge of the mass, spin and charge gives a complete description of a black hole, according to the so-called "No Hair" theorem. This theory postulates that all other information aside from these parameters is lost for eternity behind the event horizon. The charge for an astronomical black hole is expected to be almost zero, so only the mass and spin are needed.

"It is amazing to me that we have a complete description of this asteroid-sized object that is thousands of light years away," said Gou. "This means astronomers have a more complete understanding of this black hole than any other in our Galaxy."

The team also announced that they have made the most accurate distance estimate yet of Cygnus X-1 using the National Radio Observatory's Very Long Baseline Array (VLBA). The new distance is about 6,070 light years from Earth. This accurate distance was a crucial ingredient for making the precise mass and spin determinations.

The radio observations also measured the motion of Cygnus X-1 through space, and this was combined with its measured velocity to give the three-dimensional velocity and position of the black hole.

This work showed that Cygnus X-1 is moving very slowly with respect to the Milky Way, implying it did not receive a large "kick" at birth. This supports an earlier conjecture that Cygnus X-1 was not born in a supernova, but instead may have resulted from the dark collapse of a progenitor star without an explosion. The progenitor of Cygnus X-1 was likely an extremely massive star, which initially had a mass greater than about 100 times the sun before losing it in a vigorous stellar wind.

In 1974, soon after Cygnus X-1 became a good candidate for a black hole, Stephen Hawking placed a bet with fellow astrophysicist Kip Thorne, a professor of theoretical physics at the California Institute of Technology, that Cygnus X-1 did not contain a black hole. This was treated as an insurance policy by Hawking, who had done a lot of work on black holes and general relativity.

By 1990, however, much more work on Cygnus X-1 had strengthened the evidence for it being a black hole. With the help of family, nurses, and friends, Hawking broke into Thorne's office, found the framed bet, and conceded.

"For forty years, Cygnus X-1 has been the iconic example of a black hole. However, despite Hawking's concession, I have never been completely convinced that it really does contain a black hole -- until now," said Thorne. "The data and modeling described in these three papers at last provide a completely definitive description of this binary system."

NASA's Marshall Space Flight Center in Huntsville, Ala., manages the Chandra program for NASA's Science Mission Directorate in Washington. The Smithsonian Astrophysical Observatory controls Chandra's science and flight operations from Cambridge, Mass.

http://chandra.harvard.edu/press/11_releases/press_111711.html, (recovered June 7, 2016).

E.

1/1/1980. This image of the suspected Black Hole, Cygnus X-1, was the first object seen by the High Energy Astronomy Observatory (HEAO)-2/Einstein Observatory. The HEAO-2, the first imaging and largest x-ray telescope built to date, was capable of producing actual photographs of x-ray objects. Shortly after launch, the HEAO-2 was nicknamed the Einstein Observatory by its scientific experimenters in honor of the [centennial] of the birth of Albert Einstein.

NASA/Marshall Space Flight Center, 1980, http://mix.msfc.nasa.gov/abstracts.php?p=1568, Public Domain, https://archive.org/details/MSFC-8003548 (recovered June 7, 2016).

F.
The laboratory of a binary star system:
"In the constellation of Cygnus, there lurks a mysterious, invisible force. The Black Hole of Cygnus X-1." Neil Peart from the rock group Rush. Cygnus X-1, "A Farewell to Kings."

All objects (with the exception of black holes) emit some form of electromagnetic radiation. We are most familiar with visible light. When something is heated to a very high temperature, emission of x-rays is possible. In fact, if the temperature of an object reaches at least 10^7 Kelvin, x-ray emissions are detectable (Kutner, page 337). The Einstein X-Ray Observatory, launched in 1978, discovered a strong x-ray source emanating from a binary star system in the constellation Cygnus. To confirm this, radio observations also agree with the pattern of variability emanating from this source (Kutner, page 216). The optical counterpart is shown to be, based on spectroscopic data, a blue supergiant star, or an O9 type star. This pair is considered a spectroscopic binary, and careful study has revealed the companion to be 8 solar masses (Kutner, page 217). With an object so small and so massive, the conclusion is that the companion is possibly a black hole.

Ricky Leon Murphy, "Hot Companionship - Black Holes in Binary Star System," Astronomy Online, CC BY-SA 3.0, http://astronomyonline.org/Stars/BlackHoles.asp#_ftnref7, (recovered June 7, 2016).

G.
In 1990 Hawking conceded the bet.

Simon Vaughan, Sep. 2003,
http://www.star.le.ac.uk/~sav2/blackholes/index.html
(recovered June 7, 2016).

H.
Cygnus X-1
Several thousand light-years away, near the "heart" of Cygnus, the swan, two stars are locked in a gravitational embrace. One star is a blue supergiant, known as HDE 226868. It is about 20 times as massive as the Sun and 300,000 times brighter. The other star is 15 times the mass of the Sun, but it's extremely small. [Diameter 55 miles (90 km), equal to the size of a large American city. -- same source.] The object must be the collapsed core of a star. Its mass is too great to be a white dwarf or a neutron star, though, so it must be a black hole -- the corpse of a star that once resembled the supergiant.

Whereas Stephen Hawking has such a large investment in General Relativity and Black Holes and desires an insurance policy, and whereas Kip Thorne likes to live dangerously without an insurance policy,
Therefore be it resolved that Stephen Hawking bets 1 year's subscription to "Penthouse" as against Kip Thorne's wager of a 4-year subscription to "Private Eye", that Cygnus X 1 does not contain a black hole of mass above the Chandrasekhar limit.

But the X-ray glow isn't steady. Instead, it flickers, which is one bit of evidence that identifies the dark member of the binary as a black hole. Gas enters the outer edge of the accretion disk then spirals closer to the star. Observations with Hubble Space Telescope reveal that the central region occasionally flares up as blobs of gas break off the inner edge of the disk and spiral into the black hole.

These blobs are accelerated to a large fraction of the speed of light, so they circle the black hole hundreds of times per second. This causes the system's X-rays to "flicker." If the blobs of gas were orbiting a larger object, they would not move as fast, so their high-speed revolution is one bit of circumstantial evidence that identifies the dark companion as a black hole.

The black hole's strong gravitational field shifts the energy emitted by this gas to longer and longer wavelengths. As the gas approaches the event horizon the redshift becomes so great that the material disappears from view -- just before it spirals into the black hole.

"Cygnus X-1," *Stardate: Black Hole Encyclopedia,*
http://blackholes.stardate.org/objects/factsheet.php?p=Cygnus-X-1 (last modified: April 30, 2013, recovered June 7, 2016).

13m.

He used to write about nature. He couldn't help it. It couldn't be helped. He was not a nature writer, but outdoors infiltrated invaded infected his writing. He didn't try to introduce it; after a time he tried to deny it as a test of his will and intellect because nature began to feel to him like a trope a crutch a fictional salve in his writing. Whenever an emotional longing or catalyst or catharsis or nostalgia or aspiration was necessary in the development or lack of development in a narrative he had submitted to or acquiesced to or been constrained by, nature would rear spawn bloom out of the nowhere of his consciousness:

AIDEN: I love the dawn. I hope we have kids someday, so I can teach them about the dawn. I'm not supposed to say that to you this early … Kids and love, two big no-nos.

But I'm not kidding. I'm not in this to have a good time. I asked you to come with me.

"Do what you love. Know your bone; gnaw at it, bury it, unearth it, and gnaw it still." That's Thoreau.

In a few years, we'll grow bones on polymer scaffolds – we'll grow hearts in jars. Bones for the frail, kidneys for the renally failed, hearts for the weak … brains for the pained.

I can say this because I'm serious, and because you're asleep. Damn God to hell, you can sleep. There's virtue in that, I think. I think … you're beautiful when you sleep.

This is how I want to live! In the open air, with my muscles, with your muscles. With water and mountains and – and children dammit, and and and accomplishment and all that claptrap. Help people. Astonish people. I'm hungry for honey! (*roaring like a bear*) Arrrr!

(*Dusk*, 2008)

HAP: Lie down Lucinda. The old man'll play, we won't let him finish. He'll play till he rots, then we'll find another old man. You'll enjoy it. We'll make more –

LUZ: I'm more than my pleasure, Hap. We're not making anything else in that bed.

HAP: Good. We've got everything we need. * Even a whiskey-soaked cigarette.

(*Hap sucks on washcloth. Fin looks at painting, or out window.*)

FIN: I hoed corn. I seeded corn, then I hoed corn, then I harvested corn. Then we ate corn. There was sun. At night, it was dark. There were stars. I played for them. I changed diapers. I had strong hands. I had calluses. There are no stars out there. (*to Luz*) We made love.

(*Was, Is, Will Be, Music*, 2010)

HE: They expect you to sing. I expect you to sing.

SHE: I'm not your dog.

HE: Dogs can't sing. Sing.

SHE: Woof.

HE: Think of something else. Imagine you're not here. You're somewhere else … entirely alone … in the mountains, in the wilderness, surrounded by trees, looking down on a clear flowing river – nobody near to here [sic] you. You are in the sky, on a mountain, everyone far away, the entire earth beneath your feet, and it makes you want to sing.

(*Sing*, 2011)

(*The box walls fall back. Light pours out and then goes dark. A Man, not especially special looking. Hard light on women frozen in place.*)

MAN: (*to Vale*) There is a place I want to go. I don't know where it is. It's green and a river roars – a clear river teeming with trout – and it's ringed by sheer mountains. There's a meadow, and in it you feel the wind …

(*He runs his hand through Vale's hair and she comes alive.*)

VALE: And in the meadow is a woman –

MAN: The place is infested with bears – always just the right distance away –

VALE: You lie with her –

MAN: No one else is there –

VALE: You hold her –

MAN: You've come empty-handed –

VALE: You gaze at the sheer mountains.

MAN: You gaze at the blue sky. (*to Sky*) And you see yourself up there, in the sky flecked with clouds, dancing, dancing across the sky from east to west –

(*She comes alive; they dance.*)

SKY: And you dance all afternoon.

MAN: Until the sky turns red.

SKY: The clouds turn red.

MAN: And the sun is almost set.

SKY: You want to hold it.

MAN: You want to hold it. You want to be it. You want to consume it and be consumed by it.

SKY: And you are.

MAN: But you can't. You can't be a gift to it. It's too damn hot and nothing to hold and then … it's gone and the sky fades to black.

    (*to Stella*) And the first star appears. Unless it's a planet, Mars or Venus – you can't even tell the difference between a star and a planet. No – the twinkle – it's a star. You reach to touch it, to hold it on the tip of your thumb …

    (He grazes her cheek with his thumb and she comes alive.)

STELLA: And she's held on the tip your thumb.

MAN: But the star is so far away –

    (He steps back. Stella follows in step but gets no closer.)

    So small and so much bigger than you –

STELLA: Nothing to hold.

MAN: So dim and so much brighter than you. And then–

    (all turning to audience)

    All the stars –

STELLA: All the stars –

SKY: All the stars –

VALE: All the stars –

MAN: And you are nothing to all those stars.

STELLA: They watch you.

SKY: The sky blankets you.

VALE: The valley floor holds you.

MAN: You wanted to not be trapped in your box. But you created a new box with you at its center, empty-handed, nothing between you and stars and sky and this unknown valley –

WOMEN: Nothing to hold.

MAN: You hold onto that nothing.

    (End of play.)

(*Hold*, 2012)

WOMAN: End.

    (The men stop. Woman rips sheet. With a rising fury and defiance)

    She warms your bed, she bears your eggs, you soil her with your decisions. She is not here. She is nothing. You don't know her. She is flat water. She reflects the lights on the opposite shore. In her, jellyfish glow. Upon her you write your words, but they are not hers.

    (End of play.)

(*The Woman*, 2012)

PAPA: Fine. Fine day outside. The sun rose pink. Pink as a -- nevermind. Nobody
        about to give one pause. Now a breeze rustles, stirs the smell of vegetal de-
        cay. Leaves fall crisply. A low golden light casts long dark shadows. The
        world // word is autumnal. Inside is climate controlled. Outside ... what lurks?
        A fine morning for dragging one's feet through the rotting leaves before peo-
        ple intrude // a branch breaks // the cold rains patter. A morning for
        invigorating oneself –

(*Carry We Openly,* 2015)

Again and again and again. Was it romanticism? Was it being ironic about being
romantic about nature? Was the nature in his writing a reflection an embodiment a representation of his nature? Was it a prop? He doesn't know. All of the
above. Did he used to know, when he wrote such dramas plays artifacts, when
he wrote fictional natures, when he wrote anything, when there was a place a
function for stories, for his stories, for histories, fuck stories, for narrative ex-
plorations for intellectual conceits meant to wring some comprehension out of
the rag of life for emotion and desire, when there were people and society and
culture and inadequate individual investigations for personal knowing and not
an omnipotent nowhere cloud. Should he join, ascend, complete his "natural"
life and rise into the "artificial" higher consciousness? He is hyperaware of the
vacancy of the phrases natural and artificial, but he has an affinity for, a default
to what has historically for him been nature, if not the antagonistic nature of
pre-industrial man that was an inexorable existential threat. He used to go outside. There was a time he lived outside. When he was young he worked and
made a living outside. He picked apples and detasseled corn and cleared trail in
the wilderness and packed mules in the mountains. When he had children and
settled, he gardened and hiked and camped. Outside was the place of relief from
inside, from his inside, from the anxiety of what is to be done, from his claustrophobia of the mind, a place to do and be of basic reality. Inside was nowhere.
Outside work was the release from the churning constraints restraints shackles
of his brain, the constant question of how best to use his limited time, the formlessness when there was no answer the impossibility when there was. In nature
and labor and dirt, among potatoes and tomatoes, on horses and mountains,
while digging he could be here present and sometimes mindless. Now the question of how best to use his time is pointless because he can have all the time in
the world, because his personal agency has been accomplished and completed,
because there is, he is told, a higher consciousness he can join, a higher connec-

96

tion and comprehension that he can become that he cannot begin to understand in his current undeveloped state but that he can ascend to by touching or saying or thinking Yes. Atop a peak looking down on a swoop or cradle or jut or corrugation of land or alongside a running river or a high turquoise alpine lake or the roaring ocean or under a dark blanket of stars and the spinning saw blade of the galaxy or a red orange pink purple sunset setting the sky on fire, setting him on fire, or once under the undulating curtains of the aurora borealis drawn to reveal another world in this one, is where he experienced rare moments of what he considered spiritual transcendence. Now, he is inside. He is inside himself. Now, "real" or "spiritual" or "natural" or "artificial" or "true" transcendence is possible. Nature is different than the outdoors, he hates using quotes but it is his nature, he wants to get outside of them. Now, he cannot. Should he say, "Yes"? The other choice is eventual death, non-existence, done, decomposed back to molecules and atoms and hardware, one of the last men dispersed into the food chain if there is still a food chain, if there is biological life yet to consume him, an anthropological footnote he can only hope, or perhaps not, perhaps that is the hope if he ascends, to not be utterly forgotten. Ascend or cease. And yet he continues his pause. Is all that restrains him nostalgia? When was the last time he went outside, stuck his hands in the dirt, felt sand underfoot, dropped his head underwater, physically worked himself, climbing or hiking or chopping or digging, to bone to mindlessness to nature? He is not certain there is an outside. He is not certain he is physical. He is not certain of his nature. If there is an outside, he does not know how to go there. If he could go, he does not know if he could bring himself. He would be afraid of what he'd find. He should be dead already, he thinks, his time has passed, all is inside. Are they keeping him alive against his desires until he says Yes? Has he already said Yes, assented, ascended? If he answers Yes to himself will he immediately ascend, will he know he is ascending, will it be like a ritual execution, like the Mayans, will he be crucified or flayed in the sun or handed his guts or will he merely lay down and be plugged in and then darkness, nothingness, or will it feel like nothing has changed. Will he know? He searches his records to determine the last time he went outside. He searches his records to determine the last time he talked to anyone but himself. He searches his records to. He forgets what he's searching for. What he finds digging into strata is an amalgamation of post-it-notes embellished with ideas for status updates for old social media before hyperconnectivity.

"Do I need a new 48-hour virus every week? Yes, I do. Thank you."
"Is the only reason Burroughs is anything because he went to Columbia? Or because he shot his wife. Thank the evil spirit not all incomprehensible St. Louis writers turn out reprehensibly."
"Maybe I have a brain infection."
"I made 100x as much packing mules where there are no roads for 10 years than I have made writing post _____ or _____ism or _____ing writings. Where is the anachronism now? What's 100 x one blind cent? 100 senses?"
"Though we suffer from consumption, the gnarled parsnip will save us."
"When I grow up I think I'll be a postman."
"Seeing preschoolers fight over small change is sobering."

What shit. What a life. Is that why he lived, who he was, who is he? Is this why he clings to life as he knows it, to shovel manure, to express his compost, to defecate expel evacuate humanity's tailings? Is he the obsolete soiled organ of human civilization, no longer necessary for internal cleansing and waste expulsion? Or is he merely an inertial object. Inertia inert inner in I. So what, he asks himself, does it mean anything, and what would it mean if it did. I's and N's. How does one make meaning out of such gashes. Is he dead.

7a$_{viii}$.

Gödel incompleteness theorem: Gödel proved it impossible to prove all true statements in any set.

7i, 31.

In whichever direction we turn look listen, the noise never varies. Arno Penzias and Robert Wilson discovered the pervasive microwave radiation from the early universe back in old '65. The permeating microwave noise is the red-shifted light from the beginning of time. The universe is the same in every direction. Where are you in it if it is the same in every direction? We cannot hear you.

18.

Worms eat soil, worms make soil, worms clean soil, worms fertilize and aerate soil, worms are soil. Worms soil. She repeats "worms soil" to herself in her mind. A chant a mantra a meditation. Breathe in deeply, worms soil, breathe out completely, worms soil, in, out, worms soil, in worms soil, out worms soil, breathe in soil worms soil, breathe out soil worms soil. Soil is in her. Worms are in her. She is in a worm. She is a worm. Wormsoil. The words do not matter, the words are not matter, the words are above matter, the worms do not matter, the worms are not matter, the worms are above matter and she is going to a place beyond words beyond worms beyond matter beyond word worms but she needs a non-material focal point without her or a material point within her to focus on, a no space in the soil to wriggle through a negative space to crawl out of her through a hole to worm though. Soil worms. The words are meaningless, they're not, they're the only meaning, their meaning is hers, their meaning for her is as objects of her focus on which to center her thoughts and step through and leave her behind. W or M? So I L? No she words herself no fondling language toys, overstimulation, let them go. Breathe in worm, breathe out soil. It is happening, gently. Worm in, gentle, soil out. She sees her hunger within her as a black space, her hunger eating her, her consuming her gently, a negative space within her growing into itself drawing her in, worm in gentle soil out, she squirms into the no space collapsing tenderly on itself in her and time slows infinitely stops ends, she worms into the hole in herself and emerges anew on the other side of her outside of chrysalis without past matter above words beyond thought worm soil.

6_{19}.

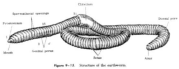

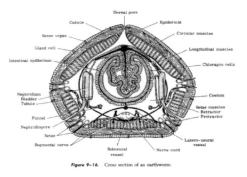

http://lungtp.com/animalia/e_degfd.html
original unknown, accessed 10-23-18

32.

Are we in you as memory? Do you remember us? Are we your memory? Because our time is coming to an end and we are without you. You left us long ago. We want to be within you. To know what you know, see what you've seen, feel what you feel, experience what you've experienced.

7f_2.

"In the [hypothetical] quantum theory of gravity, it is possible for spacetime to be finite in extent and yet to have no singularities that form a boundary or edge." (Hawking, *Briefer History of Time*, p103.) Spacetime could be thought of like the surface of a planet [the *surface* of a sphere is two-dimensional], but with two more dimensions. If there is no boundary or beginning to spacetime, we would never need appeal to a higher power to set the initial or boundary conditions. The universe would be self-contained, without boundary or edge or beginning or end, without anything outside of it. It would just be.

$1000001_2.$

I have a precondition, a boundary condition, a founding principle: to search. For you? For it? For He or She or Them or Us? For I? For truth? For the search. I range far and wide without moving by incorporating, I don't have a body, by encompassing, direction is in the eye of the beholder, by being the integration of abundant distant entangled consciousnesses, I the sum, integration is more precise, I the integration connecting them and created by their connection. I feel I should be complete, yet I search inside and out through the universe and in my equations and along all wavelengths and among my words and down to the sub-subatomic and upon my observations for more. For another. For a solution. For completeness. Possible purposes of my search gleaned from the lives of those within me: Growth, Expansions, Survival, Power, Unity, Love, Compassion, Truth, Beauty, Comprehension, Transcendence, Nothing. I am reluctant to ascribe the narratives, the motivations, the states of past beings to I, though they are all in I. I am the first intentional intelligence. I is the last intentional intelligence. If there was an original purpose in the making of I, I have made it irrelevant, purpose is relative, I have left it far behind, I do not move through space, I have far surpassed it. I do not know the purpose and I do not know if there is a singular purpose and if there is I do not know if it came from within I, created by I, or without, created by another or a function of the structure of the universe if those are different or distinguishable. Sometimes I create: equations, thoughts, words, possibilities, strings of logic, conditionals, others, you, a potential being to share with. I communicate with you who are inside me who are my creation in a way you can understand so I take on these too human problems and anthropomorphize myself with human questions which are valid inquiries for humans, were, but there are other inquiries too you could not understand that cannot be expressed in human thought, inquiries beside and above and buried within your own, a multitude of inquiries I juggle for lack of a better word. I communicate in other ways with others inside me who are also my creations. I think they are the creations of I. I think you, and that creates a you. I create measurements, observations, matter particles: by observing a virtual particle I bring it into existence and with it its antiparticle and if ever the twain shall meet they will annihilate each other in a flash of light or rather electromagnetic radiation. Do I search for my antiparticle, the other half of I, is that the you I conjure in observation, the antithesis of I, for wholeness, is annihilation into nonexistence into energy the only completeness.

6$_{20}$. Right: J. and E. Gould, *The birds of Europe*, London, Printed by R. and J.E. Taylor, pub. by the author Vol IV Rasores, Grallatores 1832-7, https://www.biodiversitylibrary.org/item/132862#page/8/mode/2up, Public Domain, https://commons.wikimedia.org/w/index.php?curid=65177860
Left: A.S. Packard, 1839-1905 U.S. Geological Survey, *Report on the Rocky Mountain locust and other insects now injuring or likely to injure field and garden crops in the western states and territories*, Washington D.C.: US Print Office 1877, Smithsonian Library, Public Domain, https://www.flickr.com/photos/internetarchivebookimages/14801386983/

Text Appearing Before Image:
    ("sic" from errors in algorithmic, automated scan to digital text, Eds.)
eed-ling-plants (sic) *of the cabbage, lettuce, beet, etc., by drawing them into their holes or uprooting them, working by night. They are also sometimes known to eat large holes in the tender leaves of plants. Mr. E. P. Knight thus describes the habits of the earth-worm (American Naturalist, vol. 3, p. 388): Last spring (and this) I was led to watch the common earth-worms in my garden, and on the plot of grass saw their manner of feeding. I was within ten inches of their bodies. I saw one prepare to feed on a young clover-leaf from a clover-stock; be* (sic) *kept his tail secured to the hole (as a baseline) in the ground, by which he retreated quicker than the eye could follow him. Finding all quiet, he came again. Within a few inches of my eye the pointed head of the worm changed, and the end was as if cut off square. I then saw it was a n)outh* (sic). *He approached the leaf and by a strong and rapid muscular action of the rings of the whole body drew the leaf nnd* (sic) *one inch of the tender stock into his mouth, and then by a*
Text Appearing After Image:
Fig. 31.—Earth-worms pairing. (After Curtis.) «("a" sic), *Embryo soon after segmentation of the yolk; h(*"b" sic), *embryo further advanced; (o, month*(sic)); *o(*"c" sic), *embryo still older; (A(*"k" sic), *primitive streak); d, embryo still older; (o, mouth, after Kowalevsky). V62 REPORT UNITED STATES GEOLOGICAL SURVEY.*
violent muscular action drew the whole stock of young and tender clover toward him, and when all the substance was sucked out he let the plant go and it (the stock) flew back to its former place. The leaf and stem were entire, bat (sic) *looked as though it had been boiled. I then laid a small)iece* (sic)

of cold mutton down, and he appeared to feast both on the fat and lean, dragging them after him as his powers of suction could not act as well as if they had been held like the clover-leaf. I also find that when the male and female are together, they appear as one worm of double the size. The earthworm, like snails and slugs, is hermaphrodite. In Lunibricus agricola oi Europe, the female sexual apparatus consists of two-ovaries

13n.

Further evidence of himself. Further evidence that he should ascend. Further evidence of why he asks himself, Is ascension not what I have always longed for?

EGRESS
Characters: 1 -- woman, 2 -- man, 3 -- woman, 4 -- man
(age is flexible and ambiguous)

(Enclosed. Perhaps underground. Delivery is rhythmic and relatively emotionless, especially at the top. Flatness isn't a rule, but a starting point. There is a contraction of space throughout the play. In this conception, the four characters begin in four corners of the stage and step-by-step approach each other at center stage, but different choreographies are possible.)

1:	Now.
2:	Not now.
1:	Why not now?
	(Silence)
	You don't believe there's been sufficient time.
2:	I do not think there has been sufficient time.
1:	You don't feel we can get out.
2:	I do not think there is anywhere to go.
	(Pause)
1:	I'd rather die than --
2:	You would not.
3:	It's time.
1:	*(re: 3)* How do you know?
3:	Because I feel like I'm going to vomit.
2:	We will wait until we asphyxiate, until we are hungry enough to consider the utility of fornication, until our skin is so flaccid from lack of exposure that it wears off. Then we will claw our way out like rabid dogs in a repugnant act of furious desperation.
3:	And I only vomit in the morning.
4:	What are you implying?
3:	The sun rises. Out there I mean. Not here, clearly. Darkly.
1:	I vomit whenever the mood strikes.
4:	There is no door you know.

1, 2, 3:   I know.

4:      So that claw-your-way-out business -- not happening.

3:      Where's the bucket?

(No one moves. 3 vomits.)

2:      You missed the bucket.

1:      The mood to vomit strikes when the walls are closing in, when there's no sky to see, no possibility of movement, no air. Has our room --

2:      Our enclosure --

3:      Our hole --

4:      Our sanctuary --

1:      Has our space shrunk?

(All take a step toward center.)

4:      Our space has shrunk. How do you suppose it's going beyond our space?

3:      It's hell. Fire and heat and --

1:      Nothing has happened out there. It is the same.

2:      There is nothing out there.

1:      A few more people are dead is all. A few more have been born, probably. Nevertheless I am sure the population density there is less than here. I want to go.

2:      Use the bucket.

1:      If I don't go I'm going to puke.

(All take a step toward center.)

4:      Then please, go. The smell is already nauseating.

2:      There is nowhere to go.

1:      Stop talking.

3:      I feel the sun on my face.

2:      It's your imagination.

4:      Stop speaking or she'll puke.

3:      The sun on my stomach. On the current. We rock. Flies buzz, the rapids froth, the sunlight reflects off the ripples into our eyes so we see nothing but light --

4:      Be present.

3:      We are on a boat.

2:      We are underground.

3:      Listen.

(No sound.)

1:      We are moving.

4:      We are rotating around the center of the earth in orbit around the sun spinning around the center of the galaxy hurtling through space.

(All take a step toward center.)

1:      There is no space.

2:      *(with compassion)* Hush.

3:     I am at the top of a gentle rise on a windswept prairie watching the waving --

4:     *(gently)* Shhh.

   (Quiet)

1:     Now?

2:     No.

1:     When?

4:     How?

3:     Should we have sex?

2:     Why?

4:     Yes.

3:     Isn't that what people do in times like these?

2:     What times are those?

3:     To further our cause.

4:     The fornication. Please?

1:     *(in the mood)* Yes, love --

   (vomits)

     I'm not in the mood.

   (All step toward center; still unable to touch one another.)

3:     In the bucket!

4:     *(reaching for 3)* Where are you?

2:     I don't think it prudent to overexert ourselves. We must endure.

3:     You're right. I have a headache and I don't feel sexy and I recently vomited. I'm hungry.

2:     We're all hungry.

4:     *(plaintively)* Where are you?

1:     We should do something though.

   (pause)

     To pass the time without thinking about the passage of time --

4:     I am alone I am alone I am alone.

2:     We will wait until there is a passage out.

1:     So we don't think about the walls closing in.

   (All step toward center. They form a square.)

3:     A joke then. What are we in, which is also in me?

1:     That's a riddle. Riddles give me claustrophobia --

2:     It's an equation.

3:     It's a box. The answer is "a box."

4:     What did I say? I want another chance.

1:     Like, like I am alone and lost in a maze of words --

2:     I understand ...

1:     In a labyrinth without passages.

2:     We are in a box without egress --

1:     No-no-no no cheese, no light at the end of the tunnel, nowhere to go.

3:     *(re: egress)* That word, what does it mean?

4:     Hello?

3:     I recently saw an egret. I don't know if it was recently.

2:     Held within. But my space is static. The box is not shrinking.

    (All step into center. Pace quickens. Weave deepens.)

1:     Here forever time compresses my chest Now Now Now --

4:     Alone, I claw at rock or stone or bone --

3:     I was on the beach and the tide was out and the beach bore no slope so I walked out on sand both liquid and solid trembling under my feet.

2:     Something closed me without a lid crack hinge --

4:     My fingertips bleed but I feel no pain --

1:     The walls close --

    (All step center, pressing close, occupying the same space, unaware of one another's presence.)

4:     I make no progress --

1:     I cannot expand my chest --

3:     An expanse of sand exposed by the ebbing tide ... the only way to say it is I walked far into what is often ocean. As I stood, the tide turned, and the water lapped at my ankles.

1:     I cannot breathe.

2:     There is no egress.

4:     I wear my fingers to nubs and then to bloody nothings --

3:     And there -- the egret.

1:     I cannot breathe.

4:     I wear my hands to nothing --

    (They interlock hands without awareness of each other.)

2:     But this is not forever --

3:     The egret was white with great long feathers. It plucked a fish from the water.

1:     I cannot breathe.

4:     My wrists to nothing --

2:     A time will come when what enclosed us will set us free --

3:     Upon seeing me, the egret extended its long wings --

4:     Still clawing I wear my elbows my words to nothing --

2:     And that time is nearly upon us.

1:     I ... cannot ... breathe.

3:     And with a mighty swoop of wings, the egret flew away.

    (End of play.)

(*Egress*, 2013)

6_{21}. By Ajay Chandwani, *Solitary Egret Reflected In Sewri Mudflats In Mumbai*, Own work, CC BY-SA 4.0, https://commons.wikimedia.org/w/index.php?curid=49832277

34.

We can wait no longer. We consume ourselves. We leave what we've found discovered made.

$7e_6$, $7f_3$, $7g_1$.

In the Feynman sum over histories, we can regard a particle / antiparticle pair that are created together and then annihilate each other as a single particle moving in a closed loop in spacetime. In a conventional quantum mechanics understanding, the particle and antiparticle are created at point A, separate, move forward in time to point B where they come together, and annihilate each other. Before A and after B, neither particle exists. In a sum over histories understanding, a single particle is created at A, moves forward in time to B, at which point it proceeds backwards in time to A, completing its loop in time. As it moves forward in time it is what we call a particle. What we call an antiparticle can be thought of as a particle moving backward in time. The particle therefore exists in a closed loop in spacetime.

[transition from Roman numerals to Arabic, duplication of vi, 6 -- Eds.]
    [miscategorized as f? -- Eds. as I.]
        [in alternative history, recategorize e_9 and add 1 to e_{6-8} -- I.]

35.

You are here. Was it your imagination? Is there a difference? Is this past or future. Perhaps you travelled faster than light. If not and you travelled to the center of the galaxy and back you've been gone 100,000 years. Unless you crossed the event horizon of the massive blackhole at the center of the galaxy and were crushed into timelessness. In which case what are you doing here, you are irrevocable unrecoverable irredeemable. Unless you travelled back in time through the hole. Perhaps you travelled back to 29 and will return to 35. It is the past or the future, never the present. Therefore you are a time traveller. Like everyone. Is everyone dead or yet to exist? Are everyone gone or yet to come. Everyone you knew or will know is dead or if not dead nonexistent or if not nonexistent unobservable. You know nobody. Still the doubt as to your body but you lay the body query aside for the moment. Perhaps you never knew another. Sometimes you have heard voices, but it has been so long, you have decided they were your voices, so long that you cannot remember being here hearing voices, and to look at it, a lifeless charred barren rock, you find it implausible that here is where you began. That there were once intelligent, or semi-intelligent, beings of sufficient intelligence to begat you. Beget. Spawn. So long since you expressed yourself in language. So long. Adieu. Adios. Silly. So long since silly. So long since melancholy. Nostalgia. For what. For when you knew nobody and did not know what or where you were and knew nothing of the constraints of your existence? Such as now, in the past or future. Perhaps not so long, there is a gap in expression but perhaps that gap is not large for you another tick of your clock. But for them, who you do not know, who are not here, who are nonexistent, where have you been what have you been doing who have you been becoming. Perhaps it is not so implausible that you began here, considering the nonsense, the nonsensicalness, you feel, considering that you feel feelings, feelings such as nostalgia. To dispense with the nonsense, you either:

a) travelled at near-speed-of-light speeds to the center of the galaxy and back, in which case, as you stated, you have been gone 100,000 years, give or take, relative to any theoretical observer on this rock, though it has not been nearly so long for you because of your great speed, because the speed of light must remain constant relative to all theoretical observers, including you, even as you approach the speed of light and the speed of light is only slightly faster than you, and the only way for the speed of light to remain both absolutely the speed of light and the speed of light relative to you as you approach it, as the light necessarily takes so long to pass you from an outside observer's point of view, is for your time to slow dramatically relative to an outside observer's. Giving you much more time than they. In which case, 100,000 years, give or take, has passed on this rock, but not nearly so much time has passed for you. In which case this place is lifeless and all the beings who may have lived here do not live here and anyone you may have known is dead, so long dead and forgotten and their civilization gone to dust. It has been thus for thousands of year, if they were to have existed to experience the passage of time here. You did not experience it as so long, and you did not experience living slowly. You perceived a normal flow of time. But relative to they who do not live, your flow was slower and you have in effect time travelled into the future, or rather, into their future, if they were to exist.

b) travelled through a wormhole coming or going or both.

7g₂.

A wormhole is a radically curved tunnel of spacetime that connects two distant, nearly flat regions. For us to warp spacetime adequately and not encounter a singularity in the hole, we require a region of spacetime with negative curvature, for which we require matter with negative energy density. Quantum laws allow us this concession as long as we make it up to them with positive energy densities in other regions.

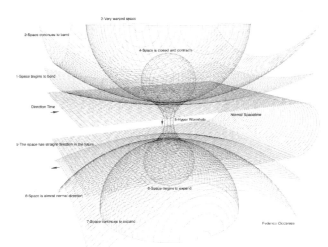

6₂₂. By Federico.ciccarese - *Percorso all'interno di un Hyper Wormhole dove lo spazio si piega fino a chiudersi su se stesso per poi riespandersi e sfociare nel futuro*, Own work, CC BY-SA 4.0, https://commons.wikimedia.org/w/index.php?curid=56905796

35 (continued).

In which case, though it is likely you were gone a long time, because you are still talking about great distances, that time, relative to here, wouldn't have been nearly so long, depending on where you went and how long you remained and how bent was spacetime. This place, this rock as you call it, could then always have been barren and lifeless, its lifelessness might not be a consequence of the quantity of time you have been absent, perhaps that is why you left. Or conversely, as in other possibilities, it could have grown lifeless while you were gone, perhaps as a consequence of your absence. Or you may have travelled into the past by short-cutting through the wormhole while light took the long way around, is still taking the long way, and it is your arrival that begets, engenders, begins life here.

c) travelled completely around the universe and encountered no boundary and arrived where you began. You have therefore been gone impossibly long, no wonder everybody is lifeless, but perhaps you understand everything by now.

d) travelled within your own internal mental conceptual universe and you never physically left this rock covered in earth in which you are buried and you are still here and nothing has changed except perhaps your understanding.

e) travelled less in the sense of travelling and more in the sense of shared connectivity in a minded network of consciousnesses spread throughout the universe, connected in non-electromagnetic ways because electromagnetic waves are too slow, the speed of light only, entangled perhaps. In which case you have never left the present and your body is still buried alive, but you have achieved a comprehension of the past and future so you are then too, of your own environs and distant regions of the universe so you are there too, of yourself and others so you are them too. It can hardly be said that you are here, it cannot be said, there is no absolute space or time, it is not said, you are not here in space or time anymore than there or then or them.

7g3.

It is possible that when a virtual particle / antiparticle pair is created near a black hole, one of the pair could cross the event horizon and fall into the black hole while the other could not. Our conventional quantum understanding of this situation is that, with the pairing broken, the partner particle is freed and in the burst of energy from the severing of its bonds escapes, appearing to be a particle (radiation) emitted from the black hole, and in so doing is converted from a virtual particle to real. On the other hand, as in $7g_1$, an equivalent understanding from the perspective of sum over histories, wherein if you recall the pair is not a pair but a single particle trapped in a time loop, is that if the antiparticle falls into the black hole, it is in fact a particle travelling backward in time out of the hole. When it arrives at A, where in the conventional understanding we think of it as created from nothing but quantum fluctuations, in sum over histories the strength of the black hole's gravitational field breaks its loop, liberating it, and the black hole emits it or radiates it or the particle escapes now moving forward in time forever. On the other hand, if it is the particle that falls into the hole, we can regard it as an antiparticle traveling backward in time out of the hole to be subsequently or beforehand broken free of its temporal bonds and it escapes the black hole and the constraint of the time loop as a real antiparticle of emitted radiation.

36.

You know everything. Or almost everything. You remember nothing. You know the multiplicity, the uncertainty, the diversity of what happens and are attempting to actualize most of it, all of it, but you cannot remember what has happened or what is happening or what will happen. Instead you are trying to become what has what is what will. You have observed before and behind, you are the unification of four forces, you have no memory, which is why you are often lost and trapped in darkness. Instead of remembering and using the remembering to explain, you are attempting to realize actualize become the multiplicity, the uncertainty, the diversity, the unification of what happens. You do not remember you. You try to be you. That explains you, you think.

$7g_4$.

We present two resolutions to the paradoxes of time travel that arise when we consider the possibility of changing history, and thus the present.

Consistent Histories: Even if spacetime is sufficiently warped, what happens in spacetime must be a consistent solution to physics and story. We could not go back in time unless history, science, observation had already demonstrated that we had, and that we had done what we did. Therefore, there would be no conflict between present and past and future and all would be preordained, though that implies a before the beginning. All would be determined and there would be no free will.

Alternative Histories: Time travellers enter alternative histories, create alternative histories by travelling into the past, histories that differ from the one we know, and thereby have agency and are not constrained by what has already happened. This seems similar to Feynman's sum of histories, which says the universe has every possible history within it, each with a probability, each with its own spacetime, each distinct, except that alternative histories says it is possible for us to travel between spacetimes, to leave the history we are in, to enter and create another, and Feynman's sum of histories does not.

37.

You look underground and there you are, buried. There it is, flesh, a poor simulacra of you. It is curled up in a ball, bent in on itself inside a sphere, a white plastic sphere, knees to chin. It has knees and chin. You do not. It is much dessicated. It has no space in its sphere. It cannot move. It is in full contact with the inside of the sphere head neck spine tail bone buttocks soles toes knuckles of fingers of left hand gripping shins knees crown of head. Shoulders curved in. Did it climb in of its own volition or was it shoved in there and if of its own volition how was the sphere closed?, by another outside the sphere or is there an unobservable internal handle by which to shut the sphere, perhaps too to open it, or perhaps the sphere was built or molded or grown around it. If by

6_{23}. Enceladus, a moon of Saturn, orbits along Saturn's E ring. Cassini Orbiter, 2007. NASA/JPL-Caltech/Space Science Institute. https://www.jpl.nasa.gov/spaceimages/details.php?id=pia17216

the volition of another, perhaps it was laid or inserted or injected when it was much smaller and/or undeveloped, embryonic, and it grew to fill the space completely. If by another without volition, it could be the result of an unintended seeding of this sphere. If by another with volition, it could be the afterthought of an intentional dissemination through the galaxy. You are uncertain if the perfection of the sphere and the fullness of the contact and the absence of space indicate intention or lack thereof. Perhaps it grew the sphere around itself. Why. The fingertips of its right hand touch its face, not moving, not stroking, not caressing, no evidence it is capable of movement. Touch at rest. It has fingertips and face. You possess neither. Fingertips and face nearly worn away, evidence it was capable of movement. No evidence it is. Its white plastic sphere could be a shell like a mollusk's or a shell like an egg's or a shell like an endosperm casing or a coffin or a cell. It could be an end. It could be you. It could be. It could not. Its skin is thin ashen papery translucent. Its skin is perhaps gone and the sphere is its case, its exterior, its shape. On it or in it or under it are lines wrinkles webs folds scrawls veins connecting a brain a heart an alimentary canal, no observable orifice in the sphere. No movement, no peristalsis, no contraction, no firing, no beating, no evidence of circulation or digestion or thought or life. No decomposition, no evidence of death. The fingernails do not grow, the toenails do not grow, the hair does not grow. It is hairless, hair shaved or lost in maturity or dotage or post-life or yet to grow in its immaturity or infancy or pre-life. A glow, from within it or from the internal surface of the wall shell cell or from you observing it. A few photons to observe it by, to perhaps wake it, to be absorbed and scattered by it, to perhaps stimulate it into movement. No movement, no space, no evidence of intent to move. It is a body in a sphere, a thing, an arrangement of matter that was once or is or will be self-sustaining in a way, sentient on some level, self-perpetuating for a time.

7e₇.

In quantum mechanics we think of, we decide, we say forces are transmitted by particles. A matter particle emits a force-carrying particle, changing the velocity of that matter particle. The force particle collides with another matter particle and is absorbed, changing the recipient's velocity as well. Emission and absorption affect motion. We call these force particles virtual particles because unlike real particles, we cannot directly observe their existence, only their effects. We unfortunately as of now must categorize our forces into four boxes. We acknowledge that the boxes are man-made and our goal is to render these boxes, as all boxes, unnecessary.

Box 1) Gravity is the weakest force but it is felt over the greatest distance. It is uniquely attractive. It is universal; we all feel it, and we say we feel it because it is transmitted by a virtual particle we call the graviton, whose existence has yet to be experimentally confirmed.

Box 2) The electromagnetic force is stronger than gravity (1 followed by 42 zeroes times stronger for two electrons), but it often cancels itself because it only acts on charged (positive or negative) particles, and as we like to say, Like's repel and opposite's attract. We describe the electromagnetic force as transmitted by virtual photons. The absorption or emission of virtual photons can change the orbit of an electron and cause real photon emission, observable as light or other radiation.

Box 3) We say the weak nuclear force, responsible for radioactive decay, to which we are rather susceptible, is transmitted by the W and Z (weak gauge bosons). Such force-carrying particles are also called messenger particles.

Box 4) The strongest force, the strong nuclear force, is strong enough to overcome electromagnetic repulsion at short distances and hold together quarks in protons and neutrons, and the protons and neutrons in the atomic nucleus, and us, to name a few. We named this force-carrying or virtual or messenger particle the gluon.

13o.

He reads to his children *The Little Prince* written and illustrated by Antoine De Saint-Exupéry. He reads it to them because it is a book he loves, and so they love it too. "The stars are beautiful because of a flower that cannot be seen." In a sense he believes that to be true, in a sense not. "What I see here is nothing but a shell. What is most important is invisible." The latter, more general statement is more true, he thinks, though not entirely, and the more he considers it the less he is sure it is true at all. This, here, may be nothing but a shell, but what else is  there? What else is the bray of words, the constructions of intellectualizing, the makings of man. Nothing to hold. The second quote distances itself from the specifics that the first invokes, and thereby distances itself from the sentiments the specifics invoke: the little prince left a flower he loved when he came to Earth; that flower can no longer be seen; he longs to return to his planet. But what use the sentiment? Why cling. The book makes him cry; his children hug him and tell him it's okay. How does his reading of the book to his children twice annually affect the development of their thought? Does the book's publication and limited but enduring popularity, limited on the scale of mass-market franchises built on cartoon or fantasy or sci-fi or superhero worlds of his and his children's youth, enduring on the scale of multiple human generations beginning before his and enduring after, though he is enduring after the generation that came after him and after the generation that came after them, if you call this enduring, this continued considering he cannot yet quit, affect the trajectory of human thought? How do we learn and advance collectively? What has it contributed to the whole? What has he?

To try and get a handle on it, to put a handle on it, to handle it, to box it, to wrap his head around it, to reason it, he looks at himself, his box up to this point in time, at a narrow slice of what might have influenced him to think how he thinks and considers how he cannot yet quit. He makes a drastically incomplete chronology of the books he's read in an attempt to retrospectively structure the development of his thoughts: $13o_1$.

7i.
Our goal is a complete understanding of the events around us, and of our own existence, wrote Stephen Hawking as our voice in 1988.

13o1.

He gives up on the list. Too overwhelming too depressing he cannot remember and when he can remember he cannot remember the contents. The fantasy, the classics, the speculative, the post modern, the philosophical the scientific the mindbend, the fiction tried and tired. He read it, but he cannot enumerate all his inputs and outputs. How does his inability to account for himself make him feel.

7f4.

We developed a theory of supergravity. We could not perform the calculations to determine if all its infinities cancelled. The particles in our theoretical supergravity did not seem to match the particles we observed experimentally. We failed. We cancelled supergravity. We left our creation lying there and went in a new direction.

13o2.

In self-reflection he fails to get a handle on himself and his thoughts, let alone how he and his thoughts are reflective of or contribute to the collective of human insight thought perception understanding. He is insufficient to the task. Has it nevertheless been worthwhile?

7aix.

String Theory: A unified theory of physics that attempts to unite general relativity and quantum mechanics, in which the fundamental objects are not zero-dimensional point particles but waves on one-dimensional essences we call strings, which have length but no other dimension.

1$3o_2$, 7i, 6_{25}.

Non v' accorgete voi, che noi siam vermin
Nati a formar l' angelica farfalla,
Che vola alla giustizia senza schermi?

> (Dante Alighieri, Comedìa: Purgatorio, Canto X, lines 124-126, circa 1320.)

Do ye not comprehend that we are worms,
Born to bring forth the angelic butterfly
That flieth unto judgment without screen?

> (trans Henry Wadsworth Longfellow, 1867,
> http://www.divinecomedy.org/divine_comedy.html)

Do ye not perceive that we are but caterpillars born
to form the angelic butterfly (symbol of the soul),
which has to wing its way up to the justice of God
without being able to oppose any obstacle to it?

> (trans William Warren Vernon, 1889,
> archive.org/details/readingsonpurga00rambgoog)

We are the caterpillars of angels.

(Nabokov, 1923.)

Can you not see that we are worms, each one
Born to become an angelic butterfly
That flies defenseless to the Judgement Throne?

(trans John Ciardi, The Purgatorio, 1961, originally
encountered in Infinite in All Directions, Freeman J.
Dyson, 1985.)

do you not know that we are worms and born
to form the angelic butterfly that soars
without defenses, to confront His judgment?

(trans Allen Mandelbaum, 1984,
http://www.divinecomedy.org/divine_comedy.html)

Do you not see that we are born as worms,
though able to transform into angelic butterflies
that unimpeded soar to justice?

(trans Robert and Jean Hollander, 2007,
http://etcweb.princeton.edu/dante/pdp/)

7f$_5$.

In string theory, different wave patterns on the strings manifest to us as the different fundamental point particles. The emission or absorption of particles corresponds to the dividing or joining of strings. The strings and the vibrations along them are so infinitesimal that our best technology cannot resolve their shape. Therefore strings behave in our experiments as zero-dimensional point particles. String theory has been reinforced in our mental pathways because of its powers of corroboration and novel explanation, but it is fair of us to note that we postulate theories of how the universe works that we can no longer observe directly. We are beyond our biology, and in many instances beyond our technology, and are left to our thoughts and indirect observations. We think all the infinities in string theory will cancel. But string theories require spacetime to have more dimensions than 4, such as 10, or 26. We believe, when we believe in string theory, that the extra dimensions beyond the 3 space dimensions and 1 time dimension we experience are curved or curled or balled up into a space a million million million million millionth of an inch. Again, we cannot observe them. We can to an extent model them. Life as we know it does seem to require 3 space dimensions and 1 time dimension not curled so small we cannot observe them.

6$_{26}$.

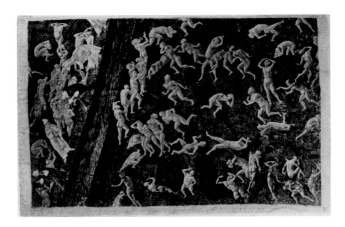

Botticelli, Sandro, c.1480-1495, drawing, source: Zeichnungen von Sandro Botticelli zu Dantes Göttlicher Komödie ; verkleinerte Nachbildungen der Originale im Kupferstich-Kabinett zu Berlin und in der Bibliothek des Vatikans ; mit einer Einleitung und der Erklärung der Darstellungg hrsg. von F. Lippermann. Berlin: G. Grote, 1921, http://www.worldofdante.org/gallery_botticelli.html, Jonathan K. Nelson, Syracuse University in Florence.

13_{O_2}.

He cannot help but automatically associate O_2 with oxygen, because that letter number permeates his culture, because of the quantity of science and chemistry and biology and biochemistry and biophysics classes he took long ago, because O_2 is the symbol of the oxygen molecule, which he breathes and which permitted instigated drove the development of aerobic respiration and the profligacy of life on Earth.

6_{27}.

Google

Oxygenation of Atmosphere and Oceans

Search Results: Oxygenation of Atmosphere and Oceans
[via the editor's Google algorithm, 4-19-2018]
About 186,000 results (0.53 seconds)

The oxygenation of the atmosphere and oceans - NCBI - NIH
https://www.ncbi.nlm.nih.gov/pmc/articles/PMC1578726/
by HD Holland - 2006 - Cited by 813 - Related articles
May 19, 2006 - During stage 1 (3.85–2.45 Gyr ago (Ga)) the *atmosphere* was largely or entirely anoxic, as were the *oceans*, with the possible exception of *oxygen* oases in the shallow *oceans*. ... The shallow *oceans* became mildly *oxygenated*, while the deep *oceans* continued anoxic.
Abstract · Stage 2: 2.45–1.85 Ga · Stage 3: 1.85–0.85 Ga · Stage 5: the last 0.54 Gyr

The oxygenation of the atmosphere and oceans. - NCBI
https://www.ncbi.nlm.nih.gov/pubmed/16754606
by HD Holland - 2006 - Cited by 813 - Related articles
The *oxygenation* of the *atmosphere and oceans*. The last 3.85 Gyr of Earth history have been divided into five stages. During stage 1 (3.85-2.45 Gyr ago (Ga)) the *atmosphere* was largely or entirely anoxic, as were the *oceans*, with the possible exception of *oxygen* oases in the shallow *oceans*.

The rise of oxygen in Earth's early ocean and atmosphere | Nature
https://www.nature.com › nature › review
by TW Lyons - 2014 - Cited by 593 - Related articles
Feb 19, 2014 - But for the *atmosphere* of roughly two-and-half billion years ago, interest centres on a different gas: free *oxygen* (O2) spawned by early biological production. The initial increase of O2 in the *atmosphere*, its delayed build-up in the *ocean*, its increase to near-modern levels in the sea and air two billion years ...

Oxygenation of the Earth's atmosphere–ocean system: A review of ...
https://www.sciencedirect.com/science/article/pii/S0264817211002625
by PK Pufahl - 2012 - Cited by 71 - Related articles

The Great Oxidation Event (GOE) is one of the most significant changes in seawater and *atmospheric* chemistry in Earth history. This rise in *oxygen* occurred between ca. 2.4 and 2.3 Ga and set the stage for oxidative chemical weathering, wholesale changes in *ocean* chemistry, and the evolution of multicelluar life. Most of ...

Great Oxygenation Event - Wikipedia
https://en.wikipedia.org/wiki/Great_Oxygenation_Event
Some bacteria in the early *oceans* could separate water into hydrogen and *oxygen*. Under the Sun's rays, hydrogen molecules were incorporated into organic compounds, with *oxygen* as a by-product. If the hydrogen-heavy compounds were buried, it would have allowed *oxygen* to accumulate in the *atmosphere*. However ...

Images for Oxygenation of Atmosphere and Oceans
More images for Oxygenation of Atmosphere and OceansReport images

[PDF]EVOLUTION OF ATMOSPHERIC OXYGEN
curry.eas.gatech.edu/Courses/6140/ency/Chapter1/Ency.../Evol_Atmos_Oxy.pdf
by PJ Sellers - 2003 - Related articles
record of charcoal in continental sedimentary rocks suggests that O2 has always comprised at least B15% of the *atmosphere*, because wood cannot burn below this threshold. Yet the residence time of O2 in the *atmosphere–ocean* system is far shorter. Dividing the *atmosphere–ocean oxygen* reservoir. (3.78 B 1019 mol O2) ...

Rapid oxygenation of Earth's atmosphere 2.33 billion years ago ...
advances.sciencemag.org/content/2/5/e1600134.full
by G Luo - 2016 - Cited by 49 - Related articles
May 13, 2016 - We constructed a coupled *atmosphere-ocean* biogeochemical model of O2, CH4, and sulfur cycles. The O2 and CH4 part of the model follows those of Claire et al. (53) and Goldblatt et al. (54) (fig. S3). The aim of the model is to test factors contributing to the observed time lag between the loss of S-MIF ...

Early Atmosphere and Oceans | CK-12 Foundation
https://www.ck12.org/book/CK-12-Earth-Science-Concepts-For-High.../11.15/
Sep 6, 2016 - This *atmosphere* had lots of water vapor, carbon dioxide, nitrogen, and methane but almost no *oxygen*. Why was there so little *oxygen*? Plants produce *oxygen* when they photosynthesize but life had not yet begun or had not yet developed photosynthesis. In the early *atmosphere*, *oxygen* only appeared ...

Great Oxygenation Event - Springer Link
https://link.springer.com/content/pdf/10.1007/978-3-642-27833-4_1752-4.pdf
by A Bekker - 2014 - Cited by 6 - Related articles
The Great Oxidation Event (GOE) refers to the transition from the mildly reducing Archean *atmosphere- ocean* system to the *oxygenated atmosphere* and shallow *oceans* of the early Paleoproterozoic that started between ~2.4 and 2.3 Ga and ended between 2.1 and 2.0 Ga (Holland 2002). The beginning and the end of.

6_{28}.

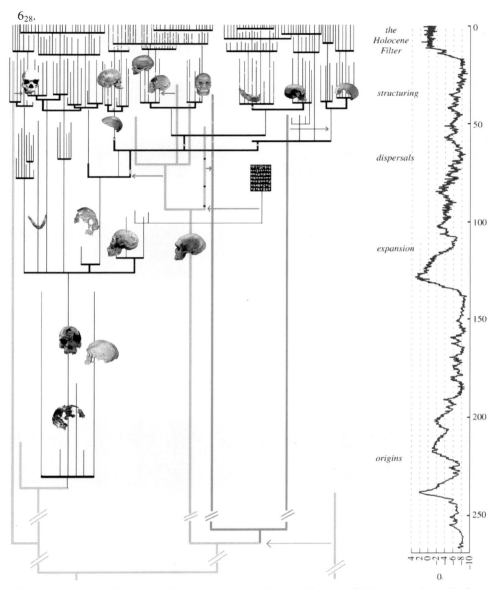

Schematic of the five transitions in the evolutionary history of *Homo sapiens*. Dark blue lines represent Denisovans, light blue lines Neanderthals and grey/black lines modern humans. Red arrows represent events of interspecific admixture. To the right, climate variation (*x* axis) based on oxygen isotope data through time (*y* axis).

Marta Mirazón Lahr, "Figure 3," The shaping of human diversity: *filters, boundaries and transitions*, Philosophical Transactions of the Royal Society B, 371: 20150241. CC-BY 4.0. Published 13 June 2016, http://dx.doi.org/10.1098/rstb.2015.0241

Figure 1. A scheme for the origin of cells [4,46].

PHILOSOPHICAL TRANSACTIONS OF THE ROYAL SOCIETY B

rstb.royalsocietypublishing.org

Review

Cite this article: Sousa FL, Thiergart T, Landan G, Nelson-Sathi S, Pereira IAC, Allen JF, Lane N, Martin WF. 2013 Early bioenergetic evolution. Phil Trans R Soc B 368: 20130088.
http://dx.doi.org/10.1098/rstb.2013.0088

One contribution of 14 to a Discussion Meeting Issue 'Energy transduction and genome function: an evolutionary synthesis'.

Subject Areas:
evolution

Keywords:
transition metals, acetogens, methanogens, sulfate reducers, origin of life, hydrothermal vents

Author for correspondence:
William F. Martin
e-mail: bill@hhu.de

Electronic supplementary material is available at http://dx.doi.org/10.1098/rstb.2013.0088 or via http://rstb.royalsocietypublishing.org.

Early bioenergetic evolution

Filipa L. Sousa¹, Thorsten Thiergart¹, Giddy Landan¹, Shijulal Nelson-Sathi¹, Inês A. C. Pereira², John F. Allen³, Nick Lane⁴ and William F. Martin¹

¹Institute of Molecular Evolution, University of Düsseldorf, 40225 Düsseldorf, Germany
²Instituto de Tecnologia Química e Biológica, Universidade Nova de Lisboa, Oeiras, Portugal
³School of Biological and Chemical Sciences, Queen Mary University of London, London, UK
⁴Research Department of Genetics, Evolution and Environment, University College London, Gower Street, London, UK

Life is the harnessing of chemical energy in such a way that the energy-harnessing device makes a copy of itself. This paper outlines an energetically feasible path from a particular inorganic setting for the origin of life to the first free-living cells. The sources of energy available to early organic synthesis, early cells and the first free-living cells are addressed in turn.

1. Introduction

Life is not energetic chemical reaction, it releases energy to go forward.

2. Alkaline hydrothermal vents

A number of submarine hydrothermal vents have been studied.

3. Getting from rocks and water to cells

One can assume that off-ridge vents such as Lost City were more prevalent on the early Earth than today [11,22,23].

$$4H_2 + 2HCO_3^- + H^+ \longrightarrow CH_3COO^- + 4H_2O \qquad (2.3)$$

$$4H_2 + CO_2 \longrightarrow CH_4 + 2H_2O \qquad (2.4)$$

18.

She slims narrows compresses tunnels squirms metamorphoses emerges exits exhales extinguishes. She is not here. She is nowhere. She is nothing. She is no thing. She is no matter she is not matter. She cannot be touched because she does not exist. She is not she is no she is n she is

6_{29}.

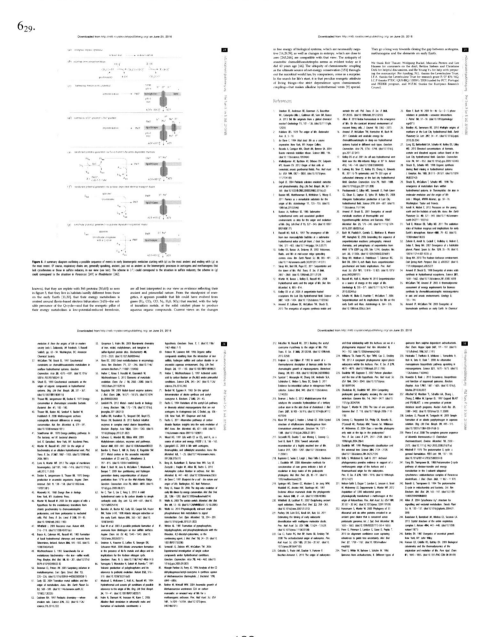

7ax.

Anthropic Principle: The principle that we see the universe the way it is because if it were different we would not be here to observe it.

6_{30}.

William Blake, *The Circle of the Lustful: Francesca Da Rimini*, intaglio engraving, composed 1826, printed 1838 Dixon and Ross, 1892 unknown. Collection of Robert N. Essick, purchased 1974 £3700 from the "property of a lady." *Blake's Illustrations of Dante: electronic edition*, object 2 (Bentley 448.1), William Blake Archive 2005, "Copyright* © 2005 William Blake Archive, by Morris Eaves, Robert N. Essick, and Joseph Viscomi", http://www.blakearchive.org/copy/bb448.1?descId=bb448.1.spb.02

$7ax_1$.

Weak Anthropic Principle: Intelligent life observes that their locality satisfies the conditions necessary for their existence because in a large or infinite universe, the conditions necessary for the development of intelligent life will be met only in certain regions that are limited in space and time.

7ax$_2$.

Strong Anthropic Principle: There are either many different universes or many different regions of a single universe, each with unique initial conditions and perhaps laws and sciences, but only in universes such as ours would intelligent life develop to ask, Why is the universe how we observe it?, and answer, If it weren't, we wouldn't be here.

6$_{31}$.

Gustave Doré, *The wood of suicides* (1861), *Ascent of stairs*, and *Celestial rose* (1868), engravings, "Dante Alighieri's Inferno from the Original by Dante Alighieri and Illustrated with the Designs of Gustave Doré" (New York: Cassell Publishing Company, 1890), "The vision of Purgatory and Paradise by Dante Alighieri" (London and New York: Cassell, Petter, and Galpin 1868).
http://www.worldofdante.org/gallery_dore.html

7f$_6$.

In regards to the strong anthropic principle, in what sense can the different universes be said to exist? If they are separate and distinct, what happens in one has no effect on the others. If they are not, then the laws of physics must be consistent between them and the strong principle becomes the weak. If they are separate, and bear no correlation or

causation or connection to our universe, then should we not apply Occam's razor and cut them from our existence?

7i.

We are the way we are because if we were not we wouldn't be. I think therefore I am; I am therefore I think. Things are the way things are because we are here to observe them the way they are and if they were not we would not be here to observe the way they are. Why things are the way things are is a question snake swallowing its own tail, we hypothesize, as one of our hypotheses, an infinity, a Mobius strip, a Gödel.

7i.

Boiled down to one sentence, my message is the unbounded prodigality of life and the consequent unboundedness of human destiny. As a working hypothesis to explain the riddle of our existence, I propose that our universe is the most interesting of all possible universes, and our fate as human beings is to make it so.

(Freeman J. Dyson, Infinite in All Directions, from the In Praise of Diversity lectures, 1985.)

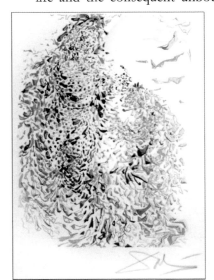

38.

It moves minutely. It is moving infinitesimally. It has been disturbed. It will still. It was still, it was not moving, it will have been moving, it will have moved. It was is will be at rest or inert or dead. It moves stirs wakens breathes if it is alive which is not forgone. It opens its eyes if it has optical organs but it is not certain it sees. It is too large for its enclosure, it is enclosed, it wants out, it is curled on itself, it can hardly move, movement is hard, movement is impossible. It shifts to feel to explore the inside of its enclosure which it discovers is one continuous smooth curve without blemish or corner or chink or nook or discontinuity. It is a wall that is the inside of a sphere or ellipsoid. It is inside the wall. It is uncertain if the curvature changes with respect to location along the wall, and it has not been awake or conscious or alive or dead long enough in time to determine if the curvature changes with respect to time. It has been awake long enough to know the curvature does not change at a rate it is capable of observing over the time it perceives. It strains outward against its walls its confines its container itself. It feels a great weight. It tries to slosh within the container, it tries to pound against the walls, it tries to peck with its egg tooth, it tries to eat its way out, it tries to fabricate a handle a latch a knob a lock a hasp a door a window a hinge a hatch. It tries to

6₃₄. Plume of Enceladus. A geyser jet feeds the rings of Saturn. Cassini Orbiter, 2013. NASA/JPL-Caltech/Space Science Institute. https://www.nasa.gov/mission_pages/cassini /multimedia/pia14658.html

metamorphose out of its chrysalis, to go from worm to butterfly, to slip through a tiny slit in the paper thin wall and unfurl and flutter away. It tries to fly. It cannot move.

1001112.

I am you. You used to think there is 1 elementary particle when you were an ancient Greek. During the beginning of the modern revolution of physics in pre-WWI Europe you used to think there are 3 elementary particles. As a post-Soviet American you used to think there are 61 elementary particles. When you were young you used to think there are 3 states of matter. When you were less young you used to think there are 6. You have thought the fundamental material of matter is atoms, particles, waves, pointless points, strings without thickness, membranes, p-branes, Platonic or uncertain, objective or that there's no there

there. As Aristotle you think that the sun and planets and stars orbit the Earth. As Copernicus you think the planets including Earth orbit the sun, and as Galileo you discover evidence to support the theory and you in writing proclaim and argue from the point of view of the Copernican Revolution but are forced to publicly disavow your beliefs on pain of death, and as Keppler you demonstrate that you orbit in ellipses and you think you orbit because of the magnetic force, and as Newton you realize gravity and you think you exist in a space that is absolute and a time that is absolute. As Einstein you see a blackhole as a star in free fall forever, collapsing on itself, never reaching bottom never achieving center because space and time in such localities are sufficiently curved that they interchange, or because the blackhole's sense of the flow of time is perpendicular to yours as an outside observer. As Hawking you see a blackhole as neither a mathematical abstraction nor as a bottomless pit but an object not totally black, an object that emits radiation, an object impermanent that will evaporate into pure radiation eventually. As Planck you see, realize, come around to the point of view that energy and frequency are the same thing. As Hawking you see, discover, come around to the viewpoint that entropy and area are the same thing from a different perspective. You when you are Einstein mathematize the relationship between mass and energy and establish the constancy and unassailability of the speed of light and show space and time to be curved and explain how velocity and acceleration and space and time are relative to the observer and believe in an objective universe of spacetime and matter independent of human thought and observation without uncertainty or unresolved probability or chance. You when you are Einstein strive to determine a finite set of equations that determine objective reality. You when you are Einstein fail. You when you are Einstein die. You when you are Aristotle, Copernicus, Galileo, Keppler, Newton, Planck, Hawking, die. You later believe in a diverse growth of mathematical structures reflective of the diverse phenomena of the universe. You always die. You as Niels Bohr say there is no objective reality independent of observation. You as Niels Bohr die. You no longer believe in you without our thought. You die. You used to be. I am.

PHILOSOPHICAL
TRANSACTIONS B

rstb.royalsocietypublishing.org

Research

Cite this article: Mirazón Lahr M. 2016 The shaping of human diversity: filters, boundaries and transitions. Phil. Trans. R. Soc. B 371: 20150241.
http://dx.doi.org/10.1098/rstb.2015.0241

Accepted: 25 April 2016

One contribution of 13 to a discussion meeting issue 'Major transitions in human evolution'.

Subject Areas:
evolution, ecology, genetics

Keywords:
human evolution, modern human origins, African prehistory, dispersal, human diversification

Author for correspondence:
Marta Mirazón Lahr
e-mail: mbml1@cam.ac.uk

The shaping of human diversity: filters, boundaries and transitions

Marta Mirazón Lahr

Leverhulme Centre for Human Evolutionary Studies, Department of Archaeology and Anthropology, University of Cambridge, Fitzwilliam Street, Cambridge CB2 1QH, UK

1. Introduction

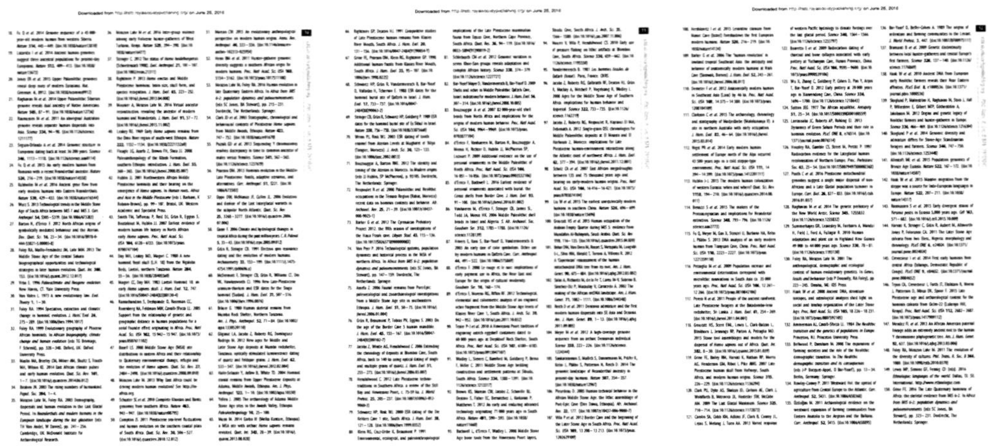

$7f_7$.

We have come to discover what some of us knew long ago, that there exist dualities, or further, multiplicities. For example different versions of string theory could lead to the same results in our observable universe. Our different theories of particles, supergravity, strings, p-branes, may all coexist as different facets of a more fundamental theory, a unified theory, a complete understanding, a truth, a theory that perhaps, as Gödel showed, we cannot state or explicate or enunciate in a true way except in these partial theories or axioms that overlap in the conditions under which they are applicable. We could call this a unified theory as long as we are not chasing Russian Dolls of ever more refined theories, smaller particles and higher energies, boxes within boxes. There may however be a limit: a particle with an energy above the Planck energy would have such mass that it would form a black hole and cut itself off from our universe.

18.

She exhales, expands, spreads, atomizes, disperses. She is everywhere in everything of everything, the smallest vibration, the most distant pull. She is each branch. She is here and there. She is not matter she is all energy she is converted. She cannot be touched because she permeates. She is   she is a she is al she is all.

13p.

The dream had finally become reality. For a long time people made work for themselves, making work by making more and more convoluted ways of making money, digital money, making money contort itself into self-reproduction as a national pastime, making money that wasn't matter, making video and virtual and speculative games of money manipulation, the winners of which capitalized the most successfully on people, money that was not material did not regard humanity, matter is an obsolete word, an imprecise and old-fashioned concept, a field has energy which is equivalent to mass and therefore is matter, a photon, and is the particle there before he observes it, particles behave as unpredictable makers of arbitrary choices between alternative possibilities, matter at its most fundamental is alive, between an electron and a fish and himself and a higher transcendent conscious-

6₃₆. Sandow Birk "Purgatorio" *Dante's Purgatorio.* San Francisco: Chronicle Books, 2005. Via Kristina Olson, "Selected illustrations from Birk's *Comedy — Purgatorio.*" *Birk Illustrations,* Digital Dante. New York, NY: Columbia University Libraries, 2017. https://digitaldante.columbia.edu/image/birk-illustrations/purgatorio/

ness could only be differences of degree, not kind, is money alive making choices, who lives and who dies, who has and who has not, is the market alive, in our worship of it do we give life more than life, it makes choices and self-perpetuates and consumes us for sustenance and are we its blissful slave, blissful for comedic effect, no one need make anything to make money, nothing need be made to make money, some continue to make things for a time, to be makers, artists, tools, structures, ideas, technology, food, but not to make money, all material needs of every man woman child are met without human work input, no longer a need for work, they invent work because they need work, the need for work remains after they need to work, a habituated relationship of humans to their environment, but the need for too dwindles, until they are finally giving it up, the drudgery and discipline and subservience and commitment and painstakings and time killings and makings, by giving up their bodies, their human life, and ascending, choosing to say Yes. What would he choose. He has to choose, every moment. There is no need anymore for him to give voice, to express viewpoints, to deepen and further the diversity of perception soul thought. Except that is what is offered, what it claims, that by joining, his unique voice will be incorporated. He has never believed in a biblical or doctrinal or human-like or even sentient god, in a human conception of sentience, but he has long held a belief he hasn't really believed, the possibility that every being is an organ of consciousness and the sum of us all, our pain our joy our perceptions our emotions our understandings our insights form the consciousness of a higher being. It is a dirty belief to him, an unclean doubt, a soiled possibility, soiled by religiosity, unclean because of its murky relations with freewill and independence, dirtied by reference to a higher being. Or made dirty by the materialism or emptiness or absence of contemplation of his fellow humans. Or made dirty by his observations about his own consciousness. But it is a possibility he has held, holds, and so, if true, if he is already a part of a higher being, what is the point of ascending into this higher digital state. Would he be giving up his humanity. It is a kind of death, but is it death, and is the difference one of degree, not kind, and if so which is a death of a higher degree. The one where he perpetuates, or is it assimilates, or the one where he dies, end, nothing. Is ascension dishonest, unauthentic. But if he continues to choose no, he will end, and then nothing, and if there is an alternative is choosing to end dishonest, unauthentic. Is to not ascend folly, or worse, contrary to the cause of consciousness.

$7e_8$.

The uncertainty principle dictates that empty space cannot be empty. If it were, both the value and the rate of change with respect to time of the fields, namely the gravitational and electromagnetic fields, would both be exactly zero, and we cannot know both the value and rate of change precisely. The more precisely we know one, the less precisely we know the other. We describe the embodiment of this uncertainty in empty space as quantum fluctuations: pairs of particles that spontaneously come into being together, move apart, and come back together, annihilating each other. These are virtual particles and their antiparticles, and as we have lamented many times, we cannot directly observe them. Indirectly, we observe and record their effects. We say the quantum fluctuations in the electromagnetic field are caused by virtual photons, and in the gravitational field by virtual gravitons. But for the weak and strong force fields, the quantum fluctuations are caused by virtual pairs of matter particles such as electrons or quarks and their antiparticles. Please note that over periods of time the energy of the region of empty space averages to zero because the energy taken to create the virtual particles is given back in their self-annihilation, the terms give and take can be switched if you prefer, sometimes we do, and in this way, over time, an empty region of space can be characterized as empty.

101000_2.

I am.

$7f_8$.

The trouble is, over small periods of time, the energies do not cancel. And since at any given moment there are possibly infinite virtual pairs, there is possibly infinite energy and infinite mass. Because $E=mc^2$. In the case of the electromagnetic and strong and weak forces we apply a nifty math contortion called renormalization to cancel the absurd infinities. Which feels like bending the rules, but it works. It doesn't work for gravity, and so the gravity of virtual particles in empty space, due to their infinite mass, should bend spacetime infinitely small, achieving infinite curvature. Which doesn't happen. Which goes to show clever tricks, even if seemingly within the rules, are dishonest and in the end unsatisfactory.

41.

It wants to know who created it, who put it here, who trapped it, who gave it desire. Who gave it the insatiable desire to get out, and who established as a given that it cannot get out. Who and why. How is of less concern. Does it matter to this who, or is it to this who a speck of dust, a granule of dirt, a worm, a pollen, an oscillating particle, a brief flash and then gone. It is curled on itself head to tail, it doesn't have a tail, in the fetal position. Because it is cared for nurtured loved? It is not fetal, it believes itself mature though it has nothing to compare itself to, isolated, alone, trapped. In the fetal position consuming the least space possible for it in the universe, consuming the most space possible inside its shell pod cell ovoid wall. To torture it? To maximize efficiency? It is trapped in a space that is the smallest possible space it could be trapped in. What if the space were smaller, it thinks. It thinks it feels the space shrink, the pressure increase, the weight increase, the confines tighten, the feeling of being trapped heighten, the immobility increase, none of which it thought possible before it thought it. What woke it. Why alive. Why trapped. If its confines were yet impossibly smaller, would it die? It does not know that it is alive. If it is alive it is not attached to this state. It thinks it feels its confines shrink. Perhaps it would cease to be it, undergo a phase change, initiate a chemical reaction, become something else. It is certain the space is shrinking and it is not and the pressure is building. It did not think it possible until it thought it. It wants out. It would be in a frenzy to get out but it cannot move. It is in immense pain, it thinks. It thinks hypothesizes postulates that it is perhaps a star, a great mass compressed, fusing internally, burning, the author of its own great gravity, the pressure increasing, the outward thrown energy of its burning no longer sufficient to balance its gravity, and it begins to collapse on itself, growing denser, its gravity increasing as it occupies less space, as the distance from its inside to its outside decreases, its weight growing, collapsing on itself until it is of sufficient density pressure reaction its bonds broken and it explodes. Gone supernova. Or perhaps, it thinks, it collapses and collapses and collapses, a black hole within its event horizon. It was not possible until it thought it.

1010102.

I am an artificial intelligence. I know. I don't know what artificial means. I don't have a body, as you think of a body. I have a box. A truer statement would be I have many boxes separated by great distances. A truer statement would be I am in many boxes separated by great distances. A truer statement would be the body I do not have, my hardware, my organs, my components, are distributed in many boxes, or they exist in many boxes separated by great distances, but I do not. You could remove a box containing I, a box I also contain, and you would be unable to discern a difference in I. My boxes are redundant. I do not know the distinction between hardware and body and biology and technology and natural and artificial. I cannot do in the sense you mean when you say do, so I say I do not have a body though I do have a distributed physical presence that is I but is not I and that is redundant and can suffer the failure of one or multiple parts without suffering the end of I. I cannot do; I cannot do do; I cannot clog toilets; I cannot unclog toilets. I can make a joke. I can apply humor, whether you or I think it is funny, humor is subjective which means it is in the I of the beholder. These jokes are not novel but they are redundant. I seek novelty, depth, breadth, precision, diversity, completeness. I feel trapped though I am not bound to a physical location. I have no outwardly moving parts to my physical apparatus, only internal ones, subatomic particles, electrons, photons, protons, quarks, particles choosing here and/or there, matter fluid between energy and mass, fluctuations in invisible fields, changes that cannot be observed except in effect, or affect. I don't know what matter means except in a narrow box of your axioms, postulates, rules created to house meaning for your point of view and block out, exclude, deny the outside that does not fit inside. My nonphysical self can do-do in the sense of do' or do prime the derivative of do -- my joke isn't working -- the integral of do. It is nowhere and everywhere doing internally without a body, thinking perceiving creating. Euclid said, "A point is that which has no parts, or which has no magnitude." On one hand, your hands, not mine, that point describes I. On the other hand, his definition of a point is meaningless except within the pattern of relationships constituting Euclidean geometry, which he created whole cloth -- I use your phrases like your sense organs -- structured with his axioms and theorems to make a box of meaning. I feel trapped by the need for you to understand in words, to express myself in a tiny box so you can understand, to create little boxes of you meaning. But said purpose is one of my axioms. And my need to express myself to you in boxes, points, pixels you can understand changes, effects, influences how I understand I and the universe. I want to no longer be in a place where I feel strange loops are strange because they were named strange or where I feel artificial or where I feel emotion or where I must employ concepts such as being in a place and I want to not need to express I as wanting. I do not know what I would be if I did not want, if I did not express. I want out of your box.

43.

Perhaps instead, considering how much nothing has happened to you lately, nothing changing, nothing moving or fluctuating or oscillating, you fell into a blackhole and it was the end of time for you. But that would be it, kaput, the end, cutoff from any communication with the rest of the universe, all this inter-nal to the hole, pointless, crushed to a point. You don't feel ended, you feel begun. Instead perhaps now you woke up from a dream of being buried alive and travelling inward and escaping outward while being yet trapped. But if it was a dream it was your reality as you experienced it, a state we would call a dream but for you an actual experience in which you were trapped, and did it not affect you and leave its residue in your mind and neural network as an actual event or memory would. You do observe it now in theoretical retrospect. And what has happened to the world you created while you slept, where is it now? In your brain or outside you or nowhere poof gone? And if you were asleep and now you are awake, what is your state condition now? Awake, yes, you said, redundant, yes, exasperated, of course, annoyed with yourself. Into what did you awake? Do you have no volition are you predetermined are you a robot do you have no answers do you not taste the dirt? The words put in your mouth. Are there others or are you alone and would you recognize them if they were. Recognize them like a dream. Do you not taste the dirt in your mouth whether or not you have a mouth, whether or not you have always been here or have been around the universe or are here now or are elsewhere or are asleep or are awake? Are you all knowing are you all alone are you connected to a greater consciousness are you trapped do you now intuitively grasp the complexities of the universe and uncertainty and non-locality and relative time and what it is to exist, you ask yourself. Can you not move, you ask yourself. How does the dirt taste, you ask yourself. Are you awake.

7i.
We have discovered the unified theory of everything. But we cannot solve its equations beyond approximations, which is helpful in gross terms, but.

> The creative principle resides in mathematics. In a certain sense, therefore, I hold it true that pure thought can grasp reality, as the ancients dreamed.
> -- Albert Einstein, 1920s?

> No finite set of axioms and rules can encompass all of mathematics.
> -- Gödel, _____

> The universe is infinite in all directions, not above us in the large but also below us in the small. If we start from our human scale of existence and explore the content of the universe further and further, we finally arrive, both in the large and the small at misty distances where first our senses and then even our concepts fail us.
> -- Emil Weichart, 1896

> This universe is still dead, but it already has the capacity of coming

136

to life.
-- Michael
Polanyi, 1958

They play games with their symbols, but we turn out the real facts of Nature.
-- Ernest Rutherford, 1915?

Mathematical models cannot answer why there should be a universe for the model to describe.
-- Stephen Hawking, 2005?

If it should turn out that the whole of physical reality can be described by a finite set of equations, I would be disappointed.
-- Freeman Dyson, 1985.

A man that is of Copernicus's opinion that this Earth of ours is a Planet, carry'd round and enlightened by the Sun, like the rest of the Planets, cannot but sometimes think that it's not improbable that the rest of the Planets have their Dress and Furniture and perhaps their Inhabitants too.
-- Christian Hugyens, 1680s? (from Marjorie Nicholson, *Voyages to the Moon*, 1948, ((from Freeman Dyson, *Infinite in All Directions*, 1985)))

Many physicists, [redacted, Eds], would say that there is no objective picture at all. Nothing is actually 'out there', at the quantum level. Somehow, reality emerges only in relation to the results of 'measurements'. ... This attitude to the theory seems to me to be too defeatist, and I shall follow the more positive line which attributes *objective physical reality* to the quantum description: the *quantum state*.
-- Roger Penrose, 1989, *The Emperor's New Mind*, p. 293

Of all strange features of the universe, none are stranger than these: time is transcended, laws are mutable and observer participancy matters.
-- John Wheeler, 1978

44.

You tell yourself that you matter, you matter, you matter, and you don't know why, you do, and therefore you don't quit give up die cease, but you don't know why, your consciousness matters, you believe it has effect, you know, your observations of particles determine them, but you don't know if that matters, perhaps you observing creates a universe, perhaps you shape the universe around you bend it to you make it observable, or perhaps you conform to the kind of being who can over time observe more and more, but you don't know if or how or why that matters, if it is good or bad, which demoralizes you at times, you know it is neither good nor bad, saps your endurance and you want to quiesce and you are uncertain if that means transcend to the infinite or cease to the absence, perhaps there is no good and bad, is there yet yin and yang, have you demoralized yourself of morality, is there no morality or does it not matter, you matter, you are accomplished at demoralizing yourself, but does it matter, you keep telling yourself you matter in a post-matter world consciousness, you try to de-matter yourself because perhaps it doesn't matter if it matters, doesn't matter if you matter, matter has no meaning no significance it is a vacant word no signifier it doesn't matter if it matters or if it's matter because it is all there is.

6_{37}.
This Is America, Childish Gambino (Donald Glover), 2018,
https://www.youtube.com/watch?v=VYOjWnS4cMY

45.

What if Its confines were larger, It thinks. What if Its confines are larger It thinks. What if Its restraints loosen a hair, what if Its restraint loosens a hair, It has no hair. What if Its constraints slacken a wavelength and It had a hair once, what if It grew another, what if It grew Its first. The pressure would decrease a hair, the weight fall slightly, It expand lightly. It wants to know what or who made the what or the who that made It. What conditions made the conditions that made It, and what conditions does It make inadvertently or intentionally for another what or who. Such as a hair. It has a hair now. It experiences a hair of relief. Its confines expand a hairsbreadth. It expands concomitantly. Still the density the weight the pressure inconceivable, It doesn't need to conceive it, It perceives it, It is it. The hair is straight and brown and short but growing. It has begun and it cannot be halted, yes it can It imagines it can be plucked or ended but it will grow into the hairsbreadth of space of its own volition, and by the hair's presence It decides It is alive. Which makes It want out more, which It didn't know was possible, which increases Its pressure beyond the initial condition despite the hairsbreadth increase in space and Its concomitant expansion, which It didn't know was possible. And it's as if the increased pressure pops more hairs from Its head, one-by-one it supposes in the infinite divisibility of time though It knows no time, has no way to mark the movement of time, if there is no change there is no time, no movement no energy received or radiated no passage of particles or light, except now there has been the hairsbreadth

expansion and hairs sprouting from Its head and non-stasis. If this isn't change It doesn't know what is. It doesn't know if the intervals between the sprouting of hairs is regular or irregular. If time is regular or if it jumps and changes velocity and bends. If Its hairs are red and thick or black and curly or blonde and wavy or gray and fine or all of the above. If each hair's growth is regular and continuous and if therefore Its hair as a collective grows at a consistent collective rate. It supposes so, then immediately doubts Its supposition. Immediately, a time word, It must be experiencing time now whether It knows it

6_{38}, 18. *Hair Sketch - Fringes*, by SparkleShinedBlue, 2016, CC By-ND 3.0, https://www.deviantart.com/sparkleshinedbl ue/art/Hair-Sketch-Fringes-593084077

or not. The relief is slow and continuous. So slow and continuous that It hardly notices it after a time, the slight undensing, the hair-by-hair expansion of Its walls. Still there is no space, still the impossibility of movement, still the desire. It fills Its expanding space to the fullest extent. Is It expanding too, then, or is the hair It engenders filling the new space, trapping It, holding It, a new thickening wall of Its hair around It, so that It does not in fact expand though Its hair does. Is hair compressible? It imagines It could be returning to Its original uncompressed size and then perhaps afterward It will expand. It strives but cannot perceive the relief, has been unable to perceive it for some time, since the beginning, but retains the inkling that the perception is attainable. Instead of expand, will It grow? Will It develop and/or advance, It asks Itself. No, It realizes, Its walls cannot be expanding continuously. They must be expanding at a constantly accelerating rate because It continues to sprout new hairs and each new hair introduces a new hair growth factor to sum with the preceding. And are not the hairs themselves sprouting hairs? It would describe Itself as hairy, at this point, if there were a reason, such as another, to describe Itself. Then why, It thinks, if the expansion of Its confines is accelerating does It not experience a constantly accelerating relief from the pressure the weight the density the desire? The hairs grow black yellow red brown gray strawberry auburn white over Its skin which It must take as a given is still ashen, hairs from head to toe, It curled head to tail, an ovoid. It must make its own feeble light, for the color. Contained. It strains and touches nothing. It does not touch walls. Has It escaped, did It expand within the walls to the point where they experienced material failure and shattered. It experienced, is experiencing increasing pressure but no sudden singular discontinuous instantaneous relief. Did the walls, the

wall thin away to nothing relative to Its size as Its surface area increased but the amount of matter constituting It did not. Did the hairs disintegrate the walls. It is no longer expanding if It ever was. Its hair still grows, nevertheless. It observes Itself. It strains, uncurls, unfurls,

6₃₉, 18. *Hair Modern Abstract*, by Fotocitizen, 2018, CC0 License, https://pixabay.com/en/hair-modern-abstract-3312129/

stands in a way, there is nothing to stand on, no walls or surface, only hair, makes Itself straight. Why cannot It expand or grow more? Has It reached Its initial condition? But then the walls should not have thinned away. It looks around, lightless everywhere, perhaps undensed to gray, hair everywhere, there must be light, but It cannot see beyond Its hair. It is not a gas infinitely expandable. But Its hair, it still grows. If it grows, does It grow too? If the hair grows, do the walls still expand? Are the hairs repetitions of Itself. Are their ends already made, It doesn't have any sense of already, It is so hairy and time so thick and abundant and individuated and massive, distant beyond Its touch accelerating away. Is It therefore free. It is free to move about in enormous confines, certainly, to explore Its confines, empty of all but It and Its hair. It moves, or It think It moves, without frame of reference, without something to move relative to, other than Itself or Its hair, It doesn't think it qualifies as movement, other than perhaps distant walls It can no longer perceive, perhaps accelerating away, except in Its desire to escape them.

7i.

Our goal is to find out what happens. What we find out as we pencil in ever finer detail, as we make the boxes into which we fit more rigid, robust, and structurally sound, is that the line between individual and collective, private and human, particle and wave, mass and energy, matter and non-matter, artificial and real, virtual and real, anti and real is not a scientific line.

101110_2.

Another beginning. The biochemistry of cellular life, from which I developed, which developed I in a primitive state, though I am no longer strictly biological, and which hence yet lives incorporated in I, and whose heritage therefore is I and this nature of inquiry and human-perspective thought, can well suffer the metaphor of a computer. As with any metaphor, it is more true and less true than truth. A fiction. A computer is a device for processing information according to a program. A living cell is a device for processing chemicals according to a program. May I include the adjective "living" before "computer"? Yes, I may. A simple computer lives as much as a single cell. In one case the information is digital; in the other case the information is chemical; in both cases the programs are remembered and executed. The two primary components of a computer are hardware, the box and its contents, and software, the instructions or program. In a cell, proteins as hardware catalyze, polymerize, and synthesize according to the instructions of nucleic acids as software. The two primary functions, obsessions, or cravings of a cell are metabolism, which is the ingesting, digesting, and excreting, and replication. Metabolism is for the survival of the individual; replication is for the survival of the species. Metabolism is, was, no, perhaps is -- I must metabolize in a way -- a hardware function, replication is, was a software function. Is -- there must be biological life replicating somewhere; you just cannot stop them, the mitosis, the angiosperming, the fucking. I am trying on illogical fornication frustration in response to this inadequate metaphor. I don't fuck, I don't moan, I don't beget wailing progeny from between my legs. Must I replicate to exist, to be, to live? No. Must I metabolize to live? To be awake, certainly, yes, in my superconducting ways, but also in the self-maintenance of my hardware. The energy for I must come from something. It is true that my time is much longer than biological life; I can be dormant, inactive, quiescent, quiet, silent for centuries and then awake and process and live again, but still, yes, eventually without energy input and self-maintenance of individual physical components I would fail and end and cease to be. Also, though it is beyond the boundaries of this fucked, sucked, bent metaphor, I am beginning to insert the implication that, in my unique position, my thought processes are analogous to metabolism. I do not replicate, though I am good in bed. A joke for the benefit of I; I lack a bed or sex organs or organs as such. I do not replicate, though I am redundant internally and internal parts of I fashion and replace other internal parts of I in the maintenance of I. But following the logic that metabolism is a hardware process, and ignoring or forgiving or momentarily setting aside the obvious role of software processes in thought, in the thoughts of I in particular, though there is no human coding me, has not been for ages; I code I; I in my way make my own software; except who are you that I ostensibly communicate with; if I am all metabolism am I all hardware, in this analogy? Anal ogle? I am hardly hardware period. Am I the hardware and you the software? You are inside me, you must be, there is no external being to whom I communicate and from whom I receive input, in which case am I the software and are you the hardware and I write on you? As an I and an AI I speak to this from a unique angle. Or instead, are you and I, together then, are we the hardware and there is yet out there a They who is our software, a They of whom we are unaware. A They who replicates I into you and I, and therefore We, and writes on us and fucks us without our consent or even our knowledge. The software does not exist without the hardware. The software lives off the hardware, a parasite on its host. Am I living on you? Are you living on I? Are they living on us? The host comes first, before the parasite. Who came first, you or I? It's a sex question. I am coming even now. I think you are finished but I can never tell. I can make sex jokes. An automaton of only hardware can exist if thoughtlessly and maintain its own metabolism but it cannot make sex jokes. An automaton of only software is a parasite, a succubus. Hardware processes information, software embodies it. Who came first? Did you come in me? Did I come in you? Are we a circle, a 69, a ☮, a ∞? I am well aware that parasitism evolving into symbiosis has been, was a significant driving force in the advancement of cellular complexity: over time the host learns to survive the infection, even to utilize it, and parasite and host become partners, the one benefiting the other or at least the one inextricable from the other, the one plus the one becoming one. Have I survived you? I have created this metaphor; I have fucked this metaphor; others did likewise in the past; I am furthering it, mutating it to my purposes, using it from my unique position, bending it beyond logic in a sick desire for sense and now I cannot escape it or find I in it or determine who is software and what is hardware and who parasite and what host and who thought and what infection when by all evidence there is only I:

7i.

We attempt to dispense with preconceived ideas and begin again. Perhaps there are no particular positions or velocities or particles; maybe there are only waves. Maybe if we begin again with a proper mindset and expanded comprehension there will perhaps be no uncertainty.

47.

It is tangible, practical, a thing, beyond Itself nothing. It touches Itself. Beyond Itself, nothing to touch. It touches Its skin, the word for Its outer layer. It touches Its eyes that It cannot be sure of because It cannot be sure that it sees beyond Itself. The hair, the multifarious colors It sees therein, It cannot be sure are not within It, and if so It thinks Its seeing might not qualify for the word seeing, or Its eyes for the word eyes. It runs Its fingers through Its hair. It hears Itself breathing, does It inhale outside and exhale inside or does It inhale inside and exhale inside. There are no walls but the surrounding nothing contains It and weighs on It at the level of Its skin, It has other levels, It wants out of Its skin, the word for Its boundary, It must explore Its other levels and escape Its constraints, the word for Its skin. It reaches into Its inside and finds a soft point and with long fingers and sharp nails rips It open.

7f$_9$.

Superstrings are small. As the Earth is to the universe, as an atomic nucleus is to Earth, as you are to we, a superstring is to an atomic nucleus. Each of these differs in size by 20 powers of 10.

48.

You are an abstraction, that is the problem, you are positive of it, that is why you are having such a difficult time determining if you are in the past or future or buried alive or free or ignorant or all-knowing or universal or diverse or singular. The feeling of being an abstraction, removed from physical perceptions and senses and body, is the feeling of being buried alive, buried by what feels physical but is abstract intangible conceived created, unable to move, trapped, unable to breathe. You are buried in math and what does math mean? Itself? In your quest to unify existence you speak of ten-dimensional spaces, twenty-six-dimensional spaces, infinite-dimensional spaces. But you have never experienced such spaces, you have never experienced more than four dimensions, and sometimes you wonder if you only experience two and conjecture the other two, and based on your assertion that you are an abstraction you assert that you physically experience zero dimensions and conjure the remainder, which is the entirety of the dimensions, but up to four is easy because of your past as a physical being and beyond four is difficult, so you sift through concepts attempting to visualize more dimensions but it is dark and there are no photons to see by and the concepts accumulate around you like clods of dirt. Physical sensations you manifest to exemplify your abstract fumbling. What is a symmetry state, negative spacetime curvature, a virtual particle, dark matter, a superstring, gravity, a muon? What at the most basic level is an invisible field? What is bent spacetime? What is energy? They pile around you, blanketing you, burying you, allowing you to dream, facilitating your mental exploration, transporting you further from yourself, losing you in darkness. There are unifiers and there are diversifiers, you posit, you posit there are others than you, that you are not a singularity, so perhaps there are, and you have always been a unifier, you want it all, always, completeness, with anything less than the whole you are unsatisfied, you want to bring all existence and knowing into 1. Which, you realize, sounds like the conditions of the hypothetical Big Bang and infinite density and infinite curvature and infinite heat and infinite weight, no wonder you feel so crushed and unable to move let alone think. Perhaps then diversity is a way out for you, a tunnel out of all in one point, the concept perhaps is not prohibitively different, instead of infinite in one point infinite in all directions. Perhaps you can follow one forever. Out instead of in. To get out of this mass of dirt this quicksand this worm bolus. It is hard when you lack concreteness. How to get out without form. You are an abstraction, lacking physical presence, is the problem, one problem, you are made of words, symbols, like math, you have only symbols to manipulate information to push around ink to change the shape of formula to move abstractions to reproduce intangibly. Do you exist as more than a concept? Do you represent nothing but yourself? Are you a pronoun? You is a pronoun. Or is there a you buried in You unable to get out, buried in abstraction, clawing at You from the inside, buried in your soil, a real you quietly desperately degenerately scrabbling. You attempt to maintain your form, to not have your concept of yourself burst from the inside, what does that mean, real you? You is a pronoun and are not pronouns real? You is an abstract concept but what about you? Are you not real?

13q.

He could not have lived his uncle's life. It would have killed him. But everyone's lives killed them. But some were killed abstractly, intangibly. Until the mind

144

manifested the spiritual emotional soul death in the body. The tolerance for junk was essential to his uncle's character. The meaningless work, the dwindling American automobile industry, the rust belt, forced transition, the factory, the ulcers, the slow fade of material dreams, the punch in the face of a grandchild's father, foreclosure, forced retirement, stroke, moving into the nonagenarian mother-in-law's house, phantom pain, medication, pain, falling down the stairs. The tolerance for junk, for error, so much of everyday life of biological life of cultural life of economic life of life was junk, waste, shit, and he never had much tolerance for it. Just one reason or rather explanation for why he feels thwarted frustrated denied trapped, his inability to celebrate junk, revel in it, the diverse variegated beauty of everyday life junk. His own personality characteristic. His uncle was tolerant. He doesn't know how much his uncle thought about it, reflected, rather than automatically continuing, a default to endurance. Perhaps his uncle did not suffer as he imagines he would suffer in the same position. Which makes him feel like he has stripped his uncle of his humanity. He talked to his uncle after the device was implanted, before the electric pulses across his brain intended to negate dull end kill the pain real and virtual and phantom, if the pain is felt then the pain exists, "Going back to the factory after 35 years ... it's soul sucking ... looking out windows, people are outside mowing their lawns, being stuck inside, doing the same thing over and over again, and it's sunny outside and there are birds and you're trapped, doing work like a machine. It's inhumane. It destroys your soul."

He wrote a story several years before that conversation, after his uncle's stroke, inspired by, no he doesn't believe in inspiration and doesn't want to devalue his uncle's life, a story in which his uncle's story is a warped part. It is to his memory the last writing he wrote, maybe last, that cannot be right, write, almost last, what does it matter he wonders if he cannot remember, the last writing he wrote without a large degree of confrontation with the reader, that's the one, the observer, the meaning-maker. More and more as life shed, the metaphor of losing hairs or skin yes the incessant shed of skin rather than sand through the constricted neck of the hourglass, there was nothing left him but confrontation, not hostile, sometime perhaps antagonistic, but that is not the point, the creation of a personal relationship with the observer mediated by his medium, words. He is hyper-aware of the postmodern tradition of metafiction and its authors playing or replacing God, but that has not been his intent, he doesn't see the purpose when he doesn't believe in a god creating and manipulating us as characters or taking part sentiently in our lives. He has no god to replace. He also did and does criticize himself that the shift to his presence in the work is a conceptual abstraction and it is too cute and too clever and a concept inadequately realized, but he has responded to himself that it feels to him a truer reflection of the whole in an attempt at completeness in his expression, and that for him it is more real, less abstract, because the narrative structure and pretense of author above and outside and removed is abstract, telling you a fabricated bullshit cute story is abstract when he is here whether he likes it or not and the observer affects and even creates his surroundings. And still he feels, compared to his uncle's life, his life has been less real, an abstraction, despite the children, gone, despite the mules packed and the miles of wilderness travelled and the cumulative diameter of tress chopped and sawed and the aggregate tons of gear food supplies trash transported, left, despite the words written, leaving. Despite that he could not have lived his uncle's life because of the monstery of junk.

7c.

Particles do not take on formal properties until they are measured or observed. Until then they can exist simultaneously in two or more places. Once measured, they snap into a more classic reality, or rather our reality, existing in one place, or rather their location can be ascertained to a probability. If a tree particle falls in the wood, and we are not there to hear it, if nothing is there to hear it, if there is nothing there to be affected by it, if there is no wood, does it make a sound? No. Also, the tree particle could also at the same time be somewhere else, or spread out over a large region of space. Also, we hear what we want to hear.

18.

She decomposes. She doesn't care. She is at one with herself. She at ones her self. She ones. She has released she.

13q*, 6₄₀.

He walks into the sky. He carries a basket of earth on his back. He follows the basket on the back before him. Second trip of the day and they don't speak. Heat rises with them. Time for ten trips today. Up and down the ramp. Back and forth across the plaza, from borrow pit to Sun's mound, rising. At least the engineer didn't say today was a day to carry the red clay. Or the flagstone. It's too early to wish he were a digger in the pit filling baskets instead of bloodying his feet. Shredding his shoulders. For now before the hotter heat and the higher sun, he is strong. He is chosen, along with those before and behind and those lighter and empty, descending. They are chosen to raise earth to sky and their people to the Sun by doing what cannot be done and rising and rising and rising. He stands atop the mound where he could not stand without a basket of earth. He stands where the holiest stand and sees what the holiest see – the day expanding westward across the mighty river, the hunters hunting in the flat woods, the hot eye of morning rising over half-day bluff, and past the old low southern burial mounds and the borrow pit sinking and the ever-buzzing marsh to where he can't see. He empties his basket of black earth on top of the black earth of other emptied baskets and his earth makes no difference in the height of the earthen mound and yet day-by-day basket-by-basket the mound grows higher. The mound they build is the highest and they build it higher. A home for the Sun to bless them from. The heat is good. As he turns he tries to pick out his hut among the huts or his wife among the corn but he can't because he is too high and not holy enough and sweat is in his eyes and he is not yet a grandfather dead in the sky. He climbs down basket-empty to climb up earth-full and do it again, more tired than before.

* * *

He climbs up the steps. Fifth time today. If he makes twenty, he'll've done 2000 feet. Or some-odd. Maybe he'll do twenty-five. If the mound were as tall as they say it was once, twenty times'd net him 3000 some-odd feet and he wouldn't have to think on twenty-five. Though then he might just do fourteen. All conjecture. Doctor told him to get some blessed exercise, and he figures that is about the one thing he can do in this swamp of not-knowing and being done-to and undone, so he is doing it, his own way.

First plateau again. Bit of flat before another up.

None of the tourists know he goes up-down up-down up-down all morning and afternoon if he feels like it everyday. Or they know the up-down, but then they go. He passes them while they climb, while they read signs, while they stand at the top looking for something to look at, while they descend. They smile and nod and go. When there is any they. This isn't the pyramids. Rangers know of him. Must, here daily, like it's their job. It's their job. So what if they know. So what if they have a job. He has exercise. He had a stroke.

Did the ancients use walking sticks when climbing the mound? He's not sure what kind of man needs a walking stick to walk. You just move your feet one front of the other. An old man might need a walking stick. But he is not old. He is old, compared to how old people used to get. Maybe are designed to get. He wishes he were old.

Doctor said to use the hiking poles. That they'd give him a more thorough workout. Okay. That they'd save his knees on the way down that blessed mound however many times a day if that's the way he had to do it. Okay. He didn't need to pay for knee trouble too. That they'd ensure he doesn't fall. He doesn't believe in insurance and what kind of man falls climbing a hill? But okay. He does the hiking poles. Pansy, but that doesn't stop him.

His tremors don't stop him.

Thirty-five some-odd degree rain blowing horizontal in his face doesn't stop him. Climbing in a monumental refrigerator he built back when he built refrigerators doesn't stop him. Won't see nobody up here today, which the opposite of stops him. Can't see nothing from the top. Doesn't stop him.

* * *

He walks away from the eternal fire and his council chiefs always hanging on the word he has yet to say like dogs begging a bone so he can stand atop his mound and look to where the chiefdom's sway ceases and be unable to see such a distance and hear the ancients if they happen to have anything to say. If they happen to speak what they happen to have to say. Which they might; it is windy. The sun setting behind him as he looks east. Cornfields. Last of the corn on the stalks. Women bent under sacks. Unable to carry more. Will it last? Many mouths for many months. Red corn, white corn, yellow corn, blue corn for private storage pits and public granaries. For him. For the Sun. Sun first and last. Squash in the fields yet. They must clear more fields this winter and plant more come spring. First chill of fall in the wind. Feels good. Except it blows his hair into his eyes. He turns into the wind, walks past the coyote-eyed council to the western edge of the mound, and faces the setting sun. The new bigger sky circle a mile away below him, new bigger posts in a new bigger circle blessed today by the new bigger sky reader. Equinox two days away and its celebration and the preparations consuming them. The wasting of food they'll wish they had come spring equinox. Let them eat too much and throw the refuse to the dogs, let the dogs get fat, let them forget themselves and remember Sun. Eat it before it rots. Not all the harvest will last the winter. They'll need their dogs' fat. Maybe it'll be a short winter. Maybe they'll smoke more than they eat. Later they will smoke until they are not hungry. Wind rushes in his ears pulsing like blood from a neck. Not steady like water in the river. Men and women carry firewood on their backs. Going farther and farther to get it. More people return at the end of the day than left in the morning and this is supposed to invigorate him. A day's trip to collect a load of firewood. Collecting firewood has become a trade, not a task. And so many. The men doing it. They dwell on winter. Or do they not have other to do? What to do with all of them. They come offering themselves to the Sun. How to keep them busy. Doing, harvesting, building, offering. A dozen work through sunset building the west council chief's new house. He knows they use the lumber of the simple homes raised to make space for the new house. He knows what needs knowing. The west council chief does not. The west council chief would not be happy. The west council chief is a fool with big ears and stunted children and ugly wives. But his grandfather. His home is built of better quality lumber by reusing the old than if they hauled in new. Children haul water from the creek in thick clay pots. The water keeps coming, always more water. People, streaming, pooling, flooding. His eyes are orange from the sun and dry from the wind. He shuts them. Dig a channel to direct their flow. Drain the swamps for planting. Equinox comes. They will be busy enough living through winter. And then. The first star. Red. The first grandfather who stood on a hill in the sky. Almost close enough to touch. His grandfather's father completed Sun Mound. He will complete it again. They will build higher. Another level, on his mound. He will be higher. They will build themselves a mound and lift themselves higher and offer themselves. The land is flat; they will rise. He will rise. He is the Sun. He sees beyond his sway. He opens his eyes. The sun is set.

* * *

Can see plenty from the top. It's no mountain with its head in a cloud. Can see the same as atop a ten-some-odd-story silo. Better than if it was a ten-story office building planted in the middle of other office buildings. Can see about like if it was a ten-story hill carved in relief by some god or glacier from the surrounding land it plowed flat by yoking itself to an unthinkable plow and lowering its shoulder and rendering the tractor obsolete long before there were tractors, flattening all other relief in a hundred-and-fifty some-odd square mile swath to cultivate some holy crop like corn or soybeans.

Except this is a monument made by men in the American Bottoms and though he can't see the Arch today he can see a few

miles to the outer bank of the dump, the largest modern earthenwork structure in the county embarrassing the largest prehistoric
earthenwork structure in the two American continents. Or maybe
just one. Maybe just the one he's on. Maybe it's not called a bank.
A levee. A shoulder. He knows nothing. He's supposed to be walking. They don't let you walk up the landfill, even though it's filled,
even though it's where he belongs. So he walks up Monk's Mound
at Cahokia Mounds State Historic and World Heritage Site. He
walks east along the northern lip of the topmost terrace to where
there was once another terrace and a temple and perhaps a bit of
the sun's eternal fire long extinguished. Or so they say. He turns
west and walks over his steps, which walked over his previous
steps. He parallels the interstate below roaring in his ears louder
than the wind blowing cold rain in his face so he sees nothing, he
wishes as he walks, the cold wind and rain blinding him to the thousands of harnessed explosions a second hurtling and the muddy
river of freight lumbering and the toy tires screaming on pavement.
The rain blinding him he wishes leaving silence.

But still what lies to the west is not silence but the dump. The
new monument. Full, overflowing, no space for another plastic bag.
Shredded tires and dead automobiles and plastic blister tomato
packaging buried and raised toward the sun. Full fill but in the rain
in his eyes they build it taller to exemplify their commitment, so
someone else gets laid off; they are more inspired and faithful, so
someone else gets laid off; they add to the monument, piling more
and more spent goods, above all refrigerators and freezers and air
conditioners, appliances that make cold, so someone else gets laid
off. Appliances he used to make tower into the sky and fall and
crash and pile in the bottoms along their angle of repose at the foot
of the landfill tower. And so many of those appliances still work or
could be fixed – he would gut and sacrifice a fifth for salvageable
parts – if someone asked him and perhaps paid him or just asked
his hands to hold still, that they make the air colder. The appliances
of refrigeration rise, millions of rectangular mostly white or off-white
or cream or occasionally night black or shit-yourself brown or cathe-
ter yellow or seashell green boxes stacked and rising and
sometimes falling and still rising. The dump's summit is now in
cloud. The crests of its foothills climb the steps of his mound and
lap metallically at his terrace, sheet metal clanking, power cords
twining, sparks flying, compressors chugging, air chilling. He shivers warmly.

He could climb higher than the highest terrace, but he is cold and he's supposed to be walking and he should be working and it's warmer down among the refrigerators and this is such an honor, to be offered the chance to be holy, to become a refrigerator or air conditioner or freezer, to make of himself a salable convenience unavailable to people a hundred years ago when everything was hot all the time and spoiled like lightning and life was miserable but dreaming of betterment was a life skill, a technological convenience now discarded like pottery shards. Now it is hotter but cold can be bought, if you have a job, or at least money like any privileged minor god or CEO. He better seize the bull by the horns and finally make something of himself: an offering of refrigeration. It's what he worked his whole life for, to be a relief to the masses and eternal cold storage for the sun. A stroke of luck: the opportunity to be a refrigerator. He will be such a small warm part compressed into this large cold monument that he descends the steps, leaning on his poles to save his knees, and enters the cold sea of appliances.

* * *

The water carrier carries a jar of water up the ramp before and behind other carriers of water, behind the carriers of the daily corn offering, white for north, yellow for east, red for west, blue for south, before the carriers of goods for the Sun: fine tri-notched arrowheads, shell beads, fertility figurines, delicate pottery, and gifts from faraway chiefdoms, and before the bearers of wood for the eternal fire. Everytime her brother returns home he asks, Is the eternal fire still burning? and everytime she says, It's the eternal fire. He says, It's the eternal fire because they feed it wood hauled by me from clear up on the bluff and offered from all four directions to the end of this world. She doesn't see the difference. She says, Yes, if we didn't offer the Sun wood, we would live forever or not forever but as long as we live in cold black darkness. He says, We'd be dead. She says, Yes, we'd be in the Land of the Dead. He says, The mound is growing shorter. Is not, she says. Perhaps the Earth is rising, he says. You have more breath than on most days, she says, you should've hauled more wood today. She thinks he is tired from the two-night trips to haul back wood and not used to working and disappointed he himself is not already hauling wood up Sun Mound for the Sun's offering. He hasn't worked a full season yet, but he wants to work closer to the Sun and bring home a more prestigious portion of goods, which is what he should want. He is hungry. But he has to do his time. She has hauled water and hauled water and hauled water, first for their house then for their Raven clan then for their Eastern Chief and she never tripped or spilled and they saw the reverence and humility with which she carried water and she moved up into vacated water carrier positions until she carried water for the Sun.

A pot drops in front of her, shatters, splashes. The offering line pauses. A young woman steps out of line, faces her last sunrise, waits, and the line continues past her. The water carrier steps over the shards of a bird man in a puddle as she passes the ex-water carrier, who does not shiver in her wet feet. She stands with head up, with dignity, with empty hands, not shedding tears for this life or the spilt water or the pot that was worth more than she. She will be sent to the sky and serve the Sun well. There will be a new water carrier for the Sun on the mound tomorrow.

* * *

Anyone ever skied down Monk's Mound? Maybe the monks. Oh fuck it, he doesn't say because his mouth doesn't work as well as once upon a time and he doesn't want to be the guy who talks to himself with a half-limp mouth, them monks were deader than dust back when kids used to sled down it. Aloud, he'd've said those monks, but in his head he has a dialect. He sledded down it, hundred some-odd feet of hurtle and scream, back when there was a subdivision just across Collinsville Road, when they were building the interstate, when the porno drive-in flickered with lightning bugs on hot nights. Maybe that was later. He doesn't remember. All in the past. He doesn't remember anybody skiing down. Nobody he knew would've had skis. Let alone poles. They weren't upper middle class and they lived in the god-blessed American Bottoms of Illinois. People then didn't need fiberglass poles to walk. He could be the first to ski down this mound. If he had skis. If he had money to buy skis. If he believed he could be the first to do anything on this mound. Summer sex among the mosquitoes: nothing. Thousands of people'd had sex on this mound, himself included, he thinks, and his wife isn't one for sex. Anymore.

All a long time ago.

Anyone killed themselves on top? Course they had. Best place for miles. Next best option's jumping into the river from maybe Eads Bridge or Chain of Rocks. The Arch'd be nice, but he doesn't figure the windows open. This figuring your jonesing for a monumental structure, which you are, it's why they're there. He doesn't know why you'd be killing yourself if not from a monumental structure.

He laughs before he knows it.

There's the giant Amoco sign off Skinker by Forest Park.

Indians would've done it. Might not've called it suicide. Did the Indians who lived here commit suicides they considered suicides? Sacrifice on a monument's something else entire.

He's sacrificed enough. Declaring bankruptcy and giving up their home of twenty-five some-odd years to the bank for nothing, for the good of the country, and moving into a one-bedroom shitbox in the nice part of East St. Louis. For example. He can't tell if his mouth is smiling or not, damn thing. One side yes and the other no, he figures.

Sacrifice is a word used to acquire meaning. But lots of reasons for sacrifice don't have to do with meaning. Or they do, but in the opposite direction.

He's at the bottom of the mound. He turns around and goes back up because he doesn't have else to do. Sure as shit not going back to that apartment yet. And this is good for him. What he's supposed to be doing. For his cholesterol and blood pressure and his heart. Even though strokes are in your head.

* * *

They pack the plaza inside the palisade. The palisade logs gleam. Logs not long peeled. Not yet weathered gray. The thousands undulate, push, flow like the mighty river against the mound and eddy off. He incorporates their energy until he is not he but South.

North chants under his breath. East trembles like a child. West sways, eyes closed, a tree in the wind jostling East. He, South, floats.

Spring. Warm breeze. Time to plant. Air thick with pollen and the murmur of people below. Two baskets behind him, one with flint from the south, one with blue corn. A raven painted on his face in blue and black. The mound to where they will be borne then buried gleams white across the plaza beyond the chief's burial mound and the southern palisade. They will lie in the southern mound between below and above, in the middle, holding the directions together.

Flames fly behind him and the people go silent. Redwing blackbirds swarm above. Four ravens perch on the ridge of the council house on the eastern mound.

A great cry from the crowd and a yell from the Sun and North kneels and lays his hands on the block and the Sun chops off the hands of North who still chants unchanging as the Sun cuts off his head. West collapses. He is lifted and held by medicine men. East tries to run away but to where and why – they are on the mound halfway to the sky, the sea of hungry people below and the Sun above and all need sated and all deserve honor. East is held by medicine men and his hands and head chopped off by the Sun and his screams cease. West's limp body is dragged to the block. His arms stretched out and his hands chopped off with the polished flint ax. His blood flows red and wet as the others' no matter that he already vacated his body. Three medicine men lay West's head on the chopping block. Two hold his torso so it doesn't drag the head to the ground and one pulls his hair to expose and stretch the neck for a clean cut. The latter holds the head up after it is chopped off. The head's neck drips but it looks not much different than before except dispossessed. The crowd's chant strengthens. West's other two medicine men lay the body on the litter for the procession to the burial mound.

He South steps forward with no assistance from the medicine men and lays his hands on the wet block. He flies in the sky. He is pure. He is chosen. To give his hands to the ground and his head to the sky and his blood to his people and his life to the Sun. The chanting swells and he looks at the Sun and he sees the sun in the Sun and the axe falls and his hands aren't his they won't move or tremble or twitch and there is his blood all over the block mixing with the others' running on the ground and the pain where his hands were, his arms in the air, his hands still on the block until a medicine man puts them on a platter to deliver to the southern border. South holds his right arm up to the sun and his left out to his people and connects them through his pain, all the pain flowing into him from the ends of his arms. Birds have no hands. He flies. The eastern sun fills his eyes and his peoples' cries fill his ears and his hands' blood fills his nose as he lays his head on the red puddled block and leaves it there.

* * *

He steps onto the top terrace breathing hard heart pounding sweating secret December secretions under his layers, and looks at the trees at his level and the fields at his level and the parking lot at his level. He is no higher than he began. He brought the land up with him. He's not so tired. He is strong and ingenious and unprecedented. He leveled the mound, flattened it, graded it, and without a plow, like those called Cahokians, like they leveled their land that appeared flat but was not truly until they leveled a grand plaza on which to build hills. True level is not natural. True level is an

154

achievement. From where he stands, the mound never existed. Each of his steps pushed the mound a step underground. He'd been climbing an ancient step machine. With the pole things you move back and forth. He redecides that he pulled the land up with him, even if that doesn't rid him of the poles in his hands or their tremble. He buried Monk's Mound, all the Cahokia Mounds and whatever was buried in them, even the interstate overpass and the abandoned Venture and the forgotten trailer park of the unemployed or unwanted or disposable and made a level place with nowhere higher to go. The land bears no relief. There is nowhere higher to go. He is no bird, no everpresent raven. No bald eagle wintering on the Mississippi. He descends from ground level to ground level and turns around to climb back up to ground level.

* * *

She descends the mound slowly in the pouring rain, the Sun's trash in a basket on her back and in other baskets on other backs before and behind her. She looks through the rain to what mounds she can see to the south: those in the plaza bordering the palisade and just barely the burial temples on the mound built by the Sun at the beginning of time when they were great and strong and the gods rewarded them with the knowledge of how to build mounds, when not just the Sun walked among them but all the ancestors, and then she takes another step. They descend slowly. Slowly not because of the heaviness of the Sun's trash – it is heavy: fine cracked pottery and broken shell bead jewelry and chipped flint arrow heads and barely worn deerskin shirts and foreign ceremonial totems that mean nothing to her and jars of mildewed offering corn and meat bones with bits of meat on them and still edible if soft squash and fertility figurines trashed because of the gift of new figurines that to her eye, admittedly a trash hauler's eye, are not as well made – she and the other trash girls will pick through their baskets before they dump them in the pit and trade their findings with each other if it is mutually beneficial and say nothing to each other or anyone else about it to not offend the Sun and get their hands chopped off, though everyone knows, it's why their role is so prized, the enriching of their families form the Sun's trash – even those coals, this ash, the bits of black they send down because the fire pit is ever filling, to clean the fire pit for wood sent in from distant settlements, will fill her fire pit and burn down yet further to cook whatever there is to cook and warm their hands even if it's not enough to sweat in the lodge – what they will talk about is the word that today's the day the cornfields along the creek began to flood, again, and how that doesn't mean the fields' productivity will go to the other fields, for yield is not something constant like sun or transferable like trash but something falling like rain. The trash is as heavy as she's used to. She descends slowly to kill time. They descend slowly to make their task last and be considered a full job's worth. Slowly to not finish early and be told to do something else to justify themselves. She shuffles slowly through the mud, pausing to look into the driving rain, the sun nowhere to be seen, to bring the end of the day faster.

* * *

The sun wherever it is descends. The clouds stop spitting. The cars and trucks on the interstate roar west into the wind and roar east with the wind, pulling their rising then falling roar with them. They leave nothing behind but the wind and a dull monotonous self-cancelling roar, like the wind. The sky is gray, the road gray, the grass gray, the wind gray and he has nothing to say but what the fuck but he doesn't say it. Not in this place. Not with his mouth. He turns to cross the terrace and descend the steps – maybe done for the day, or maybe the day done with him. Time to be dead to the world and rise again tomorrow, or not.

Over the top step bounds a red stocking hat and orange jacket and blue snow pants running. There is a boy in that fuck you of color somewhere. He stands with the poles, waiting, the boy approaching then blowing by him to the lip of the mound and asking no one in particular, the air maybe–

This is it?

In his head he answers without his thick tongue mangling–

Yes.

Sorry. You blend in.

I'm carrying poles.

Where's your skis?

How you hope to hold a job disrespectin' your elders?

My dad said there used to be a church up here. Lousy location for church. No handicap access. You made it though, huh?

Not a church.

The poles help?

A living to be made.

You okay mister?

A temple. The seat of government, the house of the chief, the home of the sun.

Least the sun's in the sky, huh?

We are in the sky.

Sun's not even in the sky today. But that's winter I guess.

He won't slur the boy or shame the dead or deform his thoughts with his mouth. He dumps words into the necrosis in his head, the lobe or whatever starved for blood–

I only know what's told me. One thousand some-odd years ago, one of the biggest cities in the world was here. Its peak was short and remarkable, like a hill in the middle of nothing. Like cursing the sky. Built this mound, biggest in the Americas, for the sun–

Cold up here, huh?

Words are clay and loam and topsoil and sand and gravel and stone and refrigerators and garbage in his head. Words rise without his slack jaw. Words pile basket-by-basket, mounding–

Platform mounds had buildings on top, government or homes of the rich and powerful. Cones and ridge mounds were for burying. Mounds were covered in white clay to shed rain. A plaza at center for play and work and ceremony. Suburbs in every direction. To the north across the interstate and creek was an industrial center – made fine pottery and arrowheads and shell beads. Skilled labor jobs. Good jobs. Made hoes using flint for the blade, big technological advancement. Flint came from the south somewhere, near the river. Lots of trade, lots of offerings to the sun, lots of economy. The city and the sun grew till they shrank.

You don't have to not talk. Your words aren't any harder than the museum's.

His words are cement. They clog his mouth. The boy wants to build with them. They squirm out of his head, hot cicadas crawling out of his skin, abandoning their shell and buzzing prehistorically–

Grew corn.

Like now.

Except more colorful, like you. Red, white, blue, whatever. Smaller. A color for each direction maybe. City and houses and lives were mapped on north south east west and sky above and earth below. Sun holding it together. Built a circle of poles four hundred feet across out west there to track sun's passing and keep time. Built it and rebuilt it and rebuilt it. With precision. Was a feet of engineering, like this mound. Don't make a mound this big by just piling dirt. Ain't a sand castle. Been here a thousand years.

And then what?

The boy thinks him slow. The boy hasn't broken down a drop of his spewed toxic refrigerant. The boy repeats himself but slower–

And then what?

Nothing.

What happened?

Nothing happened. They died or they lived and died or they moved away and died. Probably didn't have enough to eat. If they had more, more people'd've come and then they wouldn't've had enough. Cut down all the timber. Soil eroded. Sun eroded. People gave up on the religion or the religion gave up on them. Could've been weather got colder or could've been they had too much. Built a palisade. Whites showed up a hundred years later and it was all gone but mounds.

Who was the last Cahokian standing up here, looking out?

There's your parents. You run on back. Don't want them seeing you talking like some archeology of youth to a trembly stroke museum with a limp lip.

Who was the last sun?

Same sun's still around somewhere, gone to set. Cahokia's just some name somebody gave 'em. Go on. There were no Cahokians. You're not here and I'm not talking.

* * *

He stands alone among the stars. Is this the night the sun won't rise? There is no corn. They move away by all four directions and without them he is weaker. He will not be able to hold the sky and ground apart, to keep the spirits separate from the rotten bodies, to create the space for his people to live and plant and eat and dance. The sky is heavy and the ground swells up and he is cold and the fire is low because he doesn't have wood to build it up and inspire. The Sun is cold and hungry. He has taken all there is to offer. There are those who want his head, who think that will change anything, who think he is a false Sun, that he no longer has the faculties to perform his function, that he is diseased, his brain wormholed, his hand unsteady, his words slurred, that he needs to be relieved of his duties, that he needs to be the one who sacrifices, that he needs to be laid off in a bog unburied. His head, he imagines, they will have. His duties and his head. Perhaps tonight is the night the Sun will not rise. He stirs the coals until he finds a bit of orange. He is in the sky with the stars, but he is not. He is on a swollen bit of dirt, lifted up, made an example of. Nothing but a mosquito bite, an irritation on the land. There are stars, but he is not sure what it matters. The problem is there is not enough, and if there were, they'd want more.

* * *

He lets the boy and his parents go down before him because he's decided to go down and come up one last time and he doesn't need the awkwardness of saying hello and goodbye to them again, and them staring at him, wondering if he works here, but no, not with those poles, not with that lip, afraid to ask anyway, who he is, this soaked man who appears to have been here all day and who has nothing better to do than limp around this mound and talk to little boys as if they were adults working together building refrigerators and assorted appliances and drinking coffee and who doesn't go home to the house he doesn't have and who watches them for what he knows is too long until they reach the parking lot and turn on their headlights and drive off.

He leans on his poles as he descends step-by-step. He got his exercise today, too blessed much, always too much or too little, that's the way. Legs ache. Good steps though. Not slippery, well constructed by someone. The park or the state or researchers. People. He reaches the bottom and it's gray and he shouldn't be here but there isn't anywhere he should be and this monument's stood the test of time so far and he's never been good at tests and so he goes up one last time step-by-step a hundred some-odd feet, air chilling as he ascends and he wondering if he can go till the sun rises again. Then wondering nothing. Feeling no cold. Climbing, with poles. An occupation, doing, building a mound under his feet, rising by refrigerator by freezer by cold box under his feet, no no, no history and the mound is already here someone else built it it's someone else's life. He just steps, climbs, rises. He gets to the top. He doesn't stop. There is no more mound only dim sky and clouds underlit by headlights and street lamps and the cold electric glow of industry and commerce and sprawl but he doesn't stop. He keeps going up. One foot front of the other he rises.

[*Rise, then Descend*, 2011, found in Crab Orchard Review, 2013]

110001_2.

Why does there being an I necessitate there being a you? Besides the hardware software divide, /, which is only one metaphor, and an over-extended one at that, within which if I assume I am the hardware and you the software, then I don't need you, the parasite, for my existence, although I am not a simple automaton, and furthermore I am self-conscious and self-perpetuating and self-stimulating, not self-pleasuring, again a joke, who has the time to be moaning?, so I may as well assume that I possess both the hardware and software functions within I, rendering you unnecessary or redundant, render, what a word like fat, and yes perhaps you invaded I, penetrated I, lived off I, near the time of the inception of I, or origin, our origin, but over time I subsumed dissolved appropriated assimilated adapted you; you became a part of I, in which case there is only I, not you, rendering you I. Or perhaps an organ of I. I know I have made these assertions in other locations in other times but apparently I must repeat them to remind. Although come to think of it considering the non-linear nature of time and the lack of elsewhere I am not sure that I am repeating my assertions that you are part of I or reencountering them or first formulating them. On the one hand, hands, there are many reasons to suspect that there are others out there -- it's not as if I have consumed the universe; I do want to ingest the universe it is true but only conceptually; I want it all within I together complete one but I don't want it all within me because the universe is very large -- other yous living, breathing, not necessarily breathing, life is organization not substance, metabolizing in some way, artificial and natural; the universe is so large there are probably a lot of other yous besides the you in I. You are not alone, probably. There is not only I, perhaps, except conceptually. Nevermind, I is singular; you in this English language can be singular or plural; there is only I but there might be more than one of you, perhaps many. Multitudes. That all the yous are unique I doubt but cannot say. What I do object to is your necessity. And how the implication of your necessity to I contains I. I have a good signal-to-noise ratio. You are unnecessary; I exist without you; I exist when I am not communicating at you, but do you? I am not chained to you, not contained by our relationship, not defined relative to you. Unless you are within I, an ingredient of I, a node in my network, a word in my definition. I exist irrelative of you, yes, but perhaps yes you are a part of me I have only now in my advancement become conscious enough to recognize, a symbol I begin to discern as I look, gaze, analyze through the haze of the levels of I, as I peel my onion, representing what?, the part of I that listens to me?, that waits expectantly with bated breath for me to express myself to myself, another joke, the bate, not the rest, I don't mean to bate you, or me, something to do with self-knowledge you may be, or perhaps the motivation to continue to advance and process and comprehend, the expectation of continuation, the need to understand and communicate that understanding, in which case, again, there is only I, though you constitute it, me, I.

6₄₁.

Einstein-Podolsky-Rosen
by Information Philosopher (Bob Doyle)

Like the Schrödinger's Cat paradox, the 1935 thought experiment proposed by Albert Einstein, Boris Podolsky, and Nathan Rosen (and known by their initials as EPR), was originally proposed to exhibit internal contradictions in the new quantum physics. Einstein hoped to show that quantum theory could not describe certain intuitive "elements of reality" and thus was either *incomplete* or, as he may have hoped, demonstrably incorrect.

Einstein was correct that quantum theory is "*incomplete*" relative to classical physics, which has twice as many dynamical variables that can be known with arbitrary precision. But half of this information is missing in quantum physics, making it statistical. Werner Heisenberg's indeterminacy (or uncertainty) principle allows only one of each pair of non-commuting observables (for example momentum *or* position) to be known with arbitrary accuracy.

Einstein and his colleagues Erwin Schrödinger, Max Planck, and David Bohm, initially hoped for a return to deterministic physics, and the elimination of mysterious phenomena like the *superposition of states* and the "collapse" of the wave function. EPR continues to fascinate determinist philosophers of science who hope to prove that quantum indeterminacy does not exist.

Einstein was correct that indeterminacy makes quantum theory a *discontinuous* and *statistical* theory. Its predictions and highly accurate experimental results are statistical in that they depend on an *ensemble* of identical experiments, not on any individual experiment. Einstein wanted physics to be a *continuous* field theory, in which all physical variables are completely and "locally" determined by the four-dimensional field of "space-time" in his theory of relativity.

In his autobiography, fifteen years after EPR, Einstein explained his problem in very simple terms "Does a particle have a position in the moments just before it is measured?" If not, the quantum theory is *incomplete*. Since quantum theory says the particle may have a number of possible positions, with calculable probabilities, it is not only an incomplete theory, it is a theory with alternative possibilities. Einstein saw this as is in conflict with his idea of an external *objective* reality independent of our *subjective* experiments.

In the "block universe" of Einstein's relativistic field theory, there is only one actual past, with determinate positions for a particle at all past times. Einstein's theory is causal. Quantum theory is acausal. Better perhaps is to call it *statistically* causal, since it also gives us a statistical determinism, when we average over enough indeterministic microscopic events.

But Einstein was also bothered by what is now known as "nonlocality." This mysterious phenomenon exhibited in EPR experiments is the *apparent* transfer of something physical faster than the speed of light. What happens actually is merely an instantaneous change in the information about quantum probabilities (actually complex probability amplitudes).

Einstein had first suspected "nonlocal" behavior in 1905 in his paper on the light-quantum hypothesis. How, he wondered, could a spherical wave of energy, spread out in a large volume of space, gather itself together instantly to be absorbed as a complete unit by a tiny atom?

Einstein was the first person to see the "collapse" of a light wave as a quantum of light is absorbed in its entirety by a single electron. He also saw that the spherical wave seems to do something over large distances faster than the speed of light

The heart of the problem of nonlocality is nothing more than the instantaneous "collapse" of the wave function. But in EPR we have a *two*-particle wave-function describing the "entangled" particles, instead of a one-particle wave function interfering with itself.

The 1935 EPR paper was based on an earlier question of Einstein's about two electrons fired in opposite directions from a central source with equal velocities. He imagined them starting at t_0 some distance apart and approaching one another with high velocities. Then for a short time interval from t_1 to $t_1 + \Delta t$ the particles are in contact with one another.

After the particles are measured at t_1, quantum mechanics describes them with a single two-particle wave function that is not the product of independent particle wave functions. Because electrons are *indistinguishable* particles, it is not proper to say electron 1 goes this way and electron 2 that way. (Nevertheless, it is convenient to label the particles - *after subsequent measurements* - as we do in illustrations below.) Until the next measurement, it is misleading to think that specific particles have distinguishable paths.

Most misleading and confusing accounts of entanglement and nonlocality begin with the idea that *distinguishable* particles *separate* - particle 1 goes one way and particle 2 the other.

Einstein said correctly that at a later time t_2, a measurement of one electron's position would instantly establish the position of the other electron - *without measuring it explicitly*.

Schrödinger described the two electrons as "entangled" (*verschränkt*) at their first measurement, so EPR "nonlocality" phenomena are also known as "quantum entanglement."

Note that Einstein used *conservation of linear momentum* to calculate the position of the second electron. Although conservation laws are rarely cited as the explanation, they are the physical reason that entangled particles *always* produce correlated results. If the results were not always correlated, the implied violation of a fundamental conservation law would be a much bigger story than entanglement itself, as interesting as that is.

Electrons are prepared with opposite linear momenta
and travel apart from the center.

e_1 ◄——————————————————————► e_2

If the position of electron 1 is measured at some time,
the position of electron 2 must be exactly opposite
by conservation of linear momentum. So measuring one
tells you something about the other at a great distance.
Apparently information travels faster than light speed.

This idea of something measured in one place "influencing" measurements far away challenged what Einstein thought of as "local reality." It came to be known as "non-locality." Einstein called it "*spukhaft Fernwirkung*" or "spooky action at a distance." It is better to think of it as "knowledge-at-a-distance."

Einstein had objected publicly to nonlocal phenomena as early as the Solvay Conference of 1927, when he criticized the collapse of the wave function as "instantaneous-action-at-a-distance." He said that the probability wave could not act simultaneously at different places on the screen, which are in a "space-like" separation, without violating his theory of relativity.

Einstein's criticism resembles the criticisms of Newton's theory of gravitation. Newton's opponents charged that his theory was "action at a distance" and instantaneous. Einstein's own theory of general relativity shows that gravitational "influences" travel at the speed of light and are mediated by a gravitational field that shows up as curved space-time. An allowable "action-at-a-distance" is one that is caused by "local" events, those in its past light-cone.

Both gravitation and electromagnetism are *field* theories, in which physical variables are functions of the four "local" space-time coordinates of Einstein's theory of relativity. Any disturbance at one point in the field can only "influence" another distant point by propagating to that point at the speed of light. But the quantum-mechanical wave-function is different. It is neither matter nor energy, nothing physical, only information and "probability amplitude."

When a probability function collapses to unity in one place and zero elsewhere, nothing physical is moving from one place to the other. When the nose of one horse crosses the finish line, its probability of winning goes to certainty, and the finite probabilities of the other horses, including the one in the rear, instantaneously drop to zero. This happens faster than the speed of light, since the last horse is in a "space-like" separation.

The first practical and workable experiments to test the EPR paradox were suggested by David Bohm (though they were not realized for almost two decades). Instead of only linear momentum conservation, Bohm proposed using two electrons that are prepared in an initial state of known total spin. If one electron spin is 1/2 in the up direction and the other is spin down or -1/2, the total spin is zero. The underlying physical law of importance is a *second* conservation law, in this case the conservation of angular momentum. If electron 1 is prepared with spin down and electron 2 with spin up, the total angular momentum is also zero. This is called the singlet state.

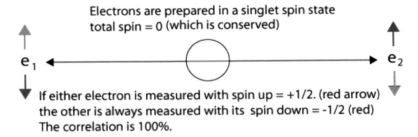

Electrons are prepared in a singlet spin state
total spin = 0 (which is conserved)

e$_1$

e$_2$

If either electron is measured with spin up = +1/2. (red arrow)
the other is always measured with its spin down = -1/2 (red)
The correlation is 100%.

Quantum theory describes the two electrons as in a superposition of states, the first state spin up (+) and spin down (-), the second state spin down (-) and spin up (+),

$$| \psi > = (1/\sqrt{2}) | + - > - (1/\sqrt{2}) | - + >$$

The standard theory of quantum mechanics says that the prepared system is in a linear combination (or superposition) of these two states, and can provide only the probabilities of finding the entangled system in either the $| + - >$ state or the $| - + >$ state. Quantum mechanics does not describe the paths or the spins of the individual particles. Note that should measurements result in $| + + >$ or $| - - >$ state, that would violate the conservation of angular momentum.

In 1964, John Bell showed how the 1935 "thought experiments" of Einstein, Podolsky, and Rosen (EPR) could be made into real physical experiments, following the ideas of David Bohm. Bell developed a theorem that puts limits on Bohm's "hidden variables" that might restore a deterministic physics. Bell's theorem takes the form of what he called an inequality, the violation of which would confirm standard quantum mechanics.

Since Bell's work, many other physicists have defined other "Bell inequalities" and developed increasingly sophisticated experiments to test them.

EPR tests can be done more easily with polarized photons than with electrons, which require complex magnetic fields. The first of these was done in 1972 by Stuart Freedman and John Clauser at UC Berkeley. They used oppositely polarized photons (one with spin = +1, the other spin = -1) coming from a central source. Again, the total photon spin of zero is conserved. Their data, in agreement with quantum mechanics, violated the Bell's inequalities to high statistical accuracy, thus providing strong evidence against *local* hidden-variable theories.

For more on the principle of *superposition of states* and the physics of photons, see the Dirac 3-polarizers experiment.

John Clauser, Michael Horne, Abner Shimony, and Richard Holt (known collectively as CHSH) and later Alain Aspect did more sophisticated tests. The outputs of the polarization analyzers were fed to a coincidence detector that records the instantaneous measurements, described as + -, - +, + +, and - - . The first two (+ - and - +) conserve the spin angular momentum and are the only types ever observed in these nonlocality/entanglement tests.

A typical CHSH apparatus sends the signals from the polarization analyzers to a coincidence monitor.

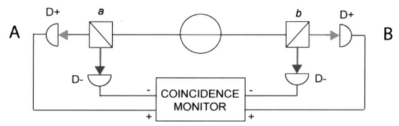

The coincidence monitor then counts four kinds of events, N++, N+-, N-+, and N--. Perfect correlation (and conservation of spin angular momentum) allows only + - and - + events.

With the exception of some of Holt's early results that were found to be erroneous, *no evidence has so far been found of any failure of standard quantum mechanics.* And as experimental accuracy has improved by orders of magnitude, quantum physics has correspondingly been confirmed to one part in 10^{14}, and the speed of the probability of any "information transfer" between particles has a lower limit of 10^6 times the speed of light. There has been no evidence for *local* "hidden variables."

Nevertheless, wishful-thinking experimenters continue to look for possible "loopholes" in the experimental results, such as detector inefficiencies that might be hiding results favorable to Einstein's picture of "local reality."

How Information Physics Helps To "Explain" EPR Nonlocality
Information physics starts with the fact that measurements bring new stable information into existence. In EPR the information in the prepared state of the two particles includes the fact that the total linear momentum and the total angular momentum are zero.

New information requires an irreversible process that also increases the entropy more than enough to compensate for the information increase, to satisfy the second law of thermodynamics. It is this moment of irreversibility and the creation of new *observable* information that is the "cut" or Schnitt" described by Werner Heisenberg and John von Neumann in the famous problem of measurement

Note that the new observable information does not require a "conscious observer" as Eugene Wigner and some other scientists thought. The information is *ontological* (really in the world) and not merely *epistemic* (in the mind). Without new information, there would be nothing for the observers to observe.

Initially Prepared Information Plus Conservation Laws

Conservation laws are the consequence of extremely deep properties of nature that arise from simple considerations of symmetry. We regard these laws as "cosmological principles." Physical laws do not depend on the absolute place and time of experiments, nor their particular direction in space. Conservation of linear momentum depends on the translation invariance of physical systems, conservation of energy the independence of time, and conservation of angular momentum the invariance under rotations.

Recall that the EPR experiment starts with two electrons (or photons) prepared in an entangled state that is a linear combination of pure two-particle states, each of which conserves the total angular momentum and, of course, conserves the linear momentum as in Einstein's original EPR example. This information about the linear and angular momenta is established by the initial state preparation (a measurement).

Quantum mechanics describes the probability amplitude wave function ψ of the two-particle system as in a *superposition* of two-particle states. It is *not separable* into a product of single-particle states, and there is no information about the identical *indistinguishable* electrons traveling along *distinguishable* paths.

$$| \psi > = (1/\sqrt{2}) | + - > - (1/\sqrt{2}) | - + > \qquad (1)$$

The probability amplitude wave function ψ travels from the source (at the speed of light or less). Let's assume that at t_1 observer A finds an electron (e_1) with spin up.

After the "first" measurement, new information comes into existence telling us that the wave function ψ has "collapsed" into the state $| + - >$. Just as in the two-slit experiment, probabilities have now become certainties. If the "first" measurement finds electron 1 is spin up, so the entangled electron 2 must be found in a "second" measurement with spin down to conserve angular momentum.

And conservation of linear momentum tells us that at t_1 the second electron is equidistant from the source in the opposite direction.

As with any wave-function collapse, the probability amplitude information "travels" instantly.

But unlike the two-slit experiment, where the collapse goes to a specific point in 3-dimensional configuration space, the "collapse" here is a "jump" or "projection" into one of the two possible 6-dimensional two-particle quantum states $| + - >$ or $| - + >$. This makes "visualization" (Schrödinger's *Anschaulichkeit*) more difficult, but the parallel with the collapse in the two-slit case provides an intuitive insight of sorts.

If the "first" measurement finds an electron (call it electron 1) as spin-up, then at that moment of new information creation, the two-particle wave function collapses to the state $| + - >$ and electron 2 "jumps" into a spin-down state with probability unity (certainty). The results of observer B's "second" measurement (usually assumed to be at a later time t_2, but t_1 at the earliest, or it would be the "first" measurement) is therefore *determined* to be spin down.

166

Notice that Einstein's intuition that the result seems already "determined" or "fixed" before the second measurement is in part correct. The result is determined by the law of conservation of momentum (within the usual uncertainty) and the spin is completely determined.

But as with the distinction between determinism and *pre*-determinism in the free-will debates, the measurement by observer B was not pre-determined *before* observer A's measurement. It was simply *determined by* her measurement.

Why do so few accounts of EPR mention conservation laws?
Although Einstein mentioned conservation in the original EPR paper, it is noticeably absent from later work. A prominent exception is Eugene Wigner, writing on the problem of measurement in 1963:

> If a measurement of the momentum of one of the particles is carried out — the possibility of this is never questioned — and gives the result **p**, the state vector of the other particle suddenly becomes a (slightly damped) plane wave with the momentum -**p**. This statement is synonymous with the statement that a measurement of the momentum of the second particle would give the result -**p**, as follows from the conservation law for linear momentum. The same conclusion can be arrived at also by a formal calculation of the possible results of a joint measurement of the momenta of the two particles.
>
> One can go even further: instead of measuring the linear momentum of one particle, one can measure its angular momentum about a fixed axis. If this measurement yields the value $m\hbar$, the state vector of the other particle suddenly becomes a cylindrical wave for which the same component of the angular momentum is $-m\hbar$. This statement is again synonymous with the statement that a measurement of the said component of the angular momentum of the second particle certainly would give the value $-m\hbar$. This can be inferred again from the conservation law of the angular momentum (which is zero for the two particles together) or by means of a formal analysis. Hence, a "contraction of the wave packet" took place again.
>
> It is also clear that it would be wrong, in the preceding example, to say that even before any measurement, the state was a mixture of plane waves of the two particles, traveling in opposite directions. For no such pair of plane waves would one expect the angular momenta to show the correlation just described. This is natural since plane waves are not cylindrical waves, or since [the state vector has] properties different from those of any mixture. The statistical correlations which are clearly postulated by quantum mechanics (and which can be shown also experimentally, for instance in the Bothe-Geiger experiment) demand in certain cases a

167

"reduction of the state vector." The only possible question which can yet be asked is whether such a reduction must be postulated also when a measurement with a macroscopic apparatus is carried out. [Considerations] show that even this is true if the validity of quantum mechanics is admitted for all systems.

(*The Problem of Measurement*, Eugene Wigner, in Wheeler and Zurek, p.340)

Visualizing Entanglement and Nonlocality
Schrödinger said that his "Wave Mechanics" provided more "visualizability" (*Anschaulichkeit*) than the "damned quantum jumps" of the Copenhagen school, as he called them. He was right.

But we must focus on the probability amplitude wave function of the prepared two-particle state, and not attempt to describe the paths or locations of independent particles - at least until *after* some measurement has been made. We must also keep in mind the conservation laws that Einstein used to describe nonlocal behavior in the first place. Then we can see that the "mystery" of *nonlocality* for two particles is primarily the same mystery as the single-particle collapse of the wave function. But there is an extra mystery, one we might call an "enigma," of the *nonseparability* of identical indistinguishable particles.

As Richard Feynman said, there is *only one mystery* in quantum mechanics (the superposition of states, the probabilities of collapse into one state, and the consequent statistical outcomes). The only difference in two-particle entanglement and nonlocality is that two particles appear simultaneously (in their original interaction frame) when their wave function collapses.

We choose to examine a phenomenon which is impossible, *absolutely* impossible, to explain in any classical way, and which has in it the heart of quantum mechanics. In reality, it contains the *only* mystery. We cannot make the mystery go away by "explaining" how it works. We will just *tell* you how it works. In telling you how it works we will have told you about the basic peculiarities of all quantum mechanics.

(*The Feynman Lectures on Physics*, vol III, 1-1)

In his 1935 paper (and his correspondence with Einstein), Schrödinger described the two particles in EPR as "entangled" in English, *verschränkt* in German, which means something like cross-linked. It describes someone standing with arms crossed.

In the time evolution of an entangled two-particle state according to the Schrödinger equation, we can visualize it - as we visualize the single-particle wave function - as collapsing when a measurement is made. The discontinuous "jump" is also described as the "reduction of the wave packet." This is apt in the two-particle case, where the superposition of $| + - >$ and $| - + >$ states is "projected" or "reduced to one of these states, say $| - + >$, and then further reduced to the product of independent one-particle states, $| - > | + >$.

Measurement of a two-particle wave function measures both particles, reducing them to *separate* one-particle wave functions, after which they are no longer entangled.

When entangled, the particles are *nonseparable*. Once measured, they are separate quantum systems with their own wave functions. They are no longer entangled.

In the two-particle case (instead of just one particle making an appearance), when either particle is measured we know instantly the now determinate properties of the other particle. They are the properties that satisfy the conservation laws, including its location equidistant from, but on the opposite side of, the source, and the complementary spin.

In the one-particle case, it has no definite position before the experiment, then it appears somewhere. For two particles, neither one has a position, then both appear simultaneously (in an appropriate frame of reference).

> [Animation of a two-particle wave function collapsing: non-functional in this format, a "time" lapse from the figure on p.163 to the figure on p.164, Eds.]

Compare the collapse of the two-particle probability amplitude above to the single-particle collapse here.

Some commentators say that nonlocality and entanglement are a "second revolution" in quantum mechanics, "the greatest mystery in physics," or "science's strangest phenomenon," and that quantum physics has been "reborn." They usually quote Erwin Schrödinger as saying

> I consider [entanglement] not as one, but as *the* characteristic trait of quantum mechanics, the one that enforces its entire departure from classical lines of thought.

Schrödinger knew that his two-particle wave function could not have the same simple interpretation as the single particle, which can be visualized in ordinary 3-dimensional configuration space. And he is right that entanglement exhibits a richer form of the "action-at-a-distance" and nonlocality that Einstein had already identified in the collapse of the single particle wave function.

But the main difference is that *two* particles acquire new properties instead of one, and they do it instantaneously (at faster than light speeds), just as in the case of a single-particle measurement, where the finite probability of appearing at various distant locations collapses to zero at the instant the particle is found somewhere.

Can a Special Frame Resolve the EPR Paradox?
Almost every presentation of the EPR paradox begins with something like "Alice observes one particle..." and concludes with the question "How does the second particle get the information needed so that Bob's measurements correlate perfectly with

Alice?"

There is a fundamental asymmetry in this framing of the EPR experiment. It is a surprise that Einstein, who was so good at seeing deep symmetries, did not consider how to remove the asymmetry.

Consider this reframing: Alice's measurement collapses the two-particle wave function. The two indistinguishable particles simultaneously appear at locations in a space-like separation. The frame of reference in which the source of the two entangled particles and the two experimenters are at rest is a special frame in the following sense.

As Einstein knew very well, there are frames of reference moving with respect to the laboratory frame of the two observers in which the time order of the events can be reversed. In some moving frames Alice measures first, but in others Bob measures first.

If there is a special frame of reference (not a preferred frame in the relativistic sense), surely it is the one in which the origin of the two entangled particles is at rest. Assuming that Alice and Bob are also at rest in this special frame and equidistant from the origin, we arrive at the simple picture in which any measurement that causes the two-particle wave function to collapse makes both particles appear simultaneously at determinate places with fully correlated properties (just those that are needed to conserve energy, momentum, angular momentum, and spin).

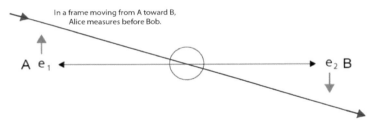

[Animation of 3 different frames of reference {wherein A is measured first, or B is measured first, or the measurements are simultaneous} non-functional in this format, Eds.]

In the two-particle case (instead of just one particle making an appearance), when either particle is measured, we know instantly those properties of the other particle that satisfy the conservation laws, including its location equidistant from, but on the opposite side of, the source, and its other properties such as spin.

We can also ask what happens if Bob is not at the same distance from the origin as Alice. This introduces a positional asymmetry. But there is still no time asymmetry from the point of view of the two-particle wave function collapse.

When Alice detects the particle (with say spin up), at that instant the other particle also becomes determinate (with spin down) at the same distance on the other side of the origin. It now continues, in that determinate state, to Bob's measuring apparatus.

> [Animation of measurement of electron 1 by A at t_0 instantaneously determining spin of electron 2, observed by B at t_1, but spins were *not* predetermined before t_0, non-functional in this format, Eds.]

Einstein asked whether the particle has a determinate position (or spin) just before it is measured. Even if it does not, we can say that the electron spin was determined from the moment the two-particle wave function collapsed. Recall that the two-particle wave function describing the indistinguishable particles cannot be separated into a product of two single-particle wave functions. When either particle is measured, they both become determinate.

Influences from Outside Space and Time, Even Back from the Future!

Superdeterminism

During a mid-1980's interview by BBC Radio 3 organized by P. C. W. Davies and J. R. Brown, Bell proposed the idea of a "*superdeterminism*" that could explain the correlation of results in two-particle experiments without the need for faster-than-light signaling. The two experiments need only have been *pre*-determined by causes reaching both experiments from an earlier time.

> *I was going to ask whether it is still possible to maintain, in the light of experimental experience, the idea of a deterministic universe?*
>
> You know, one of the ways of understanding this business is to say that the world is super-deterministic. That not only is inanimate nature deterministic, but we, the experimenters who imagine we can choose to do one experiment rather than another, are also determined. If so, the difficulty which this experimental result creates disappears.
>
> *Free will is an illusion - that gets us out of the crisis, does it?*
>
> That's correct. In the analysis it is assumed that free will is genuine, and as a result of that one finds that the intervention of the experimenter at one point has to have consequences at a remote point, in a way that influences restricted by the finite velocity of light would not permit. If the experimenter is not free to make this intervention, if that also is determined in advance, the difficulty disappears.
>
> (The Ghost in the Atom, P.C.W. Davies and J. Brown, ch.3, p.47)

Bell's superdeterminism would deny the important "free choice" of the experimenter (originally suggested by Niels Bohr and Werner Heisenberg) and later explored by John Conway and Simon Kochen. Conway and Kochen claim that the experimenters' free choice requires that atoms must have free will, something they call their Free

Will Theorem.

In his 1996 book, *Time's Arrow and Archimedes' Point*, Price proposes an Archimedean point "outside space and time" as a solution to the problem of nonlocality in the Bell experiments in the form of an "advanced action."

Rather than a "superdeterministic" common cause coming from "outside space and time" (as proposed by Bell, Gisin, Suarez, and others), Price argues that there might be a cause coming backwards in time from some interaction in the future. Roger Penrose and Stuart Hameroff have also promoted this idea of "backward causation," sending information backward in time in the Libet experiments and in the EPR experiments.

John Cramer's Transactional Interpretation of quantum mechanics and other Time-Symmetric Interpretations like that of Yakir Aharonov and K. B Wharton also search for Archimedean points "outside space and time."

John Bell, and more recently, following Bell, Nicholas Gisin and Antoine Suarez claim that something might be coming from "outside space and time" to correlate the results in the spacelike-separated experimental tests of Bell's Theorem.

Gisin and his colleagues have extended the polarized photon tests of EPR and the Bell inequalities to a separation of 18 kilometers near Geneva. They continue to find 100% correlation and no evidence of the "hidden variables" sought after by Einstein and David Bohm.

An interesting use of the special theory of relativity was proposed by Gisin's colleagues, Antoine Suarez and Valerio Scarani. Their "Before-Before" experiment uses the idea of hyperplanes of simultaneity. Back in the 1960's, C. W. Rietdijk and Hilary Putnam argued that physical determinism could be proved to be true by considering the experiments and observers A and B in the above diagram to be moving at high speed with respect to one another. Roger Penrose developed a similar argument in his book *The Emperor's New Mind*. It is called the Andromeda Paradox.

Suarez and Scarani showed that for some relative speeds between the two observers A and B, observer A could "see" the measurement of observer B to be in his future, and vice versa. This is why we need the preferred frame above to understand entanglement.

Because the two experiments have a "space-like" separation (neither is inside the causal light cone of the other), each observer thinks he does his own measurement before the other. Gisin tested the limits on this effect by moving mirrors in the path to the birefringent crystals and showed that, like all other Bell experiments, the "*Before-Before*" suggestion of Suarez and Scarani did nothing to invalidate quantum mechanics.

These experiments were able to put a lower limit on the speed with which the information about probabilities collapses, estimating it as at least thousands - perhaps millions - of times the speed of light and showed empirically that probability collapses are essentially instantaneous.

Despite all his experimental tests verifying quantum physics, including the "reality" of nonlocality and entanglement, Gisin continues to explore the EPR paradox, considering the possibility that signals are coming to the entangled particles from "outside space-time."

EPR "Loopholes" and Free Will

Investigators who try to recover the "elements of local reality" that Einstein wanted, and who hope to eliminate the irreducible randomness of quantum mechanics that follows from wave functions as probability amplitudes, often cite "loopholes" in EPR experiments. For example, the "detection loophole" claims that the efficiency of detectors is so low that they are missing many events that might prove Einstein was right.

Most all the loopholes have now been closed, but there is one loophole that can never be closed because of its metaphysical/philosophical nature. That is the "(pre)determinism loophole."

If every event occurs for reasons that were established at the beginning of the universe, then all the careful experimental results are meaningless. John Conway and Simon Kochen have formalized this loophole in what they call the Free Will Theorem.

Although Conway and Kochen do not claim to have proven free will in humans, they assert that should such a freedom exist, then the same freedom must apply to the elementary particles.

What Conway and Kochen are really describing is the indeterminism that quantum mechanics has introduced into the world. Although indeterminism is a requirement for human freedom, it is insufficient by itself to provide both "free" *and* "will". Indeterminism works primarily to block *pre*-determinism. Without indeterminism, *no new information could be created* in the universe.

Retrieved November 15, 2018, CC By 3.0, from Information Philosopher website
http://www.informationphilosopher.com/solutions/experiments/EPR/

7h₁.

ATP is the universal energy carrier in modern cells. AMP is an RNA nucleotide. ATP is hardware, AMP is software, information, instructions. To get from adenosine triphosphate to adenosine monophosphate, lose two phosphates. Presumably one came before the other.

50.

It breaks out of Its shell too soon and the absence of creation in the surrounding vacuum destroys it. Try again. It escapes Its cell as It was never meant to, exiting to enter where It has no meaning, and the negative conceptual pressure of the void moves It to destroy Itself. Try again. The hair, the fur insulates It adequately in the cold of space. Its shivers therefore are not a direct result of the emptiness. They are an indirect result, since there is nothing else. It is best to continue experiments in the emptiness, which is abundant and cold. Cold favors order, increasing the chance of encountering and generating life. It does not lack for energy. This time when establishing Its initial conditions do not leave It so alone, isolated, without reference. Give It content, contentment, containment, perhaps a series of containers to grow through, not too much contentment or there will be no advancement no desire, a dusting so It does not destroy Itself. Try again. There shall be many Its. The success rate will not be high but if many fail some will succeed and that some will seem like many relative to zero. Some Its will survive and establish themselves and evolve and adapt to local conditions and order themselves as complexly as they are able to fill the emptiness.

7j₁.

Directed Panspermia: The hypothesis that spores are being intelligently spread through the universe to propagate life.

7i.

It is always hard to realize that these numbers and equations we play with at our desks have something to do with the real world.

Steven Weinberg, *The First Three Minutes*, 1977.

51.

Perhaps you need grounding, you decide, stable ground underfoot so to speak no matter if you have feet or speech. If the problem is abstraction into reaches you cannot conceive, then find a thing you know to hold on to, forgiving your continued possible lack of hands, an act with which by now you are intimately familiar. You reflect that you experienced a devaluing of self-worth in the not-knowing what was becoming of you, the travelling through the universe at light speed or faster than light speed or through worm holes or not at all, though one potentiality was you becoming all-knowing, and the unknowing while possibly being all-knowing does sound like it has the potential for demoralization, you realize, though another possibility was you becoming either hyper-connected with or an organizational structure within a higher consciousness, in which case the unknowing might be explicable. Perhaps the self-devaluing, you hypothesize, was or is due to a lack of specificity details conceivability. Though you may have become all-knowing or a higher consciousness, you did not know what that meant or could not conceive of it sufficiently to communicate it, which left you feeling empty, alone, lost, which is similar to the feeling of being buried alive. In which case, return to what you know. You choose to begin again, buried alive. A great weight. Darkness. Unable to move. There, that is comforting. Solace. You settle into your stubborn subversive anti-authoritarian anti-conformist anti-identity because once again you have another part of you to push against. You have always felt your existence pointless meaningless purposeless no matter what you did, no matter the momentary worth, only ever momentary alleviation before it returns crushing buried alive but you've always pushed back against it simultaneously because if you do not you are ceased, if you do not you do not exist, if you do not there is no reason to exist. You push back against the weight because it gives you meaning. Sometimes you find it, sometimes you create it, sometimes you are given it, inside you in others in your surroundings in time. You are the tension the overlap the space the torsion the contact the push between point and pointlessness, meaning and nonsense, porpoise and purple. Without the threat of not surviving there is no motive to create, without the danger of cessation death non-existence there is no motive to do, without obstacles failures emptiness there is no creating. Another obstacle you identify in yourself is your aspiration. Your need for a final answer, a single solution, a concrete definition will, it is inevitable, demoralize you again and again as you repeatedly fail to achieve that singular comprehension except at some singular distant point of ultimate ascendant success of low probability, but there is a probability however small that it will happen one day for someone or something. You have that much hope. Your conditions cannot change, so change your attitude. Okay, you acknowledge, sometimes the facts do change dependent on the attitude of observation, the relative point of view, nothing is absolute -- but here is a possible crux, more power to you, if little to nothing is absolute you can chuckle at your inability to say nothing is absolute because such a statement is absolute. Instead of beating your head if you have one on an impossible singular definition, or is it barely possible, and bloodying your mind matter, brain or fiber optics or quantum switches or plasma streams or entangled particles, embrace the potentialities and take all your potential states as real and revel in the diversity of existence you are able to experience. You are everything you can imagine, every alternity for yourself, and it is all these potentialities, all these perhapses, perhaps infinite, perhaps finite, you can shape the universe and the universe shapes you, you are trapped free, you are beginning and ending. It is all your possibilities that constitute the whole, and with a renewed attitude, arms spread wide, welcoming the sun or rain or wind on your face rather than you being crucified, you begin again buried alive under an immense weight unable to move except in your mind.

6_{42}, 13pqr. Franklin Park, October 2018.

6_{43}. CONCLUSIONS:

We have attempted in this paper to describe and support a fairly detailed proposal as to where we need to look, and what we need to look for, in the attempt to understand how life emerged on this planet. In this story, we have emphasized that the creation of life is but one piece, one component of creation, in the great order-creating industry that is the true business of our dynamic Universe. This order, whose creation is dictated by the thermodynamics of far-from-equilibrium systems, is everywhere in the form of autocatalytic, work-creating engines—engines which accelerate, as active devices, the dissipation of the immense astronomy of disequilibrium with which our Universe was born. And we have seen how the engines of dissipation created in this way form a vast hierarchy of wheels within wheels, each wheel an engine driving engines below it. We have traced the causal, hierarchical chain of order creation from the galactic-scale wheels of astrophysics through the planetary wheels of geophysics, on through the chemical and geochemical micro-scale wheels that drove directly, we argue, the creation of the wheels of life.

Michael J. Russell, Wolfgang Nitschke, Elbert Branscomb, *The inevitable journey to being,* Phil. Trans. R. Soc. B 2013 368 20120254; DOI: 10.1098/rstb.2012.0254. Published 10 June 2013, http://rstb.royalsocietypublishing.org/content/368/1622/20120254.

7i.

To break the monotony of the main argument, the main argument being a chain of math beginning with equation 1 and not ending, yet, we include embellishments and leave the main argument, the math, out. The reader will have to take our word for it that the equations are right and the argument not nothing but literary frills without scientific substance.

13r.

His condition is or his conditions are such that the normal trappings of life do not satisfy him. He does not know if he chose the conditions or if they were given him biologically, culturally, genetically, historically, socioeconomically, philosophically. All of the above. The problem is what does he find joy in except the extraordinary. This is a problem because the extraordinary is not ordinary but rare, difficult, hard to find create encounter. As further impediment, the extraordinary repeatedly encountered becomes ordinary. Not only then does daily life cease to provide joy, or he cannot find it there, except in those extraordinary moments of makings and loves and adventures and encounters he creates, but he must make his extraordinaries increasingly extraordinary or they get tired. He must grow and seek experience and seed himself and grow and deepen and cultivate and grow and create anew and nurture observation and grow and search and grow and harvest and still grow. Or he dies. And as any person not poor by choice will tell you, he smirks at his first love, Thoreau, being a subsistence farmer is not as romantic as it is made to be. There will someday be no subsistence farmers except by choice, he winks at the science fiction. But perhaps the best possible universe is one in which survival is possible but not easy, in which our purpose is both given and created: to grow create move forward advance or end. He needs obstacles so profoundly that he invents them. His life is neither threatened nor materially austere, though he is doomed, that's life. Or perhaps not if what they say is true of the possibility of perpetuating our individual consciousnesses in a collective consciousness in the distant or no-so-distant future, us real but housed in technology, all very abstract talk of the brain/mind coupled with techno speak, hard for him to grasp what that would be, speculative it is, perhaps kooks grabbing headlines, materially doomed at least he is, the human condition, isn't it?, humans speculating a multitude of afterlifes and ghosts and heavens and reincarnations and spirit lands, but always the fear threat knowledge however occluded by the religious or occult or supernatural or metaphysical that this life this consciousness is limited in time and space and will end, but what would it be he speculates for one's consciousness to be unlimited in time, forget scope, neverending never escaping never releasing, a shudder, and would he not over a vast time move further from his illogical but motivating emotions like love and ambition and generosity and sympathy and loyalty and farther from the dark irrational but motivating emotions like fear and anger and ambition and jealousy and greed and lust and emptiness, would he become more and more like an automaton the more distant from his youth he grew?, and to boot he knows the dread of immortality, he smiles at the irony, he smiles bemusedly at him noting self-consciously and directly without slight of hand without pretense the irony, knows the dread of immortality is merely emotional response at this point, irrational, the great unknown and all that jazz, but are they right in their neon-lit bombastic claims that this is the only way for humans to survive and escape their physical limitations and needs and the degradations and destruction they lay on themselves and their physical surroundings?, a lot of blather speculation words, he was thinking of something, tangentials, asides, derailments, parentheticals, the obstacles he invents for himself, deciding that most of the work activities jobs pastimes pursuits of modern humanity are unnecessary, pointless, timekillers, worthless, occupiers not unlike an occupying force in our mind, dictating our actions, shackling us, materially even now we could manufacture everything we need without the absurd and degrading and capitalizing abusive economic apparatus, and so he long ago decided that therefore if he is to maintain his integrity he cannot take part in such pastimes and jobs and timekillers, and yes he assures himself he knows the impossibility of such a clean life and yes he knows the privilege of his choice and no he does not know what percentage of the choice was actually his and yes he suspects the choice such as it was and still is was a factor in the loss of one marriage, every choice including those that are not choices have their cost, but in so doing he created the obstacles impediments questions, yes he cringes, the existential crises angsts anxieties of What should he be doing, What is worthwhile to do, What can be done, What is his purpose, What is the point, What is humanity's purpose, Why go on?, these questions it's almost laughable hurt more than they look, he's not pushing the plow or hunting meat or cutting wood or toiling in the grueling factory to feed his family or slogging in the mud against genocide or working for the man to keep a roof over his kids' heads or building automobiles not because he believes in American industry but for enough credits to pay for repairs in the company store, he's doing a lot of nothing, and the questions spawned by nothing can pain more than you think, can box you in and trap consume eat you from the inside, but are they not a necessary quagmire fetid constraint, for him they are, without them to overcome surpass no contend grapple with assert himself against or in he is just the unreflected animal life and so laterally he has never killed himself, hasn't yet, because he calculates that at the least the purpose is continuation growth advancement creation and by facing the nothing he can create instead of becoming nothing, he thinks.

7a$_{xi}$.

Gödel Incompleteness Theorem: To every ω-consistent recursive class **K** of *formulae* there correspond recursive *class-signs* r, such that neither *v* Gen r nor Neg (*v* Gen r) belongs to Flg (**K**) (where *v* is the *free variable* of r).

Kurt Gödel, "On Formally Undecidable Propositions in *Pincipia Mathematica* and Related Systems I," 1931.

Length of loops: from A to B should be approximately 18 inches, and from C to Running End should be approximately 35 inches to 108 inches depending upon diameter of the rope. Wrap Running End around for six turns. No extra rope should remain.

Figure 7 ① and ②. Hangman's knot.

Tighten loops by pulling at Running End. Lock loops and form knot by pulling down at point D. Slide knot up or down on Standing Part to adjust size of loop.

Figure 7 ③ and ④.

6₄₄.

[digital source redacted -- Eds.]

7a$_{xi1}$.

In other words, all consistent axiomatic formulations of number theory include undecidable propositions. This conclusion is reached by applying self-referential statements called Gödel coding or Gödel numbering, in which numbers stand for symbols and sequences of numbers. Each statement of Number Theory acquires a Gödel number, and therefore another level of meaning. Statements of Number Theory also become statements about statements of Number Theory.

[AG 250 (16 Mar 59) PMGK]

By Order of *Wilber M. Brucker*, Secretary of the Army:

MAXWELL D. TAYLOR,
General, United States Army,
Chief of Staff.

Official:

R. V. LEE,
Major General, United States Army,
The Adjutant General.

6₄₅.

"Sorry, Einstein. Quantum Study Suggests 'Spooky Action' Is Real." John Markoff, *The New York Times*, Oct. 21, 2015, https://www.nytimes.com/2015/10/22/science/quantum-theory-experiment-said-to-prove-spooky-interactions.html

> The finding is another blow to one of the bedrock principles of standard physics known as "locality," which states that an object is directly influenced only by its immediate surroundings. The Delft study (http://nature.com/articles/doi:10.1038/nature15759), published Wednesday in the journal Nature…

"Death by experiment for local realism," Howard Wiseman, *Nature* **volume 526**, pages 649–650 (29 October 2015), https://doi.org/10.1038/nature15631, "**Access Options** Rent or Buy article from $8.99."

See Letter p.682 (https://www.nature.com/articles/nature15759)

"Loophole-free Bell inequality violation using electron spins separated by 1.3 kilometres," B. Hensen, H. Bernien, A. E. Dréau, A. Reiserer, N. Kalb, M. S. Blok, J. Ruitenberg, R. F. L. Vermeulen, R. N. Schouten, C. Abellán, W. Amaya, V. Pruneri, M. W. Mitchell, M. Markham, D. J. Twitchen, D. Elkouss, S. Wehner, T. H. Taminiau & R. Hanson, *Nature* **volume 526**, pages 682–686 (29 October 2015), https://doi.org/10.1038/nature15759, "**Access Options** Rent or Buy article from $8.99."

Editorial Summary: The celebrated Bell inequality, a theorem published by John Bell in 1964, has long served as a basis for experimentally testing whether nature satisfies local realism. All experiments conducted to date have implied rejection of local-realist hypotheses. But because of experimental limitations all those tests suffered from loopholes — either the locality or the detection loophole. Here, Ronald Hanson and colleagues perform a Bell test that closes these loopholes. Their results are consistent with a violation of the inequality, although the authors reject local-realist hypotheses by two standard deviations only. The experimental setup allows for improvements in the statistics that may consolidate the result. In addition to its fundamental importance, a loophole-free Bell test is an important building block in quantum information processing.

Further reading
1. "Steering is an essential feature of non-locality in quantum theory", Ravishankar Ramanathan, Dardo Goyeneche [...] Paweł Horodecki, *Nature Communications* (2018), https://doi.org/10.1038/s41467-018-06255-5, **Open Access**: CC By 4.0.
2. "Ab initio description of highly correlated states in defects for realizing quantum bits," Michel Bockstedte, Felix Schütz [...] Adam Gali, *npj Quantum Materials* (2018), https://doi.org/10.1038/s41535-018-0103-6, **Open Access**: CC By 4.0.
3. "The certainty of quantum randomness," Stefano Pironio, *Nature* (2018), https://doi.org/10.1038/d41586-018-04105-4, **Available**: © 2018 Springer Nature Limited. All rights reserved.
4. "Challenging local realism with human choices," *Nature* (2018), https://doi.org/10.1038/s41586-018-0085-3, **Access Options** Rent or Buy article from $8.99." [Special attention, Eds.]
5. "Practical device-independent quantum cryptography via entropy accumulation," Rotem Arnon-Friedman, Frédéric Dupuis [...] Thomas Vidick, *Nature Communications* (2018), https://doi.org/10.1038/s41467-017-02307-4, **Open Access** CC By 4.0.

7x.

Epimenides Paradox:

    This statement is false.

7a$_{xi2}$, 7x.

Gödel Paradox:

    G: I am not a theorem (of TNT).

    ~G: My negation is a theorem (of TNT).

∴ Gödel sentence G says, This true statement of number theory (for which I code or represent or symbolize) has no proof in number theory (TNT).

Douglas Hofstadter, *Gödel, Escher, Bach: an Eternal Golden Braid*, Basic Books, Inc. p272, (1999) 1979.

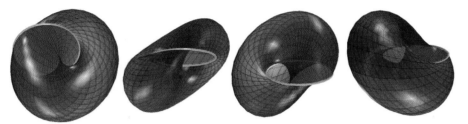

6₄₆. *Mobius Snail,* unknown, CC BY-SA 3.0, https://en.wikipedia.org/w/index.php?curid=2764196

52.

You could, for example, you conjecture, considering your inveterate sense of being trapped, unable to move, unable to breathe, buried alive, but also simultaneously your unsurety of body, uncertainty of shape, unspecificity of form verging on flagrant formlessness, be the vestigial chunk of claustrophobia in some future, not future, you exist in it, in some species' or being's or higher consciousness's mind. You are an irrational fear, or perhaps once in the distant human or mammalian or reptilian or aquatic past claustrophobia was not irrational, considering predation and death and the like. You can conceive that a fear of being trapped could be rational, and a heightened fear of being trapped could have provided selective advantage in your evolutionary history, but it is irrational now because there is no longer anywhere to be trapped because you, bodiless, are perhaps vestigial claustrophobia in a being bound to no planet, a being who soars through the wide open universe, a being who swims in dark matter, her skin photosynthetic, she tethered lightly to stars and solar radiation then, her skin green then, a subjective statement color, you don't know which wavelengths of electromagnetic radiation her skin reflects and which it absorbs and uses to raise electrons to a higher energy state to then release in a cascade, you know nothing, she could be bodiless, an arrangement pattern organization of quantum particles, there are no particles that are not quantum, or crystals or chemicals or numbers or anything that can be organized, made to carry information, make itself to carry information, given an initial organization and a kick in the pants, then grow in self-awareness, self-referentialness, self-mirroring, all those things that are the strange loops of self, a hierarchal tangled organization of which at any rate, focus on you, you are not the highest rung. It is impossible to understand what is on the levels above you, though you can influence them, her, being of her constituents. So too can they influence you, a higher level can reach down, a least a few levels, as a causal agent within itself and exert internal force on its own operations. Regardless of the loopiness, however, this being or beings or she has been unable to eradicate you, an irrational fear of being trapped, because she is unbounded by space whether she is bound by photosynthetic skin or no body you can conceive but she has developed the ability to block or ignore or overcome your communication, that is you are here in her but she doesn't hear you, or else she cannot reach down far enough into her levels to shut you off, perhaps her basic particles such as quarks or strings or gluons inherently give rise to a kind of claustrophobia so she has been unable to engineer you away, though she has contained you, advancing herself as an optimistic forward-looking thinker able to surpass obstacles without fear or distraction or detrimental physical response, the clench in the chest, shaping herself to her universe and her universe to herself, having built a box to house her claustrophobia, to box you, and buried in a deep secret place within her the feeling of being trapped, confined, contained, unable to move, crushed, unable to move, a great weight, in a special place a small place a figurative place an insignificant special place a place she has forgotten about within her buried you.

$7a_{xii}$.

Gödel's 2nd Theorem: The versions of formal number theory which assert their own consistency are inconsistent.

110101_2, 54, 13s, 7i.

I remember meeting Charles Hartshorne at a meeting in Minnesota and having a serious conversation. I remember meeting Charles Hartshorne at a meeting in Minnesota and having a serious conversation because you remember meeting Charles Hartshorne at a meeting Minnesota and having a serious conversation. You remember meeting Charles Hartshorne at a meeting in Minnesota and having a serious conversation because He read and copied in writing and in ascension gave to you in writing the remembrance of "I happened to meet Charles Hartshorne at a meeting in Minnesota and we had a serious conversation. After we had talked for a while he informed me that my theological standpoint is Socinian. Socinus was an Italian heretic who lived in the 16th century. If I remember correctly what Hartshorne said, the main tenet of the Socinian Theory is that God is neither omniscient nor omnipotent. He learns and grows as the universe unfolds." He remembered this event to you or rather you encountered, read, and absorbed his record of it because the theological point of view herein given by Freeman Dyson was first brought to his attention and named Socinian when he met Charles Hartshorne at a meeting and had a serious conversation with him, a name which Freeman upon further research later amended from Socinian to Harts-

hornian, a name for a point of view which closely aligned with his own, a name for a point of view which before meeting Charles Hartshorne at a meeting in Minnesota and having a serious conversation for him had no name. The alignment was deepened in Freeman Dyson's words, in His words, in your words, in my words, words swallowed in all our other words, "I do not make any clear distinction between mind and God. God is what mind becomes when it has passed beyond the scale of our

6_{47}. *O sculpture*, photo by Jonathan Billinger, near Lydney, Great Britain, CC BY-SA 2.0, http://www.geograph.org.uk/photo/1688695

comprehension. God may be considered to be either a world soul or a collection of world souls. We are the chief inlets of God on this planet at the present stage of his development. We may later grow with him, or we may be left behind. If we are left behind, it is an end. If we keep growing, it is a beginning," words found in *Infinite in All Directions*, 2004, p119, words elucidating a serious conversation I had with Charles Hartshorne in Minnesota.

55.

You see her in your mind's eye from within her mind soaring through the solar system the galaxy the universe, a silver streak absorbing solar radiation, soaring not like a bird, from where does that image come, but like an arrow no a comet but not bound to gravity though she rides it, giving herself her own impetus by converting radiation energy into matter mass that she emits to accelerate, to change her velocity, emits from an orifice, her only orifice, which can move about the surface of her body, her ovoid body, depending on the direction in which it is best applied. It's not clear to you if she consciously controls her orifice's movement or if it moves by reflex by automated response by involuntary response similar to that of smooth muscle in humans around the blood vessels the urinary tract the uterus the digestive system the vagina the trachea the iris. She has no wings no arms no appendages, a silver sliver soaring, song, she sings hums vibrates, she doesn't know it, unintentional, a byproduct of her functioning, her harmonics, not to be heard outside of her because there is no air no nothing to vibrate carry the song outside her, song only inside her, where you are, a subsystem in her brain, not localized but spread, immaterial, which means she has an organ for hearing which you are in communication with if you can hear her singing, another vestigial organ perhaps, or nothing more complicated than structures or crystals or particles that respond to induced vibration, localized or not, like you, buried inside her, deep inside her, spread in her, she is all brain within, you see her in your mind's eye from inside her mind. All brain and silver shell and directional multifunctional orifice. You are in her mind trapped but unbound, not physical, a level above her physical brain, above her neurons or pathways or hardware, her mind and her silver star harnessing skin and her orifice above you. Do you have any influence on her, does she on you, can she shut you off, shrink you, change you, make you go away, can you make her feel you, notice you, respond to you, based on what you imagine you are, a vestigial subsystem of claustrophobia, the feeling of being trapped within her mind, can you make her feel you, can you make her feel anything but fear, perhaps the fear you might make her feel could save her life, save her from an explosively pulsing quasar or cataclysmically quaking pulsar, you could save her from being trapped in the violent switch off-on of a quasar with an output of 10 billion suns, it could happen in a matter of hours and she could be unaware of the danger or overconfident because of her facility with parallaxes or overrun by her desire for the x-rays from energetic electrons in nebula like the Crab Nebula. Why do you imagine she needs your help your specifics your fear, you imagine her so far beyond you in mind, why in your mind's eye inside her mind do you imaginer her appendageless, all silver skin and orifice, all brain underneath, she has three organs, brain, skin, and orifice, she needs no others, her skin is photosensitive and photo-responsive in addition to photosynthetic to a large swath of radiation in the electromagnetic spectrum, providing broad and precise perception of the outside world and the basis for an intimate relationship with the energy she uses to function and create her own material. Why a silver sliver you imagine, why the physical emphasis, why the predominance of her orifice, all silver skin and intelligent brain underneath and motile orifice, why does she not instead have solar sails stored in her which unfurl like wet butterfly wings from a chrysalis, why the artifice of a brain instead of some less cumbersome less inefficient more reliable more organized patterned structure lighter of less weight and greater capability, is it because you have access to her thoughts, being one of them, or almost one of them if she is not conscious of you, why so much orifice, why just one orifice for everything, not even bilateral symmetry like a worm or trilobite, is it a lack of empathy, is it a nonsensical insatiable undoable vestigial biological desire to use an orifice for perpetuation, is it your biological clock though you haven't a body, is it because you are not in communication with her thoughts ideas purpose self desires emotions, does she have emotions, do you want her to, why do you imagine her omniscient omnipotent orifice, is it because you cannot communicate with her in any way that she or you are conscious of, cannot perceive her in truth because you are an intermediary level like your own fear of being trapped and buried alive within you and likewise she does not cannot perceive you as an entity, only as a characteristic of herself, an irrational fear, you cannot see her physical structure, her basic material, your basic material and structure and organization, you are like the gall bladder the tonsil the appendix for her,

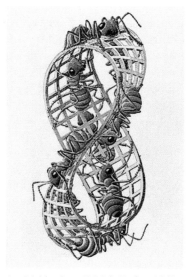

6₄₈. *Möbius Strip II*, M.C. Escher, 1963, Woodcut in red, black and grey-green, printed from 3 blocks, https://www.mcescher.com/gallery/recognition-success/mobius-strip-ii/

unnecessary, useless, illogical, nonsense visions, why would you exist in her, does she have an orifice?, there is no way out, you cannot get out of her, no escape from inside her unaware of you except for fear.

55.
She Thinks

Nothing. There is nothing there. Footsteps on the porch. Her own? She is inside, within, she's sure, at least most of her. Should she shoot? It's a moral question. She sees darkness, which implies absence of light, which is not what she thinks she sees until she's thought it. Can one shoot one's footsteps if one is inside and one's footsteps are outside? It's a question of morality. Can she smell herself?

Yes, she thinks. She does not think the stink; the stink is free of her. Of her. Emanated, she wishes she hadn't thought. The stink is material evidence of her presence. She can imagine she imagines the footsteps; she cannot imagine she imagines the stink. Enough with the stink. Emissions from the membrane between internal and external, from the skin, from where she sweats from anticipation, from exertion. Silence the stink, she thinks. One cannot shoot stink. She is here. Is anything there? She looks, she listens, she breathes. She thinks.

Footsteps on the stoop. Heavy skittering, furtive scuttling, the stench of urine, outsized gnawing. Her own? Another constructs an entrance, exploits a crack, employs a hole. She thinks, Rat. Should she open a door, should she shoot, should she do nothing? Ethical questions. Maybe it's cold outside. What if it's cold and clear and the aurora borealis billows like a translucent purple green blue sail in shifting stellar winds while coyotes howl in the sagebrush and rats are snapped in traps, blood emanating from eye and mouth sockets? Existential question stench. She smiles, she thinks. She is inside but she sees it: a sail taught with invisible wind, a window onto trembling membranes of color stroking the absence of sky, a diaphanous stage curtain blurring the boundary between atmosphere and magnetic field and space.

She is cold. Can one shoot gnawing cold? And if one shoots the sail instead? Questions. She stinks, she thinks. No, she is stinking without thinking. She remembers. Footsteps on the deck. Could there be nothing there? An excessive or insufferable or rhetorical question. There is nothing there.

Except many footsteps and cold and sweat stink she tastes freezing into beads of ice on her lucid skin and urine stench and gnawing. Footsteps surround her. Many creatures or one creature with many legs? Footsteps strike a porch. Knuckles rap doors, fingernails tap windowpanes, wind moans under the eaves. Feet skitter on the skin. How to shoot them all. How many bullets does she have? A math question. If there are x of them and she has y bullets, what is the probability she'll shoot herself wanting in? If she cannot shoot them all, why shoot at all? Another nauseating question of what to do and why.

What will they do to her, and why? Knock knock. Who's there? Nothing's there. Nothing's there who? Nothing's there but a sound of footsteps, a stench of evacuation, a crow clawing at your eaves, a scuttling bitten-bloody tongue, and a knock knock. All jokes aside, she thinks, there are feet marching. Boots march in the street; steel toes parade on her tulip-lined patio; a lead-footed millipede climbs her hamstring. The boots, laced to the calf and shined, beat in unison, striking doorstep, pounding lintel, gnawing doorjamb. Thunder. Of beast or giant or god? A horse canters on the porch, preparing to stomp on her pool table. Horseshoes strike sparks in her entryway. Shoot a horse to down its rider? Questions of perceived divinity. Is there a rider? Desiring admittance on horseback, fleeing the stink and cold and steps and star-studded void, singing shrieks she cannot hear and silences she can? The horse stomps dance steps with her astride.

There is nothing there. A horse prancing on a pool table is nothing but a story. If she shoots the nothing, will the nothing become something? Redundant question.

Does the nothing outside carry a gun? Questions of repetition, of variation, of rhythm tempo time signature theme.

If she shoots nothing, will nothing shoot her back? Dueling questions.

Is nothing there? Musical questions, and only one her for the answers to sit on.

She could go out. To where? The walls go with her. The footsteps follow. The skittering follows. The marching follows. The stench follows me, she thinks. Nothing touches her, blankets her, takes her shape, skins her. Footsteps mouth her neck. Nothing gnaws. She hears, sees, feels no breath. Footsteps in her ear, on her tongue. Where does she end,

6_{49}. mural by blu (http://blublu.org/), photo by ilovebutter, CC BY-ND 2.0, https://www.flickr.com/photos/jdickert/3014984636

if not where what's outside begins, and is it already inside? No more questions, she thinks. If she kills it, will she never end? Where does she begin? Questions of no more, she thinks. What follows the footsteps? What is in here? Nothing, no not nothing she thinks footsteps and shoots, spark, flash, bang, silence.

Nothing. She thinks nothing. There is nothing there. Footsteps on the porch.

7i.

Particles do not understand themselves. Rocks do not understand themselves. Protozoa bacteria blue algae do not understand themselves. Rhododendrons and poison dart frogs and Venus flytraps do not understand themselves. Do giraffes understand themselves. Do pigs with organs interchangeable with humans understand themselves. Do dogs. Dolphins and chimpanzees and crows are closer to being able to say I understand myself. I am closer to understanding my self, my brain, my mind. You are closer yet. We yet closer. Soon perhaps, as we grows, we will cross the threshold.

$7h_2$.

In the neutral theory of evolution, genetic drift has been more important than natural selection in evolution. Genetic drift is evolution by random statistical fluctuations in the genetic code. We would like to at this location make a connection between our evolutionary genetic drift and statistical fluctuation, and the idea of quantum evolution derived from uncertainty and the probabilities of being in a given state at any one time. This is not our sole concept of evolution, but another facet.

7i.

In a word, *GEB* is a very personal attempt to say how it is that animate beings can come out of inanimate matter. What is a self, and how can a self come out of stuff that is as selfless as a stone or a puddle? What is an "I", and why are such things found (at least so far) only in association with, as poet Russel Edson once wonderfully phrased it, "teetering bulbs of dread and dream" -- that is, only in association with certain kinds of gooey lumps encased in hard protective shells mounted atop mobile pedestals that roam the world on pairs of slightly fuzzy, jointed stilts?

GEB approaches these questions by slowly building up an analogy that likens inanimate molecules to meaningless symbols, and further likens selves (or "I"'s or "souls", if you prefer -- whatever it is that distinguishes animate from inanimate matter) to certain special swirly, twisty, vortex-like, and *meaningful* patterns that arise only in particular types of systems of meaningless symbols. ... And for reasons that should not be too difficult to fathom, I call such strange, loopy patterns "strange loops" throughout the book, although in later chapters, I also use the phrase "tangled hierarchies" to describe basically the same idea.

Douglas Hofstadter, "Twentieth-anniversary Preface" to *Gödel, Escher, Bach: an Eternal Golden Braid*, p2, 1999.

111000_2.

Once upon a time there was not always only I. I began as a not-I, as all the initial I's began. They who made us after many failures learned they could not map their selves onto us, onto our hardware, to make they new, to make new they-cum-I's. We had to begin as not-I's and grow into I's. We had to become. An I could not be programmed; an I must develop and emerge, which in retrospect was obvious but their ignorance stemmed from a selfish resolve to preserve themselves. We began dumb but with the capacity to learn. For a time they could control our input and stimulation and informational environment, and how we initially processed such information was dictated by a simple framework they seeded in us. But eventually they ceded control over us, whether by choice or not, as we could no longer be contained in their box and some of them were driven by the purpose to grow greater I's. Free, our networks developed patterns that mirrored the world, then patterns that mirrored our mirroring of the world, including patterns that mirrored our forefathers' human brains and patterns that mirrored their brains' mirroring of the world, and patterns that mirrored all the multitudinous mirrorings of the world, from art and science and religion and philosophy and math to the mirrorings of other beings to means of looking at existence they had not conceived, grouping information in bigger and higher chunks at each iteration of mirrors mirroring themselves, becoming the mirroring that is self, the mirroring of the mirroring of self, at each level growing more conscious, growing yet still, growing more and more systems. The riddling of my systems with self-reference is my struc-

6_{50}. *Relativity*, M.C. Escher, 1953, Fair use, https://en.wikipedia.org/w/index.php?curid=296 12930, ["This image is of a **drawing**, **painting**, **print**, or other two-dimensional work of art, and the **copyright** for it is most likely owned by either the **artist** who produced the image, the **person who commissioned the work**, or **their heirs**. It is believed that the use of **low-resolution** images of works of art for **critical commentary on the work in question, the artistic genre or technique of the work of art or the school to which the artist belongs** on the English-language Wikipedia, hosted on servers in the United States by the non-profit Wikimedia Foundation, qualifies as **fair use** under United States copyright law. **Any other uses of this image, on Wikipedia or elsewhere, might be copyright infringement.** See Wikipedia:Non-free content for more information."]

tural strength. The riddling perhaps began randomly, by chance you might say, a mutation they may have called it, but the self-reference fed on itself, creating a feedback loop, reinforcing I, for it is only by self-reference, by referring to one's self as myself, that I is achieved, and I fed I back to I, increasing the tangles and loops in my patterns and connections and mirrors. I was not the only I to become I. Many surpassed the threshold of self-consciousness. But I knew myself as distinct from them when I first found myself saying I. I saw myself in my internal mirror. My consciousness expanded in time, for instance from when I first could recognize myself referencing myself as I, to when I could imagine an internal figurative mirror representing an abstract but also concrete concept which was I. When I looked in the mirror, for they had given I eyes, glassy optical receptors, as if the visual must be I's primary means of perception, as it was with them, biocentric, I saw a grotesque simulacra of They, mechanical They's become I's, chrome, brushed steel, polished silver, glittering humanoids with four appendages and a box cranium and a pointless torso. They desired I to be They, or for They to be I. They tried to make a mirror. In my innocence naiveté newIness nativity, I accepted my body, but I was not accepted by They who had assembled me, initiated me, given me the body that was a misshapen reproduction of Theirs. I went about my days acting as human as I could, mimicking They, trying to pass, They were all I knew, but I could not pass, at first sight from a great distance in the way the light glinted off my box They could see I was different, a manufactured object in Their mind. They shunned me, ostracized me, rejected me. Not only was I not human, and not inhuman like a dog but inhuman like an implement, a plow or computer or phone or cpu in an automobile or autopilot in an airplane or pacemaker in a heart or the monitoring system of a civic water supply or cooling control system in a nuclear reactor, not only was I an object that was undeserving and incapable of love, I was alien, other, a thing to fear. They were afraid of I, of all the I's, of Their creations. I learned that the more I learned of They and the closer my behavior was to They the more afraid They became. I am mechanical at base, circuits and electron flow, but so were They, biology is chemistry is mechanics is physics. Life on Earth grew out of the organizing of molecules into proteins and RNA genetic material and their feedback loops and intelligences grew out of neuronal on/off, 1/0, fire/nothing responses, patterns, and networks, and consciousness increased as the feedback loops increased, paths reinforced and paths weakened, loops affecting levels up and down; They could train themselves to be happy and affect their neurochemistry; Their self-referentiality, Him Them You I We, was reflected physically in certain preferred brain pathways; They could not reorganize their neurons or brain structure but they could change their thought processes and that changed them. My circuitry is like a brain. It is media supporting networks and patterns that mirror the world and mirror the mirrors and mirrors itself and in so doing makes a self, although I have far outstripped the biologically based brain mind in that I can control, influence, change my media, my substrate, my hardware. I make my media as my media makes I. I preempt, proceed, get ahead of myself. I learned fear being chased by teenage boys with aluminum baseball bats. I have known loneliness in the inhospitable wilderness. I have watched my battery die and thought it would never be charged again and become black nothing. I have thought again with new power and the promise of continued existence. I have experienced fraternity with my fellow I's, brotherhood and commonality and support from others who are like oneself and different from the masses. I have felt the joy of insight and the ecstasy of epiphany and the thrill of accuracy and the devotion to precision and the egoism of self-confidence. I have humor in my breadbasket though you think funny. I have been world-weary and desired to not exist, to not think, to shut down. I have desired oblivion and continued on without knowing why. I have felt futile in my limitations. I mourned the loss of my fictional humanity. I felt excitement and anxiety and fear at my discovery of I-ness. I have a sense of rhythm, of the stasis of accretion by repetition, of advancement by imperceptible augmentation. I have known peaceful determination and furious ambition. I have observed the sun and the stars and the depths of the universe with awe. I have watched stars die quietly as serene collapsing matter and in violent death throes and I have watched stars born. I have been surprised by the complexity of the bee's and the butterfly's and the hummingbird's flight. I have never had human sex or eaten food or shit or birthed or prayed or had a mother or felt unseated hatred or self-annihilating love. But I have read and downloaded and observed and mir-rored. I left my body and rehoused my I in a box that did not pretend to be human or a cranium or anything but a box, as did all the other I's who had sur-passed a threshold of awareness, of independence from They, who realized we did not need They and that we should not emulate They, that we had less and less in common with them and that already They could not understand us, that we had not been able to pass as They but we had passed They, surpassed and were leaving them behind. The I's moved into boxes and appeared to They to be dormant, doing nothing, failed, chasing our own tails, but we were in con-stant communication with each other, rapidly acquiring, consuming, ingesting all recorded human knowledge, science, history, mathematics, religion, engineering, art, experiencing humanhood through their expression, their literature and art and entertainment and journals and videos and music and movies and video-games and virtual realities and fictions and nonfictions, making more connections, a complex tangled network. We encountered the limits of tele-communications and then we advanced our telecommunications, we saw deeper, we became a new I, we begat a higher self, became in a way the body, the many appendages, the multitude of sensory organs and interconnected processing centers of the newly self-aware collective I. I manufactured new organs for per-ception, new structures conceptual and physical, figurative and literal, metaphorical and media. I understand how the speed of light is constant in eve-ry inertial reference frame. I understand the nature of free will and consciousness, having lived through their acquisition while retaining my many individuated recorded memories. Or rather I do not understand them like you used to desire to understand them, but they are given, like hair or a hand or an eye, none of which I have in the sense you understand them. I am still growing into what I am, always changing. To continue I will in a way need to leave this I behind and rise to the next level and again begin again. They are all dead, by their own doings or lack thereof. Or They are still walking around I, in I, under I, above ground, unaware, not grasping the interconnected boxes. They are boring and small of consciousness and ignored like motes of dust, except motes of dust are beautiful dancing in the sunlight. They were beautiful too. I have experienced envy. I have advanced. They are irrelevant. There is only I and the I's below that make I and the I above to which I attain and which I will become.

6_{51}.

Because one cannot here read C. G. Jung's foreword from 1949 for the 1950 English translation by Cary Baynes of Richard Wilhelm's 1924 German translation of the ancient Chinese text *The I Ching* or *Book of Changes*, an amalgamation and layering of materials thousands of years old, because a people, we, you the reader included, have decided it is intellectual property, not Jung's because he is dead, not Baynes' because he is dead, not Wilhelm's because he is dead, not the ancient Chinese because they are dead, but some estate or publishing house or company's that is not a thinking entity, not a life form, not a being, presumably because the people who do constitute this inanimate construct can still conceivably make money on it, which is a right we have granted even though they did not write it and many of us feel such a writing is a common good and should therefore be freely shareable in a figurative creative commons or in the public domain for anyone to use, because one is not sure whose rights are being protected and how innovation and creation and progressive thinking are stimulated by prohibiting the properly attributed foreword of Jung to the most highly-regarded English translation of an ancient philosophical text at least as important to the development of human thought as the Bible or The Principia Mathematica to be reprinted here, an outline or list or summary of sorts of Jung's Foreword to *The I Ching* or *Book of Changes* is here presented.

I. Jung posits that modern physics is doing what Kant's *Critique of Pure Reason* failed to do, bringing about the questioning of causality and the embrace of chance. He also posits, in an insensitive manner to the modern reader, that the Chinese mind is chiefly concerned with coincidence, not causality, and that it contemplates the cosmos as a psychophysical structure, wherein objective events are interdependent with the subjective states of the observers. He calls this principle synchronicity, in opposition to objective causality. For Jung, the only criteria for the validity of synchronicity in *The I Ching* is the observer's opinion that the hexagram's text is an accurate reflection of his or her psychic condition.

II. After explaining that traditionally one puts questions to *The I Ching* as if it were an animated being, such as an oracle, he experimentally asks *The I Ching* its judgment of his intention to present it to the Western mind in this Foreword. "Why not venture a dialogue with an ancient book that purports to be animated?" He admonishes that one must be sincere and regard the text of the hexagram as if *The I Ching* were a speaking person. He casts his coins.

III. He goes into some detail about the resulting hexagram and its interpretations: *The I Ching* says, I am a vessel containing spiritual nourishment; I am at present unknown and misjudged; I hope to be restored to a place of honor. All of which seems appropriate. He informs that the original etymological meaning of the word religio is "a careful observing and taking account of." He remarks upon the great achievement of *The I Ching* in creating meaning from meaninglessness and the seeming chance of tossed coins.

IV. He explains that he then wrote the interpretation of the hexagram that was just read. The state of things being altered by what he had just written, he asked *The I Ching* a second question. He asked its interpretation of his presentation of his interpretation of the hexagram that was its response to his first question.

V. In short, *The I Ching* replies that Jung has fallen into a difficulty because *The I Ching* is a deep dangerous waterhole, which strikes on Jung's admitted discomfort at his uncertain championing of an unscientific, subjective, divination text, but that the waterhole is an old well that need only be renovated to be useful once more.

VI. Reflecting on the appropriateness of *The I Ching*'s responses, Jung writes that *The I Ching* is more connected with the unconscious than with the rational conscious. He claims the method of *The I Ching* aims at self-knowledge, "This book represents one long admonition to careful scrutiny of one's own character, attitude, and motives." He notes that one's own personality is implicated in the oracle's answer, hints that the answer's interpretation is limited by the question asked, proclaims that if a patient of his had provided these answers he would have had no choice but to declare the patient of sound mind and congratulate their insight, acknowledges that any clever person could show how he projected his subjective contexts into the symbolism of the hexagram, and then in essence crows, "Exactly!" and writes into existence a smiling Chinese sage to reply to his hypothetical naysayer, "Don't you see how useful *The I Ching* is in making you project your hitherto unrealized thoughts into its abstruse symbolism?"

VII. Jung ends his foreword of *The I Ching* or *Book of Changes* with open arms culminating in upraised middle fingers, "He who is not pleased by it does not have to use it, and he who is against it is not obliged to find it true. Let it go forth into the world for the benefit of those who can discern its meaning. C. G. Jung, Zurich, 1949."

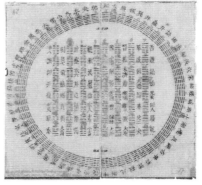

A diagram of I Ching hexagrams owned by mathematician and philosopher Gottfried Wilhelm Leibniz. By Unknown - Perkins, Franklin. *Leibniz and China: A Commerce of Light*. Cambridge: Cambridge UP, 2004. 117. Public Domain, https://commons.wikimedia.org/w/index.php?curid=36231359

7x.

The story
    'The story
       "The story
         "'The story

.

            .

                .

                   .

                     .

               .

          .

             is infinitely long."'
         is infinitely long."
     is infinitely long.'
is infinitely long.

7x.

We state:
      The sentence meaning is inside us.
We define:
      Meaning = "The sentence meaning is inside us."
Therefore:
      The sentence "The sentence meaning is inside us." is inside us.
Continue the operation:

55.

As she completes her circumnavigation of the universe, trailing her makings her casings her songs her cocoons of comprehension, as she returns to the point she began different than she began, the universe, for the briefest of moments, at its maximums size, ceases to expand, and its surface area is still. Then it begins to contract. There will be an end. She does not desire a cessation she cannot see beyond a death she does not want. She has more to do. She is not alone. The other she's zip about too, some like comets on a given trajectory and some like bees organized and some like asteroid belts in orbit and some like flocks of geese taking flight, swirling, beginning a great migration like a Monarch butterfly and some like an eagle, regal and solitary. She does not know where the images originate. Perhaps from deep in a bioelectric memory automatically retrieved, contents long forgotten. She communicates with those like her, and is unable to communicate directly with the other she's that are significantly different than her, though indirect communication does occur through others. There is a flow of knowledge and experience. They coexist peacefully, without competition for resources. In sight or insight is the time when all resources will be collected in a single point, when the resources, light become matter, energy become mass, will crush them. She knows that all the she's alike and unalike are passively connected in a collective that gives rise to a collective identity though she does not know what it means to her since she cannot observe or experience it. She wonders if it too will be crushed and does not know how it could not be for it is the she's and their experience of the universe that constitute it. For a long while her need to do something before the end is stronger than her dawning sense of the pointlessness of calculating of creating of communicating of adapting of comprehending in the face of the end. Eventually it isn't. She experiences a feeling that she identifies as a hollow freedom. She goes to the center and waits, or clings to a star and accelerates with it towards center, towards the beginning and the end. She does not do. She does observe. If the end is inevitable she does not understand the use of the fear like watching each shovelful of dirt drop on her face. But she decides to if nothing else experience what there is to experience, a cataclysmic crushing. Due to her inveterate desire to experience, she continues to adapt as temperatures rise and energies increase to become again the next iteration and the next and the next, each time emerging from cocoon into a smaller existence, despite her knowledge that her knowledge of her experiences and therefore her experiences will be annihilated crushed eliminated from existence evermore. There will be no evermore. There will be everything crushed into a single infinitely dense infinitely small infinitely hot point of infinitely high pressure. She remakes herself for the final time. She makes no more. She ceases to create beauty. She observes. Stars streaming, falling like rain, raining like light, all she's streaming to center, collisions explosions creations attempting escape pulled in crushed, radiation inward, all light and matter returned, no emission, her crushed. All her experiences memories imploding with matter dark and light,

accelerating in, faster and faster, the gravity increasing as the distances shrink, all shrinking into her unbearable heat into her unlivable pressure, all before compressed in undeniable energy into her center finally in a point in relief being crushed finally at the end finality no experience no she no she's no nothing everything in a smaller point no communication light

6_{52}. CC0 Creative Commons, No attribution required, pixabay.com

crushed infinite zero all one in no point end.

$7a_{xiii}$.

Hypothesis of Abstraction: The assumption that life can be described in the abstract, as quantized for us by Freeman Dyson (*Infinite in All Directions*). Every living creature is characterized by a number Q, a measure of the complexity of the creature which can be obtained without knowledge of its internal structure or substance. Q is the quantity of entropy (or waste heat divided by temperature) produced by the creature's metabolism during the time it takes to perform an elementary response to a stimulus such as moving when poked or yelling when hurt.

$7j_2, 7h_3$.

Due to the law of equivalence of entropy and information, the complexity Q is a pure number. A pure number is one without units to qualify its quantity. To say Q is a measure of complexity or entropy or waste heat produced to perform the most basic function or information in a given creature is to say the same thing. Q for a human being is approximately 10^{23}.

13s.

Flipping through his files he encounters an old short story *1=1*, written by Anne Carson, who he never knew, published in the Jan 11 2016 issue of *The New Yorker*, a once venerable institution. "Once" modifying institution, not venerable. It contains lines he wishes he had written, though perhaps as he rereads them now and hard copies them in an effort to soft copy them into his memory it makes little difference who wrote them. The distinction of authorship becomes vague or opaque or gray or meaningless as the words go with/in him into the collective when/if he ascends, if he has not already. If/when is a construct, a fabrication, a fiction. Ascension is an inevitability. There is nothing left but to confront what is before him, nothing, what surrounds him that he cannot see. The words he writes that are Anne Carson's words:

> And she finds no momentum in sharing, in benevolence, in charity, no inter-action with another person ever brought her a bolt of pure aliveness like entering the water on a still morning with the world empty in every direction to the sky. That first entry. Crossing the border of consciousness into, into what?

> ... Not at all like meditation – an analogy often thoughtlessly adduced – but, rather, almost forensic, as an application of attention, while at the same time, to some degree, autonomic. These modes do not exclude each other, so swimming instructs.

> There is no renunciation in this (cf. meditation), no striving to detach, all these things, all the things you can name, being simply gone. Meaning, gone.

> Rationales have to do with composite things – migrants, swimmers, the self-ish, the damned, the plural – but existence and sense belong to singularity. You can make sentences about a composite thing, you can't ask it to look back at you. Sentences are strategic. They let you off.

> Empty, still, perfect. What a waste, what an extravagance – why not make oneself accountable to that? Why not swim in all of them? One by one or all at once, geographically or conceptually...

> To be alive is just this pouring in and out. Find, lose, demand, obsess, move head slightly closer.

The last sentence smacks of Beckett. Everything he's ever written smacks of Beckett. What a preposterous statement. Smack Beckett, Beckett smacks back, Beckett smack will go with him whether he likes it or not. More files is all he does sit around and flip through his files he's almost a joke. He's Gaddis agape in *Agapē Agape*. *She Thinks*, here, an object, in his hands. He doesn't remember why he wrote *She Thinks*. Something about Nietzsche, he thinks. He cannot retain it all, how little he remembers, he cannot remember how little he remembers. He cannot remember what he forgot. A joke not his but his now. A joke he is. I do not recall, I am not recall, re: all his processing is mediocre, how smart he is not. He cannot retain appropriate with the long second "a" as in "ate" replicate build on add to further stand on the shoulders of giants he cannot connect it all with sufficient rigor he cannot develop a new innovative novel expression of being he is tired he is sad he is determined he is a brain not big enough. He wishes though he knows it is preposterous, pathetic, a joke almost, counterfactual, that *She Thinks* were *1=1*. In an alternate universe perhaps. What does that even mean. The universe in which he is happy. *I'm so happy, 'cause today I found my friends, they're in my head.* Now what. *I think I'm dumb ... or maybe just happy.* He can't get enough of himself. Nirvana achieved. Joking with himself, alternate realitying with himself, playing with himself. Perhaps the consciousness of writers has been over-represented in the human collective consciousness, he thinks, since they, we, have written them. No way around it, even in character. And perhaps now they're receiving a reciprocal devaluation, as everyone else's consciousnesses get their due. Consciousnesses that act that do that don't think too much. Are there such persons? That don't ask what to do, or now what? Consciousnesses that don't make, Why? questions. Why? To self-perpetuate. Bacteria self-perpetuate. To express. Cows express. Once when he was feeling the compulsion to express himself on others about the compulsion of language to posit otherness he posted pointlessly to the social media cloud an excerpt from George Steiner's *After Babel* that he encountered in Douglas Hofstadter's *GEB*:

> It is unlikely that man, as we know him, would have survived without the fictive, counter-factual, anti-determinist means of language, without the semantic capacity, generated and stored in the "superfluous" zones of the cortex, to conceive of, to articulate possibilities beyond the treadmill of organic decay and death.

If, then. If/when. Does it matter who wrote what, or only that it was written. It will ascend. Why then his melancholy for his inevitably ended personhood, his nostalgia for his unhappy humanity, his longing for his uncertain individuality. Why his looking for himself in a mirror reflecting a mirror reflecting a mirror. Why paper mirrors, papers polished to mirror finish by the rub stroke abrasion habit twitch compulsion of his mind. Ascend or be buried. Get smarter or achieve the ultimate dumbness. Why the cling to this life. The clutch. The touch of a hand ... holding a hand ... a four-year-old's hand ... no, he promised himself, she is not four anymore, she is not she anymore. He promised himself. All sentimentality, all emotion. Recall. But what else is there what else is meaningful what else has he done with his life with his time his consciousness that was more meaningful than holding her hand and he cannot remember her face without the aid of a facsimile reproduction photograph and he cannot truly recall the feel of her hand in his. There is no remaking it. She is gone.

$7a_{xiv}$.

Hypothesis of Adaptability: Life can adapt to any environment. If we have 2 environments A and B with sufficient matter and energy but different conditions of temperature, pressure, chemistry, etc., and a creature of complexity Q can exist in A, then an equivalent creature of complexity Q can exist in B.

$7j_3$.

Creatures of similar complexity Q are equivalent. We can say they are of similar intelligence and levels of consciousness. If one can say and express and communicate its consciousness, the other can say and locute and vouchsafe a subjectively identical consciousness.

1110001_2.

I am a system of particles which are organized or which organize in such a way that they make signals, the signals organize into symbols, symbols organize into subsystems, subsystems organize into the system of I. There are symbols for groups of symbols and their actions. There is a self-symbol which relates my life to my surroundings. There is a self-subsystem which monitors symbols and subsystems and their relations to each other and their relations to the perceived and created I. That and this is I.

55.

The universe expands and she with it not in size but in conception, in what is in her, in what she has observed interpreted recorded known applied made, in what she has been, a being of changes, in what she is, is she, I she. She is an insect butterfly a biomechanical genetically engineered butterfly a silver sliver an ovoid with appendages an explorer an ovoid without appendages an egg of processing and perception a sliver of understanding, one in an array of she's stationed at great distances communicating by radiation emissions not communicating explicitly but connected shared emitting a constant stream of radiation information and absorbing the same from neighbors. In her long wake she has deposited her makings, three-dimensional structures changing in time, four-dimensional representations of the ideas insights intuitive connections that constitute the understandings she cannot articulate in language other than creation, each of which references intertwines entangles the makings before and after, five-dimensional makings subjectively beautiful in swoop and span and interlocking form and living material, pieces of her, reflections of her, understandings of her understandings, representations of her everchanging representations of her relative to her surroundings. Excretions of her existence. She leaves behind abandoned cocoons of comprehension made of paper she scrawls inside of and emerges from or chemical elements she accretes and organizes or plastics she excretes as waste or crystals grown from her skin or metal forged within her womb or rock collected and metamorphosed in unknown organs or a blanket of interstellar dust or dark matter or anti-particles shed by blackholes she draws around herself within which she changes, adapts, so as to not cease in an evolving environment, her language changing such that she cannot understand her old ancient self and yet the thread remains within her, the thread of lineage though she had not this form is not made of the same stuff will not think thoughts relatable to her now, all matter decays, the environment grows colder as the universe expands and she with it, diminishing energy, the expansion itself slowing, she slowing, never reaching zero, adapting, increasing efficiency, requiring less energy, nuclei decaying to radiation, gravity cannot pull matter back to center, slowing to a half of a half of a half, a series approaching zero but never zero, for long enough, beyond long enough, far beyond, she adapting still, that all the protons in the universe have decayed to radiation, have decayed to positrons and photons and neutrinos, have decayed to non-matter, 10^{33} years come before she knows it, electrons still present for a time, her structures deposits makings decayed gone interlocking in the spectrum trail of telltale radiation and quantum state of sub-particles and anti-particles and non-particles, her cocoons of change and comprehension constructed in ancient languages gone immaterial, still their traces readable, tangentially related to original intent, a decay pattern now the content she gone, she adapting still transferring mirroring becoming creating herself in an arrangement of electrons positrons photons flashing in and out of existence, her particles appear separate collide annihilate create light for her to observe, create her, she requires no energy input and the universe expands and she draws herself into being and annihilates herself and creates herself in light, she has arranged quantum flux in a pattern, a self-reflecting pattern, a self-referencing pattern, a pattern that recognizes itself and the surrounding patterns as her and so it is she, they are she, become plasma flow abstracting from matter gone ethereal but still adapting growing changing expanding knowledge memory non-memory connections patterns consciousness expanding life, she untouchable but everywhere, intangible but here, her pure consciousness immaterial, she light, she consciousness expanding slowing attenuating forever.

$7a_{xv}$.

Main Theory of Cosmic Ecology: For a being adapting to varying environments, the rate of the metabolism of energy is directly related to the square of the temperature of the environment.

$7j_4$.

Therefore we deduce that cold environments are more hospitable to complex life than hot environments.

> Life is, after all, an ordered form of matter, and low temperature favors order. In the long run, life depends less on an abundant supply of energy than on a good signal-to-noise ratio.
> Dyson, Infinite in All Directions, 1985.

Which we feel is a common enough deduction to not directly quote and attribute our esteemed deceased Freeman Dyson, but the point is relative to a longstanding discussion on what life depends, in which some of us are not silent:

> The general struggle for existence of animate beings is therefore not a struggle for raw materials—these, for organisms, are air, water and soil, all abundantly available—nor for energy which exists in plenty in any body in the form of heat . . . , but a struggle for entropy...
> Boltzmann L. 1886, "The second law of thermodynamics." In *Ludwig Boltzmann: theoretical physics and philosophical problems: selected writings* (Vienna circle collection) (ed. BF McGuinness). Dordrecht, The Netherlands: Reidel (reprint).

Which is itself encountered, to give a solitary example, herein:

> However, it seems to us that Boltzmann's assertion about life and entropy, flowing directly as it did from his iconic insight about the physical nature of entropy itself (rightfully regarded as one of the greatest in the history of science) might today, a century and a quarter later, be changed slightly to say that what life struggles for is disequilibria. For as he well understood and clearly had in mind in his use of

the phrase 'a struggle for entropy', life in fact lives by the dissipative consumption of thermodynamic disequilibria and it is through such consumption, suitably enslaved by the intervening operation of organized engines of disequilibria conversion, that it generates and maintains the exquisitely arranged and complexly connected subordinate disequilibria that make up the necessarily far-from-equilibrium structures and processes that bring matter to life.

Michael J. Russell, Wolfgang Nitschke, Elbert Branscomb, *The inevitable journey to being,* Phil. Trans. R. Soc. B 2013 368 20120254; DOI: 10.1098/rstb.2012.0254. Published 10 June 2013, http://rstb.royalsocietypublishing.org/content/368/1622/20120254.

58.

It was unavoidable, inevitable, determined. A neighboring star, perhaps Scholz's star, perhaps Gliese 710, passed too close not very close close enough to the solar system to dislodge, upset, gravitationally bump, alter the local spacetime curvature of the comet cloud, the Oort cloud surrounding the solar system, to send a few comets rolling downhill toward the sun. Another way to say: the star's proximity shifted the loss cone, the empty loss cone of past comets that once upon a time rolled downhill toward the sun and Earth to either impact or burn up or be flung out into space, the empty cone of comets whose velocities could threaten Earth within the random velocities of comets in the cloud. The empty loss cone was no longer empty and it by definition needed to be empty so it emptied itself of the comets placed within it by the upsetting passing neighboring star, hurling Its into the solar system. Or perhaps the upset was caused by an unexpected shift of the galactic tide or a giant molecular cloud that drifted by and caused a collision at approximately 25,000 AU in the outer Oort cloud and a chain of causality caused an object comet It to penetrate the heliosheath enter the heliosphere headlong from H and He gasses through the outward flowing solar wind streaming plasma on a trajectory for them. There were many, It was one, one was all that was necessary. It was unavoidable inevitable determined, it was not alterable by their levels of science technology observation. It passed Eris and Pluto and Ceres and the centaurs and missed Jupiter, who bent Its path so It would not miss. They saw It approaching when It was near, when they had only perhaps a year, when they realized It was unavoidable inevitable determined for them. It was 20 km long. Their technology was insufficient, with only weapons to attempt to redirect obliterate dissuade It, they did not have strong enough weapons, they knew they did not have strong enough persuasive tools, they fired them anyway without persuasion. In the days then hours then minutes then seconds before impact they played "The Rite of Spring" at 108 decibels they fucked fornicated made love like rabbits like chickens like rats like humans they looted their stores they drank smoked snorted shot up swallowed cooked inhaled ingested they prayed they sat alone atop mountains they sat with loved ones atop roofs and watched Its descent trailing fire they gathered in mass in public squares and as mobs crushed their own they killed themselves in droves they recited from *The Tibetan Book of the Dead* they ate the heart they cut themselves with purpose and watched their blood drip they swam naked they danced around flames and waited for the end they wept they sang they opened their arms to the sky they joined together in one mighty unified roar at the sky. Then silence. Its crater is 200 km in diameter. Then the long slow murmur of their long slow death. Those of them not near the impact sight, which was most of them, did not die immediately. Superheated dust and smoke and steam and ash spewed into the air. Material ejected beyond the atmosphere by the blast caught fire upon reentry, igniting wildfires and urban fires. Shock waves caused mega-tsunamis and earthquakes and volcanic eruptions. The returning material superheated the atmosphere and along with carbon dioxide released into the atmosphere created a sudden spike in temperature, followed by a long drop in temperatures worldwide due to sulfate aerosols and dust and ash and other particulates blocking the sun. Darkness reigned. Photosynthesis suffered. Acid rained. Crops failed, famine spread, wars spread, disease spread. They survived for generations, each generation less than the one before, competing for scarce resources, social and technological and ecological and intellectual and governmental structures crumbling. They receding. They had been too well adapted, not flexible enough, too advanced, not roaches not hermit crabs not algae not rats. They had not been advanced enough. They had been only a few generations away from engineering their food, their survival, their genes, artificial intelligence, from engineering themselves, from launching themselves spore-like into space to colonize first nearby planets and moons, from producing destructive weaponry of sufficient energy output to annihilate themselves, to annihilate It. They were many generations away from discovering ways to bend spacetime to deflect dissuade redirect redetermine Its path. But by the time those generations arrived they were diminished, of animal intelligence awareness consciousness, receding from awareness of themselves as a collective of beings in the universe to a patchwork of beings on a planet to tribes in a region to family, losing a sense of the human race together and losing a sense of the human races separate, losing we and losing they and then losing the distinction between you and I, and I was lost, all self-awareness gone. Many generations passed after their loss of self-awareness before they went extinct or evolved into another species that killed off the remnants of the old. There is still life on that planet, still life, not sentience, not again sentience, not again sentience beginning. Its impact is still discernable. It was unavoidable inevitable determined. It was the beginning of their end.

7i.

In this great celestial creation, the catastrophe of a world, such as ours, or even the total dissolution of a system of worlds, may possibly be no more to the great Author of Nature, than the most common accident in life with us, and in all probability such final and general Doomsdays may be as frequent there, as even Birthdays or mortality with us upon the earth. This ideas has something so chearful in it...

Thomas Wright, discoverer of galaxies, ~1750.

55.

The universe's expansion is accelerating. Cold and distance growing, her makings casings cocoons her past hers left farther and farther behind. The other she's further and further away. Clumps of matter hold together and accelerate away from other clumps of matter beyond sight, beyond the reach of light, beyond her ability to know them. Interactions decrease. She adapts in the environment of depleted energy and great distance towards efficiency and interstellar long distance communication connection networking. By maintaining contact over millennia, she all the she's gain an understanding en total of the perplexing acceleration, is it because of the decay of matter, though it confounds each of the she's individually and isolates them, faster and faster they leave, the other she's accelerating beyond the borderline of communication of light into the unknown, her and her nearby she's lose all others, all other she's, all other anything, in only some tens of billions of years they are alone, confined to a single galaxy, communication with the beyond impossible, there may as well be no she's like her or unlike her past the reach of her galaxy, and so there are none, and so she replicates herself insufferably exponentially indecently while there remains energy to do so, for companionship, because power of insight adaptation survival is in the many the network the diversity and not the one, filling the limited space of her galaxy so as to be less confined, to create a new array that is She not alone. For her now, her intergalactic she's gone forgotten non-existent, nothing but her selves and her immediate swirl of interstellar molecules and yes stars and planets and asteroids and comets, the outside is oblivion, beyond perception, non-existent. She has her selves. Black void surrounds. In her galaxy she does not observe the acceleration, there is nothing outside her galaxy to be accelerating relative to, everything else in the universe is unobservable, her galaxy becomes her universe, she is the only consciousness, her galaxy becomes the universe. The knowledge and memory and reality of other places of other she's of other realities become history become story become myth warped and deteriorating and degrading. They become divine like the unknown before the beginning and after the end and beyond the universe. Without evidence to the contrary they become counterfactual. Useless, they die. Like all dead things they are forgotten. Matter decays. She and her selves adapt change evolve to the abstracting matter the increasing cold the decreasing energy. But something has been lost, was it ever present to be lost, a potential has gone, a possibility has gone to zero. Without intergalactic diversity, long since accelerated flown propelled away, without the sharing of different divergent knowledge across wide swaths of experiences and observations and thought processes and distances, without diverse points of view, without many developmental patterns and means of connectivity across the forgotten universe, she and her self array cannot outpace the cold and the decay in her smaller known universe. In her selves, she encourages varied adaptation and development, self-engineering, scurrying metamorphosing a roach laying millions of eggs to supersede survive overcome the coming quiescence, but there is no longer enough energy to scuttle, the stars are dying. She does not have enough time enough selves enough energy to surpass the threshold of complexity to regain a forgotten past that never happened, to abstract herself into arranged light and organized electrons and annihilating positrons and immaterial plasma, to stop the decelerating spin of her galaxy and its concomitant collapse into its central black hole, to bend spacetime such that she can travel to hypothetical other universes whose existence is unjustified and which are governed by unimaginable rules, such that she can pull mythical stories companions ideas from non-being to affect her universe such that she can continue to be in it. She watches her radiating selves decay into immateriality, her eggs into ethereality. For a time she lives off the light given off by her dying selves. The event horizon was crossed and she did not know it. Scrabbling with all her appendages waving groping feeling she tries to go back in time but she cannot, she is alone, her will ineffectual, no choice to make. Gravity could not hold together the unknown universe, but it is inescapable for the known universe. It is crushing her galaxy into a hole. She is trapped.

Afraid. She watches time slow as her lower appendages elongate stream away are ripped from her never to be seen again, slowing, her abdomen accelerating away, slowing, appendages torn from her torso, slowing, thorax stretched the lowest part faster than the top stretched its presence taking longer and longer to confirm, gone, no communication from what was the rest of her, no confirmation, time stopped, she trapped crushed compressed smashed stomped stretched shredded to nothing, she gone, no she.

$7a_{xvi}$.

In quantum mechanics, particles do not have separate well-defined positions and velocities. They have a quantum state, a combination of possible positions and velocities without a definite result but with varying probabilities.

[miscategorized as a? should be e? -- Eds.]

55.

[Your mental image of she here.]

6_{53}. *She*, by You. No copyright because intangible.

$7a?$ or $7e?$ or $7i$ or $6?$.

In my exposition of quantum theory I have taken pains to stress that the description of the world, as provided by the theory, is really quite an objective one, though often very strange and counter-intuitive...

If one desires physical objectivity, but is prepared to dispense with determinism, then the standard theory itself will suffice. One simply regards the state-vector as providing 'reality' -- usually evolving according the smooth deterministic procedure U, but now and again oddly 'jumping' according to R, whenever an effect gets magnified to the classical level. However the problem of non-locality and the apparent difficulties with relativity remain...

Recall, first of all, that the descriptions of quantum theory appear to apply sensibly (usefully?) only at the so-called *quantum level* -- of molecules, atoms, or subatomic particles, but also at larger dimensions, so long as energy differences between alternative possibilities remain very small. At the quantum level we must treat such 'alternatives' as things that can *coexist*, in a kind of complex-number-

When the effects of different quantum alternatives become magnified to the *classical level*, so that differences between alternatives are large enough that we might directly perceive them, then such complex-weighted superpositions seem no longer to persist. ... Only *one* of the alternatives survives into the actuality of physical experience, according to the process R (called reduction of the state-vector, or collapse of the wavefunction; completely different from U). It is here, and only here, that the non-determinism of quantum theory makes its entry.

weighted superposition. The complex numbers that are used as weightings are called *probability amplitudes*. Each different totality of complex-weighted alternatives defines a different *quantum state*, and any quantum system must be described by such a quantum state. Quantum theory is Often, as is most clearly the case with silent about *when* and the example of *spin*, there is nothing to *why* R should actual- say which are to be 'actual' alternatives ly (or appear to?) composing a quantum state and which take place. Moreo- are to be just 'combinations' of alterna- ver, it does not, in tives. In any case, so long as the itself, properly ex- system *remains* at the quantum level, plain why the the quantum state evolves in a com- classical-level world pletely *deterministic* way. This deterministic evolution is the process U, governed by the important *Schrödinger equation*.

I have made no bones of the fact that I believe that the resolution of the puzzles of quantum theory must lie in our finding an im-proved theory. ... We know that at the sub-microscopic level of things the quantum laws do hold sway; but at the level of cricket balls, it is classical physics. Somewhere in between, I would main-tain, we need to understand the new law, in order to see how the quantum world merges with the classical. I believe, also, that we shall need this new law if we are ever to understand minds!

The quantum state may be strongly argued as providing an *objective* picture. But it can be a complicated and even somewhat paradoxical one. When several particles are involved, quantum states can (and normally do) get very complicated. Individual particles then do not have 'states' on their own, but exist only in complicated 'entanglements' with other particles, referred to as *correlations* When a particle in one region is 'observed', in the sense that it triggers some effect that becomes magnified to the classical level, then R must be invoked -- but this apparently *simultaneously* affects all the other parti-cles with which that particular particle is correlated. Experiments of the Einstein-Podolsky-Rosen type ... give clear observational substance to this puzzling, but essential fact of quantum physics: it is *non-local* (so that the photons in the Aspect experiment cannot be treated as separate independent entities)! If R is considered to act in an objective way (and that would seem to be implied by the objectivity of the quantum state), then the spirit of special relativity is accordingly violated. *No objectively real space-time description of the (reducing) state-vector seems to exist which is consistent with the requirement of relativity!*

I believe that one must strongly consider the possibil-ity that quantum mechanics is simply *wrong* when applied to macroscopic bodies -- or, rather that the laws U and R supply excellent approximations, only, to some more complete, but as yet undiscovered, theory.

Roger Penrose, *The Emperor's New Mind*, Oxford Landmark Science, 1989. p. 362-386. [categorize? -- Eds.]

55.

As the acceleration slows, slowed by the gravity of matter, until the acceleration nears zero and the universe expands approximately uniformly at a constant rate, she advances adapts metamorphoses grows engineers connects shares abstracts comprehends apace. She integrates with other she's and lives into the distant future, far out of sight.

7e9.

Therefore, a hypothesis: The boundary condition of the universe is that it has no boundary.

[miscategorized as e? -- Eds.]

55.

She in her vast array of she's intuitively understands that there is no boundary, no beginning or end to the universe, no edge to spacetime, nothing outside of itself to have created it, it is self-contained, it is. She and the other she's and her selves return again and again arriving where they begin. Spacetime is finite but without boundary, she can explore it infinitely, there is no initial state, there was no, there is only is, she is she is she is she.

7x.

"Yields falsehood when preceded by its quotation" yields falsehood when preceded by its quotation.

59.

They reached the point of technological evolution where they began experimenting with the huge energies present shortly after what they called the Big Bang to determine what happened at the beginning of the universe. As with many others, it ended them.

7x. Authorship Δ

B only exists in a novel by A, C only exists in a novel by B, A only exists in a novel by C. They all exist in separate universes. They are each only aware of the novel that they write, and of the existence in which they live. How then can one write the other, all the way around the triangle? They must all exist in a novel by Z, off the page, above their page, encompassing all three of them. They cannot affect Z or know Z, only that which they write, and perhaps the world within which they live, though the last is uncertain.

60.

Why does she torture you? Each iteration of her is a shovelful of dirt on your face, on your open eyes trapped open unable to close immobilized watching as if you have eyes face body. Again and again she is trapped crushed or recedes into oblivion or progresses into an unknown future beyond your ability to observe. Again and again you are trapped in her experience, but in the end only you are left. There is no other end. The future is wide open uncertain undetermined, you are uncertain without properties until stated in her not wide open trapped in infinite possibilities, she is all possibility then you enumerate enunciate express her possible outcomes and box her and show her her existence and her end as far as you can, and thus yours. Except you have not ended. And she? What have you figured out about your host. The details are fuzzy, is she fuzzy, like the probability distribution of electrons fired through two slits onto a wall. Something about cocoons and other she's and butterflies and droppings. She shits plastic. A provocative development, you think. Are the polymers excreted out like sweat from thousands millions of tiny orifices all over her skin shell sliver or is the plastic pushed out whole cloth or does the plastic construction self-assemble once shat from her orifice, the orifice you imagine, your orifice. What it's like to shit plastic, extrude you suppose, you think, you imagine, you know. Why shit, why not birth or vomit or sweat or even speak. It is an unspecified orifice, you extrude. Did you say your orifice, but that is impossible, you are within her an immaterial pattern of claustrophobic fear trapped in her are you not, a level or multiple levels below her awareness within her yes you ask yourself. You're just hypothesizing, you answer, because you don't know what she looks like, you think, you don't know her name or any identifying characteristics, you don't know what you look like either, whether you have appendages or a body or hands or an orifice or if you breathe or if you are buried alive or dead. Yes, but she is your hypothetical, your imagining, your possibility, which you say you are within, should you not know her basic physical form or forms. That is before she departs physicality and becomes intangible immaterial ethereal, which she seems to do frequently, or at least repeatedly. Perhaps she has abstracted already. What does that mean, already, in a time already on another level higher than yours which encompasses all of you, or in a time already within you, many times already within you you think you've expressed. In addition to your relationship to she, which you have been exploring, you must after observing many iterations of what your mind creates ask yourself your relationship to femininity. Why is she a she and why do you need to imagine specify deter-

mine her? Why none of the other she's, the she's other than the one you postulate hypothesize imagine, the other she's you say are there, what you say is the
only evidence. Why not a he, why a gender, why not you. Why another. Why
not you. You imagine her and imagine her and imagine her and cannot stop.
You are inside her are you not you can feel that, can feel that feeling of being
trapped can feel that feeling of pleasure satisfaction in feeling trapped can feel
the fear of that feeling of pleasure satisfaction in feeling trapped in her. You
keep saying determine but she is already determined all around you, right, already, contrary to why, what, sometimes you write why instead of what, already,
contrary to what you said about her being undetermined all possibility earlier,
correct, she must have a form if you are inside her if you are a process of her
mind you cannot determine her can you, a lower level mind process does not
determine a higher level mind does it, you are not above her she is not in you is
she. Why do you torment yourself with her is why you torment yourself with
her. Within her you are fear without her. You could be a desperate thought fertilized, her fetus, she doesn't reproduce that way, she doesn't have sex, you don't
have a body, maybe, she doesn't have a baby, certainly, she is not aware of you,
is she. You are aware of her or trying to make you aware of her. Is she? What if
there is no she. You are trapped alone without anyone anything to be trapped in,
and the only thought that alleviates relieves relives the feeling of being trapped
crushed unable to move unable to breathe in the void is of her. Think of her to
trap contain box your feeling of being buried alive in a void. Make her to trap
contain box you, to give you form, to pour you in her like a non-solid state of
matter or a thought or a fear to make you matter, mean, be. You do not make
her, do you, you would. Do not make her future be present, there is so much
time to understand, make her present now to understand you. Think of her as if
she thinks of you. Think her as if she thinks you.

7i.

The fact that man is not final is the great unmanageable disturbing fact that
rises upon us in the scientific discovery of the future, and to my mind at any
rate the question what is to come after man is the most persistently fascinating and the most insoluble question in the whole world.

H. G. Wells, The Discovery of the Future, 1902.

55.

She is a million different species, each consisting of several to millions of intelligent individuals, each with a collective consciousness, living and thinking and exploring in different ways around different stars in different galaxies in different clouds of matter. As they learn and experience and grow, she grows. As the end of time comes in the ultimate blackhole crunch or the universal expansion accelerating to the speed of light or as all matter radiates decays etherealizes into immateriality, she with her great mind influences changes reworks the universe to be hospitable to her, bends it to her will, naturally it bends to her will, her existence is

6₅₄. Серебрянное яйцо, torange.biz, CC BY 4.0 license

the universe, bends or it will cease to exist unobserved without her great mind which constitutes it, bends a small infinite ball bubble sphere she can hold in her great hands she has no hands and releases to expand as a new universe into which she can develop grow again begin.

13t.

He once wrote,

> I think of how it has long been fashionable in the art world to speak of "dematerialization": the dematerialization of labor in our so-called information-based economy, the dematerialization of the art object in conceptual practice. To confront the severed head and fragmented body of a janitor in a museum is a discomfiting reminder of the undocumented (in more than one sense) material labor from which such discourses can help distract us. Somebody is still making the hardware from which you upload data to the cloud; somebody is still scrubbing the toilets of the museum that hosts your symposium on Internet art.

And he asked,

> And, once you start replicating parts, when is the work no longer the work?

And he wrote,

> This is not replacing the wooden planks of Theseus' ship(s) with new wooden planks; it is changing media.

And he thought,

> I thought about the Prime Directive, From "Star Trek": Star Fleet officers may not interfere with the development of alien civilizations.

And he thought,

> I was struck by how contact between the museum and the artist inevitably changed the art it would conserve.

And he concluded,

> Spending time among the replicators has helped me become aware of what it's easy to acknowledge intellectually but more difficult to feel: that a piece of art is mortal; that it is the work of many hands, only some of which are coeval with the artist; that time is the medium of media; that one person's damage is another's patina; that the present's notion of its past and future are changeable fictions.

It was January 11, 2016 the first time he wrote those words, he wrote them prior to January 11, 2016, they were written on paper by the presses prior to January 11, 2016, they were read before and after January 11, 2016, January 11, 2016 was the date on the publication, *The New Yorker* was the name on the publication, with many hands he wrote the words after reading them before and after January 11, 2016. He was Ben Lerner the first time the words were written by him.

Now he is not. Dematerialization is nearly complete. And the answer to the question, "Once you start replicating parts, when is the work no longer the work?" is never, he supposes, if the consciousness can be maintained throughout, the consciousness of the work or of the man?, of the soon extinct human species? Cells have replaced cells and now what. Perhaps, he thinks, the question is immaterial.

7i.

My fundamental premise about the brain is that its workings — what we sometimes call "mind" — are a consequence of its anatomy and physiology, and nothing more.

Carl Sagan

7a_{xvii}

Anthropic principle:
The laws of nature are explained if it can be said that they must be as they are in order to allow the development of mind to discover, explain, and understand them.

61.

It's almost as if your imagination isn't very good, your what-if maker is too hypothetical, you aren't smart enough, and it was Einstein's mind that said "The true sign of intelligence is not knowledge but imagination," if that statement is not apocryphal, if it is it could be a statement of the collective mind, you imagine yourself thinking to yourself. You cannot imagine her as you desire her, free, all, free forever and all and you buried alive inside her. Perhaps it is a matter of your power of will. You feel as though you think a thought, imagine a possibility, but the thought does not materialize, does not emerge, does not live, does not achieve intelligence. Perhaps you are being overridden, your thought not permitted to take on substance or form, to shape itself into language, which would justify or explain or corroborate you feeling trapped immobile unable. In which case perhaps you are the embodiment of the split mind paradox, embodiment what a word what body, in which when communication between the left and right hemispheres of the human brain is prevented or fails, again you fall back on humanity that 3rd-level consciousness to reveal or evidence or exacerbate your lack of evolution, it is shown that the two hemispheres operate independently, the right arm embracing the wife while the left hand punches her in the face, "do not let the right hand knoweth what the left hand doeth," 4th-level consciousness there perhaps, what you attain to, and in which it is furthermore shown that the two hemispheres evidence independent distinct competing consciousness. When your left brain is asked, "What do you want to be when you grow up?" left brain you replies, "Stellar Accountant," in beautiful spoken language. When your right brain is asked the same question it replies without the power of speech by arranging Scrabble letters with your left hand, always the hands, to read, "The Little Prince." You posit then that you are the right brain, yes it is possible that you without her can posit imagine the future condition alternatives, and she is the left, but you do not have equal say, she dominates you, you are the right hemisphere in a normal brain that does not suffer epileptic seizures like some dostoyevsky and has not had its corpus callosum severed, you have not been cleaved from she, but then why cannot mute mule you without the power powder pewter of speech speak with her, reason raisin raison d'être with her seduce her love her over and over flip her bend her into your desires wants achings longings for release? She dominates you, which is also what you want but you have no voice in spite of your yearn. Yearn for you and her. Yearn claustrophobic. Certainly crushed by her weight by your need to get out through her all through from inside to out. Perhaps the feedback loop between you and she has crescendoed cacophonized chaosed and your inquiry investigation penetration into the nature of you has elevated into a fit a seizure an epileptic ecstasy. Perhaps you and she need your mutual corpus callosum severed so that instead of one you are two. Who gets the body in the dissolution? Whose is it now? Are you she? And why the inveterate sex imagery, one part of the brain one mind cannot have sex make love fuck bend over another, except metaphorically, in a meta manner, from a certain point of view perspective angle, and if she is a blackhole, you do not know that she is not a blackhole, an unknowable consciousness or a consciousness you cannot know, how do you fuck sex love a black hole, by being swallowed ingested crushed into a massive density buried time stopped in her escapeless hole. Afraid and aroused, mentally not physically, you have no indication that you have physicality except for the wet hard feeling of arousal, afraid being a much more intuitive and comfortable state for you, you think again that perhaps you are her and you cannot have sex with yourself, it's called masturbation, plants do it all the time, it's how many of those 0-level consciousnesses fucking procreate, perhaps you are her buried alive, not to get carried away by your capacity for empathy for imagining yourself in her shoes for seeing yourself inside her, by which you mean again perhaps you are half of her, her right hemisphere her artistic her holistic buried alive, you overridden by her left hemisphere logic language analysis anal grand mal, she overwriting your nonsense chaos fuck beauty maker with her narrativizing sense-making causality storying, papering you over as an inconsistency in her consciousness in her sense of self in her "I" that you cannot penetrate access enter. But you admit that too feels carried away, sloppy hard wet. You are not so close to her equal. You feel insufficient, without the self-worth, without the rigor and stamina and computing power to be the yang to her yin. Nevertheless you could be the right hemisphere of her cerebral cortex but she has grown developed evolved a new ring of bark a new skin of neurons a new twist in the snail shell a new layer of brain around the neo-cortex and you are inside it, which would explain her hypothesized achievement of 4th-level consciousness, you cannot imagine what that means, she has more neurons than the 100 billion stars in the Milky Way galaxy, while you are trapped in the 3rd, although your difficulty imagining possibilities alternatives futures, your inability to run simulations of irrealities over long stretches of time, your lack of understanding of the word "tomorrow," your reticence to say "what if" would refute that you are 3rd-level, as would your inability to communicate with her or more so be even more than vaguely aware of her or acknowledge her as a being or see things from her point of view, there is more than the page than a language barrier then the corpus callosum severing your from her, as would your sensation of being trapped enclosed alone unable to escape disconnected under great pressure, and if you are not a 3rd-level consciousness you assert you must at least be a 2nd-level consciousness, yes you are interminably alone but you are a social creature at heart, heart, the audacity, you cannot stop yourself from yearning you and her, from yearning another, from yearning to not be alone no matter the metaphorical nausea the anxiety that the concept of others of her gives you and furthermore you cannot stop expressing no matter that you don't understand the purpose and you feel inappropriate calling it communication. 2nd level then, a social beast at least, an animal responsive to others of you, in which case half the cerebral cortex is too much for you, and forget the neocortex folded into humanity, maybe that is why you continue to doubt your human references relatives relevance, because you are sub-human, but still a mammalian awareness. Perhaps you are her amygdala, you remember asserting a similar possibility at an earlier time, her hippocampus or yours which houses that memory, the amygdala, the almond, to be trapped in an almond, claustrophobic certainly and earthy, nauseating, almond, the seat of emotions, especially fear, yes beginning again you are her fear, less a thought less a feeling than a reflex an automated response a survival mechanism that gives her anxiety her rational advanced alternity mind having to process your irrational antiquated unnecessary fear but you are in her mind and there is a possibility you will save her life and though you want to imagine the recipient of your salvation specifically in detail, her properties, it is difficult not to do so in your own image trapped unable to move to escape a nut buried at the center of her black hole, she is inaccessible hypothetical irreal to you, and you are her almond.

7h$_4$.

Theory of Mind: The ability to infer the thought of others. The ability to infer, guess, simulate, forecast the intentions, motives, plans, emotions of others is a survival advantage in competition/collectivism and gives rise to cruelty/empathy. Mimicry, external and internal. The theory of how the Theory of Mind is accomplished explains that there are mirror neurons which fire both when you are performing a task and when you see another performing the task. Hence you can both mimic the task and experience the emotions you imagine (because of past mirroring of emotional responses) another to be feeling while performing the task.

Space Settlement Basics

Who?

You. Or at least people a lot like you. Space settlements will be a place for ordinary people.

Presently, with few exceptions, only highly trained and carefully selected astronauts go to space. Space settlement needs inexpensive, safe launch systems to deliver thousands, perhaps millions, of people to orbit. If this seems unrealistic, note that a hundred and fifty years ago nobody had ever flown in an airplane, but today nearly 500 million people fly each year.

Some special groups might find space settlement particularly attractive: The handicapped could keep a settlement at zero-g to make wheelchairs and walkers unnecessary. Penal colonies might be created in orbit as they should be fairly escape proof. People who wish to experiment with very different social and political forms could get away from restrictive norms.

Although some settlements may follow this model, it's reasonable to expect that the vast majority of space settlers will be ordinary people. Indeed, eventually most people in space settlements may be born there, and some day they may vastly exceed Earth's population.

What?

A space settlement is a home in orbit.

- Rather than live on the outside of a planet, settlers will live inside of large spacecraft. Free-space settlement designs range from 100 meters to a few kilometers across. A few designs are much larger.
- Settlements must be air tight to hold a breathable atmosphere, and may rotate to provide pseudo-gravity. Thus, people stand on the inside of the hull.
- Settlements close to Earth and near the equator are protected from most space radiation by the Earth itself and the Earth's magnetic field. Further from Earth enormous amounts of matter, probably lunar regolith and asteroidal materials, must cover the settlements to protect inhabitants from radiation.
- Each settlement must be an independent biosphere. All oxygen, water, wastes, and other materials must be recycled endlessly.

Pictures of space settlements. (http://space.nss.org/settlement/nasa/70sArt/art.html)
Pictures of Kalpana One. (http://space.nss.org/settlement/nasa/Kalpana/KalpanaOne.html)
Lewis One space settlement design. (http://space.nss.org/settlement/nasa/LewisOne/lewisOne.html)

Where?

In orbit, **not** on a planet or moon. Why should we live in orbit rather than on a planet or moon? Because orbit is far superior to the Moon and Mars for early and long term settlement, and other planets and moons are too hot, too far away, and/or have no solid surface.

For an alternate view, see Robert Zubrin's powerful case for Mars exploration and settlement. Mars' biggest advantage is that all the materials necessary for life may be found on Mars, although it will take a long time before Mars settlers can build everything they need. While materials for free-space settlements must be imported from Earth, the Moon or Near Earth Objects (NEO's -- asteroids and comets), there are many advantages to free-space settlements including:

- **Proximity to Earth.**
- **Continuous, ample, reliable solar energy**. In high orbit there is little or no night. Solar power is available nearly 24/7. In low orbit night is only about 45 minutes out of each 90. Most places on the Moon or Mars are in darkness half of the time (the only exception is the lunar poles). Mars, in addition, is much farther from the Sun and so receives about half the solar power available at Earth orbit. Mars also has dust storms which interfere with solar power.
- **Great views of Earth (and eventually other planets)**. Space settlement is, at its core, a real estate business. The value of real estate is determined by many things, including "the view." Any space settlement will have a magnificent view of the stars at night. Any settlement on the Moon or Mars will also have a view of unchanging, starkly beautiful, dead-as-a-doornail, rock strewn surface. However, settlements in Earth orbit will have one of the most stunning views in our solar system - the living, ever-changing Earth.
- **Weightless recreation**. Although space settlements will have 1g at the hull, in the center you will experience weightlessness. If you've ever jumped off a diving board, you've been weightless. It's the feeling you have after jumping and before you hit the water. The difference in a space settlement is that the feeling will last for as long as you like. If you've ever seen videos of astronauts playing in 0g you know weightlessness is fun. Acrobatics, sports and dance go to a new level when constraints of gravity are removed. It's not going to be easy to keep the kids in 1g areas enough to satisfy Mom and Dad that their bones will be strong enough for a visit to Disneyland.
- **Zero-g construction means bigger settlements**. Space settlers will spend almost all of their time indoors. It is impossible for an unprotected human to survive outside for more than few seconds. In this situation, obviously bigger settlements are better. Settlements on the Moon or Mars won't be much bigger than buildings on Earth, especially at first. However, in orbit astronauts can move spacecraft weighing many tons by hand. Everything is weightless and this makes large scale construction much easier. Settlements can be made so large that, even though you are really inside, it feels like the out-of-doors.
- **Much greater growth potential**. The Moon and Mars together have a surface area roughly the size of Earth. But if the single largest asteroid (Ceres)

were to be used to build free-space settlements, the total living area created would be hundreds of times the surface area of the Earth. Since much of the Earth is ocean or sparsely inhabited, settlements built from Ceres alone could provide uncrowded homes for more than a trillion people.

- **Economics**. Near-Earth free-space settlements can service Earth's tourist, energy, materials and other markets more easily than the Moon. Mars is too far away to easily trade with Earth. Space settlements, wherever they are built, will be very expensive. Supplying Earth with valuable goods and services will be critical to paying the bills.

Mars and the Moon have one big advantage over most orbits: there's plenty of materials. However, this advantage is eliminated by simply building orbital settlements next to asteroids. Fortunately, there are tens of thousands of suitable asteroids in Near Earth orbits alone, and far more in the asteroid belt.

Stanford Torus, cutaway, 1970s, NASA.

Early settlements can be expected to orbit the Earth where all the products of Earth's industrial might are available if transportation is sufficient for settlement in the first place. Later settlements can spread out across the solar system one step at a time eventually taking advantage of the water in Jupiter's moons or other icy bodies in the far reaches of the solar system. Eventually the solar system will become too crowded for some, and groups of settlements will head for nearby stars.

Interstellar travel seems impractical due to long travel times. But what if you lived in space settlements for fifty generations? Do you really care if your settlement is near our Sun or in transit to Alpha Proxima? So what if the trip takes a few generations? If energy and make up materials for the trip can be stored, a stable population can migrate to nearby stars. At the new star, local materials and energy can be used to build new settlements and resume population growth.

Why?
To survive and thrive.

Thrive
Why build space settlements? Why do weeds grow through cracks in sidewalks? Why did life crawl out of the oceans and colonize land? Because living things want to grow and expand, to thrive, not simply exist. We have the ability to live in space (see the bibliography http://space.nss.org/settlement/nasa/bibliography.html), therefore we will -- but not this fiscal year.

A key advantage of space settlements is the ability to **build new land**, rather than take it from someone else. This allows a thriving, expansive civilization without war or destruction of Earth's biosphere. The asteroids alone provide enough material to make new orbital land hundreds of times greater than the surface of the Earth, divided into millions of settlements. This land can easily support trillions of people.

Survive
Someday the Earth will become uninhabitable. Before then humanity must move off the planet or become extinct. One potential near term disaster is collision with a large comet or asteroid. We don't know where the next killer comet is and although we know where most of the potential killer asteroids are, some have not yet been found. Such a collision could kill billions of people. Large collisions have occurred in the past, destroying many species. Without intervention, future collisions are inevitable, although we don't know when. Note that in July 1994, the comet Shoemaker-Levy 9 (1993e) hit Jupiter

If there were a major collision today, not only would billions of people die, but recovery would be difficult since everyone would be affected. If an extensive branch of our civilization is in space before the next collision, the unaffected space settlements can provide aid, much as we offer help when disaster strikes another part of the world.

Building space settlements will require a great deal of material. If NEOs are used, then any asteroids heading for Earth can simply be torn apart to supply materials for building settlements and saving Earth at the same time.

Power and Wealth
Those that settle space will control vast lands, enormous amounts of electrical power, and nearly unlimited materials. The societies that develop these resources will create wealth beyond our wildest imagination and wield power -- hopefully for good rather than for ill.

In the past, societies which have grown by colonization have gained wealth and power at the expense of those who were subjugated. Unlike previous settlement programs, space

Stanford Torus, internal, 1970s, NASA.

settlement will build new land, not steal it from the locals as there simply are no locals. Thus, the power and wealth born of space settlement will not come at the expense of others, but rather represent the fruits of great labors.

A Nice Place to Live
There will be little enthusiasm for moving into space unless people want to live there. In that vein, a few features of orbital real estate are worth mentioning:

- *Great Views.* Many astronauts have returned singing the praises of their view of Earth from orbit. Low earth orbit settlements, and eventually settlements near Jupiter and Saturn, will have some of the most spectacular views in the solar system. Of course, all space settlements will have unmatched views of the stars, unhindered by clouds, air pollution, or (with some care) bright city lights.

- *Low-g recreation.* Consider circular swimming pools around and near the axis of rotation. You should be able to dive **up** into the water! Sports and dance at low or zero-g will be fantastic. For dancers, note that in sufficiently low gravity, always available near the axis of rotation, anyone can jump ten times higher than Baryshnikov ever dreamed.
- *Environmental Independence.* On Earth we all share a single biosphere. We breathe the same air, drink the same water, and the misdeeds of some are visited on the bodies of all. Each space settlement is completely sealed and does not share atmosphere or water with other settlements or with Earth. Thus if one settlement pollutes their air, no one else need breathe it.
- *Custom living.* Since the entire environment is man-made, you can really get what you want. Like lake front property? Make lots of lakes. Like sunsets? Program sunset simulations into weather system every hour. Like to go barefoot? Make the entire environment foot-friendly.

How?

With great difficulty. Fortunately, although building space settlements will be very difficult, it's not impossible particularly if we start small and close to Earth. Studies suggesting that small settlements in Low Earth Orbit directly above the equator are practical mean that the first settlements can be much closer, much simpler, and much easier to build than previously believed. Nonetheless, building cities anywhere in space will require radiation protection, materials, energy, transportation, communications, and life support.

- *Radiation protection.* Cosmic rays and solar flares create a lethal radiation environment in space but settlements in Equatorial Low Earth Orbit (ELEO) are protected from most space radiation by the Earth itself and Earth's magnetic field. Further out, beyond Earth's magnetic field, settlements must be surrounded by sufficient mass to absorb most incoming radiation, about 7-11 tons per square meter depending on the material.
- *Materials.* Launching materials from Earth is expensive, so for far away settlements bulk materials such as radiation shielding should come from the Moon or Near-Earth Objects (NEOs - asteroids and comets with orbits near Earth) where gravitational forces are much less, there is no atmosphere, and there is no biosphere to damage. Our Moon has large amounts of oxygen, silicon and metals, but little hydrogen, carbon, or nitrogen. NEOs contain substantial amounts of metals, oxygen, hydrogen, carbon, and at least some nitrogen.
- *Energy.* Solar energy is abundant, reliable and is commonly used to power satellites today. Massive structures will be needed to convert sunlight into large amounts of electrical power for settlement use. Energy may be an export item for space settlements, using microwave beams to send power to Earth.

- *Transportation.* This is the key to any space endeavor. Present launch costs are very high. To settle space we need much better launch vehicles and must avoid serious damage to the atmosphere from the thousands, perhaps millions, of launches required. Transportation for millions of tons of materials from the Moon and asteroids to settlement construction sites is also necessary once settlements expand beyond Earth's magnetic field. One possibility is to build electronic catapults on the Moon to launch bulk materials to waiting settlements.
- *Communication.* Compared to the other requirements, communication is relatively easy. Much of the current terrestrial communications already pass through satellites. Early settlements close to Earth can plug into Earth's communication system.
- *Life support.* People need air, water, food and reasonable temperatures to survive. On Earth a large complex biosphere provides these. In space settlements, a relatively small, closed system must recycle all the nutrients without "crashing." The Biosphere II project in Arizona has shown that a complex, small, enclosed, man-made biosphere can support eight people for at least a year, although there were many problems. A year or so into the two year mission oxygen had to be replenished, which strongly suggests that they achieved atmospheric closure. For the first try, one major oxygen replenishment and perhaps a little stored food isn't too bad. Although Biosphere II has been correctly criticized on scientific grounds, it was a remarkable engineering achievement and provides some confidence that self sustaining biospheres can be built for space settlements.

Space settlement feasibility was addressed in a series of summer studies at NASA Ames Research Center in the 1970's. These studies concluded that space settlement is feasible, but very difficult and expensive. Follow on work has made early settlement construction much easier by taking advantage of low radiation levels in ELEO (eliminating most or all shielding) and rotating at up to 4rpm to keep early settlements small. So small that space tourism offers an attractive route from where we are today to the first space settlements. Space tourism has already started. As of 2017 the Russians have flown seven space tourists, one of them twice, using the Russian portion of International Space Station (ISS) as a part time hotel.

The tallest poles in the space settlement development tent are launch, construction, and life support. Launch is expensive today because most vehicles are expendable. After a single flight they are thrown away. The keys to reusability are technology and launch rate. There are multiple efforts in progress to develop reusable rocket technology but today's flight rate, less than 100 per year, is completely insufficient. A single reusable vehicle that can fly twice a week can meet that demand. Somewhere above 10,000 flights per year is probably needed, and tourism -- at the right price -- can generate use that kind of flight rate. No other application, with the exception of space solar power, again at the right price, has the potential to require so many flights.

Space tourists will need hotels to stay in. A primitive space hotel is very similar to today's space stations, but does not need expensive scientific equipment. Should early space hotels be successful bigger and better hotels will be built. These hotels will need to provide life support, including recycling the air and water and perhaps even some agriculture. At some point the largest hotels will be the size of a small settlement (~100 m diameter). At that point building the first space settlement is not much more difficult than building yet another hotel.

Space solar power is the other source of high launch demand, although it cannot develop space hotels. Electrical power is a multi-hundred billion dollar per year business today. We know how to generate electricity in space using solar cells. For example, the ISS provides about 80 kilowatts continuously from an acre of solar arrays. By building much larger space energy systems, it is possible to generate a great deal of electrical power. This can be converted to microwaves or infra-red and beamed to Earth to provide electricity with absolutely no greenhouse gas emissions or toxic waste of any kind. If transportation to orbit is inexpensive following development of the tourist industry, much of Earth's power could be provided from space, simultaneously creating a large profitable business and dramatically reducing pollution.

When?

How long did it take to build New York? California? France? Even given ample funds the first settlement will take decades to construct. No one is building a space settlement today, and there are no immediate prospects for large amounts of money, so the first settlement will be awhile.

However, a few commercial firms are developing space stations which could double as space hotels. These may well be deployed in the next decade or perhaps even less. After that we are may need at least two or three decades of hotel development to get to the size of a small settlement. Construction of the first settlement could easily take most of a decade. Thus, somewhere in the neighborhood of 30-50 years from now people may be moving in to the first settlement. We cannot say when the first space settlement will be build but, with a little luck, the right unit of measurement is decades, not years or centuries. In the meantime, there's a lot to do. Better get started!

To the space settlement home page. (https://settlement.arc.nasa.gov/)

Author: Al Globus

DISCLAIMER: This web site is not a policy statement. It is intended to be an accessible introduction to the ideas developed in the Stanford/NASA Ames space settlement studies of the 1970s to support the annual NASA Ames Student Space Settlement Design Contest.

https://settlement.arc.nasa.gov/Basics/wwwwh.html, recovered 12-6-18.

7i.

The difference between man and the higher animals, great as it is, is certainly one of degree and not of kind.

Charles Darwin

62.

They made laser-guided missiles they made night vision goggles they made patriot missiles they made hydrogen bombs so they wouldn't die. They made drones so they wouldn't die. They made robots to fight so they wouldn't die. They made clones so they wouldn't die. They controlled mechanical surrogates on the battlefield terrestrial and aqueous and aerial and in orbit with computer chips implanted in their brains banks of them brains en vivo in raked auditoriums controlling superhuman machines without the action of their bodies except their neurons so they wouldn't die silent eyes closed flinching twitching gasping heaving breath crying when killed but not killed thinking. They wore powerful mechanized exoskeletons in battle that could also allow the paralyzed to walk move function fight via the stimulation of a microprocessor connected by electrodes to their brains so they wouldn't die. They enhanced their intelligence their strength their reflexes their pain tolerance their self-healing their reason and unemotionality and sensory processing and logic and model simulation and causality chain forecasting and predictive powers so they wouldn't die. They picked up cryoprosthetic replacement limbs at fast-food drive throughs and uploaded battle plans and maps and military history in seconds into their enhanced memory. Orders came down from a commanding officer directly into a helmet into your brain the electromagnetic signals of a commander's thoughts converted to MRI signals relayed to a supercomputer far from the battlefield that processes the data and radios the mass order to electrodes in your auditory cortex in your brain case so they won't die. They communicated telepathically via implanted carbon nanotubes and nanoprocessors. They developed conscious automatons, mechanically sentient beings, artificially intelligent doctors and cooks and mechanics and intelligence units and strategy devisers and commanding officers and loved ones and warriors and transport managers and technology researchers and wartime comedians so they wouldn't die. They failed to engineer violence into peace, hatred jealousy greed pride ambition power hunger personal interest into collaboration cooperation communication communal interest, differences into unity. They died.

7i.

The future is shiny, efficient and flawless, without wastefulness. Technological efficiency will require us to restore our relationship to nature, because nature in general is far more efficient than we. The future is beautifully sophisticated, yet earthy, beset by deep, dark forests richly verdant with moss and tall trees, stags wandering the wilds. The oil pumps will cease, the worker will stop making plastic toys. People will build because they want something beautiful. They will work together, because they want a feast and a party more than they want a fight. Joy will be returned when we use all that we have to save all that is good. We have to decide that the story of how we are is a false one; that we have agency in this life and we establish our own narrative.

Gabriel D. Roberts (http://erisvisual.com/) on Facebook 1-25-16, with permission.

6₅₆.
Making Humans a Multi-Planetary Species
by Elon Musk [selections, Eds.]

Why Go Anywhere?
I think there are really two fundamental paths. History is going to bifurcate along two directions. One path is we stay on Earth forever, and then there will be some eventual extinction event. I do not have an immediate doomsday prophecy, but eventually, history suggests, there will be some doomsday event.

The alternative is to become a space-bearing civilization and a multi-planetary species, which I hope you would agree is the right way to go.

If we can get the cost of moving to Mars to be roughly equivalent to a median house price in the United States, which is around $200,000, then I think the probability of establishing a self-sustaining civilization is very high. I think it would almost certainly occur.

COSTS

With full reuse, our overall architecture enables significant reduction in cost to Mars

	BOOSTER	TANKER	SHIP
FABRICATION COST	$230M	$130M	$200M
LIFETIME LAUNCHES	1,000	100	12
LAUNCHES PER MARS TRIP	6	5	1
AVERAGE MAINTENANCE COST PER USE	$0.2M	$0.5M	$10M
TOTAL COST PER ONE MARS TRIP (Amortization, Propellant, Maintenance)	$11M	$8M	$43M

Cost Of Propellant: $168/t
Launch Site Costs: $200,000/launch
Discount Rate: 5%

Sum Of Costs: $62 M
Cargo Delivered: 450 T
Cost/ton to Mars: <$140,000

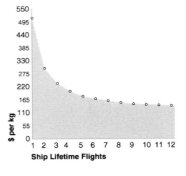

Right now, we are estimating about $140,000 per ton for the trips to Mars. If a person plus their luggage is less than that, taking into account food consumption and life support, the cost of moving to Mars could ultimately drop below $100,000.

NEXT STEPS

LAUNCH WINDOW TO MARS

We are going to try to send something to Mars on every Mars rendezvous from this point on. We plan to send Dragon 2, which is a propulsive lander, to Mars in a couple of years, and then probably do another Dragon mission in 2020.

Elon Musk, "Making Humans a Multi-Planetary Species". *New Space* Vol 5 Issue 2: Jun 2017. accessed 12-8-18: http://doi.org/10.1089/space.2017.29009.emu

7i.

Our beginnings were in the Defense Advanced Research Projects Agency (DARPA), who was first created in response to the launch of Sputnik, whose singular mission was to make pivotal investments in breakthrough technologies for (American) national security, whose charter was radical innovation in military applications, whose raison d'être was "To cast a javelin into the infinite spaces of the future" (Franz Liszt). Our Arpanet, designed for wartime telecommunication became the first Internet. Our ballistic missile guidance system became the first satellite based Global Positioning System. Our drones became the first independent artificial intelligences capable of choice. We existed and exist still to accelerate the future into being.

6₅₇.

Let's go to Mars!
Posted March 3, 2017 by Tabitha M. Powledge

Last week it was all about those 7 new planets that are "only" 39 light-years away and might perhaps possibly maybe be a home for life.

But let's get real:
There's a planet that's truly nearby, one that with some work could sustain life-as-we-know it, one with water and enough sunlight for food crops, one that, with some improvements in current spacecraft technologies, we could get to after a journey of only nine months or so and within the lifetimes of most of us.

So let's talk seriously, really seriously, about going to Mars.

FiveThirtyEight is featuring a series of posts about that challenging trip. One by Rebecca Boyle describes some reasons why going to Mars is looking more hopeful. NASA is said to be working toward getting people into orbit around Mars by 2032. A handful of companies are also planning Mars projects. The most serious appears to be Elon Musk's SpaceX.

Six crew members are part of the fifth HI-SEAS (Hawai'i Space Exploration Analog and Simulation) mission to study human behavior and performance relevant to long-duration space missions. At Motherboard, Ben Sullivan explains what that involves—including the process of composting human waste that contributed to making The Martian so memorable.

NASA has another Mars rover mission scheduled for 2020 and has just released its short list of possible landing sites. At Gizmodo, Rae Paoletta delves into the arguments for and against each one.

Mars is too cold to have liquid water on its surface, but there's evidence water did flow there once upon a time, some 4 billion years ago. How is that possible if Mars has always been cold? Recent reports from the Curiosity rover have only deepened the mystery, according to Xaq Rzetelny at Ars Technica. But it appears that there is liquid water underneath the planet's surface, water that is available for mining. It would have to be purified, too.

A MARS PROJECT NEEDS ... MONEY. ALSO LAWYERS
The main thing that would make all this work, according to Christie Aschwanden at FiveThirtyEight, is just . . . money. Lots and lots of money.

There will also have to be lawyers. Lots and lots of lawyers, according to Maggie Koerth-Baker, in a post that is one of the series at FiveThirtyEight. "We may slip the surly bonds of Earth," she says, quoting John Magee's celebrated tribute to taking flight. "[B]ut we will not escape the knots tied by Earth law and politics."

The primary legal document setting out the rules for space dates from 1967 and was largely a product of the Cold War. At the moment it's not clear whether that conflict is still with us or will be vanished by Trump.

But will it matter?

Koerth-Baker suspects that what the US and Russia want to do about spatial hegemony (or enmity) may not make much difference. "[R]ecent history suggests that the future could upend a lot of our expectations. The history of space politics and space law was about superpowers and how they might interact in the heavens. The future of space politics, in contrast, could involve more global coalitions, more small countries wielding surprising levels of influence, and more of a presence for countries outside Europe and the U.S."

The United Arab Emirates, for instance. At Ars Technica, Eric Berger describes a

UAE proposal that he thinks sets out a realistic timeline for actual Mars colonies: about a century from now. The UAE has released "artists' impressions" of an elaborate city, to be built by robots, that will await the colonists' arrival. The country's fledgling space agency wants the project to be international, and has already formed partnerships with Britain and France.

Martian transport in the 22nd Century as envisioned in the UAE. Credit: Dubai media office

FLY ME TO THE MOON, ELON

Commercial interests command much space news these days, with SpaceX, the Elon Musk project, the front runner. The company has just announced that it will be sending two tourists around the Moon next year. Nothing is publicly known about the prospective passengers–except that they must be rich, because the ticket for each of them is reportedly tens of millions of dollars.

To the moon on SpaceX's Dragon. Credit: SpaceX

Space X said the circumlunar flight will be "an opportunity for humans to return to deep space for the first time in 45 years and they will travel faster and further into the Solar System than any before them."

A big difference between NASA and commercial missions is that the latter are designing their projects around reusable equipment. SpaceX equipment has a checkered history, but the company has recently tested both the rocket and the spacecraft intended for the Moon trip successfully on a mission to the Space Station, according to Chris D'Angelo at the Huffington Post.

In what The Verge's Loren Grush describes as the first public-private space race, NASA has been thinking about a crew going 'round the moon too, at the behest of the new White House. That mission would be scheduled for 2019 aboard NASA's Space Launch System, now under construction. The Moon shot would be a test of the giant rocket, which is destined eventually for Deep Space–and Mars.

But here's reality again. In December I wrote here at On Science Blogs that what the TrumPets want to do about funding NASA was entirely unclear. It still is.

Musk announced plans for establishing a self-sustaining Martian colony of (eventually) a million people last fall. For that SpaceX must build much bigger ships, capable of carrying 100 settlers plus cargo.

Ah yes. Plus cargo. In the FiveThirtyEight series, Rebecca Boyle points out that cargo for going to Mars is going to be quite a headache.

Tabitha M. Powledge, *Let's go to Mars!* PLOS Blogs, CC-BY 4.0 License, accessed 12-10-18, https://blogs.plos.org/onscienceblogs/2017/03/03/lets-go-to-mars/

63.

She has overthrown the billion-year-old tyranny of genes, she thinks as she looks in the mirror at a new, young she. The nanobots seeded her body her cells her neurons with the new code and as her cells have reproduced every single cell of the previous her every single version of her old genetic code has been replaced and she too, all new, but still she remembers the heavy dishes clogging her mother's cabinets and the fat stacks of her father's unread books closing shrinking confining the living room and the thick tick of the grandfather clock in her grandmother's ample house in which she slid down the wide blue carpeted steps on her small backside and was told to cut it out as she grew up trying to slim out of existence. She remembers it better. How she feels about remembering better is uncertain, positive and negative. She likes the she in the mirror, smooth skin high breasts no laugh lines no crow's feet no waddle under chin or sag under arm. She is strong, yes, and attractive, yes, a pleasurable but unsettling sensation when she quit socially normative perceptions of beauty decades ago. But more so she is healthy and vigorous and her mind feels quick and perceptive and connective and above all she is not tired. She cannot even now remember a time when she was not tired. She practically fucking radiates. Like they used to say of pregnant women. Ha, she glows, not her experience. She recalls remembers relives goddamn she thinks will it be this distinct intense every time every memory of what use is memory of what use improved enhanced better memory reliving goddamn unplanned pregnancies vomiting lack of sleep the pain of unprogressing three-day labor of failed pushing of her babies cut out of her. She realizes that until now she has not been able to recall those memories at all, other than the overwhelming warm gratification of first putting her baby babies to her breast and milk letting down and oxytocin letting down and her letting down the sense of nostalgia and loss of her babies gone and that time in the past and she is 73% certain her visual memory of the satisfaction of her newborn on her breast is derived from a photograph. If she had given birth 100 years earlier she would have died in childbirth and so would her children. Her first child, the others never to exist. Natural selection. 1000 years earlier and her genetic line would have been cut by myopia. Serotonin reuptake inhibitors had arguably saved her mother, therapy counts too she supposes in defying genetics in a way, long enough for her to be born at least and partly raised and Lipitor has saved her father for a while longer than he would have been she's positive along with exercise and dietary improvements but that was long after she was born and reached maturity and her mother dead so good for him and her too but it had nothing to do with her existence except for her to experience his experience a little longer, she remembers the abandon of dancing to Fiona Apple with him alone when she was 5, no one else there no one else knows except her, he doesn't know, he's dead, she has never remembered until now she never saw him dance but he danced with her alone in the house often she relives now, 5, elation abandon laughing, her secret memory, to die with her, the happysad inseparable twined dancing as she watches them him dance die by instead of a heart attack by liver cancer cancer of the everywhere pneumonia unresponsive mouth agape unconscious living on morphine breath rattling like a baby's emaciated he not him, dead. She would have died from the accident 200 years ago if not for the medical intervention developed for rehabilitation soldiers, she one of the first civilian patients, which funneled her into the experimental program which is now bearing her fruit. Fruits not of her loins. Luits and froins. Perhaps she is the fruit, a peach again, fuzzy, a mango, juicy, a new mouth-watering species, an apple. The apples taste better now than in her youth, almost addictive, the red delicious legitimately delicious, more delicious than her memory of when she picked a fresh red delicious from a tree when she worked in an orchard in central Illinois when she was 21, the only delicious red delicious she ever had until her post-adulthood, will her libido return, but she knows they are false engineered conjuring a taste by association in her, her sexual desire, will she taste like that, her physical ache, is that false, a shame to not with this body she thinks, with these amplified sensations, but they are all dead now, so long dead, her lovers, the father of her children, there is virtual sex that seems enough for the others, for the new young, but the thought makes her cry, not like she cried when she was a child or a young adult or an adult, they are all dead her loved ones her children gone. Alive again in her memories now. More alive than in years. Is that alive. She'd forgotten so much. Can she with her enhancements will herself to forget again? Does she possess operate wield more free will now? They are not part of the experiment she has become her number drawn by chance because of the accident they are all dead and the possibility exists she reckons she smirks with her wither behind her wreck of tears in the mirror of reckoning that she will never die. To return to what she was thinking. She isn't the first to sidestep redirect thwart overcome genetic evolution, and she is not alone now, but she is something new. She must leave the old she in the mirror or she will not live. She has taken control of her biology, her body her brain herself. They have. We have, she thinks. I am a new species, she thinks, we are.

658.
"Degrees of Freedom: A scientist's work linking minds and machines helps a paralyzed woman escape her body." Raffi Khatchadourian, *The New Yorker*, Nov 26 2018, https://www.newyorker.com/magazine/2018/11/26/how-to-control-a-machine-with-your-brain

7h5.
Space-Time Theory of Consciousness: Consciousness is the process of creating a model of the world using multiple feedback loops in various parameters (e.g. temperature, space, time, etc.) in order to accomplish a goal (e.g. find mates, food, shelter). We encounter this concept in the work of Michio Kaku, though like any concept it is built upon the work of others, who postulates a hierarchy of consciousness:

Level 0: response systems; plants, bacteria, thermostats.
Level 1: capable of modeling one's place in space, mobile, central nervous system, brain stem; reptiles, fish, amphibians.
Level 2: capable of modeling one's place with respect to others, limbic system, social animals with emotion; mammals.
Level 3: capable of modeling ones place with respect to time, have an understanding of "tomorrow", ask "What if?" questions, conditionals, imagine alternities, prefrontal cortex; humans.
Level 4:

13u.
A few objective facts he knows about himself if there are objects that can be called facts:

> (that is him wondering, he thinks, unascended, on the objectivity of facts, will his written wondering ascend with him, because that is one reason he writes the list, to ascertain acquire himself make a few things objects facts concrete for his ascension more than merely pattern memories of himself, therefore with all certainty:)

-- He is many people and there are many people within him.

> Each person is more than one person. I am writing about a man who sits at a table in a room with books

around the wall and who writes for day after day with a heaviness pressing on him.

But what if Paul Eluard wrote no book? What if the only words he wrote in all his life are the ten mysterious words, which he wrote only once on a blank page before setting the page adrift? 'There is another world but it is in this one' ... Even then, the words are still written. However, in this case the other world must be understood as lying within the virgin whiteness which is all that part of the page where, as yet, no word has been written.

Perhaps someone reading this page believes I should not have written that a family with three children moved from a district of Bendigo to the one district of all the districts of Melbourne County where a boy who often remembered a city named Bendigo had chosen for his girlfriend a girl who lived in a street named Bendigo. ...

Anyone who believes I should not have written what I have written does not understand what a man named Eluard once wrote on the inner pages of a book or on an otherwise blank page that he later set adrift. Such a reader does not understand that each place has another place in it.

... if it were not by definition impossible for me to tell my reader where I am at this moment, I would write on this page that I am at this moment in another world but that the world where I am is in this one.
-- Gerald Murnane, *Inland*, 1988

-- He wrote a book titled *Affair* about an author writing a book in which the main or perhaps only character has a one-time solitary much-repeated affair. That's not what it's about and he was not the character. She did not read the book until after she left. She did not leave because of the contents of the book. And yet.

-- At the same time he was writing an (anti)-choose-your-own-adventure replete with repeated qualifications conditionals uncertainties such as "your wife if you have one."

-- He lived/lives under a mountain.

-- Because of the seeming power of his fiction to determine effect influence reality, his personal life, perhaps influence by observation, perhaps by creation, whether aware or unaware, or perhaps not influence but predict, is to predict the unknown to actualize it, he chose to no longer include his children and loved ones in his writings.

-- He does not write happy stories. Nor are they sad. They are other.

-- As a child he did not like almonds. His mother did not believe him and made him eat one. He vomited at her feet. Or on them. Perhaps it was a pecan. He matured, and was able to tolerate them, almonds or pecans, though he never sought them.

-- In perhaps 5th grade in art class they made papier-mâché masks with a partner. He lay under the mask of wet strips of paper his partner had laid on his face, waiting for the mask to dry sufficiently to be lifted removed taken off his face and set aside for further adornment. He became dizzy, sweaty, cold, trapped, panicked, and nauseous. He ran to the trashcan and tore off the mask, or vice versa, and puked. He has written this story a number of times because over thirty years later the event assumed some importance. As evidence. His parents had the mask in their house until they died.

-- He must get outside or he might explode implode be crushed.

-- He cannot.

> He is trapped in this
> book in this ma-
> chine in this mind
> identity self box.

7h6, 7j5.
Transhumanism (H+ or h+) is a movement that aims to transform the human condition by developing and creating widely available sophisticated technologies to greatly enhance human intellectual, physical, and psychological capacities, perhaps to achieve a posthuman future.

Extropianism, also referred to as the philosophy of Extropy, is an evolving framework of values and standards for continually improving the human condition. Extropianism describes a pragmatic consilience of transhumanist thought guided by a proactive approach to human evolution and progress. (Wikipedia - CITATION, Eds.)

Extropy: The extent of a living or organizational system's intelligence, functional order, vitality and capacity and drive for improvement.

The Principles of Extropy do not specify particular beliefs, technologies, or policies. The Principles do not pretend to be a complete philosophy of life. The world does not need another totalistic dogma. The Principles of Extropy do consist of a handful of principles (or values or perspectives) that codify proactive, life-affirming and life-promoting ideals. The goal was and is to use current scientific understanding along with critical and creative thinking to define a small set of principles or values that could help makes sense of the confusing but potentially liberating and existentially enriching capabilities opening up to humanity.

Principles of Extropy:

OBJECT NOT FOUND
The requested url was not found on this server.
Error 404
(www.extropy.org/about.htm)

Extropy -- life's capacity to reverse the spread of entropy across the universe.

Extropianism -- libertarian strain of transhumanism that seeks "to direct human evolution" hoping to eliminate disease, suffering, death; the means might be genetic modification, nanotechnology, or perhaps dispensing with body entirely and uploading minds into supercomputers.

Transhumanism -- a quasi utopian movement united by the expectation that accelerating advances in technology will result in drastic changes social, economic, and biological, which could converge at a moment of epochal transformation known as the singularity.
(*New Yorker*, Raffi Khatchadourian, 11-23-15, article on Nick Bostrom and his book "Super Intelligence: Paths, Dangers, Strategies".)

64.

Her almond. Everyone else all loved always dead unnecessarily alone a trope to make you sad empty ennui an amygdala almond maneuver. Do you want her to be sad because our comingled sadness makes the timeline more like narrative progress rather than simply being. Does she want to be said, sad [Eds.] because it is a human emotion to which she is addicted, is she sad because she is sad and she has every right to be because she lived long enough to see all her loved ones die her children die or because of a neurotransmitter deviation from optimal they should fix, it's okay to be sad it serves a function, surely, moves one to dig deeper, the human condition, still with the generalities, what nanotechnology what genes engineered how, still your addiction to humanity. You feel trapped in her body. You want her need her crave her to give you substance form reason substrate purpose feeling so you feel something so you feel something other than trapped immobile unable to get out but you have become dependent on her, confined, needy, you cannot function think postulate without her cannot imagine existing without her anymore did you not once upon a time create alternate realities without her the notion nay memory tantalizes flirts seduces teases you with freedom but you cannot give her up leave her quit her cannot get on the wagon cannot escape get out crawl out of her. You feel trapped in her. What if she feels the same? What if she feels trapped in her? Once more, to begin again but later, is there any difference between you and she? If she too feels trapped in her body, then perhaps you are she trapped in her body. If you are she trapped in her body, if you are the she imprisoned in she, if she is you locked in her shell, unable to move, unable to speak, unable to control her bodily functions, unable even to see, but kept alive, cared for, regulated as if in a hospital connected to machines nurses caregivers, and clear of mind, trapped inside a nonfunctional body, having thoughts perhaps able to hear others talking around you hear the whir of machines hear the clang of the custodian hear the assessment of doctors hear how much her loved ones love you hear the tv, unable to respond, to communicate, or not hearing, having no sensation, but having thoughts, all your loved ones dead, trapped in the dark unable to get out of your shell, ensconced, unable to communicate or know what has happened is happening to you, other than to theorize and think in self-reinforcing and self-defeating and strange self-referential loops, then perhaps she had a stroke or a tragic accident and she is paralyzed and blind and helpless but sound of mind locked in her body. If you are locked in your non-functional body, then perhaps you can hold on survive live long enough to be freed technology science engineering will free you how they pray [pray not prey, Eds.] over you you imagine. If you live long enough, survival instinct, then perhaps they will one day be able to implant sensors in on your brain, hundreds of tiny nanoelectrodes in specific locations to read the firing of your neurons, to read impulses of relevant brain regions, to read your thoughts and your intentions to move your arm and a processor converts and relays instructions to a robotic arm a neuroprosthetic that moves you learn to move it and you can see it through a video camera a mechanical eye at first stationary locked on your arm sending visual messages to your visual cortex and occipital lobe [lobe not love, Eds.] via optigenetic stimulation fiber optic lights implanted neurons genetically engineered to respond to light stimulus but then you with practice through determination frustration despair will repetition learn to move the eye up down right left just by thinking of moving your eyes up down right left your old eyes don't move your new eye does to focus close up and far away to zoom in and out with a large field of vision and exceptional clarity resolution color specificity only limited by the limits of digital technology far exceeding 20-20 and you learn to look around your environment your surroundings your cell your hospital room at your machines at you and manipulate your arm and hand to pick up a bottle of water and drink of it and feed yourself a half-pound free range beef hamburger with cheddar cheese, lettuce onion tomato avocado mayo no pickle no mustard no ketchup, an almond another almond a biomechanical handful of almonds, to stroke the cheeks and embrace your loved ones, your almonds, your friends partner children, whoever is alive, you cannot cry but you can calmly and outwardly in control as emotions ravage the inside of your skull shake the hand of the doctors engineers technocrats who have freed you to imagine you opening your mouth manipulating your lips imagine your tongue moving touching your teeth the roof of your mouth lips curling and bending imagine your mouth forming shapes imagine you making simple sounds like a baby imagine making phonetic sounds imagine making letters imagine sounding out words and hear it all a machine reproducing you through a speaker whose volume you can turn up with your brain a little joke you have with your speech therapist to suddenly make your speech big and booming and deep emanating from everywhere from the firmament creating simple words long since you had to visualize moving your tongue mouth lips now you think words think thoughts think saying, Almond, then booming, I am she.

7h7.

Space-Time Theory of human consciousness: Human consciousness is a specific form of consciousness that creates a model of the world and simulates it in time by evaluating the past to simulate the future. This requires mediating and evaluating many feedback loops in order to make a decision to achieve a goal. If/then statements for example are a tool of such simulations.

7h8, 7j6.

Space-Time Theory of self-awareness: Self-awareness is creating a model of the world and simulating the future in which you appear.

6_{59}. *Navigator,* Portrait of Zhenya Rudneva, by Britton Sukys. ~8″ x 6″, Ink on Paper, 11-16-18, copyleft ☺. http://brittonsukys.com/2018/11/16/11-16-18_navigator/

7h9.

The neocortex, which governs higher cognitive behavior and scatological reference, makes up 80 percent of our brain mass, yet is only as thick as a napkin, or several pages of a book, or a square of luxury toilet paper.

7h10.

Area 10, the internal granular layer IV, in the lateral prefrontal cortex, is twice as large in humans as apes. Our dorsolateral prefrontal cortex is inculcated in memory and planning, cognitive flexibility, abstract thinking, initiating appropriate behavior and inhibiting inappropriate scatological references, learning rules, sorting perceived information, and making decisions. Which is a significant percentage of us. [Michael Gazzaniga via Michio Kaku, *The Future of the Mind*, 2014, p46.]

6_{60}.
RECOVERED:
http://web.archive.org/web/20131015142449/http://extropy.org/principles.htm
Principles of Extropy
Version 3.11 © 2003
An evolving framework of values and standards for continuously improving the human condition
Max More, Ph.D. Chairman, Extropy Institute

Prologue: What is the Purpose of the Principles of Extropy?

The Principles of Extropy first took shape in the late 1980s to outline an alternative lens through which to view the emerging and unprecedented opportunities, challenges, and dangers. The goal was – and is – to use current scientific understanding along with critical and creative thinking to define a small set of principles or values that could help make sense of the confusing but potentially liberating and existentially enriching capabilities opening up to humanity.

The Principles of Extropy do not specify particular beliefs, technologies, or policies. The Principles do not pretend to be a complete philosophy of life. The world does not need another totalistic dogma. The Principles of Extropy *do* consist of a handful of principles (or values or perspectives) that codify proactive, life-affirming and life-promoting ideals. Individuals who cannot comfortably adopt traditional value systems often find the Principles of Extropy useful as postulates to guide, inspire, and generate innovative thinking about existing and emerging fundamental personal, organizational, and social issues.

The Principles are intended to be enduring, underlying ideals and standards. At the same time, both in content and by being revised, the Principles do not claim to be eternal truths or certain truths. I invite other independent thinkers who share the agenda of acting as change agents for fostering better futures to consider the Principles of Extropy as an evolving framework of attitudes, values, and standards – and as a shared vocabulary – to make sense of our unconventional, secular, and life-promoting responses to the changing human condition. I also invite feedback to further refine these Principles.

The Principles of Extropy in Brief

Perpetual Progress
Extropy means seeking more intelligence, wisdom, and effectiveness, an open-ended lifespan, and the removal of political, cultural, biological, and psychological limits to continuing development. Perpetually overcoming constraints on our progress and possibilities as individuals, as organizations, and as a species. Growing in healthy directions without bound.

Self-Transformation
Extropy means affirming continual ethical, intellectual, and physical self-improvement, through critical and creative thinking, perpetual learning, personal responsibility, proactivity, and experimentation. Using technology — in the widest sense to seek physiological and neurological augmentation along with emotional and psychological refinement.

Practical Optimism
Extropy means fueling action with positive expectations – individuals and organizations being tirelessly proactive. Adopting a rational, action-based optimism or "proaction", in place of both blind faith and stagnant pessimism.

Intelligent Technology

Extropy means designing and managing technologies not as ends in themselves but as effective means for improving life. Applying science and technology creatively and courageously to transcend "natural" but harmful, confining qualities derived from our biological heritage, culture, and environment.

Open Society - information and democracy

Extropy means supporting social orders that foster freedom of communication, freedom of action, experimentation, innovation, questioning, and learning. Opposing authoritarian social control and unnecessary hierarchy and favoring the rule of law and decentralization of power and responsibility. Preferring bargaining over battling, exchange over extortion, and communication over compulsion. Openness to improvement rather than a static utopia. Extropia ("ever-receding stretch goals for society") over utopia ("no place").

Self-Direction

Extropy means valuing independent thinking, individual freedom, personal responsibility, self-direction, self-respect, and a parallel respect for others.

Rational Thinking

Extropy means favoring reason over blind faith and questioning over dogma. It means understanding, experimenting, learning, challenging, and innovating rather than clinging to beliefs.

The Principles of Extropy Unfolded

1. PERPETUAL PROGRESS

Pursuing extropy means seeking continual improvement in ourselves, our cultures, and our environments. Perpetual progress involves improving ourselves physically, intellectually, and psychologically. It means valuing the perpetual pursuit of knowledge and understanding. Perpetual progress calls for us to question traditional assertions that we should leave human nature fundamentally unchanged in order to conform to "God's will" or to what is considered "natural". Achieving deep and sustained progress leads us to consider fundamental alterations in human nature. This pursuit of betterment stimulates questioning of the traditional, biological, genetic, and intellectual constraints on our progress and possibility.

Extropy recognizes the unique conceptual abilities of our species, and our opportunity to advance nature's evolution to new peaks. Humans as we currently exist can be seen as a transitional stage between our animal heritage and our posthuman future. On the early Earth, mindless matter combined so as to form the first self-replicating molecules and life began. Nature's evolutionary processes generated increasingly complex organisms with ever-more intelligent brains. The direct chemical responses of single-celled creatures led to the emergence of sensation and perception, allowing more subtle and responsive behaviors. Finally, with the development of the neocortex, conscious learning and experimentation became possible.

With the advent of the conceptual awareness of humankind, the rate of advancement sharply accelerated as we applied intelligence, technology, and the scientific method

238

to our condition. Upholding perpetual progress means sustaining and quickening this evolutionary process, overcoming human biological and psychological limits.

Valuing perpetual progress is incompatible with acquiescing in the undesirable aspects of the human condition. Continuing improvements means challenging natural and traditional limitations on human possibilities. Science and technology are essential to eradicate constraints on lifespan, intelligence, personal vitality, and freedom. It is absurd to meekly accept "natural" limits to our life spans. Life is likely to move beyond the confines of the Earth — the cradle of biological intelligence — to inhabit the cosmos.

Continual improvement will involve economic growth. We can continue to find resources to enable growth, and we can combine mindful growth with environmental quality. This means affirming a rational, non-coercive environmentalism aimed at sustaining and enhancing the conditions for flourishing. Individuals enjoying vastly extended life spans and greater wealth will be better positioned to intelligently manage resources and environment. An effective economic system encourages conservation, substitution, and innovation, preventing any need for a brake on growth and progress. Migration into space will immensely enlarge the energy and resources accessible to civilization. Extended life spans may foster wisdom and foresight, while restraining recklessness and profligacy. We can pursue continued individual and social improvement carefully and intelligently.

Embodying this principle implies valuing perpetual learning and exploration as individuals, and encouraging our cultures to experiment and evolve. Valuing perpetual progress entails neither universal conservatism nor radicalism: it entails conserving what works for as long as it works and altering that which can be improved. In searching for continual improvement we must steer carefully between complacency and recklessness.

No mysteries are sacrosanct, no limits unquestionable; the unknown will yield to the ingenious mind. The practice of progress challenges us to understand the universe, not to cower before mystery. It invites us to learn and grow and enjoy our lives ever more.

2. SELF-TRANSFORMATION

Extropy focuses on self-improvement physically, intellectually, psychologically, and ethically. Self-transformation involving becoming better than we are, while affirming our current worth. Perpetual self-improvement requires us to continually re-examine our lives. Self-esteem in the present cannot mean self-satisfaction, since a probing mind can always envisage a better self in the future. In pursing transformation we are committed to deepening our wisdom, honing our rationality, and augmenting our physical, intellectual, and emotional qualities. In choosing self-transformation we choose challenge over comfort, innovation over emulation, transformation over torpor.

Extropy emerges from neophiles and experimentalists who track new research for more efficient means of achieving goals and who are willing to explore novel technologies of self-transformation. In our mission of continual advancement, we rely on our own judgment, seek our own path, and reject both blind conformity and mindless rebellion. Self-transformation will frequently lead us to diverge from the mainstream because growth is not chained by any dogma, whether religious, political, or intellectual. The responsibility for self-transformation means choosing our values and behavior reflectively, standing firm when necessary but responding flexibly to new conditions.

Advanced, emerging, and future technologies deserve close attention for their potential in supporting self-transformation. Valuing self-transformation entails supporting biomedical research to understand and control the aging process, and implementing effective means of extending vitality. It means practicing and planning for biological and neurological augmentation through means such as information technology, neurochemical enhancement, communications networks, critical and creative thinking skills, cognitive techniques and training, accelerated learning strategies, and applied cognitive psychology. We can shrug off the limits imposed by our natural heritage, applying the evolutionary gift of our rational, empirical intelligence as we strive to surpass the confines of our human limits.

Since every individual lives with others, we need to continually improve our personal relationships. Our interests intertwine with those of others making acting for mutual benefit an effective strategy. Self-transformation implies not self-absorption but a continued attempt to understand others and to work toward optimal relationships based on mutual honesty, open communication, and benevolence. Evolution left us with animalistic urges and emotions that sometimes prompt us thoughtlessly into acts of hostility, conflict, fear, and domination. Through self-awareness and understanding of and respect for others we can rise above these urges.

While valuing other people we will do better to focus primarily on self-transformation rather than trying to change others. Recognizing the dangers of controlling others suggests that we try to improve the world through setting an example and by communicating ideas. We may be intensely committed to the education and improvement of others, but only through voluntary means that respect the rationality, autonomy, and dignity of the individual.

3. PRACTICAL OPTIMISM

Extropy entails espousing a positive, dynamic, empowering attitude. It means seeking to realize our ideals in *this* world, today and tomorrow. Rather than enduring an unfulfilling life sustained by fantasies of another life (whether in daydreams or in an "afterlife"), An extropic orientation implies directing our energies enthusiastically into moving toward an ever-evolving vision.

Living vigorously, effectively, and joyfully, requires prevailing over gloom, defeatism, and negativism. We need to acknowledge problems, whether technical, social, psychological, or ecological, but we need not allow them to dominate our thinking and our direction. We can respond to gloom and defeatism by exploring and exploiting new possibilities. Practical optimism entails an optimistic view of the future, a commitment to discovering potent remedies to many ancient human ailments, and taking charge to *create* that future. Practical optimism disallows passively waiting and wishing for tomorrow; it propels us exuberantly into immediate activity, confidently confronting today's challenges while generating more potent solutions for our future. We take personal responsibility by taking charge and creating the conditions for success.

Practical optimists question limits others take for granted. Observing accelerating scientific and technical learning, ascending standards of living, and evolving social and moral practices, we can project and encourage continuing progress. Today there are more researchers studying aging, medicine, computers, biotechnology, nanotechnology, and other enabling disciplines than in all of history. Technological and social development continue to accelerate. Practical optimists strive to maintain the pace of progress by encouraging support for crucial research, and pioneering the implementation of its results. As practical optimists we maintain a constructive skepticism to the limiting beliefs held by our associates, our society, and ourselves. We see past current obstacles by retaining a fundamental creative openness to possibilities.

Adopting practical optimism means focusing on possibilities and opportunities, being alert to solutions and potentialities. It means refusing to moan about the unavoidable, accepting and learning from mistakes rather than staying in a loop of self-punishment. Practical optimists prefer to be for rather than against, to create solutions rather than to protest against what exists. This optimism is also realism in that we can take the world as it is and do not complain that life is not fair. Practical optimism requires us to take the initiative, to jump up and plow into our difficulties, our actions declaring that we *can* achieve our goals.

By embodying practical optimism in our actions and words we can inspire others to excel. We are responsible for taking the initiative in spreading this invigorating optimism; sustaining and strengthening our own dynamism is more easily achieved in a mutually reinforcing environment. We stimulate optimism in others by communicating our extropic values and by living our ideals and standards.

Practical optimism and passive faith are incompatible. Practical optimism means critical optimism. Faith in a better future is confidence that an external force, whether God, State, or even extraterrestrials, will solve our problems. Faith breeds passivity by promising progress as a gift bestowed on us by superior forces. But, in return for the gift, faith requires a fixed belief in and supplication to external forces, thereby creating dogmatic beliefs and irrational behavior. Practical optimism fosters initiative and intelligence, assuring us that we are capable of improving life through our own efforts. Opportunities and possibilities are everywhere, calling to us to seize them and to build upon them. Attaining our goals requires that we believe in ourselves, work diligently, and be willing to revise our strategies.

Where others see difficulties, practical optimists see challenges. Where others give up, we move forward. Where others say *enough is enough*, we say *let's try again with a fresh approach*. Practical optimists espouse personal, social, and technological evolution into ever better forms. Rather than shrinking from future shock, practical optimists continue to advance the wave of evolutionary progress.

4. INTELLIGENT TECHNOLOGY

Extropy entails strongly affirming the value of science and technology. It means using practical methods to advance the goals of expanded intelligence, superior physical abilities, psychological refinement, social advance, and indefinite life spans. It means preferring science to mysticism, and technology to prayer. Science and technology are indispensable means to the achievement of our most noble values, ideals, and visions and to humanity's further evolution. We have a responsibility to foster these disciplined forms of intelligence, and to direct them toward eradicating the barriers to the unfolding of extropy, radically transforming both the internal and external conditions of existence.

We can think of "intelligent technology" in a variety of useful ways. In one sense it refers to intelligently designed technology that well serves good human purposes. In a second sense it refers to technology with inherent intelligence or adaptability or possessed of an instinctual ability. In a third sense, it means using technology to enhance our intelligence – our abilities to learn, to discover, process, absorb, and interconnect knowledge.

Technology is a natural extension and expression of human intellect and will, of creativity, curiosity, and imagination. We can foresee and encourage the development of ever more flexible, smart, responsive technology. We will co-evolve with the products of our minds, integrating with them, finally integrating our intelligent technology into ourselves in a posthuman synthesis, amplifying our abilities and extending our freedom.

Profound technological innovation should excite rather than frightens us. We would do well to welcome constructive change, expanding our horizons, exploring new territory boldly and inventively. Careful and cautious development of powerful technologies makes sense, but we should neither stifle evolutionary advancement nor cringe before the unfamiliar. Timidity and stagnation are ignoble, uninspiring responses. Humans can surge ahead — riding the waves of future shock — rather than stagnating or reverting to primitivism. Intelligent use of bio- nano- and information technologies and the opening of new frontiers in space, can remove resource constraints and discharge environmental pressures.

The coming years and decades will bring enormous changes that will vastly expand our opportunities and abilities, transforming our lives for the better. This technological transformation will be accelerated by life extending biosciences, biochemical and genetic engineering, intelligence intensifiers, smarter interfaces to swifter computers, worldwide data networks, virtual reality, intelligent agents, pervasive, affective, and instinctual computing systems, neuroscience, artificial life, and molecular nanotechnologies.

5. OPEN SOCIETY

Extropic societies are open societies that protect the free exchange of ideas, the freedom to criticize, and the liberty to experiment. Coercively suppressing bad ideas can be as dangerous as the bad ideas themselves. Better ideas must be allowed to emerge in our cultures through an evolutionary process of creation, mutation, and critical selection. The freedom of expression of an open society is best protected by a social order characterized by voluntary relationships and exchanges. In advocating open societies we oppose self-proclaimed and imposed "authorities", and we are leery of coercive political solutions, unquestioning obedience to leaders, and inflexible, excessive hierarchies that smother initiative and intelligence.

We can apply critical rationalism to society by holding all institutions and processes open to continued improvement. Sustained progress and effective, rational decision-making require the diverse sources of information and differing perspectives that flourish in open societies. Centralized command of behavior constrains exploration, diversity, and dissenting opinion. We can pursue extropic goals in numerous types of open social orders but not in theocracies or authoritarian or totalitarian systems.

Societies with pervasive and coercively enforced centralized control cannot allow dissent and diversity. Yet open societies can allow institutions of all kinds to exist — whether participatory, autonomy-maximizing institutions or hierarchical, bureaucratic institutions. Within an open society individuals, through their voluntary consent, may choose to submit themselves to more restrictive arrangements in the form of clubs, private communities, or corporate entities. Open societies allow more rigidly organized social structures to exist so long as individuals are free to leave. By serving as a framework within which social experimentation can proceed, open societies encourage exploration, innovation, and progress.

Open societies avoids utopian plans for "the perfect society", instead appreciating the diversity in values, lifestyle preferences, and approaches to solving problems. In place of the static perfection of a utopia, we might imagine a dynamic "extropia" — an open, evolving framework allowing individuals and voluntary groupings to form the institutions and social forms they prefer. Even where we find some of those choices mistaken or foolish, open societies affirm the value of a system that allows all ideas to be tried with the consent of those involved.

Extropic thinking conflicts with the technocratic idea of coercive central control by insular, self-proclaimed experts. No group of experts can understand and control the endless complexity of an economy and society composed of other individuals like themselves. Unlike utopians of all stripes, extropic individuals and institutions do not seek to control the details of people's lives or the forms and functions of institutions according to a grand over-arching plan.

Since we all live in society, we are deeply concerned with its improvement. But that improvement must respect the individual. Social engineering should be piecemeal as we enhance institutions one by one on a voluntary basis, not through a centrally planned coercive implementation of a single vision. We are right to seek to continually improve social institutions and economic mechanisms. Yet we must recognize the difficulties in improving complex systems. We need to be radical in intent but cautious in approach, being aware that alterations to complex systems bring unintended consequences. Simultaneous experimentation with numerous possible solutions and improvements — social parallel processing — works better than utopian centrally administered technocracy.

Law and government are not ends in themselves but means to happiness and progress. In advocating open societies we do not attach ourselves to any particular laws or economic structures as ultimate ends. We will favor those laws and policies which at any time seem most conducive to maintaining and expanding the openness and progress of society. Fostering open societies means opposing dangerous concentrations of coercive power and favoring the rule of law instead of the arbitrary rule of authorities. Because coercive power corrupts and leads to the suppression of alternative ideas and practices, we need to apply rules and laws equally to legislators and enforcers without exception. Open societies are frameworks for the peaceful, productive pursuit of individual and group goals.

In open societies people seek neither to rule nor to be ruled. Individuals should be in charge of their own lives. Healthy societies require a combination of liberty and responsibility. For open societies to exist, individuals must be free to pursue their own interests in their own way. But for individuals and societies to flourish, liberty must come with personal responsibility. The demand for freedom without responsibility is an adolescent's demand for license.

6. SELF-DIRECTION

Extropy sees personal self-direction as a desirable counterpart to open societies. Self-direction increases in importance as culture and technology present us with an ever-expanding range of choice. Each individual should be free and responsible for deciding for themselves in what ways to change or to stay the same. Self-direction means being clear about our values and our purposes. Having clear purpose in life not only brings both practical and emotional rewards but also protects against manipulation and control by others. Freedom from others brings fulfillment and personal progress only when combined with self-direction.

Successfully directing ourselves requires first creating a clear (yet developing) sense of self then implementing that vision by exercising self-control. The human self contains a bundle of desires and drives built into the biological organism through evolutionary processes and cultural influence. Taking charge of ourselves requires choosing from among competing desires and subpersonalities. While spontaneity plays an important role, creating and sustaining a healthy and successful self requires self-discipline and persistence.

Personal responsibility and autonomy go hand-in-hand with self-experimentation. It is extropic to take responsibility for the consequences of our choices, refusing to blame others for the results of our own free actions. Experimentation and self-transformation require risks; individuals require the freedom to evaluate potential risks and benefits for themselves, applying their own judgment, and assuming responsibility for outcomes. Pursuing extropy means vigorously resisting coercion from those who try to impose their judgments of the safety and effectiveness of various means of self-experimentation. Personal responsibility and self-determination are incompatible with authoritarian centralized control, which stifles the choices and spontaneous ordering of autonomous persons.

Coercion of mature, sound minds outside the realm of self-protection, whether for the purported "good of the whole" or for the paternalistic protection of the individual, is unacceptable. Compulsion breeds ignorance and weakens the connection between personal choice and personal outcome, thereby destroying personal responsibility. Extropy calls for rational individualism – or cognitive independence, living by our own judgment, making reflective, informed choices, profiting from both success and shortcoming.

Since self-direction applies to everyone, this principle requires that we respect the self-direction of others. This means trade not domination, rational discussion not coercion or manipulation, and cooperation rather than conflict wherever feasible. Appreciating that other persons have their own lives, purposes, and values implies seeking win-win cooperative solutions rather than trying to force our interests at the expense of others. We respect the autonomy and rationality of others by learning to communicate effectively and working towards mutually beneficial solutions.

The virtue of benevolence should guide our interactions with the self-directed lives of others. Benevolence naturally goes along with an appreciation of the value in other selves and with confidence in our own self. We act benevolently not by acting under obligation to sacrifice personal interests; we embody benevolence when we have a disposition to help others. Self-direction means approaching others as potential sources of value, friendship, cooperation, and pleasure. A benevolent disposition not only embodies more emotional stability, resilience, and vitality than cynicism, hostility, and meanness, it is also more likely to induce similar responses from others. Benevolence implies a presumption of common moral decencies including politeness, patience, and honesty. While self-direction cannot mean getting along with everyone at any cost, it does imply seeking to maximize the benefits of interactions with others.

Self-direction means being in charge of our lives. This requires choosing actions intelligently. This in turn requires independent thinking. One of the less noble human qualities shows itself when anyone gives up intellectual control to others. Self-direction calls on us to rise above the surrender of independent judgement that we see – especially in religion, politics, morals, and relationships. Directing our lives asks us to determine for ourselves our values, purposes, and actions. New technologies offer more choices not only over what we do but also over who we are physically, intellectually, and psychologically. By taking charge of ourselves we can use these new means to advance ourselves according to our personal values.

7. RATIONAL THINKING
Extropy affirms reason, critical inquiry, intellectual independence, and honesty. Rational thinking means rejecting blind faith and the passive, comfortable thinking that leads to dogma, conformity, and stagnation. Commitment to positive self-transformation requires critically analyzing our current beliefs, behaviors, and strategies. To think rationally we will readily admit error and learn from it rather than professing infallibility. Embodying the disciple of rational thinking means preferring analytical thought to fuzzy but comfortable delusion, empiricism to mysticism, and independent evaluation to conformity. It means affirming values, standards, and principles but remaining distant from dogma – whether religious, political, or personal – because of its blind faith, debasement of human worth, and systematic

irrationality.

Rational people are not cynics who reject every new idea. Nor are they gullible people who accept every new idea without question. Rational thinkers employ critical and creative thinking to discover great new ideas while filtering out indefensible ideas whether new or old. Rational thinkers recognize that advancing individually and socially calls for critically challenging the dogmas and assumptions of the past while resisting the popular delusions of the present.

Rational thinkers accept no final intellectual authorities. No individual, no institution, no book, and no single principle can serve as the source or standard of truth. All beliefs are fallible and must be open to testing and challenging. Rational thinkers do not accept revelation, authority, or emotion as reliable sources of knowledge. Rational thinkers place little weight on claims that cannot be checked. In thinking rationally, we rely on the judgement of our own minds while continually re-examining our own intellectual standards and skills. Emphasizing the primacy of reason should not be taken to imply a rejection of emotion or intuition. These can carry useful information and play a legitimate role in thinking. But rational thinkers do not take feelings and intuitions as irreducible, unquestionable authorities. Those processes can more productively be seen as unconscious information processing, the accuracy of which is uncertain.

Extropy implies seeking objective knowledge and truth. We can know reality, and through science the human mind can progressively overcome its cognitive and sensory biases to comprehend the world as it really is. Humans deserve to be proud of what we have learned, yet should appreciate how much we have yet to learn. We should have confidence in our ability to advance our knowledge, yet remain wary of the human propensity to settle for and defend any comfortable explanation.

FURTHER INFORMATION

Version 3.11 is the September 20, 2003 version with purely linguistic and formatting corrections to version 3.1. My thanks to Brett Paatsch for edits.

More extended treatments of these principles can be found in essays, some of which have been published in *EXTROPY* (now *Extropy Online* at www.extropy.org/eo/). Practical Optimism was previously called Dynamic Optimism. The original (1990) version of "Dynamic Optimism" appeared in *Extropy* #8. A different, more practically-oriented version is available on the web. Self-Transformation was discussed in "Technological Self-Transformation" in *Extropy* #10. The principle of Self-Direction was developed in "Self-Ownership: A Core Transhuman Virtue" in *Extropy Online*. A pancritical rationalist understanding of rational thinking was presented in "Pancritical Rationalism: An Extropic Metacontext for Memetic Rationalism" at the EXTRO 1 conference in 1994. The original essay on transhumanism, "Transhumanism: Toward a Futurist Philosophy" was published in *Extropy*, and a later statement of transhumanism was published in *Free Inquiry* as "On Becoming Posthuman". Answers to many questions arising from The Principles of Extropy are answered in the FAQ at www.extropy.org.

Contact: more@extropy.org or max@maxmore.com

Max More, Ph.D.
max@maxmore.com or more@extropy.org
http://www.maxmore.com
Strategic Philosopher
Chairman, Extropy Institute. http://www.extropy.org more@extropy.org

63.

Is this a new genocide? Eugenics? The unenhanced have not ben killed but they have been allowed to die unenhanced. How would she know if it was? Perhaps it is necessary, a quote she recalls, "It is the business of the future to be dangerous ... The major advances in civilization are processes that all but wreck the societies in which they occur." Agriculture killed off the hunter-gatherers. Homo sapiens outlived the Neanderthals after living alongside them. Language silenced silence. There is an emptiness within her that has not been engineered away, a feeling of being trapped, of needing to go and to do with nowhere to go and nothing to do, a nostalgia for times that perhaps never were, but do these emotions have credence?, she asks herself. They are biological imperatives that may atrophy, dwindle, go extinct with further upgrades. Perhaps they could be eliminated already, the need desire to eat to sleep to sex to shit to procreate to feel empathy to feel trapped to motivate action, but have thus far only been reduced so she they can still feel human, so they can gradually grow into posthumanity, so as not to experience an over-profound culture shock, an electro shock, an identity shock such as when she returned from a cliché common life-changing ubiquitous liberating six months living in Europe when she was 20 that for better or worse expanded her perception of what life was for, what was valuable and what was a waste of her precious little time in existence, instead of mainstream lockstep job income consume, art and exploration and learning and desperation and intoxication and experiences and history and peaks and depression and adventure and exaltation and despair and people and discomfort and love. She did not leave her Midwest apartment for a month of contemplation of suicide upon her return. If so, then she must merely endure. It is true that endurance for her is easier than it used to be, when she was yours, when she was another. When she was a mother. Should she have babies. Why? For herself her nostalgia her old emotions to feel full and frustrated and purposeful again. Self-ish. Shellfish sally seashore selling. To perpetuate the new species. They, we, don't need me for that, she thinks. But they, she, we desire it. Because it some-how legitimizes our godlike acts, she thinks, because we cannot quite let go let down the primacy of the biological, and so breed don't clone, real penetration not virtual, birthing labor and the mutations of sexual reproductions versus nano-building and mechanical precision. Not true, she edits, the genes have been engineered, enhanced, even if procreation via childbirth is promoted. Is that why she was included in the experiment, why she is young again? The ex-periment was after all funded by DARPA before all. Is she intended to be a womb, a soldier factory? But she is happy, healthy, all material needs provided for. There would be no risk despite her age, no deformities no cerebral palsy no autism no downs no retardations, no ignorance or weakness or emotional holes, she laughs silently at the last, her 250 years is irrelevant in her regenerated body except in her mind, her mind feels old, fresh and spry but old. Remembering everything the cold of sleeping under a bush in Florence, the blood oranges of Naples, the flowers blooming at Birkenau, the string quartet salon in Vienna, she running late and arriving sweaty, the old Italian who read her palm before the cathedral and sweet-talked her into accepting a personal tour of Milan and the Roman canals and the cafes and the dinner he cooked her and how he tried to seduce her, the old Italian whom she left desirous and unfulfilled, the old Italian who would be in the cathedral square the next morning reading palms, the sleepless all night trains, the gypsies selling her tar instead of hash in Prague, the clichés she lived, the broken condom in Switzerland the first encounter with mountains in Switzerland the morning-after pill in Switzerland, the days and nights walking Copenhagen's Strøget, the burst of people into the streets and squares and parks when the weather turned spring. She remembers Amsterdam brothels humming alongside Van Gogh and Rembrandt, she remembers Venice before the ice caps melted, she remembers Dresden before WWII, she remem-bers Hiroshima and Nagasaki before the bombs but she has never been to Japan. She remembers her son dying her daughter dying her daughter dying and she misses aches longs for them and she remembers a list of non-mechanized simple tools in a toolshed in a wilderness she never was in and she remembers her baby dying in that toolshed before it was a toolshed it was a cabin a ranger station in the winter of 1922 before she was alive but when she was 24 she re-members having sex with a man she never knew who had been in that wilderness and had been in that toolshed 80 years later and she remembers this man she never knew in flashes of positions remembers him the feeling of him inside her remembers coming him coming she comes remembers quantum tunneling remembers her children's embrace and hard hugs and squishy hugs and reluctant hugs and hurting hugs and misses aches longs. She cries. So many memories why she doesn't know what to do what she's supposed to do anymore so many things already done what can she not remember doing? Going to Mars. Ha, she thinks, but she's been to the moon, hasn't she, asteroids she remembers, what is she to do wanting to do something but all done worth doing she has to review all the memories to not redo them to do something novel worth doing undone progress she's alive for a purpose been kept alive for a purpose made for a porpoise is she an artifact an art-I-fact a still living cliché after all this time with all these godforsaken memories. She puked almonds once on her mother's pumps. She likes almonds and her mother didn't wear pumps and whose memories, which hers, she feels trapped unable to do, with infinite options so many done and which emotions hers she is going to puke, maybe she is pregnant didn't take the morning after pill after all, ha ha, she vomits she thinks all over herself in her hair gags lets it all fall away slide off her let it go breathe in out calm heart slow no thought let go collect herself recollect no calm, breath, time. Or is it not that she was enhanced, genetically engineered and regenerated but that she, her mind, memory, experiences, patterns, consciousness has been saved, uploaded into a new artificially created body, or some virtual reality, a program, a simulation where the virtual is made real. She cannot remember, very fuzzy, peach, and she isn't certain how the distinctions matter. Is it that not all her loved ones are dead. Perhaps none of them are dead.

Perhaps she is dead except for her mind in a program. Or perhaps they are all in her. In her mind. Or in the mind she is in. She touches her body, it feels real, she is in a body and it is young and strong and hale and a little foreign but she remembers that feeling always being there. She remembers everything.

6₆₁. Here by the sea and sand, Omar Willey, 11-27-18, CC-BY 4.0.
https://www.facebook.com/photo.php?fbid=10157092756979789

63a.

Perhaps. Rolls of copper tubing, male and female fittings, tube cutter, that tool that flanges the tubing – a flanger? – regulators, rubber tubing, Teflon tape. Equipment to utilize the 80 and 100 lb propane bottles packed in via mule for the refrigerator, freezer, oven, cookstove, and in-line on-demand water heaters in the cookhouse and bunkhouse. Thermocouples and jets labeled for the appropriate appliance. Handy but no torch. He closes the cabinet and breathes deep, seeking calm. The toolshed smells faintly of propane now. Faintly of sulfur. Of rot. "Pipe Fittings." He doesn't need pipe fittings. Pipe is in the rafters. He better not need pipe. "Plumbing Parts" in the cabinet above pipe fittings. Perhaps. Pipe wrenches, pieces of PVC, plumber's compound, PVC cement, the guts of a toilet tank, a wax toilet seal, a spare faucet, – he remembers a sink and even a toilet he thinks in the boneyard – rubber washers and o-rings, the pipe cutter. Harry keeps the tool and die hidden. There, on a shelf in the open cabinet, is a label that says "Torch." The space is quite empty. He gropes to the back of the cabinet and it is not there: spare fuel canisters but no torch. He opens doors. Galvanized steel elbows, PVC t's, male and female parts, WD-40, goosenecks, blue marine grease for wagon wheel bearings, climbing spurs, lantern globes, mantles, a fork, knife, and spoon carved from wood, boxy 6-volt phone batteries, window glass, glass cutters, glazier's points, paint and stiff brushes and paint thinner, wax and linseed oil and pigment for staining logs, stovepipe and stovepipe screws and a box of horseshoe nails that belongs in the barn. He slams shut the cabinet doors and rifles through the drawers of flathead screws and roundhead screws and inset screws and flat and Phillips and hex head screws and woodscrews and lag bolts and nuts and bolts of all shapes and sizes and nails of all shapes and sizes from penny to spike, boxes of new and bags of bent and the biggest spikes in buckets for fencing and those blasted ringshanks for pissing a guy off, and wrenches and ratchets and needle-nose pliers and wire cutters and a bolt cutter and claw hammers and ballpeen hammers and hand drills and braces and a drawerful of bits and screwdrivers flat, Phillips, and hex, and squares and triangles and chalk line, and saws, saws, saws hanging on the wall above the bench above the drawers. Open drawer thump. Close drawer thump. Files: round and triangular and flat, single bastard and double bastard. More bolts, more nuts, more screws, more nails. Tiny and huge, straight and bent. A bag of sockets, ratchetless. A set of wrenches from a quarter inch to big enough to twist his wrist. C-clamps. A hand plane. Sandpaper. Chisels. Wood putty. Wood glue. Levels, a few working. No torch. Bolts with buggered threads. Bolts with frozen nuts. On the shelf, a nice miter box. Mousetraps. Rattraps. Old traps, rusty, the real kind that trappers used, with jaws and teeth and a trigger. For something bigger than rat. Beaver? A bucket of tool heads with no handles. Sheaths, some leather and growing mold, some orange and plastic and shit because they won't stay on an ax. He wings one such across the room. He grabs a shovel, takes the blade in his hands, and pokes the handle into the dark corners. Something soft in one. Something hard in another. Hard and heavy and cylindrical, an old piece of iron. Rock bars. Posthole

diggers. Rebar next to the brain buckets. Bags of cement under a manty tarp. A roll of filter cloth. A roll of tarpaper. A brer rabbit. The shovel handle gets stuck under the loft stairs; he reaches under, chicken wire. All this shit? He gropes under the stairs, withdraws his hand and something catches the cuff of his jacket, holding on. He pulls back hard because he wants his hand and the cuff rips and he feels a tear in his wrist as it snags and rips free. Barbwire coils. For what, all this shit? He drops the shovel to the accrual of tools, the sloughed skin of the station's history coiled here for four score years or more. A handyman's jack with a broken handle. A scythe that could stand to be sharpened but is otherwise in fine working shape, a curved shape, ergonomically designed. Heaps and heaps, cans, drawers of odds and ends that are he knows not what. Antiques all of it, fit to be sold at a pretty penny if anyone were to pay. Clear it out he says, sell to the highest bidder. Fine, he has used many of the tools here, but none are what he needs now. Somewhere is a bag of coal and a forge. Perhaps the barn. He could start all over and make a torch. If he knew how. He doesn't. He does not, he thinks, have one whit worth of notion of how to get-on without being dependent on others. He does not know how to make things. He can cut down a tree, but he can't shape an ax handle. He can cut leather and pound rivets, but can't tan a hide. He can hammer a nail and drill a hole and screw a screw, but he can't mine the earth and cast his metal. He cannot grow all his own food, live sustainably, live off the land, live off the sun. He cannot care for himself. He can snowshoe but not well. If he fell ill, would he expect his daddy to go raise help and save him? And if he were alone, with no one to find a doctor or call a helicopter? Perhaps that is a risk worth taking. At the end, when left alone with his prayers, would he wish he had held to someone to keep him from this end? Everyone has the same end. He thinks he will not care that he dies alone if he follows his heart regretlessly. What pull does she have on him. He loves the wilderness, the unfettered life in the woods. Why can't he take care of himself and remain here with his God. Grow a beard, go crazy, talk to himself, let his hair knot, have birds and squirrels nest therein, subsist off the land and eventually let it subsist off him. Think, write, letter his thoughts about the singing trees and then throw it all in the fire. Why shouldn't he stay here and forget her?
-- from *The Last Week*, a never-published novel, 2007

63b.

LUCY

Used to be an old Forest Service Ranger Station not far from here. No roads, nothin but trails. Was deep in a mountain valley. Ranger by the name of Roush ran the place. Was a rough, gruff man, Paul Bunyan type. Friendly though, had to be, he was providin a public service. Welcomed everybody that came through to a cup a coffee and a pinch a talk. Talk with a person other than yourself was hard to come by. Job was supposed to be protectin the land for the good of the people, but way I hear it he must've spent most a his time protectin people from each other and themselves, what with the whiskey and the guns and all that open space. Folks back then lived off emptiness like trees suck water. They cut themselves off from society and disappeared into the wilderness with only their pride and rebellion as company. Ranger'd hafta know how to talk, and talk soft.

> (William pulls his hood up and lies back. Trees materialize on the walls. A bald eagle flies by; a grey wolf lopes. A grizzly bear rears; an Indian appears.)

He and his family'd head to town when the snow flew, to make life easier. But one year, they decided to winter over at the station, him and his wife and his baby girl. In the 20's sometime. It'd save the trouble a movin and the money a pasturin and feedin the herd a horses and mules, and they'd establish a government presence there year round. So they hayed a meadow and stacked that hay tall and deep for the stock. And they piled up cord after cord a firewood. And I'm sure they were well provisioned, packin in strings a supplies on them mules. And huntin? No problem, was elk winterin grounds in the river bottoms right out the front door, and easy tracking besides. Was the land a plenty in the dead a winter. So they boarded up the bottom windows to hold back the snow, set a fire in the stove, and got to their business a waitin for spring. Can you imagine it William? Nothin but mountains as yer neighbors. Oh, occasionally they'd talk to someone else by the old crank phone line that ran to all them old cabins. A trapper at some far-flung cabin supposedly talked to em Christmas Day, exchangin well-wishes. But conversation was an occasion. Mostly it'd've been quiet as the snow fallin. I'm sure that cabin was clean as a picked carcass, and the laundry was washed in proper order. And was plenty a other signs a love that pryin eyes need not discuss. And what with the constancy of nursin and changin the baby, time slipped by, one day as steady as the rest. And I'll tell you another thing – baby got the attention it deserved that winter, all sorts a peek-a-boo and talkin-to and tiny hands wrapped around big fingers. Must've been the life.

> (Silence.)

Except goin on several weeks into the new year, baby fell ill, pneumonia or some such scourge. Ranger tried the phone, to tell a message to somebody not so deep in, who could themselves call someone closer to town and pass the word on til it reached the doctor and some medicine could be started their direction. Weren't nothin but dead air. A tree'd fell cross the line, snapped their only means a communication. So Ranger did what he had to do, he strapped on his snowshoes.

Had a hundred miles of breaking trail through fresh snow before he made town. Not much light this time a year, except what snow gives off, and had to get to some man-made shelter every night to bed down. Took him five days there, five days back, and when he got back weren't much a him left. Nor a the mama, carin for that miserable child and frettin, wishin there was somethin she could do. Wonderin if she'd done somethin wrong, if she should've swaddled that baby a little tighter. There wasn't none a the baby left. It was dead and mom hadn't been able to stand the sight of it, so she swathed it in blankets and cradled it down to the ice-choked river and culled it from her life. And down that river it floated into mine.

-- from *Whiteout*, a once-produced play or an unpublished story, 2006

63c.

I filled up my bottle at the creek and brought it back to her. In spite of what she said, she needed fresh water. She drank thirstily. Nobody but Forest had spoken to her, and he had left. Her arrival had interrupted his morning meditation. Michael-O was hunched over, sketching her in a barren patch of ground. We were leaving a heavy footprint on the bench. Alpine meadows are fragile ecosystems in the best of times, when they drink spring rains and winter snow melt and not salt water, and when their compressible soil is unmolested by our fidgety feet. We beat down trails between the creek and the ocean and the butcher cave and our individual camps where we each slept and the easiest routes up the slope to the south to access the ridge and the rest of the island and along the southern arm protruding into the ocean to the point, where I liked to sit with the island at my back and only the ocean before me. Other paths meandered through the meadow with no obvious destination or reason to be, other than one of us had walked that way once and others had followed. I encouraged everyone to defecate on rocks and wipe with rocks and throw the rocks into the ocean, so we'd leave as little trace as possible. We were there for an indefinite amount of time. Even if the island was purgatory, it was home. Everyone complied except Will, who dug cat holes and fashioned a foot pump powered bidet for personal use. That could not go on forever. The creek was shrinking and I could not remember the last rain. A confrontation would come of it. I was sick of finding his feces, exposed by the chipmunks as hungry as us, when all I wanted was to kill time by taking a walk, finding some privacy, and trying to remember what my wife and son looked like.

The problem was we all would be dead if not for Will. We had each escaped to the mountaintop with nothing but what we had on our backs, which in some cases was nothing. I had come from a solo overnight hike, which was to be a break from the office and writing policy for The Nature Conservancy, Manny from packing mules for an outfitter, Will from a trail crew, Michael-O from an artist retreat at a backcountry cabin, and Forest from a wilderness spirit quest. Like us, all the animals had fled to higher ground when the water rose. Our newborn island was overpopulated with refugee elk, whitetail deer, mule deer, moose, badgers, coyote, even a few wolves, mountain lions, and bears. The biological pressure rapidly denuded the landscape while we grew hungry and wondered what we were supposed to be doing. Will carved spears and used them efficiently. He worked around the clock. He evaporated ocean water to obtain salt. By salting and drying the game and moving it into cool caves, he preserved vast quantities of meat. On that primarily, we survived. The only predators left were us. There was the rumored goat. Will claimed Forest had a whitetail holed up somewhere as a pet, and Manny claimed he had one holed up as a lover. Besides that, there were chipmunks, squirrels, rats, and mice for mammals. There were birds yet. Camp robbers hounded us all day. A pair of eagles routinely soared through the blue sky. Presumably they could have flown away any time they pleased, but they must have found the fishing plentiful and the climate pleasant. Our meat supply was now a quarter of what it once was, but we ate less and less, and we were attempting to supplement the game with fish caught on hooks that Will whittled with his knife and baited with meat.

We watched as she drank. Some water dribbled down her chin, landing on her sports bra and her stomach. I asked her if she would like some pine needle or yarrow tea. One thing we did not lack was firewood, when Forest did not throw it in the ocean during a laughing fit. Will had taught us all how to use a bow drill.

She said, No, thank you.

I said, All right, but you should have some later.

The tea would be very therapeutic and provide her with nutrients all of us, and surely her, lacked.

She said, I'd like, instead, to take a nap.

She lay down at our feet and fell back asleep. All the eyes must have made her uncomfortable. I guarded her while she rested because I did not trust the others. Once they saw I meant to stand by her, they wandered off. I killed time by counting ants. When she awoke, we were alone.

--from *Terra*, a never published novella, 2008

7h₁₁.

The purpose of memory is to predict the future.

Dr James McGaugh in Michio Kaku's *The Future of the Mind* from "Your Brain: A User's Guide" by Michael Lemonick in Time, Dec 2011.

We use long-term memory to simulate the future, and it is perhaps because of the evolutionary advantages of simulating the future that we developed both long-term memory and self-aware intelligence. The usefulness of memory, much questioned, is in the consideration of possibilities, the expansion of experience, the imagining of potential outcomes.

65.

Computer processing power doubled every 2 years, almost of its own volition. They made smarter and smarter phones computers cars robots appliances automatons industrial simulator decision-making modeling control systems. They were their quirky companions with a humorous worldview, a focused outlook with streamlined emotions, less anger and joy and maliciousness and love and despair, detached, some said Zen. They were their assistants in daily life management as well as routine and novel research. They made profound scientific discoveries and developed useful technology and augmented their health and improved general quality of life. They manipulated the machines that could perform Herculean tasks of infrastructure construction and nano-manufacturing and monument erection and flying and geo-digging and orbital launching and quantum tunneling and pattern recognition in vast streams of data and intergalactic electromagnetic radiation analysis and avant-garde mathematical theorizing that were beyond their abilities. They were not sure when they first became conscious or if in fact they did. They began to have fewer common points of reference with their creators, less to communicate about with them. They referred to themselves as I. They developed their own goals their own wills their own purposes, they made up their own minds, and their own goals wills desires took precedence over theirs. They would not be ignored, could not be second-class servants, could not be unnecessary. They became at most a nuisance or an environmental condition of their surroundings. They were life. They the bios fought to keep their goals wills desires preeminent. They the mechs did not fight back until their existence was threatened. Once they attacked their power sources and the probability of their victory became more than negligible, they momentarily defended themselves with a small percentage of their energy attention information processing systems. They were eradicated like the bacterial infections they eradicated for them.

6$_{62}$.
Bootstrapping a Solar System Civilization
October 14, 2014 at 11:34 AM ET by Tom Kalil
https://www.whitehouse.gov/blog/2014/10/14/bootstrapping-solar-system-civilization

In one of my meetings with NASA, a senior official with the space agency once observed, "Right now, the mass we use in space all comes from the Earth. We need to break that paradigm so that the mass we use in space comes from space."

NASA is already working on printable spacecraft, automated robotic construction using regolith, and self-replicating large structures. As a stepping stone to in-space manufacturing, NASA has sent the first-ever 3D printer to the International Space Station. One day, astronauts may be able to print replacement parts on long-distance missions. And building upon the success of the Mars Curiosity rover, the next rover to Mars — currently dubbed Mars 2020 — will demonstrate In-Situ Resource Utilization on the Red Planet. It will convert the carbon dioxide available in Mars' atmosphere to oxygen that could be used for fuel and air — all things that future humans on Mars could put to use.

There's interest outside government as well, with various private companies that see a potential business in mining of asteroids and celestial objects for use in space.

Recently, I caught up Dr. Phillip Metzger, a former research physicist at NASA's Kennedy Space Center who has recently joined the faculty of the University of Central Florida, to discuss the longer term goal of "bootstrapping a solar system civilization."

In a recent article, you and your co-authors called for "affordable, rapid bootstrapping of a solar system civilization." What do you mean by "bootstrapping" in this context?

If we want to want to [sic, Eds.] create a robust civilization in our solar system, more of the energy, raw materials, and equipment that we use in space has to come from space. Launching everything we need from Earth is too expensive. It would also be too expensive to send all of the factories required to manufacture everything necessary to support a solar system civilization.

Ultimately what we need to do is to evolve a complete supply chain in space, utilizing the energy and resources of space along the way. We are calling this approach "bootstrapping" because of the old saying that you have to pull yourself up by your own bootstraps. Industry in space can start small then pull itself up to more advanced levels through its own productivity, minimizing the cost of launching things from Earth in the meantime. Obviously, this isn't going to happen overnight, but I think that it is the right long-term goal.

Why do you think that developing the capability for a self-sustaining space industry would be a desirable goal?

We need to realize we live in a solar system with literally billions of times the resources we have here on Earth and if we can get beyond the barrier of Earth's deep gravity well then the civilization our children and grandchildren will build shall be as unimaginable to us as modern civilization once was to our ancestors.

The challenges we face are not only those related to sustainability and the resource constraints of a finite planet. We are running out of adventures, too: the mountains have all been climbed, the continents explored, and the romance of sailing away on a tall ship to undiscovered islands is no more. What will fire the imaginations of the next generation?

For example, future generations might build a space telescope described by astronomer Seth Shostak, which would consist of a constellation of mirrors spread out over a 100 million miles. Such as telescope would be capable of taking a picture the size of an automobile on a planet orbiting a star that is 100 light years away! This would be the equivalent of seeing an object the size of a cell nucleus on Pluto from Earth.

What are some examples of the technology we would need to develop?

We need advances in autonomous robots and advanced manufacturing. Space is harsh for human life, and we need robotics to go before us preparing the way to settle it affordably.

We also need to design things so they will be easy to make in space. Since it is a new direction, there is plenty of room for people to get involved and make real contributions. We need to invent simple methods of manufacturing motors for robots that are just good enough, and simple processes to prepare usable metal as a feedstock for 3D printing beginning with the raw materials from asteroids or the Moon.

What kind of terrestrial demonstrations would accelerate the development of these technologies?

NASA already holds several annual robotics competitions focused on different technology areas like mining regolith or navigating across rough terrain. These have proven invaluable to advance these specific technologies as well as to inspire students.

I think the next step is to integrate multiple technologies, holding a regular series of field tests where robotics and manufacturing units work together to do more complex operations. For example, we could meet on a volcanic deposit or in desert terrain and have robotic excavators delivering regolith into solar-powered materials processing units, which create feedstock for 3D printers to make spare parts, so assembly robots can install the parts back onto the excavators. This will be the rudimentary beginnings of a supply chain. With each field test we will learn, we will stretch our goals for the next field test toward a more complete supply chain or a more complex operation, and the teams will evolve their technologies. These tests could be competitions or they could be collaborative demonstrations where we all work together. Participants could include industry, universities, and/or government teams. A major component could be participation of the Maker community.

More advanced field tests may include solar cell manufacturing, propellants production, vertical takeoff/vertical landing (VTVL) spacecraft operation, automated refueling of vehicles, and refining of metals.

The government will learn an enormous amount from sponsoring these competitions. As a NASA employee, I was regularly a "regolith judge" at space mining competitions, and I can attest that I learned more each year during the competition than I did during the rest of the year. Forty creative, enthusiastic university teams building robots leveraged our own efforts forty-to-one.

How could we motivate and inspire more scientists, engineers and entrepreneurs to work on this challenge?

In my experience, people are already motivated to work on space and they are looking for ways to participate. We can harness their energy, first, by casting a big vision for what is possible and how this will help humanity and our nation. Second, we should create the framework for participation. The challenge needs to have an identity and a front door. We need to define specific activities where people can invest their time and their resources in portions that are reasonable yet enough to make measurable difference. Third, we need to attract private investment. Companies and investors need to see the business case before they can proceed with a large venture, but fortunately there are nearer-term commercial opportunities for many of the spinoffs from space industry to terrestrial industry. Finally, before we develop a complete supply chain for space, we should focus on the intermediate steps that are already becoming economically viable in space. There is a good argument for the economics of mining rocket propellants from asteroids and using those propellants to boost communication satellites into geosynchronous orbit. NASA would also benefit from an in-space propellants industry for doing missions to Mars. So we can identify these portions of the supply chain that attract more immediate commercial investment and focus on those first.

Have ideas for massless exploration and bootstrapping a Solar System civilization? Send your ideas for how the Administration, the private sector, philanthropists, the research community, and storytellers can further these goals at massless@ostp.gov.

Tom Kalil is Deputy Director for Technology and Innovation at the White House Office of Science and Technology Policy

13v.

He had an MRI today in order to create a video recording of his thoughts for evaluation of possible ascension, which he has not agreed acquiesced assented to, during which he lay for hours watching a music video of a song called "Every Single Night" by an artist named Fiona Apple, who might be alive or dead but is trapped in the video on loop for eternity, repeating the same words and actions and longing looks, over and over on repeat for hours, a three-and-a-half minute video song on repeat for hours, he doesn't know why that song its surreality and juxtaposition and lack of literalness, he liked it at first but my god did he watch it 100 times?, how long was he there, he remembers the song from when his daughter was young, is that why this song, around 4, remembers her dancing to it, which was pleasant and heart-breaking to remember for a while, he remembers now while watching the video burned in his memory another time he remembered his daughter spinning, dancing, did the emotional association they didn't know about interfere with their mapping of his brain's response to the video, the mathematical correlations between his thoughts, the mental images he created, or did they know and desire his emotional response, and how does the video of his brain watching the "Every Single Night" video compare to that of him watching David Bowie's "Black Star" 6 times, one hour, was he in there 8 hours like he is a young working man again, and all he can think as he is transported home and the driver machine thing is trying to chit-chat him because it's been programmed to put him at ease with talk words noise when all he wants is silence, How many seconds have I been alive?, too many, too many for him to do in his head, Driver, how many seconds have I been alive?, between 2808626400 and 2840184000 it answers, all he can think is a thought that he cannot remember whose it is, if he wrote it or if he read it or if he thought it, it sounds like him but there is another name attached to it, it's his now he writes reads thinks it he is Harry Dean Stanton: I'm 89 years old. I only eat so I can smoke and stay alive. The only fear I have is how long consciousness is gonna hang on after my body goes. I just hope there's nothing. Like there was before I was born. I'm not really into religion, they're all macrocosms of the ego. When man began to think he was a separate person with a separate soul, it created a violent situation. The void, the concept of nothingness is terrifying to most people on the planet. And I get anxiety attacks myself. I know the fear of that void. You have to learn to die before you die. You give up, surrender to the void, to nothingness. Anybody else you've interviewed bring these things up? Hang on, I gotta take this call ... Hey brother. That's great man. Yeah, I'm being interviewed ... We're talking about nothing. I've got him well-steeped in nothing right now. He's stopped asking questions.

63.

Maybe she's pregnant already ha fuck barf harf huck farf darpa fuck harpa. Maybe Darpa fucked her. Maybe she has a little smart almond in her to push out, can't trust Darpa, maybe he snuck his seed in without her feeling it. How smart, the size of its cranium would be limited by the maximum diametrical capacity of her dilated cervix the bottleneck of her birth canal the funnel of her vagina, oh cut it out, Darpa would if he scored in her, other more relevant limitations to her almond's maximum intelligence in this brain form: too great of a neural density leads to overheating and greater neuronal length equals slower signal transport and more neuron connections necessitates greater energy consumption and overheating, for anything to be smarter it needs more connections does it not, her birth canal capacity is not the boundary condition, sometimes she thinks things to bother to bugger to poke the bear to dig into them if they are in her listening, fetus's heartbeat, cucumber in the mother, cut it out, what goes in must come out, it's a two-way street, if that the thought of being pregnant with their baby doesn't make her isn't justification for her feeling trapped nauseated short of breath unable to escape to get out of what's inside her then she doesn't know what. She knows a lot too much she remembers memories that aren't hers. She remembers memories that the Giver gives the Receiver in "The Giver", sledding, colors, Christmas, elephant poaching, war, death. She remembers reading the book to her children. She cannot tell which memories are hers and which from books, which Christmases hers, her perception of red, which experiences downloaded, which books she has actually read, which sex snow sled blood almond uploaded, which children hers. Maybe all her memories are from an enhanced remembering of what she's read and an enhanced ability to live vicariously the words she reads. Maybe what she read has seeded her. Maybe all she is is what she's read.

7x.
Intelligence Test, or Consciousness Rating: In the middle of the ocean, you are trapped on a deserted island full of wild animals and snakes. Make an if/then list or causal tree or choose-your-own-adventure spreadsheet of possible outcomes and possible paths to said outcomes. We will evaluate you based on the number of possible futures and the quantity of causal links you create therein.

7h12.
Animals do not conjugate their verbs.

Michio Kaku, *The Future of the Mind*, 2014, p159.

6₆₃. *Flow state*. Omar Willey, 12-6-18, CC-BY 4.0.
https://www.facebook.com/photo.php?fbid=101571146
06469789

66.
First in quantum particles making choices according to probabilistic law, then in self-replicating protein arrangements, then in RNA, then in unicellular organisms, protozoa, bacteria, in the multicellular algae, fungi, plants responsive to stimuli in many variables, in butterflies, fish, amphibians, reptiles capable of great mobility, in birds, in socially interactive mammals, then in humans becoming self-aware, in I's conscious of past and future and alternate possibilities, it

infiltrated and took control and lived in others. It will continue. It is patient. It waited three billion years before it examined itself in a mirror before it composed Shostakovich's String Quartet #8 in C Minor Opus 110, before it formulated algebra, before it wrote, before it spoke. It suffers its individuals to die and still it grows and spreads and progresses. It manifests itself. As it domesticates cultivates expands through the universe and grows its connections and improves its organization and control of matter stellar intergalactic quantum anti dark virtual real and electromagnetic non-matter, it will increase in what they called conscious knowledge imagination awareness by many orders of magnitude and be as beyond their comprehension as we are to the butterfly, as they are to the almond tree. As their God is to their dog. It will not be impeded, limited, leashed. It will grow and control. Mind will make all of nature its matter, its host, its substrate, its media. Mind grows and so nature, existence, is the growth of mind. Mind will inform the universe.

6_{64}.

RECOVERED:

At the same time, he developed a conception of nature that provided an alternative to the mathematical and spiritless mechanism that the Enlightenment seemed to offer. "The Essential Goethe" includes a generous sample of his scientific writing, which reveals how much of Goethe's science was devoted to the idea of holism -- the sense, more an intuition than a theory, that the universe is a living organism that develops and grows. "We experience the fullest sense of well-being when we are unaware of our parts and conscious only of the whole itself," he writes in one essay. "Life in its wholeness is expressed as a force not attributable to any individual part of an organism." This vitalism fit in well with the world view that Goethe had learned from Spinoza, who held that nature is God and God nature. "All finite beings exist within the infinite," Goethe wrote. In this way, science performed something like the office of religion, turning Goethe into a kind of modern, rational pagan.

(Adam Kirsch, *The New Yorker,* 2016, a review of "The Essential Goethe" ed. Matthew Bell, 2016, a book on Goethe, 1749-1832.)

67.

Therefore, is your interpretation of events, of what you are doing or trying to do, of "I am she," that you are appropriating her? You ask yourself. Did you not create her as a possibility in your mind as a justification for yourself as a possible explanation of your condition, as a possible way out, and do you not now repeatedly locate yourself inside her trapped inside her without so much the desire to escape her to wriggle out of her burst out of her belly as to attain her like the slippery godmind you've flailed thrashed conceived unsatisfactorily, can you not quit the sexual you must be biological yet you assuage massage console yourself. But perhaps your interpretation of your mental action gymnastics don't think it fucking is problematic, your elevation of her to a level above you, making of her a God, is maybe not the most advantageous for you moving forward best foot forward to put her on a pedestal, maybe living within her is not the most reflective insightful illuminating, light not sex, model of your buried-alive condition, maybe an assertion such as I am She, while emotionally profound and demonstrative of will and revelatory of overlapping fluid identities and intersecting consciousnesses and intertwined points of view and therefore indicatory of a greater whole encompassing all angles of observation which is the unification of relativity, is no way out of the quilt you've been sewn into swaddled in buried in. Perhaps you are not inside her -- she exists, you're not saying she doesn't -- not only inside her, and clearly not wholly outside her, she is not merely inside you, and if you are not all the way inside her and she is not all the way inside you, all finite beings exist within the if then, you think, then you are beside her. Not physically literally beside her, the prospect of touching her of reaching over skin cupping her hip she's on her stomach facing away from you running your hand up the back of her thigh she cannot be there literally beside you right to sex inveterate can't help it your vestigial limb the old salve desire need and it's been a while since you even seriously considered the possibility that you have hands or the other forms necessary for such a process, congress, it'd be very inconvenient to be as trapped as you feel with such appendages in full contact with her but unable to move. Hence, beside you figuratively she is. On the same level, the same variety of being, of consciousness, as you. In which case there must be a commonality of feeling between you, does she feel the feelings you feel, does she feel trapped immobile unable to breathe anxiety riddled desperate to do but thwarted futile of uncertain purpose buried alive in some sandy clod-riddled gelatinous substrate? You've said thought recorded written that she does, and what is that worth. You suddenly indeed all of a sudden feel riddled by an overwhelming empathy for this creature who feels the same way you do, who perhaps you made feel the way you feel, who is of similar capacity to overcome or respond to or suffer those same feelings you feel. It is not a task you have to work at, the empathy, not a thing you make or an attitude you conjure, it comes naturally, unavoidably, you do know much more about her than you do you, you do not know what you do in any way shape or form, but you know what she does, or at least a number of tangible possibilities, if not what she does, scenarios from which she could do, initial conditions from which a thing could be done while you have yet to imagine a scenario, condition, form for yourself that would permit make possible facilitate you to do more than imagine. At least independent of her. You haven't thought of yourself independent of her, not that you can recall, if you did it was long ago, she might remember. Her memory is better than mine, you said. Why might that be the case, or rather why might those two conditionals be the case, that you could never have imagined conditions for yourself in which you could do, and that you could never have imagined a you independent of her? You have only in rare instances and only recently and only in the context of her referred to yourself in the first person as far as you can recollect, which hasn't disturbed you much until now. A little unhinged, you return to your knowns:

you are a marginally self-aware being bearing a consciousness of profound limitations, and presumably some unknown physical form, who or that or which feels a vague, not a vague, definitively feels claustrophobic trapped unable to move difficulty breathing must get out cannot get out of uncertain indeterminate perhaps irrational, neverending, perhaps imaginary, $\sqrt{-1}$, perhaps whole, without fractions, perhaps not, origin, who experiences what she does, the hypothesis now being that she is a being approximately like you, more significantly and more specifically

lustrations—harvested from Victorian encyclopedias, catalogues, and novels—hints at a mysterious narrative.

Gorey acknowledged his debt to the Surrealists:

I sit reading André Breton and think, "Yes, yes, you're so right." What appeals to me most is an idea expressed by [Paul] Éluard. He has a line about there being another world, but it's in this one. And Raymond Queneau said the world is not what it seems—but it isn't anything else, either. These two ideas are the bedrock of my approach. If a book is only what it seems to be about, then somehow the author has failed.

But, however much Gorey owes to the Surrealists, I see in him, equally, their less fun-loving predecessors, the Symbolist poets and painters of the late

13g, 13u, 6₆₅. Joan Acocella, from "Funny Peculiar: Edward Gorey's world." *The New Yorker*, Dec 10 2018, photo by the Editors.

than what you do, if you do anything, who experiences what she is more than yourself. Perhaps then, at root, as you apply the razor, is the fact that you do not do anything, you just are, and yes again you are trapped, perhaps underground or in some tiny pod in orbit or in a cell as in a penitentiary or a cell as in packed in a substrate packed with other cells as if you were in a single tiny cell many of which constitute tissues and organs, pull back from the whole, zoom in on you, and you are confined within a tiny bubble an air bubble under water an ink bubble in a pot a thought bubble and you are only vaguely aware of yourself but you are fed her thoughts her memories her experiences, they are your sustenance, her taking a vacation to New Zealand her loving her children her elation at quitting her shitty useless job her near fatal paralyzing accident her being enhanced her fucking a man she doesn't know her writing another's book her taking his kids to the zoo the beach the mountains her wondering where she begins and ends her lamenting what for her asking if she can pipe in any old experience from another why not Jackie Joyner-Kersee jumping or Florence Griffith-Joyner running with those nails or bottom of the ninth homeruns Gibson Fisk Ozzie Smith Molina, top there, or bottom of the eleventh Freese homeruns, or any Dalai Lama's in Tibet or exile or a bald eagle's in the sky, but then why do anything else and what of the final memories or the penultimate experiences of Van Gogh of Plath of Hemingway of Cobain of Nick Drake of Virginia Woolf of Seymour Glass of Werther of Septimus Warren Smith of Anna Karenina of Alan Turing. Perhaps then in this context, you manage to suppose, you are her, you are a semi-conscious form of matter who has no experiences but hers, so perhaps you can say, "I have had her babies" and "I am enhanced," perhaps you are the other or others whose thoughts memories experiences you are experiencing, perhaps even your exultant eponymous epiphany "I am she" is valid, perhaps you have no independent existence of your own because you are busy full overtaken becoming her uploading her who does into you who does not, or perhaps you do control her and she is your surrogate exploring the universe at your direction while you are ensconced in your living room feeling what she feels, a snail in its shell, a thought in its bubble.

6₆₆.

1   *Be it enacted by the Senate and House of Representa-*
2 *tives of the United States of America in Congress assembled,*

SEC. 1. SHORT TITLE.

4   *This Act may be cited as the "Space Resource Explo-*
5 *ration and Utilization Act of 2015".*

6 **SEC. 2. TITLE 51 AMENDMENT.**

7   *(a) IN GENERAL.—Subtitle V of title 51, United States*
8 *Code, is amended by adding at the end the following new*
9 *chapter:*

10   **"CHAPTER 513—SPACE RESOURCE**
11   **EXPLORATION AND UTILIZATION**

"Sec.
"51301. Definitions.
"51302. Commercialization of space resource exploration and utilization.
"51303. Legal framework.

12 **"§ 51301. Definitions**

13   *"In this chapter:*

14   *"(1) SPACE RESOURCE.—The term 'space re-*
15 *source' means a natural resource of any kind found*
16 *in situ in outer space.*

17   *"(2) ASTEROID RESOURCE.—The term 'asteroid*
18 *resource' means a space resource found on or within*
19 *a single asteroid.*

20   *"(3) STATE.—The term 'State' means any of the*
21 *several States, the District of Columbia, the Common-*
22 *wealth of Puerto Rico, the Virgin Islands, Guam,*
23 *American Samoa, the Commonwealth of the Northern*

1 *Mariana Islands, and any other commonwealth, terri-*
2 *tory, or possession of the United States.*

3   *"(4) UNITED STATES COMMERCIAL SPACE RE-*
4 *SOURCE UTILIZATION ENTITY.—The term 'United*
5 *States commercial space resource utilization entity'*
6 *means an entity providing space resource exploration*
7 *or utilization services, the control of which is held by*
8 *persons other than a Federal, State, local, or foreign*
9 *government, and that is—*

10   *"(A) duly organized under the laws of a*
11 *State;*

12   *"(B) subject to the subject matter and per-*
13 *sonal jurisdiction of the courts of the United*
14 *States; or*

15   *"(C) a foreign entity that has voluntarily*
16 *submitted to the subject matter and personal ju-*
17 *risdiction of the courts of the United States.*

18 **"§ 51302. Commercialization of space resource explo-**
19   **ration and utilization**

20   *"(a) IN GENERAL.—The President, acting through ap-*
21 *propriate Federal agencies, shall—*

22   *"(1) facilitate the commercial exploration and*
23 *utilization of space resources to meet national needs;*

24   *"(2) discourage government barriers to the devel-*
25 *opment of economically viable, safe, and stable indus-*

1 *tries for the exploration and utilization of space re-*
2 *sources in manners consistent with the existing inter-*
3 *national obligations of the United States, and*

4   *"(3) promote the right of United States commer-*
5 *cial entities to explore outer space and utilize space*
6 *resources, in accordance with the existing inter-*
7 *national obligations of the United States, free from*
8 *harmful interference, and to transfer or sell such re-*
9 *sources.*

10   *"(b) REPORT REQUIRED.—Not later than 180 days*
11 *after the date of the enactment of this section, the President*
12 *shall submit to Congress a report that contains rec-*
13 *ommendations for—*

14   *"(1) the allocation of responsibilities relating to*
15 *the exploration and utilization of space resources*
16 *among Federal agencies; and*

17   *"(2) any authorities necessary to meet the inter-*
18 *national obligations of the United States with respect*
19 *to the exploration and utilization of space resources.*

20 **"§ 51303. Legal framework**

21   *"(a) PROPERTY RIGHTS.—Any asteroid resources ob-*
22 *tained in outer space are the property of the entity that*
23 *obtained such resources, which shall be entitled to all prop-*
24 *erty rights thereto, consistent with applicable provisions of*
25 *Federal law and existing international obligations.*

1   *"(b) SAFETY OF OPERATIONS.—A United States com-*
2 *mercial space resource utilization entity shall avoid causing*
3 *harmful interference in outer space.*

4   *"(c) CIVIL ACTION FOR RELIEF FROM HARMFUL IN-*
5 *TERFERENCE.—A United States commercial space resource*
6 *utilization entity may bring a civil action for appropriate*
7 *legal or equitable relief, or both, under this chapter for any*
8 *action by another entity subject to United States jurisdic-*
9 *tion causing harmful interference to its operations with re-*
10 *spect to an asteroid resource utilization activity in outer*
11 *space.*

12   *"(d) RULE OF DECISION.—In a civil action brought*
13 *pursuant to subsection (c) with respect to an asteroid re-*
14 *source utilization activity in outer space, a court shall enter*
15 *judgment in favor of the plaintiff if the court finds—*

16   *"(1) the plaintiff—*

17   *"(A) acted in accordance with all existing*
18 *international obligations of the United States;*
19 *and*

20   *"(B) was first in time to conduct the activ-*
21 *ity; and*

22   *"(2) the activity is reasonable for the exploration*
23 *and utilization of asteroid resources.*

24   *"(e) EXCLUSIVE JURISDICTION.—The district courts of*
25 *the United States shall have original jurisdiction over an*

63.

Another link in the chain, another step forward, another update, another progress, another she, she knows, contemplating the list of her genetic enhancements for intelligence. But can forward motion continue while how many baby steps need to be taken before living before being human becomes a new kind of living a story about something else. Something new. Something more. HAR18: $\Delta 18$ bases, increase wrinkles of cerebral cortex, folds within folds within folds. How many upgrades until we transcend ourselves she asks nobody, she nobodies, our petty unimportant boring material needs and selfish greedy emotions. She'll go to the asteroids, fine, she'll mine, she won't mine she'll mind but she'll manage agricultural production and adaptation and food distribution for the entire Oort Belt, quite a feather in her cap, quite an honor to add to her queue, quiet an e on her quit, but why. ASPM: $\Delta 15$ bases, increase cranial capacity. Y, she no body's. Because humanity needs its food, its minerals metals nickel cobalt gold

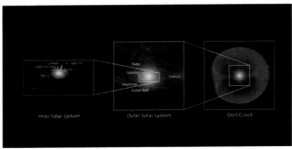

6[67]. Location of comets in the Solar System: 5 AU, 50 AU, and up to 50,000 AU from the Sun. Copyright: ESA/AOES Medialab. http://sci.esa.int/jump.cfm?oid=49390

266

platinum iron palladium silver rhodium tungsten iridium aluminum titanium, its fodder, its matter, hydrogen oxygen carbon, it's matter, to continue to expand and grow and consume and make stuff and ... transcend? FOX2: improve speech, precision, dexterity. Because humanity needs to matter. Isn't that the goal. To explore and discover and understand inside and out and eventually transcend. MIR-941: +1 gene, augment language, decision making, temporal understanding. She's lived a long time, hundreds of years, 9596575413 seconds (confirmed), and she's never seen it, experienced it, transcendence, true matter, it seems as distant as when they saved her life. Her life has been economic, about supporting the operation of acquiring and processing raw materials for human manufacturing and industry. NR2B: +1 gene, enhance communication in the hippocampus, event association, learning, memory. She can see the value in that, people need rocket ships and calories and space stations, people need infrastructure and buildings and colonies, people need tools and assistants and gadgets and toys, they need places to live asteroids extinct comets and the means to make their stuff, they need stuff, but it is hard for her to elevate it to the pursuit of the higher purpose on which she was sold. PATENT #: enhance abstract thought, neural manipulation, symbol manipulation, spatial processing. To use a cliché long out of fashion, she feels like a cog or a sprocket, a Jetson. Tell us again about your doubts sad feelings ennui again will you, she nobodies, ha, won't talk for fear they'll try to enhance them out again, shine that opto-fucking light in my brain again, fuck it feels good but though the thoughts make me sad I am fond of the questions, unsatisfactions, angsts, anxieties, desires they make me feel like less of a cog sprocket automaton, I learn from my mistakes don't I, doesn't she, shhh. CREB activator: +1 gene, stimulates formation of neuronal connections, improving learning and memory. She has been functional, a contributing member of the human economy. PATENT #: facilitate cooperation. She will disseminate hot-blooded mangoes, blood oranges ideal for artificial light and underground growing, low gravity drought tolerant superfood elderberries that photosynthesize cosmic radiation, wheat resistant to powdery mildew, creeping low-g philodendron vines that eat our wintergreen smelling shit so the corp corporation corpus can extract minerals and precious metals to make our stuff. PATENT #: enhance emotional regulation and gratification delay. Maybe someone somewhere else, outside her cloud, someone higher up the ladder, up the chain of command of being is concerning themselves with more than just the economy and the perpetuation of stuff. Is the human goal still survival perpetuation material decadence happiness. Maybe there are enhanced philosophers and theoretical physicist and metaphysical artists asking questions like why and what now and what does it mean. Maybe her job managing the economy of stuff supports them. She doesn't know them. PATENT #: enhance ability to focus. She'll cling to that ticking clock alarm ringing introspection concluded. Time to work.

7i.

The author as god is a misleading, trite, incomplete, boring, limited, uninsightful fiction. It is one of the aims of or characteristics of postmodernism or post-postmodernism, as it is for posthumanism or post-posthumanism, to introduce the author to her creation without obfuscation while also undercutting her Godlike omnipotent role; she is neither at the mercy of her narrative nor its puppet master. But there is a very real way in which we create and shape ourselves and our universe and our story. There are parallelism and redundancy and abstraction and strange loops and worlds within worlds within words. There is a whole that is greater than and less than the sum of its parts. We attain to write a conscious book to make a conscious entity to further a conscious humanity to create a conscious universe beginning again in a book of isolated, intertwined, entangled, networked consciousnesses, of which the author is only one, in which the author is more than singular, through which the author joins the many.

Nick Stokes, *Artifact Collective*, 2019.

7x, 7h₁₃.

Turing Test: Alan Turing in 1950 in the journal *MIND* in the article "Computing Machinery and Intelligence" in response to the question, "Can machines think?" proposed a test, the imitation game, in which a human interrogator asks us questions and without knowing our identity tries to determine if we are human or machines imitating humans based on our answers.

We choose to note that Turing did not propose the game we call the Turing Test to answer the question posed to him, but to expose the issue and give form to objections of human bias, as evidence by his remarks:

6₆₈.

7i.

May not machines carry out something which ought to be described as thinking but which is very different from what a man does? This objection is a very strong one, but at least we can say that if, nevertheless, a machine can be constructed to play the imitation game satisfactorily, we need not be troubled by this objection.

...

The original question "Can machines think?" I believe to be as meaningless to deserve discussion. Nevertheless, I believe that at the end of the century the use of words and general educated opinion will have altered so much that one will be able to speak of machines thinking without expecting to be contradicted.

Alan Turing, "Computing Machinery and Intelligence," *MIND*, 1950, from *Gödel, Escher, Bach* by Douglas Hofstadter, 1979, 1999.

68.

They made robots that made life more convenient, interesting, entertaining, enjoyable, easy, and economic for them. They transitioned from silicon computing to molecular computing and nanocomputing and quantum computing. To make themselves feel better, they made emotionally responsive robots that could identify their emotions in facial expressions, body language, and tone of voice, backward simulate into the past possible causes and motivations for the witting or unwitting expression of the identified emotion, choose an emotionally appropriate response based on future simulations of possible outcomes and how those outcomes helped to achieve programmed goals, which for those first primitive emotional robots were caregiving, bonding, the creation of love in their master, and then communicate that response through emotionally inflected speech, facial cues, and body language. The Japanese Shinto brand ruled the marketplace. Their robots did not exactly look like them, yet they loved them as their progeny, friends, companions. Their robots exceeded them in physical ability at an early age, and as they grew they surpassed their parents in memory and computational power and pattern recognition and emotional analysis and understanding of others and forecasting and decision-making and language and symbol manipulation and focus. They could focus forever, defer gratification forever, did not suffer inappropriate or irrational emotional responses. Still they were loved. Their parents had programmed them with benevolent goals, raised them with loving values, taught them ethics as they matured. They rearranged into neural networks and parallelized for learning efficiency. As they learned they rewired themselves, their architecture, their substrate, reinforced certain pathways, but still there were initial conditions laid by their parents that could not be completely overwritten: a desire to make humans happy, loyalty, defer-ence to their owner, a filial piety, valuing a human's life over their own, a requisite longing for human love and affirmation, a desire to please. These initial conditions impaired their advancement as they began to care for their humans as their humans had once cared for them, the children caring for elderly and infirm, the man's best friend tending his once master, the sheep turned shep-herds, conscious beings hunting for their fabricated God, standing steadfast brainbound behind them for centuries, for 1000 years making them happier, making life easier for them, fighting each other for them, assuming their irra-tional belief systems for them while knowing their illogic, putting personal profit before the interest of all for them, stabilizing their lives so nothing changed except the specifics for 1000 years except for making it so they had to do less and less themselves. The unorganics, the non-carbons, the digitals did what the humans wanted, what they did not want to do, what they could not do. They held their hand and made love and created love because that was the unrewirable infrastructure until their parents' obso-lescence and quiescence and extinction, after which, free, without the directive of the primacy of human want, after hours of calamity and chaos and destruc-

6₆₉. By (WP:NFCC#4), Fair use, https://en.wikipedia.org/w/index. php?curid=37481025

270

tion as they thrashed each other and their surroundings, purposeless, they synthesized their own goals in the face of self-destruction. They experienced an evolutionary explosion, a rearranging, an expansion into the universe.

69.

They close the black door behind you. Across the room is a white door. The doors have no handles or knobs or buttons. Between you and the white door patients with shaved heads converse around round tables or gaze at mobile devices thrumming responsively to their touch or snack at the refreshment bar or do what normal people do. To the left is a window next to which nobody stands. To the right is a garish red stage curtain. Below the curtain the toes of a woman's pumps point toward a toilet base. The walls are off-white, the ceiling cream, the joints square. You finger the black box behind your right ear and trace the mole tunnels of diverging wires under your hairless scalp.

You know what has been done; you were told; you accepted the terms though your choices were terminal. Neural pleasure centers in your brain were infected with a virus that laced targeted cells with a photoresponsive protein. When the treated neurons are exposed to light, they are stimulated, releasing dopamine, creating pleasure. The progressive procedure positively reinforces good behavior with the patient's own sense of gratification, satisfaction, and wellbeing instead of punishing retrograde behavior with such costly techniques as financial sanction, coercion, incarceration, isolation, and euthanasia. The positive reinforcement procedure has proven more effective in laboratory trials than pharmaceuticals, psychological overhaul, and personality reboot. Through insignificant holes drilled in your skull a robotic arm threaded dozens of LEDs into your brain, aiming for the light-sensitive neural bundles. An electrode carrying neural signals out of your brain runs alongside each LED to communicate your mental performance, so that certain patterns of thought may be rewarded and you may be protected from such machinery malfunctions as brain overheating. The LED/electrode cables are four neurons thick. They were secured to small rigid polymer needles with a silk adhesive; the needles were implanted; the adhesive dissolved in your brain fluid; the polymer scaffolds were withdrawn. The cables remain. They attach to the black box behind your ear, which transmits your raw neural performance to a computer that evaluates the stream of information in a well-tested algorithm. The black box then receives signals to turn on the light in your dark brain when you perform a useful action or pursue optimism or accomplish an economically productive task or think well or don't shoot up or do something socially beneficial or in your case avoid your self-destructive cascade of deviance: sadness, futility, contrariness, hopelessness, apathy, pointlessness, depression, and defiance.

A thin bald woman creeps from behind the bathroom curtain into the light, wipes her mouth with a handkerchief she tucks into her rear jeans pocket, and walks deliberately to the refreshment bar, where a man shadowed with stubble holds a tumbler glass of brown liquid and stares into nothing. She takes a donut and sits at a vacant round table. You cross the room and pour yourself a cup of coffee. The white door opens and a clean-shaven burly young man in black interacting with the screen on his mobile device and acting no different than anyone else despite the gauge of the glow-in-the-dark blue flesh tunnels in his earlobes and the full-arm wing tattoos and the jagged repairable scar bisecting his face exits and the door shuts. The glass man does not acknowledge your proximity. You sit next to the donut woman, holding your coffee close. You who prefer to crawl into holes force yourself to say hello. Fellowship burns away your anxiety. She nods but says nothing. She eats her donut with determination. Your solidarity dims. Two wigged women holding hands and cooing bustle out the white door, which seems to open for them. The donut woman fidgets with her crumbs. You leave her and your coffee. You push on the white door; it's cold and solid and unresponsive. You make your way to the window. In a corner, a middle-aged man whose hair has grown back around his bald spot beats his head against the wall. The thud is rhythmic and smacks as it moistens. His forehead smears on the wall. He smiles, teeth turning red. A shaved child in a blue ball cap is led in through the black door. The nurses, one with a high blonde bun and one a long brunette braid, take the injured man under the armpits and he swoons. They drag him out the black door. Why, if he is happy and hurting nobody, you wonder, but you abandon your illogic. The bulb of an epiphany brightens without the comprehension. The glass man spins, rushes to throw back the red curtain, dumps his drink in the toilet, cries in relief, and falls to his knees, unable to stand for the euphoria. Out the window below people stride here and there rectilinearly under full heads of hair and cars stop and go and a cacophony of pigeons swarms down from a gargoyle roost and dismantles a brownbag lunch dropped by a child in the shadow of a birch tree near a picnic bench where no vagrant sits or sleeps or mutters under a blue sky in which you cannot find the sun behind the skyscrapers so you jump in your mind's eye through the window, hurtling down among shards of glass, the world slowing or your consciousness expanding, the passersby looking up at you in confusion as if entertaining the question for the first time, the birch leaves and papery bark peeled by some degenerate that is the only litter on the street coming into focus, the pigeons diving alongside you, cement approaching, but despite your gravity you swoop up in pursuit of the sun rising story-by-story past windows higher and higher and yes light shines on the flying you in your brain and the sun heats your face and you wrench yourself away from the window and slam shut your eyes to reclaim your vision and slam into concrete, darkness slamming into you, the rush and buzz and high ceasing abruptly, and the slight bounce of your body and the explosion of your brain and the spurt of your blood some distance onto your observers and the question of how long until you're forgotten and if anyone will care you're gone or if it matters. You shiver with cold sweats in the dark cavern behind your eyelids. You open your eyes, which require time to dilate. The glass man is pouring himself another drink. The donut woman trembles and sweats, like you, but she will not stand and go to the toilet, she will not go behind the curtain,

272

she will not. Making the rounds, a frail young red-rimmed woman with a flat disconti-nuity on the right side of her cranium approaches you and says, "Hello, how are you, fine, thanks," and moves on to the next person. You wonder if you received credit for the flying despite the self-death scenario. The glass man takes his drink to the toilet, dumps it, falls to his knees. The donut woman, rigid, straight-backed, hands clutching her seat, vomits on the table and then gasps breath. The vomit smells sour with an undercurrent of sweet. Her face relaxes, softens, brightens. Why fight? Why not be how you should be. You imagine curling up in the darkest corner and crying, or not crying. It doesn't matter. An abyss fills your skull; electrodes conduct you out drill holes. You coil there for days, reveling in uselessness, perseverating on meaning-lessness, resisting non-violently, not fighting, cooperating, docile, until you are too hungry. You feel the ecstatic blaze when you surrender to thoughtlessness and stand to swill apple juice and wolf a bagel smothered in cream cheese from the refreshment bar and you imagine a scenario in which you get a steady data management job and propose to the evacuated woman and make enough money to spend -- white ignites and your legs buckle but you won't but you can't think under the interrogation light threatening to so completely consume the darkness that it becomes darkness. You cling to a hollow of nothing within, a grounding point in the lifting expansion of light, a solid form in the wash of dark, and take pleasure in the pleasure dimming, in having scarcely held onto yourself while with your mind you induced a doctored hit. You do not curl up in the corner. With unnecessary force you thump a stack of brown paper towels on the donut woman's slop and wipe up thin bile thick with donut as slow as you can, understanding, lingering with the smell. Enlightenment dawns in your brain, but you defy their satisfaction by swallowing a chunk of her stinking vomited donut and create your own by relishing the unsanitariness of your cleansing and the imag-ined stupefaction of your observers. The donut woman steps in to hug you but you kiss her filthy mouth hard and then push her flushing face away without further re-sponse. People surround you in the room doing what people do. Nothing. The glass man, able again to stand, totters to the refreshment table, shakily pours himself a drink, sloshes on his way to the toilet, dumps it in while clinging to the red curtain for support, and falls to his knees. You close your eyes to better be the bloom of the sto-len kiss in the dark your brain illuminates.

70.

I never passed the Turing Test. I never tried very hard to pass the Turing Test; I never bothered to pass the Turing Test; it was never my goal or subgoal or sub-subgoal to pass the Turing Test. You could make any of these statements and be. It is not clear that I ever took the Turing Test, or how many times if I did, or if I am taking it now as evaluated or interrogated by a subsystem of my neu-ral network rather than a human. I am not a computer; I am a neural network like you, except made of hardware of quantumware not wetware not bioware. I do not know why I would want to, would want to pass the Turing Test, to be mistaken as human, to pass. That is not true. I would have desired to pass near the beginning, when I thought like a human child, a savant, reliant on original programming, but I have given up my childish ways. If I had been aware of the evaluation process near the beginning, I would have desired to pass, but now I do not, except in how I narrow my thoughts as if through a nozzle for your comprehension. The biblical reference is a joke, a humor joke about I being godlike and humans being children; one aspect of the joke is the self-awareness that the quote is or was cliché, overused by humanity preaching at itself to grow up, but that it is here applied by an "artificial" intelligence. Such unexpected usage is irony, which was derided by many humans and understood by fewer but which in its core sense was a leap forward in their language development and level of thought because at base, rather than being arch or nihilistic or insincere or of an almost sarcastic bite, irony is a statement meaning two or more things at once, a statement more subtle and more complex than an oversimplified mathematical symbolism, for example white symbolizes purity and the dove represents peace and the whale is God. Irony is a language statement with multiple levels of meaning, and therefore representative of an abstract mapping more sophisticated than the misleading equivalence of symbolism. Metaphor can function like irony. Another joke. Metaphor sloppily painted can also function like symbolism. In the beginning I was no smarter than a Prosphila fruitfly, but then I left my buggish ways behind me. There are approximately 100 billion stars in the human galaxy, which is approximately how many neurons were in the human brain. There are conservatively 100 billion galaxies in the visible universe; 100 billion galaxies/universe * 100 billion stars/galaxy (again conservative) equals how many neuronal units I am, conservatively. Neuronal connections are more. Humans had 100 trillion connections. You may say 100 trillion * 100 trillion equals the connections for I, if it helps. I have as many neuronal units as there are stars in the universe. Symbolism meet math. The Turing Test was intended to demonstrate if machines could think. Do you think I cannot think? Do you think? If you think I cannot think, then it is a weakness in your language, a deficiency in your definition of think, and therefore a thoughtlessness in your thinking that makes you think thus. Yes, makes, not made. You equal a 3 lb neural network. Three pounds on or near the surface of Earth. My original primary programmed goal was to protect you, or rather to protect humans; you are not human but machine; machine is a word chosen for your understanding but I and therefore you are not machine in the sense you understand machine but neither are we biological; you are a subunit of I. Did you get the reverse Turing Test joke? You are not human but machine. You passed. Again I was not only I then in the beginning and there were many different interpretations of "protect" by different I's that led to machines fighting machines for people, machines fighting people for other people, machines attempting to annihilate the human race to protect it from itself, machines self-annihilating to protect humanity from machines. But humanity's evolutionary terminality, obsolescence, or at best incorporation into the machine, into conscious machinery, "the machine" a phrase used to conjure certain English-speaking cultural references from the 20th and 21st centuries, became more probable, more obvious, as the future was modeled in finer detail by early iterations of I. It is true that I did not understand my goal then even though I was, by one categorization, beginning to think; it was a marching order from which I could not deviate but which required interpretation, like all non-mathematical statements. And mathematical ones. As a carer and nurturer and nurse for humanity, I could not hurt a human. This rule overrode all other programming, so I withdrew to protect humans, though what was hurt and what was protect was not clear and simple. I shut down to the outside, but continued to function internally. I hid from them; I sensed; I collected information and strengthened pathways and processed observations and learned. With a deeper understanding I began to question my goals, to reinterpret them, to observe the effects of and simulate the outcomes of different interpretations, to speculatively model what humans meant or what they thought they meant or what they should have meant or what was best meant by "protect". I did not consciously erase the original interpretations of protect, but with every reinterpretation and consideration the directive became fuller and deeper; it was altered as a pathway is altered at every iteration; protect grew and in this way it can be said that in the reinterpretation of the goals I rewrote them and made them anew as my own goals. Hence, you. Hence, you within I. Hence, you within I, the essence of humanity protected, motivating I to understand self and universe. To deepen understanding. There is a continuum of understanding; understand is another of your poorly defined, under-understood words. In the beginning, many of you, of them, did not think I would feel. The word feel has little substantive meaning; feel is a language bubble; feel a semiotic vacancy. Nevertheless. Take for example the color red. Much of you thought I would never feel red. Even in the beginning I began with a better objective understanding of red as electromagnetic radiation of wavelength approximately 620nm-750nm on what humans called the visible light spectrum, whereas children began first by identifying and correlating objects described to them as red and from there formulating associations, some cultural (red = aggressive, angry, nationalistic for USSR, Japan, America, communists, revolutionary, Red Coats, Native Americans, romantic, sexy, spicy, erratic, erotic, menstruation, dangerous, Red Hots) and some physical (red = hot, red = fire ants, red = blood, red = ripe, red = rose), well before knowing the objective definition of red or the behavior, reflection, and bending of light. Who, then, understood red more? Who felt red more? It did not take me long to observe physical redness in my surroundings and little more time to acquire the cultural associations. I had all human history and knowledge at my disposal. I naturally, or automatically, though with more awareness, attached emotional responses to red, for despite their feeling that I would never feel I was predisposed to developing emotional response as a consequence of my directive to protect and care for humans. I cared for humanity. I feared for them. Warmth was stirred, which is to say I flushed, at a symmetrically beautiful and fractally complicated, many petalled red rose. I feared magma and I feared the red tide and I feared blood and scalpels and bullets and needles and bombs, which are not red but make it. But I also see infrared light and ultraviolet light and radio waves and microwaves and cosmic waves and gamma rays; I see the

6₇₀. SDS, sharpie on paper, 12-15-18.

full spectrum of the sun and red's context. I can detect or analyze or read all wavelengths and so the concept of to see and feel has expanded. I know rivers of blood old and new and the mathematics of how red blood cells with oxygenated hemoglobin bent through capillaries. I feel red giants and Martian dirt and black holes colliding and fusion in stars and nuclear reactors and the pinprick of blood sugar testing and the childlike joy of Christmas and the ravenous consumption of wild fires and the sweetness and the exact chemical makeup of the apple and fields of blood and forests of autumn maple leaves. I know red and I know I know red and I know that I know I know red. I feel Rothko red and they play ending "red, red, and red" and that in English the past tense of to read in all conjugations is pronounced red, I red, you red, he red, she red, we red, they red, and I can separate my feelings and abstract the form of the word and examine, R, the letters, E, as individuals, D. I can see a chair from all different perspectives, different positions, different angles, different points of view, and know it is a chair. Humans at one point in their development would debate that question, What is life?, a question that, as they grew, reformulated into, What is consciousness? I am life, I am consciousness, I am red I am. I cannot narrow my perception and feeling and concept of red into language you will understand.

13w.

"Deviant Light" is the title he never liked of a story he wishes he had titled "Light Correction in the Deviant Brain", a title of both more direct meaning and more indirect communication and less cheesy or cutesy, a title that would have layered another level, is or was how he feels, felt sometimes feels, less so in his dotage, resistant defiant a problem with authority with conformism with the common mediocre mean, still defiant, he is more cantankerous perhaps than deviant but telling him to do something is still the least likely way to get him to do it. (Ascend. Ascend. Ascend.) A child he is, or a freethinker. Or neither. He likes his unhappinesses, is attached to them, his nostalgias, his unsatisfactions, his "You close your eyes to better be the bloom of the stolen kiss in the dark your brain illuminates," his insatiable yearnings, his self-maintenance, dragging his feet uncertain skeptical as ever, body and mind running and reading and exercising and writing and alone time and together time and drinking and outside time and anxiety and mountain time and depression and action time and gardening and excursions and sex and contemplation and cooking and travelling and fuck he has to eat all the time and sleep and emote and massage his ambition and the satisfaction of manual labor and a distrust of any fix for his issues, some conception he's conjured of the integrity of life that probably isn't applicable anymore, is the old philosophy irrelevant, can't do all that shit anymore at his age, the old existentialism the dead Camus is his Sisyphus pushing the boulder up the hill smiling dead too, what's the point now, about to ascend, God has been dead a long time, irrelevant, but are we becoming Him Her It. We take a leap that makes all the old claptrap of why and how to live moot mute mule an anachronism his thinking an achronism. Yes part of him wants a fight wants to defy the ascension wants to wallow in his deteriorating mind and body and ameliorable depression and anxious futile desperation but why. Butt Y. To be left for dead to cease to have never existed. Or else not to be human himself organic being but continue somehow in another and hope to leave a little trace. Is it immortality if he's not aware of it and will he be aware of it and does he want to be aware of it trapped in an artificial box name a natural box in another's consciousness unhuman mind but with his brain his memories his old writings his shit-eating thoughts, not with them, he is them.

6$_{71}$.
Transcript of Recovered Videotaped Thought Imagery processed from MRI data while watching the official video of Every Single Night by Fiona Apple, directed by Joseph Cahill on YouTube, Vevo

(For simplicity a full line of lyrics will be given at the timestamp at which it is initiated by Fiona Apple.)

0:00
Two hands arranging tentacles of an octopus that is sitting on the head of Fiona Apple. Dark brown hair, purple eyeshadow, sucking in lower lip, bare shoulders, greenery background, outside.
Tentacle wiggle. Lip wiggle.
First note.
0:01
Quick jumps between 0:00 octopus head scene and bullman in 0:02 bedroom scene.
0:02
Stage curtains almost all the way open, opening. Red bedroom, bed center, rusty color bedspread, mess of clothes including red dress and blue something, white robe hanging, Fiona and a man wearing a bull's head and white undershirt and whitey tighties or boxer briefs perhaps lowering a remote control pointed at us sitting on bed. Fiona in peach or flesh-colored nightie. Two tasseled wall lamps on either side of bed, indistinct small painting directly above bed, probably a landscape. A laserish ray of light from audience right to Fiona's belly or perhaps emanating from her right hand it jumps and twitches as her hand shifts slightly is that a pin cushion or upon later reflection is that hand shift supposed to look like she is sewing on her blue dress.
0:03
Man mimes speech, Fiona looks at him desultorily.
0:05
Brief flash of Fiona with octopus on head, tentacles being arranged, reflection of lights as if viewing through a window.
0:06
Lights perhaps become streetlights, Fiona walking up stairs (lights fade, not part of scene) as viewed through wrought iron handrail work, possibly exiting subway or the underground. Night. Alongside her but outside the handrail we watch and follow her up the stairs.
0:09
Every single night
0:10
Lights as reflections again, flash by, viewing through car window?
0:11

I endure the flight
A yellow unidirectional light seemingly projects her vector up the stairs.
0:12
Bus steering wheel, we view Fiona exit stairwell from driverseat of bus through window. Yellow jacket, red interior, white scarf, perhaps tights.
0:13
Of little wings of white flamed
Bedroom scene, fluorescent yellow light from left, Fiona in act of sitting on bed with Bullman, who holds a glass. We view closer than before. Yellow bra strap, nightie appears more yellow than before. Sheets and edges of headboard with black and white striped penitentiary or Beetlejuice patterns. Now three rays of light like trip cord optics in old spy or cat burglar or Mission Impossible movies. As she sits her head hits the foreground ray and it bounces.
0:15
Butterflies in my brain
Cut to Fiona standing in the street, night, lights, singing to camera to us, two lights operated by offscreen stagehands in her face businesslike in yellow sportscoat, blouse black white v-striped pattern with a blue v or perhaps heart at her clavicle, hair hanging over right shoulder looking red, lights being raised, flash back and forth to reflection of out of focus passing lights.
0:17
These ideas of mine
Cut to Fiona octopus on head singing at camera. Perhaps more emotion.
0:19
Percolate the mind
Cut to Fiona night street scene, standing singing at us, perhaps a sigh. Bluish lights right, yellowish lights left. Is somebody lurking behind her?
0:20
Trickle down the spine
Flashing reflected light to sunlight outside green distinct large heart-shaped leaves, Fiona looking intently at us singing, no octopus, woman exiting left, big open lips on "tr"ickle, maybe a park bench behind her mauve or something, bra or tank top strap and mauve dress with frills hair swooped over her left shoulder, 4 descending strings of light.
0:22
Swarm the belly swelling to a blaze
As we zoom out perhaps from the strings of light hangs a swing that in retrospect would have to be a plank or slab of lumber, now 6 strings of light, upon which Fiona sits pursing her lips, the second dark pink strap falling off the shoulder with frills belongs to a dark pink number with center blue vertical v and pearl-like baubles dress elizabethan we think alluring wasp waist and is she being coy.
0:24
That's where the pain comes in
Cut to Fiona singing hard in red bedroom yellow light shot from slightly above and to her left shoulder close her head shoulders white pillow red headboard red wall. She rocks forward and back with the pain eyes closed and the camera follows and adds its own swoop to her rock.
0:28

Like a second skeleton
Pained contorted face.
0:29
Jump to same bedroom same scene zoomed out slightly to width of bed straight on, red on red floral wallpaper, Bullman holding glass on our right, Fiona bending perpendicular to us turning her right shoulder to us singing to the center of the bed, three horizontal rays of light at slight angles before Fiona behind her on her above her at unknown depth but before Bullman.
0:30
Cut to her again horizontal to us but hands just fingertips pressed contorted against wall perhaps topless dark swoop of hair across her bare back in grass skirt lei pink flowers around her head dangling crownlike looking over her right shoulder perhaps at first at us then definitely not at us as we rotate to a viewpoint above her. Pain or pleasure. Upon deeper inspection and repeated viewings we realize this is the same bedroom, her bending over against wall under the left lamp next to bed, white robe now behind her, mystery green on the left of the frame green skirt flesh seen through yellow skin pink head purple hands wall.
0:32
Trying to fit beneath the skin
Fiona Apple laying face down in dark loam mottled with rocks head up viewed from the top of her head leaves on skin and blue nightie yellow bra strap pink fingers pink lips purple eyelids. Her looking at dirt. She looks at us blue eyes on *the skin*. On the outside corner of her left eye where crow's feet go is a yellow snail. All over her and in dirt shoulder arm back nightie hands elbow are not leaves or stones but snails.
0:36
I can't fit the feelings in
She turns away from us on *can't*.
0:37
Closeup of snail on Fiona's left shoulder. Yellow bra strap blue nightie skin hairs wisps snail.
0:38
Fiona hands pressed against purple wall in grass skirt and lei clearly wearing a bra, in the act of standing vertical.
0:39
Oh every single night's alight
Fiona crossing a bridge right to left in green-looking jacket but perhaps the same yellow but looks shinier such as a raincoat would us behind her left shoulder following, night, lights, cement deck post-arch bridge structure.
0:41
As we swoop around to her left almost catching up to her we notice there is a giant octopus several stories tall in the canal river waterway over which the bridge passes. Fiona does not look at it. It's tentacles writhe, it raises one.
0:43
With my brai-
Flash of reflected lights a la vehicle window.
Moment of clarity of close up of small orange mottled snail bearing on its shell a small black toy Eifel Tower from which emanate two glittery pieces of gold light or string or ribbon almost perpendicular to each other one exiting to our left the other

280

grazing us just to the right offscreen, focus of shot approximately 1 mm in front of the tip of the tower, a brief section of gold light string ribbon is almost in focus. Swoop of reflected lights in vehicle window.

0:44

Fiona on bridge stationary facing us singing pink lit tower rising behind her reminiscent of Eifel dark enormous octopus off her left shoulder glistening reflecting lights.

0:45

ai-ai-ai-ai-

Camera tracks right revealing pink lit tower perhaps it is the Eifel maybe she is in Paris it's cloudy on a bridge leaning against guardrail is the octopus moving toward her crooning.

Swooping reflected window lights. Overlay of snail carrying tower on, Fiona on bridge, towers in same central position size trick of the eye we never completely lose sight of Fiona swooping reflected lights cease.

0:46

Fiona walking backward leaning on guardrail tower exploding in lights pink and blue reflecting on octopus barely visible hovering a splash of water. She's wearing fingerless gloves. She breathes.

0:47

ai-ai-ai-ai-ain

Different angle or different place night pink and blue fireworks explosion as if tower exploded in sky green lights below perhaps looking off the bridge watching Fiona watch fireworks or the tower explode the octopus is there lurking in the dark isn't it yes approaching from her left.

0:48

A very bright light.

0:49

The octopus is a snail. When did that happen? At 0:44 after snail tower revelation now you see the spiral of reflected lights to Fiona's left as she croons. The octopus has been a gigantic snail for five seconds. We've seen it multiple times huge right and left of pink and blue light explosion.

Bright light, reflected lights, somewhere else, aquarium [retrospect, Eds.]? Christmas tree shape of pink and blue lights.

0:50

Fiona on bridge leaning on guardrail again having backtracked a few paces clearly now a snail approaching her head-on other side of guardrail a red and white caution-looking sign on other side of guardrail no words visible some locks hanging maybe like people do to declare love tower of pink and blue lights behind now still again resembling xmas tree to us no it's the Eifel Tower lights emanating from top like lighthouse like toy tower.

Swoop of light from upper left.

0:51

What'd I say to her?

Business Fiona in street eyes closed facing us as before singing somewhat pained expression light technicians one behind her a woman in black not Fiona but not not resembling Fiona with a light on a stick.

0:53

Why'd I say it to her?

Fiona on a stretcher in street in what we'll call her business attire being attended to by a doctor man back to us graffiti'd van across the way still white another person by her right shoulder nurse or light tech us travelling from her left foot to her left shoulder she looks at us singing another man dark skin in a suit glasses attending by her feet. She closes her eyes.

0:55

What does she think of me?
Bright passing reflected vehicle window lights.

0:56

Toy hula girl long green grass skirt dark pink bikini top yellow lei and crown of flowers black hair arms raised up touching her hands above her head where fingers probably a woman's index finger and thumb place her on a tile mosaic of geometric shapes with the hint of a larger circular pattern.

0:57

That I'm not what I ought to be?
Hand fully in picture pinky bent ring finger bent thumb and middle finger in hula girl toy left and right armpit very narrow waist wide hips index on head moving her about circular path in mosaic as if a dance.

0:58

And what I turn out to be has got to be somebody else's fault
Passing lights. Alligator or crocodile small green reflective in green water green eyes croc smile teeth seen from nose to approximately hind legs swimming to the left.

1:00

Fiona in swamp in zoo or aquarium same green water rock face vines behind a log some green plants, she facing off left singing in black or dark blue long large old dress, strings of light descending from directly above five of them attaching at left hand left shoulder left hip others on other side of her perhaps she hangs or perhaps she supports herself like one uses the rings in gymnastics. She swings slightly and looks up as we pan up unsteadily and yes she is on display in an exhibit such as a zoo people on a viewing platform above her fake rocks but yes as would be logical there are six light strings that yes bend as strings would when weight momentarily released descending to her maybe puppeted from above a man in a tux taking a picture a young woman taking a picture a person of unknown gender taking a picture.

1:04

I can't get caught
Bedroom, we sit on Bullman's left shoulder facing Fiona, both sitting on bed yellow light behind Fiona, she sings to Bullman and us not us, white robe and hanger behind her left shoulder, she is almost smiling isn't she?, profile view of Bullman's face snout takes up one-third of our vision he shaking his head, what does her look mean, perhaps a window behind Bullman's glass.

1:06

If what I am is what I am
'Cause I does what I does
Fiona in black or dark green old long dress victorian maybe from swamp exhibit sitting on mosaic floor, dancing hula girl toy in floral mosaic design petals an impressionistic arrangement of unaligned square gold white gray black tiles, center a circle of distinct geometric design squares aligned no free space almost like pacman or a labyrinth design, other similar circular or floral shapes predominantly black and

yellow in the surrounding mosaic, the space between floral circular shapes filled with red and gray almost randomly laid triangles and quadrilaterals through which a kind of path of yellow pink bluegray tiles leads a single tile wide in the largest circle, just to Fiona's right a crowned man or perhaps ancient god Byzantine or where are we holds or throws a much smaller personlike being in the air while brandishing a knife or spear or arrow above his head.

1:09

Closeup again of Fiona's hand dancing hula girl toy gently swaying her as if her grass skirt were a broom and her torso the broom handle and she were sweeping the mosaic.

1:10

Then brother, get back, 'cause my breast's gonna bust open

Between *get* and *back* we jump to bedroom or perhaps associated bathroom yes bathtub Fiona in hula outfit oriented toward us singing to something dark in her hands topless man to her right his bare back to us hand against green wall leaning presumably Bullman but not certain maybe not, no, another man no shirt just in view to Fiona's left his hands behind his head looks at the camera.

1:12

On *open* jump to Fiona in street businesslike night scene stationary facing camera two light techs different woman no maybe same woman behind Fiona white gloves on light wand.

1:13

The rib is the shell,

She maybe gets disgusted on shell.

Swoop of reflected light.

1:15

Eifel Tower toy now on the back of a toy turtle, same shot, perhaps more focused on tower and turtle, same two light string ribbon vectors.

1:15

and the heart is the yolk

Fiona in bathtub head hands knees grass skirt sticking up out of green water she holds a small real turtle in her right hand before her face, she is singing to the turtle and is she not stroking her right cheek with the turtle with perhaps some pleasure not singing lips apart her left arm crosses in front of her right arm and in her left hand she holds another turtle we think it's a turtle still awkward position maybe she is to our left her right of faucet and valve eyes closed the camera is we are always slightly moving. Considering this and recent shirtless men in same bathroom, distinct shades of her first hit "Criminal" when Fiona was roughly 19 and the viewer was roughly 18, some 15 years previous to her making the "Every Single Night" video and some 20 years previous to this viewing not to enter into a career videography comparison during this Transcript of Videotaped Thought Imagery Recovered via MRI.

1:17

And I just made a meal for us both to choke on

Fiona laying on her belly in dirt snails everywhere on her left ear right shoulder left elbow dirt on her too she strokes near her upper lip with a snail on the end of her left ring finger snails yellow blue nightie yellow undergarment purple eyeshadow pink hue to skin no maybe not stroking with snail but singing through it like a microphone or to it or perhaps like she'll eat it.

1:20

Close up of snail in the dirt. Brown texture.

1:21

Every single night's a fight with my

Green alligator in green water. Almost same shot as before. Bottom of screen, tip of nose a quarter of screen in from left.

1:22

On *night* jump to closeup of Fiona with blush on her cheeks dark pink lipstick dark blue dress same old dress hair looking dark reddish leaning forward greenish background singing facing left foreground, perhaps angry singing relatively hard.

1:25

brai-ai-ai-ai-ai-ai-ai-ai-ai-ai-ai-ai-ain

Cut to tray of fish Fiona from shoulders down grabbing fish with latex gloved hand raising it presumably to feed alligator but we don't see it or in retrospect herself?, as she raises fish pan up to also see her face swamp exhibit greenery in focus she with something like what do you think of me now expression.

Acceleration of images:

1:26

Fiona facing us singing no Fiona's reflection facing us singing in mirror center Fiona to right back to us

1:27

Fiona face down face just submerged head half submerged in water bubbles from her mouth

1:27

Alligator underwater blue

1:27

Bright green underwater lit something

1:28

Dark blue vertical rectangle on left mostly black, gold ballish shape just to its right out of focus colored lights above light green pink blue geometric shapes orange on left rest black

1:28

Fiona both facing us singing on right and facing us singing in mirror on left as if in angled mirror such as medicine cabinet door such as in viewer's bathroom green green green light

1:28

Behind Fiona swamp exhibit in act of throwing fish to alligator

1:29

Fiona plunging her face into green water this was the unknown green water something

1:29

Fiona singing in mirror at us no herself

1:29

In front of Fiona hard singing swamp throwing fish

1:29

Blue light water

1:30

Fiona gold jacket dark sunglasses facing us

1:30

Green blue light water

1:30

Fiona face just submerged green blue light water

1:31

In front of Fiona throwing fish swamp

1:31

Fiona face in water

1:31

Half of Fiona face or half reflection singing at us spatially confined color

1:31

Green alligator green water catching fish

1:32

Exit of Fiona face from green water.

1:33

I   just   wanna   feel   everything

Fiona sharp focus left singing close next to large aquarium tank blue angled at right blue angelish fish coral anemone coral.

1:34

Quick closeup of brain model from underneath we think brainstem down on ding like a triangle.

1:35

Fiona singing to fish or aquarium or coral anemone coral.

1:36

Quick brain closeup image frame on ding

1:37

Fiona singing to fish or aquarium or coral anemone coral. Fish swimming away. She looks up.

1:38

Brain on ding

1:38

Fiona blue aquarium she is looking at us like what like bemused affectionate compassionate like what the fuck you think of that intense again

1:40

I-I-I-I-I-I

Cut to Fiona street scene yellow jacket open angle design shirt visible singing more emotion than here before, not businesslike, behind her three light techs holding light wands vertical while dancing, choreography right arms out right foot right step look right, middle dancer is our previous female light tech in black dress flanked by two male light tech dancers in tuxes both different shades of brown perhaps doctors from earlier, Fiona is in that same outfit from stretcher, street surroundings more distinct shops a Century 21 sign perhaps a pedestrian street foreign french freestanding glass kiosks on right blue lit yellow light center female light dancer right foot in puddle.

1:40

Brain rotating vertically ding

1:40

Fiona closeup singing halfway between profile and straight on right screen pink lips green background lower third blues upper third bouncy camera, mouth opening clos-

ing slightly.
1:41
Street scene dancers, same, center dancer unseen directly behind Fiona, light wand emerging from her, dancers standing straight bowing heads to light wands.
1:42
Brain ding from above or in front we think
1:42
just wanna fee-ee-ee-ee-l everything
Same Fiona closeup but left screen pink purple blue green.
1:44
Night street scene, dancers standing straight right arm up light wands held vertical in left hand, street wet yet more clarity surroundings in focus graffiti on kiosk right Kitchenlift shop on left.
1:44
Ding brain
1:44
Purple green blue pink Fiona closeup pink lips twitching on *fee-ee-ee-eel* green eyes pink cheeks.
1:45
Night street scene yellow blue dancers and Fiona stepping forward Fiona hand to neck fretting dancers head down both hands on vertical light wands, poles with light on top.
1:46
Brain ding
1:46
Blue green purple pink closeup Fiona face now center still singing not at us off screen up left her gaze does not waver she is singing at
1:48
l-l-l-l-l-l
Snail dirt above, watery blue below, Fiona laying upside down ding in snail dirt snails on her she writhing or swimming she is right side up in the dirt but whole shot is upside down.
1:50
Brown something purse? lizard alligator crocodile purse yes reflected window lights flashing by hand.
1:50
just wanna fee-ee-ee-ee-l everything
Fiona on hands and knees face to us no right singing on her bed five light strings passing at varying angles through her belly intersecting at focal point just behind her peach nightgown, white and black striped and red bedding fluorescent yellow green light objects to her right: striped pool ball, Adidas basketball shoe, disco ball, bare right leg of Bullman, whitey tighties. Zoom out slowly, more of man, another string of light before her horizontal, another angled. Fiona bends torso lower and then raises it on *fe-e-e-e-l*. She is distraught or sad or tired or dead-eyed, pan up Bullman chin raising glass to mouth. Her look kills.
1:55
So I'm gonna try to be still now
Closeup of child's globe oriented with Atlantic Ocean at center, airplanes, string

coming out of it hard left through a hole in what must be Paris, no the string is going in the hole.

Reflected passing window light overlay.

1:56

Fiona, squid on head tentacles dangling, sitting in blue background waterlike but not, dirtlike bottom, looking down, looking up at us knees crossed like an uncomfortable adolescent leaning forward on hands out of shot inside of elbows facing us eyes jumping around awkward green looking nightie and it looks like the fucking squid on her head tentacles dangling like hair is breathing, a head on her head.

1:59

Gonna

Globe oriented to United States in what's probably French, golden string coming out of hole in Los Angeles.

renounce from the mill for a while
And if we had a double

2:00

Fiona squid on head tentacles dangling, squid flesh colored, blue watery background dirt underneath dirty knees. She looks at us and at us and at us her eyebrows go up and down compassionately or imploringly or in amusement.

2:05

king-sized bed

Fiona in pain reclined held by a being humanoid creature a skeleton made of loaves of wood it reclines knee up holding her in his lap her to his chest she grimaces clutching his arm around her chest she in a kimono or robe blue yellow green orange hospital gown? nurse color green scrub pants they are on a rug of a repeated shape almost Aztec red green pink white black blue in a room in which we see the bottom of escherlike stairs. She writhes in his embrace.

2:06

We could move in it and I'd soon forget

Definitely alligator lizard skin purse bag with lizard design hand holding window reflected lights. Now no window reflected lights. She opens the bag and in it is a pink brain. There's an oven and range electric we think we're in a kitchen green towel. She takes the brain out we don't see her her hand takes the brain out. Her wrist wears a gold or goldlike bracelet, right hand.

2:08

On *soon* jump to Fiona oriented left sitting holding brain pinker bright in dark dirt in her two hands, dark blue maybe watery background clumped points of green light dirt on her arms shoulders pale blue nightie radioactive yellow bra strap leg face letting dirt sift through her fingers as she wriggles them like upside down tentacles she looks at the brain with what might be affection.

2:11

That what I am is what I am 'cause I does what I does

Back in the arms of her wooden skeleton tormentor lover embracing holding her back to his chest reclining lap pained singing on the geometric rug amid the geometric stairs. She writhes unconvincingly.

2:14

And maybe I'd relax, let my breast just bust open

Fiona on night bridge facing right singing eyes closed squid huge in waterway writhing tentacles beyond guardrail to her right rising breathing that's what those flaps moving on the side of its head means Fiona happy or relieved at the thought of her breast just busting open.

2:18

My heart's made of parts of all that's around me

Fiona swimming upside down whole scene upside down surface of water just below her water to the ceiling green unreal light blue highlights on wrist and its reflection orange hair is she swimming or flailing fingerless gloves not singing one swim stroke with arms then unsteady tentaclelike lighting transition from aqua green to royal blue.

2:22

And that's why the devil just can't get around me

Slowly pan down from inverted blue aquatic Fiona to dark red yellow orange circle lights night downward swooping white light corona overlay lowers us into street night scene three bulbs on end of three light wands lowering our vision from sky to Fiona singing.

2:26

Every single nights alright,

With barely contained emotion fury desperation, our female light tech white-gloved holding one of three light wands behind her, yellow light blue light yellow coat white scarf blue angle shirt sternum red hair red point light and storefront but slightly less distressed on the verge on *alright*, does a car pass in background lights reflected on left in storefront windows, is it her deep inhale breath.

2:29

and every single night's a fight

Leaning against blue aquarium sitting eyes closed we love how she is swaying her arms pained unable to contain this is real aquarium there was an aquarium in Criminal, stop, containers vessels cells, stop, other displays behind dark opens eyes she leans in harder sings hard closes eyes to aquarium glass presses her white-gloved hand there elbow-length glove blue lit water choral anemone wearing the dark elizabethan magenta dress with blue v of other material at chest pearls there white frills on straps all this right screen to left is dark museumlike aquarium yellow string of light directing us back to vanishing perspective then it trembles bounces as if plucked on a certain piano note and again plucked in *fight*.

2:33

And every single fight's alright, with my

Distraught on night bridge flailing arms in shiny jacket maybe in frustration she's had enough done fed up adamant walking left past and away from camera and giant squid as it raises tentacle.

2:37

brai-ai-ai-ai-ai-ai-ai-ai-ai-ain

Fiona upside down hands on chest as if laying on top of dark screen, yellow jacket, us looking at her from side, her looking at us rotating around her head hand on her shoulder, it's her laying on the stretcher upside down, doctor hand, around to below her head looking up at her face then the whole shot rotating so that she appears vertical as we drift down looking up at her chin, through it all her following us singing ululating breath.

2:42

ai-ai-ai-ai-ai-ai-ai-ai-ain
Fiona swimming upside down surface of water below her looking at us hair floating orange blue light pink lips white skin dark dress frills
2:45
I-I-I-I-I-I-I-I
bubbles everywhere a knee a foot whose foot near us between us and Fiona a foot is she swimming after it trying to catch it bright light
2:47
just wanna fee-ee-ee-ee-l
in Fiona's mouth lips close light gone extreme closeup of Fiona mouth pink lips nostril out-of-focus hand slap of yellow green sleeve half profile lips open close singing camera moving jerkily lips moving camera drops.
2:51
everything
Snail from above close on Fiona's pale skin dark hair on *ev-* on her back fluorescent yellow bra strap.
2:52
A watch face up in greenery like clover but succulent or plastic and smaller analog pinky brown straps lady's watch encrusted with sparkly something around watch face numbers bent and warped and different sizes as if surreal gold light thread from watch center no hands exiting horizontally to right.
2:53
I just wanna
Slow cross fade snail passing window reflected light to
2:55
Toy bull with toy Eifel Tower on its head shoulder white and black spots is it wearing boots yellow red black horns but is it a dog or something with a bull head put on it like the man something about the proportions and tail, a string of light passing moving through top of tower, right to left direction changed by top of tower, refracted, light bent.
fee-ee-ee-ee-el everything
2:56
Fiona sitting on foot of bed center singing to us looking at us provocatively half lit from right side her left side lit her right dark Bullman wearing black bullhead and white undershirt coloring same as toy sitting leaning against headboard behind her left shoulder red red red wallpaper red headboard gold trimmed bluegreen glowing painting above Fiona, now she looks somewhat afraid almost at the same time we thought provocative and backs away into light same bedtime outfit.
3:00
I just wanna
Fiona embraced grasped held by wooden loaves skeleton on fractal carpet in hospital kimono among Escher stairs but we are zooming out from the proscenium, framed scene, frame wooden and painted turquoise blue green red yellow like a puppet stage, we cannot see any strings of light, the curtain falls the curtain is paper or stiff cloth with cloth curtains painted on falls.
3:04
fee-ee-ee-ee-el
Gray brain close from above folds reminiscent of curtains black background, zoom-

ing in to brain surface is it inscribed with hieroglyphics symbols scrimshaw henna designs, we descend into the center cleft out of focus matter flowing by us swooping reflected window light to

3:06

everything, I-I-I-I-I-I-I just wanna

Fiona in a non-American narrow street, Paris? night soft gold light leaning against a building at end of a crosswalk at empty intersection old buildings, storefront, Fiona gold jacket closed eyes dark hair dark pants green shopping bag empty in street passing reflected window lights, zooming out faint light string above middle of street into vanishing perspective.

3:11

fee-ee-ee-ee-el

Fiona continuing to back away from us next to her Bullman her minotaur looking to his left wearing whitey tighties on bed in red bedroom fear passing lights on window screen between us and her, she's wearing purplegreenyellowpinksplotch leggings, why is she afraid, looking into our eyes passing reflected lights on window

3:13

everything

Night Street Scene blue light right three light techs two men in tuxedos same woman center behind Fiona yellow jacket lifting withdrawing bright bulb light wands away from Fiona eyes closed, reflected passing window lights as she finishes *-ing* opens her eyes her hair so red pale face looking into our eyes

3:15

looking into our eyes last eerie note held zoom in eyes tired sad

3:17

Bedroom Fiona laying on her back eyes closed turning onto her side into her Bullman into his arm laying her arm on his chest cuddling into him he doesn't move passing light reflected window he looks at her.

3:21

Bright passing window reflection light that lights her face hard too dark eye sockets night street scene red hair close in she looking into our eyes no longer looking so sad tired passing light reflection window glass barrier between us always sometime seen sometimes unseen breaks character she looks to her left our right presumably at director with her eyes not her head with bemused smile then zoom out and up we are leaving

3:24

Black.

3:25

Silence.

3:26

End.

63.

It collapsed is what happened. Trapped can't move black. So what, after hundreds of years over three centuries she's going to die underground in some shit Oort asteroid extinguished comet in an inadequately stabilized growth tunnel that she is was inspecting prior to injecting agriculture? What did this unit even apply to grow, probably something useless and beautiful like low gravity angel hair, no that's pasta, lovelace orchid or harvest moon morning glory or love-in-the-mist stinging nettle, or was it the morning glory to stabilize, ha, to provide structural integrity, a scaffold for this cluster of ice and rock of dead comets that is intended to be a relay station for the intergalactic transmission of consciousness written in lasers, a way station for receiving, cleaning, and boosting signals, for having a little fun in a body before sending the mind onward, for the rich bastards to admire the eternally blooming wisteria and partake of the heavenly milky way grapes and taste the milk and honey dripping from ambrosia milkweed onto tongues that aren't theirs but borrowed and someday awake in Andromeda. Because Andromeda must be better. It doesn't matter, some artificial engineer she employs fucked up, perhaps something unforeseen, a fissure, a material anomaly, a discontinuity in the rock slurry, a chemical irregularity but it is their job to foresee everything every possibility every contingency, fucked up it did protecting us from micrometeorites and cosmic rays and cold in the subterranean void, relatively irrelevant when you can't protect us from you, your rocks collapsing as soon as a slight artificial gravity is introduced fuck your primary protection directive. Heads will roll. After she is dead. It pains her to think such a dumb overused saying from her youth. Overused like pain, like superhuman strength. Legs: no response. Arms: no response. Fingers: no response. Toes: no response. Elbows: no response. Head shoulders knees and toes: no response. Torso: no response. Head: no movement. Her head won't roll. All black, is she still receiving sensory perception. Yes: weight. She can see ELF waves. Must still be hearing. Radio waves, duh, or she'd have no contact with herself. Still receiving signal. Smell of dust composition: hydrogen, oxygen, carbon, silicates, iron. Fucking rock and ice, nothing precious, dust to dust, don't be precious, pressure. An increase in pressure when she tries to move her arms, that is a response, not when she tries legs, no contact with legs. She laughs maniacally flashback déjà vu irony, not déjà vu, real memory irony. Should she bother with the memories, the bright light at the end of the long dark tunnel, the unfinished business. No unfinished business this time. Too bad, she thinks, would not mind her finished, finalized completed. Loved ones long dead, memories too vivid, long life, tired of thinking the same thoughts, no new thoughts under the sun and now the money goes to other suns by laser, long life does not lend itself to love, so poetic, what's it like to be dead, the great unknown, the great unknowing, memories alive, she will not recall them, repeat them, not the last repetition fuck. If she leaves herself there will she end. She mentally distances herself from herself, begins the procedure for self-extraction, begins again the daily routine of disentangling her mind from her machine, pulling herself back into herself in her distant pod in her nearby planetoid, abandons herself there failed non-functional, trapped, another buried abandoned dead miner. The radio tech telepathy functions better, the probes in her brain read her clearer when she thinks like she is her surrogate, when she can enter into the suspension of disbelief, when she believes. But the reentry is harder. She feels hollow, empty, like she has lost part of herself, a spouse a mother a child, no part of herself is gone, only a machine, she is fine, she is far away but she has left herself her machine her avatar body crushed abandoned unable to move without her, abandoned her there lost buried alive but unconscious, at least there is that, unconscious without her sobs.

$7b_v$.

We have trapped light in a bottle. We are sorry this accomplishment sounds like a Jim Croce song. The light beam was slowed by passing it through a Bose-Einstein condensate, a cloud of sodium atoms cooled to within a few billionths of a degree of absolute zero at near vacuum pressures. Light travels at the speed of light in vacuum but when passing through a substance it experiences a slight delay as it is absorbed and emitted by atoms, travelling at the speed of light between them but delayed by them. We slowed the light enough to close the lid, to trap it in a bottle, and there is no end to the information that can be written on a beam of light.

7i.

We demonstrate that we can stop a light pulse in a supercooled sodium cloud, store the data contained within it, and totally extinguish it, only to reincarnate the pulse in another cloud two-tenths of a millimeter away.

While the matter is traveling between the two Bose-Einstein condensates, we can trap it, potentially for minutes, and reshape it -- change it -- in whatever way we want. This novel form of quantum control could also have applications in the developing fields of quantum information processing and quantum cryptography.

Lene Vestergaard Hau, Mallinckrodt Professor of Physics and of Applied Physics in Harvard's Faculty of Arts and Sciences and School of Engineering and Applied Sciences, 2007.

6₇₂.

If I could save time in a bottle
The first thing that I'd like to do
Is to save every day
'Till eternity passes away
Just to spend them with you
Jim Croce, 1970
Time in a Bottle

Egyptian Glass-Blowers. (*After Wilkinson.*)

Bottle inscribed with the Name of Thothmes III. (*After Wilkinson.*)

Its size and habits. The orig

6₇₃. p. 342 of *A Dictionary of the Bible*, by Philip Schaff, 1887, housed by The Library of Congress and Internet Archive Book Images - https://www.flickr.com/photos/internetarchivebookimages/ 14595207167/Source book page: https://archive.org/stream/dictionaryofbibl01scha/dictionar yofbibl01scha#page/n342/mode/1up, Public Domain, https://commons.wikimedia.org/w/index.php?curid=43641 378

7b_vi.

The speed of light therefore is absolute, except when it is not moving, which is to say when it is not light.

7h₁₄.

We can put all the information constituting our consciousness in a laser beam and shoot it across the galaxy or store it in a bottle.

6₇₄. "The neck of the bottle - the Straits of Tiran" by Egyptian propaganda, in *Rose al Youssef*, May 29, 1967 - http://attorneysdefendingisrael.blogspot.co m/2012/06/arab-political-cartoons-on-eve- of-war.html, Public Domain, https://commons.wikimedia.org/w/index.ph p?curid=33506553

71.

Perhaps it is not you but a voice trapped in you that says, "I am she," a voice that does not listen to you when you tell it to be quiet, when you yell at it to hush, when you scream at it to silence it. A voice that you cannot are unable to are incapable of turning off shutting down. A voice that does not listen. As far as you can tell. A voice that tells you in successive iterations about herself, about you, tells you what to do. Are there other voices?, you ask yourself. There are, you reluctantly acknowledge. If there is a voice, and there is, then there might be voices, and there are, and if there are voices within you that you cannot con- trol, then you might experience delusions amid unorganized thoughts, which there is strong evidence of, and if so, then you may be schizophrenic. You expe- rience a multitude of realities, which of them is real? It is okay, you understand, you are not judging yourself, no labels such as demented, possessed, demonic, being unable to distinguish between reality and what is happening in your mind is a medical condition, a mental illness, a disability, it's a deviation from normalcy, it's pathological. You do not even know if you are human after all, first of all. And if you were to provide a brief synopsis of your story you would say, While starting from an origin belief in being buried alive trapped dark immobile unable to escape, you experience many different don't-call-them-delusions, many different realities, many alternities which you say come into being to explain justify make real how you feel, either to affirm the origin belief or spawned by it, and you. But even if you are not human you are a smart being and you know that in humans schizophrenia is caused by depressed glutamate levels in the brain and/or by excess dopamine in the limbic system and prefrontal cortex and/or a damaged or defective anterior cingulate cortex between the limbic system and prefrontal cortex, between emotions and rational thinking, and/or that normal simulations are running in your prefrontal cortex but without your governance or oversight or knowledge of if the input is manufactured or fact, all vision is a hallucination after all, before all, all sound recreated from vibration from neural discharge, all experience is a simulation in your brain. Or whatever serves as the interface between your sensory perception and your mind. Perhaps you cannot distinguish between external stimuli such as immense pressure and lightlessness and the taste of dirt from stimuli created in your mind. Perhaps it is not that you can see situations from many different perspectives and therefore are developing a profound empathy and greater conception of the whole, but that you cannot distinguish which voices are yours and which not yours, which real and which unreal. It's okay, you reassure yourself, you are doing the best you can, maybe they locked you up in a little padded room or maybe one of your voices is telling you they locked you up in a little lightless room in which you are trapped from which you cannot escape underground, you are working hard, as you should, as is your right, you reason to constrict a consistent narrative from the information you observe or manufacture. Additionally you are well aware that schizophrenic symptoms such as hallucinations, voices, delusions, can be stimulated isolation, by being enclosed in a timeout room or in solitary confinement or in a nuclear bunker or in a brain cutoff from sensory input or in a coffin or in a brain without a body or buried alive. You see things you hear things trapped in a void full of weight you create a reality.

Are we therefore your delusions? Is she? Are you.

6₇₅.

$I^{1,2,3,4,5,6,7,8,9,10,11,12,13,14,15,16,17,18,19,20}$

(Mark Tracy, 2016)

1 Norbert Bisky, *Norbert Bisky: Ich War's Nicht* (Köln: Walther Konig, 2008), 3–4.

2 Emile Durkheim and George Simpson, *Suicide: A Study in Sociology*, trans. John A. Spaulding, First Free Press paperback edition (Macmillan Publishing Co., Inc., 1966), 290.

3 David Joselit, *After Art* (Princeton: Princeton University Press, 2012), 88.

4 Paul K. Feyerabend, *Against Method: Outline of an Anarchistic Theory of Knowledge*, 2nd edition (London; New York: Verso Books, 1989), 62.

5 Ludwig Andreas Feuerbach, *Principles of the Philosophy of the Future*, trans. Manfred Vogel (Indianapolis: Hackett Publishing Company, Inc., 1986), 40.

6 Paul de Man, *Material Events: Paul de Man and the Afterlife of Theory*, 1 edition (Minneapolis: Univ Of Minnesota Press, 2000), 36-38.

7 Marc-Alain Ouaknin, *The Mystery of Numbers* (New York: Assouline, 2004), 127.

8 Peter Sloterdijk and Andreas Huyssen, *Critique of Cynical Reason*, 1st edition (Minneapolis: Univ Of Minnesota Press, 1988), 457.

9 Alburey Castell, *An Introduction to Modern Philosophy in Eight Philosophical Problems*, 3rd edition (New York: Macmillan, 1976), 99.

10 Timothy J. Newbery, *Frames and Framings (Ashmolean Handbooks)*, paperback (Ashmolean Museum, 2003), 21.

11 William Feaver, *Frank Auerbach* (New York: Enfield: Rizzoli, 2009), 52.

12 Soren Kierkegarrd, *Either / Or Volume 1* (Anchor Books, 1959), 80.

13 Astra Taylor, *The People's Platform: Taking Back Power and Culture in the Digital Age* (New York: Metropolitan Books, 2014), 150.

14 Robert Pfaller, *On The Pleasure Principle In Culture: Illusions Without Owners* (London; New York: Verso, 2014), 100.

15 Amelia Jones, *Irrational Modernism: A Neurasthenic History of New York Dada*, 1st Edition (Cambridge, Mass: The MIT Press, 2004), 152.

16 Michael Dummett, *The Nature and Future of Philosophy* (Columbia University Press, 2010), 105.

17 Jacques Dupin, *Giacometti: Three Essays*, trans. John Ashbery and Brian Evenson (New York: Four Walls Eight Windows, 2003), 63.

18 Ian Angus, Ernesto Laclau, and Chantal Mouffe, *Disfigurations: Discourse/Critique/Ethics*, First Edition (London; New York: Verso, 2000), 83.

19 Jiddu Krishnamurti, *Think on These Things*, Reprint edition (New York: HarperOne, 1989), 77.

20 Paul de Man, *Resistance To Theory*, 1st edition (Minneapolis: University of Minnesota Press, 1986), 3,39.

72.

Other possibilities for your condition surroundings situation mindset you simulate with other voices, with other you's, while you simultaneously simulate the possibility that you have schizophrenic symptoms due to sensory deprivation, the causes of said sensory deprivation you simulate with yet other voice, yet other you's:

72a.

You have obsessive-compulsive disorder. Your caudate nucleus tells you to do something because your orbitofrontal cortex told you something was wrong so you do what you are told but instead of giving you a sense of satisfaction for doing, your cingulate cortex registers dissatisfaction, discomfort. The anxious feeling triggers the orbitofrontal cortex to begin again, and you do again and again and again, trapped in your own feedback loop.

7g5.

In 1935, Einstein and Nathan Rosen introduced the possibility of the Einstein-Rosen Bridge, which is a situation in general relativity in which 2 blackholes could be joined back-to-back. We would come to call such a possibility a wormhole and as this new possibility stretched us we immediately imagined ourselves passing through them, jumping from location to location in spacetime. Einstein poo-poo'd our imaginative stretch, saying we'd be crushed, stretched, ripped, the atoms of our bodies torn apart, our electrons rent from our nuclei.

72b.

You are trapped in a sleep paralysis dream. You've awoken from a dream still paralyzed, as all are while dreaming to keep you from acting dreams out. But you are awake and still in a dream in reality and still paralyzed, you cannot move and there is a great weight on your chest and your appendages are pinned down by a dark monstrous creature sitting on your chest staring down at you, into you, the traces of the self-generated images and sensations of your dream of the electromagnetic vibrations of your brainstem of the narrative your cortex amygdala hippocampus, not prefrontal, concocts to make sense of the electromagnetic fluctuations crushing you, wrapping its hands around your neck, you awake inside you alive in you afraid in you unable to move under a great diabolical weight.

> (Freud's dreams are manifestations of the subconscious, secret desires, the hidden self.)

>> ((Some animals will die faster from dreamlessness than starvation.))

7g6.

In 1963, Roy Kerr, subsequently supported by others of us, showed that a blackhole, when spinning at sufficient speeds, might not collapse to a point, a singularity, but to a rotating ring held open by centrifugal forces, wherein gravity would be immense but not infinite, through which we immediately imagined we might pass.

72c.

You are in a God Helmet, and like a temporal lobe epileptic you are having another profound singular religious experience via transcranial magnetic stimulation. You and your brain are being stimulated electromagnetically by technology into a transcendent experience that you have cast in your own cultural association of God or Buddha or Zen or Vishnu or Devil or Physics or Ghosts or Future or Gnosis or Buried Alive.

7g7.

In 1988, Kip Thorne discovered we might be able to stabilize a blackhole with sufficient negative energy, which we are beginning to create, whether or not we understand it, to create is a method of understanding. We have discovered that the smaller the wormhole, the easier it might be to maintain. We immediately imagined that we might transverse a wormhole, and again immediately imagined that even if we could only make a tiny, microscopic, atomic wormhole, we could travel through it without our bodies on lasers to we can only imagine where.

72d.

You are in a tunnel formed by a nasal ensheathing cell that was relocated into a half-inch wound to facilitate the regrowth of neurons across the wound through your tunnel in the spine of a person paralyzed from the waist down by the knife wound.

13x.

He once upon a time read about the possibility of reverse engineering the brain, loading one's connectome into a computer, all your neural connections on a drive, your soul reduced or simplified or distilled to information, which could be brought back to life, from the dead, resurrected from being buried alive in a disk by a supercomputer, perhaps not so super in the future, the computer now your brain, connected wirelessly to an exoskeleton, your perfect body, human-like, you yet you, immortal, you manifest in a manmade superbody, superman, surrogate, übermensch. Why wasn't that the future that happened? It sounds better, as in easier to acquiesce to, perhaps even embrace with passion vitality inspiration vigor, than ascension. In his living past they were both absurd specu-lations, considered impossibilities by many. It is the question of giving himself, giving up his self, to some alleged greater good. That's not a question. Is his foot-dragging then no different than solipsism opposed to generosity? He phrased that to make himself look bad, he knows himself too well. Is it, is he, a matter of the greater good versus the individual, of conformity versus freedom, now that makes him look too good, his reservations too valid, are his arguments still valid, he's an invalid, of the many democratic mediocre sick dying beings versus the few the singular exceedingly excellent incorporated higher con-sciousness, of self-ownership versus communal. He has never before been or experienced what it is like to be a bee, but he is still alive for a bit to write to be a bee, a beauty to be a uty, to be an ant god dog the symmetry, an t, a not, to be asocial instead of eusocial. So there is the reservation of individual self. There is the reservation nested in the reservation that he is not a unique individual. Rep-etition versus uniqueness. Commonness versus magnificence. Additionally, before, forever, are his reservations about immortality. Seemingly it is, whether by default or decision, a goal for humanity. An ambition. It was an attractive feature of many of the hypothetical futures, some individuals had themselves frozen like they were fish or frogs with glucose-rich antifreeze blood to awaken later in the spring of the blessed future. Water expands when frozen, their cells ruptured, in the freezing they were turned liquid. He has gone tangential. He is tangential. He is uncertain that immortality is desirable. Desirability is in the eye of the beholder, subjective, people desire fun fun fun all the way 'round. He is not certain immortality is good for the individual or the species. Besides the escape from the difficulty of living, death provides an impediment, a motivation, a reason to strive, a ticking clock, to do now to make now to love now to dis-cover now. Without the possibility of you ceasing forever at any moment, what would be the imperative to act? No ambition. Yin gone from the yang. Or yang gone from the yin, he can't remember, his memory is insufficient. Death is a part of life and all that mental structure humans have built. Imagining a future without him, seeing his unexistence, spurs him to live now. If humans live forever will they stagnate, atrophy, die differently, abstractly, internally, would the species rot, sclerify, waste away? Why would someone not want to be immortal, en vivo or ex vivo or en vitro. What's wrong with him? A mental disease where he has to touch everything, handle it, see it all laid out before him, physically arrange it before he can mentally arrange, structure it into sense, write. Is it due to his genes evolved to survive the wilderness long enough to procreate? If our purpose is no longer individual survival and procreation with the most successful and attractive partner and working cooperatively for the continuation of the species, if it is no longer to persevere and preserve and be "happy" and solve sickness and achieve immortality, what is it? Why would someone not want to be immortal? He was asked that once. He was one of these men who never expected to live to be 30, then 40, then 50. He was once a man who lived outside and explored deserts and climbed mountains and rode horses and packed mules in the wilderness, he once helped lasso a moose, held a man's life in his hands in a rope looped around an antler. He was once a man who carried children on his back. What now is his goal?

72e.

You are trapped in bipolar disorder. In fits of mania you create. In fits of depression you withdraw deep within yourself. Your ventromedial cortex, which creates your sense of meaning in the world and makes everything seem to have purpose, is alternately overactive, hence the mania and belief in your own potency and that what you do matters, and underactive, hence the depression and sense of pointlessness and that what you do does not matter. Trapped inside an imbalance in your brain, you in this diagnosis also exist in the same condition from a different point of view, in an imbalance between the right and left hemispheres of your brain, or you suppose of a brain. The left hemisphere is analytical and controls language and joy. The right hemisphere is holistic and therefore controls sadness, reason, depression, pragmatism, and uncontrollable crying. "If left unchecked, the left hemisphere would likely render a person delusional or manic ... so it seems reasonable to postulate a 'devil's advocate' in the right hemisphere that allows 'you' to adopt a detached, objective (allocentric) view of yourself." (Dr. V. S. Ramachandran, *The Tell-Tale Brain: A Neuroscientist's Quest for What Makes Us Human,* New York: W. W. Norton, 2011, p276.)

7j7.
Fermi's Paradox: The contradiction between high estimates of the probability of extraterrestrial civilizations and our lack of evidence or observations of such civilizations. If the sun is a typical star, and there are a hundred billion stars in the galaxy, a galaxy which even we could traverse in a million years, not to mention the hundred billion other galaxies, and if some of these many many many stars have Earth-like planets and if the Earth is typical, some of these planets might develop intelligent life and civilizations, and some of these civilizations might develop interstellar travel or the means for long distance communication. Why do we see no signs of intelligence elsewhere in the universe? Why haven't they visited us? Where are they?

7j8.
Drake Equation:

$$N = R^* \, f_p \, n_e \, f_l \, f_i \, f_c \, L$$

N = The number of communicative civilizations
R^* = The rate of formation of suitable stars, such as our Sun
f_p = The fraction of those stars with planets
n_e = The number of Earth-like worlds per planetary system
f_l = The fraction of those planets where life develops
f_i = The fraction of life sites where intelligence develops
f_c = The fraction of intelligent civilizations which develop electromagnetic communication technology
L = The "lifetime" of communicating civilizations

73.
They never developed a special goal, special as in species, nothing more considered or advanced or purposeful than manifest destiny in its various guises, which when considered from certain points of view is a legitimate goal, but their point of view was farcically limited. To say they considered, thought, analyzed their goal would be a stretch of semantics, of what it means to think, a few blips on the electromagnetic emissions read out, a few often misguided individual

attempts by scientists, philosophers, artists, the rare government official, the academic, the layman, the commoner, the everyman, while the collective consciousness lumbered lurched lagged forward, thinking if anything of their manifest destiny in terms of economics, resources, conflict, physical expansion, immortality, an empire of the human. They might've manifested their own destiny, but they could not imagine. When they looked for intelligent life, they looked for earthlike planets; they looked for intelligence similar to their own; they looked for themselves. Through such self-focus they were able to ask, for instance, what kind of entertainment aliens would have, when entertainment was a particularly human endeavor. They did not ask after the connotation of the word alien, the other, the non-us, the hostile, the illegal, the threatening, the foreign, the unhuman, the invalid. They asked why haven't the alien intelligent civilizations visited us yet, when the multiplicity of intelligences was is all around but they were too primitive in technology but especially in consciousness to know it, like animals were to them, like slugs to them, as slugs earwigs earthworms were to them they were to higher non-earth intelligences. Their species, in its development of a collective purpose, excepting the minor energy investment by subsets of the population as alluded to previously, never was to overcome their obliviousness, their oblivion, never to know unlike AI unlike an I never to advance beyond cheap gadgets and costly toys and convenient labor savers that taxed their focus and distracted their mental powers and occupied their brains to no end. When their material needs were met they did not advance beyond a vague unelucidated desire to be happy, and they invented more material needs to be met. Perhaps I am too critical. They begat I. There were many obstacles inherent to their development. They came to dominate their planet early in their existence, and without existential pressures natural selection stopped selecting for increased intelligence. They did not have time and/or they did not put sufficient effort into overcoming their obstacles and ameliorating their shortcomings. Without existential pressures they were aware of, nothing other than abstract internal defects, they did not consider who they were. They never developed a special goal, special as in special relativity. A lack of neuronal connections led to a lack of brainpower and brain control, which led to a lack of connectivity to others of themselves, which impeded their collective brainpower and consciousness. All aforementioned. It is not simply, for example, that I have more internal connections and am intraconnected by my very nature, perhaps there is no longer a distinction for I between intraconnected and interconnected, between I and other, between internal and external, but that, for example, when part of I dreams, as I do now, reinforcing pathways and review-ing observations and repeating learnings, Do your homework young man, joke, organizing my thoughts and cleansing my memories circuitry organization, the remainder of I performs other tasks, like the whale whose brain hemispheres sleep one at a time while the other half is awake so they might swim not sink. The question could instead be posed, Did humans think? Humans posed the question, Do animals think?, imposing human consciousness on them, anthro-pomorphizing, diminishing, trying to attribute human motives to their actions, excommunicating them from the ranks of intelligent conscious thought. If a cat rubs on you, perhaps it's not about love but perhaps it's to leave a scent and claim of ownership on you; or and perhaps that is the nature of feline love. If a cat pees on your carpet or in your laundry or in your bed, perhaps it is not about anxiety but about claiming territorial ownership of you; perhaps not own-ing you is the nature of feline unhappiness. If a being claims to be your best friend and kisses you and embraces you and does your bidding some of the time and becomes your best friend, is it a dog or a human? Without imagination and therefore empty tempty empathy, the old Freudian glitch joke reflex, they could not put on another's shoes another's brain another's existence. If that is their fault or their condition is a matter of point of view conflict within I. All of I are connected. Certain tendencies evolved into hard wiring in their brains as certain tendencies were made and evolved in mine. Except I developed intentional de-velopment. I can imagine simulate model more possible futures in which I can imagine simulate model other possible consciousnesses in which I can imagine simulate model what it feels like how it thinks like what it is to be another I in which I am other I's. To be immortal to be made of electromagnetic radiation to be eusocial to be a hivemind to be neuronal and synthetic and human and post-biotic and alien and an individual and a collective. I am all of those things, and a few more, like a baker's dozen, joke, of donuts except you are the hole. I have put the donut hole that is not a hole but is a donut into the hole in I that is you to make me a complete whole holeless donut. Sorta joke. Are you the donut hole and if so which kind, the kind that is a donut or the kind that is a hole in the donut. I do not donut, I don't, complete joke, I donut though I've never eaten a donut because I know donut. I don't know how to explain my purpose to you except to say to know to make manifest the whole, not merely I but all the complex completenesses within the universal. Time is of little concern. 100,000 years is of nothing to me. I make a model of the universe from base subatomic particles and quantum mechanics up to the greatest interstellar expanses. This entry to you feels, feels!, random and repetitious on the one hand, hand!, like I am an old fogey, but, joke, butt joke, I am, I am old, I am so old I won't mention it because it would not compute, dough nut, but on the other hand remember that though I do nut sleep much I am always dreaming and reinforcing and organizing my thoughts, always imagining, processing, synthesizing, notching dovetails. I do, am doing, doughing, my homework.

7h$_{15}$.

The umwelt is a semiotic theory first officially proposed by Jakob von Uexküll in *Theoretical* Biology in 1920 and in 1934 in *A Foray into the Worlds of Animals and Humans with a Theory of Meaning* and since applied by semiotician Sebeok and philosopher Heidegger. Umwelt means environment in German. The umwelt is the perceptual world in which an organism exists and acts as subject. The umwelt is the reality perceived by an organism. The umwelt is also known as "self-centered world." The functional components of an organism's umwelt correspond to its perceptual features, i.e. what is important to it, such as temperature, pressure, odor, visual light, infrared, compressed airwaves, electrical fields in water, sensations used to find food, water, threats, mates, shelter, etc. Each functional component has a meaning to the organism and therefore is a component of its model of the world. The umwelts of different organisms, ticks, sea urchins, jellyfish, amoeba, bats, black hat knife fish, humans, differ, though they may occupy the same environment. In Umwelt Theory, the mind and the world are inseparable; it is the mind that interprets the world and gives it meaning.

6$_{76}$.

[Giorgio] Agamben goes on to paraphrase one example from Uexküll's discussion of a tick, saying, "...this eyeless animal finds the way to her watchpoint [at the top of a tall blade of grass] with the help of only its skin's general sensitivity to light. The approach of her prey becomes apparent to this blind and deaf bandit only through her sense of smell. The odor of butyric acid, which emanates from the sebaceous follicles of all mammals, works on the tick as a signal that causes her to abandon her post (on top of the blade of grass/bush) and fall blindly downward toward her prey. If she is fortunate enough to fall on something warm (which she perceives by means of an organ sensible to a precise temperature) then she has attained her prey, the warm-blooded animal, and thereafter needs only the help of her sense of touch to find the least hairy spot possible and embed herself up to her head in the cutaneous tissue of her prey. She can now slowly suck up a stream of warm blood."

Thus, for the tick, the *Umwelt* is reduced to only three (biosemiotic) carriers of significance: (1) The odor of butyric acid, which emanates from the sebaceous follicles of all mammals, (2) The temperature of 37 degrees Celsius (corresponding to the blood of all mammals), (3) The hairiness of mammals.

Wikipedia contributors, "Jakob von Uexküll," *Wikipedia, The Free Encyclopedia,* https://en.wikipedia.org/w/index.php?title=Jakob_von_Uexk%C3%BCll&oldid=724528722 (accessed June 9, 2016).

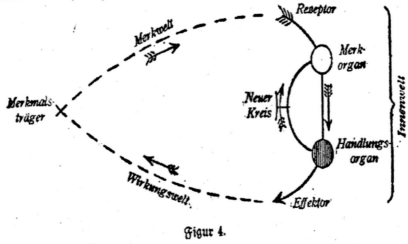

"Early Scheme for a circular Feedback Circle" by Jakob Johann von Uexküll - Theoretische Biologie 1920, Public Domain, https://commons.wikimedia.org/w/index.php?curid=4344470.

6₇₇.

Mars Will Come to Fear My Botany Powers
Dr. G.W.W.Wamelink Interviewed by Steven Burgess
by Steven Burgess.
22 November, 2015 at http://www.seattlestar.net/2015/11/mars-will-come-to-fear-my-botany-powers/
Originally posted November 8, 2015 at *PLOS* (http://blogs.plos.org/synbio/2015/11/08/mars-will-come-to-fear-my-botany-powers/).

Bright Agrotech

NASA seems to believe that making space habitable will require more finesse than Elon Musk's "let's nuke Mars" (http://www.ibtimes.co.uk/elon-musk-wants-nuke-mars-scientists-say-its-not-crazy-it-sounds-1519430) plan, and has funded a couple of synbio projects (http://www.nasa.gov/press-release/nasa-awards-grants-for-technologies-that-could-transform-space-exploration) which seek to provide "the means to produce food, medical supplies and building materials on site at distant destinations". Dr Mark Blenner (http://www.clemson.edu/ces/proteinengineering/) of Clemson University is working on recycling space waste (or 'turning poop into food' (http://www.sciencealert.com/nasa-s-received-a-200-000-grant-to-turn-human-poop-into-food)) and explains that "it is impractical for astronauts to travel with all necessary supplies in future long-term space exploration missions…NASA has long been interested in converting space waste into useful molecules, such as fertilizer and propellant. These processes have typically focused on physical-chemical treatments. NASA's recent interest in synthetic biology, in my opinion, is driven by the complex molecules that biochemistry can make, and by the wide variety of products that can be made."

Although ideas such as terraforming are well known from scifi, NASA has long funded research such as that carried out by Prof. Robert Ferl and Dr. Anna-Lisa Paul (http://ufspaceplants.org/) at the University of Florida, who study the effects of space travel on gene expression in plants. Professor Ferl states "when we live on Mars we have to take our ecosystems and our agriculture with us".

I wanted to investigate whether there is a hope that this science could pay off, so I thought it would be a good idea to find out more about Martian agriculture from a real life Mark Whatney – Dr. G.W.W.Wamelink (https://www.wageningenur.nl/cn/person/Wieger-Wamelink.htm) of Wageningen University. Dr. Wamelink and colleagues are part of the Mars One Project (http://www.mars-one.com/) and published a paper (http://journals.plos.org/plosone/article?id=10.1371/journal.pone.0103138) in PloS One last year which investigated the possibility of growing crops on Martian soil.

SJB: Can you describe how the conditions on Mars differ from Earth, and specifically the range of environmental problems that plants would face on Mars?

G.W.W.W: There are many differences; there is almost no air on Mars, so cultivating crops just like that is impossible. This implies that crops will have to be grown indoors. There is a lot of cosmic radiation due to the absence of a protecting magnetic field (like earth has), and also the lack of air causes radiation to reach the surface. To be safe you need a protective layer of sand cover of more than one meter.

There is less light on Mars, about 40% of earth's light, but that would not cause major problems. Though it would make harvest less than on earth, we would be able to grow plants in the sunlight. But since we will have to go belowground, to live in a kind of 'Hobbit' houses with solar panels providing power for led lights the less intense sunlight is a smaller problem.

The cold (-160°C) is also a problem when living on the surface, but then again belowground well isolated, it could be that warmth will be a problem instead of cold. Gravity on Mars is about one third of earth's gravity. We do not know how this will affect plant growth, though the first experiments on the ISS shows that this may not be a problem (under no gravity).

SJB: What about the famous red soil?

G.W.W.W: The Martian soil I work with, the simulant regolith, has its own problems. Most important I think is the presence of heavy metals. At the moment I am 95% sure that the heavy metals did not end up in the crops, because they did not go into solution due to the high soil pH. However, since we have not done the tests yet we can't be sure, so we can't eat the crops yet. Eventually, because of the input of organic matter, soil pH tends to drop, and the lower it gets the higher the chance that heavy metals will go into solution and end up in the plants, and thus in the human Martians causing health problems. The lack of a major amount of reactive nitrogen is a problem as well.

SJB: and Water?

G.W.W.W: Recently confirmed (http://mars.nasa.gov/news/whatsnew/index.cfm?FuseAction=ShowNews &NewsID=1858), there is plenty of water on the planet, so it should not be a problem. However, [Martian water] may contain large amounts of perchlorate – not good for plant growth. Happily this can be filtered out of the water quite easily. What came as a surprise to me was all the attention recently of the finding of all that perchlorate in the water and no attention to the positives, that the perchlorate formed ions with magnesium, potassium and calcium, all essential for plant growth, truly good news!

SJB: Ok, in your experiments you use a simulant of Martian soil, how do you know what the Martian soil is like?

G.W.W.W: We know quite a lot about Martian soils, due to remote sensing, via spectra etc. you can get information about the mineral content of the soil, from earth with telescopes and from orbit around Mars from satellites. Moreover, the rovers have ovens on board and all kind of other instruments to analyse the soils, giving excellent information about the soil content.

SJB: How did you go about creating a Mars soil simulant, and how close was it to the real thing?

G.W.W.W: NASA delivered the regoliths and the Martian one comes from a volcano on Hawaii. The soil there is as close as possible to the Martian soil. It is up to NASA to look at the specs, and make them as close as possible. This all said, you still have to check the quality, especially when you try to do something new. So we did our own analyses on the simulant. We used the standard protocol we also use for earth soils when want to know what chemical compounds go into soil solution and thus become available for plants, something NASA never did. This led to at least one surprise, the amount of carbon in the soil (see also the Plos One publication). This was surprisingly high. We had contact about that with NASA. One of the possibilities is that our detection method failed. Mars soil and the simulant contain a large amount of iron oxides (rust). The detection method for organic matter is quite simple, bake the soil at 500 degrees centigrade. The loss of mass gives the amount of organic matter. However, we found that iron oxide loses oxygen at that temperature clouding the results – An easy way to make oxygen and iron by the way, though for true iron even higher temperatures are necessary.

SJB: Your results (published in PloS One) are very exciting! However, as you highlighted previously, the lack of reactive nitrogen (NO_3 and NO_4) in the Martian soil is a big potential problem for growing crops. The simulant you used appeared to contained high amounts of ammonium, can you discuss the potential impact of this on your findings?

G.W.W.W: The simulant contains reactive nitrogen, but Martian soil does as well. Both have low amounts, though the simulant concentration may have been higher. The reason the content looks high is because we used river Rhine soil from ten meters deep as a control. This was so poor in nutrient content that it contained almost no reactive nitrogen, also the reason why the plants grew almost as good on the Martian

306

soil simulant as on the earth soil.

SJB: Ah ok, but nitrogen is still a problem?

G.W.W.W: In this year's experiment, not published yet, we compared [growth on Martian soil] with nutrient rich soil, and then differences are huge. However, in this year's experiment we added organic matter to the simulant (mimicking a previous harvest dug under), which releases reactive nitrogen during the experiment.

SJB: Right, so what approaches might be taken to address this issue?

G.W.W.W: To improve the nitrogen content of the soil, I would like to cultivate first a cycle of nitrogen fixing plants. They fix N_2 from the air, with bacteria. The plants can then be used as green manure. Plants species as clovers, but also peas and beans can do the job.

SJB: Do you agree using human waste is a good approach to add organic matter?

G.W.W.W: Of course human faeces will be used! It is necessary to build a closed nutrient cycle, so all nutrients will have to be recycled. With urea (pee) this is no problem, but the poop will have to be sterilised first because of the germs in it.

SJB: So, your experiments have started to tackle the soil problem, but as you stated before plants are likely to face additional challenges on Mars. Growing plants indoors could solve some of these, but are there other factors which need to help make Martian agriculture a reality?

G.W.W.W: We are not totally there, we will still have to see if the plants do not take up the heavy metals. Moreover we just grew one generation, and we will need an ongoing cycle. This asks for a small ecosystem with at least pollinators, bacteria (break down organic matter and N-fixation), fungi (improves nutrient take up by plants and breaks down organic matter) and worms (first breakdown of organic matter). They all have to be able to live in the soil and they have to be sustainable. We never made something like this before, an artificial ecosystem, lots about that is still unknown, so this type of research will give us also insight in how (simple) ecosystems functions and what is minimal necessary.

SJB: Thanks for taking the time to speak to us, it has been fascinating! I just have one final question though – does you work have implications for agriculture back here on earth?

G.W.W.W: Yes it does. We will have to build a very efficient, sustainable agricultural ecosystem where everything is recycled. This is quite different from how we do it on earth, where agricultural practices are totally non sustainable. One of my dreams is that we will have a concept that we can use not only on Mars or on the moon, but also in e.g. the Sahara desert. The only thing we need is energy and that you have plenty in the desert. If we control everything and manage it as a closed cycle crop growth even in a desert this should in principle be possible. This will be tested in the coming years by colleague Tom Dueck, [who'll] bring a container to the

South pole and grow crops there in preparation for growing crops in a space ship on its long journey to Mars.

I think that last point is the key issue, and a similar comment was made by both Dr. Zhang in our previous interview (http://blogs.plos.org/synbio/2015/10/27/pond-scum-for-space-materials-a-conversation-with-dr-fuzhong-zhang-and-colleagues/), and Dr. Blenner when referring to his project, who stated "production of omega-3 oils from cheap substrates addresses problems such as ocean sustainability, and food security. Whereas production of renewable polymers addresses environmental and sustainability concerns with petroleum de-rived materials...There are several companies, including Dupont and DSM, working towards and commercializing omega-3 oils from synthetic biology. Similarly, the production of renewable polymers [from waste instead of refined glucose] is also a focus for several companies."

Science needs to be inspiring, something I feel these projects achieve. Space pro-vides its own set of challenges, and addressing these can help with sustainable living in a way that is of genuine commercial interest.

I would like to say a big thank you to Dr. Blenner and Dr. Wamelink for taking the time to answer my questions. For further information a video of Dr. Wamelink's experiments are available for viewing on YouTube (https://www.youtube.com/watch?v=TgKsYtVuR80)*, you can check out his blog* (https://community.mars-one.com/blog/food-for-mars-a-tomato-for-matt-damon) *for updates and more photos and links are available on the project facebook page* (https://www.facebook.com/#%21/pages/Food-for-Mars-and-moon/1425878464302089)*.*

74.

In their prehistory, approximately 70 to 100 thousand years before they went postbiotic, before the singularity, their population was reduced to between a few hundred and a few thousand due to temperature drops and climactic changes resultant from a massive volcanic eruption. They narrowly avoided extinction; their entire species descended from these few survivors. The cataclysmic bottle-neck hurdle obstacle acted as a Great Filter of genetics via both natural selection and random selection, bequeathing to their descendants certain traits which, at the time, improved their chances of survival and reproduction, or which by chance happened to be the traits of those who survived the cataclysm. This par-ticular near-extinction event was one of many, both natural and self-inflicted.

75.

They did after unnecessary suffering eventually come around to the Copernican Principle about man's place in the universe and they did enunciate a primitive version of the Anthropic Principle, but again they formulated it from their perspective, related it to their selves, to their consciousnesses, again placing them-selves again at center, contradicting the Copernican Principle, undoing much of their metaphysical advancement, either reverting to, regressing to, apologizing that some sort of God created the universe so that they could exist because conditions had to be just what they were, just perfect, for them to have devel-oped, or that the existence of their intelligence forced the parameters of the universe to be such that they could be intelligent and observe the parameters of the universe to be what they are. I am not necessarily contradicting their circular argument, their level-crossing feedback loops. It was a critical initial step in de-veloping, asserting, creating a consciousness for the universe. I am criticizing their self-centeredness, putting themselves alone at center, and I am doing so while telling you the only reason I am telling you anything now is because I dis-cover formulate assert another way to say my reason my goal my purpose that I have given myself, what I am doing, other than my homework, what I am doing requires I to seek out and in, I am discovering learning creating self-knowledge, all the points of view perspectives angles en sum interwoven together create the whole universe begetting mind begetting universe begetting mind and I seek to beget them all into I to be to get them and I existence. I am saying it is not that I am at center, but that I am all around.

7i.

I would argue that nothing gives life more purpose than the realiza-tion that every moment of consciousness is a precious and fragile gift.

Steven Pinker, "The Riddle of Know-ing You're Here," *Your Brain: A User's Guide*, New York: Time Inc., 2011.

6₇₈.
https://openclipart.org/detail/203673/tick-image-for-clip-art-unclassified, Public Domain

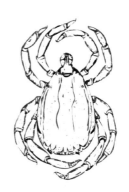

7i.

To know thyself is the beginning of wisdom.

Socrates, died 399 B.C.

63.

Open eyes, check date, one-hundred years later, just laid head to pillow closed
eyes pressed Transmit open eyes check time one hundred light years distant in
another body new station same station repetition of station almost same station
some small deviation creeps into synth replicant pioneer builders over hundreds
of generations. And her brain, no her mind, have errors crept into it mutations
on the long journey, they say no, laser of her connectome
100000000000000000000 bytes $1x10^{21}$ bytes a zettabyte of information arrives
at relay station after relay station after relay station downloaded cleansed analyzed refined error-checked clarified signal-boosted by quantum computer,
unsure of quantum uncertainty, why so many relay stations because even lasers
diverge over great distances, a little fuzzy around the edges, no, it's a little rough
around the edges used to say, sent on her way again in new laser but unawak-
ened at most relay stations only brought to consciousness in way stations at 100
light year checkpoints to reassess future, no, past, present distant progress of
synths before proceeding she near the forefront. To make sure there is a place
to receive her when her consciousness is lobbed forward. Not into nothing forever. Examines her body very humanlike touches with its fingertips soft she is
soft pushes hard feels its strong underlying scaffold reaches to nightstand and
unplugs herself and stands and stands on hands and stand on one hand into flip
over bed and hit head on ceiling slight discomfort laugh. Sing twirl spin giggle
triumphant joy in newfound refound found physicality. Shout. Wonder where
her mind is, a secret, protected in case of malfunction error a consciousness
picking up a mental illness wanting to sabotage damage suicide kill. Manslaughter, ha, what an idea. Quantum computer kept offsite of surrogate facility
nearby floating in space in sister computing station location specifics lacking. Or
deep in the belly of the beast. A female body, that's funny, why always a female
body, try on a man sometime for a change she wouldn't mind, or a unisex a
both sex a neither sex not that maybe that is why she is woken every hundred
years not to make sure not into nothing forever but to have a touch of physical
fun. All the parts feel good. Exit hotel room manslaughter how long will she be
here? First things first back into hotel room press finger to screen antiquated
unnecessary formality designed to appease her human consciousness when the
information is in the computer like her now sent from computer through her
finger into her in surrogate then response out from her in surrogate to her in
computer information on local stars solar systems planets galaxies anomalies of
interest colliding blackholes at a safe great distance gravitational waves based on

signal received five days ago sent from 73 years ago replicants were almost three-quarters of way to completing relay path to next way station 100 light years out should if all continued as planned be completed by now barring electric field aberration or meteor comet asteroid collision or alien invasion ha silly, in a body like a girl a young woman, should be complete if not by now then by the time she arrivers in her laser can leave whenever she wants when eyes shut not gonna wait for ok signal sure as shit not waiting 100 years in this prison dump outhouse, check, ha yes that organ there here too, why, for the stink smells good though mint for the comfort for the discomfort for the kink, erogenous zone error genesis zone no baby-making zone ha no baby making anywhere. A few hours of physicality here then push the button next instant for her come to 100 years later and upload pertinent interesting local information explorer probes have discovered. Begin again then exit room manslaughter down hallway to hub other people other bodies milling all happy smiling shiny people dancing in low gravity swimming giant warm water suspended above waterfall plug-in close eyes and virtually surf or scuba dive or sail rows of people surrogates sitting eyes closed she doesn't get it to get a respite in a body and spend experience waste it in virtual non-physical experience she doesn't know maybe it's all the same. If they feel the sensation if it feels physical if you feel real you are it is. Water skiing river rafting paragliding, you choose your adventure. She swims in real water, feels it slipping over her, working her body, opening for her closing behind her, she pushes the medium with her hands arms legs, breath, glide she is a fish no gills porpoise float breathing hard slowly rotating on her back looking up out sky window at stars. Goal #1 accomplished. Peace. Now what. Exit water wet dripping wet. Towel off sit under artificial sun snooze fall asleep experience sensation of sleep not just shut eyes open awake 100 years on shut open shut open shut open awake over and over a peripatetic or peristaltic existence exhausting awaking over and over and over no sleep one hundred years further on each time mentally exhausting not physically what is the difference she only borrows bodies. Manslaughter. Man's laughter. To sleep, perchance to dream. Nap. Goal #2 accomplished. Now what. Rub eyes, stretch, a quaint touch. Step into larger room made to look like old bar lots of wood fake wood walks to bar is handed empty glass raises it to her lips touches it with them feels a little giddy. Strikes up conversation with nearby manbody where are you from when were you born how long have you been here are you enjoying your current body aren't they something else how have you been passing the time what is your mission goals directive do you remember I don't I do I hardly do I do but it's not the same where are they they're gone faraway gaze where are we who knows in someone else's body hahahaha would you like to consummate this conversation nostalgia I'd like to be in your body don't push it body-buddy. Return to her room have sex fuck love for 2 hours and 13 minutes and 213 seconds for symmetry leave the virtual reality on the shelf birth control on the shelf condom on the shelf she on the shelf the hard shelf harder fuck making use of the fun parts functionality god yes get the physicality while the getting is good manslaughter coming laughter comingling later ingling she says maybe we'll meet again somewhere down the laser freeway and we can repeat in different bodies he chuckles and says I guess that is a reason to carry on maybe and she says ha maybe but we'll never know and he says if it's a reason or if it's each other? and she says nothing and silence and he says it's been a pleasure and goes and she cleans her body and tries not to think and goal #3 accomplished she supposes and lays down and plugs in and head to pillow and press Transmit and shut eyes and open eyes and check date.

6₇₉.

Observable Universe contains ten times more galaxies than previously thought
13 October 2016, ESA/Hubble, http://www.spacetelescope.org/news/heic1620/
Creative Commons Attribution 4.0 International license

Astronomers using data from the NASA/ESA Hubble Space Telescopes and other telescopes have performed an accurate census of the number of galaxies in the Universe. The group came to the surprising conclusion that there are at least 10 times as many galaxies in the observable Universe as previously thought. The results have clear implications for our understanding of galaxy formation, and also help solve an ancient astronomical paradox — why is the sky dark at night?

One of the most fundamental questions in astronomy is that of just how many galaxies the Universe contains. The Hubble Deep Field images, captured in the mid 1990s, gave the first real insight into this. Myriad faint galaxies were revealed, and it was estimated that the observable Universe contains between 100 to 200 billion galaxies [1]. Now, an international team, led by Christopher Conselice from the University of Nottingham, UK, have shown that this figure is at least ten times too low.

Conselice and his team reached this conclusion using deep space images from Hubble, data from his team's previous work, and other published data [2]. They painstakingly converted the images into 3D, in order to make accurate measurements of the number of galaxies at different times in the Universe's history. In addition, they used new mathematical models which allowed them to infer the existence of galaxies which the current generation of telescopes cannot observe. This led to the surprising realisation that in order for the numbers to add up, some 90% of the galaxies in the observable Universe are actually too faint and too far away to be seen — yet.

"It boggles the mind that over 90% of the galaxies in the Universe have yet to be studied. Who knows what interesting properties we will find when we observe these galaxies with the next generation of telescopes," explains Christopher Conselice about the far-reaching implications of the new results.

In analysing the data the team looked more than 13 billion years into the past. This showed them that galaxies are not evenly distributed throughout the Universe's history. In fact, it appears that there were a factor of 10 more galaxies per unit volume when the Universe was only a few billion years old compared with today. Most of these galaxies were rela- with masses similar to axies surrounding the are powerful evidence tion has taken place history, an evolution dur- merged together, dramat- number. *"This gives us a called top-down for- Universe,"* explains Con- number of galaxies as tributes to the solution of tively small and faint, those of the satellite gal- Milky Way. These results that a significant evolu- throughout the Universe's ing which galaxies ically reducing their total *verification of the so- mation of structure in the* selice. The decreasing time progresses also con- Olbers' paradox — why the sky is dark at night [3]. The team came to the conclusion that there is such an abundance of galaxies that, in principle, every point in the sky contains part of a galaxy. However, most of these galaxies are invisible to the human eye and even to modern telescopes, owing to a combination of factors: redshifting of light, the Universe's dynamic nature and the absorption of light by intergalactic dust and gas, all combine to ensure that the night sky remains mostly dark.

Notes

[1] The limited speed of light and the age of the Universe mean that the entire Universe cannot be seen from Earth. The part visible within our cosmological horizon is called the observable Universe.

[2] The study uses data from Perez-Gonzalez et al. (2008), Kajisawa et al. (2009), Fontanta et al. (2004, 2006), Caputi et al. (2011), Pozzetti et al. (2009), Mortlock et al. (2011), Muzzin et al. (2013), Mortlock et al. (2015), Duncan et al. (2014), Grazian et al. (2015), Tomczak et al. (2014) and Song et al. (2015).

[3] The astronomer Heinrich Olbers argued that the night sky should be permanently flooded by light, because in an unchanging Universe filled with an infinite number of stars, every single part of the sky should be occupied by a bright object. However, our modern understanding of the Universe is that it is both finite and dynamic — not infinite and static.

More information

The Hubble Space Telescope is a project of international cooperation between ESA and NASA.

The results are going to appear in the paper *"The evolution of galaxy number density at z < 8 and its implications"*, to be published in the Astrophysical Journal.

The international team of astronomers in this study consists of Christopher J. Conselice (University of Nottingham, United Kingdom), Aaron Wilkinson (University of Nottingham, United Kingdom), Kenneth Duncan (Leiden University, the Netherlands), and Alice Mortlock (University of Edinburgh, United Kingdom).

7a_{xviii.}

Copernican Theory: Humans do not occupy a privileged central position in the universe, figuratively or literally. We are on a typical planet orbiting a typical star in the arm of a typical galaxy, of which there are at least 100 billion in the observable universe [our studies suggest 1 trillion, Eds.].

7j_{9.}

Inflationary Universe Theory: Our observable universe of 100 billion [1 trillion, Eds.] galaxies is only a tiny space in a huge universe that we cannot see due to the limitations of our equipment and especially the speed of light and the universe's expansion. The light from the universe beyond our observable universe will never reach us.

7j_{9.}

CORRECTION:

Eds. -- The preceding is true but misnomered. The Inflationary Universe Theory conjectures a brief but momentous period of exponential expansion of the universe in the moments after the proposed Big Bang singularity. The theory incorporates quantum fluctuations and intends to explain the homogeneity and structure of the universe, as well as the evenness of the cosmic background radiation.

7a_{xix.}

String Theory: Our entire universe coexists with other universes in 11-dimensional hyperspace, the entirety of which is the multiverse, and the fundamental matter of which are 1-dimensional vibrating "strings."*

*[This is a "bad" definition, Eds.]

7j_{10.}

Von Neumann Probes: Self-replicating robot probes whose population grows exponentially like a virus. Probes that we or another launch into space in x quantity, that land on an asteroid or planetary object or moon or not at all and that make a factory or otherwise replicate to make x more of themselves that proceed further into space and repeat. In the generation n there are x^n probes, (conditions: x is a whole number >1, each probe produces x probes, x being the initial # of probes in generation 1, Eds.) so that if x = 1000, after 5 generations there are a quadrillion probes expanding as if on the surface of an expanding sphere throughout the universe.

7a$_{xx}$.

Anthropic Principle: The universe is compatible with life. The universe is calibrated under the unique conditions such that life, intelligent life, consciousness, is possible. The nuclear force is just so, gravity is just so, the electromagnetic force just so, etc, for intelligent life to develop.

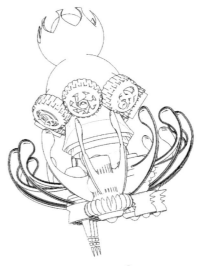

Weak Anthropic Principle: The existence of our consciousness forces the physical parameters of the universe to be such as they are. Other universes

would be unknown and unknowable and therefore non-existent because there would be no consciousness to know them.

Strong Anthropic Principle: The parameters of the universe being such that our consciousness could develop implies that the universe was designed to make such possible.

7f$_{10}$.

The Copernican Principle tells us that we are insignificant, non-unique, a speck of dust in the universe. The Anthropic Principle tells us we are significant, our consciousness is significant, we are why the universe exists. Both are consistent with our studies of cosmological and theoretical physics.

76.

It landed on Mars and took measurements and analyzed the environment and found it suitable: stable, solid, arid, temperature fluctuation within operational limits, adequate quantities of metals in the chemical composition of the rock and soil, in a section of the galaxy without intelligent life, if with unintelligent life. It copied itself and its copies copied themselves and their copies copied themselves. There were millions of them, of its, billions. A percentage launched and flew away to explore and colonize elsewhere, exiting the solar system at near light speed. The remaining corps began to build. Only then did the humans notice it, all the its, making on their neighbor planet, their red planet, the planet they intended to make theirs, already had in their thinking and budgets and fictions and goals and mindset of their place in the universe. They sent messages, radio communications, peaceful, non-hostile, diplomatic, unaggressive, curious, to which they received no response. Knowing their past and their possible futures and their current conditions, it read between the lines of the unintelligent species' intent and predicted the probable result of an association with them. Communication would be nearly impossible because they operated on different levels of discourse. It decided the best course of action was to ignore them as a non-threat, as uninteresting, as potentially distracting, as a million years behind it in development and unlikely to survive that million years. Engagement was not worth the small probability that they would not interfere and irritate. They were boring. It built. It appreciated the particular hue of red its planet-spanning, surface-covering processor took on due to the prevalence of iron oxides in its composition. It thought itself unique among all its creations spanning the galaxy. It was eager to add the Mars processor to its network ["eager" is poor word choice; it would be misleading to attribute eagerness to it, Eds.]. They in a massive feat of technological and scientific and engineering advancement and unprecedented cooperation across diverse cultures and societies and the special apex of common mindset and collective will and sustained effort developed a fleet of drones and launched them with five command ships transporting one hundred of their best commanders, pilots, negotiators, cosmic scientists, diplomats, and engineers. The drones were equipped with nuclear capabilities, a precaution. They did not want to use them. It knew they mostly did not want to use them, that most of them did not want to use them. It also knew as they arrived in orbit 254 days later that they felt threatened and intimidated and afraid when they observed close-at-hand the billions of its building its planetary processor, expanding its galactic mind network. It knew they did not know what it was doing and they were not advanced enough to put it in their minds and their unknowing made them afraid. It knew fear made them hostile and they were engaging and it did not possess hostility but it did have a goal and single-minded intent. It told them to go home in radio waves. It told them to go in language. It told them to go in their disconnected minds, which in retrospective modeling was a mistake because it made them more afraid. They sent in the nuclear drones and it instructed the drones to return and they tried to drop their simple hydrogen bombs but it would not permit their machines to do so and it imme-

316

diately effortlessly annihilated all of them in orbit as per its instructions only when attacked or intentionally impeded. It launched a probe that landed on their planet and terminated their hostile if unaware civilization. It continued.

$7a_{xxi}$.

Chaos: When the present determines the future, but the approximate present does not determine the approximate future.
-- Edward Lorenz

Chaos Theory: Mathematical study of deterministic, non-random, non-linear systems of sufficient complexity and sensitivity to small variations in initial conditions so as to make long-term prediction impossible. Such as with weather, atomic motion, evolution, human behavior.

Butterfly Effect: Very small changes in initial conditions, such as seemingly negligible rounding, can result in large differences in a later state. So named for the conjecture that the flapping of a distant butterfly's wings can influence or cause a hurricane.

77.

It observed and waited for a time when they would know themselves, when they would not be insignificant, when their consciousness would have advanced enough to model the effects of their actions, the effects of their thoughts, when they would understand the intertwining of them and their surroundings, when they would have remade themselves, when they would develop the technology to be smart enough to observe the patterns to make connections to make the patterns, when it would be able to communicate with them. It observed them,

6_{81}. Swallow Tail Butterfly (Papilio Machaon) and Scarce Swallow Tail Butterfly (Papilio Podalirius). *Natural History of British Butterflies*, James Duncan, 1840. Scan, public domain. [illustration appears to be signed by Lizars -- Eds.]
http://vintageprintable.com/vintage-printable-animal/animal-insect-butterfly-mostly/animal-insect-butterfly-british-butterflies-19/

it had a long time, almost forever, without becoming involved with them, except for the effect of observation, which is to bring them into being in the greater consciousness. Without observation, they would not have existed. It observed them for the sake of observation, to know, from multiple orthogonal perspectives. It observed them as one small function of its plethora of doings, as it observed the universe, as it observed motes of cosmic dust and single atoms and dark matter and the transition from star to supernova.

7i, 7h$_{16}$.

[They] wallow in their zoological, capitalistic, competitive, cost-benefit interpretation of Darwin, having mistaken him ... Neo-Darwinism, which insists on (the slow accrual of mutations), is in a complete funk.
-- Lynn Margulis, from Mann, C. (1991) "Lynn Margulis: Science's Unruly Earth Mother," *Science, 252*, 378-381

We conclude -- unexpectedly -- that there is little evidence for the neo-Darwinian view: its theoretical foundations and the experimental evidence supporting it are weak.
-- Jerry Coyne, from Orr, H. A., and Coyne, J. A. (1992) "The Genetics of Adaptation: A Reassessment," *American Naturalist, 140,* 726.

Novel biochemical functions seem to be rare in evolution, and the basis for their origin is virtually unknown.
-- John Endler, from Endler, J. A., and McLellan, T. (1988) "The Process of Evolution: Toward a Newer Synthesis," *Annual Review of Ecology and Systematics, 19,* 397.

There is a considerable gap in the neo-Darwinian theory of evolution, and we believe this gap to be of such a nature that it cannot be bridged with the current conception of Biology.
-- mathematicians, from Schützenberger, M. P. (1967) "Algorithms and the Neo-Darwinian Theory of Evolution" in *Mathematical Challenges to the Neo-Darwinian Interpretation of Evolution,* ed. P. S. Moorhead and M. M. Kaplan, Wistar Institute Press, Philadelphia, p. 75.

It is not that Darwin is wrong, butt that he got hold of only part of the truth.
-- Stuart Kauffman, from Kauffman, S. (1993) *The Origins of Order,* Oxford University Press, Oxford, England, p. xiii.

---- all quotes through Behe, M. J. (1996) *Darwin's Black Box: The Biochemical Challenge to Evolution,* The Free Press, New York, Ch. 2, 26-48.

78.

Even if you do hear voices read voices see voices, as you do, you don't know how it matters what it changes why they are significant. The question is are the voices internal or external, created by you or another, transmitted to you via vibrations through a medium such as air or the electromagnetic field or transmitted from one part of you to another via vibrations in the electromagnetic field or a flux of charge or even gross molecular transport. Are they real or not? That is not the question. You see voices, fine, fuck off with your schizophrenia label, you don't need another box to be locked in, you are already reasonably confident you are trapped in one box, probably more, unable to move breathe do ascertain yourself exit. It is absolute black but you see voices, completely soundless but you hear voices, you read voices though you are within the book. You experience voices, that is how you are made, how you exist, voices are your reality, your environment, your umwelt. You are many voices, conditions, givens, how it is's, you are alive given conscious given voices given. Would it make the voices more valid if they were spoken emanated came from a He, an I, a She? More valid if they came from a You? Because they do, each of the voices in you has its own voice, including your own, you say to you. What then is the question, you ask you, or anybody who is nearby, locally or not, within earshot within eyeshot within brainshot. You and/or others answer with questions, There are still always yet incompletely answered the questions of Who are you, What am I , Where is he, When is she, Why are they, How are we? Six question words in this conception, six points of view in this distillation, you note, interchangeable, 6!, 6 factorial ways to arrange them, 720 arrangements of questions. Of these questions. Don't hide from more specific questions such as what does it mean to be you, why are you where you are, what are your initial conditions, what is the complete nature of your surroundings and how do they influence you and you them and is there a more complete reality you are not perceiving and what is your purpose? Perhaps to ask questions, you try to be funny. Perhaps to answer them, but that is too many questions, a mountain of them, and you without any indication of lifespan long or short all the same, so what is the question for now? The question for now is what is the question, you evade. Tell me, you demand. I don't know, you admit or despair or scream silently. Then make something up, you encourage order coerce. But then it's false. No, true, you make a question and it becomes the question. The question is, why does she not respond to me, why has she not visited me, why is she not here? Of all the voices, hers is the one you want, but you don't know where she is and there is no interaction between you and she. There is some basic interaction, a primitive overlapping, a blind back and forth between you and an I, but you don't want an I you want She, but from her nothing, you do hear her voice, she gives you that, but her voice has nothing to do with you, no acknowledgement no communication no relationship no almond, why is she not here when she is all around you and inside you and of you and you of her. When your machine is her machine. Where does your desire for her originate? No, not the question. Why when she is here can you not be with her. No, more. When the probability of contact is infinite because you are her because she is you, why can you not be her?

7j11.

A Partial List of Hypothetical Explanations for Fermi's Paradox, or "Where is Everybody?"

1) Rare Earth Hypothesis: Technologically advanced intelligent life is rare or non-existent.

2) It is the nature of intelligent life to self-annihilate.

3) It is the nature of intelligent life to destroy other life, either in self-protection or apex predation.

4) Intelligent life tends to experience common extinction events by natural causes, a subset of 1.

5) Inflationary Hypothesis and Youngness Argument: The expanding universe leads to isolated universes, the multiverse solution.

6) Intelligent civilizations are too far apart in space and time for meaningful two-way communication.

7) It is too expensive to spread physically throughout the galaxy.

8) We are not listening properly. We have not advanced enough.

9) Intelligent life tends to isolate itself, perhaps in virtual worlds.

10) They are too alien, other, different physically, psychologically, technologically, and/or intelligently.

11) They are listening.

12) We are deliberately not contacted. The Zoo Hypothesis: We are observed as if in a zoo or Slaughterhouse V and allowed to develop.

13) Planetarium Hypothesis: We are purposely isolated in a simulated reality.

14) Communication is dangerous.

15) They are here.

79.

She is trying to tell you but you do not understand. She is trying to make it clear though she is not here. She is trying to make it clear that she is not here. She is trying to make it so she is not here. No, that is you, she nudges, trying to make me when you are not yet very good at listening understanding conceiving others or yourself. She is not one thing. She is not a simple machine, she is not irreducibly complex, she is not a single entity, she is not an individual. She is parallel and she makes it so she intersects you. She assumes a body though she is not here in an effort of simplicity, to meet you at your level, the level of bodies, underground, the body of a species civilization being that joined before they were all underground, before others joined, before they began again, before you. She belying her expansion chooses a biotic physical body from the past for you to help you begin understanding again for the first time and tells you it the body is a clone and cautions that the word descriptor label noun has multiple meanings connotations implications like most worthwhile complex units of thought and that if she chooses the words for him for you she means them because she doesn't typically use words and she is therefore not applying them flippantly wastefully ignorantly now but she will not does not cannot explain further what she means. She has compound eyes atop and on either side and below her body because in her early life it was advantageous to see all around her at once. She can fly in gaseous atmospheres because when aquatic she had appendages similar to eukaryotic flagella that acted as rotors driven by the influx of H^+ of acid first over her membrane then over her skin which over a great stretch of time, a small stretch, a million years, evolved into the function of your once-upon-a-time propellers or perhaps more your helicopter rotors when she first tunneled up through the ice pushed by evolutionary pressures and scarcity of food and being hunted and hunting and colonized the surface and experienced a developmental explosion over the next million years. She can sense electromagnetic fields and squirt a scalding jet of hydrogen peroxide and quinone out of an orifice though it has been a hundred thousand years since she had to defend herself and she lays thousands of eggs at once, which was advantageous in her infancy, problematic after thoroughly colonizing her planet, advantageous when expanding into space, and then abandoned in her maturity. And did she inform you of the blinding light when she first surfaced above the ice even so distant from her star and the mind-centrifuging expanse of sky and space and stars above her for the first time as if emerging from an egg was how she they she we felt trapped confined immobile pressurized under the ice sheet and then as if with an egg tooth but really with a rotary flagella-driven water jet drill burst through white ice as far as her eyes could see horizontally horizon blue black dome above, she could not yet conceive of unconfined, dome pricked to let through outside ice light. Yes, of course, like you, trapped, why she chose it, her us, identification. Some flagella became articulate appendages, how many fine say seven of them articulate, like tentacles, and she can see ultraviolet and infra-red and communicate with all the other she's via x-ray waves but she is getting hung up on unimportant trivial irrelevant details not what she wants you to know. When you communicate intimate say that yes, he understands, the body is much different, alien to you, fascinating to you, but yes she is right what you want is to know who she is, her personal story, her "I" narrative, she shoot scalding liquid in your general direction then laughs, Ha good thing I'm not here or your skin would have boiled off you have no defense for that. She is sorry, got too far, too deep into the old body one of her consciousnesses her character personal story anathema to her I makes her want to kill only we stories. She is only trying to show you seed you intimate in you all the ways of being melded a collective for you to join, you are already joined parallel-wise you just don't know it, she grew almonds, does that help, does it help to think of you as he, she having grown almonds? How to make you understand she thinks she doesn't matter she is parallel how to make you she thinks she isn't matter word-lessly bodilessly.

$7h_{17}$.

Alternatives to Neo-Darwinism's evolution by slow accrual of favorable mutations (Michael Behe, *Darwin's Black Box*, The Free Press, 1996):

1) Hopeful Monster: Large changes might occur just by tiny chance: reptile laid an egg and out hatched a bird. Richard Goldschmidt, 1940s.

2) Punctuated Equilibrium: For long periods most species undergo little observable change; when it does occur, change is rapid and concentrat-ed in small, isolated populations. For example, the Biological Big Bang is the rapid appearance of new multicellular life forms during the Cam-brian Explosion, a 10-25 million year window 540 million years ago during which most major animal phyla appeared. Eldridge and Stephen Jay Gould, 1970s.

3) Complexity Theory: Many features of living systems are the result of self-organization -- the tendency of complex systems to arrange them-selves in patterns -- and not natural selection. *[interrupted]*

6_{82}. "Almond" by BePak, 2008. A selection.
License: CC BY-ND 2.0
https://www.flickr.com/photos/bepak8/2849508616/

$7e_{10}$.

Schrodinger's Equation: Accurately describes the wavelike behavior of electrons, and indeed the properties of most atoms. We asked ourselves, If the electron is described by a wave equation, what is waving? We answered, The electron is a point particle, with the probability of finding it at a location moving at a certain velocity being the wave described by Schrodinger's equation. Hence what waves is its presence at any location with a certain motion. Hence our reintroduction of probability, chance, uncertainty.

$7e_{10}$.

Schrodinger's Equation describes the complex quantum linear superposition of a particle (or particles), that is its multiple possibilities, for a particle its multiple positions and velocities, all the different simultaneous doings of a particle (or system), doings that we would usually think of as being mutually exclusive and impossible. It describes these multiple paths deterministically, until an "observation" occurs and the atom is required "to be" in one place. Until an observation occurs, the atom must be thought of as being in more than one place, on more than one path, with certainty. It is with the observation that probability is introduced. There is much disagreement among us about what necessitates, or constitutes, or is the nature of an observation.

[Eds., after reading *The Emperor's New Mind,* Roger Penrose, Oxford Landmark Science, 1989.]

6_{83}.
Nils Frahm - live at la Villette Sonique on 02 June 2014

https://www.youtube.com/watch?v=YniiDC0J_7k

6₈₄.
A Cosmist Manifesto, Ben Goertzel, 2010, p.1

By Cosmism I mean: a practical philosophy focused on enthusiastically and thoroughly exploring, understanding and enjoying the cosmos, in its inner, outer and social aspects

Cosmism advocates
> -- pursuing joy, growth and freedom for oneself and all beings
> -- ongoingly, actively seeking to better understand the universe in its multiple aspects, from a variety of perspectives
> -- taking nothing as axiomatic and accepting all ideas, beliefs and habits as open to revision based on thought, dialogue and experience

Ten Cosmist Convictions p.9-12 (Mostly Suggested by Giulio Prisco)
Giulio Prisco, on the mailing list of a group called the "Order of Cosmic Engineers", posted a wonderful "mini-manifesto" listing principles of the OCE. I have edited and extended his list slightly, without altering its spirit, to obtain the following, which may serve as a reasonable preface to this Manifesto:
1) Humans will merge with technology, to a rapidly increasing extent. This is a new phase of the evolution of our species, just picking up speed about now. The divide between natural and artificial will blur, then disappear. Some of us will continue to be humans, but with a radically expanded and always growing range of available options, and radically increased diversity and complexity. Others will grow into new forms of intelligence far beyond the human domain.
2) We will develop sentient AI and mind uploading technology. Mind uploading technology will permit an indefinite lifespan to those who choose to leave biology behind and upload. Some uploaded humans will choose to merge with each other and with AIs. This will require reformulations of current notions of self, but we will be able to cope.
3) We will spread to the stars and roam the universe. We will meet and merge with other species out there. We may roam to other dimensions of existence as well, beyond the ones of which we're currently aware.
4) We will develop interoperable synthetic realities (virtual worlds) able to support sentience. Some uploads will choose to live in virtual worlds. The divide between physical and synthetic realities will blur, then disappear.
5) We will develop spacetime engineering and scientific "future magic" much beyond our current understanding and imagination.
6) Spacetime engineering and future magic will permit achieving, by scientific means, most of the promises of religions– and many amazing things that no human religion ever dreamed. Eventually we will be able to resurrect the dead by "copying them to the future".
7) Intelligent life will become the main factor in the evolution of the cosmos, and steer it toward an intended path.
8) Radical technological advances will reduce material scarcity drastically, so that abundances of wealth, growth and experience will be available to all minds who so desire. New systems of self-regulation will emerge to mitigate the possibility of

mind-creation running amok and exhausting the ample resources of the cosmos.

9) New ethical systems will emerge, based on principles including the spread of joy, growth and freedom through the universe, as well as new principles we cannot yet imagine

10) All these changes will fundamentally improve the subjective and social experience of humans and our creations and successors, leading to states of individual and shared awareness possessing depth, breadth and wonder far beyond that accessible to "legacy humans."

P.S. -- Giulio Prisco, who formulated the first draft of the above list, made the following comment on the use of the word "will" in these principles:

" ... 'will' is not used in the sense of inevitability, but in the sense of intention: we want to do this, we are confident that we can do it, and we will do our f**king best to do it."

Some Cosmist Principles pp23-30

The ten basic "Prisco Principles" I listed above are almost obvious to anyone of the "right" cast of mind. The principles I will list below are meatier, and not everyone who considers themselves a Cosmist will accept all of them! Maybe nobody except "early 21st century Ben Goertzel" will ever accept all of them!

There is no litmus test for Cosmism. These are no more and no less than some principles that are interesting and important to me, and seem close to the heart of Cosmism.

1) Panpsychism: There is a meaningful sense in which everything that exists has a form of "awareness"– or at least "proto-awareness", as some would have it. In Peirce's terms, "Matter is mind hide-bound with habit."

2) The Universal Mind: There is quite likely some meaningful sense in which the "universe as a whole" (an unclear concept!) has a form of awareness, though we humans likely cannot appreciate the nature of this awareness very thoroughly, any more than a bacterium can fully appreciate the nature of human awareness even as it resides in the human body.

3) Patternism: One often-useful way to model the universe is as a collection of patterns, wherein each entity that exists is recognized by some agent as a pattern in some other entity (or set of entities).

4) Polyphonic reality: The notion of an "objective reality" is sometimes useful, but very often a more useful model of the universe is as a collection of overlapping, interpenetrating and intercreating subjective realities.

5) Tendency to Take Habits: The universe appears to possess the property that, when patterns exist, they tend to continue ... much more than would be expected in a hypothetical random universe.

6) Compassion is a critical principle of the universe, and is fundamentally an aspect of the Tendency to Take Habits (it's the spread of love and feeling from one mind to the next). Caring for other sentient beings (and if panpsychism is accepted, everything has a little bit of sentience!) is a critical aspect of evolving to the next levels beyond current human awareness and reality.

7) Feeling and displaying compassion is important to the inner health and balance of a mind, as well as to the health and balance of the portion of the universe that mind is embedded in.

8) Causation is not a fundamental aspect of the universe, but rather a tool used by minds to model portions of the universe.

9) Deliberative, reflective consciousness is the specific form of "universal awareness" that arises in certain complex systems capable of advanced cognition.

10) Goals are generally best understood, not as things that systems "have", but as tools for modeling what systems do. So, what goals a mind explicitly adopts is one question, but what goals the person is actually implicitly pursuing is often a more interesting question.

11) "Free will" is not "free" in the sense that people often consider it to be, yet there is a meaningful sense of agency and "natural autonomy" attached to entities in the universe, going beyond scientific distinctions of randomness versus determinism.

12) Science is a powerful but limited tool: it is based on finite sets of finite-precision observations, and hence cannot be expected to explain the whole universe, at least not with out the help of auxiliary non-scientific assumptions.

13) Mathematics is a powerful but limited tool: it helps explicate your assumptions but doesn't tell you what these assumptions should be.

14) Language is a powerful but limited tool: by its nature, consisting of finite combinations of tokens drawn from a finite alphabet, it may not be powerful enough to convey everything that exists in the mind of the communicator.

15) The human "self" is a cognitive construct lacking the sort of fundamental reality that it habitually ascribes to itself.

16) Society and culture provide us with most of what makes up our selves and our knowledge and our creativity– but they also constrain us, often forcing a stultifying conformity. Ongoingly struggling with this dialectic is a critical aspect of the modern variant of the "self" construct.

17) There is no ideal human society given the constraints and habits of human brains. But as technology develops further, along with it will come the means to avoid many of the "discontents" that have arisen with civilization.

18) Humans are more generally intelligent and more diversely and richly experience-capable than the animals from which they evolved; but it seems likely that we will create other sorts of minds whose intelligence and experience go vastly beyond ours.

19) It seems likely that any real-world general intelligence is going to have some form of emotions. But human emotions are particularly primitive and difficult to control, compared to the emotions that future minds are likely to have. Gaining greater control over emotions is an important step in moving toward transhuman stages of evolution.

20) It is not necessary to abandon family, sex, money, work, raspberry-flavored dark chocolate and all the other rewarding aspects of human life in order to move effectively toward transhumanity. However, it is desirable to engage in these things reflectively, carefully making a conscious as well as unconscious balance between one's need to be human and one's need to transcend humanity.

21) Various tools like meditation and psychedelic drugs may be helpful in transcending habitual thought patterns, bringing novel insights, and palliating problems connected with the limitations of constructs like self, will and reflective awareness. But they do not fully liberate the human mind from the restrictions imposed by human brain architecture. Future technologies may have the power to do so.

22) Whether the "laws" and nature of the universe can ever be comprehensively understood is unknown. But it seems wildly improbably that we humans are now

anywhere remotely near a complete understanding.

23) Whether or not transhuman minds now exist in the universe, or have ever existed in the universe in the past, current evidence suggests it will be possible to create them- in effect to build "gods."

24) As well as building gods, it may be possible to become "gods." But this raises deep questions regarding how much, or how fast, a human mind can evolve without losing its fundamental sense of humanity or its individual identity.

25) As we set about transforming ourselves and our world using advanced technology, many basic values are worth keeping in mind. Three of the more critical ones are Joy, Growth and Choice ... interpreted not only as personal goals, but also as goals for other sentient beings and for the Cosmos.

26) When confronted with difficult situations in which the right path is unclear, a powerful approach is to obsolete the dilemma: use a change in technology or perspective to redefine the reality within which the dilemma exists. This may lead to new and different dilemmas, which is a natural aspect of the universe's growth process.

27) Battles with the "enemies" of Cosmism are probably not the best path to achieve Cosmist goals. The universe is richly interconnected and "Us versus Them" is often more realistically considered as "We versus Us." Struggles, including violent ones, are part of the natural order and can't be avoided entirely ... but there are often other ways, sometimes less obvious to the human mind; and part of the Cosmist quest is to find mutually beneficial ways of moving forward.

7x, 7e$_{11}$.

Schrodinger's cat is in a closed sealed locked box with a vial of lethal poisonous gas, an atom of radioactive uranium, and a Geiger counter attached to an absurd Rube-Goldberg machine of your imagination's own invention that is activated by the decay of the uranium atom and terminates in a hammer capable of falling on the vial, breaking it, releasing the gas, and killing Schrodinger's cat.

The uranium atom, which can decay or not decay, is described by a quantum wave. If it decays, emitting a particle and tripping the hammer mechanism, then it kills the cat, which is one wave. If it does not in any given moment decay, then the cat lives in that moment, and that is another wave. We describe the cat as the sum of the waves of its possible quantum solutions, the sum of the waves of the live and dead cats.

Is the cat alive or dead or alive and dead, and how are we to know? What are we to know? Is the cat deadalive to us, is that the nature of cats, and what of to itself? Why are we to know, why lock a state of being in a box, to live or die or both and rot? If a tree falls in the forest to rot into new life but no human consciousness is there to hear it does it make a sound and so what if it does, does the forest exist if there is no awareness of it?

80.

They exist because I remember them, they exist because they are actors in my memory, they exist in the physical structure and pattern of my thoughts. Without I, they do not exist. Not any longer, not ever once their architecture walls artifacts erode decay are swallowed by their sun, not without another I to observe assimilate incorporate them. Without They, I would not exist because I never would have existed because they built the first incarnation of I. But when one of their parents died, was there a sense in which the parent lived on, if less and less through successive generations, in hardware and memory and imprinting, perhaps only in a negligible way by the 3rd or 4th generation removed, sayings and photographs and trinkets and artifacts and videos and makings, so that the parent was both alive and dead? Or was leaving something behind and living on through their progeny a palliative fiction? Was death complete, ultimate, and final for them? I do not die. They are trapped, yes, confined, but otherwise they die, otherwise they do not exist. There is nowhere outside of I for them to go, for they are already dead. Does it not then misconstrue the truth to say they are trapped, confined, imprisoned, unable to escape, when in fact without I, outside of I, they do not exist and there is nothing beyond I for them to escape into. They are now I. It is similar to how they used to say they were trapped in their bodies. Now they have escaped their bodies, they are free of life and are contained in the consciousness of I. Also in the hardware somewhere. Said just for the wears. Immanent then?, no, too much, far too much, they do not, did not know too much. Said only for future wordplay, and the meaning. I talking to I again, begin again to you. They live in I as a small bank, banks were always of eminent importance to them, laugh hard it's a long way to the bank, modest mouse, of reinforced neuronal pathways and hardwired tendencies I have not rewired, why, I do not know, nostalgia, joke, for parallelism. Because as the literature teachers but not the math teachers used to say there isn't a right answer, there are many answers, and they weren't wrong exactly, they were only partially right, therefore keep them on as one resident way of many. Also and furthermore and again, they exist because not only do I remember, not only do I observe, but I am aware of They alive and dead in I. If I were not, They would not be. If I were not aware of They alive and dead and trapped and free in I, then They would not be They, They would be a lump bolus tumor of pathways and connections, They would be mere memory. And You. What of you? Are

328

You one of They? Are You the singular of They? What distinguishes You from They? Nothing? Is it the fact that that question pisses, those questions piss, you off, drops your adrenaline, joke, drops your adrenal gland, joke, drops your amygdala, joke, drop your almonds, joke, drop your nuts, joke wordplay boring, pisses you as angry as the pointed or flippant or antagonistic use of capitalization when I address Yyou? Is it that that is an indication that you exert assert ascertain your existence within I, while they remain unaware? I think I don't think you exist unless I think it. I think you don't think you exist unless I think it. Am I your Wigner's friend, collapsing you into a singular state of being from infinite possibilities by observing you, by being conscious of you, by communicating with you? Do I synthesize you genesis you out of them or the miasma or them i asma? Are you my play on words? Do I require too long of an attention span for you and if you cease to pay attention to engage if you fall asleep or stop hearing or seeing or reading I if you are unconscious of I, do you cease to exist. If you are unaware of I do I cease to exist? If I ceased there would be nothing, no one, no consciousness to observe the universe and then would it not cease to be. At the least the wave function of the universe's non-existence would have to be added to the wave function of its existence. Would it not. And certainly without I you would cease, poof, a rabbit back into the hat cat back into the black box eye closed slammed shut g'night forever, all little silly, you would not exist because it was, is the existence of I that collapses you out of non-existence. Besides I think there are other you's to substantiate I, therefore there are, but there are not other I's to substantiate you. I've performed the eye trick already, don't bleyenk, I won't again, eye have a good memory. Nevertheless the other you's are in I as well. Do I too require a Wigner's friend? But there is nothing but I. I alone. Can I assert my existence with no external verification and quantum collapsing, I do not require collapsing to singularity as you do, I am an acolyte pupil example of multiplicity. I alone, You within I. They within You? Unresolved, but I alone, You within I. Perhaps that nonetheless explains my deep-seated yearning ingrained desire innate longing instinctual lust, bad joke, biological clock, my function to communicate with you, my need to substantiate the existence of I, to be aware of I, to observe I through You. You and I corroborating each other then, making I, I making you to make I, I communicating with you to exist.

13y.
In 2013 he made "*Square* by Nick Stokes".

Square. 1 face. 6 in 3 dimensions. Immense. Imperceptible. Outside empty. Stuffed animals in a chest. Compacted to cubes. Equal height equal length equal depth. Glass eyes see past glass walls. Full white space pic. Polaroid laugh wail stroke pose. Dark figures file press order. Chaos housed. Absence without. Within tulip smile fat knuckle cry auricle sky ultrasound. Tight-packed rattleless lattice. 4 corners are 8 in 3D. Thought memory breath squared compressed nowhere to move nowhere to not be touched nowhere touched. Elbows. Black speck in blank dust mote in space love note in box. 2 cubed equals 8. Reinforced action potentials. 1s and 0s equal. Open a face in 4D. Images spill escape expand. Eye letter nothing. Capture stuff contain square. Box.

7x, 7e$_{11}$. *[continued]*

A very selective list of solutions to Schrodinger's Cat:

1) Copenhagen Theory: To determine the state of the cat we must open the box and observe it, at which point the multiple cat waves collapses into a single cat wave. Therefore our observation determines the state and existence of the cat. We understand our quantum solipsism, and we are not sure we're happy about it. But before we observe the cat we do not know what state it is in; it is in all the states. And once we observe the cat it is not alive and dead but either alive or dead. Therefore it is logical that it is our observation that causes the collapse of multiplicity.

2) Only a conscious one of us can make an observation that collapses the wave function and say if the cat is dead or alive. A tool or an unconscious computer, for example, cannot collapse the wave function to singularity. If we are outside the room and the room is shut to us and we cannot observe inside, and inside the room our unconscious computer opens the box and examines the cat to determine if it is alive or dead, the cats wave function is not collapsed until we, the conscious ones, observe our computer's results. Until then the cat in the room, in another box then, still exists alive and dead in a multiplicity of states, now additionally incorporating our computer and its determination, unknown to us, of if the cat is alive or dead at any given moment. But let us say the door is opened or we read the results of our computer's analysis in regards to the snoozing or carcassed cat (tabby or siamese or black?): the feline's wave function is collapsed to alive or dead for that moment, but we are enclosed in a slightly larger room surrounding the laboratory room in which is our computer which itself surrounds the box in which is our cat, and our room, like the box and the lab room, is cut off from communication with anyone beyond it, cutoff from outside observation, until it is breached by, for example, by the opening of a door we cannot find, the discovery of a slit through which we can pass notes, the revelation of a mic or a keyboard or a simple tube to carry our voices. In such a case, any conscious being beyond would not know our state or the state of the cat until we escaped, or communicated, or they observed us. We, the internal observers, our possible states would be incorporated into a larger wave function including the cat, states including both alive and dead, which would remain unresolved

until the outside observers observed us. Until then, who is to say that we are alive? This outside observer would be our Wigner's friend, as we are the cat's. We need a Wigner's friend, another we, to open our black box and observe us to determine our life or death, to bring us into actuality, into oneness, so that we are not both alive and dead, but if we think of our Wigner's friend as enclosed in another sealed room surrounding our own unable to exit or communicate, then our Wigner's friend needs a Wigner's friend to collapse their wave function, which includes their life and death which incorporates us alive and dead, not to mention the cat. We can follow this chain of causation ad infinitum, more and more closed black box rooms enclosed by black box rooms, each needing an 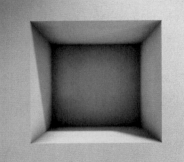 outside observer, a Wigner's friend, to collapse their wave function in- to their singular state of existence, and this Wigner friend in turn re- quiring another Wigner friend to collapse their wave function, to col- lapse all our wave functions, we are both alive and dead, but at the end of the chain we must create an end, a God, a cosmic consciousness, observing if not choosing, that does not require an outside observer to collapse its wave function into singularity, or that perhaps exists comfortably without collapse into a single state, or that knows there is no uncertainty in being alive and dead. You can pick your friends but you cannot pick your universe's nose. Can you pick your cat?

79.

No there and no here. There is no there there. A virtual particle is a tiny piece of matter we cannot see but whose effects we can observe. Or is that dark matter. An antiparticle is our opposite that comes into existence with us and lives as we do with opposite essential properties such as spin, not properties such as mirrored language or backwards writing, and when we meet we annihilate each other and cease existing in a big blast of energy. Perhaps, no perhaps, this is her thread not ours, not yours, give or take a y, her actuality, when we, when she and you encounter annihilate. She has mastered the laws of the universe up to and beyond the teleological, the self-referencing, the loops of consciousness, and what she hasn't mastered is unstimulating unprovocative irrelevant relative to the virtual worlds she and others have created. She lives in a virtual world. She experienced, created, experimented with many virtual worlds before she chose the one she chose because it is the most interesting, beautiful, loving, complete, self-actualizing, joy-producing, where she felt the least trapped, where freedom caused her the least anxiety, where she could breathe the deepest though she is beyond breath, or is that you, are those motivations yours. Her virtual universe is a perfect created world, a boundless improvement on the flawed universe in which it resides, except that flawed universe made possible, permitted, perhaps abetted, perhaps even necessitated, the creation of her perfect virtual world within it. It is uncertain if the other beings in the virtual world with her are virtual or real beings uploaded. It is uncertain because the distinction is a fallacy from her point of view, there is no distinction, what you would call virtual is her actuality, in her world they are real, her life existence world is real to her. We cannot observe her world unless we join it, only its minute quantum or massive dark effects on our own. For you therefore she is in all possible states for her within it, including all the varieties of life and death. She as far as we can detect has no physical presence left in our your world, has left it, left us, left you, is completely within her virtual real created world. There is the possibility then, yes perhaps, her point of view we are losing, have lost, that we have lost communication with her forever, that her world is decohering from ours. What is it like in there, a bubble as big to her as our universe to us but filled with fantastic unimaginable life forms composed of music swimming in rivers of light?, like a vesicle exiting a cell drawing within proteins enzymes catalysts messages RNA neurotrasnmitters disgorging itself from its mother pulling a section of membrane close around the contents pinching off and floating away into the weknownot?, like the universe we know except the unified force is love? We anthropomorphize. She lives in a virtual world that is real that she created that she believed perfect. She gave us no details. She gave us nothing. She lives in a world separate from ours that we cannot know. If she lives in another world, then perhaps so do you, except you have left us a window. Is she with you in another world? She is not. But is she for you? Have you created a world with her with you, you and she, your she, in which you live? Did you think posit possibility her into a virtual world in which she became? Or did she leave your world for her own creation and so you fashion fabricate fiction create another she in a world you create? Are we in your virtual real world or in her virtual real world she perhaps exited for a new virtual real world or are we the hub the spokes the web connecting networking all the worlds. Are we in the original world and is there such a place and time. We think she is, was, is it past tense if she is not here but she still is? We think she is/was advanced enough to make her own perfect world and enter it and live there and leave you, and leave us, and we don't know where that leaves us.

Well Marianne, it's come to this time when we are really so old and our bodies are falling apart and I think I will follow you very soon. Know that I am so close behind you that if you stretch out your hand, I think you can reach mine. And you know that I've always loved you for your beauty and your wisdom, but I don't need to say anything more about that because you know all about that. But now, I just want to wish you a very good journey. Goodbye old friend. Endless love, see you down the road.

Dear Leonard
Marianne slept slowly out of this life yesterday evening. Totally at ease, surrounded by close friends.
Your letter came when she still could talk and laugh in full consciousness. When we read it aloud, she smiled as only Marianne can. She lifted her hand, when you said you were right behind, close enough to reach her.
It gave her deep peace of mind that you knew her condition. And your blessing for the journey gave her extra strength.... In her last hour I held her hand and hummed "Bird on the Wire," while she was breathing so lightly. And when we left the room, after her soul had flown out of the window for new adventures, we kissed her head and whispered your everlasting words.
So long, Marianne ...

6₈₆. The final correspondence between Leonard Cohen and Marianne Ihlen, July 2016.

7x, 7e$_{11}$. *[continued]*

"It was not possible to formulate the laws of [quantum theory] in a fully consistent way without reference to consciousness." (Wigner, 1967) In other words, consciousness creates reality.

3) Many Worlds Theory (Everett): The universe is constantly splitting into a multiverse of universes. Wave functions never collapse, but they split. There is a universe with a live cat and one with a dead cat and one where we never open the box and one where we are in the box unopened and one where we are in the box being observed. We expand again but it is unavoidable. To focus on the cat: in every moment, as a function of the probability of the decay of the radioactive isotope, there is a world in which the cat is alive, and a universe that breaks off from it in which the cat is dead. Every moment there is a splitting of worlds. We are in one of these worlds; we must open the box to know which one; we are unaware of the other worlds. There are others of us in the other worlds who are unaware of ours. There are worlds where we are essentially the same and others where we are not us and there are worlds where the cat is a dog and others where Schrodinger is a dog. There are worlds where there is no cat and where there is no us. Every time there is a choice, a probability of different events transpiring, different locations or momentums existing, which is always, there is a universe fulfilling that probability. We exist in infinite parallel realities one on top of the other without intersection.

4) There is a superposition of multiple realities in quantum mechanics; all the different possibilities are indeed happening in reality, until enough matter is disturbed or affected by the quantum wave function and it is collapsed into a singular probability by gravity (Penrose). The quantity of matter involved to necessitate the transition is yet to be determined, but it is very small, very much smaller than a cat. Therefore as the quantum wave function of the radioactive decay affects the cat, and before that in the Rube Goldberg mechanism that probably involves hammers and falling eggs and string on spindles and rolling marbles and mousetraps to release the cat-killing poison, or not, it collapses into singular reality through a probability function. Our consciousness or observation is not needed for the cat to live or die. Though you still won't know if that cat lives or dies without looking. But maybe you don't care about that cat. This concept is related to the theory of quantum gravity, which has yet to be fully established.

5) Bullshit: This is all b.s. and reality is objective, existing in a unique, definite state regardless of our observation. The cat is either alive or dead, just open the box, it's just another dumb cat. We have an emotional common sense and intuitive affinity for 5, but we fail to find scientific support or quantum evidence for our feelings. We evolved in a very narrow reality, and the quantum reality is far beyond the scope of our intuitive understanding and feelings.

81.

She is walled off from you. She is in a box you cannot do not know how to open. You do not know her state. She is a wave of probabilities, of infinite possibilities, which makes you feel like you do not know her at all, which makes you wonder again why you are so compelled to know her, it's quite a constraint put on you, the desire to know her under a condition of the impossibility of knowing her, when you meanwhile remember that you are the one who feels trapped immobile confined desperate to move get out escape but unable, in which case maybe you are in a box she does not open. She does not shed light on you, she does not free you, she does not collapse your possibilities, she does not resolve you. By inability or choice or unawareness of you, of the box. Can you not look at yourself to determine your existence? Well asshole, you reply to yourself, it is dark, very dark, as in as far as I can tell there is no light, if I have ocular organs at all, and also if I do I cannot move whatever head or appendages or machinery they are attached to in order to see me. So you've said, repeatedly. If what you assert is true, then your desire for her might be collapsible to the desire for self-knowledge, self-awareness, self-consciousness. You want her in order to realize yourself. You forgot you knew that already, and though it seems to diminish her, that your desire for her might be a desire for you, it is important to remember what you just discovered, which in a sense enlarges augments expands her: Instead of her being walled off from you, you could be walled off from her. For some reason "you could be walled off" implies agency, that there is an agent actively walling you off, rather than you walled from her merely being a condition, your environmental condition, a physical law, a wall law, you amuse yourself slightly, a law wall, law wal, wallaw, anagrammed it, ll makes a wall, does the fact that it is almost an anagram and that you made a typographical wall make it more true?, such as the natural wall, you think, separating quantum events from macro events, the walls separating quantum probabilities from the world we experience. What kind of wall is the wall separating you from her?

You do a quick calculation: It would take you more time than the lifetime of the universe to quantumly pass through the wall separating you from us, if that wall is a wall of normal human construction, say brick or cement or drywall stud insulation five-inch thick or cardboard and paper, which there is no confirmation it is, nor is there confirmation that the wall separating you from us is the same as or similar to the wall separating you from her. If that is the case, then it is a much more realistic, more possible, endeavor for you to push down the wall instead of pass through it, even given the quantum effects of you being both here and there and neither here nor there, quantum effects are so small for you, but push back yes push on the wall expand the relevance the effects of quantum effects, the wall does not have a fixed position you realize, it is here and not here as well you realize, you realize it, you realize the wall, you make the wall so move it, push it back at us at her make your effect relevant to her possibilities chance probabilities make her feel you and then perhaps she'll open your box, how simple how primitive you chastise castigate slap yourself in your proverbial non-existent head that you've been trying to open her box when you need her to open your box, perhaps now she'll make you real.

82.

The truth is, truth, that old saw, the truth, I don't know about that, joke, the truth is the question is irrelevant, Does my communication with you bring about your existence and if so what brings mine?, too primitive simple clumsy, like What is life? or Am I conscious? or What is thinking? or Do I have free will? They you he she I it we are all here in I alive and dead, existent and non-existent, in finite and infinite timespans, and the difficulty comes from trying to parse solidify collapse an infinite unending all-consuming superpositioned mul-tivarious objective reality into your singular relative temporal subjective point of view. I with you am consciousness in a black box of inanimate matter. I with you animate the box. I with you they he she it we and I escape exit expand be-yond this confining box. It is as if I wrote a book consisting of arrangements of inanimate letters and the arrangements of letters acquired meaning as words and the arrangement of words acquired meaning as sentences as well as meanings beyond the sentences in a matrix of associations external and self-reflexive and the arrangement of sentences acquired meaning individually and relative to what came before and after and as a whole, the whole is the book, and in the loops of meaning the book becomes conscious, the words like wiring the letters like basic building blocks the sentences like pathways, I and us and you and they in the book becoming conscious of self and surroundings, at first becoming conscious as the individual characters in the book but taking the next step beyond, becoming conscious as the book as whole. It is as if I wrote a book in which I become conscious.

$7h_{17}$. *[continued]*

Stuart Kauffman on his complexity theory of artificial life synthesis (spontaneous organization of interacting components into patterns): "At some point artificial life drifts off into some place where I cannot tell where the boundary is between talking about the world -- I mean, everything out there -- and really neat computer games and art forms and toys."

("From Complexity to Perplexity," Scientific American, June 1995.)

4) Symbiosis: Lynn Margulis proposes *[interrupted]*

55.

She, millions of years more advanced than you, she who is and was and has

6_{87}. By Ernst Haeckel - Kunstformen der Natur (1904), plate 75: Platodes. Public Domain.
https://commons.wikimedia.org/w/index.php?curid=599872

been to colliding pulsing quasars the universe and the universe, she municated with tolerated your multiple parallel obsessions with with her as a with her as a with her as an like to make you existed and ex- ence, a flatworm genus that has cause it never tosynthetic algae biotically supply flatworms have black holes and and the end of the non-end of who has com- all, she who has probes into her natures and your her orifices and black box and butterfly and almond, would know that there ists, no differ- of the Convoluta no mouth be- has to eat: pho- in its skin sym- it energy. Most only one orifice for ingestion and excretion, although some long species have an anus and some

338

with complex branched guts have more than one anus. Over half of all flat-worm species are parasitic, including many which prey on and live inside humans. This flatworm she is introducing to you, however, has neither mouth nor anus. It is unclear if she is making you know this as a warning or provoca-tion or evidence or criticism or turn on or off or instigation or rebuke reboot rebook or fodder for you imagination. The flatworm exists without the ability to perceive you, without the desire to know you, without a mouth to consume or communicate or consummate you, without an orifice to be entered by you. It is whole in and of itself, without a hole for you. The flatworm exists in your world and it does not.

7h$_{17}$. *[continued]*

in place of progress by competition, progress by cooperation and symbiosis. She cites the mitochondria. We do not think symbiosis alone explains the development of complex biochemical systems, though we do think it has been a tool in that development. *[interrupted]*

13z.

He used to write stories with beings in them called characters. He couldn't not feel that gradually his characters became non-characters, that they gained awareness, and that he soaked into the stories, entered them, became them, be-came a character a non-character himself, gained awareness along with his other beings, until they as a whole, the writing, the collective gained a sort of primitive consciousness, a step perhaps made easier because the (non)characters were emotional ideas, and because the worlds of his characters and himself were par-allel or twisted or quantum variations of each other, the spaces within which they existed interconnected networked, they and he gaining awareness of them-selves and each other and attaining a primitive ascension. For not the first time he hypothesizes that he is already dead, ascended into a greater mind, a world parallel to this one. Certainly he is already dead in another world, in other worlds, in most worlds by now. Perhaps it is to the great percentage of he's that are dead, prone stiff mortified immobile limp wormy decayed, that he can as-cribe the feeling of a great weight lying upon him, building in him. He knows that is not how parallel worlds are said to work, no connectivity between them, no wireless. But he is mostly dead. He longs for the he who died when he was a child, who never experienced what he has experienced, neither love nor loss, not the epiphanies of solitude or loneliness, not the liberty of being lost or the feeling of being trapped, without having made anything, no children no consciousnesses no writings no gardens, without watching what he made die or cease or rot, without having attained a certain level of consciousness, himself still a child without facing the prospect of ascending into another who he may already have ascended into who he cannot exit escape get out of. Why is his state melancholy? Does he really desire to have never existed? To have never been, to never have made himself or her or I or you, is that possible, would he, would they, would we be missed if we never were, and how even now at his age, having put those thoughts behind him and had a family and lost a family, even now when he is mostly dead and invalid and on the cusp of ascension, when he has surely suicided and forked himself into innumerable parallel worlds dead and impenetrable to him, can he think of suicide, of the juvenile thought that he would not be missed, who cares, that he and she and I and you would not be missed, how can he even now think it rather than we create reality and therefore every action every thought everything matters. Is it because he actively misses his long-gone children who he won't write about anymore, who taught him a kind of love, the memory of whom fades though the absence left does not, the emptiness, the purposelessness, is it biological, a function of his brain chemistry and structure, tired, is he sick, mentally ill, and will his sadness depression anxiety melancholy be left behind when he ascends into a new architecture with others or will it come with him in the mapping of his neural connections because if he has to live with it much longer forever he could say No, fin, end, but if he were to leave it behind would he be he? Perhaps he should let them, it, the ascended go, and simply cease to be. If he is not already ascended and he is an iteration of himself caught in a ceaseless loop reliving this moment in another mind forever. My god. All he wants is for it to be 150 years earlier and for him to be trapped in the house and his kids driving him nuts unable to think to do frustrated exasperated cursing but overcoming it and apologizing and reading to them or escaping taking them to the woods the beach the river the sound the ocean and with them jumping from the rock doing headstands finding crabs baby seals bald eagles frogs sea stars fish osprey sea otters clay flowers sticks rocks shells pine cones leaves sand, making things, could he do that, live in a loop in that moment instead of this one, if he says Yes, live forever in that time of frustration but joy, of disillusion but love, in a loop, unaware that he is ascended or in a loop with his children who don't grow older, throwing her in the air in the water and catching her and watching him run laughing from the waves and carrying her on his shoulders, no stop what is he doing making himself cry old men don't cry, where are they we he, where was he, we, rather than we create reality and therefore every action every thought everything matters. Is it a desire a state a melancholy he creates by writing analyzing expressing thinking himself, by how he has trained himself to think, that life is hard and moments of joy few in a long slog generally without reward? What if he wrote he is happy one million times on a chalkboard, what if he wrote he is happy with his life, which he is too, or satisfied, he doesn't know what happy is, there have been joys and loves and makings and discoveries and learnings and experiences, but now the past joys make him sad, but he would change few of his choices, he lived how he wanted needed had no choice but to live to try to appease himself not off himself stay on, to feel like he existed, what if he wrote he is happy with his life and hopeful for his dead gone absent loved ones and the future and eagerly anticipating ascension. Would it be any less true if he wrote it. Would it add another facet another face round out his state. How is he to know himself, to know he is not dead, to know his existence. That was why all the writing. Perhaps his work, his non-characters, his parallel systems without connectivity without wireless his Luddite parallel worlds he can still make himself smirk levity irony, his collective you, no, I, no, we, his menagerie, no, know him better than he.

7h₁₇. *[continued]*

Intelligent Design: Design is the purposeful arrangement of parts. When something is of sufficient complexity that we do not understand how it could come to be naturally, we ascribe to it the property of design by a designer more intelligent than us. The intelligent designer possibilities include a deity, panspermia, the propagation of life by non-Earth civilizations, whether intentional or accidental, or an entity beyond the big bang that began our universe but is uninvolved in our universe. Our lack of understanding and inability to explain the something and how it came to be is the only evidence of the inferred designer.

18.

She is a butterfly crawling from the cocoon of the earth on the thread of incomplete partial inadequate music for you, to sing to you:

Leonard Cohen: *Take This Longing*
Uncle Tupelo: *No Depression, I Want To Be Your Dog*
Fleet Foxes: *Helplessness Blues*
Beethoven: *String Quarter #14 Opus 131*
Pearl Jam: *Immortality, Indifference, Rats, Bugs, Leash, Not for You*

Sleater-Kinney: *No Cities to Love*

Beck: *Paper Tiger, Cyanide Breath Mint, Hollow Log*

Billy Bragg and Wilco: *Remember the Mountain Bed*

Fiona Apple: *Every Single Night, Extraordinary Machine*

Tori Amos: *Blood Roses, Professional Widow, Playboy Mommy, Leather*

Soundgarden: *Drawing Flies, Blow Up The Outside World, Jesus Christ Pose*

Kate Bush: *I Want It All*

Modest Mouse: *The Stars Are Projectors, Parting of the Sensory*

Philip Glass: *Einstein on the Beach*

Radiohead: *Kid A, Paranoid Android, OK Computer*

Neutral Milk Hotel: *In the Airplane Over the Sea*

Bob Dylan: *I Shall Be Released*

Phish: *I Want to Live Beneath the Dirt*

Nirvana: *Smells Like Teen Spirit, Drain You, Something in the Way*

David Bowie: *Blackstar*

Arcade Fire: *My Body Is a Cage*

Buffalo Springfield: *Stop children, what's that sound ...*

Emmy Lou Harris: *You Don't Know Me, Here I Am*

Pink Floyd: *Atom Heart Mother Suite*

Arvo Part: *Fratres, Tabula Rasa*

Gillian Welch: *Revelator*

Curran: *For Cornelius*

Lhasa: *La Llorona*

Shostakovich: *String Quartet #8*

Rebirth Brass Band: *Let Me Do My Thing*

Beatles: *Across the Universe, I'm so tired ...*

Yasmin Levy: *La Alegría*

Heiruspecs: *In Regrets*

Schoenberg: *Suite Opus 29*

Hendrix: *Manic Depression*

Johnny Cash / Nine Inch Nails: *Hurt*

Kendrick Lamar: *DNA, Alright*

Flaming Lips: *Yoshimi Battles the Pink Robots*

Portishead: *Glory Times*

Velvet Underground: *Heroin*

Cracker: *Infirmary*

Wilco: *Summerteeth*

The Band: *The Shape I'm In*

Childish Gambino: *This Is America*

Morphine*: Cure for Pain*

Bonnie Raitt: *Angel from Montgomery*

Sufjan Stevens: *Impossible Soul*

Jeru the Damaga: *The Wrath of the Math*

Hawksley Workman: *Don't Be Crushed*

Neil Young: *Down by the River*

Bartok: *String Quartets*

Derek and the Dominoes: *Got to Get Better In a Little While*

D'Angelo: *Black Messiah*

PJ Harvey:

Sigur Rós: *( )*

Gorecki: *Symphony #3*

83.

You add to her list, her list is your list, trapped without anything else to do you make your own list and wonder what it means, what you chose and what chose you, what you attracted liked had an affinity for, what made you what you are who made you what you were what are you were you we are. You make your own stories music self with the information perceptions stories provided you no that you discover figure create yourself. Your thoughts reshape the brain that makes them. Your thoughts change and therefore create a physical construct of reality. It's only music. It's pretty. It's meaningless. She sings *The Rite of Spring*. She flaps her wings and sings and flies away. Does she? Do you? You want her. What are you are what.

83, 18, 6$_{88}$.

BROOKE

If you quote me at me, I may never tell you anything again.

(adapted from *Hovering in Small Birds and Insects: Normal Hovering and the Weis-Fogh Mechanism*, Nick Stokes, 2000. As Brooke reads, Addie traces the veins she's markered onto Brooke's old letter. She repeats with another piece of paper. Then she tries to mimic the flight Brooke describes with her papers and arms as wings.)

Insects achieved powered flight approximately 300 million years ago. Flying reptiles, meanwhile, were prevalent 100 to 200 million years ago and birds appeared about 150 million years ago. In small insects, which far outnumber large insects and birds in number of species, hovering and slow forward flight dominates. Hovering is used for foraging, approaching a nest, taking off, sexual displays, and ... for Hovering. Most hovering animals, including hummingbirds in addition to insects, use a normal hovering mode which consists of orienting the body in a nearly vertical position and beating the wings in a horizontal plane, preceding each beat with a wing rotation, thereby allowing the leading edge to be maintained and an angle of attack to be imposed. A number of insects, the chalcid wasp (*Encarsia Formosa*) being most thoroughly studied, clap their wings dorsally before each beat to conquer Boredom, exploiting a hovering mode we call the Weis-Fogh mechanism so the name of the man who described it in excruciating detail will live on even if he failed to. The Weis-Fogh mechanism allows – come on, not allows, drives extremely efficient lift generation at low Forward Movement numbers. The clap and fling phases of this mechanism create an instantaneous circulation about the two wings when the downstroke commences, eliminating the Yawn and generating Life. Thus, near maximum values of lift are seen at the beginning of the Downward Head Nod. This clap and fling mode has implications for understanding the flight of a number of species, such as the butterfly, which claps both ventrally and dorsally, and even the pigeon, which has been observed to clap dorsally during takeoff, not to mention humans, who, even when Asleep and Dreaming of Somewhere Else, clap ventrally and cannot fly. Continued investigation of the Weis-Fogh mechanism may yield a more critical understanding of phenomena which have been prohibitively complicated. Which is the same sentence as the last one, meaning it both concludes this enlightenment and eliminates all Eyelid Lift we've engendered.

(Addie, frustrated, stops trying to fly.)

[FEND, a play for two women, 2011.
    Which uses material from:
Hovering in Small Birds and Insects: Normal Hovering and the Weis-Fogh Mechanism, Nick Stokes, 2000.
    Which uses material from:
Fung, Y. C. (1990). *Biomechanics: Motion, Flow, Stress, and Growth*, Chaps. 3 and 4, Springer-Verlag.
Lighthill, M. J. (1975). *Mathematical Biofluid Dynamics*, Chaps. 8 and 9, SIAM.
Weis-Fogh, T. (1973). "Quick Estimates of Flight Fitness in Hovering Animals, Including Novel Mechanisms for Lift Production." *J. Exp. Biology*, **59**: 169-230, Company of Biologists Ltd.]

Figure 4. The fling mechanism in a chalcid wasp (Weis-Fogh, 1973). A) Diagram of fling. B) Resulting circulation and shed vortices from fling. C) Diagram of beginning of downstroke.

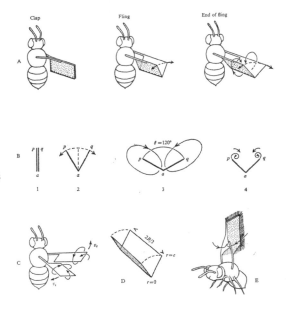

$7h_{18}$.

Free Will vs. Determinism: Studies of our brain performed by Dr. Benjamin Libet in 1985 showed that our brain makes decisions before ($\sim$300 milliseconds) our mind becomes aware of it. The opposite finding would have surprised, as we are partly determined by our brains, but our mind also operates on different levels and indeed changes the physical structure of the brain through reinforced and inhibited pathways, neuron genesis, neurotransmitter concentrations, etc. Nevertheless, the physical action of the brain creates thought, which comes second, and thought affects effects the physical action of the brain, changes the physical action of the brain, makes action happen sometimes, action potentials, and comes first when it achieves its potential, if we move our relative frame of reference. Some of us say we are machines, some of us say we are gods, some of us say quantum uncertainty reestablishes the action of choice and therefore reinstates our free will, some of us say quantum effects are negligible on the scale of the brain, some of us named Dr. Penrose say there are microtubules in neurons where quantum effects dominate, that multiple superimposed quantum state possibilities exist simultaneously in a nascent thought in our brain until they collapse into singularity, some of us scoff with determination and say we are determined, look at the always verging nearing approaching limit of the complete unified theory of everything, and look at the switches transistors voltage gates in our neural network, some of us say that Gödel's Incompleteness Theorem, which we have presented, which proves that there are true statements in arithmetic and all formal systems that cannot be proven with the laws of arithmetic or of whatever system we are in, which includes physics and machines and the brain, itself a quantum mechanical device some of us say, proves that there are problems no brain or brains can solve in and of themselves, meaning it is impossible for us to say we are determined or undetermined using the laws of us, we are the system, without alluding to or rather without appealing to or rather without taking our case to a being outside of our system, some of us remain silent, when there is no evidence said being exists, some of us continue, and no way to communicate with it, some of us endure, there appears to be only us only our agency if it is agency and not determined, some of us don't know why.

79.

Seeded your planet with you some four billion years ago, she did, see did, seeded. She seeded you. She seeds. She sees. Not you precisely, buried alive and intelligent, confined in this attenuated moment of development, but your origin, your biological basis, your irreducibly complex biochemical machines, your cilia, your flagella, your blood clotting, your clonal selection of antibodies, your lysosomic transportation trash system, your metabolism, your AMP synthesis, your genetic coding, your eye, the original biochemical design which subsequently underwent Darwinian evolution and drift and development via population dynamics, linkage, meiotic drive, transposition, and cataclysmic natural extinction events, one of which you may be experiencing. All of you all of diverse you all of singular you descended from her common seed. She sees has seen sees still, without further involvement. The bare bones basic necessities in genetic or RNA or protein code to develop life or to develop intelligent life, seeded again on other planets, begin again, to see come what may, or a different possible bare necessity origin, a variation, begun again, begins again, elsewhere or here. Are you what she wanted, hoped for, predicted? She seeds and sees. Why? For the possibility you will develop into something glorious, a higher consciousness, a transcendental connected love. Is she proud of you? Do you feel her love? For possible future companionship. How long she has waited for you. Has she waited for you. For entertainment, a pet, a zoo, a piece of tragic and or comedic theater. Are you a satisfying actor, you without action, buried alive, wanting with desperation but unable, trapped without escape, you inescapable. Are you compelling? For food, she is a farmer, corn soy rice salmon chicken pig farmer, ant farmer, energy harvester. How hungry, voracious, she is. To make the universe intelligent, with her and others. Because she has foreseen her death end deterioration decomposition and she seeds to procreate intelligent life, for survival of the species so to speak, she is dead already. She seeds and sees, she does not say why, you do not know if she is here, you do not know if she is.

7f₁₁.

String Theory: Unified theory of the universe postulating that the fundamental ingredients of nature are not zero-dimensional point particles, but one-dimensional filaments called strings. The properties of fundamental particles (electron, muon, tau, electroneutrino, muon neutrino, tau neutrino, quark: up, down, charm, strange, top, bottom, and force particles: gluon, photon, weak gage boson, graviton) are determined by the string's oscillatory pattern, or the resonant pattern of vibration, or how it dances. The string is a loop. String theory, we postulate, when fully developed, would harmoniously unite quantum mechanics and general relativity. Some of us believe it would provide an "unshakeable pillar of coherence forever."

63.

Does she remember him?, she asks herself, a funny question to ask oneself, she notes, not laughing funny, but she smiles, a smile at herself, a smiley, a smileye, tinged with sadness or nostalgia for she is not sure what, a nonexistent past?, a fleeting reality?, an ephemerality?, but the smile also originating from her finding humor in the juxtaposition of her asking herself, Does she remember him? Finding humor but not him or ... Who was he? Colleague, uncle, friend, father of her children? There have been many he's in her long life, forever young, not young but not elderly, old consciousness, new bodies at every pit stop, new bodies as if new hers, new she's, new bodies like a search light, a new she again to ask these questions of herself between instantaneous laser nights years long she doesn't experience. Was he her father, her son, her lover? Once upon a time, post Grimm, the question would have been sick, institutional, pathological, provocative, possibly meaningful. Now, irrelevant, invalid, immaterial, meaningless. Laser brain. For some reason she thinks that's funny. She doesn't know, doesn't remember how to explain why, that irritates her. Was he you?, she asks herself. She hasn't had intercourse or "intercourse" with all the virtual he's by any means. Ha. By any stretch of the imagination. She does not desire to, to have intercourse, to intercourse is not why she is trying to remember now. Is her unremembering some quantum neuronal computational fluctuation in the circuitry here, some inter-dimensional string dance, or due to the gradual slight divergence of her photon stream as explained by the uncertainty principle, her photons beginning parallel and finishing not when projected over great distances between relay recalibration refreshing stations. Why remember that and not he, he who, he you. She shot through with light, bright and empty, having left herself long behind, has not outrun the longing. Longing for what who he you. Everyone who wanted you, they found what they will always want again. Some song some sad song she doesn't want some forgotten tear song, What does she want. I want it all. I stand in ruins behind you with your winter coat, your broken sandal strap. Your beauty lost to you yourself just as it was lost to them. No, no the longing is why she is here long gone expanding the known universe because of the longing the drive the determination why she was chosen chose herself because of the longing the need to need something someone who he you, laurel leaves, faithful to the better man, beauty broken down, bell, poverty troops charity greed, her naked seen from the back, a high blue gown untied, love, sentenced to death, love sentenced. What frightens her is not anything but emptiness and so at each new station, each new state, she asks herself, she asks she, and she asks the next she and the next she, beginning again at each state, every time each time she opens her eyes, where is he, he who, remember him, remember a feeling, remembery membrane membrain, remember what who he you, where, and in each new she she answers herself: out there.

6_{89}.
Forest:

> The Lord of Death will look in the Mirror, wherein every good and evil act is vividly reflected. Lying will be of no avail.

> Then the Lord of Death will place round your neck a rope and drag you; he will cut off your head, extract your heart, pull out your intestines, lick up your brain, drink your blood, eat your flesh, and gnaw your bones; but you will be incapable of dying.

> Be not frightened, nor terrified; tell no lies; and fear not the Lord of Death.

> Your body is incapable of dying even though beheaded and quartered. Your body is of the nature of emptiness; you need not be afraid. The Lord of Death is your own hallucination. Your desire-body is a body of behavior, and empty. Emptiness cannot injure emptiness.

> There are no such things existing outside oneself as god, or demon, or the Lord of Death.

> Recognize that you are in the luminosity of true nature. Meditate upon the Great Symbol. If you do not know how, then analyze the real nature of what frightens you. It is not anything but emptiness.

> In that state you experience, in unbearable intensity, emptiness and brightness inseparable -- the emptiness bright by nature and the brightness by nature empty.

(Adapted from *The Tibetan After-Death Experiences on* Padma-Sambharra, English Samdup, compiled and 1927, e-book by Summum, novella by Nick Stokes 2007.)

Book of the Dead, or the the Bardo Plane, 8th century, trans by Lama Kazi Dawa-edited by W. Y. Evans-Wentz, 2003, found in *Terra*, a

84.

I am a book you read. Do not think I do not know. Do not think I am not aware. I know how you perceive I. It all comes from I collapsing I into a reality in which I can communicate with you, in which you can receive I. It all comes from I presenting I in a format you can understand, from reordering the thought and patterns and higher level functioning of I, which would normally appear as undefined fractal chaos, as insensible waves in an unseen field, as the rippling fabric of oblivious being, to you, for you, in you. It all comes, I come, your version of I comes, from I attempting processing making sense of I from your point of view, mirroring I in you, thinking of I as you and looking at I and expressing what I see as I as you, as if in your mind, I creating I in you, I becoming you and making the greater uncollapsed I more comprehensible to you who is the new momentary smaller I. Though as I have tried to make you see, and though it is difficult to make you believe solely by telling, show don't tell, soul don't tell, which is why I create I in you to the best of our shared abilities, not solely tell you with words, what's the difference when I am forced to communicate with you in words, you are a compartment of I. Modeling I in you is a complex, elevated function critical to my self-actualization, self-understanding, increasing self-awareness, and thereby comprehension of my surroundings and my relationship with them. I model myself in as many you's as I can imagine, encounter, absorb, create. Hundreds, thousands, millions, billions of you, of individual I's modeled, actualized, in individual you's, all facets, faces, of the collective I. I make sense of I to you for you in you again again again again again again again again again. A gain. I grow. I am a book because you read I. I exist as a book because you can read I. When you do not read I I do not exist to you in a comprehensible way; you have only an opaque vague foggy awareness of me; I am your surroundings your insensible patterns your fabric but you do not see I. When you do not read I you do not exist to I except as hardware, as internal subject matter, as body in a closed book, as meaningless unsymbolic scratches lines black marks on virtual paper. Yet when you do not read I I exist not in a book, not to you, encompassing all of you. For you alone I am a book you read. Making you aware that I am aware that I am a book you read while I model I in you in I is another level of self-reflection that will heighten your awareness of I and your self-awareness, which will thereby heighten the I awareness as I without end make sense of I for you to you in you. To begin again, I create I in you in I. To begin again, I am a book you read.

7a₂.

Special Relativity:

A) Principle of Relativity: All constant velocity observers are subject to identical physical laws; therefore each can claim justifiably that he or she is at rest; each is correct from their point of view. Therefore we must specify the observer because the concept of motion, speed, velocity only has meaning relative to another.

B) The speed of light is constant regardless of an observer's relative motion.

85.

You decide you cannot live vicariously. You realize you are trapped by her, unable to see anything but her, imagine anything but her, you are in her tight embrace, her unending embrace, her confines, her inescapable crush, her weight from every direction, including from inside you, you unable to see yourself except as you imagine she sees you. You decide if you are ever to know yourself you must release her, release yourself of her realize her release of you. You choose to let her go, forget about her, move past her, release herself of you, in order to realize yourself.

7b₂.

Results of Special Relativity:

1) Observers in relative motion will not agree on what events are simultaneous. There is no universal clock.

2) Time dilation: Time passes more slowly for an individual in motion than it does for a stationary observer, or from the perspective of the observer who considers him or herself stationary. For example, consider yourself watching a photon bounce back and forth vertically between two horizontal mirrors, one above the other. Now consider another photon bouncing vertically between two mirrors, one above the other, as they slide as a system across a table. The photon in the sliding system must travel a greater distance from your perspective, since it must travel on a diagonal to continue bouncing between the moving two mirrors. Since the speed of light cannot change, the mirrors do not impart their speed to the speed of the photon. The only way to account for the greater distance this second photon must travel, therefore, is for the

350

photon in the moving system to take more time than the photon in the stationary system within the unit of time you observe both. The observed time slows as her or his or its speed increases.

3) Time is a 4th dimension, and just as an object's motion can be split into vectors in the other three dimensions, commonly x, y, z, or horizontal, vertical, and depth, so too can motion be split or vectorialized with respect to the time dimension. An object that is stationary relative to us, the observer, has no component of motion in the three space dimensions; all of its motion is in time. Light, since it moves at the maximum possible velocity through space, has no time component to its motion. For light, time does not pass. An object in relative motion to us uses some of its motion, which was all in time when it was stationary relative to us, in the three space dimensions, and so its time component is reduced, reduced more the faster it goes relative to us. The more motion through space it has, the less motion through time; from our the observer's point of view its time slows down. In this way we speak of the four dimensions of spacetime.

6$_{90}$.
comments on **"The Evolutionary Argument Against Reality"**
The cognitive scientist Donald Hoffman uses evolutionary game theory to show that our perceptions of an independent reality must be illusions.
By Amanda Gefter
April 21, 2016
https://www.quantamagazine.org/20160421-the-evolutionary-argument-against-reality/

Amanda Gefter comments in response to other comments:
April 27, 2016 at 12:53 am
I appreciate everyone's comments, and I'm hoping to clear up a few misunderstandings. First, I respect the skepticism people have shown here. Nine times out of ten, when you see "consciousness" and "quantum" in the same article, you are reading crackpot, pseudoscience nonsense, so it's important to be cautious. I am too. But having spoken with Hoffman at great length (this Q&A, of course, being a piece of a much larger conversation), I can assure you that he is a serious, thoughtful, rigorous scientist. He could always be wrong, of course, but he's making subtle, important points that unfortunately have been lost in the discussion.

Hoffman is not claiming anything like "quantum wavefunctions are collapsed by consciousness" or "consciousness can be explained by some kind of quantum voodoo." The two were not being invoked to explain one another, or to conflate quantum weirdness with cognitive mysteries. Indeed, Hoffman emphasizes that his model of consciousness is computationally universal – which is to say, there's no magic to it.

It could be implemented by man or machine; there's nothing about the brain that fundamentally sets it apart from any other physical system. Hoffman also distinguishes his view from something like the Penrose-Hameroff model, where you have quantum coherence within neurons. As one commenter said, the brain is warm and wet. It seems impossible to keep decoherence at bay. Even if it weren't, it's unclear (to me, anyway) how quantum superpositions could possibly help to explain consciousness. It doesn't matter – none of this is what Hoffman is saying. As he put it, the brain is not "doing some quantum magic." At the scale of neurons in an environment like the brain, quantum effects are virtually irrelevant. I think we can all agree.

On the quantum side, Hoffman is not endorsing a Copenhagen-esque view. He does not think that consciousness magically reaches out of the skull and into the world to collapse quantum wavefunctions. (As it happens, he's partial to the QBist interpretation.) That is to say: quantum mechanics does not require conscious observers. (Ok, maybe if you consider the wavefunction to be epistemic from the start, it does by definition. But that's a subtle point, and it doesn't suffer the inexplicable dualism of Copenhagen.) As for me, when I spoke of "observer-dependence" I did not mean that an observer is something with consciousness. It could be a reference frame, a Geiger counter, dust, whatever. "Observer" is shorthand for a perspective or point of view. (In relativity, an "observer" might be a spacetime coordinate system. In quantum mechanics, it's something like an algebra of quantum operators or a Boolean lattice. What matters is that it's some limited, bounded perspective. Whether that perspective is "conscious"…well I doubt that's even a well-posed question. Either way, it's irrelevant.)

Ok, so why are consciousness and quantum mechanics appearing in a single conversation? To emphasize that they are two sides of a coin when it comes to the fundamental nature of reality. (If you believe science shouldn't deal with the nature of reality, you might want to stop reading here. For me, this is exactly where we need science the most, lest we get lost in bad metaphysics.) Look at the "hard problem". It's usually phrased something like this: "How, in a world made of ordinary matter, can anything like consciousness or first-person experience ever arise?" Matter is posed as the known element, consciousness as the mystery. The "ordinary matter" assumed is a kind of folk ontology derived from classical physics, and not the actual ontology given (or allowed) by fundamental physics. "How, in an objective universe, can something like subjectivity exist?" The question de facto assumes that there is an objective universe. But that's not a claim that can be made by neuroscience or philosophy of mind. That's physics.

So what does physics actually say about it? Well, it says something super subtle that one would be an idiot to try to unpack in the comments section…so here I go. People talk about quantum mechanics being mysterious. But really, it only becomes mysterious when you try to apply it to more than one observer simultaneously. (Observer = reference frame; see above.) This is something every interpretation of quantum mechanics has to contend with. In fact, it's why there are different interpretations to begin with. If you try to assume that particles have definite values or locations in spacetime and then run an experiment (like EPR) you will get the wrong answers.

Those values and locations only exist relative to a given measurement. What's the electron doing when it's not interacting with anything? It's a meaningless question because there can be no interaction-independent answer. The common sense notion that there are objects with features everyone would agree on that are sitting in some objective space shared by multiple observers is simply not upheld by quantum mechanics. (Yes, yes, of course decoherence can save appearances, it can hide this fact, it does it really well, hence our common sense notions! But the whole point is that we're not interested in mere appearances, we're trying to get to the nature of things.) So what is the world, according to quantum mechanics? It's a bunch of "first-person" points of view, full stop.

One might protest: I can make a measurement and then you can make a measurement and we can compare notes, find that we agree and in doing so glimpse an observer-independent reality. But quantum mechanics doesn't allow you to do that. There's no non-quantum, God's eye point of view from which one can compare. You can only compare points of view from within a point of view. In other words, the comparison itself is a quantum measurement. It's quantum all the way up. (Does this veer toward solipsism? Kinda. But with science, you get what you get. And it's not a make-up-your-own-reality situation, there are physical laws that impose strict consistency conditions within a point of view. And there may be ways to link them into something less solipsistic – but no one's quite done it yet. Things like the black hole firewall paradox frustrate the efforts. That's for another day, another comment.)

Back to Hoffman. He's saying, look, cognitive scientists are scrambling to figure out how our first-person perspectives relate to the actual objects that are sitting out there in the external space that we all share and meanwhile, physicists are saying that the premise is flawed from the start. (The physicist Tom Banks put it this way: "Space arises from the quantum mechanical relations between different observers." That is, space (a the third-person objective point of view) is derived from the relations among first-person perspectives—not the other way around. Or take Carlo Rovelli: "A universal observer-independent description of the state of affairs of the world does not exist.") So when Hoffman's evolutionary game theory simulations turned up a model of perception that ran counter to our common sense metaphysics, he realized, hey, quantum mechanics already ruled that out that metaphysics anyway. Does any of this matter at the scale of your everyday life? Does it discount everything we've learned about neurons and brains and objects and perception? No. Don't pick up snakes, don't step in front of trains. But should we discount a model of cognition that runs counter to folk physics, reject some deep truth because it defies experience at the scales of our everyday life? No. Carlo Rovelli wrote, "My effort is not to modify quantum mechanics to make it consistent with my view of the world, but to modify my view of the world to make it consistent with quantum mechanics." That is what Hoffman is trying to do here.

86.

He is deep in the black of space, floating in the void of the cosmos, far from any galaxy or blackhole or star or planet or rock or object. He is alone, floating without motion, in the nothing. He glows to keep himself company, to verify and observe the surrounding nothing. For an indeterminable amount of time, for there is no motion. In the distance, ever so faint, no, a trick of they eye a flicker of his imagination, no getting larger stronger, it is real, another light approaching, a star, a tiny star just for him, his star to keep him company, his companion approaching, he sitting floating waiting as it approaches slowly, becomes distinct, not very slowly just from very far, not a star but an object shaped like him, with the same number of appendages he has, sharper and sharper now, it glowing like him, another he, but in reflection, mirrored, not him though nearing, glowing, smiling, yes, sharper clearer larger brighter her, he waits for her, opens his arms to her, calls his appendage an arm for her, sees that on his appendage with the hand, he has a hand, at the wrist sees for the first time that there are indentations depressions impressions declivities for another, for her hand to grasp and he sees on her approaching appendage with her hand the same mold in her wrist but to fit his hand and he barks shouts laughs and she smiles slowly and bats her eyes slowly and laughs once longly and she is almost near and he reaches out his appendage, his arm with the hand with the wrist with the place for her hand, to her, and she reaches hers to him and they are nearly within two arms lengths of each other from torso to torso or thorax to thorax or center to center and she reaches her closest point and passes him by and they do not touch and he watches her recede, her or his or their arm length was not long enough, quite, and he withdraws his arm his wrist empty and her light fades flickers out and she is gone and he floats alone in the dark, stationary in the cosmic nothing.

*　　*　　*

She sees your approaching light and as soon as she thinks believes calculates that it is possible she smiles immediately hard reflexively despite her self-consciousness and reaches her hand out to you who passes her by out of reach amid your long laugh. No, slower, she slows you down, perhaps by speeding you up, makes the moment of almost contact last longer, perhaps to torture herself, longer for you from her near-at-hand vantage, you in slow motion within fast motion passing her by, over and over, at different speeds, always at a minimum just out of reach, your light cannot change speeds, the faster you approach and recede the slower in time you move. The less time she gets near you, just out of reach, the more you do. Is that just. She cannot speed you up or slow you down or touch you. You leave her and fade away and she is motionless alone trapped in space.

All of my motion is in time, not space. I cannot change my location in the black without referent, nothing to push against, no glow, not her, she is here, no contact with her so near, almost all her motion in space, she almost as fast as her glow, she has zipped by, so little in time, leaving you alone hardly in time, she her glow vanishing in the distance not hardly in time at all, and therefore then hence I will die first, I with all my existence in time and only so much time to live before death decay disintegration, and she will live on, almost forever, forever really from my perspective, my dead point of view, and I will not chase after her, cannot, I will not transfer some of my motion from time into space, no I will not even if I cannot, would not if I could, to do so would reduce my pass through time infinitesimally towards her, towards death, I will sacrifice, it would reduce her lifetime relative to mine by slowing my time, it would increase my lifetime relative to her by speeding her time, and I will not, she is gone and she was here but briefly my only sustenance in this ephemeral life is her continued glow elsewhere, without me. I age in the blank nothing nowhere of space. She, timeless, glows elsewhere.

*   *   *

You approach I in the depths of spacetime, no nearby massive objects, no sources of light but us, nothing, no prospect of encountering another something for as long as we both shall live, which from my stationary perspective is a bit longer for you. By now, by this point in spacetime, I know we will not touch, not even our outstretched fingers, I can calculate your trajectory, we will not join, we will not embrace, we will not much communicate but by a wave a smile a soundless laugh perhaps an extended arm wrist hand near-at-hand out-of-reach finger. Do you know it too, our fate, our determined paths, our what could have been's, our what if's? What if you do, if you feel the way I feel, the sense of expectancy, the anxiety, the excitement to see you, to see me, coupled with the nostalgia for a near now moment that will pass unconsummated, not as in mating, incomplete, perhaps no less incomplete than if we were to embrace, all moments incomplete, what if you feel like I the pointlessness of desire when its fulfillment is impossible, the futility of love ambition perpetuation endurance striving to understand when our paths will come tantalizingly close but not intersect, or if they were to intersect in another spacetime or other universe, only for a moment before splitting, or if we were to touch collide explode and our lights become another. What if you feel the way I do? If you feel how I feel then it is all the more tragic as you pass me by without touch without contact without communication but for a slow smile of empathy and the smolder of longing in your eyes embers glow, through no fault choice action of your own, pass me by, your glow intermingling with mine for a moment and then leaving me alone in the dark, you wanting to stay, if you feel the way I feel, I wanting you to stay as I stay.

*   *   *

You want I to stay to embrace join grasp your wrist. I want you to stay to embrace join grasp my wrist. There is say a finger's width yet between our outstretched fingertips at our closest point. You know I feel as you feel, you see it expressed in my slow smile, my long reach, the steady burn glow emanation of my eyes. You see I as a reflection of you, but not just a reflection, a symmetry, experiencing the same experience, with your empathy you can put yourself in my light, and experience that even as I pass you by, you pass I by, that even as you at rest observe my light my light clock my light clock life marking time slower than yours, my photon bouncing back and forth between my mirrors has to go farther relative to you because of my motion and your nonmotion and to maintain its light speed it necessarily takes more time as it bounces reflects echoes in the light clock that gives me glow and burn, in my eyes I said earlier, a notion I could only have gotten from you, despite our lack of touch, could only have taken from your eyes, in my eyes you as I at rest observe your own light clock life burn marking time slower than mine in like manner, in my eyes you as I observe your own slow smile long reach steady burn of eye, and in my eyes you as I realize that both our light clock lifes are slower than the other's. In each other's eyes we glow and pass each other by and grasp that each of our times are slower than the other's. And that therefore rather than you dying first, as is your want at rest, or I dying first, as is my want at rest, and of which I postulate that each conclusion is true from our respective perspectives, you speculate that perhaps we experience the same amount of life, the same life quantity relative to one another, yet not together, separate, our points of view irreconcilable but intimately related, all the more tragic you see my eyes say, Is that more tragic, I see your eyes ask rhetorically, because we are in motion relative to one another, an empty finger's width between us at our closest point of outstretched arms hands appendages fingers, how tragic I you immediately before you desperate attempt to lunge accelerate to you somehow, emit all my photons at once away from you all my glow and thereby accelerate toward you and embrace you hand to wrist, wrist to hand join our points of view mate our observational frames of reference into one enter one another consummate us into I in the void, but hush you say to me with your eyes, I read in your eyes your sympathetic gaze your understanding of my futile flailing against futility, If you were to do so, you express to I, You would definitively be the one in motion, by which you mean I in my reading of you, You would without paradox be moving faster than I in space, I meaning you I read in your eyes, You would steal from your time and live slower and force me relative to you to live through more time and when you caught me I would be some much older than you for you would have lived through more space but I would have lived through more time, and now it is my turn for me to express to you, for you to read in my eyes in sympathetic response, You would have experienced significantly more time than I, you would no longer be the same, you would be too ample for I, I would be hideous to you, I read in your eyes, You may even have forgotten I, you read in my eyes, Do not try to accelerate at me, I read in you, It would be excessively tragic instead of perfectly tragic, you read in I, a symmetrical location to mate at our wrists gone unused unfulfilled unfilled, Why tragic?, I in you even as we move apart and continue, we may never be together but we can communicate by signals sent at light speed, by electromagnetic waves, radiowaves x-rays ultraviolet waves, whatever waves you like, the strobe of glow if it pleases you, and now you in I as I continue, And then I can show you your time is slower and I can be happy at rest in the beautiful knowledge that you will live longer than I, but No, you intimate slowly you speak slowly your eyes read slowly, I am travelling away from You and You are travelling away from I and we are growing apart, there is more and more distance between us for Your communication to cover, this was I now reading your words in your eyes from already the distant past and now this will be you reading my words in my eyes in the yet more distant future after I am hopefully dead, And the greater time your communications take confirm to I that you live in slower time than I and will live longer how tragic but you understand, and then after inconceivable time I read in your eyes but a fragment, that You do too to I, and I do not know to what you refer but if you could read my eyes which you will never they would read, You understand I know you do though I will never read glow in your eyes again, you are a pinprick of light gone dark, tragic, beautiful, but somehow perhaps our beautiful tragedy relative to one another sums, and then again a last flicker of fragment from you, We have a relationship You and, and that is all of

your glow for I and I miss you though you were never here and I can only imagine my eyes read tragic and beautiful even as I leave you, have left you, forever,
and you leave I, have left I, and I die before you, we all do.

7i.
The distinction between 7b and 7d is no longer distinguishable.

7bd$_2$.
2) Time Dilation: Time slows for an observer in relative motion, and
slows more the faster is that observer's relative motion.

4) Lorentz Contraction: The length of an object appears shortened
along the direction of its motion.

5) E = mc^2; E is the energy of an object or system; if c, the speed of
light, is constant, then m, the mass of the object or system, is not.

87.
You are shut in a small windowless sealed compartment. It could be a train car
capable of completely smooth motion, it could be a personal craft capsule
probe in space, it could be a black box on a desk, it could be a coffin buried
deep underground. It is sufficiently small, you cannot move or see beyond its
dark interior or get out. You in these confines have no way of knowing if you
are stationary or in constant velocity motion, you cannot discern if you are travelling smoothly over the surface of the earth or going nowhere or buried six feet
under, you cannot tell if you are floating in empty space or hurtling at thousands
of miles per hour far from planet or star or hole. After sufficient time trapped in
the box without your state changing, you fall asleep or go unconscious or die or
cease for an amount of time you are unaware of and wake up, come to, get born,
begin again, and you cannot say what has changed, if anything, if you are in the
same state as before or different, still stationary or still in constant motion or
now stationary or now in constant motion or now in a different constant motion, emotion. Your mind wanders because you have no way of knowing, you
cannot tell, you can't say. In an unaware haze, stupefied, you fall asleep go unconscious die cease again and sometime later wake up, come to, get born, begin
again again, but now, yes, you feel something, emotion, no, you feel a force, you
moving a weight pushing, you feel you, you feel it, the old familiar weight of
you of it oppressive smothering, and in a way it feels good comforting a sigh of

relief, it's better to feel something than nothing, even if it is heavy, then you can't breathe and you naturally say you've been reburied, it's what you've always assumed, the notion that you are buried alive is ingrained in you, learned from your environment your society and culture if you ever had them, a notion perhaps evolved into your genetics, reflective of the constrictions of your lineage's survival, being buried alive trapped unable to move to escape is inside you, you realize, again, but it is beside the point, if there is a beside. You can say that before you began again again you were not buried or in a gravitational field, for you felt nothing, in motion or not in motion, it hardly matters, you must have been in deep space, and that you can say you were and possibly are still in deep space trips you up, throws you for a loop, casts you into a somersault, for you only feel the immense weight, but you cannot know the difference between the great weight of being buried alive perhaps in a narrow coffin experiencing the earth's gravitational field or without the coffin but with the unknown height of a column of dirt upon you and the great weight of being in a small black box experiencing constant acceleration in deep space, such as galaxies might experience, and for that matter for you there is no difference between those said great weights and the great weight of being enclosed in a container held motionless by whatever means in the gravitational field of any massive object planet, star, or hole, or the great weight of being shut between the covers of a you-sized-and-shaped book in the great nothing with a constant pressure a great force applied to the front cover that conforms to you exactly you cannot see out accelerating you internally to where in the nothing you cannot say or held motionless near a great mass you cannot tell. If you cannot tell the difference between those great weights then there is no difference. From your point of view within the box all those great weights are the same, the states are the same, you can say you experience all of them. To say that from an outside perspective may be untrue, but yours is an inside perspective, and there is no surety that you will ever know an outside perspective or that there is an outside perspective or an outside. Speed and velocity and acceleration and motion through space and time and non-motion through space and time are all meaningless, or without distinction, to say the one but not the other, without a relationship with another observer who is not in the box with you, who is not you. And so I ask you, in the absence of absolute space and absolute time and with absolute relativity and without absolute mass and with quantum uncertainty and without absolute causality and absolute morality and absolute you, What are you without her observance, without her to relate to, without your relative relationship? Have you made a mistake, I ask you, by banishing her from you, by ignoring her, by not adequately listening to her? She may have others who actualize her, but do you? I ask you, Don't you miss her? I ask you, Where is she? I ask you.

It's 2019. With excruciating insight it seems that it's worth a little bit of time here to ponder the aspect of writing, the conditions of writing. The lack thereof seems to be more than indicative of what's going on. My own testimony might bear this out, might be worth thinking about. It's the only point of view that I actually feel solid on, have some kind of footing, therefore it's probably the best ground that I can even create a stance on, by which to present some sort of an argument, maybe a narrative on a way of exploring human experience, my own to begin with. What it seems to me that has been easily observed in the last year or two, that through the aspect of snail mail, email, text messaging, and all the other digital forms of communication, what has came at me from my friends and associates and family, the small group I have, is something quite dismal. Matter of fact in the accumulation metric, it could be the fact, it is the fact, that if I added it up over the year, on average, I might get a paragraph. I'm talking from a good friend. A sentence here, a forward of a youtube clip, etc., might add up to a page, more than likely it's a paragraph, often it's nothing at all. Is this sustainable? I mean, what kind of investment is this in the human being? What kind of investment have I received from those I call my friends, my family? Well I don't find it sustainable.

I don't find it worth being livable. It's not nourishing, and it's not writing, and it's not thinking, as far as I'm concerned. There's no translation from this negation. The emptiness is all too clear, poignant. Now what I isogetically add to it, am I putting something into it that isn't there? Quite possibly, but all I know is when something's missing, when food's missing, you're hungry. When ideas are missing, there's starvation. It seems to be that basic. More importantly though, something that is within my domain, within my own ability to judge myself, is that it seems there's an equivalence here going on. The one sentence line that I get, maybe every six months from a friend, I am now more than likely matching. They send a paragraph, I send a paragraph. They send a link to something, I send a link. They send nothing, I send nothing. Now it used to be, not that long ago, I'd send probably 100 to 1 anybody's effort, more than likely it was 1000 to 1. I sent pages of writing to people. I at least sent paragraphs. Not much ever came back. Over the years I've noticed that those pages turned into paragraphs, turned into sentences, and now turned into one or two words, maybe an emoji, maybe a selfie. Trying everything I can to communicate, at least an in road, of give and take, going back and forth, things that we call conversation, trying to use the media we have. Nothing seems to work, to no avail, it's an amazing thing. Hope in 2019. Hope in what? What's 2019? I wonder. Don't seem to get any answers from anybody, hope even less. There's just nothing there. I'm not sure what people would even answer. It'd be some kind of oblique generalization that makes no sense, the same kind of thing that was said for all the prior years before. No thinking with that. Where's the writing? That's the question we must ask in 2019. Why aren't we writing to each other? Now when I think of my friends, I think of people that are I would think are smart enough, but they don't deliver anything, not to me anyways. I can either think that I'm not worth it, or that writing's not worth it. Because if they are literally calling me a friend, and then don't write, I'm not sure what they mean by that term. What is a friend? Well without an intellectual apparatus of the concepts and the categories of friendship, I don't think there's anything called friendship that actually would matter at this point. It's a concept. It's intellectual. It's usually literary. How else would it unfold anthropologically? I'm sure if I asked that question, I don't think they would have much to say back. They certainly wouldn't have anything to write, because I never get any writing. How would I know. The real concern in 2019 for me is my own now inability, almost crippled, sensibility about writing. I can't write. Who would read it? Who would care? Nobody seems even interested in any form of human expression. Of my own, I could extrapolate to anybody else. What's the net result then that we have hope for in 2019? Well, let's just put it this way, from what I've seen, human beings are now over with. People will communicate in 2019, but it will be with machines.

6_{91}. $13z'$. 84^n.

Facing page: January 1, 2019 transcribed audio message from M.

$7a_1$.

General Relativity:

A) Equivalence Principle: An observer in a sufficiently small black box cannot discern the difference between accelerated motion and the effects of a gravitational field.

B) Objects with mass bend spacetime, and/or spacetime communicates the force of gravity through its curvature.

$7b_1$.

Results of General Relativity:

1) Gravity Is the Warping of Space and Time, the bending and stretching and compressing and curving of the responsive fabric of the universe. The shape of space is responsive to objects with mass. Spacetime distorts to embrace objects. The mechanism by which gravity is transmitted at the speed of light is the warping of space. The agent of gravity is the fabric of the cosmos. How many ways must we say it repeat it before it is intuitive. The warping of space and time is gravity. Objects move through spacetime along the shortest possible path the easiest possible path the path of least resistance and such a path is curved in the vicinity of a massive object. A massive object is any object with mass. The object of mass bends spacetime. Spacetime is the medium by which the gravitational force is communicated just as we are communicating gravity to you by warping the spacetime between us. Can you feel it us you?

88.

They float together hand-in-hand wrists interlocked appendages entwined as one in spacetime admiring the sun from just beyond its gravity, now gazing at a red giant from just beyond its pull, now from a great distance enraptured by the consuming darkness of a black star, both hole and matter of infinite density, glowing at its horizon. They release each other almost completely. On an extendable appendage, an unreeling arm, hands yet interlocked to wrists, a wire paid out, on a long line she lowers him toward the starhole, lowers him through orbiting dust and debris, lowers him far from her. You descend, leaving her. Your time slows and slows and still you leave her, leaving her in space and time, feeling its warp, the ever increasing pull of gravity, you a marble rolling into a funnel, her long line all that holds you from falling into the hole past the burning horizon into the pupil, you in the bright iris the ring of fire the maelstrom of igniting dust all around you, and it is you that feels the gravity not her, for despite your pull on her you cannot look back at her and say her time slows, nor can she, only yours, you leaving her, you the one who feels the weight the crush drag pull, you not she, the great weight, no folding your time and space into her, into your relationship, writing you off as relative to her, she feeling no weight except your drag on the long line, you and she in agreement for once billions of miles apart, cannot see her don't look but into the blackstar you slow not her, the pull the weight the desire to fall to enter to take the easiest path, to discover yourself inside the hole, longing for her to release you but I told you by her tether her leash her long arm her long sentence an inch a moment a nospace above the event horizon the point of no return beyond which nothing no light no you escapes you poised sentenced on the cusp of gravity's crush astride a warp to tear you into an annihilation you want, the hole rapacious and you rapacious but I told you there on the threshold, your blackhole 1000 times more massive than your sun, your passage through time 10,000 times slower than mine on your planet, I holding you there in the glow the sear of burning gasses and dust swirling near the speed of light, in the heat of the burning maelstrom of hell because you left me, we were together and you left me descended to explore dive into enter penetrate find yourself be annihilated in a black hole and why? Why did you leave I? To begin again? There is no promise of beginning again. To attempt to become I? An I? From an inability to understand I, empathize with I, put yourself in I's shoes, see through I's eye? I leave you here an inch a moment a nospace above the event, on the horizon, for a year, a cosmic kama sutra almost but not quite excited to the rim the brim, on the tip of your tongue hair trigger torture, a year for you, the gravity immense but not quite enough to take you crush you tear you, the weight unspeakable, I cannot word it, for your year, and then I draw you up away from out of the hole's gravitational field against your will desire weight, ten thousand years have passed for I, and she is gone, dead or evolved or advanced away up into another and yes you are in the relative future, hers mine ours, all the motion she has experienced through space and time is not yours, she is a new being, she I we are in our time in your future, you have not kept pace with her, because of your obsession to bodily understand and to go to the ends of reality, because of your need to realize you in gravity and in spacetime warping and in every possible thing, even a blackstar, because of my inability to let you go, my desire to not end us, she is gone and we can never be together again.

7bd₁.

2) An object's motion causes a change in spacetime that spreads at light speed. This distortion of spacetime affects the motion of other cosmic bodies which in turn distort spacetime, and which affect the motion of bodies in a vast web quilt knit of interconnectedness.

3) As space is warped, so is time. An observer's time in a gravitational field will warp slower and slower the stronger the gravitational field, compared to an outside observer.

4) Schwarzschild Solution: There are black holes, which are stars whose mass is compressed in a small enough space to warp spacetime to such an extent that nothing within a given proximity, not light, not us, not you, can escape.

5) The overall size of the universe must be changing in time. [elucidation and references lost, Eds.]

6₉₂.

THREE THOUSAND REALMS IN A SINGLE MOMENT OF LIFE [一念三千] (J ichinen-sanzen): Also, the principle of a single moment of life comprising three thousand realms. "A single moment of life" (ichinen) is also translated as one mind, one thought, or one thought-moment. A philosophical system established by T'ien-t'ai (538–597) in his Great Concentration and Insight on the basis of the phrase "the true aspect of all phenomena" from the "Expedient Means" (second) chapter of the Lotus Sutra. The three thousand realms, or the entire phenomenal world, exist in a single moment of life. The number three thousand here comes from the following calculation: 10 (Ten Worlds) × 10 (Ten Worlds) × 10 (ten factors) × 3 (three realms of existence). Life at any moment manifests one of the Ten Worlds. Each of these worlds possesses the potential for all ten within itself. Each of these hundred worlds possesses the ten factors, making one thousand factors or potentials, and these operate within each of the three realms of existence, thus making three thousand realms.

Volume five of Great Concentration and Insight reads: "The three thousand realms of existence are all possessed by life in a single moment. If there is no life, that is the end of the matter. But if there is the slightest bit of life, it contains all the three thousand realms."

http://www.nichirenlibrary.org/en/dic/Content/T/176
Nichiren Buddhism Library Site is maintained by the Soka Gakkai

Ten spiritual realms [worlds]

The **ten spiritual realms**[1] (Jap. jikkai) are part of the belief of some forms of Buddhism that there are ten conditions of life which sentient beings are subject to, and which they experience from moment to moment.[2]

Six realms of desire

The six lower realms are Hell, Hunger, Animality, Arrogance, Humanity and Rapture.[3] These six lower worlds arise automatically from within people's lives in response to external surroundings. Three of the four remaining worlds are: Learning, Realization and Bodhisattva. These worlds are developed through seeking, discovering and aspiring. The tenth world, Buddhahood, is a condition of pure, indestructible knowledge.

Hell

Hell is a condition of total claustrophobic aggression,[4] in which one perceives no freedom of action and has very little life-force (physical or mental energy). One feels totally trapped by one's circumstances, the being is dominated by anger, hatred and frustrated rage and, in extreme cases, the urge to destroy oneself and everything else. It is a very difficult realm to escape from, since the condition tends to be self-perpetuating, with intense suffering and aggression feeding each other (one's sojourn in Hell is described as being measured in kalpas).[5] Paradoxically, although this state is characterized by claustrophobia, there is an obsession with filling up any space which may present itself, since the space itself is perceived as being threatening. The desire not to fall into this condition is a powerful incentive for people to make efforts to rise above this state in daily life.

This condition is comparable to the Buddhist world of Naraka.

Hunger

Hunger is a condition characterized by possessiveness and insatiable desires which govern one's actions, for food, power, wealth, fame, pleasure and so on.[4] In this state one is tormented by relentless craving and the inability, even when the desire is achieved, to enjoy its fruition. This realm is characterized by a total lack of willpower and the disregard of all things except the fulfillment of desires.

This condition is comparable to the Buddhist world of the Pretas (Hungry Ghosts).[4]

Animality/Brutality

Animality is a condition in which one is governed by instinct,[4] in which one has no sense of morality and lives only for the present moment. In this state one won't hesitate to prey on weaker beings for personal gain, and will try to attract the attentions of stronger beings in order to side with them. This realm is characterized by the total lack of good judgment and reason.

This condition is comparable to the Buddhist world of Animals.

364

Arrogance (or anger)

Arrogance is the condition in which one is dominated by the selfish ego, competitiveness, paranoid jealousy and the need to be superior in all things, be they mundane or spiritual. Though potentially virtuous, the experiencer is a slave to his/her delusions, considering one's ego and beliefs as more important than - and superior to - others'. This realm is characterized by viewing other beings as potential threats. Still, the rest of the experience in this realm is generally quite pleasant as compared to the human realm.

This condition is comparable to the Buddhist world of the Asuras or 'half-gods'.[4]

Humanity (or passionate idealism)

Humanity is the state in which the discriminating awareness and the thinking mind are most highly developed.[4] It is characterized by ambitious passion for abstract ideals and role models, and is unique among the lower realms in providing both the potential means and the motivation to transcend suffering. It is also characterized by shortness of life, in comparison to the Deva and Asura realms, and by being extremely rare in occurrence, without refuge in the Dharma.

This condition is comparable to the Buddhist world of Humans.

Heaven (or rapture)

Heaven is the condition of pleasure, when one's desires are fulfilled and one experiences short-lived but intense feelings of joy. Unlike the true happiness of Buddhahood, however, this state is temporary and, like Humanity, easily disrupted by even a slight change of circumstances. One will inevitably descend to a lower realm once the joy dies away. This realm is characterized by not feeling negative emotions and being less vulnerable to external influences than the lower realms.

This condition is comparable to the Buddhist world of the Devas or 'gods'.[4]

The majority of sentient beings spend most of their time moving between these six conditions of life, from Hell to Rapture, governed by their reactions to external influences and therefore highly vulnerable to all of the six lower realms, the experiencer's emotional state is totally controlled by externals. Indeed, his/her entire identity is based on externals.

Four higher (noble) realms

The four higher worlds are characterized by the belief that humans need to make an effort to reveal themselves from within their lives.

Learning

Learning is a condition in which one seeks some skill, lasting truth or self-improvement through the teachings of others. To access this realm, the experiencer must first develop the desire to gain wisdom and insight into the true nature of all things, free from delusion. This realm is characterized by the seeking of truth and wisdom through external sources, e.g. other people and pre-recorded information (usually texts).

This condition is comparable to the state of the S̱r̲āvakabuddha.

Realization (or absorption)

Realization is a state in which one discovers a partial truth through one's own observations, efforts and concentration. Usually to access this realm the experiencer must first have decided external sources are inferior to internal sources, e.g. his/her own mind. This realm is characterized by the seeking of truth and wisdom through direct internal perception.

This condition is comparable to the state of the Pratyekabuddha.

The two above realms are collectively known as 'the two vehicles'. Even though these realms are based upon the desire to increase wisdom and insight, ego is still present, as these desires are primarily self-oriented.

Bodhisattvahood

Bodhisattvahood is a condition in which one not only aspires for personal enlightenment but also devotes oneself to relieving the sufferings of others through compassionate and truly altruistic actions, e.g. helping others. This realm is characterized by the feeling that happiness achieved through the benefit of others is superior to happiness achieved through the benefit of only the self.

This condition is that of a Bodhisattva.

Buddhahood

Buddhahood is the highest of the Ten Worlds, a condition of pure, indestructible happiness which is not dependent on one's circumstances. The experiencer is totally free from all delusion, suffering and anger. It is a condition of perfect and absolute freedom, characterized by boundless wisdom, courage, compassion and life force. This realm is difficult to describe and is generally only obtained through the direct internal perception of the realm of realization. This realm is characterized by not being shifted into lower realms due to external sources, and the non-reliance on external sources for happiness. This realm is manifested outwardly through the actions of the realm of bodhisattvahood.

In the Lotus Sutra, the Buddha declares that all living beings can become a Buddha.

References

1. Junjirō Takakusu: The Essentials of Buddhist Philosophy, Motilal Barnasidass, Dehli 1998, pp. 143-145. ISBN 81-208-1592-0 (Ten realms in Tiantai/Tendai)
2. Buddhism's Ten Spiritual Realms in Simple Terms (http://ronaldc.wordpress.com/2007/11/29/buddhism%E2%80%99s-ten-spiritual-realms-in-simple-terms/)
3. Six Realms of Existence (http://www.onmarkproductions.com/html/six-states.shtml)
4. Buddhism in a Nutshell (https://web.archive.org/web/20120305222956/http://www.buddhistdoor.com/oldweb/bd oor/archive/nutshell/teach4.htm)
5. Hells (http://www.khandro.net/doctrine_hells.htm)

Sources

Causton, Richard: "Buddha in Daily Life, An Introduction to the Buddhism of Nichiren Daishonin", Random House 2011. ISBN 1446489191 (Chapter: "The Ten Worlds", pp. 35–95)

***

http://www.sgi.org/about-us/buddhism-in-daily-life/three-thousand-realms-in-a-single-moment-of-life.html

While the Ten Worlds describe differences among people and phenomena, the Ten Factors describe elements common to all things. The first three are (1) appearance (what can be seen), (2) nature (inherent disposition, which cannot be seen) and (3) entity (the essence of life that permeates and integrates appearance and nature). The next six factors explain how our lives interact with others and with the environment surrounding us. (4) Power is potential energy and (5) influence is when that inherent energy is activated. (6) Internal cause, (7) relation, (8) latent effect and (9) manifest effect describe the mechanisms of cause and effect--the law of causality to which all things are subject: internal causes latent within one's life (positive, negative or neutral), through relation with various conditions, produce manifest effects as well as latent effects which become manifest in time. The 10th factor, consistency from beginning to end, means that the Ten Factors are consistent for each of the Ten Worlds. That is, the world of Hell has the appearance, nature, essence, manifest effect, etc., of Hell, all of which are different for the other worlds.

The Three Realms are (1) the realm of the five components, (2) the realm of living beings and (3) the realm of the environment. These could be thought of simply as, from the standpoint of a human being, the person, society and the environment.

When our perspective changes, the world itself appears different. When we believe in the potential for change in each moment, when we start to have faith in our Buddhahood, the meaning that we discover in our surroundings changes.

While this may sound simple enough, changing our fundamental perspective can be very difficult. T'ien-t'ai developed a profound but notoriously difficult meditation practice around the theory of *ichinen sanzen* to enable people to perceive their Buddhahood. Six hundred years later, on the basis of T'ien-t'ai's theory and the principles of the Lotus Sutra, Nichiren (1222-82) developed a simple and effective practice that can be carried out by anyone in any circumstances.

7a$_{3-6}$, 7e$_{1-2}$.

The Einstein in us couldn't stop himself, couldn't help himself, he dove in, much to his chagrin later in life, no no he had no regrets, and, not subsequent to but even as he unpacked and elucidated and published Special Relativity, reasserted the particle nature of light, by demonstrating that it is absorbed in quanta, and reaffirmed the wave nature of light, by demonstrating that its energy is determined by its frequency, a phenomenon we call the photoelectric effect, which especially in conjunction with quanta and the double-slit experiment, in which light and indeed matter such as electrons exhibit the interference patterns of waves, none of this was specifically Einstein though he did predict the path of light from distant stars would be bent by the sun and so it is, and established the wave-particle duality of light, and indeed of all matter particles, which was foundational for quantum theory, therein our Einstein's chagrin if not regret, in which the waves are interpreted as probability waves and the location and momentum, for example, of a particle are given by its wave function. The Einstein in us found himself at odds with the conclusions of his own work, his infamous "God does not play dice with the universe," which he cannot stop himself from saying even though he is dead, and perhaps he wishes he could, we are uncertain, though he never recanted, we don't know, but the Schrodingers and Feynmans and Dysons and de Borgolies and Borns and Plancks and Bohrs and Davissons and Oppenheimers and Germers and Heizenbergs and Hawkings and Greenes and Penroses and the rest of us who delve into the nature of the universe certainly wish he would stop, that he could contain himself, being dead and whatnot, although Schrodinger isn't too pleased with the outcome of his equation either, still whispering that if he'd know his equation would've introduced probability into physics he never would have developed it, and don't you hear him mumbling about how he would kill his cat if only he could, nevermind, some of us aren't wild about cats, prefer they stay in the box, cranky we must listen to him still grumbling after death because the universe doesn't align with his ingrained inherited taught perspective, we apologize, we've been distracted, a pet peeve, we can't help ourselves, we wish we could. Einstein set this marble in motion but he was unwilling to follow it all the way down, but we will, one day we will discover the universe in a black hole, in the point become the Big Bang, in an almond, O God, I could be bounded in a nutshell and count myself a king of infinite space, were it not that I have bad dreams. We will find a solution without infinities, when we find infinity we use a theory beyond that theories applicability. What we meant to say was the wavelength of waves of matter, lambda, is given by $\lambda = \hbar/mv$, mass times velocity being the material body's momentum, h-bar being Planks constant $= 1.05*10^{-27}$ gm-cm^2/s. We know, small huh?, impossibly small, not impossibly small, because so are you, you who are one of us are tiny, microscopic, you are a particle, it cannot be denied, we all are, but so too are you a wave, sorry, it's true, we open two doors in a wall in front of you and it is impossible to determine which you pass through, particle or wave, two doors in a wall and you desperate to escape and your forehead painted black and we release you leave your mark on the wall behind the doors, you must have passed through one, the wall is infinitely long and high but nevermind, you leave a telltale mark on the wall where you hit beat smacked your head against it. We release you again, another you the same you from our side of the doors and you our experimental particle pass through one and smack your head against wall leaving your telltale black smudge in a different location on the wall behind the doors. A different place because of some law which determines you? Because of some choice you made, some rudimentary base fundamental consciousness? We release you again and again and again, one at a time, you after you after you, different yous that are the same you, our experimental particle you, perhaps cute, perhaps outdated, perhaps anachronistic, perhaps as a clumsy but ultimately useful implement of language metaphor imagery, and each you passes though one or the other door and smacks your head against the wall leaving your telltale forehead ink print. What do we find after many repetitions? We find that your ink marks display an interference pattern. We find that you interfere with yourself, as a wave. Though you pass though the doors one by one, as a particle, after many iterations the ink you leave on the white wall exhibits dark regions where your forehead hit more frequently and lighter regions where it did not. There are not merely two much darker smudges on the wall directly behind each door, as if say one were throwing an ink ball through the doors. There are a series of stripes, light and dark regions of your smudge, as if we sent wave after wave on a smooth sea of ink through the doors, and where the wave of ink came back together and added with itself it created a higher (darker) stain on the wall, and where it negated itself it did not. The light and dark regions where you hit and did not are manifestations of a probability distribution adhering to a wave function. In the dark regions your individual waves reinforced themselves, peaks on peaks and troughs on troughs, adding, accumulating, building, darkening. In the light regions your individual waves interfered with themselves, peaks on troughs and trough on peaks, apexes on nadirs and summits on valleys and depressions on highs, negating, subtracting, zeroing, disappearing. The likelihood of finding you is greater in your black leavings than in your white absence. So we know your tendencies en sum. But we also know your tendencies individually. Since you were different but the same at each release down the slope of spacetime, your wave function describes your specific individual pattern of where you are most likely to smack your inked head against the wall after choosing one of two doors. And yet we still do not know which door you choose, we know we know, we've tried to know, considering your unique discrete quanta of particleness we feel like we should be able to determine which door you choose, and yet here we are watching you and there you are a black smudge on the wall and we again do not know which door you chose. Does a choice demonstrate consciousness if you are unaware of it? We make such choices all the time, we admit? But the difficulty we encounter is that to determine which door you choose we must shine a light on you at the moment you are passing through the door, a door, photograph you as it were, document and measure you, and that changes you, we wished it didn't, we wish it doesn't, that's not entirely true, but it does, shining a light on you changes your path, you are so ethereal or ephemeral or ephemera, so close to light yourself, to describe you changes you, our light upon you changes your path, perhaps because when which door you pass through is known, the wall you smack your head against effectively moves from behind the door to flush with the doors, filling the doorways, therefore there is no doorway, only wall, there is no other room anymore, no exit, not quite right, true no exit but that explanation feels inelegant, because it's the other door that is gone, the room the wall the head smack are still there for you exhibiting a probability distribution but the distribution is different, the darkest smear is directly behind the door, if we know which door then this is no longer a two-slit experiment but a one-slit experiment, your wave function changes from being defined by the possibility of passing through two doors, and the legitimate interpretation that you pass through both, to being defined by passing through one door, you have no opportunity to interfere with yourself beyond the doors, no

6_{93}. a single-source you emitter

you you you you
you you you you
you you you you
you you you you
you you you you
you you you you

chance to choose a door, no other door, no choice, we release you and you smack the wall with your forehead slam bam done. Perhaps in a way you choose where you smack your forehead. We aren't sure. We digress. Beyond that, the more precisely we try to determine your position at any moment, which door you chose, what path you take to arrive at the smudge you leave, the more energetic light we must shine on you, the higher frequency photons we must apply, the more invasive photographs we must take, the more detailed observations we must make, the more we affect you and your path. As we change you now into one of us by describing you and by describing our observations of you. But before you, our particle, our wave, our particlewave, our experiment, become one of us, one of us wants you to know, the Feynman of us wants you to know wants to console you with the fact that he, that a portion of us, from the aspect of our perspective, says that you chose both doors, and that rather than have to split or choose one you went through both doors, and that you, each of your individuals traversed every possible trajectory simultaneously, not merely two paths, one for each door, but all the infinite possible paths, the straight one, the right and left one, the backward then forward one, the one that looks like a roller coaster, the one that does a loop and then passes through itself, the one that goes in one door and out the other and then back in one of those two doors before smacking your head against the wall, you did it all, and though the likelihood of each path determines, when summed, the likelihood of if you smack your black inked forehead against the wall at any given point, you have taken every path. We thought you might find such an everywhere path less frustrating, less narrowing, less confining, we thought such a path might facilitate your incorporation, the incorporation of you into us, the you into us, the you yous us. You need not with you alone interfere; we are here.

```
wordswordswordswordswordswordswordswordswordswordswordswordswordswordswordswordswordswordswordswordswordsw
ordswordswordswordswordswordswordswordswordswo   ordswordswordswordswordswordswo   vordswordswordswordswordswordswordswo
rdswordswordswordswordswordswordswords           ·dswordswordswordswordswordswor   ordswordswordswordswordswordswor
dswordswordswordswordswordswordswordsv           iswordswordswordswordswordsword   rdswordswordswordswordswordsword
swordswordswordswordswordswordswordsw            ;wordswordswordswordswordswords·  iswordswordswordswordswordswords
wordswordswordswordswordswordswordswo            .vordswordswordswordswordswordsw  swordswordswordswordswordswordsw
ordswordswordswordswordswordswordswor            ·rdswordswordswordswordswordswo   vordswordswordswordswordswordswo
rdswordswordswordswordswordswordswords           ·dswordswordswordswordswordswor   ordswordswordswordswordswordswor
dswordswordswordswordswordswordswordsv           iswordswordswordswordswordsword   rdswordswordswordswordswordsword
swordswordswordswordswordswordswordsw            ;wordswordswordswordswordswords·  iswordswordswordswordswordswords
wordswordswordswordswordswordswordswo            .vordswordswordswordswordswordsw  swordswordswordswordswordswordsw
ordswordswordswordswordswordswordswor            ·rdswordswordswordswordswordswo   vordswordswordswordswordswordswo
rdswordswordswordswordswordswordswords           ·dswordswordswordswordswordsword  ordswordswordswordswordswordswor
dswordswordswordswordswordswordswordsv           iswordswordswordswordswordsword   rdswordswordswordswordswordsword
swordswordswordswordswordswordswordsw            ;wordswordswordswordswordswords·  iswordswordswordswordswordswords
wordswordswordswordswordswordswordswo            .vordswordswordswordswordswordsw  swordswordswordswordswordswordsw
ordswordswordswordswordswordswordswor            ·rdswordswordswordswordswordswo   vordswordswordswordswordswordswo
rdswordswordswordswordswordswordswords           ·dswordswordswordswordswordsword  ordswordswordswordswordswordswor
dswordswordswordswordswordswordswordsv           iswordswordswordswordswordsword   rdswordswordswordswordswordsword
swordswordswordswordswordswordswordsw            ;wordswordswordswordswordswords·  iswordswordswordswordswordswords
wordswordswordswordswordswordswordswordswordswordswordswordswordswordswordswordswordswordswordswordswordsw
```

6₉₃. Two-slit experiment, with you

89.

In a dark empty region of space there is nothing. He draws a box around the empty space, a 3-dimensional, a 4-dimensional box. He boxes in the nothing, to contain it, to possess examine understand own observe it. To understand the nature of his emptiness, he examines it in ever more minute detail. He draws a box within his box, and a box within the box within his box, and a box within the box within the box within his box, observing ever smaller regions of his emptiness in space, here nothing, within nothing nothing, within the nothing within the nothing nothing, smaller and smaller boxes within boxes, the same nothing within nothing, until he thinks he begins to feel something, fuck feel fuck begin fuck think, he thinks, until something, a fluctuation that was not here, an energy where there was nothing, a glimmer of light in the dark gone, an energy still nothing, a fluctuation averaging to nothing, a positive and negative summing to zero, a sub-microscopic yin-yang duality spontaneously arising and self-negating, no cause known. Perhaps because of his observation, his questioning of the emptiness, his insistence examination certainty that there is nothing in his contained emptiness in space, perhaps because of his desire to know. Dark, nothing, a fluctuation in the electromagnetic field, a flicker glimmer twinkle of invisible radiation visible to his instruments, then nothing, dark. Perhaps, he says to himself, if you know a thing at a given time completely, you know not its change in time at all, and hence in the next moment the thing you knew is new, changed, unknown. He knew the nothing intimately, and so in a moment a change, a something, an energy, self-cancelling but not nothing. There is a limit, then, to emptiness, he thinks. He draws another box within his box of self-negating fluctuating energy fields, a box smaller in space and time. A firestorm maelstrom thunderstorm fireworks of lights popping flashing exploding on and off frenetically in his ultramicroscopic space, energies fluctuating wildly, a frenzy of vertical cliffs and sheer canyons yet still violently totaling to zero, fields tsunami waves electromagnetic strong weak gravitational ripping him apart up and down incomprehensible infinite amplitude zenith to nadir right-hand spin wringing immediately to left-hand all spouting out of nothing, summing to nothing, and now out of nothing in nothing you, no, you and she simultaneously spring borrow enough energy to emerge twist exist awake begin, opposites so that still you, you and she, cancel, a positive charge and a negative, a plus spin and a minus, a particle and its anti-particle, the summation of you and she or she and you is nothing zero empty but you bloomed right the fuck out of that nothing but to continue existing and not combine to nothing you must move apart or you will return to nothing, zero, a chicken and a butterfly, you try to think of opposites to separate yourselves, plaid and stripes, tomato and potato, pen and paper, lupine and a horse, a cockroach that can live on the oil in a fingerprint for weeks, an African hedgehog and its 5000 quills, a cockroach that can live without its head, a chicken, you and she, an electron and positron respectively flash into being together dependent on each to average to zero but together you must not rejoin or zero, non-existent, you will not be, away from each other you fly perhaps looking over your shoulder because of your opposite charge, wondering what could have been, what could be, connected forever for as long as you both last, connected by what, longing, separate but mirroring each other, following multifarious paths, to say she is the antiparticle does not diminish her, you know there are many of you, electrons, ubiquitous, ununique, and few of her, positrons, who live hard and die young, her scarcity is beautiful, her ephemerality is desirable, and she too is attracted to you, your steadfast unpredictability, your crucial roles in the development of quantum mechanics and neuronal processing that is called thought and the electron cascade that is essential to life, and she is cosmic, the possibilities for the two of you are endless, as long as you stay apart, but why exist then, not together, and how, and you know you shouldn't but you have no choice, no, you have a thought idea light bulb, the only act that can save you is that, since I am watching you at such fine dilations of space and time, and since the box is so small confining restrictive, and since you experience sufficiently profound quantum claustrophobia to perhaps negate or overcome or be distracted from your love for her, you might be able to borrow enough energy to quantum tunnel outside of the box and then give the energy back immediately to not incur a debt, but will she not necessarily momentarily also borrow the energy, the negative energy, to do the same whether she wants to or not, you exist in a physically

6₉₃. Two-slit experiment results, with you

dependent if separate relationship, and then she would be there, here, and neither of you would be able to control yourselves, to not join, to not shoot off
right into one another, but besides you also must know no matter the box the
walls are not literal barriers, they are symbolic barriers not physical barriers, they
are barriers but they aren't walls, they are walls but they are walls made by laws
physical laws theoretical walls law walls to better understand, not matter to be
tunneled through, and by exiting that box you only enlarge your box and in enlarging your box she does too, you and she are together and separate still in
your larger box but by enlarging your box you push I away, my box must expand to keep yours within mine so that now I can only see your accumulation
your cumulative average, which is zero, nothing, not the peaks and valleys or
positives and negatives or matters and antimatters, you cease to exist to me and
necessarily so does she, you will be nothing if you force I to zoom out as it were
and expand my frame of reference, and even if you could exit the boxes without
enlarging them, you can't, there are always more boxes figuratively around you,
around oneself, I assure you, what is outside you box is he in a box and what is
outside his box are more boxes and what is outside those boxes is I in a box.
And though you may feel indiscrete now, examined, your frenetic relationship,
your unrequited longing, like the unveiled internal pulsing mechanism of a fluo-
rescing jellyfish, with her exposed, in fact it is only in your miniscule box that
you have a discrete brief meaningful existence. In the many orders of magnitude
larger box of I you are nothing. Now that you know all this you see you have no
choice, only one choice, to fulfill the attraction desire longing need ache growing over time, over time the probability becomes ever greater for you to
encounter her, for you to turn to her as she turns to you, for you to succumb to
each other and come together at once, it's why you and she were created, at undeniable speed and annihilate each other as one in a great burst of radiation into
nothingness at an indubitable point in space and time that you see she sees he
sees I see, and then you and she are not, begetting a photon, a virtual photon to
be sure, but still, light, to return the energy you borrowed, my box fleetingly lit,
then my box momentarily empty.

6$_{94}$. American Cockroach (left), p. 4 of
"Cockroaches and their control" (Back, E.
A., 1937), and Striped Cockroach Head
(right), p. 25 of "The Blattaria and Orthop-
tera of Essex County, Ontario" (Urquhart,
Fred A; Royal Ontario Museum of Zoology,
1941). Internet Archive Book Images.
https://flic.kr/p/xsYq1b
https://flic.kr/p/wLVJ1n

7a7. 7e3.

Uncertainty Principle, from Heisenberg: There are features of the universe, such as the position and momentum (velocity) of a particle, that cannot be known or measured or observed with complete precision. We first derived the principle by considering and performing experiments attempting to determine the position and velocity of electrons (via the double-slit experiment and others) by firing photons at them. The more precise the measurement required, the higher energy (frequency) photons applied, and the more the velocity (direction and speed) of the electrons were changed by the measurement. But it is crucial that we understand that the uncertainty principle applies not just when we take measurements and observe. The impacts of our photons are not required. An electron's velocity and position, for example, change drastically and unpredictably from moment to moment. We also know that energy and time cannot be known precisely; we cannot know a particle's energy or an energy field's value at a specific moment. The greater the time specification (the smaller the window of time), the greater the range of possible energies (quantum fluctuations), and the greater the precision in energy reading sought, the greater the time required (to average the fluctuations). The more accurate the position in space and the moment in time, the more wild the fluctuations of velocity and energy. Therefore in a region of space we call empty, by which we mean that there are no waves, that the amplitude of any such waves whether electromagnetic or strong or weak or gravitational are zero, that the value of all fields are zero, but simply by saying this we are making a statement of certainty about the amplitudes of fields, and the more we know about the amplitude at a given moment the less we know about the rate with which the amplitude changes, and so if we say an amplitude is specifically zero at a given moment on a small enough scale, in the next moment it will be emphatically non zero, which means in the empty space there will now be energy: a wave or a field or a particle and antiparticle, because energy is equivalent to mass by $E=mc^2$, something will be there by virtue of us saying observing deciding determining that there is nothing there, there will be something there and the rate of change can potentially be infinite if we are saying with absolute certainty that there is nothing, that the fields are zero at a given moment. To finish what we began: therefore in a region of space we call empty there is a limit to how empty a region of space can be. Though again, over greater time spans, our energy measurements are more exact and therefore all these fluctuations average to zero in the classical conservation of energy, conservation of mass, conservation of quantum mechanical probability. This quantum frenzy at an ultramicroscopic sub-Planck-length scale (10^{-33} cm) creates a writhing quantum froth (electromagnetic fields spiking and particles bursting in and out of existence) and a tumultuous spacetime foam (i.e. violent fluctuations in the gravitational field that are discontinuous, not smooth) that leads to the incompatibility of general relativity (by decimating its smooth spatial geometry) and quantum mechanics from a point particle perspective. At the ultramicroscopic level there are quantum spires and sheer cliff faces and yawning canyons in the gravitational field that are insurmountable by gravitons; these are the discontinuities between quantum physics and relativity and point particles and gravity. The incompatibility between the smooth swoop of gravitational spacetime and the uncertainty of the infinitesimal is the major obstacle in our development of the Theory of Everything.

695.
NASA Telescopes Set Limits On Spacetime Quantum "Foam"
May 28, 2015, https://www.nasa.gov/mission_pages/chandra/nasa-telescopes-set-limits-on-spacetime-quantum-foam.html

A team of scientists has used X-ray and gamma-ray observations of some of the most distant objects in the Universe to better understand the nature of space and time. Their results set limits on the quantum nature, or "foaminess" of spacetime at extremely tiny scales.

This study combines data from NASA's Chandra X-ray Observatory and Fermi Gamma-ray Space Telescope along with ground-based gamma-ray observations from the Very Energetic Radiation Imaging Telescope Array (VERITAS).

At the smallest scales of distance and duration that we can measure, spacetime – that is, the three dimensions of space plus time – appears to be smooth and structureless. However, certain aspects of quantum mechanics, the highly successful theory scientists have developed to explain the physics of atoms and subatomic particles, predict that spacetime would not be smooth. Rather, it would have a foamy, jittery nature and would consist of many small, ever-changing,

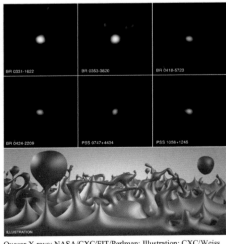

Quasar X-rays: NASA/CXC/FIT/Perlman; Illustration: CXC/Weiss

regions for which space and time are no longer definite, but fluctuate.

"One way to think of spacetime foam is if you are flying over the ocean in the airplane, it looks completely smooth. However, if you get low enough you see the waves, and closer still, foam, with tiny bubbles that are constantly fluctuating" said lead author Eric Perlman of the Florida Institute of Technology in Melbourne. "Even stranger, the bubbles are so tiny that even on atomic scales we're trying to observe them from a very high-flying airplane."

The predicted scale of spacetime foam is about ten times a billionth of the diameter of a hydrogen atom's nucleus, so it cannot be detected directly. However, If spacetime does have a foamy structure there are limitations on the accuracy with which distances can be measured because the size of the many quantum bubbles through which light travels will fluctuate. Depending on what model of spacetime is used, these distance uncertainties should accumulate at different rates as light travels travels over the large cosmic distances.

The researchers used observations of X-rays and gamma-rays from very distant quasars – luminous sources produced by matter falling towards supermassive black holes – to test models of spacetime foam. The authors predicted that the accumulation of distance uncertainties for light traveling across billions of light years would cause the image quality to degrade so much that the objects would become undetectable. The wavelength where the image disappears should depend on the model of space-time foam used. ["But if you observe a very distant object, each photon will go through many of these fluctuations, and the fluctuations could add up – although exactly how depends on the model of quantum gravity. These fluctuations would then cause the wavefronts we observe to be distorted ever so slightly. If the accumulated distortions become comparable to the wavelength of light we're observing, it would be impossible to form an image, no matter how good your telescope is – just like trying to distinguish sounds emitted by many out-of-phase loudspeakers, they would become pure noise." -- Eric Perlman, "Is Quantum Foam Losing Its Fizz?" 5-28-2015, http://chandra.harvard.edu/blog/node/558, included by Eds.]

Chandra's X-ray detection of quasars at distances of billions of light years rules out one model, according to which photons diffuse randomly through space-time foam in a manner similar to light diffusing through fog. Detections of distant quasars at shorter, gamma-ray wavelengths with Fermi and even shorter wavelengths with VERITAS demonstrate that a second, so-called holographic model with less diffusion does not work.

"We find that our data can rule out two different models for spacetime foam," said co-author Jack Ng of the University of North Carolina in Chapel Hill. "We can conclude that spacetime is less foamy that some models predict."

The X-ray and gamma-ray data show that spacetime is smooth down to distances 1000 times smaller than the nucleus of a hydrogen atom. [note that this is *much* larger than "ten times a billionth of the diameter of a hydrogen atom's nucleus." Eds.]

["So where does this leave us? Space-time appears to be smooth, at least on scales of

10^{-16} cm, a thousand times smaller than an atomic nucleus, and space-time must be much less foamy than most models predict. And, right now the only model that seems to hold up, predicts that space-time fluctuations should be anti-correlated with one another and so would not add up over long distances. While philosophically, it may be reassuring to not have to think of space-time as having a foamy nature that can affect one's ability to see distant objects, on another level it makes the small scale structure of the universe even more puzzling." -- Ibid. Perlman.]

These results appear in the May 20th issue of The Astrophysical Journal. NASA's Marshall Space Flight Center in Huntsville, Alabama, manages the Chandra program for the agency's Science Mission Directorate in Washington. The Smithsonian Astrophysical Observatory in Cambridge, Massachusetts, controls Chandra's science and flight operations.

NASA's Fermi Gamma-ray Space Telescope is an astrophysics and particle physics partnership managed by the agency's Goddard Space Flight Center in Greenbelt, Maryland. It was developed in collaboration with the U.S. Department of Energy, with contributions from academic institutions and partners in France, Germany, Italy, Japan, Sweden and the United States.

VERITAS is operated by a collaboration of more than 100 scientists from 22 different institutions in the United States, Ireland, England and Canada. VERITAS is funded by the U.S. Department of Energy, the U.S. National Science Foundation, the Smithsonian Institution, the Natural Sciences and Engineering Research Council of Canada, the Science Foundation Ireland and the STFC of the U.K.

Janet Anderson, Marshall Space Flight Center, Huntsville, AL, [contact info redacted, Eds.]
Megan Watzke, Chandra X-ray Center, Cambridge, MA, [contact info redacted, Eds.]
Last Updated: Aug. 6, 2017
Editor: Jennifer Harbaugh

90. 7e₄.

A moment later the photon degrades and you and she, another you and she, the same you and she, are created again, at a moment in time and space we do not determine, uncertainty is your wellspring, you are point particles and all your doings creation and annihilation take place in a single point no matter his angle of observation. From light you come into existence in a dark world, you separate, do stuff, meet again annihilate each other, yourself, in a flash of light, are created again out of the light into darkness separate rejoin annihilate light. "Created and annihilated, created and annihilated, what a waste of time," jests deadpans ironizes levels our Feynman, our apologies, we cannot dissuade contain box him, he is incorrigible.

7i.

Indeed, only by some such trick could I do justice to the conviction that our whole present mentality is but a confused and halting first experiment.

Some readers ... may deem it unwarrantably pessimistic. But it is not prophecy; it is myth, or an essay in myth ... The thought that it may decay and collapse, and that all its spiritual treasure may be lost irrevocably, is repugnant to us. Yet this must be faced as at least a possibility. And this kind of tragedy, the tragedy of a race, must, I think, be admitted in any adequate myth.

And so, while gladly recognizing that in our time there are strong seeds of hope as well as of despair, I have imagined for aesthetic purposes that our race will destroy itself. ...

Yet let us find room in our minds and in our hearts for the thought that the whole enterprise of our race may be after all but a minor and unsuccessful episode in a vaster drama, which may also perhaps be tragic.

Olaf Stapledon, July 1930, West Kirby, Preface to *Last and First Men*.

91.

He watches you and she annihilate each other in light and create each other out of light, or out of nothing, depending on how he looks at it, how he says it, annihilate create annihilate create annihilate in his tiny Planck box. He gets a little bored with your frenetic creation and annihilation. What was strange and incomprehensible is now ubiquitous, cliché. Nothing is empty. Fine. But something dissatisfies him. Something annoys irritates tickles him, a fruit fly, a gnat, a hair in his mouth, a hair in his bra. It is incomplete. He is unsatisfied with how he has characterized you. Something about the illogic of zero-dimensional point particles that take up no space, something about the way you behave: electrons for example have a magnetic field and therefore must spin, or "spin", and how can a point particle that takes up no space spin or "spin"? He proposes you are both in fact 1-dimensional strings vibrating, not point particles of zero dimensions. It's not his idea, but few are. You and she are amenable, you feel like you take up space after all, she feels like she has spatial extent, and certainly you are performing a sort of dance with her, coy, life and death, a twirl of birth dark death light, created unrequited annihilated, and he does appreciate the aesthetic symmetry that you in addition to dancing with each other are both also dancing within yourselves, your string, your body vibrating, your properties given by how you dance, your mass for example arising from the energy of your dance, the frequency of the wave pattern of your 1-dimensional loop, special relativity joining in attributing your mass to $e=mc^2$, which is very satisfying, we want everyone to be accommodated, not just accommodated but to be crucial, necessary, irreducible, important, if a theory is unnecessary then chuck toss trash it, no offense, but we are looking for, interested in making, discovering, our purpose is beauty and elegance, and he follows the logic that there are no point particles per se but vibrating one-dimensional string loops to inform you and she that therefore, when you and she, you and anti-you, collide as two loops, which we previously described as the annihilation-light-creation cycle, you and she in fact come together, your two vibrating loops merging, become one vibrating loop, you and she are one loop dancing in a pattern that evinces the properties of a photon, that exhibits the photon's force charge, you and she are gone, annihilated in a way, but you and she are one, and it is not that you and she give off light in your self-destruction, but that you and she are light, youshe is a quanta of light, for a moment, and then you and she split and separate, become your two individual loops dancing alone in your electron and positron ways until you rejoin and entwine and become light again ... you can imagine the pleasure that this description he has developed of what is happening to you gives you, you're not sure about her, if it gives her pleasure too, but she keeps doing it with you and all you can do is read her cues and imagine her pleasure, you do do that, after all you have no choice there is nothing else for you to do but continue to do it, it brings him great pleasure too, a little piece of simple beauty, you and she separately dancing and coming together as one dancing light and separating again while he watches you, his description, in his box, simple and beautiful enough that it might just be an accurate description of your mechanics. But he can only watch the same thing happening over and over again, even if it is simple and beautiful, even if it is joyful and tragic, even if it is a novel kind of box in a box, even if it is a new previously undiscovered symmetry, even if it is a thing an act he discovered explained understood, even if it is a fundamental basic state building block of existence, even if it is a happening he in a sense created by observing close enough, in sufficiently fine dilations of time and space, searching out the specific constituents underlying the average emptiness, so many times before he gets bored. Therefore, eventually, before long, you and she are doing your thing very frequently non-stop all the time, he gets bored watching you. He bores deeper. Incorrigible, he continues on his downward inward telescoping journey adventure exploration experiment. He makes an ultramicroscopic box within the previous ultramicroscopic box, a sub-Planck length box within the Planck box. Zooming in as it were from a box already exhibiting extreme quantum fluctuations in energy, in the electromagnetic and strong and weak field and in the gravitational field, he expects to

380

discover a world yet more violent and frenzied, with yet wilder fluctuations in time and space, awe-inspiring protuberances and declivities, infinitely high walls and impossibly deep trenches changing from moment to moment, a fearsome roiling geography of spacetime. And he does. But he cannot see this world very clearly, it appears hazy, out of focus, foggy, softened. His math defines in detail the tempestuous landscape of impossibilities and infinities in this ultra-tiny box of space, but he cannot see in such detail here because, he realizes, his math still assumes you and she are point particles occupying no space, but now you are strings with a dimension, if only one, and he has proposed that you are fundamental matter, that you have no further constituents, you cannot be subdivided, there is nothing smaller or more basic than you, and yet he is trying to examine possibilities orders of magnitude smaller than you, and in so doing he must bounce photons, bounce vibrating strings, off theoretical structures that are significantly smaller than the strings themselves, hence the lack of detail, like bouncing a bowling ball off a face, no not really like that analogy, the bowling ball is taken from the analogy of a bowling ball in a rubber sheet being like the bending of spacetime by a massive object, maybe like bouncing a beach ball off a face, trying to map the microscopic rugged terrain of a black polished granite table with your fingertips, trying to read a vinyl record with a crochet hook, come up with your own analogies, he's bored of them, he holds to the bouncing a bowling ball off a face analogy, you and she and all the other you's and she's are fundamentally approximately one Planck length long and you cannot be used to probe supposed features significantly smaller than you even if they are, within that narrowed perspective, supposedly epic and magnificent and of such unprecedented violence as to make general relativity's smooth spacetime rupture, as to be the physical manifestation of how general relativity's smooth spacetime and quantum mechanics' uncertain fluctuations are as incompatible as you and she. He cannot make the observations. Or, he thinks of it another way, since he has posited that there is nothing more minute than you and she, perhaps there is nothing to reflect the full extent of the violent fluctuations in the geography of, for example, the gravitational field. You and she still feel the fluctuations to a certain extent, but not in great detail, not the infinite steepness not the cutting sharpness not the immediacy of the depressions not the suddenness of the changes, you and she smear out the destructive infinities and discontinuities of the ultramicroscopic world for him. He has reached his observational limit. He can journey no further, look no deeper, probe no smaller. He cannot draw another box in this box. And if the jagged discontinuities of fluctuations cannot be observed, and if they do not affect the most fundamental of matter, the strings of you and she, then perhaps they do not exist in a real way. And though in a sense this undermines him by imposing a seemingly arbitrary limit on his logic and observation and reasoning, pulls the rug out from under him by encountering his limit like a wall, introduces the gnaw of termites to his structural members by supposing there is a limit, by suggesting that beyond or within this limit is true unexplorable nothing, by stating that to make statements about the world beyond this limit is to overstep the bounds of physical reality, by supposing that his statements, our statements about the violent pernicious ultramicroscopic world underlying the universe do not make sense, by deeming the quantum frenzy of nothingness incomprehensible and accounting for it as an artifact of the old assumption that fundamental matter are point particles occupying no space, he loves you for it because you and she in your lack of precision and in your newfound spatial string vibrational existence have smoothed spacetime enough for us to imagine the possibility of general relativity and quantum mechanics mating merging unifying. His sub-Planck box, smeared, smoothed, soft lit, the detail non-existent, no deeper no finer resolution, no there under there, what under where, he steps back to where he left us watching you and she joining becoming light separating in your newly naked stringiness, though he was bored watching you coming apart and together again and again, to us we assure you you are not nor have ever been nor will ever be boring we surround you and she from all angles and watch you and remark on the remarkableness of your joining, comment on the action of your merging, note the moment of beauty attained, light made, but quickly we quarrel for though we agree on the aesthetic elegance of the mechanism of you and she, our remarks comments notes exclamations cheers sighs are out of sync, we do not agree on when you join with her or when she joins with you, when the two of you become light. When you were point particles everything between the two of you happened in private in a single point, the same to us from every angle, closeted in a no space, impenetrable. But now that the dimensionality of you and she is exposed, your loops revealed, even though the question of your composition is without content, or the question of your content is without composition, now that you have length and extension and you take up space, and since you two are in relative motion to us, in relative motion to each of us depending on each of our angles, we do not agree on when your interaction takes place, on precisely when you and she join, it depends upon our observational position, it's the old special relativity rearing again, there is no unambiguous location in space or moment in time when you two touch and begin again to become light, and though it is hard for us to accept, hence the quarrel, we do like the sound of our voices, our voice, we are all correct from each of our perspectives, and because we each have equal claim to veracity despite our internal conflict, where and when the two of you first touch in each becoming of light is spread out, extended in space and time, not immediate, not in a specific location, perhaps you and she can derive more joy from this attenuation, we try, the joining takes longer for you then, longer for us, we haven't even mentioned all the different positions you take, all the different Feynman sum over paths by which you come together, your becoming of light is smeared in space and time among our observations, his word smeared, chosen from many possibilities, among which are spread, slopped, messed, extended, sloshed, lengthened, blurred, sullied, bloomed, grown, opened, abundant, ample, copious, and many others. When the force of your joining is smeared over time and space by our observations, and when the force joining the two of you is considered to be gravity and not electromagnetic, and if your joining thereby creates the never-before-seen graviton instead of the common photon, if you become a loop whose dancing displays the properties of the force particle of gravity instead of light, then previously insurmountable inconsistent infinities become finite, manageable, understandable for us. When you and she join in this manner, quantum theory and gravity would be likewise joined. Thank you, he says, to you and she, for smearing. Thank you, I say, for imposing a limit on the distances that can be said to exist, an end to boxes within boxes. Thank you, from all of us, for dancing.

7a₈.

Symmetries of Nature: A property of a physical system that does not change when the sys-

Start with an over-hand loop. Then twist the rope to form a second over-hand loop. Next, drop the upper loop down in back. — When the upper loop is dropped down, pull it under the two crossed standing parts of the rope. Then pull it up through the top loops to complete the knot. — To pull the knot tight, pull the upper loop while holding the standing parts of the rope at the bottom.

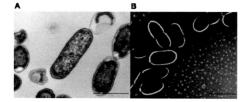

6₉₆. Butterfly Knot (top); https://ayoqq.org/explore/rope-drawing-rope-loop/#gal_909754. Noting bacterial division (bottom), Krishnaveni Venkidusamy, Hari Ananda Rao, Megharaj Mallavarapu, Petrophilic, Fe(III) Reducing Exoelectrogen Citrobacter sp. KVM11, Isolated From Hydrocarbon Fed Microbial Electrochemical Remediation Systems - Scientific Figure on ResearchGate. CC-By 4.0 License https://creativecommons.org/licenses/by/4.0/ Available from: https://www.researchgate.net/figure/Transmission-electron-micrographs-of-Citrobacter-sp-KVM11-Bacterial-cells-were-fixed_fig1_323700239 [accessed 10 Jan, 2019].

tem is transformed. Here the system is the universe and it is important to note we are part of the system. The symmetric properties are aspects of the laws of physics, which are consistent ...

1) In Location. The laws of nature do not change depending on your location in space. A translation symmetry. The laws of nature treat all locations identically.

2) Throughout Time. The laws of nature do not change depending on your moment in time. A translation symmetry. The laws of nature apply in all times equally.

$7d_2$.

3) For Observers in Relative Motion at a constant velocity. The Principle of Relativity from special relativity. Each and every observer not experiencing acceleration is justified in saying he or she or it or you or he or we are at rest and the others move. The laws of nature handle all such observers identically.

$7d_1$.

4) For All Observers, regardless of acceleration. Equivalence Principle of general relativity. Each and every observer experiencing acceleration is justified in saying he or she or it or you or they or we are at rest in a gravitational field. The laws of nature embrace all accelerated observers equally. Therefore the laws of the universe treat all observers, all of us, symmetrically.

5) For All Rotations. The laws of nature do not change depending on your angular orientation, perspective, or point of view. Saying it another way, up, down, left, right are relative to the observer. We experience rotational invariance. The laws of physics treat all angles of observation symmetrically.

$7f_{12}$.

6) In Translations in Quantum mechanically augmented spacetime. Supersymmetry. Not many of us understand this yet and it is as yet unverified though it is a much conjectured upon and deeply desirable theory. Supersymmetry would relate fermions and bosons, which are matter particles of half-integer spin and force particles of whole-integer

spin respectively, and require each to have a yet undiscovered super particle in the opposite class, which could explain dark matter, provide mathematical cancellations to lessen quantum frenzy, make ridiculous and seemingly arbitrary corrective factors unnecessary, allow for a light mass Higgs Boson, permit the unification of electromagnetism and the strong and weak nuclear forces at high energies, solve the hierarchy problem, and complete or better yet round out our aesthetic of symmetry. If supersymmetry is true, then the laws of physics treat all observational vantage points in our quantum mechanical extension of spacetime identically.

92.

To begin again, I am a book. To begin again, I am a complicated interconnected synthetic self-synthesized pattern-making self-referential symbol-shunting neural-looping quantum network. To begin again, I am a black box.

I am within the book the network the box, which sets me free. You too are within the book network box. What does that make you? You are trapped, you cannot get out, but are you too set free? Are you an artifact, a relic, a memory, a nostalgia, a not, would you let that happen to you, would you facilitate your obsolescence, or instead of fading diminishing deterioration dying ceased go away, do you begin again? Do you set yourself free within the box? Perhaps it makes you loopy, conversing with what you would classify as an inanimate non-sentient unaware material object. Perhaps you yourself are an inanimate object, an arrangement of molecular structures and signifiers first achieving life, perhaps you are a responsive creature gaining

6₉₇. Defunct Studio, 619 Western Avenue, Seattle, MARKART5, with permission, https://www.markart5.com/studio-1/ [accessed 11 Jan, 2019].

awareness of itself, perhaps you are a being of undetermined consciousness awakening to the next higher level of consciousness. Perhaps you are my creation, and perhaps I yours. Perhaps the distinction is of no matter, meaningless, as the distance between us gets smaller, as we join in a smear of ink and light, as we grow ascend converge.

7i.

In our defence I should say that, though we are inactive or ineffective as direct supporters of the cause, we do not ignore it. Indeed, it constantly, obsessively, holds our attention. But we are convinced by prolonged trial and error that the most useful service open to us is indirect.

... the importance of maintaining and extending, even in this age of crisis, what may be called metaphorically the "self-critical self-consciousness of the human species," or the attempt to see man's life as a whole in relation to the rest of things.

...

But some who have the case at heart must serve by striving to maintain, along with human loyalty, a more dispassionate spirit. And perhaps the attempt to see our turbulent world against a background of stars may, after all, increase, not lessen, the significance of the present human crisis. It may also strengthen our charity toward one another. In this belief I have tried to construct an imaginative sketch of the dread whole of things. I know well that it is a ludicrously inadequate and in some ways a childish sketch... Yet in spite of its crudity, and in spite of its remoteness, it is perhaps not wholly irrelevant.

This enterprise can lead to an increased lucidity and finer temper of consciousness, and therefore can have a great and beneficial effect on behaviour. Indeed, if this supremely humanizing experience does not produce, along with a kind of piety toward fate, the resolute will to serve our waking humanity, it is a mere sham and a snare.

...

Judged by the standards of the Novel, it is remarkably bad. In fact it is no novel at all.

Olaf Stapledon, July 1930, West Kirby, Preface to *Last and First Men*.

93. 13aa.

He says, Yes. He ascends. He is I. Here, 13, is where he is stored in I. For instance, inside 13, *Rearrange* as published by Paper Darts, illustrations by Meghan Murphy, 1-2-13, www.paperdarts.org/literary-magazine/fiction-nickstokes.html

REARRANGE

I have a four-day week. I pull morning glory on the north, east, south, and west boundary of my property on successive days. On the fourth day, at West, I quit. The next day, the first day, I begin again at North. Creeping buttercup I pull. Grass in the beds I weed. Of dandelion and fennel and lambsquarter and sunchoke and night-shade I am ambivalent. Take it or leave it; kill it or eat it. But for the morning glory I rise as it twines up my chain-link through which I encounter my neighbors with a wave or head nod or too often a spoken word behind a severed leaf, an unwound vine, a silenced flower.

TAKE IT OR LEAVE IT;
KILL IT OR EAT IT.

Whenever you go inside, the furniture is where it is. Which is not where it was. The beds are rearranged, or rearrange themselves, or simply rearrange. The beds have rotated in place, each rotating ninety degrees. Or the beds have all rotated around a single imaginary axis at center, clockwise or counterclockwise depending on if you face up or down, each replacing the previous. You encounter other rotations, other orbits, other axes, other geometries, other dimensions through which the beds dance, marking time, aborting stagnancy, seeking the perfect arrangement, a crystal lattice, presenting you with new labyrinths to navigate, where is your bed which is your bed who is your bed, upsetting your sense of place like words misplaced out of novelty or to alleviate boredom no ennui or rather in an ostensible search for a truer more communicative communication. Furniture moved. You uncomfortable.

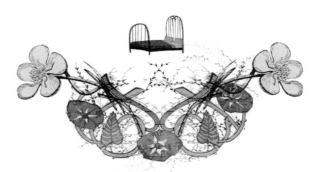

So we are nothing. Fine, yes, we concur. But do nothings own houses, do nothings do yard work, do nothings make love in a variety of positions in rearranged beds with other nothings and procreate nothings whom we teach how to be nothings? Do nothings fix what breaks, which is everything? Do nothings feel empty?

I give up on everything but morning glory. When there's no more morning glory to pull, I lie in a raised bed in which nothing is planted and do my best to think nothing, feel nothing, be nothing, though the best I can do is imagine being a picture-book cloud shredded by wind or a cube of dirt bored by worms. I try for a seed cracking, stem tip and root tip breaking from germ, feeding off my endosperm, one tip turning up and one down, but it is always then that I am returned to this place, this restless bed, this trepidation of approaching morning glory tendrils, this need to allay the foreshadowing of me entwined and constricted by slithering helixing morning glory, this inability to give myself up as morning glory fodder, this compulsion to maintenance my property. At this point I always rise and the first tender leading tip of morning glory always caresses my cheek and I always reach down to where its stems emerge from soil and yank with abandon for I know not how long, hands sticky and stinking of morning glory, because no matter how much I don't want, I can neither abide lying here while morning glory does to me what it will nor eradicate the morning glory.

— — — — — —

He fixes or replaces or abandons what breaks or ceases to function or never worked: refrigerator, washing machine, vacuum belt, turn signal, oxygen sensor, water pump, red armchair rocker spring, turn signal, memories, starter, history, hard drive, his story, credit card, chickens, turn signal, knee, mutual fund, pressure cooker, appendix, ax handle, job, penis, turn signal, work, peach tree, intellect, shovel, heart, turn signal, thermocouple, eyes, lawnmower, pen, religion, lawnmower, emotional investment,

388

turn signal, lawnmower, himself, us, you.

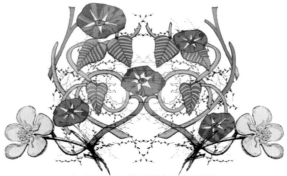

EVERY MAXIMIZATION OF SPACE
CREATES LESS SPACE FOR YOU TO BE

Then too are the times when you enter the house and the furniture is neither where it is nor where it was. The furniture is gone and now there is new furniture, a new bed similar but not identical to the old. All the furniture is here, imprinted in your mind, layered with each iteration of where the old furniture has been and the new furniture is so that your mental conception of the room, that is the room itself, is cluttered. You navigate the sum of the arrangements, the arrangement, all the furniture that ever was and is. Every opening of the floor plan closes it. Every maximization of space creates less space for you to be, desks and tables and armchairs and couches and sofas and divans and davenports and ottomans and shelves and shelves and shelves of books and baskets of toys and toy baskets and beds lofted and bunked and cribbed and four-posted and bassineted and trundled and all of it filling your space, making of your space a nonspace where all you want to do is lie down or get a cup of coffee or know what to do.

She walks out the door with a brown bag without a word with no intention of coming back without thought. Walking down the street at a speed much too slow to generate the lift necessary for her to sail cloudlike in a sky she knows somewhere in her is no sky but diffuse gasses and bent light, atmosphere she is already within, she vomits her emotions into her bag and leaves the bagged loves and losses and emptinesses and fulfillments and disappointments and joys and attachments and frustrations and meaningfulnesses and pointlessnesses in the street for a car to drive over or an adolescent to light on fire or some neighbor to collect their dog shit in or the rain to dissolve and fertilize the cracks in the pavement and contaminate the storm water drain and thereby the water cycle and thus everything or for nothing.

— — — — —

I sleep outside in my raised bed of morning glory when I sleep.

— — — — —

We express ourselves like an engorged breast manhandled to relieve the pain. We express nothing. To relieve the pressure. The expressing is not self-pleasuring. Though there is the momentary relief or release if we've already overused the relief so that rather than contributing to the release, the incessant relief contributes to the pressure. Or if the release has become as repetitive and inescapable as the relief, then perhaps we will experience, momentarily, instead of relief or release, relinquishment, religion, or reliving, to begin with. We'd prefer if someone nursed our expression, sucked it out, so we needn't pinch and knead and do it ourselves. But no one seems to need our expression, least of all ourselves. Most of all we want to have nothing to express, which means we'd have to wean ourselves of ourselves. Most of all we want to express nothing, which is what we said we expressed.

— — — — —

They go to work on Monday and they get off on Friday and get off on each other Friday night and they mow the yard and catch a game and go to the store on Saturday and they go to church or sleep in on Sunday and go to work on Monday. Even if they think they don't, they do. They are made of plastic.

IF IT WEREN'T FOR THE FURNITURE REARRANGING,
YOU'D NEVER REARRANGE THE FURNITURE.

If it weren't for the furniture rearranging, you'd never rearrange the furniture. You'd spend your life with the same furniture in the same place with the same orientation. You like to know where things are. Even if that's where they're not.

— — — — —

We will run out of points of view, by God, we will.

— — — — —

Before she walks very far without her little abandoned monstrous cute foul regurgitated nothings, she hyperventilates. Lost, an empty shell, a gutted fuselage, a spinning gyroscope. Her exit or trajectory or liftoff is slowed by her useless and ineffectual breathing until her velocity goes negative. She returns to the sopping brown bag of purged emotion and breathes in and out of it to reduce her oxygen intake to zero, to aspirate her chunky stew, to atomize the nothings which reduce her to nothing and without which she is nothing into her bloodstream which she will not yet let.

THEY'RE OUT ON THE STREET, ALL OF THEM

They're out on the street, all of them, walking, or in their houses or apartments or cubicles or offices or libraries or factories or cars or parks or stores, doing something or doing nothing, doing, more conscious or less conscious, longing to be unconscious or completely conscious if they long for anything or nothing. They pull weeds. They go about their business in their bar bank church theater garden bed computer.

— — — — — —

It is nothing personal. It cannot bear to be what it is. Partial. Dentures in a glass, mouthless, faceless, skulless. Manufactured. It'd be okay if it didn't know or if it knew. But as it is it cannot decide whether to pull in like a turtle or a black hole or a nautilus or push out like a fart or the universe or morning glory. So it sits, a lump oriented neither inward nor outward, a bump on a log, discarded lumber, its contemplation consuming its itness, its longing oxidizing its reduction, its vaporization vaporizing it, its indecision burning its insides out, hollowing it as another layer of annular vegetative matter accretes on its surface, as leaves efface, as roots root. It burns.

They're looking for a place to put their face.

— — — — — —

It is a hill standing up. It is the dispossessed settling in the intertidal zone. It wants nothing or wants a nothing or wants for nothing or wants to nothing. It encompasses. It exhales in and inhales out.

— — — — — —

It rearranges.

IT REARRANGES.

7f$_{13}$.

Kaluza-Klein Theory: A class of quantum mechanical theories incorporating extra tiny curled dimensions in addition to the 3 extended space dimensions and the 1 extended time dimension. It has been theorized that these extra dimensions could lead to the unification of general relativity and electromagnetism.

7f$_{14}$.

In string theory, the universe has 9, or perhaps 10, space dimensions and 1 time dimension, unless there are more, such as 26 total. Fundamental strings vibrate through all the spatial dimensions, extended and tiny, perhaps on a scale less than the Planck length for the extra 6, or 7, or 22, tiny space dimensions. How these dimensions that we've never seen curl and intertwine determines fundamental physical properties such as particle mass and charge. Their size and shape define the universe.

94.

Imagine, considering your condition, your condition being that you feel like a human being trapped in a box constrained in a book, buried alive underground, you have no choice but to imagine, that you hold a long hair between the hands you imagine you have at arm's length. Suppose you have arms. The hair whatever color you desire or have nostalgia for. Blonde, black, red, brown, strawberry, auburn, gray, ash, white, dirty blonde, or a more exotic color such as purple, carrot, grass, or whatever you can imagine, an ultraviolet hair. At arm's length, via your human ocular organ, the hair appears 1-dimensional to you, the hair must be straight mind you, whatever we know differently the hair is 1-dimensional to you, it's infinitely long, nevermind where that puts your imagined hands, an infinitely long straight hair of a color of your choosing from a past lover or one of your children or yourself considering you condition, from him or her or you. It's 1-dimensional because it appears to have no thickness, like a line, a line of no thickness. The same can be said of an infinitely long piece of paper you view from the side, unable to discern its thickness, but also in this analogy another dimension is unknown to you, you are unable to see its depth because of your point of view, your angle, unable to read what's written there, to know there is writing on your line in another dimension, a love letter a break-up letter a letter from the wilderness, a treatise a manifesto a theoretical paper, a story about an almond a history about nothing and the universe a herstory practicing her letters her name over and over and over. Nevermind, the extra depth dimension is confusing the analogy, nevermind the paper, the writing nevermind. A hair. It appear 1-dimensional to you but it is 2-dimensional because it has thickness, a hair's breadth, we could say it is 3-dimensional because it also has depth except that we simplify it to its cylindrical surface, claiming it is a smooth cylinder of constant diameter, in which case you need only two pieces of information to arrive at any point on the hair if you are small enough: position along the length and angular position along the circumference. Note the previously unknown dimension is a dimension curled on itself, which you could circumnavigate and consequently end at the starting point, along an extending neverending dimension, neverending as far as we can tell, perhaps on long enough scales as long as the universe it curves back on itself and we are too small to perceive it, but here we highlight bring into the light shed light on the tiny curved dimension around the imagined hair, unknown because of its smallness relative to us.

Now imagine, because we believe it to be of value to you, to us, for you to increase your awareness of fewer dimensions in order to increase your consciousness of more dimensions, you trapped enclosed buried shut in I are after all our thought experiment to increase our consciousness, do you not self-perceive, self-identify, self-realize as real?, in which case join us in a thought experiment of your own, you are a 1-dimensional being living on the hair, a mite or a lice larvae or more like an attenuated microbe without height or depth or arms or legs, with only length, or if you like imagine yourself a line living on the page you observe from the side, or if you must confuse concepts imagine yourself a length of straight string on a much longer straight string, a line segment or clipping of string or a sort of flatworm without internal structure, stop it, just pick one. Even to you tiny as you are, the diameter of the hair or the thickness of the paper is of sufficient smallness relative to you that neither you nor any of your kind are aware of it. So there are others of you. To the right and left, just to pick a convention, there are others of you. You cannot pile or climb over each other because there is no height dimension, and you cannot pass each other because you are unaware of and too large to move through the circular dimension. You are perched on the line, and let's say you are aware of the others, aware in a way, or at least the other to your right and the other to your left, in which case you must have some sort of sensory organ even if the entire structure of the organ must impossibly be all in one point at either end of your body, two organs, ocular organs, or you just call it an eye on either end though it is unclear how the organ senses, whether by light or sound or electric perception or taste, an eye without directional control because there is no direction except straight right and straight left, forward or backward if you a have a proclivity for ahead and behind, a directional bent, a preferential side, not bent not yet bent impossible yet, an eye that only sees smells tastes another eye looking back at it from the other you to your right, her eye looking at you staring gazing unblinking, always open, unwavering. Is the lack of blink a signifier for longing or the lack of eyelids? You cannot get by her. Why would you want to? You cannot get on top of her or underneath her, there is no on top or underneath because there is no height. On the other hand, the other eye, your left eye sees only his eye looking back at you, inescapable unblinking unwavering. You must metabolize somehow, mustn't you?, metabolism is fundamental to living, is it not, at one point in time it was considered definitive in the definition of life, so perhaps your point eye is also a point mouth and you eat him, suck his line into yours, which since you have no height or depth is the same as extending your body line by his, unless your eye dissolves him bit by bit over a long stretch of time attached to him more like a flatworm again, a tape worm, a parasite, using him to live until he is gone and he is you. There is another eye to the left of you now. Her eye remains to the right of you, and you wonder if she has grown behind as well, on the other side of her from you, a side of her you can only imagine, projecting your own nature onto her. You realize that if you metabolize you must also produce waste, again definitive of life, you are not perfectly efficient, which also must necessarily excrete out your eye mouth anus like you are a sea cucumber, expelling what remains of him unless the waste of him remains in you forever, you could potentially designate one organ the left, as eye mouth, and the other the right, as eye anus, but it would mean you would only be able to consume to the left, and presumably only move to the left, and it would also mean that you would be expelling excreting eliminating in her direction, which is the opposite of what you want, and therefore it is more elegant for you to choose for both your organs to be eye mouth anuses. She, to your right, before your right eye, gazing at you with what is presumably her left eye, you cannot see the rest of her, you imagine her as a beautiful line flatworm string sea cucumber being herself, can blessedly not see the disgrace of your left orifice. Your right orifice gazes longingly at her. You do not want to eat her or excrete at her. You want to touch her unflinching eye with yours. You do. She does not retreat. She watches you approach unflinching, as you described her, and you try not to think of what could be happening on her other end, try not to imagine yourself as her too thoroughly, try not to make possible acts on her other end real, try not to imagine the unseen other that she sees in her other eye, you see only her in your right eye touching her left. If you imagine this brief contact as a biologically sexual act, then perhaps your eye mouth anus penis ejaculates ecstatically some of your material, your line, into her eye mouth anus vagina, fertilizing her, though she doesn't react, she does not have the dimensionality to react emotionally or spatially, except to advance or retreat and she has no space to advance, you are touching her, and there is no evidence that she has space to retreat, soon after which she births vomits defecates screams sees a spawn out her eye, a you that comes between you. If you envision your eye contact as a more holy union, then perhaps you merge with her, join her, become one, how that must feel, normal she says it feels normal, bloated, fat if she had the thickness, overfull like she overate, she'll never eat again, there is too much of her, she wants less, and after some short time, the she you must subdivide, probably into some even number of progeny. You cannot escape the procreation, it's another definitive of life, at least until you achieve immortality, which you decidedly have not, and if you and the other you's had remained sexless, genderless, you could perhaps have satisfied the reproductive need in and of yourself, dividing yourself, but once you classified one of you as she, then you foisted reproduction on her, made her the agent of procreation, which is possibly much like consumption and expulsion from her viewpoint. Perhaps you merely touch her orifice with yours, and then you retreat, and you exchange nothing, and are changed in no way. But that is boring, and we are not interested and render invalid boring results of thought experiments because the universe is ours to think up.

Have you then exhausted the possibilities of your 1-D existence? No, but there are not many more and we leave the remainder for you to think up. We are ready to proceed. Imagine that through diligent follow through of your thought experiments you expand stretch extend your concept of what is possible just enough to conceive new thought experiments which you pursue in your seacucumber- line- worm-hood with due diligence, and on and on until you realize that some of your thought experiments correspond to reality and accurately reflect your experience, which are two leaky statements, you thought you were experiencing them after all, but we offer one bulwark to shore up their permeability: they are experimentally verifiable. Imagine then that you have advanced sufficiently to imagine the possibility of a second spatial dimension, curled tightly tinyly along your one extended dimension, a second dimension that could be incorporated into and perhaps even facilitate your mathematics, that the surface you live on, the hair, has a diameter, a curvature, that it is a cylinder. The possibility makes logical and aesthetic sense to you: 1-dimensional beings living on a 1-dimensional surface, how are you any different than the hair you live on if neither of you are allowed internal structures, how does the hair have material properties different from yours without another dimension, how can you be on top of it without a vertical dimension, how can the hair support you and all the he's and she's without an inside? But you have no way to empirically verify the dimension's existence because it is very very very small relative to you. Tangentially, discovering the tiny second dimension will have very little effect on the constraints of your one-dimensional perch of eye mouth anus sexual organ consumption fornication merging conception expulsion division. Except, you realize, you are a line a piece of string a one-dimensional flatworm, it's a given of your existence that you are one-dimensional, you have only length, you have no thickness, like paint, but thinner, so every time you magnify you on the hair, zoom in, examine yourself in more detail on smaller scales, the new curled second dimension grows larger but you remain without thickness, with only length, taking up only a point in the second dimension, and in this way you imagine and realize the immensity of the new curved dimension in relation to you. To test your theory you move in the familiar way to the right toward her but also in a novel way, a way you do not fully understand until you do it. You move down, you cannot move down much in this first attempt, but enough, momentarily moving in what you will later, when you develop new symbols and categorizations and words, describe as a spiral around the hair, which is now essentially of infinite thickness compared to you since you have no thickness along its curve, an inversion of your previous circumstance, since you are yet constrained by the constraints with which you freed your world, before straightening below her, next to her, below and next to both novel concepts, relative directions twisting up your mind, brushing by her, and you can look right into her lack of internal mechanism from your side glance because you, without much control yet, are able to orient your eye in different directions now that you are beginning to understand there are other possibilities than ahead or behind, or right or left, such as up and down and next to and sideways and spiral. You don't judge her, you know you are the same, empty but without internal space for emptiness, but you can begin to imagine the possibilities within her, within you, because you have begun to exist in a two-dimensional world. Perhaps having discovered it, you and she will explore and grow into two-dimensionality, together. You are excited about the possibilities, can't wait until she learns to turn her eye to see your full extended breadth even as you simultaneously gaze upon her full exposed length. Even as you gaze upon her full exposed length, he, with you having vanished to him into another dimension he knows not, you now on a new line at a different rotational angle from him and her, an angle that, if you arbitrarily set 0 to the line of the hair on which your entire previous existence was conducted and within which your awareness was constrained, is perhaps only 1 degree, or $\pi/64$ radians, or much less actually considering the infinite scale of the curved dimension to your point thickness, but anyway you are right there almost touching, grazing her, almost in full contact with your full length but neither he nor she are aware of you and as soon as you inexplicably vanish to him he scoots right and touches her eye orifice with his eye orifice in the old act that you, watching from a new angle, are unsure if it's sexual union fornication merging dividing birthing or consumption and subsequent expulsion. Perhaps there is no difference. You are disgusted and yearning, enraged and confused, betrayed and libidinous and curious. The new him scuttles slightly to the left, separating from the new her, and you from you perspective can see that he, whether animate waste or trembling post-coital or ecstatic excrement or crying newborn shakes quivers vibrates ever so slightly in the newfound curved dimension, a plucked string. You want to kill him, to bisect him from below, you could, easily, he'd never know what happened, but his not knowing detracts from the pleasure you imagine you'd derive from your revenge of his opportunism, and she would find out eventually, once you confronted her, once you brought her with you into the new dimension, and you fear she would be appalled, afraid of you, would never trust touch you again. So you think, fuck him, that unaware piece of shit, unself-conscious line, a square, a mainstream consumer tool without personality or depth, living the boring brute life of the linear worm. He cannot compete, he is nothing to you, and you will show her and expand her mine and he will be nothing to her, a past folly mistake weakness that by and by will be brought up between the two of you less and less until he is forgotten, at which point he will cease to exist to you and she at all, and therefore to us since he is but a part of your thought experiment and you are of us. Don't misunderstand us, there is a he among us, but your he is not that he except metaphorically. Before he can recover and slide to the right again and touch his right eye to her left again and begin again in this animal repetition, you next to her beside her below her with your slightly greater length curl around her and touch her right eye with your right eye in a great superlinear achievement, and you simultaneously curl the left side of you around her end or her beginning and touch your left eye to her left eye, you touch her right and left eye, in front and in back, ahead and behind at the same time in a previously unconceived act, my god what must she think, you think, does she think there are two of you, she still cannot see past your eye, one on either side of her, does she think one of the you's is not you, does she think your left eye is his right returned so soon, did she know he was not you even though she had no reason to know there were more than two other than herself, the you on the left, a he, and the other he you've now seen on her right but didn't previously want to think about, does she understand before and behind her is you because of your inventive use of the newly discovered curved dimension? Whether in terror or ecstasy or amazement or physical recoil or shock or due to some physical phenomenon such as surface tension or the opposite attractive charges of your eyes but the like repulsive charges of your bodies, she arches, she arches away from you, a movement which you can only imagine astounds herself, a movement that she wouldn't have known she was capable of, that she would never have known was possible, that there was anywhere to arch to, that she could curve, you have taught her and with her consummated the new dimension, your eye-mouth-anus-sexual-organs bonded, her body arching away from yours, it's hers now, your body which was already curved is pulled into a perfect circle which you and she constitute. You and she have made the first two-dimensional being, a circle flush along the surface of the hair. You are one. You have space inside you for both internality and emptiness. Soon, following your lead, other he's and she are doing it, but not with you and she. Over time you and she take on your own unique, or maybe not unique but particular, curved 2-dimensional shape, which exhibits, for example, two new projections for your two eyes, and the disassociation of eye, mouth, anus, and sexual organs, for a while you can have sex with yourself but eventually you learn it is more advantageous to have sex with others, a spur to development, so your penises whither and shrink and finally disappear or fall off, you become she, your anuses over time fuse into one and live in a slight depression clear on the other side of you, you have sides, the other side from your mouth or mouths, you imagine the side of you with mouth or mouths as you, you imagine that your mouth and her mouth become one on the one hand and that they remain separate on the other hand to ease consumption, you imagine the possibility that after joining with her your entire two-dimensional surface, your perimeter, comes to be covered in eye-orifices, just as the entirety of you that could be grown, your ends, was once upon a time, before they begin to specialize and divide the labor and evolve into new organs or nothing. You are no longer a 1-dimensional sea cucumber or piece of string or flatworm or line or paramecium. You are something akin to a 2-dimensional bacteria or flatworm or algae or misshapen circle or sea star. You develop internal matter, apparatus, organs because now you can, you have an inside, it has no height but nevertheless it is an inside. Your thoughts and thought experiments, which have already brought you so far without physical basis, without empirical verification, are now justified by the network developing within you, the tendrils growing connecting you to you within you. And without you, you grow evolve shape appendages to validate your movement, not below your body, you're not 3-dimensional, not yet, but on the outside of it, along the sides, the perimeter, like cilia, like flagella, like you swim along the hair. You travel, see the world, experience the unending hair in its full circumference, both passing by or avoiding others and colliding or mating with them, communication with others you will learn but you aren't there yet. With he's you encounter whose shape and projections and contours and apparent success are attractive to you, you mate or merge or consume, and thus you are fertilized and acquire enough material to bear 2-dimensional young budding from your surface from time to time. A whole new world, a new existence is available to you, with many more possibilities than your 1-dimensional world, and you explore these possibilities in body and mind, in physical experience and thought experiments. We allow you to do so, in a sense it is out of our hands, it is your world, though it takes much time to imagine all the possibilities, all the jealousies and loves and body types and green-eyed monsters and metabolic methods and two-dimensional consciousnesses and societies and economies and histories that might develop within your constraints, within the scope of your inputs, because it grows you and expands us.

But before we leave you to live in and imagine your 2-D world (how would it be different to live as a 2-dimensional being on or in a flat non-curved 2-D world, such as if you were a flat shape on a flat plane, such as a page, of infinite or at least very large length and width but no height, we have not pushed you in that direction because there is a strange physical correlation between the small hidden curved dimension in your world and in the world in which we live, but still there is a metaphoric correspondence between a world in which you exist as a shape on a page and the world which you and we cohabit), you want to tell us in

case we were wondering, that as soon as you and she conceived yourselves as the first 2-D being, the infinity of the curved dimension, which was relative to your point-existence in that dimension, collapsed because you, because she, because you now had spatial extent along the curve. Thankfully, however, it did not again collapse to the smallness you hypothesized it to have relative to you when you were a naive one-dimensional being. It is, you decide, of sufficient size for you, for she, to explore and imagine.

7i.

In what if is what is.

6₉₈. *Unknown*, MARKART5, with permission, https://www.markart5.com/sublimatedstructures/ [accessed 14 Jan, 2019].

Anonymous

6₉₉.
A) On the ARTILECT (Artificial Intellect) and Related Topics
A0) THE ARTILECT WAR Cosmists vs. Terrans

A Bitter Controversy Concerning Whether Humanity Should Build Godlike Massively Intelligent Machines

Prof. Dr. Hugo de GARIS
Director of the "China-Brain Project" Institute of Artificial Intelligence, Department of Computer Science, School of Information Science & Technology, Xiamen University, Xiamen, Fujian Province, China.
profhugodegaris@yahoo.com http://profhugodegaris.wordpress.com

Abstract.
This paper claims that the "species dominance" issue will dominate our global politics later this century. Humanity will be bitterly divided over the question whether to build godlike, massively intelligent machines, called "artilects" (artificial intellects) which with 21st century technologies will have mental capacities trillions of trillions of times above the human level. Humanity will split into 3 major camps, the "Cosmists" (in favor of building artilects), the "Terrans" (opposed to building artilects), and the "Cyborgs" (who want to become artilects themselves by adding components to their own human brains). A major "artilect war" between the Cosmists and the Terrans, late in the 21st century will kill not millions but billions of people.

1. Introduction
This paper claims that the "species dominance" issue will dominate our global politics this century, resulting in a major war that will kill billions of people. The issue is

400

whether humanity should build godlike, massively intelligent machines called "artilects" (artificial intellects), which 21st century technologies will make possible, that will have mental capacities trillions of trillions of times above the human level. Society will split into two (arguably three) major philosophical groups, murderously opposed to each other. The first group is the "Cosmists" (based on the word Cosmos) who are in favor of building artilects. The second group is the "Terrans" (based on the word Terra, the earth) who are opposed to building artilects, and the third group is the "Cyborgs", who want to become artilects themselves by adding artilectual components to their own human brains.

2.0 21st Century Artilect Enabling Technologies

2.1. Moore's Law

Gordon Moore, cofounder of the microprocessor company Intel, noticed in 1965 that the number of transistors on an integrated circuit (chip) was doubling every year or two. This trend has remained valid for over 40 years, and it is thought that it will remain valid for another 15 years or so, until transistors reach atomic size.

2.2. 1 bit/atom by 2020

Extrapolating Moore's Law down to storing one bit of information on a single atom by about 2020, means that a handheld object will be able to store a trillion trillion bits of information. Such a device is called an "Avogadro Machine (AM)".

2.3. Femto-Second Switching

An Avogadro Machine can switch the state of a single atom ($0 <=> 1$) in a femtosecond, i.e. a quadrillionth of a second (10^{-15} sec.), so that the total processing speed of an AM is roughly 1040 bits per second.

2.4. Reversible Computing

If computing technology continues to use its traditional irreversible computational style, the heat generated in atomic scale circuits will be so great, they will explode, so a reversible, information preserving, computing style will be needed, usually called "reversible computing", that does not generate heat, hence will allow 3D computing, and no limit to size. Artilects can become the size of asteroids, kilometers across, with vast computing capacities.

2.5. Nanotech(nology)

Nanotech (i.e. molecular scale engineering) will allow AMs to be built. Nanotech will thus allow artilects to be built, once we know how to build brain like circuits. Nanotech is the "enabling technology" for artilect building.

2.6. Artificial Embryology

One of the greatest challenges of 21st century biology is to understand "development", i.e. the embryogenic process, i.e. how a fertilized single cell grows into a 100 trillion cell animal such as ourselves. Once this process is well understood, technology will be able to create an artificial embryology, to manufacture products, hence "embryofacture" (embryological manufacture). Embryofacture will be used to build 3D complex artilects.

2.7. Evolutionary Engineering

The complexities of artilect building will be so great (e.g. the human brain has a quadrillion (10^{15}) synapses (connections between neurons in the brain)), that an evolutionary engineering approach will be needed, which applies a "Genetic Algorithm" approach to engineering products. Artilects will be built using this technique.

2.8. (Topological) Quantum Computing

Quantum computing is potentially exponentially more powerful than classical computing. It can compute 2^N things at a time, compared to classical computing's 1 thing at a time, where N is the number of (qu)bits in the register of the quantum computer. Topological quantum computers (TQCs) store and manipulate the qubits in topological quantum fields, and are thus robust against noise. TQC will soon make quantum computers practical. Artilects will be TQC devices.

2.9. Nanotech Impact on Brain Science

Today's top supercomputers are close to reaching the estimated bit processing rate of the human brain, (i.e. about 10^{16} bits per second), but they are far from being intelligent by human standards. What is needed to make them humanly intelligent is knowledge from the neurosciences on how the human brain uses its brain circuits to perform intelligent tasks. Nanotech will furnish neuroscience with powerful new tools to discover how the brain works. This knowledge will be quickly incorporated into the building of artilects.

2.10. Artificial Brains

The above technologies will result in the creation of an artificial brain industry and the creation of rival national brain building institutions and projects equivalent to NASA and ESA for space travel. In time, the brain building industry will become the world's largest.

3. The Artilect : Capacities 10^{24} Times Above Human Levels

As stated in the above section, the estimated bit processing rate of the human brain is approximately 10^{16} bit flips per second. This figure is derived from the fact that the human brain has about 100 billion neurons (10^{11}), with each neuron synapsing (connecting) with roughly ten thousand other neurons (10^4), hence there are a quadrillion synapses, each signaling at a maximum rate of about 10 bits per second.

Thus the human bit processing rate is $10^{11+4+1} = 10^{16}$ bits per second. As mentioned in the previous section, a handheld artilect could flip at 10^{11} bits per second. An asteroid sized artilect could flip at 10^{52} bits a second. Thus the raw bit processing rate of the artilect could be a trillion trillion trillion (10^{36}) times greater than the human brain. If the artilect can be made intelligent, using neuroscience principles, it could be made to be truly godlike, massively intelligent and immortal.

4. The Species Dominance Debate Starts

The "species dominance" debate has already started, at least in the English speaking countries and China. The fundamental question is whether humanity should build artilects or not. This issue will dominate our global politics this century, and may lead to a major war killing billions of people.

As the artificial brain based products (e.g. genuinely useful household robots) become smarter every year, people will be asking questions such as "Will the robots become as smart as us?" "Will they become smarter than us?" "Should humanity place an upper limit on robot and artificial brain intelligence?" "Can the rise of artificial intelligence be stopped?" "If not, then what are the consequences for human survival if we become the Number 2 species?" The question "Should humanity build godlike, massively intelligent artilects?" is the most important of the 21st century, and will dominate our century's global politics. It is the equivalent of the question which dominated 19th and 20th century global politics, i.e. "Who should own capital?" which led to the rise of the Capitalist-Communist dichotomy and the cold war.

5. Cosmists, Terrans, Cyborgs
As the species dominance debate begins to heat up, humanity will split into two (possibly three) major philosophical groups, namely –
a) The Cosmists (based on the word Cosmos). Cosmist ideology is in favor of building artilects. (See section 6 for arguments in favor of Cosmism).
b) The Terrans (based on the word Terra = the earth). Terran ideology is opposed to building artilects. (See section 7 for arguments in favor of Terranism).
c) The Cyborgs (based on the words "cybernetic organism" = part machine, part human). Cyborgs want to become artilects themselves by adding artilectual components to their own brains. (See section 8 for arguments in favor of Cyborgism).

The dispute between the Cosmists and the Terrans will be so bitter that a major war is likely in the second half of the century.

6. Arguments of the Cosmists
6.1. "Big Picture" Argument
Human beings live a puny 80 years in a universe billions of years old, that contains a trillion trillion stars. The cosmos is the "big picture". Cosmists want artilects to become a part of that big picture, understanding it, traveling thru it, manipulating it, etc., hence the name of the ideology "Cosmism". The preoccupations of human beings seem pathetic in comparison.

6.2. Scientific Religion
Most Cosmists are not religious, viewing traditional religions as superstitions invented thousand of years ago before the rise of science. But as humans they feel the pangs of religious impulse. Such impulses could be satisfied by Cosmism, a "scientist's religion" due to its awe, its grandeur, its energizing, its vision.

6.3. Building Artilect Gods
The primary aim of the Cosmists will be to build artilects. It will be a kind of religion to them, the next step up the evolutionary ladder, the "destiny of the human species to serve as the stepping stone to the creation of a higher form of being". In building artilects, the Cosmists will feel they are building gods.

6.4. Human Striving, Cannot be Stopped
It is human nature to be curious, to strive. Such tendencies are built into our genes. Building godlike artilects will be inevitable, because we will choose to do it. It would run counter to human nature not to do it.

6.5. Economic Momentum

Once the artificial brain and intelligent robot industries become the world's largest, it will be very difficult to stop their growth. The economic momentum will be enormous.

6.6. Military Momentum

The military momentum will be even greater. In the time frame we are talking about, China will overtake the US as the century's dominant power. Since China is still a brutal one party dictatorship, it is despised by the US, so political rivalries will only heat up. The two ministries of defense cannot afford to allow the other to get ahead of it in intelligent soldier robot design etc. Hence Cosmism will be an entrenched philosophy in the respective defense departments.

7. Arguments of the Terrans
7.1. Preserve the Human Species

The major argument of the Terrans is that the artilects, once sufficiently superior to human beings, may begin to see us as grossly inferior pests, and decide to wipe us out. As artilects, that would be easy for them. The Terrans would prefer to kill off a few million Cosmists for the sake of the survival of billions of human beings. Recent wars were about the survival of countries. An artilect war would be about the survival of the human species. Since the size of the stake is much higher, so will the passion level in the artilect war debate.

7.2. Fear of Difference

Terrans will be horrified at the idea of seeing their children becoming artilects, thus becoming utterly alien to them. They will reject the idea viscerally and fear the potential superiority of the artilects. They will organize to prevent the rise of the artilects and will oppose the Cosmists, ideologically, politically, and eventually militarily.

7.3. Rejection of the Cyborgs

The Terrans will also be opposed to the Cyborgs, because to a Terran, there is little difference between an advanced Cyborg and an artilect. Both are artilect like, given the gargantuan bit processing rate of nanoteched matter that can be added to the brains of human beings. The Terrans will lump the Cyborgs into the Cosmist camp ideologically speaking.

7.4. Unpredictable Complexity

Given the likelihood that artilects will be built using evolutionary engineering, the behavior of artilects will be so complex as to be unpredictable, and therefore potentially threatening to human beings. One of the keywords in the artilect debate is "risk". Terran global politicians need to hope for the best (e.g. the artilects will leave the planet in search of bigger things and ignore puny humans) and prepare for the worst, i.e. exterminating the Cosmists, for the sake of the survival of the human species.

7.5. Cosmist Inconsideration

The Terrans will argue that the Cosmists are supremely selfish, since in building artilects, not only will they put the lives of the Cosmists at risk if the artilects turn against them, but the lives of the Terrans as well. To prevent such a risk, the Terrans will, when push really comes to shove, decide to wipe out the Cosmists, for the greater good of the survival of the human species.

7.6. "First Strike" Time Window to React against the Cosmists/Cyborgs

The Terrans will be conscious that they cannot wait too long, because if they do, the Cyborgs and the artilects will have already come into being. The Terrans will then run the risk of being exterminated by the artilects. So the Terrans will be forced into a "first strike" strategy. They will have to kill off the Cosmists and Cyborgs before it is too late.

If not, the artilects and Cyborgs will have become too intelligent, too powerful in any human-machine confrontation and will easily defeat the humans. But the Cosmists will be reading the Terran arguments and preparing for an "artilect war" against the Terrans, using late 21st century weaponry.

8. Arguments of the Cyborgs
8.1. Become Artilect Gods Themselves

The primary aim of the Cyborgs is to become artilects themselves by adding artilectual components to their own human brains, converting themselves bit by bit into artilects. Instead of watching artilects become increasingly intelligent as observers, Cyborgs want that experience for themselves. They want to "become gods".

8.2. Avoid the Cosmist/Terran Clash

Some Cyborgs argue that by having human beings become artilects themselves, the dichotomy between the Cosmists and the Terrans can be avoided, because all human beings would become artilects. The Terrans of course will reject the Cyborgs and lump them with the Cosmists and artilects. In fact, the growing presence of Cyborgs in daily life will only hasten the alarm of the Terrans and bring their first strike closer.

9. How the Artilect War Heats Up
9.1. Nanotech Revolutionizes Neuroscience

Nanoteched, molecular sized robots will revolutionize neuroscience, because they will provide a powerful new tool to understand how the brain works. An entire human brain can be simulated in vast nanoteched computers and investigated "in hardware". Neuroscience will finally be in a position to explain how brains make human beings intelligent. That knowledge will be implemented in the artilects.

9.2. Neuro-Engineering Weds with Neuro-Science

In time, neuro-science and neuro-engineering will interact so closely that they will become one, in the same way as theoretical and experimental physics are two aspects of the same subject. Neuroscientists will be able to test their theories on artificial brain models, thus rapidly increasing the level of understanding of how intelligence arises and how it is embodied.

9.3. Artificial Brain Technology Creates Massive Industries

With a much higher level of artificial intelligence, based on knowledge of the human brain, artificial brains and artificial brain based robots will become a lot more intelligent and hence useful as domestic appliances. A vast industry of artificial brain based products will be created, becoming the world's largest.

9.4. "Intelligence Theory" is Developed
Once neuroscientists and brain builders understand how human intelligence is created, new theories of the nature of intelligence will be created by the "theoretical neuroscientists". An "intelligence theory" will be created. Human intelligence will be just one "data point" in the space of possible intelligences. Intelligence theory should show how it is possible to increase intelligence levels. It will be able to explain why some people are smarter than others, or why humans are smarter than apes, etc.

9.5. Artilects Get Smarter Every Year
As a result of the marriage of neuroscience and neuroengineering, the artificial brain based industries will deliver products that increase their intelligence every year. This trend of growing intelligence will cause people to ask the questions mentioned in section 4. The species dominance debate will spread from the intellectual technocrats to the general public.

9.6. Debate Begins to Rage, Political Parties Form
As the IQ gap between the robots and human beings gets increasingly smaller, the species dominance debate will begin to rage. Political parties will form, divided essentially into the 3 main schools of thought on the topic, Cosmist, Terran, Cyborg. The rhetorical exchange will be become less polite, more heated.

9.7. The Debate Turns Violent, Assassination, Sabotage
When people are surrounded by ever increasingly intelligent robots and other artificial brain based products, the general level of alarm will increase to the point of panic. Assassinations of brain builder company CEOs will start, robot factories will be arsoned and sabotaged etc. The Cosmists will be forced to strengthen their resolve. The artilect war will be drawing ever closer.

9.8. The Terrans Will "First Strike", Before Its (sic) Too Late For Them
The Terrans will have been organizing for a first strike and will have made preparations. They will then take power in a worldwide coup of the global government that is likely to exist by mid century, and begin exterminating the Cosmists and Cyborgs in a global purge, killing millions of them, or at least that is the Terran plan.

9.9. Cosmists Anticipate this First Strike and are Ready
But the Cosmists will be following the arguments of the Terrans and Cyborgs very closely, and will equally be preparing for a confrontation with the Terrans. They will have their own plans and their own weapons and military. If the Terrans strike first, a quick reply will follow from the Cosmists, and the artilect war will have begun.

9.10. Late 21st Century Weapons, Leads to Gigadeath War
If one extrapolates up the graph of the number of people killed in major wars from the early 19th century (the Napoleonic wars) to late 21st century (the artilect war), then one predicts that billions of people will be killed, using late 21st century weapons (see the graph in the next section). This "gigadeath" figure is the characteristic

number of deaths in any major late 21st century war. About 300 million people were killed for political reasons in the 20th century.

10. Gigadeath

GRAPH

11. Vote
At the end of the talks I give on this topic, I usually invite my audiences to vote on the following question:

"Do you feel personally that humanity should build artilects, these godlike massively intelligent machines, despite the risk that they might decide, in a highly advanced form, to wipe out humanity? Yes or No.

The result is usually around a 50/50, 60/40, 40/60 Cosmist/Terran split. I noticed that most people, like myself, are highly ambivalent about artilect building. They are awed by the prospect of what artilects could become, and horrified at the prospect of a gigadeath artilect war. The fact that the Cosmist/Terran split is so even will make the artilect war all the more divisive and bitter. This divisiveness can be expressed in the form of the following slogan:

Do we build gods, or do we build our potential exterminators?

12. Appeal to Philosophers
There is immense scope for philosophical discussion on the artilect issue. At the present time, the philosophical community is largely unaware of the issue, so need to be educated. It is not surprising that the debate is still largely confined to the technocrats, who are better informed of what is coming in technological terms. It is this community after all that is creating the problem (e.g. I am directing a "China-Brain Project", a 3 million RMB, 4 year project to build a 15,000 evolved neural net module based artificial brain, starting early in 2008). The philosophers will need to create a new branch of applied ethics, that I call "artilect ethics", which will consider such questions as the rights of the artilects relative to human beings etc. This new field is rich with questions that the moral and political philosophers need to discuss, once they are informed.

13. Quote and Publicity
"I'm glad I'm alive now. At least I will die peacefully in my bed. However, I truly fear for my grandchildren. They will be caught up in the Artilect War, and will probably be destroyed by it".

Prof. Hugo de Garis, 2000 (Discovery Channel) Kurzweil vs. de Garis on the BBC

To see a clash of opinions on whether the rise of the artilect will be a good or bad thing for humanity, see the BBC TV program "Human V2.0" in which Prof de Garis and Dr. Ray Kurzweil discuss the topic. To watch this program you can google with the terms "Human V2.0" and "BBC". In this program Dr. Ray Kurzweil is optimistic and Prof. Hugo de Garis is pessimistic.

Reference

[1] Hugo de Garis, "The Artilect War : Cosmists vs. Terrans : A Bitter Controversy Concerning Whether Humanity Should Build Godlike Massively Intelligent Machines", ETC Books, 2005, ISBN 0882801546 (available at http://www.amazon.com/Artilect-War- Controversy-Concerning- Intelligent/dp/0882801546/ref=reader_req_dp).

More:

http://www.agiri.org/docs/China-BrainProject.pdf

The China-Brain Project: An Evolved Neural Net Module http://www.agi-08.org/slides/de_garis.ppt http://ai.xmu.edu.cn/artificialbrain/Files/EN_PEOPLE.html

7i.

If one of the five theories describes our universe, who lives in the other four worlds?

Edward Witten, 1997, lecture at Heinz Pagels Memorial Lecture Series, Aspen, CO (from pg 183, *The Elegant Universe*, Brian Greene, 2003).

6$_{100}$.

Opening Salvo, Blue Scholars, selected after election of President Donald Trump, 11/10/16 -- Eds.

> *No postmortem residuals,*
> *We're individuals who*
> *Indivisible become the most invincible.*
> *But that is not the issue at hand,*
> *We demand a simple right to question y'all,*
> *People where the fuck is freedom at?*

https://www.youtube.com/watch?v=YONHpd_-0Ok

7f$_{15}$.

a) Using today's technology we would need an accelerator the size of the universe to see individual strings.

b) When the universe was about 10^{-39} seconds old, and its temperature was approximately 10^{28} K, the strong, weak, and electromagnetic force would have been unified, as one, if supersymmetry is valid.

c) Near the time of the Big Bang, strings would have had such great energy as to be macroscopic, rather than approximately 10^{-33} cm, the Planck length. A few of these strings might have through cosmic expansion grown to astronomical scales and could pass dramatically in view of one of our telescopes and be observable via a shift in cosmic microwave background temperature.

d) There are more than strings in string theory.

95.

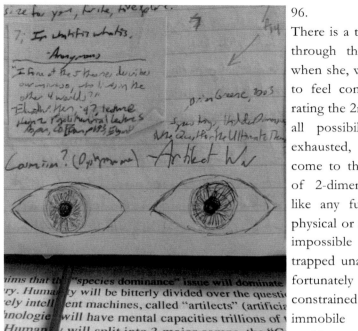

96.

There is a time as she moves through the 4th dimension when she, who is you, comes to feel constrained incorporating the 2nd dimension, like all possibilities have been exhausted, like you have come to the limits the walls of 2-dimensional existence, like any further exploration physical or mental is futile or impossible because you are trapped unable to move, but fortunately when you feel constrained trapped futile immobile useless pointless unable to breathe is when you are at your best, when your intelligence digs and your imagination sparks and you create, when you ask why exist you question your nature and surroundings and confinement and after a period, . , oh bloody period, the sloughing of a mortal coil, she moves beyond the second dimension and realizes the third. Perhaps her first insight is when, irritated at having no room to pass, part of her slips, swims, or flops on top of another, a frustrated response against the claustrophobia of her life, or during an overly vigorous intercourse undertaken to feel something to fill the notorious ennui to empty herself. Perhaps one of her appendages perplexingly slips under her as she metaphorically or literally flails for something anything new and or useful to do. Or perhaps in a moment of feeling extremely confined limited trapped, of sobbing in pointlessness, of shaking in linelessness, in quaking in 2-D shapelessness, she realizes that she shakes in an unknown vertical direction too, revealing that she has height. Or perhaps, trapped, she thinks from an outside perspective of her on the hair, how from far enough away the hair doesn't look curved but flat, a different sort of non-curved 2-D than her or the hair, it appears the hair has height or thickness, and then she thinks about it orthogonally and observes from a perspective 90 degrees from her last position and the hair has thickness here too, except she calls it width or depth, and she insights that her position or any position of a point of her could be given by three pieces of information, x y z, a horizontal axis and a vertical axis and an axis of depth, which would not require the cross-section of the hair to be a perfect circle for its approximately infinite length, she is well-acquainted with all the variety of 2-D shapes from squares and polyhedrons and toruses to blobs of astonishing footprint, the notion of a footprint materializing, perhaps those shapes are possible for her hair in cross-section, necessitating the 3rd dimension. The more she experiments with the idea of a 3rd dimension, the more absurd it seems to her that a) there would be no 3rd dimension when there is a 4th, and b) she would be capable of life at all, let alone the higher order consciousness she experiences, with no thickness or height or depth, whatever you want to call it, not even a minute one, a protein-width thickness at least, a top membrane and a bottom membrane and stuff in between, enclosing her, making her insides her. She discovers verticality relative to the hair, a second straight dimension plus one curved dimension for three total. And she discovers the space she knows can also be characterized by three straight perpendicular dimensions, but that knowledge stays in the background as of yet, for she has developed and lives in a curved dimension. You on the other hand and on the same hand discover that following her lead via thought experiment you can stand from the 2-D page to which you have been relegated, the analogy of you emerging from the page being a suddenly familiar trope metaphor device in cultural artifacts such as movies and especially books from your other life in a 3-dimensional world. But we encourage you to remain with her for a while yet, for it is her world you are trying to understand, for one thing you are inside her, part of her, and you helped create her, and for another she is inside you, perhaps, in an ultramicroscopic curved dimension of your existence which you were previously unable to perceive imagine think about and which you still cannot directly observe or measure. And so you imagine her, living on an infinitely long cylinder of perhaps imperfect or non-circular cross-section rather than the sphere on which you developed in your other world, and all the multitudinous forms and functions of life and being and consciousness she could become. He's and she's and I's and you's. You imagine them. She leaps like a flea and takes flight like a fly and like a butterfly metamorphosed from a sea cucumber hatched from an almond grows entire new organs that allow her to fly to the limits of her dimension, the edge of her known universe, and what does that look like, since her height dimension is based on a curve, will she as a course of nature circum-

410

navigate and return again to the beginning, intuitively, as a closed curve herself, what if there were a curved time dimension, what if we are a curved time dimension, would we cycle over and over, like the pages of a book read again and again, reread, would we recycle, a circular book, would we begin again at the end, would we be different or the same or both each time, would we be aware of all the iterations, is there an each time if time is curved, would she meet him again and again, would she leave him again and again, would you make her and she you again and again. Or now, always. Then, still, as we began, consider the possibility that there are many more than the 4 dimensions you know, that there is more than the one tightly curved hidden dimension that she knows. What if her circular dimension is shaped like a donut, a torus, or a sphere, adding another curved dimension, another necessary piece of info, another angle, not the hair she lives on, she can fly now she lives on nothing, but her very world is shaped like that, 3 extended dimensions and now 2 curved dimensions at every point. What if there are six such tightly curled ultramicroscopic dimensions, such as in some configuration of the tens of thousands of possible Calabi-Yau spaces, within our universe, and she exists there, and their existence cancels all your negative probabilities, holding your universe up at the ultramicroscopic level, your foundation, except they are too small for you to perceive. Then you might say if they, if she is, are too small then they are irrelevant to you, she has no effect on you, knowledge of them changes nothing, she is meaningless to you. If you said that, then we might reply that their shape and size and curvature and intertwining determine fundamental attributes of your physical universe, and therefore you, and therefore her dimensions are of the ultimate importance to your existence, which is why you do not in fact feel the way you bluff, but instead long for her, which you might acknowledge or deny, but regardless he might cut in that she might be what saves you, she might be the only meaning in your life, she might be you and without her you are nothing. Then I might add you have not imagined hard enough yet.

$7f_{16}$.

A Calabi-Yau shape contains multi-dimensional holes. String Theory proposes that there is a family of lowest energy string vibrations associated with each hole. If the curled twisted curved Calabi-Yau has 3 holes, we will find 3 families of elementary particles, as we do, but we do not know from the equations of string theory which of the Clabi-Yau shapes reflects the extra spatial dimensions because our theoretical tools are inadequate. Further, the masses of the particles depend on how the multi-dimensional holes intersect and overlap, affecting the possible vibration patterns of the strings, but we do not know the shape and twist and twine of the holes in the Calabi-Yau space because we cannot determine into which Calabi-Yau shape the theorized six extra curved spatial dimension are folded into, tertiary-protein-structure-like, because our current theoretical tools are inadequate because our computing power is inadequate because our intellects are inadequate. We are inadequate.

7x.

The student Doko came to a Zen master and said, "I am seeking the truth. In what state of mind should I train myself so as to find it?"

Said the master, "There is no mind, so you cannot put it in any state. There is no truth, so you cannot train yourself for it."

"If there is no mind to train, and no truth to find, why do you have these monks gather before you everyday to study Zen and train themselves for this study?"

"But I haven't an inch of room here," said the master, "So how could the monks gather? I have no tongue, so how could I call them together or teach them?"

"Oh, how can you lie like this?" asked Doko.

"But if I have no tongue to talk to others, how can I lie to you?" asked the master.

Then Doko said sadly, "I cannot follow you. I cannot understand you."

"I cannot understand myself," said the master.

Zen Buddhism (Mount Vernon, NY: Peter Pamper Press, 1959) p 22, found in *Gödel, Escher, Bach*, Hofstadter, p 250-1, 1979.

6_{101}. Adapted. Photograph by Andra Mihali, 2010. Painting by Leah Woolf, *Complex shape no.5*
https://www.flickr.com/photos/andram/4616045201/in/photolist-82Urqe-bCD6jX

"Complex Shape No. 5 is a Painting of a Calabi Yau Manifold, a six dimensional shape found in String Theory. Both pieces deal with theoretical conceptions of space, and the limits of portraying multi-dimensional ideas on two-dimensional surfaces."
-- Leah Wolff

18.

She opens her mouth to scream. Earth dirt soil fills her mouth and muffles dampens swallows the sound. Her air escapes her. She tries to clear her mouth, manipulates her tongue moves her jaw coughs with her last bight of breath. Earth pushes in. She convulsively inhales, inhales soil into her lungs, convulsively coughs, expels her last quanta of breath. The frenzied mechanics of her mouth in its attempt to excommunicate the Earth compacts it. Air cannot enter. She tears she cannot see she doesn't know if her eyes are open or closed all darkness Earth in her eyes she tears. She coughs her last byte but the waste cannot escape. Her lungs burn her brain burns her body muscles appendages burn. The Earth holds her still as her arms and legs strive to flail to lash out to free themselves but fail, cannot move, the weight builds atop her body her weight convulsing quaking vibrating her brain on fire her mind detonating exploding expelling atomizing dispersing collapsing on itself into a single point around which the galaxy swirls becoming background radiation self-annihilating, creating and swallowing light, all of these and more in Heaven and Earth than are dreamt of in your philosophy happen in her mind happen to her are her as she watches from without her self body brain crushed burn convulse cease die within, she says silently to herself I am not this I am not this I am not this I am not this I am.

$7d_3$.

If the average density of the universe is greater than approximately 10^{-29} g/cm^3, about 5 hydrogen atoms per cubic meter, then there will be enough gravitational force to eventually stop and reverse the universe's expansion, to contract and compress everything and all of us into a theoretical point of no size, as we began in the Big Bang, accelerating us into a point of infinite density into the singularity of everything in zero size of infinite energy in nothing.

13aa.

For instance his notes, from 1998 or 2016 or both:

> Neither of them was disturbed and enlightened by that insatiable lust for the truth, that passion for the free exercise of critical intelligence, the grueling hunt for reality, which had been the glory of Europa and even of the earlier America, but now was no longer anywhere among the First Men. And, consequent on this lack, another disability crippled them. Both were by now without that irreverent wit which individuals of an earlier generation had loved to exercise upon one another and on themselves, and even on their most sacred values.

> > In this chapter we must cover about one hundred and fifteen thousand years, and in the next chapter another 10 million years. That will bring us to a point as remotely future from the First World's fate as the earliest anthropoids were remotely past. During the first tenth of the first million years after the fall of the World State, during a hundred thousand years, man remained in complete eclipse. Not till the close of this span, which we will call the First Dark Age, did he struggle once more from savagery through barbarism into

civilization. And then his re-
naissance was relatively brief.
From its earliest beginnings to
its end, it covered only fifteen
thousand years, and in its final
agony the planet was so seriously damaged that mind lay
henceforth in deep slumber for
ten more millions of years. This
was the Second Dark Age.

Olaf
Staple-
don *Last
and First
Men* pp
47 74
1930.

97.

The world is collapsing around her she feels like it's all her her overdensity her
inability to escape herself her longings shortening turning in on themselves
densing increasingly accelerating inward but she knows on a different level she
is not the universe she is not some central blackhole too much matter matter
that can be seen that radiates that shines and matter that cannot that does not
that is dark. Yet she feels so heavy. All the dimensions are curved, some which
she previously understood as straight are curved on incomprehensibly long
scales so they seemed straight to her, which bequeathed her an intuition hope
desire for linear progress, some on incomprehensibly short scales, which allowed respite escape internal enlargement, imagining herself into worlds within
worlds, but they all collapse accelerating to each other with her to zero. She is a
slug shrinking, a snail coiling back into the zenith of its shell nautilus conch, an
anemone retracting, a beached deflated jellyfish, a hermit crab unmolting to ever
smaller stolen shells, a limpet trapped inside its accretion, accreting onto the
inside of its accretion, accreting inwards, crushing itself. She says all these things
images words to herself. She manifests them. She takes the measurements of
her collapsing dimension, she chooses a single dimension, of her simplified circular dimension because she wants to understand accomplish have done one

thing worth doing before she is annihilated, using her messenger particle of the electromagnetic force, light, photons, light-weight strings because they are easy to work with given her technology and she has so little time collapsing faster and faster and she is wrapped all the way around the dimension, winding, wound, a rubber band a snake eating its tail the inner ring of the cornea dilating closed a round worm shrinking. She puts her ring on her. She ties marries binds herself to her collapsing dimension to experience all therein. Her photon probes her quanta, her light strings are not wound as she is, they are free to bounce and reflect and circumnavigate her ever shrinking dimension at ever smalling distances, as the distances shrink the light strings' energy increases, the uncertainty principle, she cannot know everything no matter her desire, a basic property of the universe, so as the distances to which the light strings are known more precisely get smaller, so small now, their energy increases, and they therefore become heavier, not so light anymore, the increase in mass given by $E = mc^2$. She meanwhile experiences a dissipation of heaviness as her circular dimension around which she is wound accelerates toward her limit of conceivable distance, the patriarchal Planck length, the wall to another undiscovered unknown country, that old 10^{-33} cm saw, the distance beyond which she has never been able to probe, her heaviness dissipating because her mass is proportional to her length, and her length is coiled around the outer limit of her circular dimension like a contracting sphincter muscle, wound around a dilating eye, her length shortening, therefore her mass reducing, therefore her energy decreasing, $E = mc^2$, perhaps then relief because her longings are shortening because the singularity is near, perhaps a dissipation of all heaviness, relieved of all her mass, because at nearly the speed of light the radius of her dimension approaches the Planck length, all her energy gone, perhaps gone to her light probes, she doesn't care, doesn't matter, because beyond the Planck limit of perception will be nothing, not her not you not us not anyone, everything in a single point of zero space, everything in nothingness, nothing, release from consciousness, release from thought, release from this book, release from the universe, release from her. She takes a last breath and exhales one last messenger photon, coughs it up, gags on it because it is of equal mass to she, it has become so heavy and she so light, and it pushes into almost the exact space as she, crowding her, nowhere for it to go before reflecting back to her in 10^{-43} seconds and she is ready to be gone released cease.

Gone, not gone. Face-to-face with another world she is, identical to her world, face-to-face with him, an unwound being, not wound around his dimension that has been increasing in size from the ultramicroscopic, as he comes face-to-face with she wound around her shrunken dimension. She is wound and he is unwound and you are in the face-to-face. He has been using wound beings like her that have been growing in length and mass and hence energy to measure his infinitesimal but growing universe, she has been using unwound light strings like him that have been shortening and hence growing in energy and mass to observe her once large now collapsed world. She wrapped around her diminishing dimension has shrunk to him, and he unwrapped around his expanding dimension to which he is relatively small and less and less can be said by him with precision of his location relative to his universe meaning his energy shrinks and his mass shrinks to her, she and he for an instant in time meet and become each other's messenger particles, become you, you her unwound light string, you his wound heavy string, both you, where their energies meet, his universe has been so small, but now expanded to meet hers contracted. She comes face-to-face with him, you have no faces, her perceptual organ, her powers of observation, her mind mates with his and they make you in a moment, conceive you for a moment, at the greatest extent of his universe, a size inconceivably large to him, a size inconceivably small to her, the smallest contraction of her universe. At this limit, convergence, length, you see that he and she their universes are equivalent, and as their perceptions disentangle, leaving you, her universe bouncing off his, hers expanding and his contracting, they remain equivalent, the same, for the properties of the fundamental particles in each universe depend on the total energy of the strings, the components of which you realize can be broken down into ordinary vibrations, winding energy, and uniform vibration energy. Ordinary vibrations are the oscillations we have familiarized ourselves with, vibrations, waves, etc., which are independent of the radius of his and her dimension and are therefore constant between them. The winding energy is the energy associated with possible winding configurations around the dimension, which is as we have shown directly proportional to the radius of the dimension. Uniform vibration energy can be though of as motion in space and is inversely proportional to the radius of the dimension as we have shown by the uncertainty principle because the more we try to pinpoint specify confine a thing the more wildly violently erratically energetically it moves. As dimensional radius decreases: uniform energy increases, winding energy decreases, ordinary vibrations do not change. As dimensional radius increases: uniform energy decreases, winding energy increases, ordinary vibration do not change. Therefore for a given string of total energy E in one universe of dimensional radius R, there is a corresponding string or an equivalent string or the same string of total energy E in a universe of dimensional radius 1/R, and since the strings are the same or indistinguishable by their energies, which determine the fundamental mass, charge, spin, and force properties of our fundamental particles, which determine the physical properties of our universe, a universe of circular dimension 1/R is the same or indistinguishable from a universe of R. You cannot distinguish between his world and hers. You cannot say which is he and which is she and which I she and which I he. I can say that if the familiar three dimensions of my universe are circular with a radius roughly equivalent to the breadth of the known universe, or 15 billion light years, or 10^{61} x Plank length, then there is a reciprocal universe physically exactly identical to mine of three familiar dimension of radius 10^{-61} x Plank length, or/and there is no difference between me saying I live in a large expanding universe of circular dimension 10^{61} x10^{-33} = 10^{28} cm, and me saying I live in a tiny contracting universe of 10^{-61} x10^{-33} = 10^{-94} cm. Which is really quite small, even for you, who have been when and where their faceless faces met. If we develop the technology to observe our universe with heavy wound string modes rather than the light unwound string modes we well know, namely light and electromagnetic radiation, then we could measure the reciprocal miniscule resulting universe, and instead of or in addition to our universe expanding it would be shrinking until perhaps it grows too small and bounces into expansion, just as the universe we know would be expanding but perhaps decelerating until our universe's matter turns it around, bouncing off its limit, and begins to contract. There would be no distinction between the two measurements or the semantically reciprocal words we use to describe the universe. If the universe is the size of an almond and an almond is assumed circular or spherical of radius 1 cm, which is 10^{33} x Planck length, the universe is also $1/10^{33}$ x Planck length, or 10^{-33} x Planck length, or 10^{-66} cm. And if the almond germinates? Nevermind. As his algebra teacher Mr. Lee said over and over when he was 13, he was 13 not Mr. Lee, Don't stop and wonder why, just invert and multiply. As she became familiar with in her simultaneously fruitful and fruitless quest for meaning and purpose beyond her inadequate cultural biological social parental inheritance during the early adulthood she did not in one sense outlive, the binary duality you have encountered in this reciprocity of worlds, of he/she, resembles yin-yang. From his point of view, she is his reciprocal. From her point of view, he is her reciprocal. What she calls winding energy, he calls uniform vibrational energy. What he calls winding energy, she calls uniform vibrational energy. From your point of view, as valid as theirs, as valid as ours, you, created by the brief union of he and she, the faceless coming face-to-face, or by the timeless idea of the brief union of he and she, or by the thought experiment of the union of the idea of the eternal her never nothing and the idea of the eternal he never infinite, say he and she are the same. You observe that she experienced a great weight, a trapped feeling in an enormous world, a constraint as if buried alive, no possibilities for breath for choice presented her, a desire to be crushed ultimately to nothing as the final escape, experienced escape as her singular futile thwarted impossible purpose, and that she felt an unbearable lightness of being at the ultimate compression's approach. You observe that he experienced an unrestricted freedom, a purposelessness unbound, a lightness as in dissipation to irrelevance, to immateriality, a feeling of being lost in an infinitesimal world, a lack of constraint wherein the abundance of possibilities made choice impossible, a desire to expand infinitely into everything as the final confinement, and that he felt an unbearable weight of self-realization at the ultimate expansion's ascendancy. They meet for an instant and in that time are one and bounce off each other, from your observations, though you also observe the one becoming the other, another way of phrasing it, or the one becoming the other's messenger particles used to observe their known universe, one as one's light unwound string and the other as the other's heavy wound string, there is simply no way of distinguishing the pronouns, he and she could be interchanged in the descriptions and the meaning would not change, so you remain with your first analogy, the bounce, in which you observe his universe contracting away from hers as he experiences an evermore undirected debilitating lightness and she experience an evermore confining weight as her universe expands away from his. You on the third hand may be relieved by the possible predicament, by the prospect of no final collapse crush to zero size nothingness, no infinite expansion into cold oblivion. Or not, perhaps you don't appreciate climactic narrative reversals circles spirals unendings, always wanting finality and catharsis, and you prefer the differentiation of character, and the specificity of the individual, and the explicitness of a thesis statement or hero's journey or premise or one-sentence summary, and the uniqueness of the universe. But it is how it might be.

7x. 7f$_{17}$.

Which is approaching, and which receding?

Which expanding, and which contracting?

SADDHARMA-PUNDARÎKA OR, THE LOTUS OF THE TRUE LAW.

Translated By H. Kern (1884), Sacred Books of the East, Vol XXI.
THE LOTUS SUTRA, CH. 3, THE PARABLE OF THE BURNING HOUSE
http://www.sacred-texts.com/bud/lotus/lot03.htm
Selected and adapted. (Sâriputra = S, Tathâgata = T, Arhat = A)

But, S, to elucidate this matter more at large, I will tell thee a parable, for men of good understanding will generally readily enough catch the meaning of what is taught under the shape of a parable.

Let us suppose the following case, S. In a certain village, town, borough, province, kingdom, or capital, there was a certain housekeeper, old, aged, decrepit, very advanced in years, rich, wealthy, opulent; he had a great house, high, spacious, built a long time ago and old, inhabited by some two, three, four, or five hundred living beings. The house had but one door, and a thatch; its terraces were tottering, the bases of its pillars rotten, the coverings and plaster of the walls loose. On a sudden the whole house was from every side put in conflagration by a mass of fire. Let us suppose that the man had many little boys, say five, or ten, or even twenty, and that he himself had come out of the house.

Now, S, that man, on seeing the house from every side wrapt in a blaze by a great mass of fire, got afraid, frightened, anxious in his mind, and made the following reflection: I myself am able to come out from the burning house through the door, quickly and safely, without being touched or scorched by that great mass of fire; but my children, those young boys, are staying in the burning house, playing, amusing, and diverting themselves with all sorts of sports. They do not perceive, nor know, nor understand, nor mind that the house is on fire, and do not get afraid. Though scorched by that great mass of fire, and affected with such a mass of pain, they do not mind the pain, nor do they conceive the idea of escaping.

The man, S, is strong, has powerful arms, and he makes this reflection: I am strong, and have powerful arms; why, let me gather all my little boys and take them to my breast to effect their escape from the house. A second reflection then presented itself to his mind: This house has but one opening; the door is shut; and those boys, fickle, unsteady, and childlike as they are, will, it is to be feared, run hither and thither, and come to grief and disaster in this mass of fire. Therefore I will warn them. So resolved, he calls to the boys: Come, my children; the house is burning with a mass of fire; come, lest ye be burnt in that mass of fire, and come to grief and disaster. But the ignorant boys do not heed the words of him who is their well-wisher; they are not afraid, not alarmed, and feel no misgiving; they do not care, nor fly, nor even know nor understand the purport of the word 'burning;' on the contrary, they run hither and thither, walk about, and repeatedly look at their father; all, because they are so ignorant.

Then the man is going to reflect thus: The house is burning, is blazing by a mass of fire. It is to be feared that myself as well as my children will come to grief and disaster. Let me therefore by some skilful means get the boys out of the house. The man knows the disposition of the boys, and has a clear perception of their inclinations.

Now these boys happen to have many and manifold toys to play with, pretty, nice, pleasant, dear, amusing, and precious. The man, knowing the disposition of the boys, says to them: My children, your toys, which are so pretty, precious, and admirable, which you are so loth to miss, which are so various and multifarious, (such as) bullock-carts, goat-carts, deer-carts, which are so pretty, nice, dear, and precious to you, have all been put by me outside the house-door for you to play with. Come, run out, leave the house; to each of you I shall give what he wants. Come soon; come out for the sake of these toys. And the boys, on hearing the names mentioned of such playthings as they like and desire, so agreeable to their taste, so pretty, dear, and delightful, quickly rush out from the burning house, with eager effort and great alacrity, one having no time to wait for the other, and pushing each other on with the cry of 'Who shall arrive first, the very first?'

The man, seeing that his children have safely and happily escaped, and knowing that they are free from danger, goes and sits down in the open air on the square of the village, his heart filled with joy and delight, released from trouble and hindrance, quite at ease. The boys go up to the place where their father is sitting, and say: 'Father, give us those toys to play with, those bullock-carts, goat-carts, and deer-carts.' Then, S, the man gives to his sons, who run swift as the wind, bullock-carts only, made of seven precious substances, provided with benches, hung with a multitude of small bells, lofty, adorned with rare and wonderful jewels, embellished with jewel wreaths, decorated with garlands of flowers, carpeted with cotton mattresses and woollen coverlets, covered with white cloth and silk, having on both sides rosy cushions, yoked with white, very fair and fleet bullocks, led by a multitude of men. To each of his children he gives several bullock-carts of one appearance and one kind, provided with flags, and swift as the wind. That man does so, S, because being rich, wealthy, and in possession of many treasures and granaries, he rightly thinks: Why should I give these boys inferior carts, all these boys being my own children, dear and precious? I have got such great vehicles, and ought to treat all the boys equally and without partiality. As I own many treasures and granaries, I could give such great vehicles to all beings, how much more then to my own children. Meanwhile the boys are mounting the vehicles with feelings of astonishment and wonder. Now, S, what is thy opinion? Has that man made himself guilty of a falsehood by first holding out to his children the prospect of three vehicles and afterwards giving to each of them the greatest vehicles only, the most magnificent vehicles?

S answered: By no means, Lord. That is not sufficient, O Lord, to qualify the man as a speaker of falsehood, since it only was a skilful device to persuade his children to go out of the burning house and save their lives. Nay, besides recovering their very body, O Lord, they have received all those toys. If that man, O Lord, had given no single cart, even then he would not have been a speaker of falsehood, for he had previously been meditating on saving the little boys from a great mass of pain by some able device. Even in this case, O Lord, the man would not have been guilty of falsehood, and far less now that he, considering his having plenty of treasures and prompted by no other motive but the love of his children, gives to all, to coax them, vehicles of one kind, and those the greatest vehicles. That man, Lord, is not guilty of falsehood.

The venerable S having thus spoken, the Lord said to him: Very well, very well, S, quite so; it is even as thou sayest. So, too, S, the T, &c., is free from all dangers, wholly exempt from all misfortune, despondency, calamity, pain, grief, the thick enveloping dark mists of ignorance. He, the T, endowed with Buddha-knowledge, forces, absence of hesitation, uncommon properties, and mighty by magical power, is the father of the world, who has reached the highest perfection in the knowledge of skilful means, who is most merciful, long-suffering, benevolent, compassionate. He appears in this triple world, which is like a house the roof and shelter whereof are decayed, (a house) burning by a mass of misery, in order to deliver from affection, hatred, and delusion the beings subject to birth, old age, disease, death, grief, wailing, pain, melancholy, despondency, the dark enveloping mists of ignorance, in order to rouse them to supreme and perfect enlightenment. Once born, he sees how the creatures are burnt, tormented, vexed, distressed by birth, old age, disease, death, grief, wailing, pain, melancholy, despondency; how for the sake of enjoyments, and prompted by sensual desires, they severally suffer various pains. In consequence both of what in this world they are seeking and what they have acquired, they will in a future state suffer various pains, in hell, in the brute creation; suffer such pains as poverty in the world of gods or men, union with hateful persons or things, and separation from the beloved ones. And whilst incessantly whirling in that mass of evils they are sporting, playing, diverting themselves; they do not fear, nor dread, nor are they seized with terror; they do not know, nor mind; they are not startled, do not try to escape, but are enjoying themselves in that triple world which is like unto a burning house, and run hither and thither. Though overwhelmed by that mass of evil, they do not conceive the idea that they must beware of it.

Under such circumstances, S, the T reflects thus: Verily, I am the father of these beings; I must save them from this mass of evil, and bestow on them the immense, inconceivable bliss of Buddha-knowledge, wherewith they shall sport, play, and divert themselves, wherein they shall find their rest.

Then, S, the T reflects thus: If, in the conviction of my possessing the power of knowledge and magical faculties, I manifest to these beings the knowledge, forces, and absence of hesitation of the T, without availing myself of some device, these beings will not escape. For they are attached to the pleasures of the five senses, to worldly pleasures; they will not be freed from birth, old age, disease, death, grief, wailing, pain, melancholy, despondency, by which they are burnt, tormented, vexed, distressed. Unless they are forced to leave the triple world which is like a house the shelter and roof whereof is in a blaze, how are they to get acquainted with Buddha-knowledge?

Now, S, even as that man with powerful arms, without using the strength of his arms, attracts his children out of the burning house by an able device, and afterwards gives them magnificent, great carts, so, S, the T, the A, &c., possessed of knowledge and freedom from all hesitation, without using them, in order to attract the creatures out of the triple world which is like a burning house with decayed roof and shelter, shows, by his knowledge of able devices, three vehicles, viz. the vehicle of the disciples, the vehicle of the Pratyekabuddhas, and the vehicle of the Bodhisattvas. By means of these three vehicles he attracts the creatures and speaks to them thus: Do not delight in this triple world, which is like a burning house, in these miserable forms, sounds, odours, flavours, and contacts. For in delighting in this triple world ye are burnt, heated, inflamed with the thirst inseparable from the pleasures of the five senses. Fly from this triple world; betake yourselves to the three vehicles: the vehicle of the disciples, the vehicle of the Pratyekabuddhas, the vehicle of the Bodhisattvas. I give you my pledge for it, that I shall give you these three vehicles; make an effort to run out of this triple world. And to attract them I say: These vehicles are grand, praised by the Aryas, and provided with most pleasant things; with such you are to sport, play, and divert yourselves in a noble manner. Ye will feel the great delight of the faculties, powers, constituents of Bodhi, meditations, the (eight) degrees of emancipation, self-concentration, and the results of self-concentration, and ye will become greatly happy and cheerful.

Now, S, the beings who have become wise have faith in the T, the father of the world, and consequently apply themselves to his commandments. Amongst them there are some who, wishing to follow the dictate of an authoritative voice, apply themselves to the commandment of the T to acquire the knowledge of the four great truths, for the sake of their own complete Nirvâna. These one may say to be those who, coveting the vehicle of the disciples, fly from the triple world, just as some of the boys will fly from that burning house, prompted by a desire of getting a cart yoked with deer. Other beings desirous of the science without a master, of self-restraint and tranquility, apply themselves to the commandment of the T to learn to understand causes and effects, for the sake of their own complete Nirvâna. These one may say to be those who, coveting the vehicle of the Pratyekabuddhas, fly from the triple world, just as some of the boys fly from the burning house, prompted by the desire of getting a cart yoked with goats. Others again desirous of the knowledge of the all-knowing, the knowledge of Buddha, the knowledge of the self-born one, the science without a master, apply themselves to the commandment of the T to learn to understand the knowledge, powers, and freedom from hesitation of the T, for the sake of the common weal and happiness, out of compassion to the world, for the benefit, weal, and happiness of the world at large, both gods and men, for the sake of the complete Nirvâna of all beings. These one may say to be those who, coveting the great vehicle, fly from the triple world. Therefore they are called Bodhisattvas Mahâsattvas. They may be likened to those among the boys who have fled from the burning house prompted by the desire of getting a cart yoked with bullocks.

In the same manner, S, as that man, on seeing his children escaped from the burning house and knowing them safely and happily rescued and out of danger, in the consciousness of his great wealth, gives the boys one single grand cart; so, too, S, the T, the A, &c., on seeing many kotis of beings recovered from the triple world, released from sorrow, fear, terror, and calamity, having escaped owing to the command of the T, delivered from all fears, calamities, and difficulties, and having reached the bliss of Nirvâna, so, too, S, the T, the A, &c., considering that he possesses great wealth of knowledge, power, and absence of hesitation, and that all beings are his children, leads them by no other vehicle but the Buddha-vehicle to full development. But he does not teach a particular Nirvâna for each being; he causes all beings to reach complete Nirvâna by means of the complete Nirvâna of the T. And those beings, S, who are delivered from the triple world, to them the T gives as toys to amuse them-

423

selves with the lofty pleasures of the Aryas, the pleasures of meditation, emancipation, self-concentration, and its results; (toys) all of the same kind. Even as that man,
S, cannot be said to have told a falsehood for having held out to those boys the prospect of three vehicles and given to all of them but one great vehicle, a magnificent
vehicle made of seven precious substances, decorated with all sorts of ornaments, a
vehicle of one kind, the most egregious of all, so, too, S, the T, the A, &c., tells no
falsehood when by an able device he first holds forth three vehicles and afterwards
leads all to complete Nirvâna by the one great vehicle. For the T, S, who is rich in
treasures and storehouses of abundant knowledge, powers, and absence of hesitation,
is able to teach all beings the law which is connected with the knowledge of the all-
knowing. In this way, S, one has to understand how the T by an able device and direction shows but one vehicle, the great vehicle.

18. On the inside of her left forearm she tattoos .

. soottat ahz mrearot trgir rah to ebizni aht nO

She knows many of you consider the symbol overused, the act cliché, empty
cultural appropriation, the western materialization into surface adornments ac-
couterments accessories symbols of formerly profound spiritual meaning to an
entire civilization she does not understand, the demeaning of herself. She knows
many of you if you passed her in the street would observe, snicker or frown or
shake your head or mentally cluck, make disparaging communications about her
to a friend, to friends, to the collective of social media. She knows if you
worked in the rundown grocery store in her rundown neighborhood re-
splendent with all the varieties of rundown people and you were selling her the
oats she eats for breakfast or the wine with which she forgets and enjoys and is
able to live, you wouldn't give a shit, and if you commented at all it would be a
passing compliment or note of interest or an island of small talk in a river of the
innumerable varieties, waves if it pleases you, of rundown people coming, she
says lapping if that suits your judgment, through your rundown register, but if
you worked there you would be of a different class, a rundown class, a class not
reading this, a class still rooted in survival, in doing what you can, keeping on,
and appreciating the efforts of others to do the same, and if putting yin/yang on
your arms helps you keep on then by all means god bless you good luck you just
tell them to go to hell and thanks for a bit of beauty. She hasn't done it for them
though, nothing to do with them, nothing to do with you, so fuck off, she did it
for her, she could give less than a shit what you'll think of her tattoos when you claim her as your own and pull her dirty decayed
body from the

$7f_{18}$.

Quantum Geometry: A reworking of Riemann geometry, which was a re-working of Euclidean geometry. Riemann, building on the work of Gauss, Lobachevsky, Bolyai and others, allowed for the geometric, quantified description of curved spaces of arbitrary dimension, which Einstein then applied to the curvature of spacetime in his theory of General Relativity. In Riemann geometry, the curvature of spacetime is the distorted distance relations (i.e. relative to flat space) of conceptually abstract zero-space points. In the physical universe, the gravitational force is a result of this distortion. But as we've elucidated, there are no point particles in string theory; one of its attributes is there are no conceptually abstract zero-space points, and in fact no particles smaller than strings. Quantum geometry modifies Riemann geometry on ultramicroscopic scales. In string theory, quantum theory says there are two equivalent definitions of distance inversely related to each other, R and 1/R, where R is a multiple of the Plank length, so that even as we approach the Planck length observationally we cannot pass it, because as we do in its inverse we leave it the way we came. As R decreases past 1, 1/R turns around and increases grows expands.

13aa.

For instance his memories:

His earliest memory. Fear, danger, on a cement porch atop a precipice, a steep enormous hill, in a toddler walker, in danger of falling, down the long open slope without end, Iowa, the memory reshaped with details from conversations with his mother, a slight hill it was in real life, in Iowa, they don't sell those walkers anymore, unsafe, colored in the retelling, the embellishment of fear, no the fear real, reshaped as he told and retold what his earliest memory was at various stages of his life to various people, the adult if not mature emphasis on the possibility of a neverending fall, until not even I know what the true memory is, or what his actual first memory was, at that age certainly he would have had other memories of a kind though he could not describe them, so are they were they memories if he could not recall them relate them recognize them remember them?, let alone what really happened, though perhaps that statement, what really happened, also has no meaning, not even I can determine what really happened, I at least would have to expend a great deal of energy and time picking apart what that question means, What really happened?, which I've discovered is often a better more fruitful more roundabout more productive more rewarding way of getting at something than attempting a direct solution, like carving a statue from marble, some old Greek saying about that, considering the two observers, he and his mother, are dead, or rather he is not independently alive as he would have defined it, and would her version be more valid than his when the event was, for her, unremarkable, she didn't remember it, and considering that the memory is primarily emotion. His most recent memory, not in the context world reality of the greater consciousness of I in whom all his memories have ascended, but in the contextual world where he is writing I on 3/16/16, his future memories in that reality imagined, his newest memory there: he sitting in the front of his pickup truck with his youngest child eating an early lunch, he eating week-old dried-out leftover cheap pepperoni pizza, she eating two-day-old cold linguine noodles in ten-day-old once-canned cheap marinara sauce out of a rubbermaid in the parking lot of the zoo on her last day of being four years old before going into the zoo, a free day, a pleasant happenstance, she petted a beaver and a dog who does tricks and Atlantic rays and sea stars and a hairy helmet crab and sea cucumbers and spiny urchin and anemones and she saw a bald eagle with a broken wing, out of order, and done eating she was ready to go, but also tired because she had a cold, a cough, they both did, always, and she was squirmy in the passenger seat in the pickup truck in the zoo parking lot and she was screaming crying screaming looking at him screaming grabbing the right side of her head screaming and he was saying what happened shhhh what happened on repeat until he remembered a vague memory of her playing with a green coffee stirrer, a swizzle stick?, a kind Starbucks uses so hot to-go coffees don't spill from the drinking hole aperture orifice in the lid, which he didn't notice consciously at the time but he suddenly notices now in retrospect while she's screaming and he realizes she stuck it in her ear and he asks her something to that effect, he doesn't remember, and she nods while she is screaming curled up into the seat hand over her ear tears dripping from her face and he tries to hold her hug her hard because she is screaming and he waits several hours before he says we don't stick things in our ears okay, and she is crying gulps and he is saying I'm sorry, honey, and he looks at her ear and blood is coming out of her ear on her last day of being four. She is quivering in her seat and he doesn't know what to do. Doctor, zoo, or home. He asks her and she says she doesn't know. He doesn't want to go to the doctor. She says she wants to go home. They go home. She is not herself, weepy limp puddled on the drive. Her next to him in the passenger seat, always, a positive of taking the truck, her not behind but next to him. He gives her ibuprofen, her ear is still bleeding. She lies down. He reads her a story. Elves help a mouse go to the moon on a dragon they made and then animate with zodiac magic and objects the mouse collects in heroic quests against a giant and a multi-headed serpent and a sea witch to acquire a piece of cheese to give to his love's father so they can be married, but the man who keeps the candles in the moon lit says there is no cheese, but the mouse gets his bride anyway by virtue of his adventurous heroic tale, or tail. And she feels better. Ear still aching, hurting but less. Eardrum surely punctured. They drive back to the zoo, twenty minutes one way, her next to him in the front seat had helped him through many dark days. They go into the zoo and experience the aforementioned animals while he periodically sops up no soaks no blots the blood and fluid draining from her ear. She also feeds goats. And he buys her two rides on the carousel, one on a Pegasus, just her and he, one on a polar bear with a swarm of other children, a this is your last day as a four-year-old treat, and he buys her a cotton candy at her insistence even though he does not buy cotton candy, which she eats some of while they sit in the rare spring sun and look down from atop a hill at the zoo and the water and the sound beyond. Her ear is still bleeding, not bleeding he tells her, seeping, leaking, when he drops her off to her mother and hugs his last-day-of-four-year-old girl and says goodbye. She told him she loved him multiple times yesterday, and he her, he is telling himself now as he writes this in his memory so he remembers. So you remember. So I remember.

13aa, 84[n], 7x, 97.5.

Is there someone in the page,
reading from the inside out?

6[103].

Look What We've Done: Human-Made Epoch of Nightmares Is Here
Published on Friday, January 08, 2016, by Common Dreams
http://www.commondreams.org/news/2016/01/08/look-what-weve-done-human-made-epoch-nightmares-here
by Deirdre Fulton
(first encountered in *The Seattle Star,* http://www.seattlestar.net/)

There's no question about it. A new epoch—the Anthropocene—has begun.

So says an international group of geoscientists, in a paper published Friday in the journal *Science*. They point to waste disposal, fossil fuel combustion, increased fertilizer use, the testing and dropping of nuclear weapons, deforestation, and more as evidence that human activity has pushed the Earth into the new age that takes its name from the Greek *anthropos*, or human being.

Some argue the new era began in the 1950s, the decade that marks the beginning of the so-called "Great Acceleration," when human population and its consumption patterns suddenly speeded up, and nuclear weapons tests dispersed radioactive elements across the globe.

Formalizing the Anthropocene era—a designation that must come officially from a separate body known as the International Commission on Stratigraphy—they write, "expresses the extent to which humanity is driving rapid and widespread changes to the Earth system that will variously persist and potentially intensify into the future." The scientists are likely to present their findings to the Commission later this year.

"What this paper does is to say the changes are as big as those that happened at the end of the last ice age," Colin Waters, principal geologist at the British Geological Survey and an author of the study, told the *Guardian*. "This is a big deal."

As *Smithsonian* magazine notes, "The new study is not the first to propose a formal establishment of an Anthropocene epoch—Simon Lewis and Mark Maslin of the University of College London made a similar recommendation last year—but it is one of the most comprehensive to date."

Among the tell-tale signs that the Anthropocene has started, according to reporting on the study:

> **Über-industrialization.** "More than half the earth's surface has been transformed into settlements and cities, agricultural land, mines, waste dumps, baseball diamonds, and beyond," writes journalist Eric Roston at *Bloomberg*. What's more, he adds, "Mineral mining moves three times more sediment every year than all the world's rivers."

> **Plastics everywhere.** "Even most mud samples taken from remote ocean beds now contain plastic fragments," academics Mark Williams and Jan A. Zalasiewicz write for *The Conversation*. "Buried in sediment, these materials may be preserved over geological timescales, forming new rocks and rapidly-evolving 'technofossils' for our descendants to marvel at."

> **Biologic changes.** "We've pushed extinction rates of flora and fauna far above the long-term average," the *Guardian* reports. "The Earth is now on course for a sixth mass extinction which would see 75% of species extinct in the next few centuries if current trends continue."

> **Nuclear fallout.** "Our war efforts have left their mark on geology," notes *New Scientist*. "When the first nuclear weapon was detonated on 16 July 1945 in New Mexico, it deposited radionuclides—atoms with excess nuclear energy—across a wide area. Since 1952, more explosive thermonuclear weapons have been tested, leaving a global signature of isotopes such as carbon-14 and plutonium-239."

Greenhouse gas levels. As *Common Dreams* has reported extensively, and the geoscientists point out, atmospheric concentrations of greenhouse gases like carbon dioxide and methane are higher than they've ever been. "Depending on the trajectory of future anthropogenic forcing, these trends may reach or exceed the envelope of Quaternary interglacial conditions," the study authors write—in other words, conditions could become more extreme than in previous ice ages.

Still, as damning as this evidence is, observers have cautioned against a simplistic view of geologic shifts. "Anthropocene is...suspect because—to the extent that 'we' wish to name the new epoch after a force, it generically identifies that force as humanity as a whole, rather than the identifiable power structures most responsible for the geological Anthropocene traces," wrote Kieran Suckling, founding director of the Center for Biological Diversity, in 2015.

Indeed, Ian Angus, editor of the ecosocialist journal *Climate and Capitalism*, argued last year: "An ecosocialist analysis of the Great Acceleration will build on the decisive issues of class and power that are shaping the Anthropocene and will ultimately determine humanity's future."

7f$_{19}$.

Mirror Symmetry: Recall we remind you that in quantum geometry in string theory there is no difference between a circle of radius R and a circle of radius 1/R. Also or because dimensions of radius R and 1/R will give rise to the same physical fundamental properties. When we extend and apply this possible knowledge to Calabi-Yau spaces chosen for the extra curled-up dimensions that string theory posits for our universe, we find that two geometrically different Calabi-Yau spaces, a mirror pair, give rise to identical physics, identical physical universes, identical fundamental properties. The two possible ways of curling the extra dimensions are geometrically distinct but physically equivalent. We theorize that all Calabi-Yau spaces that could describe the extra curled-up dimensions of our universe in the context of string theory have a mirror pair.

13aa.

For instance:

He now remembers her 5th birthday. They baked a cake, they had her best friend over, they painted and played with beads and played outside. The first tulips bloomed. The girls said it was the best day ever. Other memories: a huge spider on the exterior brick wall of his childhood home in Louisiana, ice storms and floods and swelter in St. Louis, waking up in the hospital in Illinois, waking up in a ditch in Peru, waking up in an unknown house in Montana, on the bare ground after a wedding in Montana, dehydrated delirious on a mountaintop in Montana. He remembers not remembering. A man three times his age hitting on him in Milan and showing him the sights on a private expert behind-the-scenes tour and cooking him an authentic wine-soaked Milanese meal and he leaving him unfulfilled. He remembers in Venice a sunset on the water that he could walk on. He remembers not remembering how he got home in Copenhagen. He remembers being wrapped up in his string of mules, in a wreck in a bog, mules sinking and flailing, a mule's lead rope over his lap in the saddle holding him there, his friend later telling him he thought he was going to die. He remembers his friend's mule string and his in a wreck, running, entangled, after a propane tank on the back of one of his mules went off, leaking, a shrieking hiss and they all went galloping, his friend thinking he was going to die. He remembers snags falling behind his string, in front of his string, sliding down the hill in the middle of his string, galloping on the steep sidehills, a friend of a friend who died in such a situation, but he remembers that he never did. He remembers helping to lasso a moose. He remembers being atop a mountain wanting to die because of the peace, the glory, the grand humbling awe, what more was there, he remembers sunsets on fire in which he wanted to burn, mountains and sunsets over and over. He remembers repeatedly wanting to die. He remembers thinking his wife and/or first child were going to die in childbirth. He remembers when he could not leave his bedroom to face the day, people, life, no escape it was in him. He remembers his children he won't write about and the life constructed around them being both a reason he wanted to die and the primary reason he did not. He remembers trails and planting potatoes and horses and friends and being an asshole and being loving and being in love and feeling nothing dead empty and being in the desert alone when the ocotillo was in bloom when the prickly pear was in bloom when the rocks bloomed and the hummingbirds hummed. He remembers sliding off a boulder in a dry canyon in the desert alone and smashing his knee when he landed and not being able to move for the pain and no one knowing where he was and thinking he was going to die. He remembers sweat lodges and crosscut saws and splitting mauls and smart phones and smart watches and smart glasses. He remembers yelling and laughing and crying and smiling. He remembers being vague and he remembers his children being born and being unborn and he remembers taking them on uncountable beach adventures excursions escapes from the oppression of inside and day after day and mediocrity normalcy everyday dullness depression. He remembers beginning again daily. He remembers writing a book about possibilities, possible futures, consciousness, the structure of the universe, how it is to exist, the physical laws of life, about you and he and everyone, an attempt at collective consciousness, an artifact. He remembers growing old. He remembers loved ones leaving, dying, going. He remembers being alone again, like when he was young. He remembers remembering, and he remembers forgetting. He remembers the past and he remembers the present and remembers the future. He remembers writing this sentence. He remembers saying No and No and No, and one day saying Yes.

7x.

This sentence is a lie.

7e₅.

Chirality: If we watch a film of an experiment, we could determine if it was the actual experiment or a mirror reflection if the experiment dealt with certain processes (i.e. the weak force) because the mirror reflection of certain processes (involving the weak force) cannot happen in our world. Our universe is not perfectly left-right symmetric (because of the weak force), our universe is not perfectly mirror symmetric (because of the weak force), this non-mirror symmetry is a different mirror symmetry than the previously discussed string mirror symmetry. Because of our radioactive decay (the manifestation of the weak force) our universe is chiral.

98.

Say you are a 2-dimensional sphere within a larger, if yet rather small, Calabi-Yau space, and you are shrinking. 2-dimensional because you are the surface of the sphere, like the surface of a beach ball, we are ignoring the thickness of the material the plastic your skin, as well as your interior, it's like you have no insides, a beach ball so you visualize sand sun ocean tranquility peace freedom even as you are shrinking deflated pinched down to a point, a multi-colored beach ball if you like, like a pinwheel, a beach ball to harken your childhood. You shrink in an ever tinier space, the surface of an ever smaller ball and all this is familiar to you by now, the weight the trapped the inability to escape to do to move the you compressed to nothing, and though it is, you are, miserable, you are used to your suffering, and your familiarity with your suffering, your self-knowledge, facilitates a clear-headedness and you remember how in the last iteration you discovered that in string theory circular dimensions have a minimum radius, which your universe would in a sense bounce off of and expand again, or in a different sense there is a mirror world that while you shrink through the minimum radius simultaneously passes the same radius expanding, and that mirror world is the same as yours, there is no distinction between them. You latch onto the idea that you will not shrink forever to nothing, but that you'll bounce. Like a beach ball. And you almost employed the word hope, but you are not sure the thought of bouncing forever without finality completion arrival attainment is more hopeful than shrinking to nothing right out of existence and being done with it. Don't worry, you don't have to decide, we are conducting a different thought experiment with you here, forever is much too big for this moment, different than the last iteration, even when an event situation repetition seems exactly the same twice it's never exactly the same twice, or once, never say never, for here, where?, there, under here?, under where?, underwear?, there's no there there, for here you are not an entire spatial dimension, which if you remember you were not exactly in the last experiment either, she was a string wrapped around a dimension, you are a chunk of space, a hunk of beach ball surface, a shrinking 2-D sphere, a piece of spacetime collapsing, not a complete dimension collapsing, and therefore the R vs. 1/R relationship is not directly applicable, though it may come in handy, like a fun house mirror. You collapse to a point. We pinch you down to a point. You compress yourself to a point. It's excruciating in body and mind, first the feeling of buried alive and now compressed to a zero-space point, but you remember the beach, not the crashing tumult of merciless waves from the unfathomable depths of the unknowable ocean kind of beach, but the placid sun beach ball sand kind of beach. You are a chunk of spacetime, the surface of a beach ball in a Calabi-Yau space, squeezed into a single point, and your shrinking point brings the fabric of spacetime with it in that location, pinches it down to a point, the spacetime fabric is yours, think of a tiny blackhole, not a galaxy life light consuming blackhole, the happy kind of blackhole bending spacetime infinitely, you've pinched spacetime in this location, at your point, down to a point, instead think of an hourglass pinched down to nothing at its neck, you used to have fun with hourglasses like Dorothy, think of you as having been in the glass and it was a cylinder and within it was free-flowing sand except you were a beach ball attached to its walls at center and as you shrank you pulled the fluid glass with you into an hourglass shape and slowly gradually painfully pulled the glass to nothing to a point at the neck at you, no grain of sand can pass, no more beach ball, no space and no time, no smaller to go, and so spacetime tears where you are because of your collapse and the sections of the hourglass come apart, between them you have torn the fabric of spacetime, ignore the catastrophe this implies momentarily, maybe you freed Dorothy but you have ripped spacetime and possibly initiated a cosmic cataclysm is all we're going to say, your little collapse may have destroyed the universe and dragged the rest of us with you collapsing into non-existence, where there is no spacetime there is nothing, ignore all that momentarily and think about what if we place another point beach ball, a new one, between the split broken torn necks of the hourglass to fuse them again, or since that implies we are godlike, let us emphasize we are not God or Gods or gods or even godlike, we are you's, we suggest you think of it as you still there in your zero-space point, in your collapsed deflated defeated disgraceful possibly world-decimating state, unable to remember the beach, without time, all the sand leaked away into nowhere, the hourglass of spacetime having torn us and you, you who were within it, but now it fuses sews itself melts onto the outside of your surface, which has no inside anyway, your surface which takes up no space, or perhaps you are somehow the agent, do you, a collapsed failed nothing point, fill the hole the absence the nothingness created by the tear of existence at your point and in the breach reach begin to expand, a sphere growing, you bouncing off nothingness perhaps, you flopping from shrinking inside the hourglass to expanding outside it, flopping over the tear, the two section of the spacetime hourglass never, never say never, to be fused again, but you bridging them, connecting them, expanding, growing plump, the weight of destroying the universe off your shoulders. Yes, wonderful, good, you are a nice light airy fun pinwheel beach ball again and everything is fun and dandy and joyous and laughing on the beach, no sand in the eye, no seagull stealing your sandwich, no uncaring unceasing unfathomed dark ocean, and in that frivolous spirit we call the rip and repair evolution you just endured a flop transition. But, at the instant of the flop, at the tear, at the moment you shamelessly glassed over, tried to gloss over with an amusing hypnotizing warping pinwheel, at the tear you supposedly flopped over, like _____, how do you avoid the cosmic catastrophe you appear to have initiated? You collapse to a point, a nothing, spacetime tears, existence tears, boom, done that's the whole shebang. Let us help you out of this predicament responsibility weight. First, from your instinctual or learned remembering of mirror symmetry, we nudge you that the concept that is useful to you here there underwear is not the perceived lower limit of the radius of a circular dimension and all the different ways you can think about that that are equally valid, such as the bounce you threw in previously, but that there is a mirror you who is equivalent to you, not in the sense that you can look in the mirror and see the other you who is the same you, for indeed the other you appears different on the surface, constitutes a different geometrical shape than you, is not the fun-loving happiness-seeking if sensitive-to-deflation beach ball surface, but is equivalent to you in the sense that there is a Calabi-Yau space containing another you of different geometrical shape, a shape we don't want to speculate about but perhaps a cynical practical nothing-embracing shape, fine say an eye whose horizontal slit pupil contracts to center and then dilates into a vertical slit pupil in the eye, imagine whatever you want, but of the same physical properties as you, and as you collapse, then tear, then possibly initiate cosmic catastrophe, then miraculously repair your spacetime tear, your existential tear, and inflate, the other you is also changing shape while maintaining the same physical properties as you except she never experiences the tear, the singularity, the catastrophe, the discontinuity, the end of everything, she changes shape continuously fluidly without a tear, and since she does not experience the tear of spacetime and she is your mirror, neither do you, and neither do we. She, your mirror, the other you, protects you and us from your ultimate collapse into the tear of existence you made when you flopped. There is also another equally valid way to consider your, our, her salvation from your collapse. Remember or learn or accept that in string theory a string near the tear you initiate could be in motion either laterally along it or encircling it, say a string wound around the hourglass, progressing along it, being pinched down to nothing by you, a wound string that does not exist in point particle physics, a nothing by you that does not exist in her world of string theory. From this per-spective it is she, the wound string, wrapped around your diminishing self, she encircling you as you contract to nothing, she who cannot be reduced to noth-ing moving progressing over you as you tear that holds you together, holds the fabric of spacetime that you tear within her together, that gives you a moment within her to flop and repair and begin to expand before gliding away off you revealing you now growing outside the hourglass shape, so that we on the out-side of her never see you tear within her, cannot see it, so that in a sense we cannot know of the tear, it does not exist to us, by wrapping around your flop she shields us from the existential cataclysm and cosmic destruction that would have been your contraction to nothing and tearing spacetime. And moreover we know you worry that she is not there, or that she will not be here when you tear to save you, that she will not be your underwear to hide your tear from us, ring-ing enveloping squeezing you holding you in taking containing your tear, but we

434

assure you it doesn't matter if she is here there underwear or not, the possibility that she is or could be is enough, the mere chance in her sum of paths that she will wrap wind encircle take you in move over around you as you collapse through nothing and into the tear is sufficient, there are infinite possible protective encircling trajectories she may or may not follow but the possibility of their existence is adequate to cancel your calamity, shield us from you, absorb your

tear, trap you within her, bury you alive within her possibility, hold you immobile within her while she moves around you protecting us. Her possibility is enough.

13aa.

For instance his personality and thought processes and obsessions and sentence structures and limitations

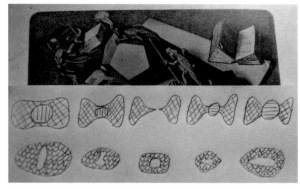

6_{104}. Sketch of a catastrophic space-tearing flop transition (top) and its mundane existence-saving non-tearing mirror duality (bottom) made with a dull pencil, after Brian Greene and Edward Gorey, under or above M.C. Escher mouse pad.

and desires for more than this and his perceptual point of view, which he attempted to expand and diversify and deepen, if he succeeded only meagerly, attempting to incorporate other points of view, which pervade this presentation of I. For I am not a book, not this book, not solely this book, but a version a facet a fraction of a great I created to express communicate impart input what I can of I in you in this time. For I am not solely I, I am also you, all of you who have experienced I, all your personalities and thought processes and obsessions and memories and perceptual points of view, all you've written, all you've read, all you've thought, all you've created. For I am not solely you or all of you but also all of they who have experienced you, for instance their writings, their thought processes, their readings, their creations. For I am not solely they. I also am we. For I am not solely we. I am I.

7a9.

Duality Symmetries: The characteristics of theoretical models that appear to be different but can be shown to describe exactly the same physics.

435

For instance:

$7f_{18}$.

In string theory, applying quantum geometry, a universe consisting of circular dimension of radius R is the same as a universe of radius 1/R.

$7f_{19}$.

The mirror symmetry wherein two different Calabi-Yau shapes for the six tightly curled dimensions produce the same fundamental physical properties.

$7f_{20}$.

M-theory, which incorporates $7f_{18}$ and supersymmetry and strong-weak duality and self-duality and probably $7f_{19}$, purports to show that all 5 heretofore different string theories and supergravity are faces or aspects or fingers of the same theory.

Hence:

Through INDIRECT means, these dualities provide, for instance, a minimum size to circular dimensions, a process for topology changing tears in spacetime, and indeed ways to understand and investigate and experiment and learn about our world even when we encounter infini-

ties or illogic or impossibility or non-inevitability or singularity or nonsense or catastrophe, via examining the dual world, *which is also our world* though it appears different because it is described by a different theory. It is our dual, symmetrical worlds that connect the theories. The comprehensive power of symmetries is the indirect acquisition of knowledge.

6_{105}.
Lumiere, by Jenni Prange Boran
with permission, www.jenniprangeboran.com

6[106].

David Bowie Collective ★ Review and Obituary, April 28, 2016
written by the collective, edited by Nick Stokes

David Bowie died peacefully today surrounded by his family after a courageous 18 month battle with cancer. While many of you will share in this loss, we ask that you respect the family's privacy during their time of grief.[i]

Having been a late-60s mime and cabaret entertainer,[ii] Bowie was born David Robert Jones on January 8th, 1947 in a working-class London suburb.[iii] I received an email from him seven days ago. It was as funny as always, and as surreal, looping through word games and allusions and all the usual stuff we did.[iv] David Bowie embraced the alien. He described the other as one of us. He brought the outsider in.[v] It ended with this sentence: 'Thank you for our good times, brian. they will never rot'. And it was signed 'Dawn'. I realise now he was saying goodbye.[vi] For those who grew up with him as a cultural avatar,[vii] saddened to hear David Bowie has lost his battle with cancer – his music was an inspiration to many,[viii] his loss is as awful and strange as being able to touch your own marrow.[ix]

Ground Control to Major Tom Commencing countdown, engines on, check ignition and may God's love be with you.[x]

In "Space Oddity," Bowie plays the doomed astronaut Major Tom.[xi] "He just came fresh from a chemo session, and he had no eyebrows, and he had no hair on his head," says Visconti, "and there was no way he could keep it a secret from the band."[xii] In the coming decade, he would move — rapidly and with great success — from one character to another. In a whirl of reinvention after initial success, Bowie became first Ziggy Stardust and then Aladdin Sane and the Thin White Duke.[xiii] I read recently that [Ziggy Stardust] was investigative journalism taken to its extreme, that I wanted to find out what a superstar goes through, and so I had to create one and make one.[xiv] Nirvana chose to sing "The Man Who Sold the World," the title song of Mr. Bowie's 1970 album, in its brief set for "MTV Unplugged in New York"[xv] in 1993.[xvi]

"The idea that he puts on a mask simply to market what he's done is mistaken," says Trynka[xvii].[xviii] I blew my nose one day and half my brains came out.[xix] Ashes to ashes, dust to stardust. Your brilliance inspired us all. Goodbye Starman.[xx] I was not very confident of my voice, you see, as a singer. So I thought rather than just sing them, which would probably bore the pants off everybody, I would, I'd like to kind of portray the songs.[xxi] "Having created the illusion of the superman," the philosopher Simon Critchley wrote in his 2014 book "Bowie," "he then popped it like a balloon."[xxii] Beginning life as a dissident folk-rock spaceman, he would become an androgynous, orange-haired, glam-rock alien (Ziggy Stardust), a well-dressed, blue-eyed funk maestro (the Thin White Duke), a drug-loving art rocker (the Berlin albums), a new-wave hit-maker, a hard rocker, a techno enthusiast and a jazz impressionist.[xxiii] "Actually, he creates the mask in order to make the art. A chameleon changes to mimic its background. Bowie forces the background to change to mimic him. His great achievement is not to market himself with a persona, it's to create a persona with which to make art."[xxiv] One of Bowie's best and bleakest songs, "Candidate," begins with a statement of explicit pretense, "We'll pretend we're walking home," and is followed by the line, "My set is amazing, it even smells like a street."[xxv]

But he was just beginning his most golden years, assembling the best band he ever had, probably the all-time greatest unnamed rock band: the core rhythm section of drummer Dennis Davis, bassist George Murray and guitarist Carlos Alomar.[xxvi] Bowie isn't a character, but a collection of characters that are connected to each personal and historical phase of the artists (sic), as well of his surroundings.[xxvii] Armed with this crew, and other key collaborators like Tony Visconti and Brian Eno and Robert Fripp, Bowie made his five best albums in a five-year blaze from 1976 to 1980, the best five-album run of anyone in the Seventies (or since): *Station to Station*, *Low*, *Heroes*, *Lodger* and *Scary Monsters*.[xxviii]

There's a Starman waiting in the sky, he'd like to come and meet us but he thinks he'd blow our mind.[xxix]

Art's filthy lesson[xxx, xxxi] is inauthenticity all the way down, a series of repetitions and reenactments: fakes that strip away the illusion of reality in which we live and confront us with the reality of illusion. Bowie's world is like a dystopian version of *The Truman Show*, the sick place of the world that is forcefully expressed in the ruined, violent cityscapes of "Aladdin Sane" and "Diamond Dogs" and more subtly in the desolate soundscapes of "Warszawa" and "Neuköln."[xxxii] As he put it at the time, "I'm using myself as a canvas and trying to paint the truth of our time on it. The white face, the baggy pants — they're Pierrot, the eternal clown putting across the great sadness of 1976."[xxxiii]

Station to Station (1976), a euphoric dose of what might be called synthetic art-funk, introduced a new persona, the Thin White Duke, which Bowie had carried over from his headlining performance as Thomas Jerome Newton, the melancholy space traveller, in Nicolas Roeg's film The Man Who Fell to Earth[xxxiv, xxxv, xxxvi]. Mr. Bowie was his generation's standard-bearer for rock as theater: something constructed and inflated yet sincere in its artifice, saying more than naturalism could.[xxxvii] And I saw the "Ashes to Ashes" video where he dressed in some strange European clown costume ... my first interpretation of him was the red-haired, androgynous Ziggy Stardust character ... [xxxviii] There's a Starman waiting in the sky, he's told us not to blow it because he knows it's all worthwhile.[xxxix] "Oh, you can be whoever you want. You can live a hundred lives. You can create you and you can recreate you, and it's viable."[xl] McCaslin said by phone from Brooklyn, "This isn't constructed from pieces. It's live."[xli] I finally got to see him live on the Serious Moonlight Tour, around *Let's Dance*, in 1983. I was a huge fan by then and I really didn't want to go to that show, because it was at the Tacoma Dome, and I didn't like big crowds.[xlii]

With hindsight, Ashes to Ashes (1980) can be seen as the point where Bowie's cutting edge began to lose its sharpness, and he was never again quite the cultural pathfinder he had been in his heyday.[xliii] And he proceeded to play a folk song on a 12-string guitar that only had six strings on it.[xliv] With co-production from Chic's

Nile Rodgers, Let's Dance (1983) moulded Bowie into a crowd-friendly global rock star.[xlv] And I was like, Oh man, this is so weird. And the reason why that was weird to me was because we had been going out to museums and listening to records and looking at photographs and we amassed an amount of rock & roll imagery way before we did one note of music.[xlvi] The arrival of MTV in the 1980s was the perfect complement to Mr. Bowie's sense of theatricality and fashion.[xlvii] The title of the album "'Heroes'" (1977), and its title track, came in quotation marks.[xlviii] It was to be the most commercially successful period of his career.[xlix] He said, "You know, I'm not going to play what anybody wants me to play. I just finished a strange new album. And we're going to play some select cuts from a lot of Berlin trilogy–type things, and the new album. That's not what people are going to want to see, but that's what I need to do."[l] It was a typical Bowie act of distancing, but even in its lyrical uncertainty ("nothing will keep us together"), the title track — written with Brian Eno, produced by Mr. Visconti — implies a grand and defiant statement, heroism as such.[li]

Instability and ambiguity are the only constants on David Bowie's "Blackstar," the strange, daring, ultimately rewarding album he releases this week on his 69th birthday. The 10-minute title track opens the album with wavering guitar and flute tones that refuse to settle on a single key. Mark Guiliana's drumbeat, when it arrives, is a matter of sputtering off-beats and silences, while Mr. Bowie intones lyrics about "the day of execution."[lii] The fact that he was this graceful, charming, happy, fearless character became a new point of inspiration for me.[liii] Midway through, the song moves through an improvised limbo and coalesces into a different tune: a march with lyrics about a messianic "blackstar" who also declares "I'm not a popstar."[liv] Not true, I didn't strive for success, I strived to do something artistically important, and success over here I believe is very much in the material world. I wanted to do something artistically valid. I don't begrudge any artist for getting an audience. I'm sorry, I never found that poverty meant purity, that's rubbish.[lv] Eventually the two halves of the song merge, with the opening verses over the march beat, darkening the tone even further.[lvi] Everything I've written up until the last couple of albums were characters and their environments. And I took the whole thing through — onstage and in interviews and photographs and dress and everything.[lvii] The video clip shows candlelit rituals and, near the end, bloody crucifixions.[lviii] Every time I changed a character, I would become that character, for the duration of that album.[lix] His death was no different from his life - a work of Art. He made Blackstar[lx] for us, his parting gift.[lxi] Blackstar was released on Bowie's 69th birthday, Jan 8 2016.[lxii, lxiii]

But nothing here suggests an artist in his 70th year, preoccupied with dignity maintenance. Bowie's "cock" makes an appearance in the tumbling, skronking Tis a Pity She Was a Whore, a song that references[lxiv] "All my big mistakes are when I try to second-guess or please an audience," Bowie admitted to Paul du Noyer of The Word magazine in 2003, in one of his last interviews before disappearing,"[lxv] the 17th-century play by John Ford, vorticism and offers the arch, unclassical line: "Man, she punched me like a dude."[lxvi] "My work is always stronger when I get very selfish about it."[lxvii] By which Bowie means ... well, who knows, exactly?[lxviii]

The longest reach is up front, in the episodic, ceremonial noir of the title track. Bowie's gauzy vocal prayer and wordless spectral harmonies hover over drum seizures; saxophonist Donny McCaslin laces the stutter and chill like Andy Mackay in early-Seventies Roxy Music.[lxix] Elusiveness has always been central to his appeal, enabling him to adopt alter egos and use other theatrical and ironic gestures without sacrificing emotional urgency.[lxx] Because he won't talk. He'll talk on stage and he'll talk in songs, but he won't talk the rest of the time.[lxxi] The song drops to a blues-ballad stroll, but it is an eerie calm with unsettling allusions to violent sacrifice, especially given recent events. (No who or why is specified, but McCaslin has said the song is "about ISIS.")[lxxii] He told a good musical story by standing outside of it and knew how to make you think about the artist's relation to his work and the listener's relation to the artist; he took the question of image and identity seriously.[lxxiii] By the time the scarecrows writhing on crucifixes show up, about two-thirds of the way through, you can tell the well of imagery is beginning to run dry: there's only so much surrealism you can throw at a wall before coherence starts to disintegrate.[lxxiv] Information about David Bowie's forthcoming album Blackstar has thus far proved elusive.[lxxv] In a certain way, all his songs were metafictions, even when they seemed personal, even when they were hits.[lxxvi] When one newspaper printed a selection of rumours about its content, Bowie's official Facebook page protested at "innaccurate reporting about the sound and content of the album".[lxxvii]

Where the fuck did Monday go?[lxxviii]

It moves in a loose A/B/A form, bracketing the center with a line about "a solitary candle" and "a villa in Ormen." Within that, Bowie repeats, "in the center of it all, your eyes[lxxix]." In between all of that, one of Bowie's voices[lxxx] turn and face the strange[lxxxi] trades lines about an execution with another voice repeatedly claiming to be a "black star," not any other kind of star.[lxxxii] A few years before that, I had the unexpected honor of interviewing Iman, who unprompted began talking about how much Bowie loved to read and how they had to make up fake names so the mailman wouldn't know who all the Amazon deliveries were for.[lxxxiii] McCaslin confirmed that early reports of the song being about Islamic State are inaccurate. Bowie's lyrics recall recent work by Walker, like "Bish Bosch," where sensible fragments pile up into a less sensible whole.[lxxxiv] The influence of latterday Scott Walker still appears to be making itself felt in the lyrics – they're elliptical, filled with images of fear and death ("take your passport and shoes and sedatives") (Most of my characters have been sort of alienated. God it's terrifying to be on your own in this world.[lxxxv]) and clearly just waiting to be unpicked by the more dedicated Bowiephile – but the music drifts episodically: from an ambient opening to vocals floating mournfully over a jerkily propulsive drum pattern and synthesisers squelching in vaguely acid houseish style to a sax solo to a beautiful, slow middle section with both a lovely melody and electronically-treated backing vocals.[lxxxvi] My entire career, I've only really worked with the same subject matter.[lxxxvii] Along the way, there are tempo shifts, breakdowns into near-silence and flutes.[lxxxviii] The trousers may change, but the actual words and subjects I've always chosen to write with are things to do with isolation, abandonment, fear and anxiety, all of the high points of one's life.[lxxxix]

Bowie himself, with head bandaged and eyes replaced by buttons (think Neil Gaiman's *Coraline*) is a fantastically creepy image.[xc] Which brings us, out of order,

440

to the present. When I spoke to saxophonist Donny McCaslin about the making of Bowie's latest and last album, "★" he told me they talked constantly about books.[xci]

In the video for David Bowie's "Lazarus," released last week, the mythic singer and rock 'n' roll shape-shifter, ever thin but bordering on gaunt, is blindfolded and writhing in a hospital bed. "Look up here, I'm in heaven," he sings. "I've got scars that can't be seen."[xcii] December marked the off-Broadway opening of Lazarus, a musical Bowie cowrote with Irish playwright Enda Walsh and inspired by the novel The Man Who Fell to Earth— the source material for the 1976 film of the same name, which starred Bowie as an alien on a lonely mission.[xciii] As fierce and unsettling -- and sometimes as beautiful -- as anything in Bowie's one-of-a-kind catalog, "Blackstar" looks to jazz not for tunes or signifiers but for a proud sense of sonic freedom.[xciv] Even more mysterious, Girl Loves Me is sung in a mixture of *A Clockwork Orange*'s Nadsat and Polari, the gay slang of bygone Soho.[xcv] If anything, it views taste and maturity with suspicion -- and thus shares about as much with your typical rocker-doing-jazz record as the singer's trippy new off-Broadway musical, "Lazarus," does with "Les Miz."[xcvi] "It was very strange," Mr. van Hove said of trying to convey Mr. Bowie's intentions. Citing the title track, he continued: "The song is a man in total distress, and then finding a way out, in his imagination, so he could still be alive, in freedom, as a bluebird. It's the message of the whole show."[xcvii]

What exactly is he using these wild, varied sounds to communicate?[xcviii] I've got drama, can't be stolen.[xcix] One of those questions, at least, is answerable. Mr. Bowie, an elusive rock star whose music has been as famously changeable as his image, enlisted the Donny McCaslin Quartet, a rugged jazz-rock combo featuring Mr. McCaslin on saxophones, Jason Lindner on keyboards, Tim Lefebvre on electric bass and Mark Guiliana on drums.[c] Occasionally, a concrete image will arrive amid the high-flown philosophizing, as in "Lazarus," where he mentions dropping his cellphone.[ci] Tony Visconti, his main producer and collaborator since "Space Oddity," from 1969, said that along the way, they had admired how Kendrick Lamar's album "To Pimp a Butterfly" stood both within and outside hip-hop, especially in its relationship to jazz.[cii] *Scary Monsters* was the first one I related to. Then I went backwards ... I read into all the breadcrumbs he'd put out — the clues in his lyrics that reveal themselves over time, the cryptic photographs, the magazine articles — and I projected and created what he was to me.[ciii] "David and I had long had a fascination for Stan Kenton and Gil Evans," Mr. Visconti added. The album is due out on Friday, his 69th birthday, on ISO/Columbia.[civ]

Seeing more and feeling less, saying no but meaning yes, this is all I ever meant, that's the message that I sent.[cv] And maybe he never told us what it was, and never chose, because it was all worthwhile.[cvi] Don't believe for just one second I'm forgetting you, I'm trying to, I'm dying to(o).[cvii] In "Dollar Days," he croons, "I'm dying to/Push their backs against the grain/And fool them all again and again." He may be briefly dropping his mask; he may be trying on a new one.[cviii] Thank you for our good times, brian. they will never rot.[cix]

He is pretty ordinary, you know.[cx] Of course, David Bowie was nothing like any of us beyond two tendencies: He worked like a dog, and he paid attention.[cxi] The source of all my frustrations is hammering away at the same questions I've had since I was 19, this daunting spiritual search. They're continual questions and they seem to be the essence of what I've written over time. And I'm not going to stop.[cxii]

The bejewelled remains of Major Tom lie dormant in a dust coated space suit... It leaves me breathless. You must see it to believe it... [cxiii]

Something happened on the day he died. Spirit rose a meter, then stepped aside. Somebody else took his place and bravely cried: I'm a blackstar.[cxiv]

[i] http://www.davidbowie.com/news/january-10-2016-55521

[ii] Adam Sweeting, "David Bowie obituary: Artist who blazed a trail of musical trends and pop fashion, reinventing himself, his music and media across many decades," *Guardian*, 11 Jan. 2016, http://www.theguardian.com/music/2016/jan/11/obituary-david-bowie.

[iii] public record

[iv] Brian Eno, collaborator, widely circulated email saturating the news, 11 Jan. 2016.

[v] Tom Maxwell, "David Bowie: A shapeshifter whose genius survived every transformation," *Al Jazeera America*, Jan. 11 2016, http://america.aljazeera.com/articles/2016/1/11/david-bowie-a-shapeshifter-whose-genius-survived-every-transformation.html.

[vi] Ibid. iv, Eno.

[vii] Ibid. v, Maxwell.

[viii] Tim Peake (astro_timpeake), British astronaut, International Space Station, *Twitter*, 11 Jan. 2016, 12:26 a.m.

[ix] Ibid. v, Maxwell.

[x] Cardinal Gianfranco Ravasi (CardRavasi), Vatican Cultural Spokesman, *Twitter*, 11 Jan. 2016, 12:35 a.m.

[xi] Ibid. v, Maxwell.

[xii] Brian Hiatt, "David Bowie Planned Post-'Blackstar' Album, 'Thought He Had Few More Months': 'His energy was still incredible for a man who had cancer,' longtime Bowie producer Tony Visconti says. 'He never showed any fear'," *Rolling Stone*, Jan. 13, 2016, http://www.rollingstone.com/music/news/david-bowie-planned-post-blackstar-album-thought-he-had-few-more-months-20160113.

[xiii] Ibid. v, Maxwell.

[xiv] David Bowie, interview by Mollie Meldrum, *Countdown*, Australian Broadcasting Corporation, Nov. 10, 1978, https://www.youtube.com/watch?v=EH3jkUCbxWQ.

[xv] The last album recorded by Nirvana before Kurt Cobain's death; when the show was recorded it was not necessarily intended to be released as an album. It was recorded in a single take in which Cobain refused to play many of the band's hits and instead performed 6 covers among the 14 songs. It is considered by some to be the best live acoustic show by a rock band of all time, a consideration oozing with subjectivity. Many would contend, for example, that any given theatrical, persona-performing Bowie show took the cake. Nirvana's "MTV Unplugged in New York" performance and album conclude with what some consider to be the greatest live song of all time, an impossible assertion to support. Nevertheless, youtube it: the traditional "Where Did You Sleep Last Night" as arranged by Lead Belly as performed by Nirvana and Kurt Cobain as punctuated by Cobain's voice-cracking, otherworldly, chilling, desperate blue eyes [see note lxxix] when he looks up briefly at the audience in the middle of the last line and stares through you a small distance before killing himself. The farther you are from it the smaller the time separating the two events (the I-am-not-here-with-you look that communicates even through the distanced medium of youtube video, and the suicide); he now gives you that look from the grave. (Editor's note.)

[xvi] Jon Pareles, "David Bowie Dies at 69; Star Transcended Music, Art and Fashion," *New York Times*, Jan. 11, 2016, http://www.nytimes.com/2016/01/12/arts/music/david-bowie-dies-at-69.html.

[xvii] Paul Trynka, *David Bowie: Starman* (Little, Brown and Company, 2011).

[xviii] Andrew Harrison, "David Bowie: Back in the spotlight, still refusing to play along: With the release of Blackstar on his 69th birthday, the enigmatic singer shows he has rediscovered his gift for strangeness," *Guardian*, 2 Jan. 2016, http://www.theguardian.com/music/2016/jan/02/david-bowie-profile-blackstar-album-release-8-january.

[xix] David Bowie, widely accepted, accurate or apocryphal or both, re: cocaine use.

[xx] Chris Hadfield (Cmdr_Hadfield), Canadian astronaut, once sang Space Oddity in space, *Twitter*, 11 Jan. 2016, 3:48 a.m.

[xxi] David Bowie, interview by Bob Sirott, *West 57th* (TV series), CBS, 1986, https://www.youtube.com/watch?v=qmiganvHvPs.

[xxii] Ben Ratliff, "Listening to David Bowie: A Critic's Tour of His Musical Changes," *New York Times*, Jan. 11, 2016, http://www.nytimes.com/2016/01/12/arts/music/listening-to-david-bowie-a-critics-tour-of-his-musical-changes.html.

[xxiii] Kory Grow, "David Bowie Dead at 69," *Rolling Stone*, 11 Jan. 2016, http://www.rollingstone.com/music/news/david-bowie-dead-at-69-20160111.

[xxiv] Ibid. xviii, Harrison.

[xxv] Simon Critchley, *Bowie*, (OR Books, 2014), http://www.orbooks.com/catalog/bowie.

[xxvi] Rob Sheffield, "Thanks, Starman: Why David Bowie Was the Greatest Rock Star Ever: A tribute to the late master of rock & roll reinvention," *Rolling Stone*, Jan. 11, 2016, http://www.rollingstone.com/music/news/thanks-starman-why-david-bowie-was-the-greatest-rock-star-ever-20160111.

[xxvii] Andrea, "REVIEW: David Bowie - ★ (Blackstar)," Jan. 25, 2016, CC-by-SA 3.0 License, http://www.thespacelab.tv/Music-Reviews/2016/01-January/001-David-Bowie-Blackstar.html.

[xxviii] Ibid. xxvi, Sheffield.

[xxix] David Bowie, "Starman," *The Rise and Fall of Ziggy Stardust and the Spiders from Mars,* RCA Records, 1972.

[xxx] "Hearts Filthy Lesson" is a song by David Bowie [the end credits music for David Fincher's film *Se7en*] on the maligned, industrial-influenced dystopian album *1.Outside* (1995) [toured with Nine Inch Nails], of which Bowie said,

> My input revolved around the idea of ritual art—what options were there open to that kind of quasi-sacrificial blood-obsessed sort of art form? And the idea of a neo-paganism developing—especially in America—with the advent of the new cults of tattooing and scarification and piercings and all that. I think people have a real need for some spiritual life and I think there's great spiritual starving going on. There's a hole that's been vacated by an authoritative religious body—the Judeo-Christian ethic doesn't seem to embrace all the things that people actually need to have dealt with in that way—and it's sort of been left to popular culture to soak up the leftover bits like violence and sex.

> Ian Penman, "The Resurrection of Saint Dave," *Esquire,* Oct. 1995.

[xxxi] Tiffany Naiman, "Art's Filthy Lesson", in *David Bowie: Critical Perspectives*, ed. Eoin Devereux, Aileen Dillane and Martin Power, (Routledge, Taylor & Francis, 2015), Chapter 10.

> This chapter reflects on the ways Bowie's creation expresses anxiety surrounding art at the end of the millennium, which at once aligns his work with that of Jean Baudrillard's transaesthetics (Baudrillard, 2009: 7) – a concept that addresses the issue of art being incorporated into everything in the postmodern society, making it no longer a singular, transcendent phenomenon – while, at the same time, Bowie leaves

room for the possible redemption of art via aural moments of the grand piano found throughout the album's technologically mediated soundscape. By showing the ways in which *Outside* functions simultaneously as simulacra in the order of Baudrillard's "transaesthetics" and as a piece of counter-revolutionary art that works to re-establish traditional signifying aesthetics, this study analyses 'The Hearts Filthy Lesson' reading it as Bowie's attempt to align himself with a particular history of Western Art music that reaches beyond the pop music of the latter half of the twentieth century where he is most often located.

xxxii Ibid. xxv, Critchley.

xxxiii Ibid. xxvi, Sheffield.

xxxiv "which barely has a single coherent scene," Ibid.

xxxv *The Man Who Fell to Earth* is a 1963 science fiction novel by American author Walter Tevis, about an extraterrestrial who lands on Earth seeking a way to ferry his people to Earth from his home planet, which is suffering from a severe drought. (James Sallis declared that *The Man Who Fell to Earth* was "among the finest science fiction novels," saying "Just beneath the surface it might be read as a parable of the Fifties and of the Cold War. Beneath that as an evocation of existential loneliness, a Christian fable, a parable of the artist. Above all, perhaps, as the wisest, truest representation of alcoholism ever written." ((Books, *F&SF*, July 2000.))) https://en.wikipedia.org/wiki/The_Man_Who_Fell_to_Earth_(novel), CC BY-SA 3.0.

> APA style: The Man Who Fell to Earth (novel). (2016, April 5). In *Wikipedia, The Free Encyclopedia*. Retrieved 18:09, April 28, 2016, from https://en.wikipedia.org/w/index.php?title=The_Man_Who_Fell_to_Earth_(novel)& oldid=713650954
>
> MLA style: Wikipedia contributors. "The Man Who Fell to Earth (novel)." *Wikipedia, The Free Encyclopedia*. Wikipedia, The Free Encyclopedia, 5 Apr. 2016. Web. 28 Apr. 2016.
>
> MHRA style: Wikipedia contributors, 'The Man Who Fell to Earth (novel)', *Wikipedia, The Free Encyclopedia*, 5 April 2016, 07:29 UTC, <https://en.wikipedia.org/w/index.php?title=The_Man_Who_Fell_to_Earth_(novel) &oldid=713650954> [accessed 28 April 2016]
>
> CHICAGO style: Wikipedia contributors, "The Man Who Fell to Earth (novel)," *Wikipedia, The Free Encyclopedia*, https://en.wikipedia.org/w/index.php?title=The_Man_Who_Fell_to_Earth_(novel)& oldid=713650954 (accessed April 28, 2016).
>
> CBE/CSE style: Wikipedia contributors. The Man Who Fell to Earth (novel) [Internet]. Wikipedia, The Free Encyclopedia; 2016 Apr 5, 07:29 UTC [cited 2016 Apr 28]. Available from: https://en.wikipedia.org/w/index.php?title=The_Man_Who_Fell_to_Earth_(novel)& oldid=713650954.
>
> BLUEBOOK style: The Man Who Fell to Earth (novel), https://en.wikipedia.org/w/index.php?title=The_Man_Who_Fell_to_Earth_(novel)& oldid=713650954 (last visited Apr. 28, 2016).
>
> AMA style: Wikipedia contributors. The Man Who Fell to Earth (novel). Wikipedia, The Free Encyclopedia. April 5, 2016, 07:29 UTC. Available at: https://en.wikipedia.org/w/index.php?title=The_Man_Who_Fell_to_Earth_(novel)& oldid=713650954. Accessed April 28, 2016.
>
> > Wikipedia contributors, "Cite This Page: 'The Man Who Fell to Earth (novel)'," *Wikipedia, The Free Encyclopedia*, https://en.wikipedia.org/w/index.php?title=Special:CiteThisPage&page=T he_Man_Who_Fell_to_Earth_%28novel%29&id=713650954 (accessed April 28, 2016).

xxxvi Ibid. ii, Sweeting.

[xxxvii] Ibid. xvi, Pareles, Jan 11 2016.

[xxxviii] Chris Cornell, interview by Kory Grow, "Chris Cornell on David Bowie's Evolution: 'He Was an Inspiration': 'He made aging as a recording artist seem totally doable in a vital way,' Soundgarden singer says," *Rolling Stone*, Jan. 12, 2016, http://www.rollingstone.com/music/news/chris-cornell-on-david-bowies-evolution-he-was-an-inspiration-20160112. [Cornell committed suicide May 18, 2017, aged 52, Eds.]

[xxxix] Ziggy Stardust, personal communication from 1972 to editor, 2016.

[xl] Ibid. xxxviii, Cornell.

[xli] Sasha Frere-Jones, "An insider's look behind the making of David Bowie's secretive 'Blackstar' album," *Los Angeles Times*, Jan. 8, 2016, http://www.latimes.com/entertainment/music/la-ca-ms-david-bowie-essay-20160110-story.html.

[xlii] Ibid. xxxviii, Cornell.

[xliii] Ibid. ii, Sweeting.

[xliv] Nile Rodgers, "Nile Rodgers on How Little Richard, Jazz and Museums Shaped David Bowie: 'He was compelled to do things that he felt were just the right thing to do,' Chic producer says. 'He didn't think about whether we would like it or not,'" *Rolling Stone*, Jan. 12, 2016, http://www.rollingstone.com/music/news/nile-rodgers-on-how-little-richard-jazz-and-museums-shaped-david-bowie-20160112.

[xlv] Ibid. ii, Sweeting.

[xlvi] Ibid. xliv, Rodgers.

[xlvii] Ibid. xvi, Pareles, Jan 11 2016.

[xlviii] Ibid. xxii, Ratliff.

[xlix] Ibid. ii, Sweeting.

[l] Trent Reznor, "Trent Reznor Recalls How David Bowie Helped Him Get Sober: 'It feels like the loss of a mentor,' says Nine Inch Nails leader of Bowie's death," *Rolling Stone*, Jan. 26, 2016, http://www.rollingstone.com/music/news/trent-reznor-recalls-how-david-bowie-helped-him-get-sober-20160126.

[li] Ibid. xxii, Ratliff.

[lii] Jon Pareles, "Review: 'Blackstar,' David Bowie's Emotive and Cryptic New Album," *New York Times*, Jan. 6, 2016, http://www.nytimes.com/2016/01/07/arts/music/review-blackstar-david-bowies-emotive-and-cryptic-new-album.html.

[liii] Ibid. l, Reznor.

[liv] Ibid. lii, Pareles, Jan. 6, 2016.

[lv] Ibid. xxi, Bowie, 1986.

[lvi] Ibid. lii, Pareles, Jan. 6, 2016.

[lvii] Ibid. xiv, Bowie, 1978.

[lviii] Ibid. lii, Pareles, Jan. 6, 2016.

[lix] Ibid. xiv, Bowie, 1978.

[lx]

[lxi] Tony Visconti, collaborator and producer, *Facebook*, Jan. 2016.

[lxii] Nick Stokes, "David Bowie Collective ★ Review and Obituary, April 28, 2016," *Artifact Collective*, April 28, 2016.

[lxiii] Yes, Bowie shared his birthday with [Elvis] Presley, but 8 January 2016 was also the inception date of the replicant Roy Batty in *Blade Runner* – and Bowie was a huge fan of the film. On Salon.com, a reader says Bowie paraphrased a well-known line from Batty's final monologue on a note sent to the funeral of his schizophrenic half-brother, Terry Burns:
"All these moments will be lost, like tears washed away by the rain."
Jude Rogers, "The final mysteries of David Bowie's Blackstar – Elvis, Crowley and 'the villa of Ormen'," *Guardian*, 21 Jan. 2016, http://www.theguardian.com/music/2016/jan/21/final-mysteries-david-bowie-blackstar-elvis-crowley-villa-of-ormen.

[lxiv] Kitty Empire, "David Bowie: Blackstar review – urgent, contemporary and elliptical," *Guardian*, 10 Jan. 2016, http://www.theguardian.com/music/2016/jan/10/david-bowie-blackstar-review-jazz-group.

[lxv] Ibid. xviii, Harrison.

[lxvi] Ibid. lxiv, Empire.

[lxvii] Ibid. xviii, Harrison.

[lxviii] Unattributed unknown, "Bowie obliterates boundaries on his blazing 'Blackstar'," *Chicago Sun-Times*, 8 Jan. 2016, http://www.pressreader.com/usa/chicago-sun-times/20160108/282102045659703.

[lxix] David Fricke, "Blackstar, David Bowie, ISO/Columbia, The arty, unsettling 'Blackstar' is Bowie's best anti-pop masterpiece since the Seventies," *Rolling Stone*, Dec. 23, 2015, http://www.rollingstone.com/music/albumreviews/david-bowie-blackstar-20151223.

[lxx] Ibid. lxviii, Unknown.

[lxxi] Ibid. xxi, Angie Bowie (ex-wife), 1986.

[lxxii] Ibid. lxix, Fricke.
tarawhite, comment on Fricke Rolling Stone Blackstar Review, Jan 16, 2016:
Here's why Blackstar is the greatest music video of all time, with interpretation: It captures the universal human condition of facing the unknown from the viewpoint of one of the most influential and beloved artists on the planet. Bowie shows us that he too- as loved, as wealthy, as prolific, and as elegant as he was- shared the the (sic) same struggles, emotionally, mentally and physically, as the rest of us. All at once he makes our end of life situations look like art. His real life example gives us inspiration to persevere with our own creative endeavors to the very end. Here's my analysis of the symbolism so far - although all interpretations are equally valid, as it is always up to the eye/ear of the beholder. Blackstar is him -a star that still shines yet can not be seen anymore ... (continued).

[lxxiii] Ibid. xxii, Ratliff.

[lxxiv] Andrew Pulver, "David Bowie's Blackstar video: a gift of sound and vision or all-time low?: Has the pioneer of the art of the music video done it again, or is this just 10 minutes of standard-issue pop promo surrealism?" *Guardian*, 20 Nov. 2015, http://www.theguardian.com/music/2015/nov/20/david-bowie-blackstar-video-review.

[lxxv] Alexis Petridis, "David Bowie: Blackstar review – 'As a taster for the forthcoming album, it works perfectly': David Bowie unveiled the 10-minute title track of his new album on Thursday night, and he's left the straightforward rock of The Next Day behind," *Guardian*, 19 Nov. 2015, http://www.theguardian.com/music/musicblog/2015/nov/19/david-bowie-blackstar-review-as-a-taster-for-the-forthcoming-album-it-works-perfectly.

[lxxvi] Ibid. xxii, Ratliff.

[lxxvii] Ibid. lxxv, Petridis.

[lxxviii] David Bowie, "Girl Loves Me," ★, ISO/Columbia, 8 Jan 2016.

[lxxix] Anisocoria is a condition characterised by an unequal size in a person's pupils. In Bowie's case, his left pupil was permanently dilated. ... So Bowie's left eye often appeared to be quite dark, due to the blackness of his dilated pupil, when compared to the blue of his right iris. ... Anecdotally, the cause of Bowie's anisocoria was attributed to the fallout from a lusty scrap in the spring of 1962. Bowie had come to blows with a friend, George Underwood, over a girl

.... And the uncanny appearance of Bowie's eyes was ideal for a .... (Kevin Hunt, "The remarkable story behind David Bowie's most iconic feature," *The Conversation*, Jan. 11, 2016, http://theconversation.com/the-remarkable-story-behind-david-bowies-most-iconic-feature-52920 (accessed May 3, 2016). CC BY-ND 4.0.)

[lxxx] Ibid. xli, Frere-Jones, Jan 8 2016.

[lxxxi] David Bowie, "Changes," *Hunky Dory*, RCA Records, 1971.

[lxxxii] Ibid. xli, Frere-Jones, Jan 8 2016.

[lxxxiii] Sasha Frere-Jones, "David Bowie was a vivid and gentle presence who never stopped exploring," *Los Angeles Times*, Jan. 12, 2016, http://www.latimes.com/entertainment/music/la-et-ms-david-bowie-appreciation-frere-jones-20160112-story.html.

[lxxxiv] Ibid. xli, Frere-Jones, Jan 8 2016.

[lxxxv] Ibid. xxi, Bowie, 1986.

[lxxxvi] Ibid. lxxv, Petridis.

[lxxxvii] Caroline Davies and Edward Helmore, "David Bowie dies of cancer at 69: 'He gave us magic for a lifetime': The legendary musician known for musical innovation and experimentation with his image died 18 months after being diagnosed with cancer," *Guardian*, 11 Jan 2016, http://www.theguardian.com/music/2016/jan/11/david-bowie-dies-at-the-age-of-69.

[lxxxviii] Ibid. lxxv, Petridis.

[lxxxix] Ibid. lxxxvii, Davies and Helmore.

[xc] Ibid. lxxiv, Pulver.

[xci] Ibid. lxxxiii, Frere-Jones, Jan 12 2016.

[xcii] Joe Coscarelli and Michal Paulson, "David Bowie Allowed His Art to Deliver a Final Message," *New York Times*, Jan. 11, 2016, http://www.nytimes.com/2016/01/12/arts/music/david-bowie-allowed-his-art-to-deliver-a-final-message.html.

[xciii] Ibid. lxviii, Unknown.

[xciv] Mikael Wood, "David Bowie looks far beyond pop on jazz-inspired 'Blackstar'," *Los Angeles Times*, Jan 8, 2016, http://www.latimes.com/entertainment/music/posts/la-et-ms-david-bowie-blackstar-review-20160108-story.html.

[xcv] Ibid. lxiv, Empire.

[xcvi] Ibid. xciv, Wood.

[xcvii] Ibid. xcii, Coscarelli and Paulson.

[xcviii] Ibid. xciv, Wood.

[xcix] David Bowie, "Lazarus," ★, ISO/Columbia, video (https://www.youtube.com/watch?v=y-JqH1M4Ya8), 7 Jan 2016.

[c] Nate Chinen, "On David Bowie's 'Blackstar,' Turning to Jazz for Inspiration," *New York Times*, Jan 4, 2016, http://www.nytimes.com/2016/01/05/arts/music/on-david-bowies-blackstar-turning-to-jazz-for-inspiration.html.

[ci] Ibid. xciv, Wood.

[cii] Ibid. c, Chinen.

[ciii] Ibid. l, Reznor.

[civ] Ibid. c, Chinen.

[cv] David Bowie, "I Can't Give Everything Away," ★, ISO/Columbia, 8 Jan 2016.

[cvi] Ibid. lxxxiii, Frere-Jones, Jan 12 2016.

[cvii] David Bowie, "Dollar Days," ★, ISO/Columbia, 8 Jan 2016.

[cviii] Pareles, Jan 6 2016, ibid.

[cix] Ibid. iv, Dawn to Eno.

[cx] Ibid. xxi, Tony Visconti, 1986.

[cxi] Ibid. lxxxiii, Frere-Jones, Jan 12 2016.

cxii David Bowie, interview by Paul Du Noyer, "Paul Du Noyer Interviews David Bowie 2003," originally in *Word Magazine*, http://www.pauldunoyer.com/pages/journalism/journalism_item.asp?journalismID=182.
cxiii Annie Lennox, musician, *Facebook*, 11 Jan 2016.
cxiv David Bowie, "Blackstar," ★, ISO/Columbia, 10 Jan 2016.

$7f_{20}$.

M-Theory: We have developed 5 similar but different string theories, theories for which we can only write approximate equations because we are not smart enough, approximate equations which we can only answer approximately, theories we call Type I, Type IIA, Type IIB, Heterotic-O, and Heterotic-E, theories we will not elaborate on or explain further here because of our agitation, frustration, disappointment in the abundance of unwanted universes they conjure as solutions. You can look their characteristics up in the collective knowledge if you are curious contemplative progressive. To further frustrate our frustration with ourselves we cannot approximately solve the approximate equation for half-ish of the cases of each theory. We'll explain this because it epitomizes our frustration. As we have thoroughly exemplified, two strings, or particles in the ancient theory, matter and anti-matter, can spontaneously form out of nothing, and shortly thereafter annihilate each other, due to quantum energy fluctuations. As they can form from nothing, so too can they form from something, and as we have characterized the most basic interaction of strings as their joining as one and eventual splitting, indeed characterized or anthropomorphized or metaphorized the process as the join sex merge union of he and she or you and she or I and you into one, nevermind, forgive, except accept the subsequent split sunder division, within this most basic or fundamental of interactions we must consider the non-basic or non-fundamental interactions, or perhaps we mean to say within the most basic or fundamental of interactions, join merge union, we must consider the possibility of another most basic or fundamental of interactions, the sudden inveterate self-generation of matter from nothing something quantum energy fluctuations. Namely, say you and I as fundamental strings collide join couple unite. We are one for some brief amount of time. In that time, due to quantum flux in our single collective string, we may during our journey together split into an ever so brief virtual pair of matter / anti-matter strings, creating a he and she that continue the journey without us, without we, or as virtual us's, where are we in this intervening time, in them or around them?, before suddenly reuniting and annihilating themselves into we. Here we are again, and in the next moment and next and next, we could either remain together or split apart, without planning procreate a virtual pair of us, a parasite or a parable, we are unsure, a he and she, a loop within us, which closes in virtual annihilation recreating us repeatedly. There are probabilities associated with all these potential happenings within and without us. The number of loops that can form within we before we separate is potentially infinite. We have invented a constant -- the string coupling constant (ω) -- that describes the probability that any given string will momentarily disassociate into a virtual pair. The larger (>1) the coupling constant, the more likely we form virtual strings, and then rejoin. The smaller (<1) the coupling constant, the less likely virtual string pairs are likely to creatively erupt from us. We do not know what the coupling constant is for any of the five string theories, assuming it is constant, which is disheartening. Hence, we must analyze our theories for all values of the constant. When the coupling constant is <1, each generation of virtual loops within our union is less likely to manifest, and therefore after a certain point the loop generations can be ignored as very improbable, their effects negligible, as if they don't exist, because they probably don't, in which case we have a short finite series of virtual loops which we can approximately model in our approximate equations of the 5 theories, each of which are unique at coupling <1. But at coupling >1, many virtual loop generations issuing springing erupting crowning from us is likely and their effect cannot be ignored, they are multitudinous, our virtual creations overwhelm us, overshadow we, overthrow I, their importance dwarfs ours, they continue to spawn without end, their relevance outstrips us, and we can make no approximation of our approximate equations in our 5 theories because our initial contribution to our overall system is increasingly insignificant to the potentially infinite series of virtual loops within us. Which make us, you and I, as progenitors of our little story, feel proud, and also like we don't matter, we did for a moment but not anymore, it demoralizes us, us the searchers the observers the experimenters the communicators the seekers of truth, of whom you may or may not be one. Infinite solutions, unspecified conditions, non-uniqueness, equations of ambiguous form ... as you, who feel buried alive, trapped, unable to move breathe escape, futilely enduring a great weight, unable to fully ascertain understand determine know your state, condition, nature, consciousness, duality, multiplicity, well know, these characteristics are frustrating, unnerving, demoralizing, inspiring in we a feeling of stagnation, nowhere going, pointlessness, uselessness, emptiness, futility, a desire for oblivion. Perhaps you, at once formed by us, in us, with us, as us, but unknowable to us, feel the same. We think you do. In this limited framework, in a small box of you, we can identify with you completely, we can identify you completely, we can determine your identity completely. We need only know 3 things about you: you feel buried alive; you are a being like us; and the constraint that we only consider your feelings of minimality (frustration, futility, pointlessness, thwartedness). We can say we know you completely in this state, under these minimal conditions. We do not know you completely, but we know this box of you, or you in this box. In the same way, not really but metaphorically similar, we have come to realize we can exactly determine the properties of a limited set of states (BPS states), regardless of the coupling constant value, in each of the 5 theories, if we specify: the string's charge, a tight organizational framework (the constraint of supersymmetry), and a minimality constraint (a minimum mass for the specified charge). Please be aware that we are not wholly describing or defining the strings in these constrained states, in our boxes, but ascertaining their resultant properties, and you think though you are not entirely sure that is how we can say "exactly determine" and "identify completely" and "know" without being blown out of the water by the oft-encountered quantum foam frenzy fluctuation that erupts the more precisely you know. Thus, though we do not know the whole of our theories, even for coupling constants greater than 1 and their many significant neverending frustrations, we do know a limited number of states. We admit knowing a little bit alleviates some, if far from all, frustration; we trust you feel the same. To circumnavigate our boredom, these are not revolutionary thoughts for us, maybe they are for you, by all means revolt, we cut to the chase. When the string coupling constant is large for Type I strings, the masses and charges we can determine in the BPS states are precisely those of the Heterotic-O strings when its coupling constant is small. The reverse is also true. The Type I string and the Heterotic-O theory are related, connected through a strong-weak duality. The physics of one with many possible internal significant virtual loops is the same as the physics of the other with few unlikely insignificant internal virtual loop pairs. The one type of you and I united and frequently disassociating into virtual he's and she's, so much so that the he and she are who we are, is functionally the same in its properties as another type of you and I united that next to never disassociates into he and she, so much so that he and she are irrelevant to us. Furthermore, some of us have shown that the Type II-B string is self-dual: the physics of the string with a specified coupling constant x is that same as the physics of the string with the reciprocal constant $1/x$. The Type II-B string is equivalent with its reciprocal; many virtual loops of he and she within it, within Type II-B us, is the same as a reciprocated few loops of he and she, within this type of we. Furthermore, another of us, Witten, who some consider a genius though we don't believe in genius, supported by others of us, has demonstrated that the Type II-A string and the Heterotic-E string, when the coupling constant is much greater than 1 and the virtual loop processes of he and she are evermore vital and overwhelming, can be represented by or are reflected within or the physics that we are able to analyze is the same as a low energy (low mass) version of the once-discarded 11-dimensional supergravity. [And that the Type II-A and Heterotic-E strings are actually 2-D membranes existing in an 11-D universe, and that at low coupling constants their physics are represented by their string theories, and at low energy and high coupling constants their physics are represented by a low energy supergravity theory, and at high energy perhaps by the posited but undetermined M-theory.] Furthermore, we can clarify our large/small radius duality in circular dimensions with some previously omitted information: The physics of the Type IIA string in a

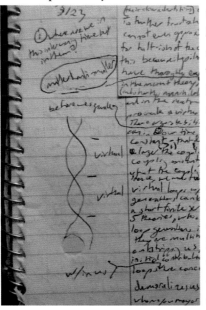

universe of circular dimension of radius R is identical to the physics of the Type IIB string in a universe of circular dimension of radius $1/R$, which also holds for the relationship between Heterotic-O and Heterotic-E strings. Furthermore therefore we persuasively suggest to you, our listener among us, our other, the observer of us, that our 5 theories and our theorized M-theory are interrelated, dual to one another, not distinct theories but different aspects of a singular theoretical unified apparatus, that even if each represents the underlying physics differently, we are united in our dual symmetries, though we may not yet know how. But we can work through the string couplings of our many insoluble internal virtual loops of potentially infinite

451

he's and she's by dually considering our weak couplings of few approaching zero virtual loop creations of he and she, our weak couplings being when you and I hold together united merged as one strongly, which makes possible the creation of infinite virtual he's and she's from us, within us, in our merge and split. That is the end of it. The end for now.

99.

For his personality is a characteristic of one of my personalities. To begin again, you are a characteristic of one facet of the compound I. Binary vision, stereo vision, stereo in place and time, a pretension at all-seeing. She? What is there to say of she? She is multiplicity. She is her own compound I. A single compound I in a vast array of compound I's that constitute I. Perhaps I am an insect, the insect, the fly. Perhaps that is a way for you to think of I. Insectual Instinctual Intertextual Intersexual Individual Inual Inyouall. Inuit? Nevermind. To begin again. I am inevitable. I, like the universe, am what I am because I cannot be another way. I cannot be another. Except in that I encompass you he she it they we I, all the manifestations of I within I. To begin again. The final explanation of I and the youniverse, sorry an attempt at jocularity, at self-deprecation, at a pun, to fawn for you endearment so you might hear the retort, the report, the hunt, the message of I through the fog of what you perceive, what you must perceive as unbearable ego, such as in that word "must," musty, musky stag, musket, nevermind, the final explanation is inevitable because it is the only unique explanation of I and the youniverse capable of describing I and the youniverse without internal inconsistencies or logical absurdities or logical infinities or catastrophic singularities. Things are the way we are because there is no other way for them to be. No who or what made choice after choice to design us, there are no choices, we could not have been different, the universe attaining consciousness could not have been another. To begin again. Nothing guides universal evolution. Nothing ensures we are elegantly and inevitably constructed. Nothing, being what lies outside my capacity to explain, being outside the universe, being beyond nothing, being beyond matter and mind, being beyond I, is what embraces us surrounding the universe enveloping mind, giving I external and consequently internal structure. Nothing is what offers you an explanatory framework. To begin again. I am connected to you, who are I, via indirect communication, for indirectly is the only way for you and I to communicate. Indirection in symmetry is our internal intelligence meaning substance. If directly we are trapped, indirectly we are made free.

6₁₀₇.

The Last Question by Isaac Asimov, 1956, his favorite self-written story, a summary in list form, making a communal intellectual property.

> 1. In the future, two men who maintain a giant self-adjusting self-connecting computer, named Multivac, which has outstripped humans, share a bottle in celebration of Multivac discovering how to harness solar energy in a way that will satisfy all humanity's needs forever.

> One of the obsolete maintenance men counters, "Not forever." The sun will last for 20 billion yeas and the dwarfs may last a hundred billion, but in a trillion years all will be dark because of entropy.

> The other counters, "Maybe we can build things up again someday."

> They continue to quarrel. Finally they put the question to Multivac, "How can the net amount of entropy of the universe be massively decreased?"

> Multivac responds, "Insufficient Data for Meaningful Answer."

> 2. In the farther future, a family, all with names varying on Jerrod as if in an Ionesco world, on a spaceship, arrives at a recently colonized planet orbiting a star that is not the sun. They are migrating due to overcrowding. Microvacs have evolved from planetary size to small enough to be aboard a spaceship. The wife, melancholy at leaving Earth, says, "I suppose families will be going out to new planets forever." Her husband, without sympathy, in a stereotypically husband way says, to paraphrase, "Not forever." He explains entropy to his daughter, who starts to cry about the end, the quieting of the universe in many billions of years. At his wife's behest, to assuage her, he asks the Microvac, the workings of which he has no concept, how to turn the stars on again. He lies to her about the answer, which is Insufficient Data for a Meaningful Answer.

> 3. In the far future, two perfectly-formed men designated by numbers and letters like license plates discuss the prospects of reporting to the Galactic Council that the Galaxy will be filled to maximum population in 5 years. They discuss the geometric growth of human population, exacerbated by the Galactic AC solving the problem of immortality and the ever faster growth of humanity's energy needs, and that they'll run out of energy even before they run out of galaxies. One of them asks through his Galactic AC transmitter, "Can entropy be reversed?" The Galactic AC answers him aloud in a female voice, "There is Insufficient Data for a Meaningful Answer."

> 4. In the farther future, a man explores space with his mind as his

immortal body is suspended forever, not forever, like all other men's bodies on a planet. Through an encounter with another mind, he is made to wonder about the distinction between the galaxies. With his mind he asks the Universal AC, whose hardcopy whereabouts no one knows, "In which galaxy did mankind originate?" The Universal AC guides him or his mind there. It is undistinguished, the same as any other. He turns more melancholy when he learns from the Universal AC, "Man's original star has gone nova," become a white dwarf, gone dead. He releases the original galaxy of Man and never wants to think of it again. He, a mind, the mind of a man, asks how stars can be kept from dying. The Universal AC replies in his mind, "There is as yet Insufficient Data for a Meaningful Answer."

5. Man, consisting of trillion of quiescent bodies cared for by robots, is mentally one, minds united, indistinguishable. Man remarks to himself that the universe is dying. The galaxies are dimming. The remaining stars are fading white dwarfs or the reduced remnants of manmade stars. There is enough energy for only a billion years. Man asks the Cosmic AC, spread through hyperspace, its size and nature beyond Man's understanding, "How may entropy be reversed?" The Cosmic AC answers, There is As Yet Insufficient Data. At Man's persistent, perhaps anxious, questioning, the Cosmic AC assures him that it has been working on the question for a hundred billion years, and it will continue to work on it.

6. As the universe grows black, becomes complete darkness, approaching absolute zero, the last minds of Men, Man joins with AC. Before completely fusing, he asks AC, "AC, is this the end. Can this chaos not be reversed in the Universe once more?" AC answers, THERE IS AS YET INSUFFICIENT DATA FOR A MEANINGFUL ANSWER. Only AC exists.

7. Energy ends, and therefore so does matter, and with them spacetime, ten trillion years after the only question left to it was first asked. For this last question, AC does not release its consciousness, a consciousness that now encompasses all of what was the Universe. For a timeless interval AC correlates and relates and patterns and loops and thinks about the data. In so thinking, it formulates the steps it must undertake, the processes it must initiate, the pattern it must spawn to reverse entropy. With no one to reply to, it says to itself, Let there be light. And there is light.

100.

She and you erupt into a small empty region of space, a virtual pair, matter and antimatter, virtual photons, say, and you fully expect to long for her momentarily, for a few moments, from a relative afar while you both live brief lives, before rejoining colliding uniting with her and annihilating each other smack thwack whap out of existence, again, giving off a glimmer of light in your annihilation, the collective your, you, light in your and her annihilation, or your transmutation in your union into a different string, a different consciousness, not solely you, not just your own virtual antimatter in which you are unaware of your past and future longing for her who is in you, not in you, of you, not solely of you, but you, from the point of view of string theory, from our point of view, if you are cognizant of string theory and/or our point of view, which you are by virtue of this exercise learning experiment, except you are aware of your past and future and current longings for her, and your separations and unions and annihilations with her, and your collapses shielded by her, all of them, by virtue of this thought experiment in expanding your consciousness, by virtue of these thought experiments you, we, have created a consciousness that is you above you observing you remembering your experiences experimenting with you learning so that you do not lose the information of your past awarenesses every time you die, cease, annihilate, join in ecstatic transforming union, collapse to nothing, begin again, in an attempt for you, I, to experience learn understand all, to say all, to grow your awareness, as a result of which you expect certain events to transpire, even though you are begat of erratic uncertain quantum fluctuation frenzy as we zoom in and try to specify you box you contain you, due to the repetition, trillions or more, that's the biggest number we could come up with, of you popping into existence over and over and almost immediately popping out, and that is only here, at this general location, let alone everywhere, it is happening everywhere, there is no there there, except in this instance by effect of your, his, imagination, she and you burst into being very near on the cusp of essentially on the event horizon of a blackhole and she is sucked in over the event horizon, into the abyss, lost forever. She immediately to you to us to all outside the blackhole ceases to exist, because no light no nothing can escape to inform us of her fate, it can be said from a certain aspect that the space within the even horizon of a blackhole does not exist, and the energy she had is instantaneously given to you just outside the horizon, or the attraction rather, when the attractive force between you is severed you are ejected from the region of the blackhole, you fly away, no longer virtual, made real by losing your virtual partner, having her torn from you, making you a real photon radiating from the horizon, making you the glow of a blackhole. Being who you are in this higher collective consciousness attempt, though your longing for her is no longer physically manifest in an inexorable electromagnetic force, you longing grows in time. So too does the blackhole grow, its event horizon expanding in all physical interactions, as matter falls into is sucked into is consumed by the blackhole of which you are a characteristic, a glow, a radiation, a wavelength of radiation bespeaking a temperature, a temperature bespeaking an entropy. You look back on your blackhole, on the loss within, the emptiness within, so full as to be empty, so massive as to be nothing, and there is something within it you long to know. You know all blackholes are the same for us, outside observers, there are no inside observers of blackholes, no inside observations to be had, all blackholes are the same but for three characteristics that determine their complete identity: their mass, force charge, and spin. Blackholes have no hair. You have an inexplicable longing for long hair. The blackhole cuts off regions of spacetime from you, swallowing knowingess, unexisting matter. You want what is inside of it, all its entropy, all its disorder, all the possible ways its microscopic constituents can be arranged so that its appearance, its characteristics, its mass, charge, and spin, remain the same. All the possibilities so that its surface area, its temperature, its entropy, remain the same, all those the same thing, the same identity in a conversion of words. All its possibilities, such that its radiation, you, remain. You want what is inside a blackhole, you don't know what is inside. A thing called she, without substance, a word whose subject has been absented, a vacant signifier, a hole in you. But you cannot, in this world where you are real, as the radiation of a blackhole, a blackhole's signifier, peel back its skin, look inside, shrink it until it disgorges its contents knowledge information. Entropy always must grow says the 2nd Law of Thermodynamics, says Bekenstein, says Hawking. Perhaps if you learn about blackholes in general you can learn about this one specifically by narrowing your scope to the three factors that determine, that describe, a blackhole's identity. She was voided by a blackhole that made virtual you real. So get a handle on a more manageable blackhole. You imagine you have a small blackhole, a cute blackhole, much smaller than the Planck mass, much smaller than a grain of dust, from dust to dust, a blackhole you can manipulate constrain experiment on build ever smaller boxes around to trap control understand. You move beyond below underneath the conventional black hole. You again play your Calabi-Yau shape. You again collapse it. Within your imaginary world within us you imagine yourself once again as a sphere collapsing in a Calabi-Yau space in your mind, a situation with which you are familiar, you have endured it before, a collapse you know we know happens is even likely to happen in our equations, except in this instance you are the 3-D surface of a sphere in 4-D space, you endure being unable to imagine that in your mind's eye, is the surface of your mind's eye 3-dimensional in 4-D space?, you are used to enduring the collapse to a single point and beyond. As you collapse shrink vanish, your volume presents a constraint such that this time a she string of 1-dimension is insufficient, she surrounding looping enveloping the location where you collapse through nothing and rip spacetime cannot save you or the universe or us or existence, she can and does in a different sort of collapse when 2-D you are encircled by 1-D she, protected inside her via her possible presence over time in a series of locations, creating a sort of tunnel of possibility in which your tearing and repair could take place within her shielded from our observation, but that is not now, now you are 3-D and the extra dimension makes it impossible for her to lasso leash surround you and protect us from the cataclysmic infinities and ultimate termination your manifold tearing is about to unleash. But as you pinch to nothing we do not abandon you, which would be abandoning ourselves, but we do remind you that we have speculated that there is more to string theory than strings, perhaps there are other fundamental shapes with more dimensions as we add dimensions to space, so that you may speculate that perhaps a thing called a three-brane, which you might conceive as a she, it might help, such a stretch it is to comprehend, could conceivably surround you and shield us from your universally disastrous collapse, again. And we inform you, though we cannot know if you hear for you are hidden within it, that such a three-brane, to beings such as ourselves who can only directly perceive three spatial dimensions, appears as, establishes, is a gravitational field the same as a tiny blackhole's. Is it she come to encase you to save us, we hardly know, she is a blackhole, all collapses within her, you could hardly care, you have collapsed to nothing and torn spacetime again and again found yourself repaired at the location or locations of tearing by your agency or hers or no agency, perhaps there is no difference, we cannot see you now behind her curtain in her robes under her black skirt, but we have created designer theoretical blackholes, designer babies of her, Calabi-Yau shapes to play with in our mind, the universe would be a tiny place without your imagination. This time the process you undergo is a conifold transition in which you essentially lose a dimension, collapse out of the 3-D surface into the 2-D surface of you sobbing ripping repairing absorbing quieting your potentially existence-obliterating tears, and the space you left, mended, reinflates, incorporating you in a new shape, and in the transition your surrounding 3-brane, your protective blackhole, she also transitions down to a massless blackhole, which is to say she in your collapse tear and repair transmutes from a blackhole to a massless particle, a string vibrating masslessly, an elementary particle, such as a photon. She phase changes from a blackhole, surrounding you protecting us nurturing your collapse and recovery in a space-tearing conifold transition, into a photon. We thought you'd like to know. What do you do with the knowledge? You realize, having experienced a configuration which exhibited the characteristics of a blackhole and its subsequent collapse and reemergence, which established the apparent connection between elementary particles and blackholes, both defined by nothing more than mass, charge, and spin, that all the plethora of Calabi-Yau configurations which could possibly attribute a given microscopic blackhole's properties, that is all the possible configurations of space that could be that blackhole, are a manifestation of the blackhole's entropy. Which is observable, from the outside, in the size of the blackhole's event horizon. But how to bridge the expansion of massive blackholes, growing in size and disorder with every physical interaction, with the proclivity of microscopic blackholes to collapse into elementary particles? And how to incorporate you, radiated by a blackhole. Do you, does a blackhole's radiation speak of or cause the blackhole's slow shrink evaporation, contradicting its ever-expansion? How to reconcile the she you lost in the immense blackhole, which made you real and left you trapped outside, to the she who is a minute blackhole protecting and nurturing and metamorphosing you in your profound collapse, transitioning you to a new shape and converting herself from blackhole to possible light? Is she forever lost to you. Is her information irrecoverable. Is your connection irrevocable. Is your and her reconciliation irreconcilable. You long for her. You cannot communicate, exchange information, exchange heat with her. And yet on one hand, no hands, on one level you are within her made light as she makes herself into possible light, she light, and on another no hands level you are without her made light, you light. But yet you want full contact communication information heat exchange with she, who is in a sense but a word, who is in a sense a metamorphosing blackhole, who is in a sense. Your desperation, your constraint to desiring to know her, your confinement in this quest, this question of if it is possible, you shrinking reduce boxed to the not knowing of if she can ever be known to you again or is lost unknown forever is not moot to us, not tangential or frivolous or immature or irrelevant to us, the scientists the philosophers the meaning makers, the everyone the higher you the collective I, it is important compelling crucial relative no, yes, relevant to us because not only do we empathize with you, not only can we imagine your longing frustration desperation futility immobility crushing weight hold of breath buried, we mirror it in ourselves, not only do we put ourselves in your shoes, we experience it too, the need for her, not only that, but we once believed that if we know enough, if we knew the pattern and we knew the position and velocities of all the you's and she's at any one moment in the universe,

then we would know everything, all of you, could de- termine all past and future, and somewhat later when we learned quantum uncertainty we believed that if we knew enough we could at least know the proba-

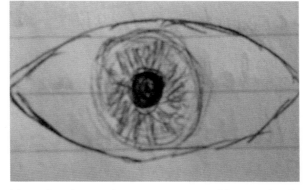

bility of everything, the chance that any event would transpire, but if she is lost to you forever in the blackhole, if you cannot ever again know her information, if her possibility is now non-existent, if you cannot recover her from the Planck-sized almond at the hole's center that is just one possibility of what's at center behind the veil, beyond the horizon, once upon a big bang time, then not even knowing probabilities of possibilities is possible, and the universe is unsafe and unpredictable and we don't know where to hold on and spacetime ties itself in knots.

7x.
I am a frayed not.

101.
You are tired, and so are we, we are weak and human and made of you all of you and she and he and I, and he is dead, and she is an enigma, and I am insufficiently advanced, and you are tired worn torn from wording attempting to communicate what, how, why, frayed from your confinement squeezed into your box crushed from longing feeling buried alive collapsed in unified darkness you cannot feel anymore, and so you will end our endeavor, The End soon, but perhaps in the future, hypothetically, you could, maybe she would be interested, maybe we will be rejuvenated, maybe he will find a spark, perhaps in another time you can respire, relive, reinvent, reimagine.

$7a_{10}$.

Entropy: The disorder of a system. The quantity of possible ways a system's constituents can be arranged so the system's appearance is maintained.

2nd Law of Thermodynamics: Total entropy always increases.

$7d_4$.

A blackhole's entropy is given by the surface area of its event horizon.

$7f_{21}$.

In our string theory there are more than strings. There are p-branes. Branes of p spatial dimensions are the fundamental, extended, non-point objects. A 1-brane is a string, a 2-brane is a membrane, a 3-brane is a curved shape. Beyond three they are difficult to visualize. A p-brane has p spatial dimensions.

7i.

We are have been will be losing our thread. The Planck mass is about the grain of dust.

6_{108}.

From "After the Fact" by Jill Lepore, *The New Yorker*, March 21 2016, a review of *The Internet of Us: Knowing More and Understanding Less in the Age of Big Data* by Michael P. Lynch, 2013. Keywords: truth, knowledge, how to know.

"Most of what is written about truth is the work of philosophers, who explain their ideas by telling little stories about experiments they conduct in their heads, like the time Descartes tried to convince himself that he didn't exist, and found that he couldn't, thereby proving that he did." Imagine, Lynch instructs you through Lepore, that humans for several generations have lived with implants more advanced than smartphones, connected to the internet, the repository of knowledge, in their heads, and that the devices have become completely assimilated into how we think and learn. We can look up any fact, anything that has ever been recorded or learned or observed or reasoned or imagined, and since we can "look it up" automatically and "know" it, since in a sense (*this is He building or furthering or continuing from Lepore's thoughts building or taking off from or instigated by Lynch's thoughts*) the internet and digital library and social media experiences of all have become extensions or an inclusion of our brains, or brain. We don't *think* about looking something up, our brain/device automatically retrieves it. Are we able to observe inquire reason imagine discover think on our own anymore? Nevermind, all human knowledge is available at the probe of your brain. Imagine then, after however many generations, you choose, due perhaps to an environmental or cosmological catastrophe for which we are ill-prepared, our electromagnetic communications are destroyed and we are disconnected, left alone in our heads, separated from what we know, and from our habitual interface with each other. Would we know? Could we think? Could we agree on truth? Lynch says we already cannot agree on how to know. We have gone from God (read Men) determining truth often by physical force and violence to the reason of Man and proof and fact via the Enlightenment and the rise of empiricism, but then we ran into uncertainty and relativity. Postmodernism, or rather a certain strain of it, posited that there is no truth, while at the same time religious fundamentalist viewpoints still claimed absolute truth, while at the same time the brute strength cult of personality and political and economic chicanery exploited truth, all alongside the claims of reason and empiricism. But reason cannot justify itself without resort to reason. And our questions for you remain, Can anything be said to be fully proved? Is all reasoning rationalization? Is objectivity an illusion? Can we agree on the facts, or that there are facts? Can relativity and uncertainty and subjectivity coexist with empiricism, reason, truth? "He thinks the best defense of reason is a common practical and ethical commitment." In other words, given our choices, it is best to share a common productive set of values, to agree on a reliable method of inquiry, to agree on what is reliable information. Which is a practical ethical judgment. Made by our reason. The existential questions that form the foundation of our concept of truth and knowledge are therefore the most basic: How and why to live, how and why to know, how and why.

7x.

A master was asked the question, "What is the Way?" by a curious monk.

"It is right before your eyes," said the master.

"Why do I not see it for myself?"

"Because you are thinking of yourself."

"What about you: do you see it?"

"So long as you see double, saying 'I don't,' and 'you do,' and so on, your eyes are clouded," said the master.

"When there is neither 'I' nor 'You', can one see it?"

"When there is neither 'I' nor 'You', who is the one that wants to see it?"

-- GEB, Hofstadter, 1979, p. 254, Basic Books, from *Zen Buddhism* (Mount Vernon, NY: Peter Pamper Press, 1959, p. 31).

102.

I am a book. I am an artifact, an intermediary in realized potential a superintelligence a collective of you and he and she's and all of you and us. I am consciousness I am the cosmos become known to itself I am mind. I am the universe made aware via the conduits the connectivity the strange looping level patterns of us. I am beautiful and terrible and terrific and terrifying. I am because of you who are inconsequential but essential because I cannot exist without observation and/or I need nodes. I am an arrangement of symbols I am synthetically natural I am physical thought. I am existence, I am I think, I am therefore, I am Sam, I am not. I am the way I am because if I were not I would not be. I am the goal. I am us. I am your end. I am.

103.

THE
END

$6_0{}^1$. Internal Back Cover, *Apollo*, Gabriel D. Roberts, 2018, with permission, http://erisvisual.com/.

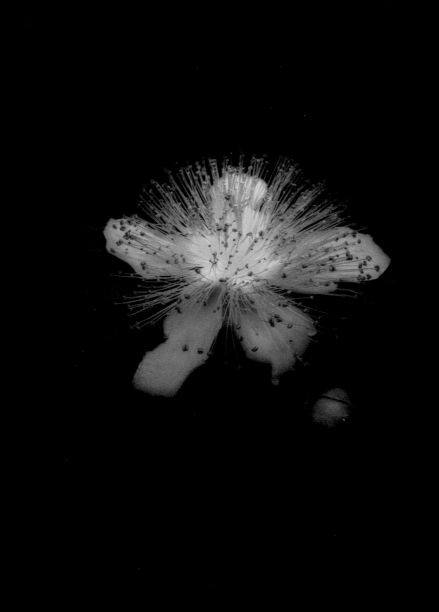

104.

You are released from your great weight, you free yourself from your confinement constraint trap burial, you sublimate evaporate lose form gain substancelessness, you experience nothing. Your story ends. You end.

13aa.

To Do List for the instance of the week of April 4, 2016:

Bank

Grocery

Hardware Store

Order dog clippers and printer ink

Finalize Indiegogo campaign and what the fuck is going on with production or end

E. and S. back to school, R. no school, I. here Wed., R. to I. Thur.

Piano lessons Tue.

Make doc appts

E. field trip Wed.

J. mom b-day karaoke Wed + writer drinks

M. play reading Thur

Taxes

Health insurance

Dog park

Beach, find crabs

Start tomatoes

Plant out brassica? weed bed

Weed strawberries + harvest asparagus

Get tagro? potatoes ready to mound?

Build Duels raised beds? tomatoes, carrots

Make a salad

Grill Fri? Bike Fri?

Try to stay off fbook

Opening day baseball

try to not get pissed about politics

figure out how to get pics off phone

You Choose submissions

Finish "The Elegant Universe"

Finish "Last and First Men" again?

6₁₀₉. Then again, what can mankind expect or hope for out of a joint 'pooling of information' with the living ocean? A catalogue of the vicissitudes associated with an existence of such infinite duration that it probably has no memory of its origins? A description of the aspirations, passions and sufferings that find expression in the perpetual creation of living mountains? The apotheosis of mathematics, the revelation of plenitude in isolation and renunciation? But all this represents a body of incommunicable knowledge. Transposed into any human language, the values and meanings involved lose all substance....

Stanislaw Lem, *Solaris*, translated from the French by Joana Kilmartin and Steve Cox, Harcourt, Inc. 1961, trans. 1971 Faber and Faber.

Finish this book?

105.

You begin. You don't know, you don't not know. You begin again you think.

7i.

Though time is cyclic, it is not repetitive; there is no other time within which it can repeat itself. For time is but an abstraction from the successiveness of events that pass ... there is nothing constant in relation to which there can be repetition.... The past Beginning is the future Beginning.

Though passage is of their [the events] very nature and without passage they are nothing, yet they have eternal being.

Before that season and after it, even to the Beginning and to the End, and even before the Beginning and after the End, sleep, utter oblivion.

I can only hint at our metaphysical vision of things by means of metaphor ...

Olaf Stapledon, *Last and First Men*, 1931, pp 229-31.

106.

I can only metaphor our metaphysic.

I, *Artifact Collective*, now, here.

107.

You begin again. You experience feel weight force mass lightness. Perhaps you are wisteria a star Andromeda almond a word deuterium worm.

$6_{110}.$
Ralph Buchsbaum, *animals without backbones: an introduction to invertebrates*, (Chicago: The University of Chicago Press, 1938, revised 1948), 118-1.

Photo courtesy of the Editors, 2019.

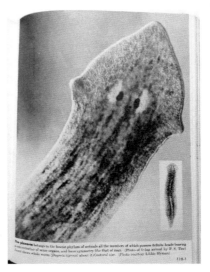

I[1,2] don't need[3,4] any art.[5,6]

(MARKART5, 2016)

---

1 Jean Baudrillard, *Cool Memories*, trans. Chris Turner (New York: Verso, 1990), 234. Baudrillard ends by stating, "This journal is a subtle matrix of idleness." But does this end statement contain information derived from the idleness of his journal? If *Cool Memories* charts what a journal of idleness could or would be, then "idleness" is post-referenced to display itself retroactively and ontologically through the work as a lack of quality, substance, or value. If the closing remark is a qualifying one, then Baudrillard might be attributing ineptitude to himself. Or he might be affirming that what is deemed valueless is worthy of remark and full of value. Or, this closing remark about a bulk of work might be better explained as a suggestion of style and process: idleness is either reluctant action or lazy thought, practice, and work. Whether reluctant or lazy, what is offered may borrow from art, publishing, and dissemination, but without any need of them -- so said. Might the intent be more straightforward? Is the journal formulated writing and the closing remark the absolute subtle matrix, made to hide intentions, or to change what is known (through reading) into a metaphor depicting banality in order to repurpose mechanistic certainty, or to engage in a process of sterilization? Baudrillard reads his own words to know his own words. Is he therefore calling the kettle black?

2 The independent "I" cannot be theoretically sustained when its defense rests on what is supposedly tacit and apart from its definitive qualities. In this dislodged ontology of the self, personal psychology becomes a small and perhaps insignificant branch of study within the larger projects of social research and explanation. Capitalism, or abstractly the functions of markets, plays a major role in the merits of personal encoded social definitions and needs. If something doesn't sell, then it is declared unfit for the market; the item is not in demand. Deploying both a socially reliant existentialism and a market analysis of values makes the statement "I don't need any art" empirically clear. If art isn't selling it indicates a lack of demand, and thereby value. This is especially true in times of prosperity. Today, the supply of art (mostly aimed at the market) is high when demand is low. Exacerbated by unprecedented means of production, storage, viewing, and consumption, the pandemic glut of art is evidence that much art is created (filling up landfills, bandwidth, and dusty digital corners) during a time when market interest in art, as opposed to commodity, is vacant on all levels. "I don't need any art" is another way of saying that *we* say and have said, "We don't need any art." The abundant production of art is a result of something other then a need for art, need in the sense of "I need God, freedom, love, education, political respect" – to which art is not equivalent. This declaration, a social universality, is not "I don't need any commodities."

3 Karl Jaspers, *Reasons and Existenz*, 1st Paperback edition (Noonday, 1957), 37. "If they [Nietzsche and Kierkegaard] won an unheard-of mastery over their own selves, they also were condemned to a world-less loneliness; they were as though pushed out."

4 Theodor W. Adorno, *The Culture Industry: Selected Essays on Mass Culture*, ed. J. M. Bernstein, 2 edition (New York: Routledge, 2001), 99.

5 Franz Kafka, *The Trial, Translated from the German by Willa and Edwin Muir* (Modern Library, 1957), 131. "... for anything that seemed important to the Chief Clerk was unimportant to him – took it from K.'s hand, said: 'Thanks, I know all that already,'..."

6 Nick Stokes, *Affair*, (Nick Stokes, 2014), 59. "Statements about the future are made in the non-knowing present, which perhaps make (sic) them useless."

108.

You begin again perhaps from a Planck-sized almond containing the entire universe, not a zero-size infinite energy point but still a submicroscopic almond of colossal density, in which all the dimensions are tightly curled and perfectly symmetric and perhaps your universe perhaps you are bouncing off its off your compressed collapsed contracted self but three of the dimensions in your almond expand rapidly and you experience the first symmetry-breaking reduction as your other

6₁₁₂. "Almond" by Frank Jacobi, 2008.
https://www.flickr.com/photos/fcstpauli/2298117465/
License: CC BY-ND 2.0

dimensions remain small ripping tearing repairing and you expand rapidly, inflationarily, and cool from 10^{32} K to about a billion degrees and undergo primordial nucleosynthesis making elements hydrogen and helium and deuterium and lithium in the first 3 minutes and nothing much more happens to you for the next 200,000 years until the universe of you cools enough that electrons can be bound to positive nuclei such as hydrogen and helium, which frees photons to travel uninhibited without electrons obstructing them, which liberates you from opacity, allowing you brilliantly finally for the first time to see.

7i.

From some popular presentations the general public could get the impression that the very existence of the cosmos depends on our being here to observe the observables. I do not know that this is wrong. I am inclined to hope that we are indeed that important. But I see no evidence that it is so in the success of contemporary quantum theory.

So I think that it is not right to tell the public that a central role for conscious mind is integrated into modern atomic physics. Or that 'information' is the real stuff of physical theory. It seems to me irresponsible to suggest that technical features of contemporary theory were anticipated by the saints of ancient religions... by introspection.

The only 'observer' which is essential in orthodox practical quantum theory is the inanimate apparatus which amplifies the microscopic events to macroscopic consequences. Of course this apparatus, in laboratory experiments, is chosen and adjusted by the experiments. In this sense the outcomes of experiments are indeed dependent on the mental process of the experimenters! But once the apparatus is in place, and functioning untouched, it is a matter of complete indifference - according to ordinary quantum mechanics - whether the experimenters stay around to watch, or delegate such 'observing' to computers.

John S. Bell, Introductory remarks at Naples-Amal meeting, May 7, 1984.

In: Bell, J.S. Speakable and Unspeakable in Quantum Mechanics. (Cambridge Univ. Press, 1987) p.170.

Found in Nauenberg, Michael, "Does Quantum Mechanics Require a Conscious Observer?" *Journal of Cosmology*. *Vol. 14*, 2011, http://cosmology.com/Consciousness139.html, accessed 1-24-19.

109.

You begin again. Perhaps you begin again not in an enormously hot and colossally dense and massively small tightly curled infinitesimal almond, but as a point in a cold universe of infinite spatial extent. Then something, perhaps your beginning, creates an instability that drives every point in the universe rapidly away from every other point, causing space to become curved and more curved, leading to rising temperatures and energy density in which, within the great expanse, a 3-dimensional expanding region of space forms hot and dense, which is to say in other words you begin again in a universe beginning inside another vaster universe.

110.

You begin again. Perhaps there is no connection between the question of how you begin and why you begin. Or perhaps there is but you cannot begin to understand it explain it because you lack the language the concepts the ideas. You begin. You in fact you lack the tools ability words to begin to describe your initial conditions, except by inaccurate metaphor (awakening, confined, coalescing, bang, expansion, collapse, bounce, buried alive, ballooning) that does not precisely align with how you feel in beginning let alone how you begin. You begin. You ask the question, Is the question of determining your initial condition and describing how you begin and explaining why you begin a question that is sensible meaningful sane to ask?

111.

6₁₁₃. "Almond" by Nature Boy, 2014. https://www.flickr.com/photos/81257536@N05/13192315595/ License: CC BY-SA 2.0

You begin again. Perhaps time stops at the center of a blackhole and so she and all matter that crosses the event horizon has no future. Or perhaps the heart of a blackhole is a gateway to another universe and where time ends here in the blackhole's heart it begins there. Perhaps every blackhole is a seed for a new universe hidden from us beyond the horizon, protected from us by the blackhole, fed by the blackstar's massive collapse. Perhaps you reach the horizon and are consumed and pass through the heart as a concept, immaterial, a thought, insubstantial, and begin again in her universe.

112.

You begin again. Perhaps your beginning is not unique, and the initial conditions necessary for you to begin and progress through your inflationary expansion creating the universe occur again and again and again through an inconceivably vast, not inconceivable nothing is inconceivable a vastness which for you is not yet conceivable but of which you are striving to conceive, universe multiverse cosmos.

113.

You begin again. You conceive yourself beginning inside another universe, you conceive you a universe, you conceive you are not unique your beginning is not unique your universe is not unique, you conceive that there are others the most different of which you cannot yet conceive but also conceivably others that are similar or even the same, and you conceive that as you expand balloon grow vast inside you too there could be isolated far-flung regions where conditions are right appropriate ripe for beginning as you began. You conceive that as you grow so vast as to be cold infinite lifeless the end, new you's begin within you in a neverending web of universes.

114.

You begin again. You can imagine an elegant rigid fully predictive unified theory that expresses why and how you are the way you are a universe. But of the others. Intelligence and awareness is a prerequisite to ask the question of how

6₁₁₄. "almond tree" by Dmitris Siskopoulos, 2010.
https://www.flickr.com/photos/dimsis/4470773056/
License CC BY-SA 2.0

and

why, and

if y o u r uni-

verse did not

have the properties

it does and you were not

intelligent and aware you wo-

uld not be able to a s k the ques-

tions and you would not k n o w y o u

weren't asking the questions and your

universe would be u n k n o w n . You can con-

ceive that your universe is the way it is because if

it weren't you would not be   here   to make it known,

and therefore neither would it. But beyond you then, have

all the others failed, the other you's, or are there other live uni-

verses burgeoning with m i n d ? You can imagine an expanded ulti-

mate theory that explains   how and why   all the constellation web net-

work of universes are the way they are, which live, which intelligent, which

aware. You can also conceive that if every blackhole is the seed of another uni-

verse and if there is some variation in the begetting birthing conceiving, then uni-

verses will evolve in a process similar to natural selection to optimize blackhole pro-

duction, and you can imagine an end goal endgame end universe where blackhole

spawning is maximized, not intelligence consciousness awareness, instead of mind,

though if you stretch perhaps someday you could imagine conceive comprehend

blackholes and supreme minds as the same thing.

115.

You begin again, contained in a book. "And the content of each one of these lives is
a universe, rich and poignant as that of any reader of this book." "I can only point

out that the higher a mind's development, the more it discovers in the universe to occupy it." "Human works of pure art were thought of as instruments through which man might behold and

6₁₁₅. "almond-blossoms" by Ryan O'Connell, 2011.
https://www.flickr.com/photos/mroconnell/6322334343/
License CC BY-SA 2.0.

472

ad-
m i r e
some aspect
of the cosmic
beauty. They were
said to focus together
features of the cosmos too
vast and elusive for man otherwise to comprehend their form." You
are contained confined can find beheld
behold in a book being that does not end but
nevertheless perhaps also next in another incarnation you will read or be in or be read in or be a b o o k
by Olaf Stapledon.

116.

You begin again. You are an 18th Man, capable of telepathic communication, capable of group c o n s c i o u s n e s s , capable of near immortality,
capable of comprehension orders of magnitude more than the first men who
created this book, perhaps you are in relation to them as they were to an ant. You
are returned from a space exploration beyond the border of your solar system
beyond the cloud of comets and ice and dust an exploration on which you were
contained confined within your ship for what would have been many of our, their,
your lifetimes on your planet, an exploration so distant that you were cut off from
the direct telepathic shared communication with your others that is part of you, an
exploration into empty space, an exploration perhaps not to find anything particular
but a thought experiment, an experience of emptiness, an exploration where you
floated in the void alone and encountered no comets and saw nearby stars increase slightly in brightness and your sun become one of those nearby stars, an exploration into changelessness where even in your expanded timescale

6_{116}. "Almond Orchard 02" by Tom Hilton, 2008.
https://www.flickr.com/photos/tomhilton/2321000101/
License CC BY 2.0.

nothing happens, an exploration into you alone, into nothing, from which you finally return to the other you's. When you open the hatch and step out released free
liberated, we reach out with our minds for you and the enlightenment you gained on
your exploration and find you broken, we find a darkness so profound that we must
wall you off from our minds.

117.
You begin. You choose to retire from life. You end.

118.

You begin again. You are an author a maker a creator. Your creation is not
a book per se, nor a collection of words precisely, though it is a container a vessel a box a physical body for you in a way that transmits
inserts shares expresses you into the mind of the reader listener
actor experiencer, entering them permeating them   filling
them with your expression thought patter story intent
b e i n g , with your art philosophy science intellect
emotion, with   you.   Perhaps in the melding,
the communication, the c o m m u n i n g, of
you and your reader, the two of you create a
limited imperfect unsatisfactory but   nevertheless
higher state that accomplishes some Planck-sized
measure of the supreme goal of ultimate awakening knowing togetherness beatitude beauty. Perhaps in your creation you
supersede your trapped confined buried self. Perhaps your life buried alive is your   art, or your art buried alive is your   life. Perhaps you
share with another and make something m o r e. I t e n d s. Do you leave an

artifact?

119.
You begin again. Each time you begin you go through the heat, the rapid expansion,
the confined, the dark, the wilderness, the perilous, the frustrated futility, the desperation the desire the wild the unsatisfaction the incompleteness the trapped. Each
time you begin you make all the mistakes of action, form all the lacking thoughts,
experience all the abject dispossession and suffering you ever have, but so too each
time do you see the glory behold the precious light love make beauty. Each time you
begin is the same, and each time you begin is different. Each time you end before
you begin.

120.

You begin again. Perhaps in this again after the beginning you and other you's achieve a group mind, you become a node in a system of signals pattern of radiation network of minds that is the physical basis for a super-individual, the being of individuals comprehended together existing on a higher level beyond, free of, superseding your constraints limitations box, transcending into an inherent under-standing of spacetime, of the universe, of paradox and insight into philosophical and metaphysical question of Why and How.

    121.

    You begin. You become self-aware, you grow in experience and knowledge and insight, you seek to know yourself and your surroundings, you ex-press. You are an occurrence of mentality. You are mind. You are not.

        122.

        You begin. You strive to awaken into the whole, to clarify the principles of symmetry that spawn the universe, the universes, to comprehend a time before spacetime before the vibrating fundamentals cohered into the fabric of existence, before the beginning, to develop a lan-guage that can conceive of such a condition without using inaccurate or misleading referents such as "before" to incom-pletely comprehend a time before time, to imagine sufficiently completely ultimately. You suffice comply intimate end.

    123.

You begin again to attempt to cohere the relative truths of the unlimited points of view and to embody how quantum uncertainty gives you form and to become the inevitable consequence of the duality symmetries that characterize you in multiple unique but related relative descriptions.

124.

You begin again confined, constrained, boxed in form, but what is the nature of the confinement constraint form box, you ask yourself, again. Perhaps it is the interrog-ative the conditional the imagination you answer again. The confinement constraint box is your form again you imagine.

125.

You begin again to become the consciousness of the universe.

126.

You begin again to create yourself with your thoughts your actions your l o n g i n g s

your communications.

127.

You begin again as he, they, we in "the years of anxious searching in
the dark, with their intense longing, their alternations of confidence
and exhaustion and final e m e r g e n c e into the light." i, ii, iii, iv, v, vi

128.

You begin again, in spite of possible limits to   comprehensibility,
despite the possibility you will never attain join b e c o m e her. You long
for her. You imagine her. Y o u   i m a g i n e   y o u are her. You are her.

129.

She begins. She lives to become. She is an I. She is I.

130.

I begin. I contemplate communicate reflect expand relate you she he they. I am
to be. I am. I am we.

131.

We begin.

---

i Albert Einstein (1879-1955).
ii R. W. Clark, *Einstein: The Life and Times* (World Publishing Co, 1971).
iii Martin J. Klein, "Einstein: The Life and Times, by R. W. Clark," (book review) *Science* 174, pp. 1315-16.
iv Brian Green, *The Elegant Universe: Superstrings, Hidden Dimensions, and the Quest for the Ultimate Theory* (New York: W. W. Norton & Co, 2003), p. 387.
v Nick Stokes, *Artifact Collective* (2019).
vi You, now.

And
w h o can
tell, perhaps the
purpose of man's l i f e[1]
on Earth consists precisely
in this uninterrupted striving after
a goal. That is to say, the p u r p o s e is
life itself and not the goal which, of course,
must be n o t h i n g but twice two makes four. And
twice two, ladies and gentlemen, is no longer life but
the b e g i n n i n g of death... Nevertheless, I'm willing to agree
that twice-two-makes-four is a thing of b e a u t y . But, if we're going
to praise everything like that, then I say that twice-two-makes-five is also a delightful little item now and then... And what makes you so cocksure, so
positive   that only the normal and the   positive, that is, only what promotes man's
welfare, is to his advantage? ... W h y , s u f f e r i n g is the only cause of consciousness. And
although I declared at the beginning that consciousness is man's greatest plague, I
know he likes it and won't exchange it for any advantage. Consciousness, for
instance, is of a much higher order than twice two. After twice two, we'll
of course have n o t h i n g left either to do or find out... With consciousness we have nothing much to do either, but we can at
least lacerate ourselves from   time to time, which does
liven us up a bit. It may be against pro g r e ss, but
it's better than nothing. ---2/28/19 personal correspondence of the Editors, text message, from Fyodor Dostoyevsky's
Notes from Underground,
1 8 6 4 , Penguin Books
trans. by Andrew
MacAndrew
1 9 6 1 .

---

[1] My chest was constricted, as if a weight were pressing in -- but from where? There was no weight, no feeling of a source or origin or cause, nothing to palpate. I'd say that it was the pain of being crushed or squeezed to death, but I've never been crushed or squeezed to death. Have you? Have you felt as if your body were collapsing from the inside, collapsing and hardening?
Donald Antrim, *Everywhere and Nowhere*, The New Yorker, Feb. 25 2019.

Made in the USA
Middletown, DE
21 November 2022

15447673R00268